Anna brought...
from N.E. Kingdom
6-27-15

The WHITE PINE Chronicles

Hilda Stahl

OLIVER
NELSON

THOMAS NELSON PUBLISHERS
Nashville • Atlanta • London • Vancouver

Published in Nashville, Tennessee, by Thomas Nelson, Inc., Publishers, and distributed in Canada by Word Communications, Ltd., Richmond, British Columbia.

The individual novels in this omnibus edition were originally published in paperback by Thomas Nelson, Inc., as follows: *The Covenant* copyright © 1990 by Hilda Stahl. *The Inheritance* copyright © 1992 by Word Spinners, Inc. *The Dream* copyright © 1993 by Word Spinners, Inc.

The Bible version used in this publication is THE NEW KING JAMES VERSION. Copyright 1979, 1980, 1982 Thomas Nelson, Inc., Publishers.

Library of Congress Cataloging-in-Publication Data

Stahl, Hilda.
   [White Pine chronicles (1996)]
   The White Pine chronicles / Hilda Stahl.
     p. cm.
   Contents: The covenant — The inheritance — The dream.
   ISBN 0-7852-7405-7 (cb)
   1. Family—Michigan—History—Fiction. 2. United States—History—Civil War, 1861-1865—Fiction. 3. Michigan—Fiction.
I. Title.
PS3569.T312W48   1996
813'.54—dc20   96-1757
                                   CIP

Printed in the United Stated of America.

1 2 3 4 5 6 — 01 00 99 98 97 96

1997 BLC 24510 24.99

Contents

Foreword

Hilda Stahl was a wife, mother, grandmother, writer, speaker, and teacher. Over the years she's grown to be one of the most loved authors for children and adults. But she didn't get there overnight.

From the time she first began writing short stories, Hilda dreamed of greater things. Few people encouraged her in this, but that didn't stop her. She was determined. From the sale of her first book in 1972 to the publication of her final book, *The Women of Catawba*, in 1993, Hilda believed in her dream.

The biggest moment for her, though, was when she received approval for writing The White Pine Chronicles, her first long adult series. The titles alone—*The Covenant, The Inheritance*, and *The Dream*—spoke of her own struggles through life and of her belief that God was able to see her dreams fulfilled.

Hilda's dream wasn't just to write but to reach people all over the world through her books—that they could identify with her characters and see there was a solution to every problem with God's leading. Hilda knew she'd achieved her goal again and again from all the beautiful fan letters she received over the years.

Our mother used to tell us that if there was something we desired to do, do it and never give up . Keep striving no matter what the odds. Her favorite scripture was, "I can do all things through Christ who strengthens me." The odds were against her, having seven children to care for, but that didn't stop her.

Hilda Stahl may be gone from this world, but her dream will live on in the hearts of every man, woman, and child who has read her books and learned from them. We pray that the legacy she's left behind will continue for many years to come.

We, her children, would like to thank all her faithful readers for making our mother's dream come true.

With Appreciation,

Jeffrey Scott Stahl

Laurie Ann Stahl Murray

Bradley Allen Stahl

Mark August Stahl

Sonya Lorraine Stahl

Evangelynn Kaye Fordham Stahl

Joshua Jay Stahl

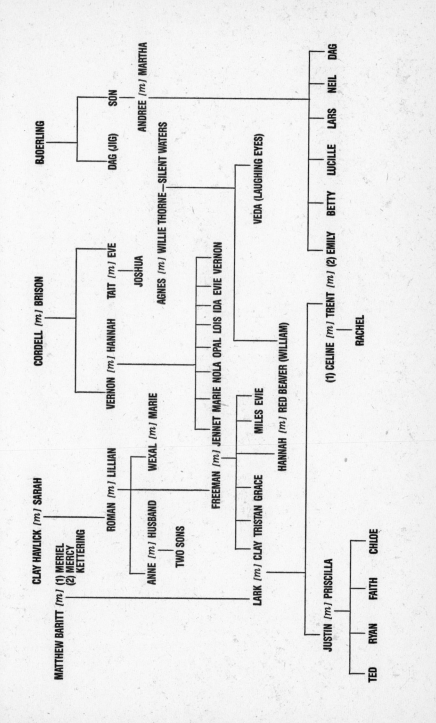

CHAPTER
1

♦ Jennet Cordell trembled with excitement and a touch of fear as she tucked the folded linen handkerchief that she'd hand stitched for Wexal Havlick in the frayed cuff of her brown serge work dress. She flipped her thick chestnut-brown braids back over her narrow shoulders. She was used to dressing in the dark, but this morning she'd felt all thumbs as she had buttoned the patched muslin petticoat at her narrow waist and slipped her dress down over her tall, hard-muscled body. She picked up her patched leather shoes, which she'd carefully stuck under the foot of the bed she shared with Marie. It was too dark to see the pegs on the wall where they hung their clothes or the chest or the three beds that almost filled the room.

The gentle snores of her six sisters told Jennet they were still asleep. She crept between the beds to the open stairs. Her heavy skirts swayed against her legs only inches below her knees. She'd tried to tell Ma that she'd grown too big for her dresses, that she needed a dress that covered her ankles since she was fourteen, soon to be fifteen, but Ma didn't hear. And when she'd tried to tell Pa he'd brushed her aside. Lois mumbled something, and Jennet jumped, then breathed a sigh of relief. Lois was talking in her sleep. She'd started doing it just after Ma had taken to her bed three months ago when Baby Vernon had died. Jennet bit her lip. Would Ma ever get over the death of her son? After seven girls she'd been pleased to present Pa with a boy, only to have him take sick and die when he was a month old.

Jennet stepped lightly down the stairs of the two-story cabin, avoiding the treads that creaked. It was almost dawn, and everyone would be up soon. For as far back as she could remember on every farm where Pa had worked, they'd all crawled out of bed at dawn, worked till dark, then fell into bed at night to sleep till dawn, except in the winter, when farm work let up some. Then she and her sisters, as each got old enough, sat at the kitchen table, and Ma taught them to read and write and do sums. Ma had planned to be a teacher before she'd married Pa and education was important to her.

This morning Jennet had to see Wexal before anyone was stirring here or over at the main house. She smiled. Her wide blue eyes sparkled at the very thought of Wexal Havlick.

As she reached the bottom step, the smell of the slop bucket next to the back door hit her and turned her stomach. She could barely make out the shapes in the room from the tiny glow of a heavy log smoldering in the huge stone fireplace. Chairs sat at both ends of the trestle table with a wooden bench at either side. Just beyond the table was the spinning wheel that Grandma Brison had given Ma as a wedding present sixteen years ago. A work table for preparing meals stood beside the cast-iron cookstove.

From the tiny space that Pa had partitioned off as a bedroom, Jennet heard Pa's loud snores and Ma's quieter ones, and she breathed easier. Since Baby Vernon's death, Pa had not slept well. It was still hard for Jennet to walk through the cabin and know that her little brother wasn't sleeping in his cradle but was, instead, in the wooden box Pa had made and buried in the frozen ground under an apple tree nearby.

Impatiently Jennet pushed aside thoughts of the baby. She'd see Wexal, then get the cows in before Pa had a chance to leave the cabin. He'd never know about her secret meeting with Wexal. Nor would Wexal's pa, she vowed silently.

Jennet slipped her shoes over her long wool socks and lifted the wooden latch of the heavy door. Chilly May air rushed in, and she shivered. She got her black wool work coat from a peg near the door and stepped into the predawn darkness. An owl screeched from the woodlot behind the barn. Granger ran to her, whining and wriggling with happiness. She knew he wouldn't bark. He'd been taught to bark only to warn the family or to herd the animals.

"Hello, Granger," she whispered, patting his thick neck and rubbing his pointed ears. "You stay put and wait for Pa."

Granger whined but sank to the ground near the back door.

Flinging her coat around her, Jennet ran lightly across the grass, bright green from April showers and now wet with dew, to the path that led past the two oak trees just budding. Pa had always said when the oak leaves were the size of a mouse's ears it was time to plant corn. He and the other workers on the Havlick farm were hurrying to get the fields ready to plant.

The entire farm had once been covered with hardwood trees and a few evergreen trees, but each year Roman Havlick cleared off more land to farm. He used some of the wood to build his buildings and to burn for firewood, then he piled up the rest of the timber and the tree roots and burned them to get them out of his way. Only the big woodlot remained. Jennet liked walking deep into the woods just to be alone with her thoughts, but she couldn't do it often.

Jennet ran along the barnyard fence toward the big red barn made from black walnut trees. She'd taken the same path many times during the past four years that Pa had worked for Roman Havlick. She glanced southeast of the barn toward the huge two-story farmhouse, but no light flickered in the windows. She knew that Kit, the hired girl, would soon be up to start the fires and cook breakfast for Roman, Lillian, Wexal, and Freeman when he was home. Jennet saw a tinge of light gray in the eastern sky and knew she had to hurry.

She raced along the last few feet of the board fence. Wexal would be waiting for her inside the barn, and she wanted as much time with him as possible. She knew he'd never forget their meeting. Her heart leaped, and she almost laughed aloud for gladness. She slowed as she reached the barn.

Suddenly a work-roughened hand closed over her arm and brought her up short. She stifled a scream, then giggled. "Wexal," she whispered. "You scared me out of a year's growth!"

"How'd you know it was me?" he asked with a low chuckle. "It could've been Free."

"Is your brother home again?"

"Came in last night." Wexal led Jennet inside the barn, closed the wide doors, and lit a lantern that cast a soft glow around them. For a moment the smell of sulfur covered the pungent odors of old hay and manure. The cooing of pigeons in the haymow floated through the early morning stillness. Wex hung the lantern on a peg in the huge hand-hewn support beam, then turned to Jennet. He was a few inches taller than she and lean with hard muscles from working the farm all his life. He wore dark heavy trousers with a gray collarless shirt buttoned to his throat. His head was bare, and he'd brushed his dark brown hair back off his narrow forehead. "Morning," he said softly.

She smiled and her blue eyes brightened. "Happy birthday, Wexal."

"Thank you, Jennet." He stepped closer to her but didn't touch her.

"I got a gift for you," she said breathlessly.

His dark eyes flashed and he chuckled. "Could it be a kiss?"

"No! You know not to ask for a kiss yet. When I'm sixteen, I'll give it some thought."

"That's not for two more years!"

"One year from next month!"

"Oh, so it is!" He grinned and reached for her, but she pushed him away.

"Do you want your gift or not?" she asked sharply.

"Yes." Wex flipped her chestnut-brown braid over her thin shoulder. "But I'd rather have a kiss."

She held out the handkerchief. "It's not much, but I stitched it myself. And look. I stitched a 'W' with white thread in the corner."

He ran his calloused finger over the fancy "W." "I'll treasure it forever, Jen."

Jennet gripped her coat tighter around her thin body. Two of the buttons were missing, and the collar was badly frayed. "You'll get better gifts from your family but not given with more affection. Oh, but I wish I could've given you more!"

"Having you remember is more than enough!" Wexal sighed. "This is just another work day to Pa. He won't remember it's my birthday. Ma won't make a special occasion of it unless Pa says she can." He hunched his broad shoulders, then smiled. "But Freeman brought me a knife and gave it to me last night. And Anne will remember, I'm sure. She'll drive over today unless the baby is cranky or she has another meeting to go to."

Jennet had heard the change in Wexal's voice when he

spoke of his sister's meeting. "I thought you were proud of the work she's doing."

"I am. But it's not right that she can go around making speeches to stop slavery and Pa won't even let me join the army." Wex's dark eyes flashed. "I want to be a Union soldier and help win this war!"

Jennet gripped his hand, and her blue eyes filled with sudden tears. "You know two of the Cross boys went and were killed in the swamps of Virginia! I don't want that to happen to you!"

"I don't either. But I don't want the South to win! Here it is the third of May, 1863, and the fighting is still going on! We all thought it would be over in '61! Nobody thought it would take so many men." Wex lifted his chin. "I don't want anyone to say that Michigan wouldn't fight to stop slavery."

"We've been saying we're against it for as long as I can remember, Wex."

"Saying is not doing! There's another call for Michigan men. I saw it in the Grand Rapids paper yesterday. I want to be one to go!"

Wex's voice rose and Jennet glanced around nervously. "Shh! If your pa heard us in here, he'd whip the daylights out of you."

Wexal's face hardened. "I wish I could be like Free! Pa wouldn't dare whip him."

"But he's twenty, not seventeen. And he doesn't live here like you do."

"I know. He lives in the woods." Wexal scowled. "Sometimes I think he should've been born sooner. He even dresses like the old woodsmen. He would've fit right in as a fur trader with Grandpa Havlick."

"Why's Free home now?"

"Money. He says he knows how he could make a fortune. But Pa is tight as skin on a hog."

"Forget about Free. Your Pa might let you quit early."

Wex rubbed his finger down the side of her face. "He won't," he said, shaking his head.

Roman Havlick owned the huge farm and had several workers, but he worked as hard as all of them. And he made sure his son did too.

"I don't guess my pa will remember my birthday next month what with Ma being how she is, and the spring planting." Jennet stepped closer to Wexal.

He caught her hand and held it. "Your pa would beat you if he knew you were meeting me, wouldn't he?"

Jennet didn't want to think about it. Lately Pa whipped her if she looked at him cross-eyed. She tugged her hand free. "I better get the cows in so he won't suspect I had this time with you."

All at once the barn door was thrown open. Roman Havlick stood framed in the doorway, his eyes blazing with anger.

Jennet wanted to run, but she couldn't move. She felt the tension build in Wex and she wanted to reach out to him, but she kept her hands at her sides. Blood pounded in her ears.

Wexal tried to act as if he wasn't frightened, but Jennet saw perspiration pop out on his upper lip, which was just showing signs of growing hair.

"I caught you two!" Roman unbuckled his wide black belt and jerked it off his thick middle. He folded it and slapped it against his leg with each step he took toward them. "I warned you to stay away from her! I warned you both!" Roman grabbed Wexal's arm, swung the belt, and struck Wexal hard across his backside.

Jennet caught at Roman's thick arm, but he brushed her aside as if she was a pesky fly. "Don't!" she cried. "I only brought him a birthday present!"

"Stop your lying tongue, girl!" growled Roman, his face red as he swung the belt again and struck Wexal a blow that almost sent him to his knees.

Wexal groaned but didn't cry out.

Finally Roman released Wexal and let him fall to the dirt floor. He turned to Jennet, his rage white-hot.

"We were only talking," whispered Jennet with a catch in her voice. "I gave him a birthday gift."

Roman grabbed Jennet's arm and raised the belt. "I told you to stay away from my son! I don't want the likes of you to entice him into sin!"

"I wasn't! I wouldn't do that!" Jennet struggled, but Roman's fingers bit unmercifully into her arm.

With an oath that burned Jennet's ears, Roman swung the belt and struck the top of her leg. Pain exploded inside her, and she cried out before she could stop herself.

Roman's loud, angry words filled the barn as he got ready to use the belt again.

Suddenly the belt was wrenched from Roman's hand. Through her scalding tears, Jennet saw Freeman toss the belt to the floor. A puff of dust rose around it. He pried Roman's fingers from Jennet's arm and pulled her tightly to his side. She smelled his buckskin shirt, heard his rough breathing, and felt the anger in him. Her leg was on fire, and she knew Roman had left a big welt on it.

"Don't strike her again, Pa!" Freeman's voice rang out with authority. He was tall and thin but as strong as the huge pine trees he always talked about. His skin was almost the same color as his leather shirt and breeches stitched together with rawhide. A long knife hung from the heavy black belt circling his lean hips. His dark eyes bored into Roman. "Leave her be! She's not yours to whip!"

"This is none of your affair, Free!" bellowed Roman, doubling his massive fists at his sides.

Jennet pressed closer to Freeman. Her heavy skirts brushed against the welt on her leg, and she almost cried out again. She glanced down at Wexal, who lay curled on his side. She wanted to go to him and comfort him, but she knew she'd better not move.

"I'm making it my business, Pa." Just seeing Pa raise a hand to the thin, frightened girl had sent Freeman's temper flaring. Pa was a hard man, but he had no call to whip a girl that wasn't even his to whip. "If you want to keep these two apart, let Wexal join the Union army like he wants."

"Never!" roared Roman. He kicked Wexal's heavy work shoe. "Not when I need him here." Roman pointed to Wex as he ordered, "Get your breakfast, then go finish plowing the oat field!"

Wexal scrambled to his feet and ran awkwardly from the barn without looking at Jennet or Freeman.

Roman watched Wexal until he was out of sight, then he glared at Jennet. "Your pa will hear about this."

"There's no need for that," snapped Freeman. He didn't want the girl to get yet another beating from Vernon Cordell. The man had always been too hard on her and, from what Wexal had said, was even harder now that his wife had slipped over the edge.

Jennet pulled away from Free, and he reluctantly let her go. She wanted to walk right up to Roman, look him square in the eye, and tell him what a fine son Wexal was to him and that he should appreciate him and trust him, but she couldn't find the courage. "I'll get the cows," she mumbled. Freeman's eyes locked with hers, and she blushed, ducked her head, and hurried from the barn. Perhaps later she could thank him for saving her.

The field hands who worked only during plowing, planting, and harvesting rode in on a wagon, stopped near the toolshed east of the barn, and jumped out to get the plows and horses. It was later than she'd thought.

Inside the barn Free took a step toward Roman. "Let that girl be, Pa. She works hard for you without pay. She and Wex are friends. No more than that." Freeman narrowed his dark eyes. But was that true? Maybe Pa should be concerned.

Roman buckled his belt around his thick middle as he

muttered, "How I treat that girl is *my* concern." Changing the subject, he said, "I thought you were leaving this morning."

"I need the money, Pa." Free hated to beg, but he was desperate. "I can get the land at a good price."

Roman's voice had a harsh edge. "You get that crazy lumbering notion out of your head. Work the farm. That's what you know to do. Not lumbering the white pine."

Free's jaw tightened. They'd had the same argument since Grandpa Havlick had told him of the money to be made off lumbering. "I will lumber the pines, Pa!"

"Not if you don't have money to work with." The reply was all-too-familiar to Free.

"I'll find a way to get it!" Free strode from the barn, anger churning inside him until he thought he'd explode. He'd been so sure that Grandpa had left money to him, but Pa had said different. "I'll get money," he vowed as he jerked open the back door of the house. He'd eat and then ride out. This time he'd not come back!

Several minutes later Jennet let the three cows in the back door of the barn, fed them grain, and milked them. Wincing from the pain in her leg, she carried each bucket of foamy milk to the milk house that stood almost in the shadow of the granary, strained it through the big strainer, lined in the bottom with cheesecloth, into several pans, and set it to cool on the wooden shelves chilled with a block of ice. Kit took most of the morning's milk to town to sell to special customers. Jennet skimmed the night's milk and set aside some of the cream; Kit or Lillian made the rest into butter. They made some of the skimmed milk into cottage cheese, and Jennet fed the rest to the hogs.

Finally Jennet washed the pails and lined them upside down on the wooden racks to dry. For the last three years this had been one of her jobs. Wexal had told her he'd had the job before her, Freeman before that, and their sister Anne before that.

Stepping outside the milk house, Jennet looked south across the rutted road to the hogpen, then east to the big farmhouse. Was Free inside with his mother, or had he already left?

The May sun felt pleasantly warm against her face and head as she walked toward the path leading between the granary and the barnyard. Her stomach growled with hunger. She knew her sisters would have breakfast waiting for her.

Jennet pushed back wisps of chestnut-brown hair that had escaped her braids. As she passed the barn on the way to the cabin, she relived the terrible happenings earlier. Had Roman told Pa yet? she wondered. She hoped Pa was already out in the field plowing.

Suddenly Pa came around the corner of the granary, and he stopped short at the sight of her. She wanted to run away from him and his anger, but she knew that would only make it worse for her when he caught her.

"Roman told me what you did!" roared Pa as he whipped off his thick black belt that kept his heavy red flannel shirt tucked into his patched trousers.

She looked down and plucked nervously at her dress. "I didn't do anything wrong, Pa," she said through a bone-dry throat.

"I heard different, girl!"

She tried to tell him of her innocent meeting with Wexal, but he cut her off.

"I won't listen to lies, Jennet! I told Roman I'd take care of you, and I aim to do just that!" Pa hauled her roughly out of sight of the men plowing the fields, sat on a stone, and turned her over his knee. She wanted to fight him, but she'd learned long ago not to or she'd be spanked harder. She closed her eyes and tried to pretend she was off by herself deep in the woodlot with birds singing above her.

Oh, where was Freeman now? If only he could stop Pa as he'd stopped Roman!

She felt the first whack of the belt and bit her lip to keep from crying aloud. Muttering angrily, Pa whipped her until she thought the skin on her backside would break and bleed. The pain was worse than when Roman had struck her, worse than the other times that Pa had whipped her. She tasted blood from biting her lip, but she didn't cry out. Yet she couldn't hold back the tears streaming down her ashen face. Finally he let her go, and she fell to the ground, unable to stand.

"That'll teach you to stay away from young Wex!" Pa almost shouted as he hooked his belt back in place. He straightened his hat and brushed at his thick beard and mustache. "Get the rest of your chores done. And don't you talk to Wexal again. If you do, Roman swears he'll turn us off his place. How would your ma feel if she had to leave little Vernon's grave? You think on that next time you're tempted to go against Roman's order."

Pa hauled her up, and she yelped from the pain of it. "Now get!" He walked away from her with long, angry strides.

Jennet's whole body ached. She knew she wouldn't be able to sit down very soon. Rage at Pa and Roman Havlick rose inside her, rage that would last long after her bruises and welts disappeared.

She walked slowly by the barn, her fists doubled at her sides. Just then she heard someone whisper her name. She stopped and looked around. Wexal stood just inside the barnyard. His eyes were red from crying, and he looked as angry as she felt.

"I'm sorry, Jen," he whispered as he pulled off his hat and worried the brim.

She lifted her chin and her eyes flashed. "We will always be friends! We promised we would—no matter what!"

"I heard your pa beating you. I wanted to stop him, but I couldn't."

"I know."

"Free's gone or he would've."

Her heart jerked. "Gone?"

Wexal rubbed an unsteady hand over his jaw. "I wanted to go with Free, but I couldn't."

"I know." She knew Wex was too frightened to leave. He couldn't make it on his own away from the farm. He wasn't like Freeman. "I'm real sorry your birthday turned out this way."

He nodded. "I better get to the field before Pa sees me.

"You better."

Jennet smiled and Wexal smiled back. She watched him trudge away.

A few minutes later she stepped into the two-story cabin that Free had told her they'd lived in until eight years ago when his pa had built a big, fancy home more befitting a wealthy farmer.

Smells of cooked food and coffee filled the room. Talking and laughing, the six girls still sat at the trestle table that Ma had insisted stay highly polished. Jennet knew with Pa out of the cabin they could do that. Three-year-old Evie was eating, but the others had finished. Ma wasn't there. Jennet knew Ma would be in her bed, staring up at the ceiling logs. She never heard what anyone said, and she spoke only to ask about Baby Vernon. At times she remembered he was dead.

Her braids bobbing, Marie jumped up and hurried to Jennet as she washed her hands in the basin. Marie was twelve and helped Lillian Havlick with meals when the field hands were there. "Are you all right, Jen?"

Jennet nodded, drying her hands on the damp towel. Her face, hands, and forearms were tanned bronze from hours of outdoor farm work.

Marie lowered her voice to keep Ma from hearing. "I heard Roman tell Pa what you did."

Jennet knotted her fists. "I only gave Wex a birthday gift!"

"I heard Pa say he'd beat you."

"He did," said Jennet grimly.

"I'm real sorry, Jen." Marie ran her hand down her patched, faded apron and fingered the end of her dark brown braid. "I kept your breakfast warm for you. Sit down and I'll bring it to you."

"I'll stand and eat it."

"Oh, Jen! Does it hurt that bad?"

Jennet nodded again. Marie handed her a plate filled with hashed brown potatoes, ham, eggs, applesauce, and two thick slices of homemade bread. Jennet wolfed down the food without tasting it. She drank two glasses of milk, then wiped her mouth with the back of her hand. "Shouldn't you be at the main house, Marie?"

"I'm on my way, but I wanted to see that you were all right before I left." Marie pulled off her apron and hung it on a peg. Lillian Havlick had a nice apron for her to wear.

Jennet set the heavy white plate on the work table. Five-year-old Ida and six-year-old Lois washed the dishes and cleaned the cabin. Nine-year-old Opal and eleven-year-old Nola cooked the meals, baked the bread, washed the clothes, carried the water, and chopped the wood. Jennet helped them if she finished early doing chores for the Havlicks.

Jennet glanced toward Ma's room. "How is she today?"

Marie shrugged. "The same. She wouldn't let me wash her or change her sheet."

Jennet sighed. She had to slop the hogs, feed the chickens, gather the eggs, then clean and sort them so Kit could sell them in town. When those chores were done, it would be time for dinner. After that she'd clean the barns and do evening chores, eat supper, and fall into bed.

With heavy steps Jennet followed Marie out the door.

CHAPTER

2

♦ Freeman Havlick left his hired horse at the livery in Big Pine and strode down the plank walk past the blacksmith and across the sawdust-covered street. As his eyes swept the area, he could see stumps of white pine trees beyond the buildings and the giant pine the town was named for. The pine was about five feet across and reached, arrow straight, at least a hundred and fifty feet into the sky with long sweeping green branches low enough for Free to touch. The needles were over four inches long with five in a blue-green bundle. The gray bark was thick and deeply furrowed into narrow scaly ridges. Once the whole area was covered with giant pine trees, but George Meeker had lumbered them off, making a small fortune. Many a man made his fortune from the trees.

Free knew Grandpa Clay would want him to invest in lumber just as Grandpa had invested in fur trading. They were one blood, born to explore and take chances and fight to survive in the Michigan wilderness. Pa, Ma, and Wex took to farming and Anne to town living. Freeman shook his head. Not him. He wanted life in the wilderness.

A leather sheath on his belt held the knife Grandpa had

given him years ago and had taught him to use in the woods for survival. Although the woodsmen didn't carry guns or knives, defending themselves instead with their feet and hands, Free couldn't give up his knife. It was a frequent reminder of his special times with Grandpa.

For the last two winters Free had chopped down the giant white pines for two different lumbermen. Last summer he'd helped set up camp, but this summer he had a chance to work with Willie Thorne, timber walker, also called a cruiser by some, a man who walked the woods, looking for the timber to cut that would provide the most board feet. Willie had said there was a good chance Free could work with him for George Meeker. But Free didn't want to work for a lumberman. He wanted to be one! Pa should've lent him money to buy timberland, but he wouldn't.

"You stay on the farm where it's a sure living," Pa had said in his gruff way. "Don't get wandering feet like your Grandpa Clay had."

"I thought Grandpa left me money," said Free. Studying Pa carefully, Free wondered, *Would Pa even tell me if he did?*

Pa had pulled his hat lower over his forehead and snapped, "You think I wouldn't tell you if he had left you anything? You think I'm that kind of man?"

Impatiently Freeman forced back thoughts of Pa and watched two men go into the boarding house, a two-story white clapboard building with a peaked cedar-shingled roof. It looked about three times bigger than Pa's house. Off-white muslin curtains hung at the row of windows on the second story. The wide front window on the first story shone as if it had been freshly washed.

The noon sun burned down on Free, making his dark brown hair wet with sweat under his hat. He recalled his first year as a shanty boy in the lumbercamp. One of the men had demanded that he sing a song or tell a story or they'd put him up. He didn't know that putting a man up meant throwing him over the big beam that supported the building they all bunked in while one man held down his feet, another held his head, and yet another pounded his backside with a bootjack. After that he'd gladly told a story or burst into song when asked. He got so he liked the sound of his own voice and sang even if he wasn't asked.

Horses pulling buggies and wagons clip-clopped past him. Big Pine was a small but growing town, busy during the fall and winter when the shanty boys were cutting down trees and during the spring when the river hogs, men wearing high-laced boots with hobnails on the soles to give them a better grip on the logs, floated the logs downriver. Already the river hogs had floated the logs away from Big Pine and on to Grand Haven. It was somewhat quiet during the summer when only the local sawmill was busy and the men setting up camp for the coming winter were around.

Free stepped into the crowded dining room, took off his hat, and rubbed his damp hair. Inside were two long tables with backless benches, and several small round tables with banister-back chairs pushed up to them. All the tables were covered with white tablecloths that looked freshly laundered. Most of the tables were jammed with roaring, swearing, sweating, laughing shanty boys with their red sashes, river hogs whose hobnail boots marked the puncheon floor, and mill workers coated with sawdust. Freeman had made plans yesterday to have dinner and a talk with Willie Thorne. His hat in his hand, Free looked around for Willie.

During a lull, silverware clattered against thick china plates. Smells of coffee, roast pork, and fresh baked bread made Free's stomach growl with hunger. He hadn't realized he was hungry. Since he'd walked away from Pa two days ago, he'd been too angry to think about eating more than a handful of dried corn and some fatback he carried in his pack.

The image of Pa bringing his belt down on Jen flashed

across his mind, and he bit back a groan. He'd wanted to save her from Pa, but he knew he couldn't do more than stop the whipping. Wex should've stood up to Pa and put a stop to the beating. Wex was a fine boy but too scared of Pa. Wex said he loved the girl, but he didn't do anything to protect her. *How could that be love?* Free wondered.

Abruptly Free switched to thinking about his own situation. He had to find a way to make money so that he could buy the sections of timber he wanted to lumber.

Just then he spotted Willie's bright red head. Free made his way through the crowded room to Willie Thorne, seated at the long table. In his late twenties, free as a bird and the best timber walker around, Willie could tell the cash value and board feet of a tract of timber within pennies of the real value. George Meeker paid him well. But Willie had said it was his last year when Free had talked to him yesterday. He wanted to get married and settle in one place to raise a family. He said he'd teach Free everything he knew. Free already knew a lot about timber, and he was willing to learn more.

"How do, Free," said Willie as Freeman sat down. "I already ordered today's special and it'll be here directly."

"Thanks, Willie."

Willie's brown eyes flashed as he smiled. His skin was tanned to a fine teak. His red hair was parted in the middle and combed back on either side of the part. "I talked to George Meeker. You got the job if you want it. It don't pay much, since you're mostly along for the walk. But when you take over from me, it'll pay a whole sight better."

A big-boned woman brought two heavy plates loaded with food and set them down before Willie and Free. They did not speak while they ate. The noise of the place pressed against Free, and he longed to be in the supreme silence of the woods. After finishing two big mugs of coffee and half an apple pie each, they strolled outdoors to the pleasant spring afternoon. Free let the breeze blow through his hair for a minute, then clamped his hat in place. He and Willie crossed the street to the dock where several small boats and canoes were tied.

"Abel Witherspoon is trying to take over some of the property George Meeker wants," said Willie in a low voice for Free's ears alone. "It might get to court, I hear. Meeker wants us to nose around a bit and put a stop to it."

Free trembled with suppressed excitement. He knew how bad some of the fights could get, and the way he was feeling right now he wanted to be in the middle of a big one. It just might help get rid of some of his anger and frustration toward Pa. "What'll we do?" he asked, making sure he didn't sound too eager.

Willie stopped at the water's edge. "I went in this morning and filed. Witherspoon said his timber cruiser filed before me and the clerk wasn't paying close attention."

"Then it's your word against Witherspoon's timber walker," said Free as he watched the water rush along and listened to the frogs sing.

"What he don't know is I always keep two records. The one I file at the clerk's office and the other one with Meeker's lawyer Justin Bracken. If he sold out to Witherspoon, I'll know it. And if it's not him, it's the clerk getting paid off by Witherspoon." Willie pulled out his pocket watch, studied the big face, and finally dropped it back in his pocket. "Mr. Bracken should be in his office. Let's go have a confab with him."

The newly constructed courthouse still smelled of sawed lumber. A man standing in an office doorway puffed at a stubby cigar and nodded slightly as Free and Willie passed him. A sign hung on the wall just inside the wide doors for all to see: HOBNAIL BOOTS NOT ALLOWED. In the silence of the building their boots sounded loud against the wooden floor polished to such a high sheen that Free could see his reflection as they walked down the wide hallway to the third door on the left.

Justin Bracken had his name etched into the glass on the door. Willie pushed it open without knocking, and Free followed him into the large office with walls of wide walnut boards.

Bracken looked up with a scowl. He had a heavy dark beard and mustache and thick hair that reached just below the collar of his suit coat. The room smelled of the pipe that hung from the corner of Bracken's mouth. "What're you doing here, Willie?"

"Witherspoon's timber walker said he already filed on that section Meeker wanted," Willie replied.

"You don't say!" Bracken paused. "When did he file?"

Free saw the lawyer's dark eyes staring intently at Willie.

"This morning when the clerk opened for business."

"Then you filed last night just as the clerk closed for business," Bracken stated flatly.

Willie grinned and nodded. "Right."

Free stiffened. He felt as if someone had hit him in the stomach.

Bracken looked Free over, then turned back to Willie. "Who's that?"

"Free Havlick. Going timber walking with me."

Free moved restlessly from one foot to the other.

Bracken locked eyes with Free. "You closemouthed?"

Free's mouth was so dry he couldn't answer. He shrugged.

"You better be." Bracken pushed himself up and walked around his big desk. "This is a dangerous business, Havlick." Bracken's forehead wrinkled as he thought a minute. "Havlick. Hmmm. Havlick. Ever hear of Clay Havlick?"

"My grandpa."

"You don't say!"

Free nodded.

"You in charge of his tracts of timber?"

Free hadn't heard about the tracts, but he didn't want

Bracken or Willie to think he was stupid about business matters. "My pa is."

"Too bad. We could've worked something out with George Meeker. He's buying timberland as fast as Willie here can find it and claim it. But maybe your pa would want to sell."

Free finally found his voice. "I doubt it. He hangs on tight to what he's got."

Willie laughed and slapped Free on the back. "That's why Free here has to work. He wants to be a lumberman, not a timber walker."

Bracken rubbed his smooth, pale hands together. "I'd like to get a hold of that lumber on Clay's land."

Free didn't want Bracken to approach Pa about any lumber business.

Willie cleared his throat. "Time's a wasting. Let's get on over to the file clerk."

Bracken picked up his pen, dipped it in black ink, and wrote in a ledger. He blew on the ink, blotted it, snapped the ledger closed, and tucked it under his arm. "Ready."

The clerk's office was just down the hall. Three men waited in line at the clerk's window, but Bracken pushed open a gate and walked around to where the clerk stood in front of a huge map.

Free watched them talk quietly. Bracken showed the clerk the ledger, and the clerk nodded. He wrote out a paper and gave it to Bracken.

"I'll get word to Witherspoon that I made an error," Free heard the clerk say as he dabbed sweat off his forehead with a big sweat-stained hankie.

"You do that," said Bracken, chuckling.

Free nudged Willie. "You see what he did?"

Willie frowned at Free. "Keep your thoughts to yourself."

"But he cheated."

"You want a tree to fall on you when you're not looking?

Don't say another word about this deal. I thought you understood how it worked."

Free could hardly believe all he had witnessed. They were cheating Witherspoon! Something told him he should walk away and forget about timber walking with Willie Thorne.

"Don't let Bracken know you're squeamish about cheating," whispered Willie gruffly.

Bracken walked back to Willie and pushed the paper into his hand. "There's your claim deed."

Sweat pricked Free's skin. Pa and Grandpa had taught him to be honest. He scowled. Being honest didn't get him the cash he needed, though. He had to have money. He hadn't done anything wrong; Willie and the lawyer had. He'd keep his mouth shut and he'd go with Willie.

Outdoors several minutes later Willie lifted his pack on his back and checked Free's to see that it was secure. "Get ready to learn how to be a cruiser, Free. The pay is good if you can stay alive and if you can beat the other walkers to the clerk's office."

Free grunted an answer as he walked with Willie toward the trail leading through the stumps into the deep timber. He was going to make money to buy timberland, and right now he didn't care how he did it.

CHAPTER

3

♦ On her fifteenth birthday, June 12, 1863, Jennet stood outside the barn and watched Roman and Lillian Havlick drive onto the dirt road that led to Grand Rapids. Their matched team of grays stepped cautiously, and the buggy bumped along over the ruts. Jennet knew they'd be gone until dark, and she forced back a cheer of freedom. Yesterday when Wexal had whispered that they could meet she'd almost flung her arms about him. This time they could spend time together without getting caught. Even Pa was gone for the day to pick up the gravestone for Baby Vernon.

Jennet felt the warm morning sun on her head and shoulders. Her brown serge work dress felt heavy and hot against her. Her stockings, bloomers, and petticoat were damp with perspiration. Suddenly it didn't matter. Today was her fifteenth birthday! She was practically a grown woman. Maybe now Pa wouldn't take his belt to her if she made him mad.

She watched the daisies along the fence row sway in the gentle breeze that blew the smell of the hogs across the fields and away from the yard. The windmill squeaked as it pumped water into a tank for the horses and cattle. Chickens clucked and scratched in the yard. A rooster crowed, then crowed again.

"Jennet," said Wexal from behind her.

She spun around, smiling. "Wex!" He stood just outside the barn with his hands resting lightly on his lean hips. His blue collarless shirt was buttoned to his chin and the cuffs rolled up on his forearms.

Her braids bobbing, Jennet ran to him. He caught her hand and pulled her inside the barn away from the prying eyes of Kit, the house maid, or any of Jennet's sisters who might be outdoors working.

The barn seemed pitch-dark to Jennet after the bright glare of the sunlight. She closed her eyes tightly, then opened them and was able to see the shadowy stalls and the huge support beams.

Wexal held her work-roughened hands. "Happy birthday, Jen!"

"Thank you! Marie is the only one who remembered." Jennet threw back her head and laughed, and the sound rang to the rafters of the barn. "But I don't care a whit! I remembered and you remembered! And I'm but a year from being sixteen."

Wexal dropped her hands and stepped even deeper into the barn's darkness. "I have news."

She froze at the tone in his voice. The neckline of her dress suddenly seemed too tight. "News?"

"Anne helped me."

"Your sister helped you do what?"

"Enlist. In the Union army."

"No!" The cry tore from her body, and she flung herself against him. She pressed her face into the sweaty front of his rough shirt and gripped his arms with calloused hands. She felt the thud of his heart and heard the sharp intake of his breath. "You can't go, Wex! You can't!" she cried against his chest.

"I must!"

"No! I read the list of the dead in Pa's newspaper yesterday! So many have died in the past two years! And always President Lincoln says the fighting won't last much longer!"

"I am going, Jen."

She lifted her face and saw the set of his jaw. He looked much like Freeman at his most stubborn.

"I'll write to you, Jen. Anne said I could send the letters to her in Grand Rapids and she'd see that you got them."

"I can't let you go! You'll be killed!"

"I must go." Gently he held her from him and looked down into her ashen face. "The president has sent out another call for men. They need me. And I can't stay here any longer to have Pa beat me if I even look at you."

"But what of me? I can't live without you!"

He pulled a folded bit of linen from his pocket. "Take this handkerchief that you stitched for me and keep it close to your heart. It's my promise that I'll come back to you."

"Oh, Wex!" She pressed the folded hankie to her lips and tears filled her wide blue eyes.

"I have more news," he whispered. "This is about you."

Trying to calm herself, she tugged at the high collar of her work dress and pushed damp wisps of hair back against her braids.

"Anne knows a woman in Grand Rapids who is looking for someone to take care of her three children. I said you would want the job."

"But how can I leave my family with Ma the way she is?"

"Marie is a fine, big girl. She can manage."

Jennet finally nodded. "Yes. Yes, she can."

"I told Anne that you'd take the position."

Jennet closed her eyes for just a moment, her head

whirling at the daring thought, then she opened her eyes and said, "Yes. Yes, I'll do it!"

"Good." Wex trailed a finger down her sun-browned cheek. "I'll miss you, Jen."

"Oh, Wex!"

"I leave two days hence, and I will take you to Grand Rapids with me. Anne will see that you get to the family she knows."

Jennet's heart almost burst. "Two days!"

"You can be ready."

She looked at him uncertainly. "I can't picture how it will be not to work the farm!"

"Anne said you will have time to read and to sew. You'll have one day off a week, and your wage is very generous." He named the sum and she gasped, her head spinning at the thought of such wealth.

"I've never had my own money," she said.

"Anne said they provide your clothing and your room and board. Your money will be yours to use in any way you choose."

Jennet sank back against a stall. A barn cat rubbed against her ankle, mewed, and ambled off toward the open door of the tack room. Dust particles floated in the air around her. A barn swallow swooped in, around the great rafters, then out. "Money of my own! Is it a dream?"

Wex caught her hand and held it to his heart. "When I return, I want you as my wife."

"Your wife!"

"I love you, Jen. You know I do. I signed up for three years, but talk is that the war will be over before 1863 draws to an end. When I return, we'll be wed."

She tugged her hand free. "What of your pa?"

Wexal's face drained of color, but he lifted his chin a fraction. "He'll not be able to stop me."

"He will," she whispered.

Wex hung his head.

Jennet rubbed his hankie against her cheek. "I'll keep this with me always. When you return, we'll see."

"But you will wait for me? You won't marry another?"

She laughed breathlessly. "Who would I marry?"

"When you live in town, you'll meet available men, men who will see your beauty and charm."

She flushed. "Beauty? Charm?" She didn't know she had either.

He laughed and pulled her to him. "Since I might not be with you on your sixteenth birthday, may I have a kiss now?"

Her lips tingled with the thought, but something held her back. She laughed shakily and pushed away from him. "You are too bold, Wexal."

"Only one kiss, Jen."

She shook her head.

Anger flashed in his eyes and she thought he would take a kiss, but the anger faded and he smiled and shrugged. "I will wait."

He led her to the wooden bench in the tack room where he'd sat many times to oil and repair harnesses. He held her hand as he talked of the war and how he planned to fight. "I will make Michigan proud! I will make you proud, Jen." He smiled and looked off into space. "And even Pa."

"I will indeed be proud of you," Jennet whispered. She couldn't imagine traveling so far away. She'd lived her whole life in Michigan on farms in the Grand Rapids area. Pa had worked on several farms, and the last four years on Roman Havlick's, one of the largest farms around.

They sat in silence a long time, and finally she asked him more about what the woman would expect of her. He told her all that Anne had told him. Butterflies fluttered in Jennet's stomach.

"I will meet you Sunday morn in the woodlot behind

your cabin," said Wexal as he traced a scratch up the back of her hand to her rolled-up frayed cuff. "Have your things ready, so you can go with me."

"Oh, do I dare?"

"You must! I want a better life for you. I don't want your pa to beat you ever again." Wexal gently squeezed her hand.

Right then she decided that she would give him a good-bye kiss. She would not wait until she was sixteen and old enough to wed! The daring thought almost took her breath away. She smiled a slow, secret smile. He would take her kiss with him to war as her promise to him. He would have it just as she had his handkerchief.

For the rest of that day and the next, Jennet smiled each time she thought of her bold decision. Once Marie asked her if she had a secret, but she wouldn't tell. Oh, but Marie noticed too much!

On Sunday evening Jennet returned to the cabin for supper. Granger ran to meet her, wagging his tail. She patted his head and started to speak to him, then stopped when she saw a horse and buggy hitched to the rail.

Just then Pa and another man walked into sight from behind the cabin. "Uncle Tait," she muttered. He'd probably come to collect the money Pa had owed him for over a year now. She knew he wouldn't get it this time either, for Pa had used it to buy the gravestone for Baby Vernon.

"Jen," called Pa. "See to Tait's horse."

Jen wanted to refuse, but she didn't dare. She hated being near Uncle Tait.

Tait pulled his pipe from his mouth and grinned. "Hello, Jen." He was almost forty, three years older than Pa. They looked alike with the same dark unkempt beard and mustache. But they dressed differently. Tait owned a store in Prickett, a settlement in the pines north of Grand Rapids. His white shirt and dark suit showed that he was a well-to-do merchant.

He eyed Jennet up and down, then slapped his thigh. "I swear, Jen, you growed more since last I saw you."

"I am fifteen now," she said.

"You don't say!"

Jennet quickly unhitched the horse and led it to the small barn where Pa kept his horse and wagon. She took as long as she could feeding and watering the horse. Leaving the barn, she looked at the woodlot where she was to meet Wexal at dawn. In the morning her new life would start! Finally she walked to the cabin, her steps a little lighter.

Jennet hesitated at the door. Maybe she could go right upstairs to bed without eating so that she wouldn't have to see Tait. But her stomach reminded her of how hungry she was.

She pushed open the door and went in. Tait's pipe tobacco smoke clouded the room. Supper was on, and the girls sat at the table along with Tait and Pa. The girls ate in silence while the men talked about the war and how they'd both go if they were younger and didn't have responsibilities. Jennet slid into her spot and filled her plate with a thick slab of roast beef, several chunks of potatoes covered with rich gravy, and a mess of dandelion greens. She buttered two slices of bread and filled her cup with milk. Several times she caught Marie looking oddly at her. Marie couldn't know that she was leaving with Wexal before dawn, could she?

Suddenly Jennet realized that Tait would be sleeping the night on a pallet near the fireplace. Could she leave without waking him? What would she say if she was caught with her bundle of clothes? Oh, she was too tired to think! Come dawn she'd know what to do.

The next morning Jennet crept around the beds in the darkness. She'd decided to leave her things. Marie could have them. Thoughts of sneaking past Tait pushed aside the terrible feeling of leaving her family. Later she'd find a way to write to them about her wonderful job and her life in town.

At the top of the steps, Jennet stopped dead. The sound of low voices told her Pa and Tait were already up! She went down a step or two until she could see Tait in Pa's chair and Pa on a bench, his right arm snaked across its back.

Jennet's heart hammered hard against her rib cage, and her tongue clung to the roof of her dry mouth. What could she do? Her head spun as she tried to think.

Maybe she could go outdoors as if she was headed to the outhouse. Maybe they wouldn't give her a thought.

She breathed easier as she walked down the steps. She knew the lamplight was too dim for them to read the fear on her face.

Jennet immediately sensed the tension in the room. She turned to run back upstairs, but Pa looked up and spoke her name. Trembling, she approached the long trestle table where they sat.

"Good morning," she said stiffly. Oh, she had to get to Wexal! Would he leave if she didn't meet him before sunrise?

Tait turned to Pa. "You want to tell her?"

"Tell me what?" asked Jennet, suddenly too frightened to stand. As she sank to the empty bench, she heard a sound overhead and knew the girls were dressing. She glanced frantically toward the door. Wexal would be wondering where she was.

Pa rubbed a large hand over his mustache and beard. "Jen, you're going with Tait to work for him."

Her mouth dropped open, but she snapped it shut as she shook her head in disbelief.

"It's all settled," said Tait. He jabbed Pa's arm. "Vern, I'll put it in writing that your debt is settled."

"Pa?" she said with a questioning look.

He scowled at her. "This'll keep Roman from throwing

us out, and it'll settle my bill with Tait. You work for him until the bill is paid."

"But I can't!"

"Mighty sassy girl there, Vern."

Pa reached across the table and grabbed Jennet's arm. "You watch your mouth, girl! This very day you will belong to Tait."

"Belong to him?" she whispered.

"Indentured slave," said Tait. He prided himself on knowing all kinds of facts.

"A slave? But Michigan won't allow slaves," she said.

"This is different," snapped Tait.

But Jennet couldn't see how.

"I own you until the debt is paid. You can't leave me until then." His eyes hardened. "If you try, you'll be sorry. It's legal to beat indentured servants who don't obey their masters."

Jennet looked helplessly at Pa, hoping for a sign that would show her he wasn't serious. But he kept his eyes on the papers in front of Tait.

Pa cleared his throat. "You write it down there that Jen works for you only three years. And no more than that! I won't have you work her all her life."

Tait chuckled. "So be it, Vernon." He scribbled on one paper and pushed it toward Pa. "Sign it and date it."

A bitter taste rose in Jennet's mouth and her stomach rolled. "What about Ma? What will she say about me being gone?" asked Jennet.

"She won't notice," said Pa bitterly.

Jennet glanced toward Ma's room, then back at Pa. "When do I go?" she asked hoarsely.

"Now!" announced Tait.

"Now?" she said in agony.

"Let the girl eat first," said Pa.

Tait pulled out his gold pocket watch, then shrugged his broad shoulders. "I could use some food too."

"What about my chores?" asked Jennet weakly.

"Marie will do them," said Pa.

Jennet locked her icy hands behind her back. Pa had all the answers. Oh, what was to become of her?

Pa strode to the stairway and called, "Girls, get down here and get breakfast on the table." He turned to Jennet. "Gather your belongings so you'll be ready to go when you're done eating."

Jennet looked at him, her eyes wide in horror. Could her pa actually sell her? Did he hate her that much? She left the table. The girls scurried into the room and she stopped Marie with a look.

"I heard," whispered Marie, close to tears.

"Tell Wexal," whispered Jennet.

"I will."

"Tell him now. He's in the woodlot."

Marie cocked a dark brow, but Jennet didn't answer her unspoken question. Marie nodded and whispered, "I'll tell him."

"Thank you!"

"I'll miss you, Jen."

"I'll miss you. Try to get Ma out of bed."

"I will." A tear ran down Marie's cheek, and she quickly brushed it away.

Upstairs Jennet tied her change of clothes into a gray shawl that she used on chilly days. She pulled Wexal's hand-stitched handkerchief from inside her bodice and held it to her face. Would Marie find Wexal to tell him what had taken place? Had he seen the light in their cabin and left without her? The morning that had held such promise had turned into a nightmare.

Jennet tucked the hankie against her heart and picked up her bundle. Back downstairs the others sat around the table eating. She looked longingly at the door. Could she make a run for it? She and Wexal could ride away where neither Tait nor Pa could find her.

Marie nodded slightly when Jennet caught her eye, then left the table and went outside. Maybe after Wexal heard what was to become of her he'd rush to her rescue.

Her shoulders slumped. Wexal was not Freeman. She couldn't escape, and she might as well stop thinking about it.

She tiptoed into Ma's room and sat on the edge of the bed. Morning light already shone through the window. Ma didn't look at her but kept her glazed eyes on the ceiling. Her chestnut-brown hair hung in tangles, and the room smelled of sweat and body odor. Jennet picked up Ma's lifeless hand and held it firmly. "Ma, I'm going away," she said softly. "Pa sold me to Uncle Tait." Her voice broke. "I must stay with Uncle Tait for three years and work off Pa's debt. Oh, Ma, please hear me! Stop Pa from doing this!"

But Ma wouldn't hear, and Jennet finally leaned over and kissed the pale face. "Good-bye, Ma."

Jennet joined the others and ate without talking. The girls silently watched her. Pa and Tait discussed the war and how much the government was pushing to get more Michigan men to join the army. Jennet thought unhappily of Wexal's being one of those men.

A few minutes later Jennet forced back her tears and told her sisters good-bye while Tait went to hitch the horse to the buggy. The girls cried a little, but Pa hushed them with a hard look and harsh words.

Pa followed Jennet out the door. She glanced around for Marie. Probably Wexal was long gone, but had Marie seen him before he left?

"I want to say good-bye to Marie, Pa," said Jennet.

"I'll say it for you," Pa said coldly without looking at her.

Her heart sank. How she wanted to cry and scream and refuse to leave! Instead she climbed up beside Tait in the buggy. He grinned broadly and sat with his shoulders square, a tall beaver hat on his head. He was proud of having become prosperous.

"So long, Vern," said Tait, laughing. "I was beginning to think you'd never be out of my debt."

Pa turned away without answering him.

Jennet's eyes filled with tears, but she wouldn't let them fall as the buggy rolled away from the cabin and out to the dirt road. Oh, how she wanted to leap out and run where Tait couldn't find her!

"Buggy's too rough," Tait declared. "River is my way of traveling." He gripped the reins tight as if he wasn't used to the feel of them in his hands. "I'll leave the buggy when we get to the Thornapple River. We'll take a canoe up the Thornapple to the Grand to Prickett."

Tait rode in silence by the grain fields and around a tree-covered hill. He passed the turn-off that led to Irving where Kit sold milk and eggs. Then he cleared his throat and said, "Your pa says you can read and write and do sums."

"I can," she managed to say as they rode into the shade of several tall oaks.

"You can help with the books as well as keep the store clean. We work long days."

Jennet was used to that, but she wasn't used to working indoors or being away from home. When Tait turned off on the road that led to the Thornapple River, she asked, "Where will I live?"

"Alone in a room in back of the store."

How would it feel to have an entire room to herself? She'd always shared a room with her sisters. "Where do you live?" Her voice sounded strained even to her ears.

"I have a place," he said, looking sharply at her from the corner of his eyes.

Pa had said that he lived with a Pottawatomie squaw, but Jennet didn't ask about that.

"I have a dress for you, one that don't smell like a cow barn."

Jennet's jaw tightened. She hadn't realized she smelled.

She didn't like his sweaty body odor or the stench of his pipe, but she didn't tell him.

Within an hour Jennet saw other buggies and wagons near the bank of the Thornapple River. Farmers stood talking and laughing outside a general store that looked cluttered on the inside as well as the outside. Jennet wrinkled her nose at the fishy smell of the river. Along the opposite shore mallard ducks caught her attention.

After returning the hired buggy to an old man leaning against a wooden fence to the left of the store, Tait spoke to a couple of men inside the store. They came out and loaded his supplies in a wide birchbark canoe. Two Indians were ready to paddle them to their destination.

The canoe swayed as Jennet stepped in, and water slapped against its sides. She moved easily with the pitch of it and carefully sat on the middle seat. Boxes covered the floor in front of and behind her, situated just right for balance. Tait sat beside Jennet without a word to her. He talked to the Indians as they pushed off. They answered back with short, gruff sentences.

Jennet held back the cries of despair that rose in her as the canoe shot through the water, taking her further away from her family and the only way of life she knew. She heard the birds singing in the trees lining the river, but she didn't look at them. She kept her eyes glued to the Indian's back.

The day felt like one long painful blur. She barely noticed when they left the Thornapple to go into the Grand River.

Just after midday the Indians docked between two boats at Prickett. Across the rutted street a big wood frame building painted white displayed a huge sign above the door: TAIT'S PLACE. Farm implements stood on one side of the building. A large white warehouse occupied a lot on the other side. Through the store's open door, Jennet saw an old man talking to a woman with a basket on her arm. Goods of all kinds lined shelves and were stacked in the wide front windows that badly needed washing. Down the street on the same side as the store, another building was labeled TAIT'S SHOE FACTORY. Several yards away from the docked boats a stone building bore the sign TAIT'S GRISTMILL. Jennet frowned. Uncle Tait owned much more than she thought. There were other buildings, but they didn't carry his name.

Tait stepped to the dock and said to the Indians, "Unload the supplies and take them across to the store. Old Gabe will pay you in supplies."

Jennet carefully climbed from the canoe, her bundle in her hand. She felt as if she were still swaying in the water, but she soon found her legs and crossed the street with Tait.

They went around to the back of the building. A small barn and an outhouse were just beyond the back door of the store. Tait led her into a room that smelled closed in and dusty. Jennet saw a small greasy cast-iron cookstove, a cot, a dresser, one chair, and a small wooden table scarred with scratches and burns crammed into the tiny space.

"The man who worked for me slept here," Tait said.

"Where'd he go?"

"Killed by a bear. Left me shorthanded."

His matter-of-fact tone made Jennet look at him uneasily. Just as she dropped her bundle on the cot, a mouse zipped across the room and into a hole in the wall.

Tait ignored the fleeing creature. He pointed to her bundle. "Those clothes clean?"

"Yes."

"Put 'em on so you don't smell the place up." He looked down at her feet. "Got shoes without manure on 'em?"

"Only these."

He peered down at them, taking the measurement with his eyes. "I have a pair you can wear, but that'll be added to your bill. Anything you cost me will be added on to your time here."

Jennet bit back a response. He really was going to treat her like a slave!

Tait opened the connecting door to his store. "I'll get your shoes," he said and walked away.

Her head down and her eyes wet with scalding tears, Jennet thought, *What is to become of me? If only I'd been able to go to Grand Rapids with Wexal!*

In a few minutes Tait came back with a pair of black shoes and a gray dress of a lightweight fabric. He dropped them on the cot beside her bundle.

"I'll be out there working," Tait said, jabbing his thumb toward the connecting door. "You come in as soon as you change. And make it snappy."

Jennet barely nodded.

Tait closed the door behind him, and she stood alone in the room that reeked of tobacco and liquor and dirt.

She sank to the chair and moaned desolately. She pulled Wexal's hankie out and ran her finger over the "W" she had stitched. Tears again filled her eyes and slipped down her cheeks. A spider dangled from its web near her face and she swatted it away, sending the web and spider flying across the room.

Finally she closed the outside door, shutting out sounds of the water slapping against the dock and the men shouting at one another on the boats. She found fresh water in a pitcher, washed, changed her clothes and slipped on her new shoes. They felt strange on her feet but fit fine. The high-necked dress tucked in at her narrow waist, then billowed out to hang almost to the floor. She touched the black piping that went around the neck and down either side of the row of black buttons. She glanced down at her feet and noticed that her ankles were covered. She brushed out her hair, rebraided it, and pinned the braids across the back of her head instead of leaving them hanging over her shoulders. She patted Wexal's hankie that she'd tucked in her bodice. Suddenly she remembered that she'd never had the chance to give Wexal her kiss. He had nothing of hers to see him through the war.

"Oh, Wexal," she whispered brokenly.

She took a deep steadying breath and with a heavy heart entered Tait's store.

CHAPTER

4

♦ Jennet walked uncertainly down the crowded aisle toward the front of the store where Tait was talking with the man he'd called Old Gabe. The strange combinations of smells of the fabrics, leather goods, tools, and the black licorice sticks in the jar near the cash register made Jennet's stomach turn.

"Well, well," said Tait, eyeing Jennet up and down. "You clean up real good." He turned to the white-haired man beside him. "Old Gabe, this is my niece, Jen. She'll be working for me for some time to come. You get on back to the mill. Tell Park I'll be there before closing."

Old Gabe grinned a toothless grin at Jennet and limped out without a word. Wide gray suspenders kept his heavy baggy trousers up high on his skinny hips and his faded blue shirt tucked in. He stuck a floppy-brimmed hat on his balding head.

Tait pulled out a big gray and white feather duster from behind the counter the brass cash register sat on. He shoved it toward Jennet. "Run this over the shelves, and then you can walk down the street to the boarding house and get yourself some supper."

"I never ate anyplace but home," she said as she gripped the feather duster.

"Nothing to it!" Tait spread his hands wide. His whiskers moved as he talked. "You walk in, sit down, and somebody will ask you what you want to eat. You tell 'em and they bring it to you. You eat it and pay for it and walk out."

"Pay for it?"

He reached in his pocket, pulled out a coin, and flipped it to her. She caught it easily and looked down at it, wondering how anyone could spend so much on a plate of food.

"Get to work. And be quick about it! One thing I can't stomach is a dawdler." Tait turned away to open one of the wooden boxes that he'd brought on the canoe.

Jennet laid the coin on the counter. She started at the end of the first aisle that held piles of men's shirts and trousers and brushed the feather duster over the exposed wood of the shelf and across the top items. She climbed up a ladder to reach the top shelf nailed to the back wall and dusted kerosene lamps of various sizes, glass flower vases, and decorative cans to use in a pantry for foodstuff to keep out the bugs and mice. "This is not like cleaning a barn," she muttered to herself.

From her high perch Jennet glanced around. The main room was a little bigger than Pa's cabin. Tait's office was even smaller than the room he had given her to live in. The store walls were wide boards and had aged to a deep brown. A potbellied stove stood in the center of the room with a rocking chair and a short bench beside it. The stovepipe ran up through the ceiling to a brick chimney. Counters with shelves reaching the ceiling lined the walls, breaking only for the doors. An L-shaped shelving unit stood between the front door and the stove. Could she survive working here for three years after being so used to outdoor work?

Jennet swallowed hard as she climbed down the ladder. She had no choice. She had to survive.

Canned goods, jars, tools, rifles, axes of different sizes,

knives, crockery, cooking pots and other utensils, shoes and boots, folded shirts, ladies' clothes, yard goods, and items Jennet couldn't begin to name—everything was coated with dust, and cobwebs hung from the ceiling. Several times she stepped out on the plank walk to shake the dust off the big feathers. The man who'd been killed by a bear must not have dusted in a long time.

When she finished, she stuck the duster back under the counter and said just above a hoarse whisper, "I'm done."

Without looking up from his bookwork in his office, Tait said, "Don't dawdle over your food either."

"I won't." She wondered when he'd eat, or if he'd even take the time. Would his squaw have supper waiting for him?

Outside the store Jennet looked up and down the street. A man on horseback rode silently past, a muzzleloader resting across his legs. A bulldog in front of the gristmill rose to its feet, watched the rider, then settled back in the sunlight. The river splashed against the dock, rocking the boats. Over the sound of the water Jennet heard children laughing and shouting, but she couldn't see them. Would she meet someone her age? She frowned. Tait wouldn't let her take time to make friends, so why even think about it?

She headed toward the weathered frame boarding house on the far side of the shoe factory. A warm breeze blew smells of the river and the pines to her. Suddenly she stopped and looked helplessly back at the store.

"Ma, why did you let this happen to me?" Jennet chocked back a sob. "Pa, how could you sell me?" The day's events tumbled through her mind. Just then a man and a woman walked out of the boarding house, letting the screendoor close with a sharp bang. The noise jarred Jennet from her thoughts. She knew she better hurry up and get a meal.

Inside the boarding house several woodsmen sat along one side of a long table. Two middle-aged women encased in big white aprons waited on them. Ladder-back chairs were turned upside down on the small square tables along the wall. A stone fireplace covered the far end of the room, the hearth blackened from use. The wide wooden boards of the floor were scarred with bootmarks but seemed clean. Pencil drawings of a lumbercamp and of trees were framed and hung on the unpainted wide boards of the walls. Smells of ham, beans, bread, and coffee made Jennet's stomach growl and her mouth water. But she wasn't sure where she should sit and her face burned with embarrassment.

"Look at that purdy girl!" cried one of the men no older than Free.

Jennet looked around for the girl he was talking about, but she couldn't see one. She glanced at the man to find him staring at her. He'd called her pretty! How strange!

The man walked right up to her. "How about sittin' with me, purdy girl?"

The smell of whiskey on his breath turned her stomach as she jerked back. "Get away from me," she whispered.

"Leave her be, Pike," said an older man.

"Not till I get her to sit with me." His black hair was cut short, making his ears seem extra big. He hiked up his gray trousers as his dark eyes sparkled with laughter. He pushed his face up to hers, and she jumped back to get away from him. When he caught her arm and pulled her toward him, she doubled her fist and punched him square in the nose. Blood spurted, and he yelped and covered his nose.

The other men cheered. One man yelled, "A real wildcat! That Tait's one lucky man."

Jennet's face flamed. "I am his niece," she said as calmly as she could. "And I work for him!"

"That's sure good to know," said a man with bright red suspenders. "We thought you was his woman. Can I come calling?"

Jennet scowled at him. "I am promised to a man off fighting to set the slaves free," she said. It wasn't exactly the truth, but close enough.

"Don't tease the girl," said a tall man with blond hair and a scar running from the corner of his right eye down to his jaw.

Smiling, one of the women walked up to Jennet. She had gray hair and wrinkles lined her face. "My name is Midge Dooley. Don't mind these men. They're not around unattached females much. They don't remember their manners at times. Sit right down and I'll get something for you to eat."

The kind voice brought tears to Jennet's eyes. She ducked her head and blinked them quickly away, then sat at one end of the long table away from the rowdy men.

The ham, beans, bread, and milk took away her hunger, but she couldn't enjoy the food with the men watching her every move. She turned down the cookies, paid for the meal, and walked out. The sun was low in the sky. Would Tait think she'd dawdled?

When she walked into the store and around the aisle, Tait glared at her. How she wanted to turn and run from him!

"News travels fast around here, girl." Tait slapped a piece of leather strap against his leg. "I heard you bloodied Pike's nose. Made a real spectacle of yourself. I won't stand for that."

"He wouldn't leave me alone!"

"Don't sass me, Jen Cordell!"

She saw the anger in his eyes, and she turned away without another word.

"Don't you turn away from me before I'm done talking to you! Your pa might've spoiled you, but not me! You don't back talk me and you don't walk away from me till I give you leave!" Tait swung the leather strap and caught Jennet on the backside. She cried out in pain and backed away from him until she bumped into a counter of material. Tait slapped the strap against his hand. "That's only a warning. Next time it'll be worse."

Jennet moaned as she thought of three years of Uncle Tait. Maybe she should run away into the wilderness and try to survive there, despite the wild animals. But she knew she wouldn't. She and Wex were just alike. Neither of them had the courage to stand up and fight or to run away. But Wex had found the courage to join the army.

Had he really gone, or had his pa learned his plans in time to stop him?

"Unload them boxes onto them shelves and be quick about it," said Tait as he motioned to the boxes.

Jennet stacked canned goods on the shelves and worked until it was dark out.

"I put together some groceries for you so you don't have to spend time or money at the boarding house," said Tait as he carried a box to her room. "Don't go eating it all in one day. What I gave you has to last a week."

That night after she'd used the outhouse and carried in a bucket of water from the well, she sank to the edge of her cot. The lamp cast a soft glow around the room. She'd locked both doors, but still she felt afraid. It was so quiet! Were her sisters already sound asleep for the night? Could she sleep without hearing them nearby?

Tears trickled down her face as she slipped into her nightdress. She washed with the cold water and dried with a towel that Tait had given her.

Jennet heard a dog bark and a man yell at it. She looked at the lone window covered with shutters. "I can't stay here," she whispered. "I can't! Not for three long years! Not even for three days!"

She crawled between the scratchy blankets on the cot and rested her head against the pillow. How different the cot felt! Oh, how could she sleep without Marie beside her?

After a long time Jennet drifted into an uneasy sleep and

woke the next morning with a start. She thought she'd overslept and Pa would beat her for not milking the cows on time. She sat up and realized she was at Tait's store, not the Havlick farm. Her heart sank. "No! It's not a bad dream!"

She lit the lamp, started the fire, quickly boiled a pot of water, and made cornmeal mush that she ate with maple sugar. It was a far cry from the breakfasts her sisters fixed for her.

She had just finished washing and dressing when someone knocked lightly and a little hesitantly on her back door. Who could that be? Cautiously she opened the door a crack. It was light out already, but the sun wasn't up yet. An Indian woman younger than Ma stood there with a basket in her hands. She was dressed as a white woman, but her straight black hair hung to her shoulders and a headband was tied around her forehead. Jennet stared at her in surprise.

"Don't be afraid of me," the woman said.

"What do you want?" asked Jennet uncertainly.

"I brought you milk and bread and butter," said the woman in a soft, pleasant voice.

"Why?"

"I knew you'd need them."

Jennet stepped aside for the woman to enter.

"I am Eve," said the woman. Her dark eyes sparkled as she smiled.

"Eve?"

"A white woman's name, I know. But I am called Eve because I am a follower of Jesus Christ. I am Tait's wife."

Jennet gasped in surprise. "His wife?"

"He calls me his squaw because he is ashamed that he married a Pottawatomie." She talked as she set the jar of milk, a loaf of bread, and a large chunk of butter onto the table. "He said you came back with him. I was afraid he wouldn't take good care of you. I brought you this while he is still asleep. It would be better if he does not know what I did."

"Thank you very much." Jennet rubbed a hand down her dress. "I'm sorry if I seemed rude, but you took me by surprise."

"I know," said Eve. "We live in a cabin a short walk from here. If you need me, I will be there."

"Thank you."

"But don't tell Tait that we have met. He likes to think that I spend my days in his house away from people." She laughed, and Jennet found herself liking this gentle woman.

Jennet smiled. "I'm glad you came."

"I must get back and milk the cow before it's time to make breakfast."

Jennet didn't want to see her leave. "Will you come again?"

Eve nodded. "Each morning just after dawn."

"Thank you! I am so lonely!"

Eve wrapped her arms around Jennet and held her close.

Jennet stiffened, but it felt so good to be held that she relaxed. It had been a long time since Ma had hugged her.

Eve smoothed Jennet's hair and gently patted her back. "May you learn to lean on Jesus my Lord. He will take away your loneliness and your pain."

Jennet had read Ma's Bible, but she didn't know that Jesus could take away loneliness or pain. "I have no Bible to read to learn about Jesus."

Eve stepped back from Jennet but caught her hands and held them tightly. "The preacher gave me one, but I can't read. I will share it with you."

"Thank you."

"You are very welcome." Eve smiled, pulled her shawl tighter around her slender shoulders, and walked away with the empty basket.

Jennet watched until Eve was out of sight, then quickly

sliced off a great hunk of bread, buttered it, and ate it. The crust was crunchy and delicious, the inside soft and yeasty. The butter was sweet and lightly salted, as good as any she'd tasted at home. She drank all the milk because she had no place to keep it cool during the day. Now, she felt as if she'd had enough for breakfast. She tucked the bread and butter away so that Tait wouldn't see it if he entered her room. She'd eat it before she went to bed.

A few minutes later she started to work in the store. She'd try not to do anything that would make Tait angry enough to whip her. He'd said he'd show her how to work the cash register and wait on customers. Once she'd learned that, he wanted to teach her to keep the books for the store, the shoe factory, and the mill.

Jennet thought of what he'd do to her if she couldn't learn as quickly as he wanted her to and she groaned. She unlocked the front door and looked at the quiet river. Not a boat or a canoe was in sight. "Wex, come get me," she whispered.

She turned away with her head down and her eyes burning with unshed tears. Wex wouldn't get her. Not even Free could save her this time.

CHAPTER

5

♦ His heart hammering, Free ducked around a giant pine out of sight of Driscoll's timber walker Keith Kirkwood. If Willie Thorne knew that Kirkwood was marking off the same section as they were, he'd see that a heavy branch fell on him and pinned him down for a while or maybe even for good.

Free pulled off his hat and wiped sweat from his forehead and hair. His shirt felt too tight and his trousers too hot. And it had nothing to do with the steamy September weather. During the summer, he'd learned how far Willie went to get land for George Meeker.

Willie just might be desperate enough to kill Kirkwood. Free's jaw tightened. He didn't want any part of murder. He wanted money in a bad way—but not that bad. A few times he'd thought of leaving Willie, but he couldn't seem to do it. He frowned. He had to admit that fear was part of it, and he didn't want to lose the money he'd earned for the summer's work even though it was only twenty dollars.

Mosquitoes buzzed around Free, but he ignored them as he pulled out his compass and carefully charted the direction. If he walked to the creek and went northwest, he could meet up with Willie to lead him away from the section Kirkwood was marking, then they could head for Big Pine to file before Kirkwood did. As payment Willie Thorne received a quarter of the land he found for George Meeker. Willie had told Free he wanted as much as he could get so he could live in comfort for the rest of his days. Free wanted to make that kind of money, too, and more, but not if he had to kill and steal for it.

Squirrels chattered from high in the pines. A blue jay scolded, then flew away. Usual smells of the woods were covered by the heavy aroma of pine.

Free slipped from one giant tree to the next until he was too far away from Kirkwood to be spotted. In an hour he reached the riverbank where he and Willie were camped. Free lifted his brows in surprise to find Willie already there.

Seeing Free, Willie hoisted his pack on his back. His red hair stood on end and looked bright against the dark bark of the trees. "Get a move on, Free. We got to hotfoot it to Big Pine now. We can't wait till morning like we planned."

"What's happening?" asked Free as he gathered his things. He kept his face carefully masked to keep Willie from reading anything in it.

"I caught sight of Witherspoon's timber walker not more than an hour ago. I got this gut feeling that he plans to claim them sections upriver that we marked three days ago. They're the best we saw yet and I want 'em."

Free kept his mouth shut about Driscoll's timber walker, Keith Kirkwood, as he fell into step beside Willie. There was no need for Willie Thorne to know about Kirkwood.

Pigeons by the score rose from the trees and almost blocked out the sun. Many times at home Free had gone out at night with a long pole to knock the pigeons out of the trees to feed them to the pigs. That made him think of Pa and Wex and even Jen. What was happening with them? Maybe he should write home just to let Ma know he was still alive.

Free frowned as he jumped over a stream swollen from last week's rain. Let them think he was dead! They didn't care anyway. But Wex did, he knew. And so did Ma. Maybe he would write when he got to Big Pine.

Just then Free saw movement several feet away. Was it Witherspoon's walker? Or maybe Kirkwood had seen him and decided to race them to Big Pine. Last month Free had seen two timber walkers racing to file. When they saw they'd reached town at the same time, they fell on each other in the street outside the courthouse and beat each other to a bloody mass, figuring the winner would file. While they rolled on the ground in combat, Willie Thorne walked right in and filed those tracts of land. He still had a good laugh over that one.

Suddenly Willie stopped short and motioned for Free to do the same. Willie gestured toward his left where Free had seen the movement. "Bear," mouthed Willie.

Free's stomach tightened. He was more afraid of bears than wolves. Once, three years ago, he'd come up on a black bear that had attacked him when he'd walked too close to her cub. He still had a scar on his shoulder from it. A stranger had suddenly appeared and chased the bear away.

Willie crept forward with Free close behind. The bear rooted at the base of a tree and didn't seem to notice them as they passed. Free breathed easier, then his breath caught in his throat as a man stepped into sight, a .50 caliber muzzleloader aimed right at Willie. The man had dark matted hair, which hung low on his wide forehead. His dark eyes flashed as he looked from Willie to Free. His big gnarled hands were encrusted with dirt. A ragged gray shirt hung on the man's big frame and over leather breeches. He wore beaded moccasins and had a pack on his back.

Free heard the sharp intake of Willie's breath as the man pulled back the hammer of his muzzleloader. The click seemed to echo through the trees.

"I told you, Willie Thorne, never to set foot in these here woods," said the man in a gruff voice with an accent that Free could barely understand.

Willie shook his head and laughed, but sweat popped out on his upper lip. "I heard you was dead, Jig."

"Not dead. Close to. But not dead. Not dead even from your knife, Willie Thorne." Jig turned his eyes from Willie to study Free from under matted brows. "You I have not seen before."

"Freeman Havlick," said Free.

"Havlick. Clay Havlick?"

"My grandfather."

"Ah! So, what is Clay Havlick's grandson doing with this man who kills?"

Free shot a startled look at Willie before he turned his attention to the old man. "Did you know my grandpa?"

"I was a young man when Clay Havlick's name was a legend among the fur traders and trappers. For many months I shared his camp and his food. I am Dag Bjoerling from Sweden, but Jig I am called." The wrinkles in Jig's face deepened. "Clay Havlick would hurt deep in his heart if he knew you walked the same trail with this one." Jig nodded his head toward Willie.

"He's a man who can make up his own mind," snapped Willie. "He wants money, and I gave him a chance to get it."

"What does Clay Havlick's grandson need of money made the way this one makes it?"

"To become a lumberman," said Free. Jig's piercing look made him uneasy. It was the same look that Grandpa had given him each time he'd told a lie or let fly a swear word.

"What of Clay Havlick's land?" asked Jig, frowning slightly.

Free's hand trembled as he gripped the strap of his back-pack. This was the second man who'd mentioned Grandpa's land. Maybe Pa hadn't told him the truth. "Where is my grandpa's land?" asked Free in a tight voice.

"North and east of here." Jig motioned with his head.

Free felt as if he'd been kicked in the stomach with hobnail boots. Was it possible that Grandpa had left him land instead of money? But wouldn't Pa have told him? Free frowned. Pa wanted to keep him on the farm, so he might've kept the information to himself. "I don't know about any land," said Free, "but I'll check into it."

"George Meeker will pay big for it, Free," said Willie, sounding eager. "We'll make you a fair offer."

"Never!" barked Jig as fire shot from his dark eyes.

"You're as crazy as ever, Jig." Willie brushed his red hair back, then settled his hat in place. "Free, let's get away from him. He don't know his right hand from his left."

"What about the land, Willie?" asked Free.

"He's telling a tall tale," said Willie. "Ain't that right, Jig?"

Jig hunched his shoulders.

"You see, Free?" Willie took a step forward. "Time's a wasting!"

Free started to follow Willie, but Jig stopped him with a look.

"Stay, Clay Havlick's grandson!" Jig turned his eyes on Willie. "Because of Clay Havlick I will let you, Willie Thorne, go on your way. But, Willie Thorne, if you walk where I walk again, I'll fill you with lead." Jig eased back on the hammer but kept the muzzleloader aimed at Willie's heart. "Walk away and don't return."

Willie wiped sweat from his brow. "This is my last season, you old scoundrel, so don't think you're chasing me off."

"Your pride is false pride, Willie Thorne, but claim it if you must to keep from seeing a true image of yourself."

Willie swore under his breath as he walked away. Free nodded to Jig and started after Willie only to have Jig pull him up short again.

"Clay Havlick's grandson will not walk where Willie Thorne walks," said Jig. "You will walk with me."

"But I won't get paid if I don't go with Willie," said Free.

Jig shook his head. "So, what of pay? Can it buy you pride in yourself? Can it meet your heart's cry?" Jig thumped Free's chest and shook his head again. "Clay Havlick's grandson will walk where I walk. He must keep his pride."

Willie called over his shoulder, "Come on, Free. Don't let that crazy old wolf-bait fill you with lies."

Jig squared his broad shoulders. "Jig does not lie."

"Jig, I have to go with Willie," said Free.

"Clay Havlick's grandson cannot choose. He will walk with me. Clay Havlick would want that."

Free could see in the man's eyes that he wouldn't let him follow Willie. "What do you want of me?" Free asked hoarsely.

"You will stay with me for a spell. You will rid yourself of Willie Thorne and his bad ways."

"And if I don't want to?"

"You cannot choose," said Jig in a deadly calm voice. "From this day forward you will not walk where Willie Thorne walks."

"Get a move on, Free," urged Willie. He had stopped about twenty yards away to wait on Free.

Free sighed heavily. He had to go with Jig if for no other reason than to learn what the old man knew about Grandpa's land. "Willie, I'm going with Jig," called Free.

Willie's face darkened with anger. "Don't expect no pay from me or from George Meeker if you don't come with me now."

"I won't," said Free. He hated to lose the money, but he couldn't see a way around it.

"Clay Havlick's grandson does not need money," said Jig.

Willie strode away, muttering angrily to himself.

"Come," said Jig, motioning with his head to Free.

Free walked with him in silence. For the first time in the months since he'd joined up with Willie Thorne, Free felt like his old self, the man Grandpa Clay would've been proud of.

Jig led Free to an Indian trail that was about six inches deeper than the other part of the ground, three feet wide, and covered with pine needles clumped together five in a bundle.

Over an hour later Jig stopped in a clearing near a stream to look in on an old friend, he said. A tiny shack nestled in the giant trees. The Indian trail took up again on the far side of the stream. A smell so bad that Free's stomach turned rose up around the shack.

Jig laughed and slapped Free on the back. "Clay Havlick's grandson gets sick from the smell of my friend Old Windy's work."

"What is it?" asked Free. He wanted to cover his nose and mouth against the smell, but pride kept his hands at his sides.

Jig showed Free the carcasses of freshly skinned animals that lay on the ground near partly gnawed piles of bones. A wolf inside an iron cage bared its teeth. "Old Windy's a trapper. He uses the she wolf as bait to draw he wolves. He kills 'em and skins 'em and gives the animal in the cage the carcasses." Jig jabbed a dirty thumb toward the red-eyed slavering wolf. "Then he sells the pelts and collects ten dollars' bounty on each pair of ears. Keeps him from having to set traps and walk a trap line. It's a far cry from the fur trading Clay Havlick did, but it's a living for an old man." Jig walked to the door of the shack and stuck his head inside. "You here, Windy?"

There was no answer, so Jig closed the door. "Must be he got over the chills. I look in on him regular like until they pass."

"I have to get away from the smell," said Free, fighting against the bile that burned in his mouth.

"Not yet," said Jig as he clamped a gnarled hand on Free's shoulder as they walked away. "You learn this, Clay Havlick's grandson. The sins of man are a stench in God's nostrils. Each man must choose who and what he is. If Willie Thorne and George Meeker gave off smells for what they did, they'd be worse smells than this." Jig tapped Free's arm. "The same smell would cover you if you walked longer with Willie Thorne. Clay Havlick would be ashamed. Sin God hates, but you, Clay Havlick's grandson, God loves."

In the back corners of Free's memory he could hear Grandpa telling him how important it was to walk upright and honest before God and man. During the past few years, he'd been so angry with Pa and so determined to become a lumberman that he'd set aside much of what Grandpa had taught him.

Walking and listening to Jig brought back the longing ache for Grandpa that Free had thought was gone for good. It had been five years since Grandpa had died, five long, lonely years.

Suddenly, without warning, Willie Thorne leaped from behind a tree and with a bloodcurdling yell swung a thick branch at Jig's head. Reacting almost instinctively, Free fell against Jig and knocked him to the ground just in time to escape a bashed-in skull. Free rolled away from Jig and leaped up just as Willie swung the branch at him. Free sprang aside. Willie's face turned red with rage.

"Is this the way you want it, Free?" roared Willie. He stood with his feet apart and his knees bent as he held the branch ready to swing.

Free's eyes locked with Willie's. "Back off, Willie. Go on your way and leave us be."

Willie swung again, barely missing Free's skull. Free jumped at Willie just as he swung again. Free ducked, and

the branch snagged a strand of his hair and jerked it out.
Free heard Jig shout something just as he jumped high and
kicked Willie in the chest with both feet. Willie's breath
whooshed from his lungs and he fell backward in a bed of
pine needles. Free landed with a thud near him, but in the
flash of an eye bounded to his feet and stood over Willie.

"You got him now," said Jig with a low chuckle.

Groaning, Willie moved and opened his eyes. Free stuck
his right foot on Willie's chest and leaned down. He smelled
his own and Willie's sweat and blood.

"Willie, get on to Big Pine and leave us be."

Willie fought for air and finally gasped, "You'll never
work as a timber walker in these parts, Free Havlick. I'll
see to that."

"You, Willie Thorne, will not threaten Clay Havlick's
grandson," said Jig as he pulled the hammer back on his
muzzleloader. The sound sent a chill down Free's spine.

"Don't shoot him, Jig," said Free firmly.

"I will shoot him if he tries again to kill me. Or you."

Free lifted his foot off Willie's chest and stepped back a
few paces. "Get up and be on your way."

Willie pushed himself up and swayed weakly. "I won't
forget this, Havlick."

"See that you don't," said Free gruffly.

Willie glared at them, then turned and stumbled away.

"Willie Thorne is a dangerous enemy," said Jig.

"I'll watch out for him," said Free. He turned to Jig.
"Are you all right?"

"It would take more than Willie Thorne to put me under." Jig chuckled as he straightened his pack. "Come with
me. I have something else to show you."

Much later Jig stopped at the bank of a clear sparkling
stream that rushed over rocks. He pointed across it at a
stand of virgin white pines such as Free hadn't seen before
in all of his days as a woodsman or even in the miles of travel
away from the Grand River and along the Muskegon River

to the shores of Lake Michigan during the summer as a timber walker with Willie.

"See the beauty of it," said Jig just above a whisper.

Free nodded as he looked up, up the rough bark of the tree trunks that had to be at least five feet across, to the dark green pine needles. Just in themselves the trees were magnificent, but calculated to board feet they meant thousands of dollars to the owner.

Jig stepped closer to Free and said softly, "God sees greater beauty when He looks on a man with a pure heart."

Free asked solemnly, "Is there a man with a pure heart? There is no man without sin." It was as close as he could come to admitting that he had not led a pure life and he knew it.

Jig rested his muzzleloader against a tree and dropped his backpack beside it. "When a man asks Jesus to forgive him of his sin, then God looks at that man in all his beauty, a beauty of more value than the timber you see."

Free eased his pack off, then sank to the ground beside Jig to feast his eyes on the timber as he thought about what Jig had said.

"Now, you are free to go, Clay Havlick's grandson."

Free looked deep into the old man's eyes. "I will never go back to work for Willie or for George."

Jig smiled, slowly stood, then waved his arm wide to take in the pines. "All of this is Clay Havlick's land," said Jig.

Free shot to his feet. "Can it be?"

Jig nodded. "Ten sections."

"Ten!" A section was 640 acres. Free saw the fortune in the trees, and his heart beat so hard he was sure Jig could hear it even over the call of the birds and the rushing of the water in the stream.

Had Grandpa left the land to him? If he asked Pa about it, would he tell him the truth? Probably not.

Free jumped across the stream to measure a tree. From what he'd learned from Willie Thorne, Free knew just that one tree would have well over 10,000 board feet. All of them together boggled his mind. "I have to see if this is my land and if these are my trees!" he cried.

Free thought of Grandpa's lawyer, Lem Azack. He'd talk to him and learn the truth just as soon as he could get to Grand Rapids. By river he could make it in a couple of days. His head spun with the fortune that might be his. He turned to call to Jig. But Jig, his pack, and his rifle were gone.

"That's strange," said Free as he looked around for Jig. "Where'd he get to? Jig! Where are you? I need to ask you more about Grandpa."

Free waited several minutes for Jig to return but finally had to admit he wasn't coming back. Free pulled out his compass to find his way to the nearest settlement so that he could hire a boat to take him to Grand Rapids.

In Grand Rapids, Free hesitated as he walked past the newspaper office on the way to the barber. Maybe he should stop in and ask Tunis Bowker what he knew about Grandpa's will. Tunis and Grandpa had been good friends for years. Free scowled. Today he couldn't put up with Tunis trying to get him to understand and be patient with Pa.

Free strode into the barbershop, got a shave, paid for a bath, and changed into a clean tan shirt and dark brown pants, then walked to the courthouse. A muscle jumped in his jaw as he walked down the quiet hall, into Lem Azack's office, and right up to the heavy walnut desk where a big white-haired man in his fifties sat. He wore a dark suit that stretched tight across his shoulders and arms, a white shirt and collar that seemed too tight around his thick neck, and a short black tie.

"I'm Freeman Havlick," said Free, fighting to keep his voice from shaking. "I came to hear about Clay Havlick's will."

"Have a seat," said Lem Azack with a broad smile and a flash of interest in his blue eyes. "I figured you'd be in here sooner or later to see about Clay's will."

Free sat down on the edge of an oak armchair. Blood pounded in his ears.

Lem Azack pulled out Clay's will from an oak file cabinet and scanned it as he sat back down. He found the place that pertained to Freeman, then grinned across the desk at Free. "Here we go. I have it here in legal terms, but I'll just say outright what is yours." Lem Azack cleared his throat and Free grabbed the arms of the chair. "Clay left you fifty thousand dollars, a house here in town, and land."

All the strength flowed from Free's body. Fifty thousand dollars! It was too much to comprehend. A house in town! "Where is the land?" he asked weakly.

"North of Big Pine near the Muskegon River," Lem Azack told him, then showed him on a map that he pulled from a drawer. It was the very place that Jig had showed Free!

"Does Pa know about this?" asked Free, his muscles tighter than the chain wrapped around logs on a skid.

Lem Azack nodded. "Told him just after Clay died."

"That's been five years! And he never told me!" Anger rushed through Free until he thought he'd explode. How dare Pa keep the money and the property from him? "How soon can I get the money and the deed to the property?"

"That could be a problem, Free," said Lem.

"Why?"

"Clay didn't exactly leave the timber to you."

Free leaned forward. "What do you mean?"

"He left it to your wife."

"My wife?" Free snapped.

Lem cleared his throat. "And you can't get the money until you're twenty-five or until you marry, whichever comes first."

Free's jaw tightened. "I'm almost twenty-one! And I have no wife and have no intention of getting one! I need the money now to timber off the land! Isn't there a way around the will?"

Lem shook his white head. "Sorry, Free. Clay wanted you to know your own mind. He didn't want anyone to take advantage of you."

Free shot from his chair and towered over Lem at his desk. "I thought Grandpa cared about me!"

"He loved you, Free. He talked about you often to me."

"Then why did he tie up my money?"

Lem folded his hands over the will. "Clay never realized how important his family was to him until his wife died and his son didn't want anything to do with him. He spent twenty years of his life fur trading. Roman was about your age when Clay finally settled down. He'd missed all those important years with his own son." Lem shook his head, his blue eyes sad. "Clay knew you didn't know the importance of family because of how he was and how Roman is. You told him often enough that you never wanted to marry and have a family. But Clay wanted you to have a wife and children and be a part of their lives. Love them and enjoy them, that's what he said." Lem paused. "When you do have a child, you inherit this section of land here." Lem pointed out several more tracts of timberland north of Big Pine, adjoining the land Jig had showed him.

Free's head spun. He'd wondered why that land hadn't been lumbered off already. It belonged to him! After he married. After he had a child.

"There's no getting around the will, Free," said Lem softly.

Anger churned inside Free. How could Grandpa have done this to him? Free knotted his fists at his sides. "I don't need Grandpa's money or his timberland! I'll make my own money to buy my own timber. I will become a lumberman in any way I can!" He strode from the office with Lem Azack's plea to calm himself ringing in his ears.

CHAPTER
6

♦ Shivering with cold, Jennet bent over Tait's books on her scarred table and carefully printed the amounts coming in and going out for the month of January, 1864. Her back ached from a day spent cleaning and stocking shelves. The old year was gone and a new one was beginning. The days and months since she'd left home had become dark blurs.

Jennet laid aside her pen and suddenly realized just how cold it was. She jumped up and pushed wood that she'd split earlier into the small stove. She yawned as she sat back down to the books. She'd brought them to her room so that she wouldn't have to work in Tait's unheated office. He wouldn't allow her to build a fire in the store's stove after closing time.

It was very late at night, but she had to finish the books before she could go to sleep. Her hair fell in dirty tangles around her shoulders, and her navy blue dress hung on her too-thin body. By the end of her first week with him, Tait had taught her how to keep the books for his three businesses. She'd been doing it on her own for over four months now. If she was late or did something wrong, he whipped her. So, she'd learned to finish on time and to do it right.

Jennet rubbed her eyes and knew she had dark circles under them. Tait had one looking glass in the store, and she used it to fix her hair each morning before he came to work. In that looking glass she'd watched her healthy glow turn to a sickly pallor.

At times Tait was kind to her. At times he even teased her to try to make her laugh. He was a hard worker and an honest businessman, she had to give him that.

At last Jennet closed the book and stood, her hands pressed to the small of her back. Her stomach growled with hunger, but she was too tired to find something to eat. She'd already finished the daily supply of bread and milk that Eve had brought at dawn.

"Wex," she whispered, then frowned. Just when had she taken to talking to Wex? She shrugged. Talking to him sometimes pushed back the terrible loneliness. "Wex, where are you tonight? I am waiting, longing for the day when you'll come for me." She bit her lip and closed her eyes. "Oh, Wex! I will marry you! I will give you all the kisses you want! Just come take me away from here! Will you come tonight? Please!"

Jen opened her bloodshot eyes and looked around the small room that smelled of wood smoke. Wex wouldn't come tonight, just as he hadn't last night or the night before or the night before that.

Every week she'd carefully read the list of casualties that Tait posted beside the front door of the store, holding her breath until she was sure Wex wasn't listed. She didn't know where he was fighting or what regiment he was with. Each time customers talked about the fighting she listened intently as she went about her work.

With a heavy sigh Jennet picked up the books, then lifted the lamp to light her way through the dark store to the cubbyhole Tait called an office. She sat the lamp on his desk and opened the drawer to lay the books inside, then realized she'd opened the wrong drawer. Just as she started to close it, she caught a glimpse of her name in handwriting she recognized. Marie's! Frowning slightly, Jennet gingerly picked up the envelope only to find three others with it. Marie had written to her, and Tait had not given her the letters! All along she'd thought no one from home had remembered her or even cared about her. She'd written letter after letter to them, and when they hadn't answered, she'd thought Pa had refused to let anyone write. But they had written, and Tait had kept the letters from her! Oh, what a cruel, cruel thing to do to her!

Jennet held the letters to her racing heart, then sank to the stool and placed them near the lamp to see them better. They were still sealed! She started to rip one envelope open but stopped short. If she opened them, Tait would know that she'd been in his desk and he'd whip her. She laid the letters back in the drawer. Tears burned her eyes as she stared down at them. She *had* to read them!

Quickly Jennet slipped the books in place, grabbed up the precious letters and the lamp, and carried them to her room before she lost her nerve. Tait wouldn't come back again tonight, not with the wind howling and the snow falling so heavily. He was all settled in his own place.

The silence pressed against her but no longer frightened her as it had the first several weeks after she'd arrived. Jennet was glad for quiet after the hours during the day of listening to customers and Tait, who couldn't find anything good to say about her work. Yet he continued to pile it on. The rage inside her had built until at times she wanted to take one of the guns from the case and shoot him. It was a horrible thought that she knew she'd never act on because Ma had taught her not to harm other people, not in word or in deed. Oh, but she wanted to forget what Ma had said and act on her feelings!

Jennet held Marie's letters, closed her eyes, and tried to

call up the sounds of her sisters in the two-story cabin. Off in the far reaches of her mind she heard them, and gradually the sounds returned until she could almost pretend that she was right there with them, talking and laughing. Even Ma's voice rang out in laughter as she told one of her funny stories. But Ma hadn't laughed or told a funny story since before Baby Vernon was born. She'd been too weak and too sick.

Jennet opened her eyes and kissed the top letter. Her cold hands shook as she carefully broke the seal so that she could reseal it to keep Tait from learning she'd read it. She saw the date: December 10, 1863. She whimpered as she realized the letter had been hidden over a month while the terrible loneliness had grown inside her until she thought she'd lose her mind.

Lovingly she spread out the letter, but before she would allow herself to read it, she opened the others and put them in order according to the dates written in Marie's neat hand. The first one was dated June 25, not long after she'd left. The second one, August 12; the third, October 24; and the last, December 10.

Tears welled up in her eyes and slowly overflowed to slide down her pale cheeks, which once had been rosy red from good health and fresh air. Now, the only time she was outdoors was to chop the wood, carry in the water, or walk to the boarding house for an occasional meal.

Impatiently Jennet brushed away her tears. She must get control of herself and not waste her valuable time crying. Taking a deep, ragged breath she started to read.

> *Dear Jen,*
>
> *It is so strange here without you. Ma is the same. I tried to get her out of bed like you said to do, but she wouldn't budge. The girls don't laugh as much as they once did. Pa never laughs at all. But you already know he hasn't since Baby Vernon died. He never*

*yells at us anymore, and he hasn't lifted a hand to
strike any of us since you rode away with Uncle Tait.
I know Pa is sorry that he let Uncle take you, but he
never says anything about Tait or about you. He
won't let us talk about you or even speak your
name when he's around.*

*I know you're anxious for word of Wex. I did meet
him in the woodlot. He was so upset about you that he
wanted to steal you right away from Uncle, but he
decided he couldn't do that. I told him that I would
write to him. We talked for a few minutes. He was
excited about going to war, but he was scared too. I
tried to make him feel better. He rode away, sad about
you, but excited about the life ahead for him. Roman
was in a rage when he learned that Wex had joined
the fight, and Lillian cried for days. Roman said
Anne can't come to the house because she helped Wex.
That made Lillian feel even worse. When Roman
isn't around, she talks to me about Wex. Finally I
told her about seeing him the day he rode off. Every
chance she gets she begs me to tell her every detail of
our meeting. I feel so sorry for her.*

*I did your chores for a while, but Lillian said she
couldn't get along without me up at the house, so
Roman hired a boy named Tim to do them. He sleeps
and has his meals up at the main house. He's nice.
You'd like him. Roman tried to take his belt to him
once for spilling a pail of milk, and Tim said he'd
walk out if Roman even dared touch him. I was
surprised, but Roman backed right down. Sometimes
I wonder if he's sorry for being so hard on his boys.
And on you. He won't ever talk about you or Wex or
Free. He looks older every time I see him. And he's
sad. He works himself even harder than he did before.
I'd feel sorry for him if it wasn't partly his fault for
your being gone.*

It's different here without you and Wex.
I miss you a lot and so do the girls. I hope Uncle
is treating you well.

Your loving sister Marie

Jennet read the letter again. Would Ma ever get better? If she did, what would she do when she realized Pa had indentured her to Tait?

Pa! Oh, but she hated him! She hoped he never laughed again as long as he lived. He and Roman could work themselves into the ground for all she cared.

Wex had wanted to steal her away from Tait! "Oh, Wex, why didn't you?" she whispered hoarsely.

Finally she put the letter aside and read the next one dated August 12.

My dear sister Jen,
I have heard twice from Wex. He is in Tennessee.
He says it's very different there. He almost killed a
Confederate. He said he was glad he missed. He
wants to come home, but he won't. He asked about
you. I told him I haven't heard from you. Oh, Jen,
when will you write? We long for word from you!
Ma has come to the table twice in the past week.
She even let me wash and brush her hair. She held
Evie for a while, then went right back to her bed. She
won't go look at the gravestone Pa bought for Baby
Vernon. That big, fancy angel cost a lot of money.
The little girls say the angel is watching over Baby
Vernon. I wonder if that's true.
Pa has really taken to the hired boy Tim. He makes
Pa smile and that sure helps around here. Pa usually
walks around with a sad face. I learned that Tim is
fourteen and has no family. Pa brings him home for
supper most nights. The girls love Tim. He always
teases them and tells them great stories. He gives

*Evie, Ida, and Lois piggyback rides and they like
that. Opal wishes she wasn't already ten and too big
for a ride. But Tim takes time for her in other ways.
Nola and I have been teaching him to read and write.
He's slow, but he is learning. In the winter we'll have
more time to teach him.*

*Why haven't you written, Jen? Won't Uncle even let
you write home? I asked Pa, but he got so angry that
I never asked him again.*

*I have grown so much that I'm as tall as you by
now. Unless you grew more, that is. Did you? I miss
you, Jen! Please, please write!*

> *Your loving sister Marie*

Jennet groaned. She had written a letter a week, and Tait
had said he'd send them. Had he hidden them away somewhere in the store? Or had they gotten lost between Prickett and home? She'd hunt around his office and the store for
them.

She read the letter again, savoring every word as she
pictured Marie talking right to her.

Jennet laid the letter on top of the first one and picked up
the one dated October 24.

Dear Jen,

*Pa said he was going to town, so he said for me
to write a quick note for him to mail. That sure
surprised me because he still won't let us talk
about you when he can hear.*

*Pa wanted you to know that Ma is better at last.
She talked to all of us today. She even walked out to
see Baby Vernon's gravestone. Jen, it made me cry to
see her kneeling at his grave, tears pouring down her
cheeks. When she came inside, she asked about you
and Pa said that you'd agreed to go help Uncle Tait,
but he didn't tell her that you're indentured to Uncle*

*for three years to pay off his debt. He doesn't think we
know, but we all do. I told the girls not to tell Ma
because it might make her sick again. When she is
well, I'll tell her and maybe she'll make Pa get you
back from Uncle.*

*I got another letter from Wex. He killed three boys
and he said he cried when he did, but he had to kill
them before they killed him. I cried, too, knowing how
much it hurt Wex to take a life. He wants to come
home. He said it's better to be home, even though his
pa beats him, than to be there. He never has enough
to eat, and he has to share a blanket with another
boy. It hurts me to think of him being cold and
hungry. I write to him every day.*

*Why don't you write, Jen? Are you angry? Please,
please, please write!*

Marie

Moaning, Jennet touched the letter and rocked back and
forth, back and forth. Pa had told Marie to write to her!

She knotted her fist beside the letter. It was way too late
for him to be sorry!

As she read the letter again, jealousy stabbed her when
she reached the part about Wex writing to Marie and her
writing back. "Wex, did you ever write to me? Do you remember that you want to marry me? Do you remember you
said you loved me? I think of your words all the time and it
keeps me going."

Finally Jennet picked up the last letter dated December 10.

Dear sister Jen,

*Christmas is coming soon and we want you home.
Pa says there's no way for you to come home, but Ma
told him to find a way. I wish he could!*

Ma has some bad days, but most of the time she's

*all right. She is too thin and we've been trying to get
her to eat more. She gets tired when she does even a
little work. She sure does like Tim. I think it helps
her forget about Baby Vernon to have Tim around. He
loves Ma a lot. I think he pretends that she's his ma.*

*In three days Nola will be twelve. She looks very
grown up, and she says she's in love with Tim and
will marry him as soon as Pa will let her. I think
Tim likes her too. He treats her special. It sounds
funny to have Nola talk about getting married.*

*Did you think of me on my birthday last month? I
am thirteen as you know. Wex sent me red and yellow
ribbons for my hair. Pa let the girls bake me a cake.
It was a fine birthday, but I wanted you here to share
it.*

*Wex says he can't wait to come home to see me. I
can't wait to see him either. He says there is a chance
he'll come home in the summer. I hope he can.*

*Pa says the war is going to last a whole lot longer
than anybody thinks because of those men in the
White House. I heard him tell Ma about some
runaway slaves that he helped hide on their way
to Canada. I didn't know Pa would do that,
but I'm glad he did.*

*I miss you, Jen. Why don't you ever write? Please
don't be so mad at Pa that you forget about the rest of
us. If you can't come home for Christmas, Merry
Christmas from all of your family!*

> *Your sister Marie*

Jennet covered her face with hands now blue with cold
and cried because Nola was big enough to talk about marrying Tim, Wex had bought Marie ribbons for her birthday,
Ma was better, and Pa had helped free slaves even while
she was a slave to Tait. She cried because on Christmas
Day she'd worked just as hard as any other day only there

hadn't been customers. She'd worked the whole day doing
bookwork, cleaning, and stocking shelves without seeing
anyone or talking to anyone. Finally she'd pretended Wex
came to see her, and she'd talked to him about their wedding and about how happy they'd be. Tait hadn't given her
money to eat at the boarding house, so she'd eaten food
that she'd heated on the stove. Eve wasn't able to get away
from home and bring her even bread and milk. That night
Jennet had cried herself to sleep.

After a while Jennet read each letter again, then
smoothed them lovingly as if she was rubbing Ma's cheek.

Oh, she couldn't part with the letters! But she couldn't
keep them or Tait would know. What could she do?

Suddenly she jumped up. "I'll copy them!" Her words
rang across the room, startling her. She ran to Tait's office
to find paper that he wouldn't notice was missing, and in a
careful hand she copied each letter so that she'd be able to
read them anytime she wanted to. She tucked them inside
her pillowcase where they'd be safe from Tait's prying
eyes. Then she carefully resealed Marie's letters and stuck
them back in Tait's drawer. She searched for the letters
that she'd written home but couldn't find them. Maybe Tait
had burned them, or maybe he'd taken them to his house.

Anger rushed through Jennet. She wanted to tell Tait that
she knew about the letters, but she knew she'd never dare
tell him or show her anger.

Jen went back to her room, got ready for bed, blew out
her lamp, and sank exhausted to her cot. The crinkle of the
letters comforted her aching heart. Somehow she'd find a
way to send a letter to her family without Tait's learning
about it. Sighing heavily, she closed her eyes and fell into a
deep, deep sleep.

The next morning she was awakened by a knock at her
door. She peeked out to see that Eve was standing in the
snow with the basket she brought each morning. She was
shivering even with her big coat on. Snow covered the roof

of the barn and the outhouse. Jennet threw open the door and Eve stepped inside, bringing icy air with her. Chunks of snow from her booted feet dropped onto the floor.

"I overslept, Eve!" cried Jennet.

"Are you sick? You look pale, and there are dark rings under your eyes."

Jennet wanted to tell Eve about Marie's letters, but she couldn't take the chance. "I'm fine, Eve," she said as she shook the grate in the old potbellied stove and quickly started the fire.

"I had to circle around to get here so Tait wouldn't see where my footprints led."

"Oh, but you take too much of a chance!"

Eve smiled and shook her head. "Did you learn another Scripture to tell me?"

"No. I'm sorry." In the past few months Jennet had read the Bible Eve had given her, then quoted a Scripture to Eve each morning and helped her memorize it. "I'll have one for you tomorrow."

"Thank you. I must hurry back," said Eve as she quickly unloaded her basket and walked to the door. "I, too, am late this morning. But I could not leave you without food."

"Thank you!" Jennet hugged Eve close and kissed her cold cheek. "Tomorrow I'll walk to your house to get the food."

"No! Tait might see you, and he would beat us both."

Jennet signed heavily. "Why do you stay with him?"

"He is my husband."

"And I am his slave," Jennet added. "We both are, it seems. If I could, I'd take you and run away."

"That is foolish talk, Jen."

Jennet kissed Eve good-bye, then quickly dressed in a warm dark green dress with black piping around the collar and the cuffs and down the front to the waist.

Later just as Jennet unlocked the front door of the store she saw Tait coming up the snow-covered walk toward her.

She thought of the letters he'd hidden from her. How she hated him!

Forcing her hands to stay steady, Jennet twisted her uncombed hair into a bun and quickly pinned it in place before Tait stepped through the door. "Good morning, Jen," he said, sounding cheerful for once.

"Good morning, Uncle." She wanted to spit in his face, but she kept her voice pleasant so that he wouldn't slap her for being sassy or rude.

"I'm going to Grand Rapids today."

Jen bit her lip to keep from begging to go along with him to see her family.

"I just might go see your pa and tell him how you're getting along."

Words welled up inside her, but Jennet forced them back. Maybe if she acted like she wasn't interested, he might take her along. "Have a pleasant trip," she said, almost choking on her politeness.

"Do you have a message for them?" he asked, eyeing her carefully as he stroked his beard.

Her heart raced and she lifted her chin a fraction. "Give them my love." *But not Pa! Tell him I will never love him and never forgive him!*

Tait laughed and slapped his leg. "And I'll tell them I made you into a fine woman with good manners." He looked around the store. "Where's the heat?"

"It's taking a little longer to warm up in here."

"Shake down the ashes and fix the fire," Tait said with a scowl.

Jen hurried to the black cast-iron stove, shook down the ashes with the shaker handle, and opened the door. Flames licked up the sides of the stove as she pushed a few chunks of wood inside. She didn't dare tell Uncle that she'd been late starting the fire. He liked it warm when he came so he could stand with his back close to it while he gave her orders for the day.

Tait hung his coat and hat on the hooks just inside his office, then walked to stand with his back to the stove. "I'm going with Rusty Zimmer on his sleigh. He figures with his team and sleigh he can make it through the snow. If Pete Stillman comes in while I'm gone, you tell him to pay his bill. Don't give him more credit till he does."

Jennet nodded.

"I have money in my desk. Get it for me."

Jen started toward his office, but he stopped her.

"Never mind. I'll get it myself."

Jennet knew he remembered the letters and knew she'd see them. He'd forbidden her even to open the desk drawers except for the one holding the books. Why hadn't he burned her letters? Did he have a conscience after all? If he did, he kept it well hidden.

After telling her a list of things to do and things to remember, Tait checked over the books. Finally, he closed them and pushed them back in place. "I'll be gone three—maybe four—days. You keep things going while I'm away and don't try to pull a fast one on me. If the men come in from the lumbercamp, you see that they pay with cash. No credit. None!"

Jennet nodded, immediately feeling her spirit lift. Three or four days without him! What wonderful freedom! It almost made staying behind worthwhile.

Just then the front door opened and a man named Kelso walked in. He was short and squat and wore a heavy bearskin coat that reached below his knees. He pulled off his bearskin cap, revealing a shiny bald pink head, and stopped in front of Tait near the counter. Kelso shook his thick finger at Tait and roared, "I tell you it was John Morgan that kilt the most people when he cut a sweep through Kentucky, Indiana, and Ohio with about 2,500 mounted cavalry."

Jennet rolled her eyes. The arguments about the war between Kelso and Tait were a daily ritual.

Before Tait could speak, Kelso bellowed, "It could be

that one of these days some of them raiders will make it right up here to Michigan." Kelso brought his fist down hard on the counter. "Lee's army is boasting about moving north to fight on northern soil!"

Jennet shivered at the horrifying thought as she picked up a man's work shirt and refolded it.

"Idle threat!" cried Tait, his beard moving in agitation.

"So you say," muttered Kelso.

"I read about William Quantrill again in last week's paper. He's an ugly son-of-a-gun!" barked Tait as he tugged at his beard. "He killed folks in Kansas and Missouri like they was flies!"

A shirt clutched to her chest, Jennet bit back a cry of alarm. Was Wex near Kansas or Missouri?

"You'd think all them Michigan boys that went to fight would make a difference," said Kelso.

"Maybe you and me should go show 'em how to fight." Tait laughed and slapped Kelso's thick shoulder.

Jennet didn't think the war was anything to joke about, but she kept her thoughts to herself, as usual.

"I'm ready to sign up when you are!" Kelso tipped back his shiny pink head and laughed hard.

"I'm in a hurry, Kelso, so you be on your way now. Talk to me when I get back."

Kelso tugged his bearskin hat down over his head and walked out the door without another word.

Tait pulled on his coat and cap and strode out into the brisk winter morning toward the mill. Jennett longed to call after him to take her along, but she clamped her hand over her mouth to keep back the words. If he did take her along to see her family, it would be too painful to leave them again.

About an hour later Jennet stood in the doorway and watched Tait ride away with Rusty Zimmer in a sleigh pulled by two powerful chestnut draft horses. Their harnesses jangled and bells on the harnesses jingled.

Jennet closed the door against a fierce blast of icy air. She suddenly felt as light as a feather on the duster she used daily. Tait was gone! A smile tried to break through, but it faded before it reached her lips.

All day she worked as if Tait was there, but after she closed the store in the evening, she slipped on a heavy coat and hat and walked out the back door and through the trees to Tait's house to see Eve. The bitter cold had reddened Jennet's pale face by the time she reached the front gate.

Tait lived in a one-story white frame house with a white wooden fence around it. A barn and an outhouse were in back. Two tall pines stood in the front yard and several behind the house on the far side of the fence.

Jennet knocked on the door and finally it opened a crack. "It's me, Eve," said Jennet softly.

"Jen! Come in!" Eve opened the door wider, smiling in surprise and happiness. "Tait said not to let anyone in while he was gone. But you, I let in."

Jennet stepped into the cozy room and stood beside the mirrored hall tree, which held coats, umbrellas, and boots. A fire crackled in the stone fireplace, sending a glow over the brick hearth and onto the maple rocking chair next to it. A horsehair couch sat against a wall between two windows covered with ruffled muslin curtains with the kitchen area beyond that. Jennet smiled at Eve. For the first time since fall had turned into winter she saw Eve without a coat. "Eve, I didn't realize you were this close to having your baby," said Jennet.

Eve smiled and nodded. "He will be born tonight."

"Tonight?" cried Jennet in alarm.

"Yes. But don't be frightened. I'm not. I've helped many women birth their babies. And the pain is not too bad."

"What a terrible day for Tait to be gone!"

"No." Eve closed her eyes for a minute and pressed her hand to her stomach. Finally she smiled again. "It will be soon. That is why Tait went away. He was very angry to learn about the baby. When I told him this was the day for the birth, he found a way to be gone. But I'm glad!" Eve sucked in air and closed her eyes tightly again. When she opened her eyes, she said, "If you don't want to witness the birth, leave now."

"No! You shouldn't be alone!" Jennet hung her coat on a hook on the hall tree and dropped her hat on the seat. She could tell that Eve's pains were very close together. "I've been around birthing of Ma's babies and the animals on the farm. I'll stay."

In the kitchen area Eve perched on the edge of a chair at the table and waved for Jennet to sit down. "I can do this alone, but I am happy you are here with me. Did you bring a Scripture for me?"

"Yes. I wrote it out for you." Jennet hurried to her coat and pulled the paper out of her pocket. She'd written the Scripture for Eve to help her when Tait was mean to her, but now it seemed to suit even better. "Psalm 32:7. You are my hiding place; You shall preserve me from trouble; You shall surround me with songs of deliverance."

Between the obvious labor pains, Eve repeated it after Jennet. Right in the middle of saying the verse alone Eve stopped and gasped. "The baby is coming now," she said softly.

Jennet waited for her to go to the bedroom and give birth on the bed the way Ma always had, but Eve went to a spot in the kitchen where she'd fixed a special pallet of blankets with a white muslin sheet over them. She pulled off her dress and slipped on a gown. She squatted near the pallet, and with low groans and a mighty push she delivered the baby on the pallet.

"I'll cut the cord," said Jennet as she looked at the dark baby lying on the blood-and-water-covered sheet.

"I will do it," said Eve. Without Jennet's help Eve cut and tied the umbilical cord. "It is a boy," said Eve proudly.

She lifted the baby by his tiny feet and held him upside down. He gasped and cried, then cried louder. Eve held him out to Jennet.

"He sounds healthy," said Jennet as she wrapped a soft blanket around him. "You take him while I clean up the afterbirth."

"I will do it," said Eve. "You take care of the baby."

Jennet held the baby close to her heart while Eve cleaned up the afterbirth and dropped the pallet in a tub of cold water, then took care of herself.

"You lie down while I bathe him," said Jennet.

"Yes, I will rest now," said Eve, smiling. "You bathe him. I am tired."

Jennet looked at the tiny red-faced baby who was part of Tait. For just a minute hatred rose in her but just as quickly vanished as the baby squirmed in her arms.

Several minutes later Jennet sat at the edge of the bed while Eve cuddled the baby to her breast.

"His name is Joshua, and he will be a man full of God's strength and love."

"What about Tait?" asked Jennet hesitantly.

Eve's face hardened. "If Tait raises a hand to beat Joshua, I will leave him. That I promise myself and my baby."

Jennet nodded. She knew Eve didn't mean a spanking to discipline, but the kind of beating that Tait gave her. "I'll help you leave," said Jennet as a solemn vow. She would do all in her power to keep the baby safe from Tait, but maybe he'd look at Joshua and love him like he'd never loved anyone before, like Pa had Baby Vernon.

Jennet glanced around the small bedroom at the bed, chest of drawers, commode, and looking glass made of oak. The headboard of the bed was hand carved with swirls and leaves and acorns. She looked back at Eve to find that she and the baby had fallen asleep.

Jennet went back to the kitchen, fixed the fire, and banked it for the night. She found a bright block-work quilt and feather pillow in a chest beside the bedroom door and curled up on the horsehair couch and fell asleep.

CHAPTER

7

♦ Jennet carefully wrote June 11, 1864, on Tait's books, then gasped. Tomorrow would be her sixteenth birthday! Almost a whole year had passed since she'd been indentured to Tait. How could that be? But she knew how it had happened. She'd worked long, hard hours without a letup, and time had slipped away before she had even known it. Months had passed since Tait had whipped her. He was happy to think he'd turned her into the type of woman she should be, hardworking, submissive, and silent.

Jennet thought of the stolen moments with Eve and Joshua, and she smiled grimly. A couple of times she'd slipped off into the very edge of the woods just to absorb the serenity there. Tait would be surprised to find that a different kind of woman was developing behind that submissive facade. She did whatever she wanted after store hours.

The warm afternoon breeze blew in the open door of the store, bringing with it the smell of the river and the dust from the mill. Men's voices floated in from across the street at the dock. Jen heard Tait's voice above the others, and she peeked through the window to see who was making him angry. A trapper walked past the window and blocked her view. Quickly she turned back to her work to finish it before Tait returned.

When Tait walked in with a man following, Jennet pushed the finished work in the drawer and closed it. She touched her braids, which had fallen over her shoulders, and brushed dust from her gray summer dress. She walked to the counter in case Tait wanted her to wait on the customer. Jen glanced past Tait to the man behind him.

Her heart jerked to a stop, then leaped into life, hammering so hard against her rib cage that it hurt. The man was Freeman Havlick! Instead of the leather shirt and pants that he'd worn the last time she'd seen him, he wore a lightweight gray shirt buttoned to his chin and tucked inside heavy blue trousers. His face was clean shaven, and a hat covered his dark hair and shaded his brown eyes.

Jennet sagged weakly against the counter, her icy hands limp at her sides. Freeman Havlick stood only a few feet from her! But maybe it was her imagination since she desperately wanted to be rescued from Tait.

When Freeman saw the woman behind the counter, he frowned slightly at the intensity of her stare, then his eyes widened in shock. Could the thin, pale woman be Jen? But what would she be doing here? This woman looked much too old and tired to be the farm girl he knew with flushed rosy cheeks and flashing blue eyes. But it was Jen! Had she run away when Wex went off to fight?

Jennet wanted to cry out to Free, but her voice was locked behind the tightness in her throat. Finally he pulled his gaze away from her without saying a word to her.

Turning to speak to the man who'd brought the canoeload of supplies, Tait scowled at the way he and Jennet were staring at each other. Tait didn't want to lose Jen to any man who took a shine to her. He needed her at the store, and he wasn't about to see her marry and leave him. He shot a look at Jennet and said sternly, "Get on back to your room."

Jennet hesitated, not wanting to leave in case Free vanished, but crept away before Tait could snap at her again. She wanted to beg Free to take her with him, but she slipped inside her room and left the door open so she could hear them.

"Who is she?" asked Free, looking past the cold potbellied stove toward the open door.

Tait knew he couldn't be too rude to the man. He owed him money and right now cash money was tight. "Jen Cordell. My niece. She works for me."

"Cordell." With a great effort Free kept his anger hidden from Tait. "Her pa, Vernon Cordell, works for Roman Havlick."

Tait lifted his brows in surprise. "You're right. You know them?"

Freeman nodded, but he didn't want to go into his private life with this man he'd instantly disliked. Tait knew him only as Free. He'd been forced to take on different kinds of jobs, the latest being to sell supplies along the river to any business that would buy them. He'd brought a load of supplies to Prickett to earn more cash on his way to an area where he was checking on a job as a timber walker. So far Willie Thorne had made sure no one hired him as a cruiser, but he kept trying. Not everyone could be influenced by Willie Thorne. Free pushed his hat to the back of his head. He glanced toward the door Jen had walked through, then back at Tait. Free wanted to call Jen out to talk to her, to make sure she was all right, but he didn't have time for her or her problems. He shrugged impatiently. "It's getting late. I'll take my money and head out."

Tait cleared his throat and pulled at his thick beard. "Thing is, Free, you caught me at a low time. Short of cash money."

Free's response was curt. "Then I'll take the supplies and sell them to someone who has money." He turned to go.

"Just hold on." Tait couldn't let Free leave. He needed the supplies. He strode toward the back of the store and barked, "Jen, get out here now!"

Jennet took a deep breath and walked on unsteady legs through the connecting door. Oh, she hated for Free to see her looking so haggard and old!

Free saw her whipped dog look and balled his fists at his sides. Tait was probably as quick to beat her as her pa had been.

Jennet didn't look at Free but kept a wary eye on Tait. "Yes, Uncle."

"You get them books figured?"

"Yes." Jennet heard Free move, but still she couldn't look at him.

"And?"

Jennet hesitated. She knew he wanted her to tell him that the books were wrong and that they did have money coming in soon. "The same," she whispered.

Free could feel the fury building in Tait and see the fear on Jennet's face. Free took a step toward Jennet but stopped. This was not his affair.

Tait glared at Jennet, and she shrank back. Anger shot through Free as he watched Jennet cringe away from Tait. From the look of him the uncle might be worse than Jen's pa.

Tait stepped toward Jennet, his fists doubled. He needed the blankets and clothing and the stock of food that Free had brought. Finally he turned back to Freeman. "You'll get your money, but not today. Come back in a couple of weeks."

Freeman needed his money now. "I can't wait. I'll take the stuff to Deerhop. Gene Littleton will pay cash for it." He started for the door, and Jennet's heart sank to her toes.

"I'll trade for the stuff," said Tait, sounding desperate.

Free turned and eyed Tait. "Trade what?"

Tait thought fast. What would Gene Littleton be short of that he had? "I need what you brought and could be Littleton needs things that I got." Tait looked around, his head spinning. "Jen, name off some things that Littleton could use."

Jennet looked helplessly at Tait. Her mind wouldn't function with Free looking as if he'd walk out and leave her behind. "Traps? Tools?"

Without warning Tait slapped her hard across the face and the sound rang through the room.

Jennet fell back against the counter, her hand at her burning cheek.

Freeman leaped forward and caught Tait's arm before he could strike Jennet again. Free forced himself to hold Tait's arm steady and not jerk it back and up to break it. "You got no cause to hit her," said Free in a voice he managed to keep dead calm.

Jennet stared at Free, remembering the other times he'd rescued her. A glimmer of hope flickered inside her.

"She's my business," snapped Tait. "Indentured to me. I can do what I please with her."

Fire shot from Freeman's dark eyes. Indentured! "Just how much money is owing?"

"None of your concern." Tait gave each word equal emphasis.

Jennet eased away from Tait until she was out of his reach. She wanted to hide in her room, but she couldn't bear the thought of being away from Free.

"I'm making it my concern," said Free in a cold, hard voice. Suddenly seeing to Jen was more important than making money. The thought surprised him. "How much time does she have left?"

"Two more years," said Tait gruffly.

Hearing that Jennet was supposed to be with the quick-tempered store-owner for two more years turned Freeman's blood cold. How had Wex let her get in such a fix?

Free's mind whirred with ideas, but he knew only one would work. "You take your supplies, Tait, and I'll take the girl."

Jennet gasped, her hand to her heart. Maybe she'd be home soon where she could wait for Wex to be discharged from the army, then they could be married.

Tait shook his head. He knew he couldn't get along without Jen. She worked harder than any man he'd ever had, harder even than he himself worked. "She's not for trade," said Tait sharply.

"Then I'm off," said Freeman. He walked toward the door, his back straight. He'd learned how to read a man, and he was sure he'd read Tait correctly.

Jennet's breast rose and fell as if she'd run ten miles without stopping. Blood pounded in her ears, and she had a sick taste in her mouth. Would Free just walk away without her?

"Wait!" cried Tait.

Freeman turned slowly, his brow cocked.

Jennet bit her bottom lip. Free wouldn't leave her after all. She could see that Tait had more than met his match.

"Leave the supplies and come back in one week, and I'll pay you," said Tait desperately.

Freeman turned and walked out the door.

Jennett sagged weakly against the counter. Freedom had been so close!

On the board sidewalk outside Tait's store the warm wind blew against Free, who listened for Tait's next move. Free's stomach knotted, and for a minute he wondered if Tait would let him walk away. He knew he couldn't leave Jen, no matter what Tait did.

Feeling defeated, Tait ran after Free. "Bring in the supplies."

Free said, "You'll trade?"

Tait nodded. "I can always get Old Gabe to help me a while."

Her nerves as tight as a snagged fishline, Jennet stood in the doorway of the store. Her legs trembled, and she almost dropped in a heap to the floor she'd kept swept and scrubbed every day for the past year.

Free glanced at Jennet. Hopeful anticipation shone in her wide blue eyes. The desire to help her grew even stronger, and Free turned back to Tait. "Sign her over to me and I'll unload the boat."

Tait reentered the store and stormed toward his office. As Jennet ducked out of his way, she saw a pleased look cross Free's face before he masked it.

Free followed Tait inside and waited near the front counter. He stood there wondering what he would do with Jen. He couldn't send her home to be overworked by his pa and beaten by her pa. Wex was still off fighting the war. And he couldn't leave her with Anne even if she'd agree to it. With Anne's work in the underground railroad anyone near her would be in grave danger.

Tait struggled with the hard spot he was in. Finally he grabbed Jennet's paper from a drawer in his desk and signed her over to Free. Then Tait walked to the counter and told Free, "You're making a bad deal."

Free looked over the paper and tucked it inside his shirt. "Get your things, Jen," Free said to her without taking his eyes off Tait.

Jennet could hardly believe what was happening. Her life was taking yet another turn. But this time it was for the better. This time she'd be happy.

Jennet darted a look at Tait, saw his rage, then sped to her room. With jerky movements she gathered up the letters from Marie, the Bible Eve had given her, and her few clothes.

Eve! How could she leave Eve and Joshua without saying good-bye? She couldn't leave a note because Eve couldn't read. Would she dare ask Free to let her see Eve one last time?

Jen peeked out to see Free and Tait unloading the supplies. Taking a deep breath, she crept out the back door and raced to Tait's house. She burst in without knocking and found Eve washing the noon meal dishes.

"What is wrong?" asked Eve in alarm as she grabbed a towel for her hands.

"I'm leaving," said Jennet, rubbing her sleeve over her sweaty face. "Right now!" In as few words as possible she told Eve what had transpired. She hugged Eve close. "I hope to see you and Joshua again someday. I will never forget your kindness to me."

"I will never forget your love and your help," said Eve as tears welled up in her eyes. She kissed Jennet, then scooped up Joshua from his cradle, and thrust him into Jennet's arms.

Jennet held him close and kissed his flushed cheeks. His dark eyes sparkled, and he plucked at her hair with his fat little fist. Reluctantly she held him out to Eve.

"Go with God," whispered Eve.

"Good-bye," said Jennet around the lump in her throat. She hugged Eve one last time, then ran out the door, past the tall pines, and along the path to the store.

A few minutes later she stood beside the canoe while Free and Tait finished unloading the supplies. She watched Free's shirt tighten against the muscles in his arms as he worked. She was afraid to take her eyes off him in case he vanished in a puff of her imagination.

Once the men had cleared the canoe, Tait stopped in front of Jennet, his dark eyes narrowed, and shook his finger at her. "Your pa will hear about this, Jen," said Tait menacingly.

Before Jennet could say a word, Freeman replied, "The debt her pa owed you is paid. The girl is mine now. You tell her pa that."

Tait glared at Free. "Just what do you plan to do with her?"

"She's my property now, and I don't have to answer to you!" Free dropped Jennet's bundle in the canoe, then turned to Jennet.

Jennet froze. His property? What did he mean?

Free felt Jennet's hesitation, and he frowned. Didn't she want to leave with him after all? He held his hand out to her, and she immediately slipped her hand in his. A tingle ran over him from her touch. He handed her into the canoe, waited until she sat on the middle seat, then he took his place. Quickly he lifted the paddle and pushed away from the dock.

Freeman didn't speak until they were out of sight of the Prickett landing. Instead of heading toward Deerhop he turned toward Grand Rapids. He saw the droop of Jennet's shoulders. Just what was he going to do with her? "Are you all right?" he asked.

Jennet shrugged slightly. She wanted to ask Free what he meant when he'd said she belonged to him now, but she couldn't force the words out.

"Did you want to stay with him?"

Jennet shook her head hard enough to make her braids flip, but she didn't speak. She watched a duck fly up from the water and disappear in the bright summer sky. The fishy smell of the river and a faint smell of smoke from the chimney of a cabin nestled in the trees near the riverbank filled her nostrils.

Free frowned out across the water as he paddled along the shaded side of the river. When he'd left Grand Rapids this morning at dawn, he'd expected to return with money in his pocket. He needed it to add to his nest egg so he could pay for the tract of timber he was buying. What would he do now? Suddenly he thought of Grandpa's will. Freeman felt as if he'd been kicked in the stomach by a river hog's hobnail boots. If he married, he'd inherit money enough to buy many tracts of land. He could marry Jen. But should he marry her? What of Wex? The last Free had heard, Wex had planned to marry her.

Jennet felt Free's eyes on her back. He seemed different than the times she'd talked with him while he still lived at home.

His head spinning, Free watched a great blue heron fly away from the river. He focused his attention on the water and where he was going. If he paddled too close to shore, he knew he'd hit a snag. Almost against his will he looked at Jennet again. Here was his chance to become a big lumber baron. Why should he consider Wexal's feelings? Or Jennet's?

Jen sat quietly as he paddled down the Grand River. They rode past a landing where boys were fishing. The boys waved and shouted, and Free waved back. Jennet managed to lift her hand. What did Free expect of her?

Just before dark Free paddled past the Grand Rapids dock where a row of fishing boats, steamships, a dugout canoe, and a few birchbark canoes were tied up. Men talked and laughed and shouted to one another as they unloaded a huge steamship. Horse-drawn buggies, drays, and carts rolled along the sawdust-covered street beside the dock. A group of rowdy barefoot boys ran past, shouting and laughing.

Jennet watched Free tie the canoe to a tree at a landing near the livery. Her mind was a jumble of thoughts. *Will he just leave me stranded in Grand Rapids? If he does, I can walk home in the morning even though it will take hours. What will Pa say if I suddenly turn up?* Now that Ma was better she might be able to convince Pa to keep her. It had been almost five months since she'd gotten a letter from Marie. And still Marie begged to hear from her, so somehow the letters that she'd sneaked past Tait hadn't reached home.

What if Free planned to keep her to work off her two years? Just what was he going to do with her? He'd saved her life. Surely he wouldn't harm her. Maybe he would let her go home. She'd wait for Wex and then they'd get married. She bit back a sigh, then, her legs trembling, she stepped to the sandy ground.

Freeman took Jennet's bundle from her and his hand brushed hers, sending sparks through him. Could he tell her his plan?

"I don't know if Pa will pay for me," said Jennet with a catch in her voice.

Her pa? How could she want to return to him after the way he'd treated her? "I won't give him a chance," replied Free evenly.

Jennet bit her bottom lip as she followed Free up the hill to the livery. Horses nickered in a wooden pen outside the building. A wagon drawn by draft horses rumbled past, leaving a cloud of dust behind it. The smell of the river below and the horses manure from the livery above mingled in the air. Jennet waited to speak until she reached the top of the hill. "I don't have any money. I can't pay you," she said weakly.

Free couldn't look at her in case the agony in her blue eyes made him change his mind. He watched a coon dog settle down on the porch of the old blue frame house beside the livery. "You can," he said gruffly.

Her stomach knotted. "How?"

His mouth was so dry that it was hard to speak. He gripped her bundle tighter. "Marry me."

Jennet stopped short and stared at him. Had she heard him right? "What?" she whispered in alarm, her eyes wide in her ashen face.

Free looked into her eyes and almost lost his nerve "Marry me."

"Do you want to marry me?" she asked in surprise.

"No! I don't *want* to marry you. But I need a wife."

She touched the hankie near her heart. "What of Wex?"

"What of him?" Free looked angrily away from her just as a rider stopped outside the livery door and called to the owner. Free looked back down at Jennet. "Wex didn't do anything to help you. He's off fighting to free slaves and left you just as bad off as a slave!"

"I promised I'd wait for him," whispered Jennet.

"It's a promise you'll have to break," snapped Free.

"Don't make me," she whispered as she pressed her hands to her cheeks and stared at him fearfully.

"Don't look at me like that!"

"How can you force me to marry you?"

Yes, how could he? He looked away from her and said bluntly, "I need a wife."

Freeman walked her toward a clump of maple trees where they could have privacy and told her quickly about his grandfather's will. "I'd give you a place to live."

"I can't," Jennet whispered hoarsely.

Freeman's stomach knotted. Was his dream going to slip through his fingers again? In frustration he pulled the paper from his shirt front and shook it at her. "This paper says you belong to me. You marry me, or I'll take you straight back to your uncle."

The look of horror on her face tore at his heart, but Free clamped his mouth shut and waited for her to give in.

Jennet groaned, but what little fight was left in her vanished when she saw the set of Free's jaw and the anger on his face. She didn't have the energy or strength to fight him. Besides, he owned her.

At last Jennet tipped her head in agreement.

"I won't ever beat you," Free told her.

"Does it matter?" A tear spilled down her cheek, and she let it drop to the sandy ground.

"We'll get married and see Grandpa's lawyer and get it settled this night."

Jen backed away from him, stumbled, and he caught her arm to steady her, then quickly released her.

"We'll hire a buggy and be on our way."

Jennet couldn't move.

"Let's go!" Free walked toward the livery. Finally she hurried to catch up to him.

At the livery Jennet stood near the wide door while Free paid for a horse and buggy. In silence Free drove to a church that he'd attended a couple of times with his sister Anne. The minister lived in the house next door, and Jennet stiffly waited on the church steps as Free knocked on the door to get the minister.

A few minutes later, with shaking legs, Jennet stood before the minister and in a blur listened to the words he spoke over them. Her dress was dirty and sweat stained, her hair in tangles. Could this really be her wedding day?

At one point Free almost backed out, but he hardened his resolve and let the man finish the short ceremony.

After Jennet signed her name under Freeman's, he took the certificate of marriage and tucked it away in his shirt with her indenture paper.

Next Free drove them several blocks away to Lem Azack's home because his office was closed on Sunday. Jennet hung back, but Freeman took her arm and they followed the maid across the wide room to a half-open doorway.

Freeman and Jennet Havlick stepped into a large study lit by several lamps. Overstuffed leather chairs, a huge mahogany desk, and a leather sofa were arranged around the room, which was bigger than Tait's store. Jennet trembled, and Free's grip on her arm tightened. A white-haired man sat in a high-backed red leather armchair behind the carved desk. As they walked across the highly polished hardwood floor, Lem Azack hoisted his dangling wide black suspenders back up on his broad shoulders and pushed himself up.

"Hello, Mr. Azack." Free dropped his hand from Jen's arm and cleared his throat so his sudden attack of nerves would not show in his voice. He felt Jennet beside him, but he couldn't look at her for fear of backing out even at this late date.

"Free," said Lem Azack as he held out a hand that was white and soft from working indoors all his life. "What a pleasant surprise." He smiled, then turned his attention to Jennet.

Jennet felt dirty and ragged and wanted to run from the man's steady gaze.

"Mr. Azack, this is my wife, Jennet." Free's voice trembled slightly, but he forced himself to continue. "I came to claim my inheritance." He handed the certificate of marriage to the lawyer.

Lem took it, glanced over it, his eyes stopping to reread the date, and then handed it back to Free. Lem held out a big hand to Jennet and reluctantly she held her small one out to him. "Hello, Jennet. I am pleased to meet you."

The older man's kind voice eased the pain around Jen's heart just a little. She couldn't find her voice to answer him back the way Ma had taught her a lifetime ago, so she only nodded.

"Please, sit down," said Lem, motioning toward the dark red leather sofa against a wall covered with family pictures.

Jennet perched on the edge of the sofa and locked her trembling hands in her lap. Free sat beside her but far enough away that they didn't touch. She could smell his sweat as well as the leather of the sofa.

Lem sat on a matching leather chair beside an occasional table that held a coal oil lamp with flowers painted on the glass bowl and globe. "So, you got married."

Free nodded and Jennet bit back a moan.

Lem ran his finger under his collar and smoothed back his white hair. "Free, I'll meet you at the bank in the morning at nine and see that the money is turned over to you."

"I'll be there."

"Your house is furnished and stocked with canned food if you choose to go there tonight."

Free shrugged. The house was nothing to him. The money and the land were all-important.

Lem smiled at Jennet. "Free's grandfather left a house here in town on Grove Street for the two of you, Jennet. It's small but pleasant and has a stable with a horse and buggy. A woman keeps it aired and dusted to be ready at a moment's notice. I'll get the key." Lem went to his desk, looked through a drawer, and finally held up a long brass key. He handed it to Free as he told him where the house was located.

Jennet's head spun and for a minute she thought she'd faint dead away, but she managed to hold on and listen to the rest of the men's conversation.

Later, in the buggy Jennet locked her hands in her lap and kept her eyes down as Free drove away from the attorney's house and down the darkened street. After a few blocks a horrible smell made her nauseated.

"It's the tannery," Free said, turning onto Monroe Street. "It takes getting used to." But the few times he'd smelled the stinking rot of animal skins and carcasses he'd never gotten used to it.

Lights shone from the huge three-story brick house that Galen Norcross had built for his Dutch wife six years ago. At Grove Street, Free turned left, drove past five large houses with wide, sweeping lawns, past a stand of hardwood trees, and pulled into the driveway of a small white house. Suddenly he realized that Grandpa's friends Tunis and Nina Bowker lived close by. In the dark he couldn't tell which house was theirs.

Free stopped beside the barn and just sat there. He heard Jennet's gentle breathing and the wild thud of his heart. Jen was his wife and this was his home. Suddenly his hands dampened with sweat. His wife! His home!

Free stepped from the buggy, and it moved under his weight. Wordlessly he helped Jen to the dirt driveway. The moon was bright enough that they could see their way to the front door. Freeman unlocked the door, found a lamp, and lit it, leaving a smell of sulfur that soon disappeared.

The front room was pleasant and held the fragrance of wild roses.

"I've never been here before," said Free as if he was talking to himself. He lifted the lamp high to show a brick fireplace with a wide wooden mantel, an oak rocking chair, comfortable cushioned chairs, and a deep blue sofa at the side of a wide window with heavy brocade drapes. "Let's look at the rest of it," said Free in a voice that didn't sound like his.

Jennet hesitantly followed him through the front room and into the dining room that held a long oval walnut table with six banister-back chairs pushed up to it. A long hutch full of dishes stood against a flowered wallpapered wall with a matching corner hutch built into the wall next to a window. The beauty of the room took Jennet's breath away.

Reluctantly she followed Free into a big kitchen that had a hand pump built right into a counter, a cookstove, table and chairs, and more cupboards than she'd ever seen in a house. A kerosene lamp sat in the middle of the round table. They opened a door that led to a pantry and another that led to a back shed where split wood was stacked. From the shed door they saw the outhouse and the barn with the hired buggy sitting beside it. A horse nickered and the hired horse answered. From a neighbor's yard a dog barked.

Suddenly Jennet yawned, then yawned again. "I'm sorry," she said, flushing with embarrassment.

"You're worn right out, aren't you?" asked Free.

Jen ducked her head. "I am tired."

"You get right to bed." Possessively he took her arm and led her down the hallway behind the kitchen, past two small bedrooms, one on either side of the hall, to a large bedroom with a canopy bed. He found a lamp on the dresser and lit it. It cast a soft glow over a portion of the room, showing a humpbacked trunk against the wall beside a dresser and a dark pink chaise. "We can talk in the morning after you've rested," Free said gently.

Helplessly Jennet looked at him. "Are you leaving?"

He nodded, wondering if he could walk away from her. She was his wife, and he had every right to stay! "I want to take the buggy back, and I have to check out a few things."

Dare she ask him his plans for her? Jennet tried to stop the frightened beat of her heart. "Will you be back to-night?" Oh, she wished she knew what to expect of him!

"I plan to."

"Oh."

Free saw her fear and a muscle jumped in his jaw. "I won't wake you. I'll sleep in another room."

He walked to the door. "See you in the morning," he said without smiling.

Jennet nodded and watched him leave. Before she could move, the door opened and he handed her bundle to her. Their hands brushed and sparks leaped between them.

"Try to rest," he said hoarsely.

She looked at him, trying to take in all the events of their day together.

"Good night," he said just above a whisper.

"Good night," she mouthed, unable to bring up even a whisper. She could barely breathe as Freeman Havlick walked out, closing the door behind him.

CHAPTER

8

◆ Jennet sat bolt upright. She'd overslept! Tait would beat her until she couldn't move. Sunlight already shone through the three partly open windows. A warm breeze puffed at the muslin curtains. She glanced around and frowned at the unfamiliar sight of the canopy bed, the chaise lounge, and the chiffonrobe against the wall to the left of the bed. With a start she remembered that she was in a house that belonged to Freeman Havlick. She was no longer Jennet Cordell, but Jennet Havlick!

Shivering even though the breeze was pleasantly warm, Jen swung her legs over the side of the bed, expecting her feet to touch the floor. The bed was not close to the floor like the narrow cot at the store. She'd become so used to the cot she'd slept on only a small part of the bed last night. Jennet picked up Wex's hankie off the pillow next to hers where she'd laid it last night and rubbed it over her cheek. "Wex, I married your brother. What will you do when you find that out? I know I said I'd wait for you, but I couldn't." Jennet's voice broke.

She slid off the bed and stood up. The carpet felt soft under her feet, and she couldn't help smiling as she traced around the design of a large cabbage rose with her bare toe. In awe she touched the pink muslin canopy that matched the pink ruffled curtains at the three tall windows. Never had she slept in such a room! The cream-colored wallpaper was covered with small pink-and-red rosebuds intertwined with rich green English ivy. She ran her fingers across the mahogany commode beside the bed and looked around at the matching chest, quilt rack, and dresser, and then gasped at the sight of a framed full-length looking glass standing on a carved base. She saw her bare feet and the ragged hem of her once-white nightdress that hung around her ankles. She tilted the glass to show her thin body and her pale face. Her braids had come loose in the night and tangled chestnut-brown hair hung limply to her thin shoulders. She pushed strands of it from her forehead, then met her wide blue eyes in the mirror. Oh, but she was ugly!

Jennet turned away and sank to the edge of the chaise lounge.

Just then Free knocked on the closed door and said, "Jen."

Jennet leaped back in bed and pulled the cover to her chin. "What?" she answered.

Freeman opened the door and walked in. He wore a dark blue suit and white shirt. His stomach tightened at the frightened look on her face. Why, she was as afraid of him as she had been of her pa and uncle! The thought made him want to beg her forgiveness for forcing her to marry him. Abruptly he pushed the thought aside and said, "I'll be gone most of the day, so you'll be on your own."

On her own for a whole day with nothing to do! Never had she had a day to herself!

Jennet's relief hurt him and that surprised him. "You'll find a tub in the kitchen beside the stove. I put water on to heat for your bath."

A bath with water that she hadn't carried and heated! A bath that she didn't have to hurry through!

"There's food for you too." Freeman turned away, then said over his shoulder, "I'm using the horse and buggy today, but otherwise it'll be for your use."

Jennet could only stare at him. Was this a dream? Could she walk out the door and hitch up her own horse to her own buggy and go to a place of her choice? "Could I see my family tomorrow?" she asked in a weak voice.

Free hesitated. Did he want her to see her family? They might find a way to get her out of the marriage and back with them. He had to talk to Lem Azack to see if there were any loopholes in the marriage. "We'll talk about it when I get back." He walked to the door and once again turned back. "I left a bundle of clothes for you on the kitchen table."

Clothes!

"If they don't fit, I'll return them." Free walked out, closing the door quietly behind him. He stood outside her door. What had he done? Jen was frightened of him and probably hated him. But could he blame her? He'd forced her into this marriage.

Free lifted his chin defiantly. She was certainly better off with him than with Tait or with Vernon Cordell! She wasn't capable of taking care of herself.

Jennet waited until she heard the outer door close, then she scurried down the hall to the large kitchen. A copper boiler full of hot water bubbled on the cast-iron range, and a round galvanized washtub sat on the floor in front of the stove. Three open windows with white ruffled curtains and green tiebacks kept the kitchen from being too hot for comfort. The wooden cupboards built into a wall between two of the windows and against the wall between the kitchen and dining room were stained a pleasant green. A big round table with four chairs pushed up under it stood almost in the middle of the room.

With a low laugh Jennet touched the red-handled pump.

She'd never seen a pump in the house before. How much time and backbreaking work it would save! She pumped cold water into a five-gallon bucket that she'd found beside the counter and poured it into the washtub. She added hot water from the boiler until the tub water felt comfortably warm. She filled the large bucket with warm water and hung a dipper on the side, then knelt beside the tub and washed her hair. She wrapped a small towel around her head, added a little more hot water to the tub, stepped in, and thankfully sank down in the water.

Several minutes later Jennet stood beside the table with a big white towel wrapped around herself and looked through the bundle of clothes that Free had left for her. She blushed scarlet as she found pantaloons, a soft cotton chemise, and two full gathered underskirts that he should never have looked at, but quickly she slipped them on, then pulled the blue cotton dress over her head and let it fall down over her, almost to touch the floor. She buttoned the long line of hidden buttons up the front, making the dress nip in at her narrow waist. The bodice fit snugly against her instead of hanging loose like her other dresses had. The small collar and the narrow cuffs were ruffled. She almost ran to the bedroom to look in the looking glass.

Oh, the dress was beautiful, just the blue of her eyes! The two underskirts made it bell out at the bottom becomingly. With shoes on, it would be the perfect length. Jen brushed her hair, which suddenly looked soft and luxurious, then tied it back with a blue ribbon that had been in the bundle. She stared at herself in the mirror for a long time, then finally whispered, "I *do* look pretty! Oh, Wex, I wish you could see me now. You'd be surprised, but happy."

Next Jennet emptied the tub, a bucketful at a time, on the ground beside the barn. As she walked back toward the house, she heard a sound behind her. She spun around to see a slender woman with graying hair, kind blue eyes, and a warm smile walking across the wide expanse of lawn. The older woman wore a light gray dress with darker gray piping and a high collar and a cameo at her throat.

"Hello! Mrs. Havlick?"

Mrs. Havlick! Jennet barely nodded. "I'm Jennet . . . Havlick." She felt awkward, fixed all fancy as if she were somebody important.

"Don't be frightened. I'm Nina Bowker, a friend of Free's, and I live next door," she said, pointing to the white frame house to the west. "I saw you and Free come last night, and I saw Free leave earlier. I wanted to make sure you were comfortable and see if I could help you."

"Help me do what?" asked Jennet in a weak voice as she set the bucket down.

"Get used to your new home and new surroundings."

"Oh." Jennet couldn't imagine anyone helping her. "Do you know Freeman?"

Nina smiled. "Yes. For years. My husband Tunis and I were best friends with Free's Grandpa Clay and Grandma Sarah. We made a promise to Clay before he died that we'd always watch out for his grandchildren. Clay bought this house next door to us for Free so we could do just that."

Jennet locked her fingers together. She'd never had anyone watch out for her since she was five years old. Just what did it entail? "I've never lived in town before," said Jennet.

Nina laughed with delight. "Then I'll show you around. Where to buy vegetables and meat. Clothes. Just everything!"

Jennet nodded.

Nina patted Jennet's arm. "But not today, dear. You'll want today to yourself, I'm sure. Today you rest and enjoy your new home and your new husband."

Jennet was at a loss for words. "It's all very different," she finally managed to say.

Nina Bowker smiled as they walked to a wooden bench

beside the back door of the house and sat down. "Tell me about yourself, dear."

Jennet hesitated. She didn't want to tell a stranger what had happened in her life, but she didn't know how to tell her that. As quickly as she could Jennet told about her family and about working for Tait. She did not tell Nina that she'd been beaten or indentured to Tait. She went into detail about Eve and Joshua, then skimmed over the part where she had married Free.

"You are a very remarkable young woman," said Nina.

The praise warmed Jennet's heart. "Thank you."

"I shall call you Jennet and you call me Nina. I hope we'll become close friends."

Jennet smiled. She felt the same kindness in Nina that she'd felt in Eve. "I hope so too. Mr. Azack said someone took care of the house. Was that you?"

"I had my housekeeper dust and keep it aired out. My gardener took care of your yard, the barn, and the horse."

"Will they keep doing it?"

"Only if you want them to. It's your decision."

Her decision! The thought was heady. "I'll take care of it myself then," she said.

"I'll tell them," said Nina. "But if you ever want their help, let me know."

"Thank you. I will." But why would she need help taking care of such a small place? One horse, one barn, one house, one yard. She could do that and still have time left in a day. "I don't see a garden."

"There's a spot for one on the far side of the barn. It's a little late to put one in this year, but you could plan for next."

Jennet's stomach tightened. She hadn't thought that far into the future. Would she be here next year?

"I'm going back home now so you can get on with exploring your new place." Smiling, Nina caught Jennet's hand and squeezed it. She walked back to her yard and the large house surrounded by several maples and oaks. A large barn stood behind the house with a wooden fence around the barnyard.

Jennet looked all around. She smelled the roses she saw climbing on a trellis at the side of the house and heard birds singing in the trees around her place and those of the neighbors on either side as well as across the street. All the houses were far enough apart to have room for barns and barnyards for their horses. A breeze ruffled Jennet's hair and pressed her skirts against her legs. No one was here to tell her what to do or beat her if she didn't work!

Jennet ran to her barn and pushed open the heavy door. Dust particles danced in the sunlight. A calico cat stretched, ambled over, and rubbed against her ankle. She lifted the cat in her arms and held it close. It purred and snuggled against her. "You're a nice cat. Do you have a name?" The cat purred louder.

The barn was clean and empty except for the cat. She saw the spot for the buggy and the stall the horse had been in. She peeked in the tack room and saw a wooden bench in the middle of the floor and pegs on the wall for harnesses. A saddle was flung over a special rack, and a bridle hung from a peg beside it. Jennet walked to the back door of the barn. A tank filled with water stood next to the barn, and a wooden fence enclosed the lush grassy barnyard. Trees shaded part of the barnyard and wild flowers grew here and there, dotting the green with bright blue, yellow, and orange.

With the cat in her arms Jennet walked all around the outside of her house. Before she went back inside, she put the cat down with a pat. She inspected each room again. The lawyer had called the house small, but to Jennet, it seemed gigantic for only two people. Could this entire house belong to her to do with as she wanted? It was too strange to be true.

Then she thought of Freeman. She was married to him

and had to do what he told her. She wasn't as free as she'd thought.

Jennet sank to a rocking chair near the front window. She rocked back and forth and tried to stop the wild beat of her heart.

Frowning, Free stopped outside the newspaper office. GRAND RAPIDS NEWS was printed in black block lettering on the dirt-streaked window. Should he go in and talk with Tunis Bowker? Free brushed dust off his arm as he glanced toward the barbershop where he'd had his hair cut. Maybe he should get another haircut and forget about talking to Tunis. Could he face Tune after his angry outburst the last time they'd met? Tune was always trying to get Free and Roman to understand each other. He said he'd promised Grandpa Clay. Free scanned the street as horse-drawn buggies, carts, drays, and wagons passed by, harnesses rattling. A small dog barked at the heels of a barefoot boy running down the sidewalk.

Free looked in the wide window of the newspaper office. Maybe he should walk away. But now that he lived right next door to Tune and Nina he couldn't just ignore them. He missed the special talks he and Tune used to have. He almost filled the empty place that Grandpa Clay had left when he died. Finally Free made up his mind.

As he pushed open the heavy door, the smell of printer's ink hit him. The noise of the printing press, which almost filled the room, made his ears ring. A man wearing an ink-stained apron stood watching paper pass through the giant machine. The scarred plank floor was covered with scattered newsprint. Another man sat at a high counter facing the wall as he proofread the pages in front of him. Signs and advertisements hung on the bare wood walls.

His hat in his hand, Free walked through the front room and back to Tunis Bowker's office. Tune sat in his shirtsleeves behind his big desk. Gray hair on his balding head stood on end as if he'd rubbed his fingers through it and hadn't smoothed it back in place. He looked up from his work and, on seeing Free, smiled warmly, got up, and strode around to hug Free. The smells of ink and sweat, which he had always associated with Tune, surrounded Free as surely as the older man's arms.

"I'm glad you came, Free," Tunis said in his deep voice.

Free twisted the brim of his hat as he sat down. "I was very rude to you the last time we talked."

Tunis sank back against his desk and crossed his ankles. His baggy gray pants hung on his long frame. "It's over and done."

"I am sorry."

Tunis smiled and spread his big hands wide. "Forgiven and forgotten!"

"Thank you." Free sighed heavily. "I was so angry with anyone connected with my father. You and he are friends, and in my mind that made us enemies."

Tune leaned forward, his brow cocked. "But now you've decided differently?"

"Yes. I guess I grew up some."

"So has your father."

Free frowned.

"He's sorry for forcing you out of his life. And I think he's beginning to understand that you want a different life than he has. And that it's okay."

For the past eight years that Tune had been part of their lives, he'd tried to help Roman understand that he needed to let his children choose their own destiny. He'd also tried to help Roman understand and love Clay while he was still alive. It hadn't worked. Clay had died with Roman still angry and resentful.

"So, he listened to you at long last?" asked Free.

Tunis shrugged. "Somewhat." He smiled slightly, walked around his desk, and sat back down. "Your father has a lot of anger to work through. But I think he's doing it."

Free didn't believe that, but he didn't say so. "Tune, the reason I stopped by. . . ." Free's voice faded away.

"Out with it, Free. I love you, boy, and I'll do anything I can to help you. You know that."

"It's about Grandpa Clay's will."

"What about it?"

"Do you know what's in it?"

"Yes. He told me."

Free leaned forward with a frown. The noise from the other room seeped through the walls and the heavy glass on the closed door. "Why didn't you tell me about it?"

Tunis lifted his bushy brows. "But Roman said he told you."

"He didn't!"

"Well, well." Tunis rubbed his long fingers through his hair and then brushed the strands down with the palm of his hand. "That explains a lot of things."

"Not to me," said Free gruffly.

"Your pa has been acting very, very guilty lately when I've talked to him about you. I couldn't understand why. Now I do." Tunis brushed at his wide nose. "I always wondered why you didn't talk to me about the will. The way Clay left it and all."

"I can't understand why Grandpa said I had to be married to inherit his money and land."

"Didn't Lem explain?"

"Yes. But it sure didn't help. It doesn't seem right that I had to get married to get what Grandpa wanted me to have."

"He wanted you to have much more than what money could buy. He knew you wouldn't marry just to get the money. He knew you had too much integrity for that."

Free forced back a flush.

"Clay loved you more than you'll ever know, Free." Tunis moved pencil and paper out of his way and put his elbows on his desk. "He loved his family—all of you very much. But he didn't realize that until late in his life, too late to give all of you the things he wanted to give you."

Tears burned the backs of Free's eyes. He'd loved Grandpa with a fierceness that he'd never understood, and he'd felt the same love from Grandpa for him.

"Clay wanted you to value family, Free. He wanted you to know love was more important than great wealth, great success, or even great power."

An ache that felt as if it would take his life away started in the very pit of Free's stomach and spread through him. Since Grandpa had died, no one really seemed to love him. Now, he had a wife who didn't love him. Instead she was frightened of him and had married him only because he'd forced her into it. How could he ever expect love from her?

"What's wrong, Free?" asked Tunis softly.

Embarrassed, Free choked back tears. He was a man, and Pa had said more times than he could count that men didn't cry. "I miss Grandpa."

"I know." Tunis laced his fingers together and looked very serious. "Your grandpa learned of God's love late in life, and he wanted to share that love with his family. Clay had material wealth to leave behind, but he felt his spiritual wealth was of more value. He wanted each of you to personally accept Jesus."

In the back of his mind Free could hear Grandpa saying the very same words. When Free was about fourteen, he'd prayed with Grandpa, and he'd asked Jesus to be his Savior. But after Grandpa had died and after he'd left home in anger, he'd pushed that commitment aside.

Tunis brushed a hand across his face, then leaned forward again. "Free, you can have all the timber, all the grainfields, all the money you can spend, but if you lose your family, all of it means nothing."

Free stared down at his hat as he wondered if he believed Tunis. Free wanted timber and he wanted money.

Tunis cleared his throat. "I never told you this, Freeman, but today I'm going to tell you."

"What?"

"Your grandpa and I had a pact. A covenant we called it. He read in the Bible about the covenant that David and Jonathan cut together. It's as though two people become one— they look after each other's property and family." Tunis brushed moisture from his eye. "Clay and I were as David and Jonathan. Their covenant was never broken; each generation renewed it. I will not break my covenant with Clay. That's why I'm now looking after you and your holdings."

Free rolled the brim of his hat tight.

"Clay and I promised each other that we'd always watch out for each other. What was mine was his. What was his, mine. I promised him that I'd take care of all of you after he died. And, Free, I've tried to do it. That's why I butted in to get Roman to change. That's why I tried to make you understand your pa. And that's why I've been watching over you after you left home to live in the woods."

"I never knew," Free said solemnly.

"Remember the time the bear attacked you? I'd asked a woodsman who worked the same area to help you if ever you needed it. He chased away the bear."

Free rubbed his shoulder where he still had the scar.

"And I told Jig, that old woodsman who spends more time talking to God than he does anything else, to get you away from Willie Thorne."

Free sank back in his chair and stared at Tunis as if he'd never seen him before. "I never knew," he repeated.

"I'm glad you listened to Jig and quit working with Willie."

"Me too."

"And if I'd known you didn't know about Clay's will, I

would've told you. I love you, Freeman. I love you like Clay did."

Free quickly brushed a tear from his sunbrowned cheek. He'd known that Tune cared for him, but he had never understood how much.

"Now you're married, and Nina and I mean to watch out for Jennet like I've been watching out for you. I'm sure she's a wonderful girl."

Free looked down at his hat. He could never let Tune know the truth! "She needed me," he said hoarsely. "I guess we needed each other."

"So I understand from what she told Nina this morning."

Free realized from the look on Tunis's face that Jennet had not told the whole story. "I'd appreciate it if you kept your eye on her when I go to the lumbercamp in September."

"We'll be glad to."

"Tune, this covenant thing . . ." Free's voice trailed off.

"Yes?"

"I appreciate it."

"So do I, Freeman." Tunis nodded slowly. "There's even more to it."

Free lifted a brow questioningly.

"God cut a covenant with all of us through His Son. When we accept Jesus as Savior, we've entered into that covenant with God. All that is His is ours. All that is ours is His. It's an awesome truth. It's greater than the covenant that Clay and I have, even greater than the one between Jonathan and David. God Himself is a covenant partner with us!" Before Tunis could continue, a man knocked on his door, stuck his head in, and said, "I need a word with you, Tune."

"Be right with you, Wallis."

Free stood. "I have to see Lem before I go home. Thanks for taking time for me, Tune."

"My pleasure."

"Tune, I'd like you to keep my marriage to yourself. I want to personally tell my family."

"Sure thing." Tunis hugged Free tight and let him go. "See you at home."

"Yes. At home." Free clamped his hat in place and strode from the office.

Jennet slept away part of the afternoon, something she'd not done since she was a baby. She ate when she wanted, then she sat again in the rocker and waited. Without anything to do, the day seemed to last a lifetime.

When Free finally drove in about seven o'clock, shivers ran up and down her spine as she waited for him to take care of the horse. Through the kitchen window she watched him walk from the barn to the house. He carried his suit coat over his arm, and he looked tired.

Free walked in the back door and stopped short when he saw her waiting for him. He stared in surprise at her. He hadn't realized that she was beautiful. "Hello," he said, suddenly losing the other words he'd planned to say.

Jennet locked her hands behind her back. "Did you decide about tomorrow? Can I go visit my family?"

He draped his coat over a kitchen chair but couldn't look at her. "Maybe."

"I want to see them. I want to know if Ma is well. I want them to know I'm here where they can come see me."

"I'll think about it," Free said as he noticed how shiny her hair was and how pretty it looked hanging down her back. The dress he'd chosen for her fit just right and matched her eyes as he'd wanted it to.

Jennet gripped the back of a chair. Why was Free looking at her so intently? "And I want to find out if they've had word of Wex. When Marie last wrote, she said he might come home this summer. Have you heard?"

A muscle jumped in Free's jaw. "I spoke with my sister a

while ago, and she said that he wanted to come home for a short leave."

Jennet's eyes lit up and she smiled. "It will be so good to see him again!"

Free stabbed his fingers through his dark hair. "Just remember that you're married to me now."

The sparkle left her eyes and Jen nodded. "Do you want supper?" she asked stiffly.

"I ate with my sister."

"I'll go feed and water the horse."

"I already did."

Jennet rubbed the back of her hand and studied her blunt cut fingernails. "I'm not used to being idle. I don't know what is expected of me," she whispered.

Free walked to the stove and back to the table to stand beside her. "You have only yourself to tend. When I'm home, you can see to my meals and my clothes." His throat almost closed over at what he planned to say next. "When we have a family, you'll tend them."

A family! She flushed painfully.

Lem had told Free that they must have a true marriage so that Jennet's family couldn't have it annulled if they so desired. He didn't think they'd want that, but maybe Wex would if he came home this summer. And Wex was not going to have Jen! He wasn't man enough for her! Had he even tried to make her life better? Had he even tried to protect her?

Free cleared his throat and moved restlessly. He'd asked Lem not to tell his family about his marriage. "Anne said she'll come see you."

"It's been a long time since I've seen her."

"Pa still won't let her go to the farm. She hasn't seen the family since Wex left." Free turned away with a frown. He didn't want to talk about Wex. "What did you do while I was gone?"

"I met Nina Bowker from next door."

"She's a fine woman. Grandpa thought a lot of her and Tunis." Free led Jennet to the front room where they sat facing each other in the overstuffed chairs. Free told her about Grandpa Clay, the covenant that he'd cut with Tunis, and how Tunis had watched out for him. He told about the bear and about Jig. In the past Jennet had heard many stories about Clay from Wex as well as from Free, but Clay had died the year before her family moved to the farm, so she'd never met him.

Jennet listened without speaking, but a part of her mind was on the frightening time that was coming in bed with Free.

Later in her bedroom Jennet held Wex's hankie to her cheek and whispered, "I have a nice house to live in, and I don't have to work hard, but I am still a slave. This time to Free. He bought me, and I have to do what he says. I'm sorry, Wex. But I have to do what he says."

Just then the door opened and Free came in. Jennet jumped and dropped the hankie. Before she could pick it up, Free did. He held it out to her, then his eyes fell on the fancy "W" and he jerked it back. Jealousy shot through him, and fire flashed from his dark eyes.

"Whose hankie?" asked Free sharply.

"Wexal's," Jennet whispered.

"What are *you* doing with it?" Free's voice was thick with anger.

"I made it for him for his birthday," she said weakly. She sank to the edge of the bed. "He gave it to me when he went away."

"And what did you give him?" asked Free coldly.

She thought of the kiss that she'd wanted to give him, and she blushed to the roots of her hair.

Free scowled at the sight of her blush. Had she given herself to him? Had Pa been right about her after all? Free pushed the hankie in his pocket. "Forget about this hankie and forget about Wex. You're my wife!"

Jennet wanted to grab the hankie back and put it near her heart, but she didn't move and didn't say the angry words burning inside her.

"Get ready for bed," said Free in a low, tight voice. "I'll give you a few minutes alone, then I'll be back."

Her eyes wide in fear, Jennet watched him stalk out of the room.

CHAPTER

9

♦ In September, Jennet stood beside the open front door, held the satchel of clothes out to Free, and said dutifully, "Take care of yourself." She wanted to say, "I hate you for forcing me to marry you! I hate you for forcing me to share a bed with you!" Her body was used to him now, and at times when he was especially gentle and loving, she responded to him even though she tried not to. She'd actually enjoyed listening to his plans and dreams just as she had in the past before he'd left home. And that she couldn't allow! She wanted to stay angry with him. She wanted him to know she was angry and would never forgive him. How glad she was to see him leave a day earlier than he'd planned! A band tightened around her heart.

Free's mind was full of the wonderful adventure ahead in his lumbercamp, but he saw the relief in Jennet's eyes. Wouldn't she miss him at all? He had seen to her every need. He'd kept her safe and protected. What more did she want? Abruptly he pushed the thoughts away. He couldn't think about her feelings now. Finally he was a lumberman by name, and soon he'd prove he was a lumberman by reputation. He managed a smile. "I'll see you in the spring. Be sure to get someone to help you so you don't have to do heavy work in your condition."

Jennet barely nodded. She hated having him say anything that reminded her that she was going to have his baby in the spring. It was one more mark to show her that she was Free's slave. She had not wanted to share a bed with him, had not wanted to have a part of him growing inside her body. But she'd had no choice because she belonged to Free and he had a paper to prove it.

Free looked possessively down her slender body to the toes of her black shoes, then up to the pulse that throbbed in her neck. He liked the way she looked in her pale pink dress. A pink ribbon held back her long dark hair. He wanted to see her smile. "Nina and Tune will watch out for you," he said."

"They told me." She loved both of them, but she wasn't a child who needed to be "watched out for."

Glancing at the hired wagon stopped on the street, Free turned back to Jennet. She suddenly looked too young to become a mother. He should've sent her home in June, but he couldn't stand to think of her pa whipping her or his pa working her too hard. Her family didn't deserve to see her! Free watched the breeze blow a strand of hair across her smooth cheek that was once again rosy and healthy. He'd hated the thought of her seeing Wex again. Free hadn't wanted Wex around her. "Are you sure you'll be all right?" he asked softly.

Jennet nodded. Why didn't he leave?

Free wanted to pull her close and beg her to be happy. He wanted to take away the agony he saw in her eyes. He had so much to say to her, but all he said was, "I don't want you riding out alone to see your family." Free didn't want them to convince her to move back home.

Jennet pressed her lips tightly together to hold back a rush of angry words. She'd wanted to see her family since she'd been there, but Free would never take her and wouldn't allow her to go alone.

Free moved restlessly. A gust of wind blew in the door bringing in a faint smell of the Grand River several blocks away. The man in the wagon whistled as he waited. Although Free wanted to be on his way, he realized that he'd miss Jennet.

Jennet wanted him to leave, not say another word to her, but he just stood there as if he didn't want to leave. His white shirt buttoned to his throat made his brown hair seem even darker.

Free wanted to kiss her good-bye, but he'd never kissed her except in bed. Why shouldn't he kiss her when he wanted? He was her husband! He pulled her to him. She fit in his arms as if she'd been made for him.

Jennet felt Free's heart beat against her as he held her tightly to him. Her heart fluttered strangely.

Free pressed his lips to hers in a long, hungry kiss.

The kiss sent a tingle through Jennet, and she stiffened.

Free let her go with a slight frown. He saw the rigid set of her shoulders and the bleak look in her eyes. "Good-bye," he whispered.

"Good-bye," she said hoarsely.

Free strode from the house to the wagon. He felt frustrated and angry and didn't know why. He forced his mind off Jennet and onto the tracts of land that he'd be lumbering. This time the camp was his, the men were his, and the logs were his. He'd filed his logmark at the courthouse and each of his logs from now on would carry that mark—F and H hooked together inside a circle.

"Morning, Havlick," said the driver. "Great day, eh?"

"Sure is," said Free as he climbed on the wooden seat beside the driver. Free wanted to look back at Jennet, but he kept his eyes on the draft horses.

Clenching her fists angrily, Jennet watched Free ride

away with the man he'd hired to take him on the hard two-day trip to his lumbercamp. She closed the front door with a bang. How she wanted to tell him that she hated him, that she wanted to be married to Wex, but she'd kept her feelings and her words to herself.

Jennet brushed at her mouth, trying to rub away the feel of his lips on hers, then groaned because she suddenly realized she would miss having him with her. She trailed her finger over her mouth. How would it feel if she did try to love him, did try to talk to him and tell him her thoughts and feelings? Oh, that was impossible! She'd never care for Free!

With a long sigh she walked outdoors to feed and water Acorn. Since June, she'd learned to love the sorrel mare, and when Free didn't have her, Jen had taken her for rides, astride her or hitched to the buggy. A few times Free had taken Jennet for a buggy ride and talked to her about his dream of being a prosperous lumberman.

The pleasantly warm breeze pressed Jennet's long pink skirt against her legs. Just outside the back door near the bench the calico cat rubbed against Jennet's ankle, and she picked him up and brushed her cheek against him. He smelled of milk and dust. She'd learned that he was the mouser for the house and barn and no one had named him, so she had called him Cal, short for Calico.

"Cal, did you catch that mouse I spotted in the barn yesterday?" Jennet asked. Her voice sounded strained. She cleared her throat and forced herself to relax.

Cal mewed and Jennet laughed softly.

"Good morning, Jen," called Nina from next door as she walked across the wide yard, carrying her hat. "I haven't seen much of you lately."

"I'm sorry," said Jennet. When she'd learned from the doctor that she was going to have a baby, she'd kept away from Nina and Tunis as much as possible. Jennet didn't want to tell anyone, not even the kind woman and her husband who had become her good friends.

Nina hugged Jennet briefly. "I saw Free leave. The next seven months he's away will be lonely for you both. Maybe you could visit him."

Jennet shook her head. She'd never do that!

"What will you do with your time now?" asked Nina.

"I don't know." Jennet looked across the yard to the trees behind the barn. What was she going to do with her time?

Nina patted Jennet's shoulder and smiled. "It's up to you. You only have yourself to answer to."

The realization hit Jennet so hard it took her breath away. She didn't have to answer to anyone but herself for seven long months! Not Pa. Not Roman. Not Tait. And not Free! Was that possible?

What *would* she do? Suddenly she knew. She'd visit her family! She'd see Ma and the girls and maybe meet Tim. But she would not speak to Pa! All summer she'd wanted to go, but Free hadn't let her. Now he was gone, and she could do as she pleased. And if she wanted to go alone, she would! He wasn't around to tell her what she could do or what she couldn't do!

Her blue eyes sparkling, Jennet smiled at Nina. "I will visit my family," she said with more assurance than she felt.

"That'll be nice for you," said Nina as she set her hat in place on the carefully arranged gray hair. The fluttering wide blue feathers matched the blue of Nina's eyes.

Jennet nodded. "Yes. Yes, it will."

"It'll be strange for you to see them again since you're a married woman and not their little girl any longer."

Jennet frowned slightly. She had never been their "little girl," but it would be strange to know that she didn't have to put up with Pa's anger.

"And will you visit with Free's parents?" asked Nina as she brushed at the wide sleeves of her dress.

"No."

Nina caught Jennet's hand and held it as she looked in concern at her. Jennet had told her about her life on the farm. "Jen, don't let anger and unforgiveness keep you from learning to love your new family."

Jennet bit her bottom lip. "I don't think of them as family."

"But they are." Nina squeezed Jennet's hand. "With God's help you can learn to care for them."

She didn't want to argue with Nina. "I'll see you when I return, Nina."

Nina smiled and laugh lines fanned from the corners of her blue eyes to her gray hair. "Enjoy yourself, Jen. I'm on my way to meet Tunis for breakfast. He's taking me to the new restaurant that opened last week." Nina smiled and touched her hat to make sure it was on straight. "You're welcome to come along."

"Thank you, Nina. Maybe another time."

"I'll see you when you return." Nina hugged Jennet, walked to her waiting buggy, and drove away. At the corner she waved and Jennet waved back.

Feeling as light as dandelion fluff, Jennet went inside to the bedroom and changed into the blue dress that Free had bought for her. She wore only one petticoat to make driving easier, then forced herself to put on the hat that Nina had helped her buy. She glanced in the mirror with a frown. Her family would think she was putting on airs if she wore such a fancy hat. She agreed. Wrinkling her nose, she dropped the hat back in its box. Jennet quickly braided her hair in one long, thick chestnut-brown braid, coiled it loosely at the nape of her neck, and pinned it in place. She packed to spend the night and walked to the barn with her case. Cal ran along at her feet and almost tripped her. A blue jay scolded from the top of a tall maple. The smell of wood smoke drifted through the air and on up to meet the fluffy white clouds dotting the blue sky.

Just as Jennet finished harnessing Acorn she thought she heard a strange noise, almost like a baby crying. She cocked her head. Was she hearing things? She listened, but Acorn rattled the harness and covered any other sounds.

With a shrug Jennet led Acorn from the barn. Walking back to close the door, she caught a flash of movement from the corner of her eye.

"Is someone in there?" Jennet asked in a shaky voice. There was no answer. With all the courage she could muster she stepped into the barn and looked around. Trying to sound firm, she said, "I know you're in here. Come out right now!"

Finally a ragged colored girl carrying a bundle emerged from the shadows. She was about the same size as Jennet but younger. Her eyes were full of fear. Pieces of hay stuck in her tight black curls and on the sleeve of her faded brown dress. "I's come for help," she said weakly.

Jennet frowned. "Who are you?"

"Dacia, ma'am. The white lady tole me to come." Dacia thrust out a paper. "I's to give this to the man called Free dat lives here."

Jennet gasped as she quickly read the note: "I know you must leave tomorrow, but Dacia needs help. I'm being watched and can't get her to the next station. Please take care of her." It wasn't signed, but she knew it was from Free's sister Anne.

Jennet stared in shock from the paper in her hand to the runaway slave girl. Free had never breathed a word about helping his sister get runaway slaves to Canada. But Free was gone! "You'll have to go back to Anne. To the white lady who gave you the note."

Dacia shook her head as giant tears welled up in her eyes. "I's can't go back. I's never can't go back!"

Just then the low cry of a baby came from the bundle

Dacia held. Tears sparkled in her black eyes. "My Colin is hungry, ma'am."

Jennet pressed her hand to her throat. Finally she said, "You'd better come in the house."

"I's scared, ma'am."

The baby cried harder, and Dacia shook the bundle gently and crooned soothingly as Jennet peeked out the barn door. She knew Nina and Tunis were gone. The other neighboring houses were hidden among trees. No one was in sight.

"Come with me," said Jennet, taking Dacia's stick-thin arm. Jennet kept Dacia close to her side as she walked to the back door and stepped inside. Smells of breakfast coffee still hung in the air. It was not yet eight o'clock, but it seemed like an entire day had passed since Free had left.

Dacia set the bundle on the table, pushed aside the rags inside, and lifted out a tiny crying baby that Jennet could see was only a few days old.

"Sit down here," said Jennet, pulling a chair out from the table. "Feed the baby while I get you something to eat."

Sighing, Dacia sank to the chair and nursed the baby.

From the pantry Jennet brought bread, cheese, and ham. She poured a tall glass of milk and set the food on the table.

While the baby nursed, Dacia ate as if she hadn't seen food in a long time.

"What am I going to do with you?" asked Jennet, more to herself than to Dacia.

Dacia lifted startled eyes. "You won'ts send me back, will you, ma'am?"

"No."

Dacia gently burped the baby before she set him back to nurse again. "Dey knew I was gonna have a baby. Dey planned to take him right out of my arms after I had him and make me go wait on old Mas'r Jacob again. I begged 'em to let me keep him. And I didn't want to be sent back to Mas'r Jacob. But dey was gonna take my baby, no matter how much I begged. And dey was gonna send me back to Mas'r Jacob, no matter what he did to me." Dacia shuddered as she bent her head over her baby. "I run. I run fast as I could. When I gots North, but not to Canada, I had Colin right out in a field."

"When was that?"

"Prob'ly six days now."

"And you've been traveling ever since?"

Dacia nodded. "He's my baby. My Colin. I won'ts let nobody sell him. I run. I run and folks helped me. We gots to get to freedom land. We gots to be free!"

Jennet knew Dacia's anguish firsthand, and she determined to think of some way to help. Suddenly she thought of Pa and his help with runaway slaves. She'd take Dacia and the baby to Pa and let him see that they got to the next station. She knotted her fists in her lap. She'd ask Pa to help Dacia, but she wouldn't have anything more to do with him.

She glanced at Dacia and the baby. There were bounty hunters looking for runaway slaves. If she was caught with one, she'd be sent to prison. She'd just have to make sure that she didn't get caught!

Jennet jumped up and told Dacia, "You finish with Colin, and then you're going to wash that travel dirt off and dress in my clothes. We're going out in the country where someone else will help you to freedom."

Dacia caught Jennet's hand and pressed it to her cheek while tears filled her eyes. "Praise be to God! You be an angel, ma'am."

"I'm not," said Jennet dryly. "I'm Jennet Havlick."

Later in the bedroom Jennet helped Dacia change into the green calico dress. "You're a very pretty girl, Dacia."

Dacia ducked her head. "I be ugly on the outside. But inside I be beautiful like Jesus."

Dacia stepped close to the looking glass and stared and stared. "I feels like a old lady, but I looks like a little girl."

"How old are you?"

'Fourteen.'

"You are a little girl! Do you have a husband?"

"No. Mas'r Jacob put that baby inside me." Dacia motioned to the baby asleep on Jennet's bed. "I wanted to rid myself of him, but I knowed I couldn't kill him just 'cause I hated Mas'r Jacob." Dacia ran a finger gently down Colin's light brown cheek. "I loves this baby. I won't let him be no slave to nobody!"

Jennet pressed her hand to her still-flat stomach, suddenly feeling the same way about her baby. She'd been forced to do what others had said all of her life. She would not let that happen to her baby!

Jennet found a basket, placed a blanket in it, and carefully laid Colin inside. She covered him lightly with a cloth to make it look like a picnic basket. Anyone pursuing Dacia might look for her *and* a baby since she was so close to delivering when she ran away.

"Let's go, Dacia," Jennet said softly.

Just then a new idea occurred to her. "Dacia, I'm going to dress you in Free's clothes and cut your hair. Folks will think you're a boy."

"I's do anything to reach freedom land, Miss Jen!"

Later, Dacia did indeed look like a boy. She stared at herself in the looking glass. "Ain't nobody can tell it's Dacia," she said, giggling slightly.

Their eyes met in the looking glass, and they both smiled. Jennet announced, "We'll call you Abe." That was the name of her butcher and the first name that popped into her mind.

"Abe." Dacia giggled harder.

A few minutes later Jennet sat beside Dacia in the buggy with Colin in the basket at Dacia's feet and drove down the sawdust-covered street. She passed several large homes, a furniture factory, a blacksmith, and a livery. As men in buggies and wagons lifted their hats to her, Jennet felt apprehensive: *Would they wonder about Dacia?* Dacia stiffened, then relaxed when nobody barked out a command to halt.

The sun sent warmth through the buggy's black canvas top. Several children played in one yard they passed, and Jennet heard their laughter and their shouts. Finally they reached the road leading to the Havlick farm. At the pace they were going, they would reach the farm just after noon. Birds sang in the giant trees that shaded the rutted road. She hesitated, then flicked the reins for Acorn to walk faster.

Jennet's heart skipped a beat at her daring plan.

"That man Free, he your husband, Miss Jen?" asked Dacia.

Jennet said very quietly, "Yes."

"You don't much like him?"

Jennet shot Dacia a startled look. "I didn't say that!"

"I's feels things, Miss Jen."

"He's all right, Dacia, but I planned to marry someone else."

"Why didn't you."

"He's off fighting in the war."

"Is your husband too old to fight in the war?"

"No. He wanted to stay here and be a lumberman." Jennet knew there was another reason that Free wouldn't talk about. She knew he wasn't afraid to go, but she had no idea what secret reason was locked inside him.

"Does he beats you?"

"No."

"You best forget about the man you ain't married to and love this man called Free."

Jennet's heart jerked strangely. "Why do you say that?"

"He be your husband, Miss Jen."

Jennet pressed her lips tightly together.

"I's didn't mean to make you feel bad, Miss Jen."

"I know." Her eyes full of pain, Jennet said, "Do you mind if we talk about something else?"

"We's can talk about anything you wants." Dacia smiled broadly.

Just then a man on horseback rode around them, dust puffing around the bay's hooves. The man glanced back at them, then looked again when he spotted Dacia.

Jennet saw his look and shivers ran down her spine. She heard Dacia's sharp intake of breath.

The man pulled in the bay and turned around, right in the way of the buggy. Jennet wanted to slap the reins down hard on Acorn and make a run for it, but she knew she couldn't. She had to act as if everything was normal.

"Please, move," she called to the man.

"A word with you, miss," he said as his bay sidestepped nervously.

Jennet pulled back on the reins and said, "Whoa, Acorn." She didn't dare look at Dacia, but she felt her fear.

The man brought the bay up next to Jennet, all the time watching Dacia. "I'm looking for a runaway slave girl. I thought maybe you and your darky might have seen her."

Jennet lifted her chin and tried to look years older than she was. "Sir, Abe and I are going to visit my family. We aren't out looking for runaway slave girls."

"Abe, you say?"

Jennet scowled at the man. Oh, what would she do if Colin started crying? "Abe. He's riding with me to see my family. My husband, Freeman Havlick, doesn't want me riding alone."

"Havlick." The man nodded. "I was at Roman Havlick's farm a few days ago."

"He is my husband's father."

"And is your husband off fighting to free the slaves?" asked the man with a sneer.

"He's a lumberman," said Jennet steadily. "Now, let me be on my way."

"I'll ride along with you since I'm going that way."

Jennet's heart beat so loudly she thought the man could

hear it. It took all her courage to say, "I would like to be by myself. I have much to think about."

"But you're not by yourself. Abe here is with you."

"I consider that being by myself, sir!"

The man laughed and slapped his thigh. "I'm sure glad to hear you don't call them colored folks equals like a lot of these Michigan abolitionists do."

Jennet fought against the panic rising in her. "I must be on my way!"

"Not so almighty fast there!" The man leaned over and looked right into Dacia's face. "You got them papers to show me who you are?"

Dacia shrugged, but Jennet knew she was too frightened to speak.

Forcing her hands to stop trembling, Jennet lifted her handbag. "I have his papers." Could the man even read? She'd show him the letter she'd started to Marie. If he could read, she'd think of something else. If he couldn't, they'd be safe. She fumbled with the drawstring on her bag. She pulled out the partial letter and thrust it at the man. "Here! See for yourself!"

He took the paper, scowled at it, and muttered, "Free." Finally he gave it back to her. His hand was dirty, his thick fingernails chipped. "I plan on finding that runaway girl."

Jennet glanced down at the letter, saw that she'd mentioned Free's name, and realized the man could read only the one word. She turned an icy stare on him. "You saw what you wanted, now get out of my way."

The man tipped his hat, turned the bay, and rode away in a cloud of dust.

"I's gonna faint dead away," whispered Dacia.

"Me too," said Jennet, closing her eyes to make the world stop spinning like the top her sisters had.

Colin cried a short, sharp cry, then was quiet.

Jennet laughed breathlessly. "I'm glad he didn't do that while that man was here."

"I's prayed he wouldn't," said Dacia, smiling. "Thank you, Jesus. You is one big miracle worker!

Jennet smiled as she slapped the reins against Acorn. "I hope nobody else stops us. I don't have enough strength or courage for that."

"We's got all the courage we's need, Miss Jen! Colin and me, we's gonna make it to freedom land! I jest knows it!"

"I'm sure my pa will help you," Jennet said with more confidence than she felt. She frowned at the thought of seeing Pa and talking to him about Dacia as if nothing had happened between them. What if Pa wouldn't help Dacia?

Jennet pulled back on the reins and slowed Acorn. Fields of tall corn stretched for miles where once giant hardwood trees had stood.

"What's you scared of, Miss Jen?" asked Dacia.

"It's been months since I've heard from home." Jennet told Dacia a little about herself and her family. "What if Ma is sick again or maybe dead?" Jennet groaned. "Maybe I should turn around and go home." She saw panic reappear in Dacia's eyes. "I'm sorry, Dacia. I won't turn back!" she said with such force that Acorn pricked her ears.

About noon Jennet watched a wagon driven by a stout, bearded farmer approach them. The man lifted his hand in a wave, and Jennet did the same. She felt his stare but kept her eyes straight ahead.

"They's all stare at me," said Dacia with a loud sigh.

"We're almost there," said Jennet.

Several minutes later Jennet drove along the stretch of road between the pigpen and the farmyard and turned into the drive. Everything looked the same. Pigs still rooted and squealed in their pen. Cattle grazed in the fields next to the cornfields. It was too early to harvest the corn, and the wheat and oats and hay were already done, so there were no workers around. Pa and Roman would be in the woodlot cutting firewood for the winter. Next to the main house wash flapped on the clothesline stretched between two trees. Bright zinnias and marigolds swayed in the breeze along the front of the large white frame house. The house looked deserted even with several windows open, but Jennet knew Lillian Havlick would be inside, probably knitting wool socks for Roman for the coming winter. Kit, the hired girl, would already be starting supper, even though she'd probably just finished cleaning up after dinner. A chicken squawked and ran out of Acorn's way.

Jennet glanced back toward the road, longing to turn and drive away as fast as she could, but she continued past the big barn and the granary, and back along the narrow lane to the two-story log cabin. Butterflies fluttered in her stomach as she stopped Acorn. "We're here," she said weakly.

"Don't be scared, Miss Jen," said Dacia, patting Jennet's hand.

Jennet tried to smile but couldn't.

Jennet climbed carefully from the buggy, stiff from sitting so long, and tied the reins over the rail that she'd helped Pa split about three years ago. Where were the girls? Why didn't anyone step outside to see who had driven up? Maybe all of them were in the woodlot helping with the wood. It took a lot of wood for the cabin and the main house. She'd helped split and stack wood as long as she could remember.

With a quick look around, Dacia jumped to the ground, then reached for the basket. Colin didn't make a sound. "What you want me to do, Miss Jen?"

Jennet hesitated before answering, "You wait in the barn until I find Pa." Jennet walked Dacia to the barn, found a hiding place behind a pile of hay, and gave her a drink of water from the well. "Make yourself comfortable and I'll be back for you later."

"I's be just fine here, Miss Jen. Me and Colin will be."

Jennet made her way toward the cabin. Would the family be glad to see her? Would they guess that she was going to have a baby? How she longed to slip out of sight with Dacia!

Jennet glanced at the angel that stood over Baby Vernon's grave, sighed heavily, and walked to the cabin door. Blood pounded in her ears. What would Ma say when she learned that she was married to Freeman Havlick? Was Ma even alive?

Just then the door opened and Ma stepped out. She wore a faded gray dress with tiny faded red-and-yellow flowers all over it. She stopped short when she saw Jennet.

"Ma?" Tears filled Jennet's eyes. Ma looked young, healthy, and pretty!

"Jen! It's me. Marie! Not Ma!"

"Marie? Is it really you?" Jennet laughed and hugged Marie hard. Marie smelled like yeast and soap. Jennet stepped back from her. "You look just like Ma!"

"I know. It's funny, isn't it?" Marie fiercely hugged Jennet again, then let her go. "I heard someone drive up, but I thought it was the others coming in with a load of wood." Marie brushed tears from her eyes and laughed shakily. "Oh, Jen! It's really you!"

Jennet hugged Marie again as she struggled with the scalding tears that threatened to overflow. Marie had grown up while she was gone and she'd missed seeing it happen! It just wasn't fair! Jennet caught Marie's hands and held them tightly. "Where are the girls?"

"Still in the woodlot, but they should be back soon."

Jennet could barely get the next question past the hard lump in her throat. "And Ma?"

"With the girls and Tim."

Jennet's heart leaped with gladness. "Then she's all right?"

"Oh, yes! She's back to singing and telling stories!"

Jennet brushed a tear away. "I'm glad she's well again."

Marie looked Jennet up and down. "You look so different! So grown up!"

"So do you." Jennet flushed. What would Marie say if she knew about Free and the baby?

Marie squeezed Jennet's hand. "Jen, you're so pretty!"

"So are you."

Marie blushed, making her rosy cheeks even rosier. "Thank you. Come inside and I'll get you a cup of water and something to eat."

"Wait" Jennet's eyes darted toward the barn, then across the field to the woodlot.

"What?"

"Pa. Where's . . . he?"

"In the woodlot." Marie brushed back a strand of dark hair. "He's . . . he's changed, Jen."

"Oh?"

"He looks so old! He lost the spark he had. He took it real hard when you left."

Jennet clenched her fists at her sides. "He sold me!"

Marie nodded. "Try to forgive him."

Fire flashed from Jennet's blue eyes. "I can't! Please, let's not talk about it." She watched a grasshopper jump from one tall blade of green to another. "I would like the drink you offered."

"Oh, Jen." Marie wrapped her arms around Jennet and held her close. "He hurt you so much!"

"Yes. He did. But let's not talk about it. Please!" Hand in hand they walked inside. Jennet looked around the room and shook her head. "It still looks the same. I thought it would be different, but it's not."

Marie filled a glass with water and handed it to Jennet. She watched her finish it before asking, "Why didn't you write? Why are you here now? Where's Uncle Tait?"

"First, I have to see Pa."

Marie lifted her dark brow questioningly. "He'll be here soon. Just tell me how you came to be here."

"It's a long story." Jennet laughed as she sank to the bench at the table, the spot where she'd always sat. Who had taken her spot when she left over a year ago? "Marie, I did write. I wrote lots of letters."

"But we never heard from you!" Marie sat in Ma's chair and leaned toward Jennet.

Jennet told Marie about her life with Tait. Marie bristled with anger that intensified with each detail Jennet shared. After she described finding Marie's letters, Jennet added, "I still have the copies." Finally she took a long, steadying breath and said, "I'm married."

"Married!"

"To Freeman Havlick, and we live in Grand Rapids."

"Married to Free?" cried Marie.

"Yes. He stopped at Uncle's and saw me there." Jennet kept her eyes lowered. She couldn't tell Marie the whole truth! "He paid Uncle what was owing, took me to Grand Rapids, and married me."

Marie pressed her hand to her mouth, unable to take the whole story in. "Does Roman know?"

"No."

"I know Lillian doesn't or she would've told me. We're very close." Marie blushed and giggled nervously. "She likes me. I'm going to be . . . to be her . . . daughter."

Jennet's eyes widened in shock and her stomach knotted painfully. "Daughter?"

Marie nervously brushed a strand of hair off her flushed cheek. "Now that you're married to Free, I don't feel so guilty about this."

"About what?" whispered Jennet hoarsely.

Marie swallowed hard. "Wex and I are going to be married when his time is up."

"Married?" whispered Jennet. Pain ripped through her, then anger at Marie forced back the pain. "Just how did this happen?" Jennet asked coldly.

"We've been writing to each other, and we fell in love." Marie lifted her chin. "It's very romantic."

The wood in the cookstove snapped, sounding like a shot inside the cabin.

Jennet laced her fingers together and forced back the blackness that she felt washing over her. "What does Roman say about that?"

"Nothing. He likes me too. He's not as hard as he was, Jen. Both he and Pa have changed. Pa is easier to live with, and Roman doesn't get angry over everything. He feels like he lost both his sons. And Anne won't even visit him."

"He won't let her," said Jennet sharply.

"He won't? That isn't what Lillian says. She says Anne is too angry with Roman to step foot on the farm, and she won't let them go to her house."

Jennet shook her head. "Free said different. Maybe Roman told Lillian that just to keep her from taking it out on him."

"Do you suppose?"

"It wouldn't surprise me." Jennet glanced out the back window at the barn. She'd forgotten about Dacia! She'd be wondering what had happened. Jennet pushed aside her anger and jumped up. "Marie, I have to see Pa right now!"

"Is something wrong, Jen?"

"I just have some business with Pa."

"You could drive out to the woodlot if you wanted."

"I'd better," Jennet replied, dreading the thought of facing Pa again even though Marie had said he'd changed.

Her legs trembling, Jennet walked to the door.

CHAPTER

10

♦ Nearing the woodlot, Jennet spotted Pa trimming branches off a felled oak with quick swings of his ax. His shirt tightened across his back muscles as he worked. Sunlight flashed on the shiny ax blade.

Jennet's hands tightened on the reins. It wasn't too late to turn back. She forced herself to concentrate on her all-important errand, though, and urged Acorn on. She stopped near Pa's wagon. She hadn't seen Ma and the girls because of the thick growth of trees, but she had heard their shouts and laughter. She knew they'd be loading wood. She didn't want to see Ma until she finished her business with Pa.

He looked up and saw her and slowly lowered the ax. Gray that hadn't been there before streaked his beard and hair. His shirt was stained with sweat under the armpits and down his chest. Wide green suspenders held up his dark blue pants. His pant legs were stuffed in his heavy high boots laced tightly with leather thongs. Even though Pa stood at six feet, he looked small next to the giant tree beside him. Light leaped into his blue eyes, and she frowned. How dare he act like he was glad to see her?

Jennet heard the ring of another ax as she climbed from the buggy. Suddenly a picture of Pa swinging her high in his arms and laughing flashed across her mind. She'd forgotten that he once had laughed and played with her. Impatiently she pushed the memory aside.

"Jen," he whispered as he took a hesitant step toward her.

"Hello, Pa," she said coldly.

He seemed to devour her with his eyes. "Where's Tait?"

"Not with me," she said harshly.

Pa stabbed his thick fingers through his gray-streaked hair. The wind's rustling of the leaves and a crow's cawing filled the awkward silence. Pa leaned the ax against a branch and took another step toward Jennet. "Did you run away?"

Jennet shot an answer at him. "No, but I should have!"

His beard worked and finally he spoke. "How is it you're here?"

Jennet wanted to lean against the buggy before she collapsed, but she stiffened her legs and her spine. "I wanted to see Ma and the girls." But not you, never you, the expression on her face said.

Pain flashed across Pa's face, then was gone, but not before she'd seen it and been glad for it.

"But not me?" he asked gruffly.

"No!" Her abrupt response was louder than she meant for it to be.

He grabbed his hat from the ground where he'd tossed it earlier and rammed it back on. "Then why are you here talking to me?"

Jennet looked intently at him. It was hard to read his eyes now that his hat shaded them. "I have business with you."

Pa cocked a dark brow and fingered his beard. His trousers hung on his lean frame and would've fallen except for his suspenders. He had lost weight!

Jennet plucked at her skirt. "I brought a runaway slave for you to take to the next station."

"Quiet!" Pa barked as he looked around fearfully. He strode to stand before her, close enough that she could feel the heat of his body and smell his sweat. "What do you know of runaway slaves?"

Jennet wanted to run from him, but she stood her ground. "I brought a girl and her baby for you to help," she said.

Pa glowered down at Jennet, and she trembled with the same fear that she'd always felt when he looked at her that way. What had happened to her resolve to be strong before him?

"You say you brought a girl and her baby? Where are they now?"

"In the barn, hidden behind the hay."

Pa gripped her arm and she winced. "You get yourself to the barn, and you hide them in a safer place until dark."

"But where?"

Pa looked around, then lowered his voice even more and lightened his grip. "I have a hidden room in the tack room in the barn."

Jennet's eyes widened in surprise.

Pa wiped a shaky hand across his face. "There's a ring up where the harness hangs. Pull on the ring and the peg that holds the harness, and the door will swing open. It's a tiny room, but I've made it comfortable." He groaned. "Jen, Jen, what've you got yourself into?"

Jennet's heart turned over at the look of concern for her on Pa's face. "Shall I tell Dacia you'll take them out tonight?" Jennet asked.

"Yes."

"I'll have to see that she has food."

"I'll see to it! Once you put her in that room I don't want you near it. You hear me, Jennet?"

She nodded. His urgent tones made her even more aware of the serious nature of their undertaking.

"Did you run across anybody who questioned you on the way here?"

She told him about the man on the bay, and the color drained from his face.

"Blue Newmeyer! He's trouble," said Pa, stepping back a pace from Jen. "But since he was here a few days ago, he probably won't be around for a while."

"Does he suspect you, Pa?" Jennet asked, suddenly frightened for him.

"No. He was just looking for runaways. Somebody told him Roman hires coloreds at times."

Jennet turned back to her buggy, but Pa stopped her with a hand on her arm.

"Be careful, Jen."

"I will," she said stiffly, her heart thundering. Was he actually concerned about her?

"Take care of the girl and then we'll talk about Tait."

She pulled away from Pa. "No! We won't talk! I came to see Ma and the girls. Not you!"

"What about Tait?"

"What do you care? You sold me to him!"

His eyes darkened with grief. "I'm sorry, Jen. I'm so sorry!"

"It's too late for that!" Shaking with emotion, she stepped away from him and added, "I plan to stay the night."

"Fine."

"I'm surprised you'll let me."

"Aw, Jen . . . don't break my heart!"

"What heart?" Jennet climbed in the buggy and drove away from him before she did something she didn't want to do—talk to him, understand him, even forgive him.

At the barn Jennet found Dacia curled up and burrowed

partway into a pile of hay with Colin tight against her breast. They were both fast asleep. Jennet knelt down and gently shook Dacia's stick-thin arm. Dacia awoke with a start, then relaxed when she saw it was Jennet.

"Miss Jen, I's havin' a dream that we was free!"

"You will be, Dacia! Come with me. Hurry," said Jennet in a low voice. She knew Ma and the girls would be coming with a wagonload of wood any minute. "Pa said to hide you. He'll take you after dark."

"You be mad at your daddy, Miss Jen? You be glad you gots a daddy. Mine be sold away from me when I was nine. Colin won't never gets to see my daddy. Not now and maybe not never till we gets to heaven."

"Oh, Dacia, I'm so sorry!"

"Nobody's never gonna sell me away from Colin!"

"We'll make sure of that." In the empty stall Jennet found the ring that Pa had told her about and opened the hidden door, amazed that she'd never noticed it before. The small dusty-smelling compartment was big enough to hold three men if they stood side by side with their backs pressed to the back wall. Dacia could easily sit or lie down. A horsehair blanket was folded in the far corner. With the door closed Jennet knew no light would shine in it. "Pa will be in later to bring food and water for you. Will you be all right?"

"I's been in hell, Miss Jen," whispered Dacia, her dark eyes wide. "I's can stay in that nice room as long as I needs to."

Jennet wrapped her arms around Dacia and Colin. "I'll never forget you, Dacia."

"I's won't forget you, Miss Jen. You think on what I's said about your man named Free. You learn to love him."

"I'll think about it."

"And you love your daddy!"

Jennet kissed Colin's warm cheek. She would never love Pa again!

Jennet set the basket beside Dacia in the small room. "For Colin," she said hoarsely. "Good-bye, Dacia. Enjoy your freedom."

"I's will, Miss Jen. Colin will always be free. Thanks to you, Miss Jen."

Jennet closed the secret door. She stood for a long time, her eyes full of stinging tears and worry wrinkles creasing her forehead. She hoped they would be all right.

Finally she unhitched Acorn, rubbed her down, watered her, and let her out to pasture. Acorn kicked up her heels and ran from one side of the fence to the other, then settled down to graze on the lush grass.

Back in the house Jennet found Marie working over the hot cookstove. Smells of porkchops and sweet potatoes made her mouth water. Jennet remembered that she hadn't eaten anything since breakfast on this remarkable day. "What can I do to help?" she asked.

Marie laughed, looking even more like Ma. "I bet you don't know how to sit and be company, do you?"

"No." Jennet washed her hands at the washbasin and dried them with the rough towel.

Marie lifted the heavy lid off the porkchops and carefully laid it on the work table. She faced Jennet, the long meat fork in her hand. "Did you find Pa?"

"Yes."

"And?"

Jennet frowned. "I talked business with him and that's all! I told him I'm staying the night, and he said I could."

"I'm glad." Marie turned the porkchops. Grease spattered and sizzled. She turned back to Jennet. "Jen, Pa has changed. Honest. I know how hard he was on you, but he's sorry. I know he is. Can't you forgive and forget?"

"No!"

"Don't let your anger stay all bottled up inside you like Pa did or it might come out like his did."

Jennet thought of her baby, and she knew she'd never

beat him. She'd spank him when he needed it, but she'd do it out of love, not anger or hatred or frustration. "Can't I do something to help?"

"I guess you don't want to talk about Pa."

"You're right."

"It's still early, but you can set the table if you want."

While Jennet set the plates around, she tried to think of a way to bring up Wexal without showing her feelings for him, but she couldn't find the words.

Marie laid down the long meat fork and turned to Jennet. "Would you like to read my letters from Wex?"

Jennet's heart leaped, then dropped to her feet. "I don't know. They're probably too personal."

Marie grinned and shrugged. "I don't mind."

Jennet couldn't stand the thought of seeing Wex's words of love to Marie. "Just tell me how he is."

"He was wounded three months ago."

"No!" Jennet sank to the bench, her hand at her throat. "How bad?"

Marie dashed away a tear. "A bullet in the shoulder. It healed all right but left a scar. He said in the army hospital he saw boys with their arms and legs sawed off. He smelled their rotting skin. And he saw lots of them die."

"Oh, why didn't he stay here like Free did?" cried Jennet.

"He couldn't," whispered Marie, brushing away more tears. "He said he had to *do* something. He couldn't stay here while others were dying to keep the North and South together. And he had to help set the slaves free! That's just how Wex is."

Jennet tried to imagine Wex being strong enough to face danger without running, but she couldn't. He couldn't even face his own father without cowering like a scared pup. Free had stood up to his pa. Yet, Free hadn't joined the fight. She couldn't sort it out, and right now she didn't have the energy to think about Free or Wex. She heard the wagon drive up. Ma and the girls!

Jennet ran outdoors with Marie right behind her and watched as Ma stopped the wagon at the side of the barn where they'd unload the wood into the lean-to.

Ma caught sight of Jennet, and joy flashed across her face. She leaped from the wagon and ran to Jennet while Marie held the girls back to give Ma and Jennet time alone.

"Jen! Oh, Jen!"

Ma looked years younger than she had when Jennet last saw her. Her chestnut-brown hair was neatly pulled back in a bun, and her cheeks were rosy with health. Her blue serge work dress fit her well instead of hanging on a too-thin body. She hugged Jennet tight. Just the touch of Ma's skin, which smelled like a warm rose, raised Jennet's spirits, and she once again felt love flowing from her. Tears ran down Jennet's cheeks, and she clung to Ma as if she'd never let her go.

Finally Ma held Jennet from her but kept her hands curled around Jennet's arms. "Oh, Jen! You've grown so! You are beautiful! I've longed to see you. How I've missed you! Your pa said he'd go get you from Tait's before winter. But here you are!" Ma pulled Jennet close again and held her fiercely. "I've missed you so!"

"I've missed you, Ma," whispered Jennet through her tears.

"Are you here to stay?"

Jennet forced out words around the lump in her throat. "Only for the night."

Ma's face clouded over. "Must you go back to Tait?"

Jennet struggled with the desire to tell Ma just what Pa had done to her but couldn't bring herself to say anything that would bring sorrow back to Ma. "I don't work for Uncle any longer."

"You don't?"

Jennet shook her head. Her stomach fluttered nervously. "I am married, Ma."

"Married?" whispered Ma. "Married?"

Jennet nodded. "To Freeman Havlick." She couldn't find the courage to tell Ma about the baby.

"Does Roman know? Or Lillian?"

"No."

Ma smoothed back Jennet's hair that had come loose from her braid. "You've left me speechless. Married! Without a word to us!" She glanced at the girls who were bursting in their excitement to greet Jennet. "I'll try to come to grips with it while you talk to the girls."

Jennet touched Ma's soft cheek with her fingertips. "Ma, I don't want you to feel bad. It was all so sudden, and there wasn't time to talk to you about it."

"Is Free here with you?"

"No. He's away at his lumbercamp."

"I want to know everything!" Ma kissed Jennet's cheek and let her go. "You go see the girls before they explode."

Jennet ran to the girls, and they laughed and talked and hugged her in turns. They'd all grown so much that she couldn't believe they were the same girls she'd left behind.

After the noisy greetings Jennet helped them unload the wood from the wagon. Suddenly she felt as if she'd never left. All her life she'd helped bring in wood for the winter.

"We have to haul another load yet," said Ma. "Girls, go to the well for a drink, then jump in the wagon."

With shouts and laughter the girls gathered around the well.

Before Jennet could say that she'd help with the load, she saw Blue Newmeyer riding toward them. She felt his eyes on her, and she knew he recognized her. She fought the urge to run and hide. Since Pa was still at the woodlot, she'd have to find out what Newmeyer wanted—and she'd have to do it alone.

"Who is that man?" asked Ma with a frown.

"Pa knows him," said Marie. "I saw them talking together."

"I'll deal with him," said Jennet as she looked at Ma and the suddenly quiet girls. Newmeyer was still far enough away that he couldn't hear her. "You go get the next load while I take care of this."

"Are you sure, Jen?"

"I'm sure, Ma." Jennet made her voice sound strong and sure.

Ma nodded and climbed in the wagon while the girls scrambled in behind. "See you in about a half an hour," said Ma.

"See you then," Jennet answered.

"I'd better check on supper," said Marie. She hurried to the house and slipped inside.

Blue Newmeyer reined in the bay and tipped his hat to Jennet. "We meet again," he said.

Jennet barely nodded.

"Where's the negra boy?"

"Out and about."

"I want a word with him."

"My pa's out in the woodlot chopping firewood. He could be out there helping him."

"Your husband's daddy is Roman Havlick. Who is yours?"

"Vernon Cordell."

"Ah."

Jennet felt panic rising in her, but she forced it down. She kept her hands loosely at her sides. The warm breeze pushed her skirts against her legs and feathered loose strands of her hair over her cheek. She waited for Blue Newmeyer to speak.

His bay moved restlessly and Blue pulled him up short. "You say that colored boy is with your pa?"

"He's around here somewhere. Pa might know where he is. Abe's a hard worker."

"You read his papers?" asked Blue Newmeyer.

Jennet frowned. "You read them! He was born of free parents in a free state."

"Then he shouldn't be afraid to answer some questions. Should he?"

Blue Newmeyer pulled off his hat, scratched his head, and dropped his hat back in place. Without another word he nudged the bay toward the woodlot.

Jennet knew Pa would send Blue packing, but she shivered as she thought about what would happen to her and to Pa if they were caught helping Dacia.

Suddenly a terribly wonderful idea occurred to Jennet. What if she told Blue Newmeyer about Pa's work with the Underground Railroad? Pa would be punished just as he deserved to be for selling her to Tait.

Her head whirled as she thought about Pa getting punished worse than he'd ever punished her. Then she frowned. Pa would probably be hung. She certainly didn't want that to happen. Ma and the girls would have to fend for themselves. Besides, she really didn't want Pa to stop helping runaways.

Jennet gazed across the acres of corn as Pa's look of delight at seeing her burned into her heart. How could he be glad to see her when he hated her as much as he did?

Impatiently Jennet pushed thoughts of Pa out of her mind. She'd spend time with Ma and the girls, then go home. Maybe she could take one of the girls home with her to help her and keep her company while Free was gone. Would Ma part with one of them for that length of time? Probably not, but she'd make the suggestion anyway.

Several minutes later they all sat down to supper, with Jennet in her old place. She took in the whole scene and realized once again how much she had missed her family. The girls still giggled at the least little thing. They were clean with neatly brushed hair even though their clothes were faded and patched. Ma looked as healthy as she had

before Baby Vernon. Pa smiled down the length of the table
at Ma with such love in his eyes that Jennet had to look
away. She'd forgotten the love between Ma and Pa. A desire to experience that kind of love welled up inside Jennet,
taking her by surprise.

Now that Ma was back at the table, they prayed before
they ate. To Jennet's amazement, Pa asked the blessing on
the food. She'd never in her life heard him pray. A warm
feeling wrapped around her heart, and she wanted to reach
out and touch Pa the way she had as a little girl. But a picture of him whipping her when she'd innocently given Wex
the birthday handkerchief flashed across her mind and
stopped her. The anger she felt toward him replaced the
warm feeling.

Pa ended his prayer with, "Thank You, Jesus, for bringing Jennet back to us today. Bless her and keep her.
Amen."

Jennet wouldn't look at him as she lifted her head.

"We are thankful to have you home, Jen," said Ma from
her end of the table.

"Ma, I'm glad you're well again," said Jennet, smiling
around Nola and Lois at Ma.

"We all are," said Pa, smiling at Ma with such love that
Jennet blushed with embarrassment.

As they ate, Jennet tried to answer all their questions.
She told them about Eve and Joshua, but she didn't say
anything about Tait overworking her or beating her. She'd
leave that for Pa's ears alone so that he'd know just what
he'd done to her. She saw the startled look on Pa's face
when she said that she was married to Freeman Havlick.
She didn't tell them that she was expecting a baby or that
Free had married her so he could get his inheritance.

Darkness had fallen by the time they finished eating, and
the lamp cast a soft glow over the room. Jennet couldn't
remember when she had talked so much. Her mouth felt
dry, and weariness was overtaking her. She tired quicker

than she had before expecting a baby. She listened to her sisters tell her what they had been doing.

Pa pushed himself away from the table and stood up. "Me and Jen are going outside for a talk," he said, walking to the door and holding it open.

Jennet started to object but thought maybe he wanted to say something about Dacia and Blue Newmeyer, so she followed him.

Granger ran to Jennet and sniffed her, then wriggled all over the way he had as a puppy.

"Aw, Granger, how've you been?" Jennet rubbed his neck and between his ears and kissed the top of his head. To her surprise, Pa waited patiently without snapping at her for being slow.

They crossed the yard to a tall maple. Standing with her back pressed against the tree, Jennet glanced toward the dark shape of the barn where Dacia and Colin were still hiding. Then she turned her attention to Pa, who had bent over to pat Granger.

Pa cleared his throat. "Blue Newmeyer was mad as a hornet that he couldn't talk to that colored boy Abe." He continued to pat Granger, keeping his eyes on the dog.

"What'd you tell him?" she asked.

"To get out of here and leave us alone. I said Abe didn't have to see him or talk to him." He didn't even try to disguise his contempt for Newmeyer.

"When will you take Dacia and the baby away?"

"Later tonight."

She could tell that Pa had something else on his mind, but she didn't want to know what it was. She wanted only to tell him just how much she hated him. Nevertheless, the thought of the love she'd seen in his eyes kept the words from pouring out.

"Jen, you be careful of Blue Newmeyer! He's dangerous. Don't do anything else to help runaways."

His well-intentioned warning sounded like an order to Jennet. She told him, "I will help if *I* want, Pa."

Pa sighed heavily. "Don't do it just to get back at me."

"You can't tell me what to do any longer, Pa. I will do as I please, and it pleases me to help runaways." Jennet glared at Pa, daring him to say more. Maybe she'd be able to tell him just how she felt about him after all!

Pa persisted. "I'll get word to Free to stop you from such dangerous work."

"It's dangerous for you and you still do it," she challenged.

"But I can protect myself."

"I am not a child, Pa. You saw to that!"

He growled deep in his throat. "Forgive me, Jen! I can't sleep or eat with the guilt resting on my shoulders."

So, he had suffered! Good! He deserved to! A cloud uncovered the moon, and Jennet saw the anguish on Pa's face. She smiled grimly. She wanted to relish every detail of his pain.

"I have only myself to blame," Pa said just above a hoarse whisper. "You brought out my anger because you were always so sure of yourself, so strong. No matter how hard you had to work, you were cheerful. I couldn't be that way, and seeing you made it bad for me. Then when your ma got bad sick, I took it out on you. I need you to forgive me."

"He beat me, Pa," Jennet hissed. How could he think she'd forgive him? "Uncle beat me if I made a mistake. A mistake! He worked me hard." She took a step toward Pa, her face pale in the moonlight. "And he didn't give me much to eat."

Pa held his hands helplessly out to Jennet. "Jen, Jen. It's too much to bear!"

"And it's because of you, Pa!" Jennet shook her finger at him.

"I know!" Pa looked down at his hands and groaned from deep inside.

Jennet leaned toward him, her voice rising. "How can I forgive you, Pa?"

"I don't know. Only with God's help."

Without another word Jennet turned on her heel. She would not forgive him, not even with God's help!

The next morning Ma walked Jennet to Baby Vernon's grave. Ma touched the angel, but Jennet couldn't bear to see her with it. She looked up at the bright blue sky.

Ma squeezed Jennet's hand. "Jen, I've come to grips with losing Baby Vernon. I had forgotten that I could find peace in God." Ma smiled as she slipped her arm around Jennet's shoulder.

Jennet leaned into Ma's warmth and looked into her dear face.

"Jen, Baby Vernon is in heaven with Jesus, and I'll see him again someday." Ma blinked tears from her eyes. "Baby Vernon's body is buried here, Jen, but he is in heaven. We didn't need this angel and I told your pa so, but he'd already paid for it and had Baby Vernon's name on it."

Jennet felt the familiar rage building inside her, and she quickly turned away from the angel to look toward the barn where she'd hidden Dacia and Colin. Pa had secretly told her before breakfast that they were safely on their way to Canada.

Jennet turned back to Ma. "I'm going home soon, Ma. I wanted to ask if I could take one of the girls to stay with me a while."

Ma frowned slightly, considering the request. "Marie?"

Jennet knew Marie would talk constantly about Wex and she couldn't abide that. "No. You need Marie here."

"I do. And so does Lillian Havlick. She's come to depend a lot on Marie."

Jennet didn't want to hear how the Havlicks' felt about Marie. "What about Nola?"

Ma shook her head. "It would break Nola's heart to leave Tim."

Jennet hadn't meet Tim yet, but Nola had said she'd take her to the barn to introduce them while Tim was doing chores. She'd told Nola they'd go after her talk with Ma.

Ma brushed a tear off her cheek. "You could take Opal. Or Lois. But she'd have to be home in October before winter set in."

Jennet lifted Ma's hand to her lips and kissed the back of it. "Could you come? Oh, Ma, I need you!"

Ma pulled Jennet close and kissed first one cheek, then the other. "My dear daughter, I long to be with you, but I can't leave the girls and your pa. You can understand that, can't you?"

Jennet nodded slightly.

"Why don't you stay here, Jen?" Ma laughed in delight. Her light brown eyes glowed. "Yes! Stay here until Free comes home!"

Oh, but it sounded wonderful! Jennet's heart leaped. She could be with Ma and the girls every day! Then she thought of Pa and Roman and she frowned. She would not live under the same roof with Pa or on the same farm with Roman!

Jennet shook her head. "I can't stay, Ma."

Ma's face fell, then she smiled. "I know you want your own home. But if you change your mind, you're welcome to stay."

"Thank you, Ma." Jennet forced back the hot tears stinging her eyes. If only she could tell Ma what Pa had done to her! "I'll go find Nola so I can meet this famous Tim I've heard so much about."

"He's a fine boy, Jen. We love him as our own."

Jealousy flashed through Jennet, but she forced it away as she walked back to the cabin with Ma.

Later in the barn, when Jennet shook hands with Tim, she liked him immediately. He was tall and thin with red hair and freckles. He had an excitement for life that reminded her of Free. Abruptly she pushed thoughts of Free away and listened to Tim talk about the farm.

Just as Jennet was leaving the barn, Roman Havlick strode up. He wore dark work pants held up by a wide black belt—the same belt he'd used on her. Remembering his harsh treatment of her, Jennet flushed with anger. Roman stopped short at the sight of her. His face darkened, but she didn't know if it was from hostility or guilt.

"Jen," he said sharply. "This is a surprise."

"I'm on my way home now," she said coldly.

"With your uncle?"

"No. Your son Free." She waited until she saw the shocked look on his face. "He and I are married." How she loved to see his anguish!

Roman swallowed hard a few times and finally said, "Then he has a good wife."

Jennet couldn't believe her ears. Where were the enraged outbursts that she'd expected?

Roman glanced around. "Is he with you?"

"No. He's at his lumbercamp."

Roman responded predictably then. "What does he know of the lumber business? He was raised a farmer!"

"He has been working at lumbercamps since he was seventeen. He is a lumberman!" Why had she said it with such pride? Was it for Roman's benefit or Free's? She didn't know the answer and didn't want to sort it out.

"Come to the house with me to tell Lillian. She'll be pleased to learn that Free is married to you."

Jennet scowled. What was happening here? She was so sure that the Havlicks would be furious. She shook her head. "I'm leaving now."

"Do you live in Grand Rapids?"

"Yes."

Roman brushed an unsteady hand over his face. "Could we visit you?"

Jennet doubled her fists at her side. She wanted to tell

Roman she never wanted to see him again as long as she lived, but instead she said, "You can visit in the spring when Free is home."

Roman pulled his hat low, said good-bye, and walked toward the main house with the steps of a tired old man.

Her heart hammering, Jennet left Nola with Tim and hurried to the cabin to tell Ma and the other girls good-bye.

Suddenly she wanted to be home alone in her own house where she had to think about only herself and her feelings. She didn't want to share her quiet house with anyone, not even one of her sisters.

At the cabin Jennet saw that Acorn was already hitched to the buggy with a saddled horse tied to the back. She frowned.

Just then Pa came around the corner of the cabin. He smiled when he saw Jennet. "You can't go home alone," he said. "It's not safe. Especially with Blue Newmeyer nosing around. I'll drive you and ride back."

Pa's kindness left her speechless. She just nodded before entering the cabin.

CHAPTER

11

♦ Jennet peeked from the corner of her eye at Pa beside her in the buggy. His hat was pushed to the back of his head, and Acorn's reins dangled between his fingers. He looked deep in thought. Was he going to make the entire trip to Grand Rapids without speaking? Jennet moved restlessly, taking her eyes off Pa and watching Acorn pick her way around the deep ruts in the road. She had to admit Pa kept a nice rein on Acorn, not too tight and not too loose.

The buggy swayed and bumped as the large wheels rolled in and out of the ruts. With each bump the wooden seat bounced on its heavy steel springs, causing Jennet to grab the seat and brace her feet on the wooden floor. The black canvas top of the buggy shielded them against the hot morning sun. Pa's horse tied to the back of the buggy easily kept pace.

After driving almost an hour, Pa suddenly chuckled, and Jennet shot him an astonished look. Pa had chuckled right out loud!

Pa glanced at her, and she saw his blue eyes twinkle, actually twinkle! It almost sent her reeling. "Jen, I was just thinking about the time you were six and we went fishing together. I caught a few bass and you caught a perch no bigger than five inches, but you were proud of it."

"It was the first fish I ever caught," she said stiffly. She brushed dust off her skirt. "I'm surprised you remembered."

Pa pushed his hat further back on his head and smiled. "I remember a lot of good times we had."

"I remember the bad ones." She did remember some of the good times when she was least expecting to, but she wouldn't admit it to him.

Pa looked down the long stretch of road, then over at Jennet. With high-pitched cries flocks of grackles flew from the tops of the trees. For a minute the whir of wings covered the clip-clop of the horses' hooves. Pa smiled wider, showing a flash of white teeth. "I remember another time. An important time in your life."

"When?" Jennet asked, then could've bitten her tongue for doing so.

"When you were nine years old. Your ma read in her Bible that God loved you so much that He sent Jesus to die on the cross for you and you started to cry. She told you all about Jesus. You said you wanted Him to be your Friend and Savior. Ma prayed with you, and you accepted Jesus into your heart."

Jennet frowned. "I remember that you were angry."

Pa shook his head and clicked his tongue. "I was too dumb to know any better. But now I do. Because August last I asked Jesus to be my Savior."

Jennet stared in shock at him. She never thought she'd hear him talk that way. He'd always made Ma keep what he called her religion talk between her and the girls.

"When your ma got sick and Baby Vernon died, I almost hit bottom. But when I let you go with Tait, I hit below bottom. I wanted to go hang myself."

Jennet stared at him as if she'd never seen him before. Was this really Pa?

Pa groaned and his beard twitched. "I was a hopeless case. Hopeless! And then one night in a dream Jesus came to me and told me He loved me. He said He wanted to put my life back together again." Pa rubbed an unsteady hand over his moisture-filled eyes. "I woke up, and I felt as if Jesus was standing beside the bed. Right then I asked Him to forgive me and take my life and make it into something good." Pa cleared his throat and couldn't speak for a while.

Jennet's heart beat fast. It was hard to keep from reaching out to Pa or snuggling close to him the way she had when she was a little girl.

"I looked at your ma sleeping restlessly beside me. She had always said Jesus was a miracle worker. Right then I put my hands on Hannah, and I prayed for her. I didn't know how to pray, but I stumbled over some words. Jesus knew my heart. From that day on she started getting better." Pa slowed Acorn until the buggy was barely rolling. "Jen, I prayed that God would give me a chance to help you. Now He has. Let Jesus work a miracle in your life. Let Him take away the bitterness and anger you feel."

She felt herself softening and she almost nodded.

"Let Jesus help you forgive me and Tait."

"That's asking too much, Pa!" A black cloud settled over her, and she felt as if her heart had turned to stone.

"Jennet, Jennet. You've always been strong willed. Don't let what I did to you keep you from God." Pa waited until he passed a creaking wagon full of hay. Dust floated behind it, blocking out the bright sunlight for a while. Pa cleared his throat. "I learned that I have an enemy. It's Satan. He does all he can to wreck lives. I was letting him wreck mine! That made me mad, but it helped set me free. I was not going to let the enemy steal my wife, my family, or our happiness."

Suddenly Jennet remembered the Scripture she'd helped Eve memorize that said Satan had come to steal, kill, and destroy. And Jesus had come to bring life more abundantly. Eve had told her that when she stepped into the enemy's territory, he had the freedom to harm her, but when she stayed close to God and obeyed His Word, Satan couldn't hurt her. "Satan will tempt you to do wrong," Eve had said. "It's up to you if you give in to that temptation. When you give in, that puts you right in his territory and he tries to make you as much a slave to him as the colored folks in the South are to the white folks."

Eve's words seemed to echo inside Jennet. She knew she was in Satan's territory when she remained angry and unforgiving.

"You're awful quiet, Jen," said Pa softly.

"I have nothing to say!"

"I've been praying for you."

Pa had prayed for her! She quickly brushed away a tear that slipped down her cheek.

The buggy swayed harder and Pa's leg bumped Jennet's. What Pa had said played over and over in her mind. She *was* tired of being a slave—first to Pa, then Tait, now Free. Was she a slave to Satan?

Jennet thought of the book of Romans that she and Eve had memorized together. She remembered that as a child of God, no matter what came against her, she couldn't be separated from the love of God. Only she could bring that separation by sinning. She knew very well that unforgiveness was a sin.

But could she forgive Pa? She saw tears running down his sun-darkened cheeks into his beard, and her heart almost broke in two.

Pa stopped Acorn at the side of the road. He turned to Jennet and took her trembling hands in his. "Jennet, I love you. I want you to be free to be happy again."

Jennet gripped his hard, work-roughened hands. "Pa, you don't love me or you wouldn't have sold me!"

"I do love you!"

"You sold me!"

He bent his head, and his broad shoulders shook with sobs. "I am so sorry for the wrong I did to you. Please believe me! Please forgive me! Your ma has."

Jennet dropped Pa's hands and looked at him in disbelief. "But I never told Ma anything about . . ." Jennet couldn't go on.

"Last night your ma asked me why you were so mad at me, and I told her the whole truth."

"Oh, Pa!"

"But she forgave me, Jen." Pa swallowed hard and sniffed. "She forgave me! And she said she'd pray that you'd forgive me too."

"Oh, Pa," whispered Jennet. Dare she believe him? Had he told Ma, and had she really forgiven him?

"I did wrong, Jen. I'd take it all back if I could. But I can't!"

Almost against her will, Jennet flung her arms around Pa. Tears flowed up and out and down her cheeks to wet the front of Pa's jacket. Her voice muffled against him, she said, "I forgive you, Pa. I do!"

Fiercely Pa held her to him as he sobbed out his anguish for what he'd done to her, then he lifted her face and kissed her damp cheeks. His beard felt strange against her but brought back the memories that she'd hidden deep inside her of the times he'd rubbed his beard against her cheeks and neck just to make her laugh.

"Your ma will be glad to hear of this," he said in a husky voice.

"God answers prayer," whispered Jennet, brushing fresh tears off her cheeks. A warmth spread through her, and she realized all her anger and hatred toward Pa had melted away.

Just then Jennet saw a rider coming fast down the road toward them. "Pa, it's Blue Newmeyer! What'll we do?"

"Act normal," said Pa, but his voice shook a little.

"We'll tell him Abe left during the night and I wasn't going to wait around for him to come back."

"Good," said Pa, patting her arm.

Blue Newmeyer reined so quickly to a stop beside them that his bay reared and snorted. Acorn bobbed her head, and Pa quieted her with a firm, but gentle word.

"Where's the colored boy?" snapped Newmeyer without wasting any time on pleasantries. He didn't bother to tip his hat.

"I refused to wait on him! If he wants to get back to Grand Rapids, he'll have to do it on his own," Jennet said matter-of-factly.

Newmeyer barked out an ugly laugh and slapped his leg. Dust rose from his gray trousers. "You got the right idea, missy. Too bad more people don't see it that way. Let the niggers do it on their own. Then we'd get 'em for sure. All abolitionists should be hung!"

Blue Newmeyer's wild look frightened Jennet. She was glad that Pa had insisted on driving her home.

"We're a free state, Newmeyer," said Pa coldly. "We have the freedom to be against slavery."

Newmeyer's eyes thinned to slits of blue steel. "But you don't have the freedom to help runaways!"

Jennet sat very still while Pa and Newmeyer stared each other down. Finally Newmeyer kicked his bay and rode away.

Much later Jennet showed Pa through her house and gave him some food and a tall glass of cold well water. It would be suppertime before he got back home. She walked to the barn with him to get his horse. Suddenly she didn't want him to go. The feeling surprised her after being angry with him for so long.

"Pa, come see me when you're in town," she said, trying to keep her voice normal.

"We will. Your ma and me. But it'll be a while before we can get back."

"I know."

"Come see us again," he said. "But, Jen, don't come

alone. Who knows just how long Newmeyer will stay in the area." Pa caught Jen's hands and held them tightly. "We'll be praying for you and you pray for us, Jen."

"I will, Pa." Tears glistened in her eyes.

Pa hugged her close, then swung into the saddle.

Calico rubbed against her and purred. Jen picked him up and held him as she watched Pa ride down the street past the neighbors' houses and out of sight.

"Jennet!"

Nina was crossing the yard at top speed, her rose-colored dress bouncing around her ankles. "I'm so glad you're back!" Nina reached out and hugged her. Looking closely at her, she announced, "Something's different. I can feel it."

Jennet smiled. "Come inside and we can talk."

Jennet opened the windows to let in the pleasant breeze, then sat in the front room in a soft chair across from Nina. She told Nina about her visit, all except the part about Dacia and Blue Newmeyer. It wasn't safe to let even a good friend know that she'd helped a runaway.

"Tunis will be delighted to hear your news," said Nina. "He spends a lot of time praying for you and Free."

Just then someone knocked on the door. Jennet lifted her brow in surprise. Who would visit her aside from Nina?

Jennet peeked out the window and saw Free's sister, Anne, standing there, her face pale. She was short and slight with Free's dark hair and eyes. Jennet glanced at Nina. "It's Anne."

"She was here yesterday to see you," said Nina. "She came to ask me if I knew where you were. I told her and I mentioned that you'd probably be back today."

Jennet opened the door and Anne walked right in. "Jen, I just learned Free left Monday instead of Tuesday. . . ." She stopped short when she noticed Nina. "Hello, Nina."

"Anne, I hope everything is all right," said Nina.

Nervously Anne pulled off her hat. "Nina, I must speak in private to Jennet," said Anne. "Please excuse us."

Nina nodded. "Of course. I'll go home and leave you girls alone. But if there's anything I can do to help, let me know."

Jennet frowned slightly at Anne as she held the door open for Nina. What was wrong with Anne? It wasn't her place to send a guest home.

Anne waited until Jennet closed the door again, then she said, "Jen, I sent someone here for Free to help."

"I know, Anne. I took care of Dacia and the baby."

Anne sank to a chair, her hand over her heart. "You did? Oh, I've been beside myself!"

Jennet sat in the rocker and quickly told Anne about finding Dacia and taking her to someone she knew would help. She didn't say that it was Pa. "Dacia and her baby are well on their way to Canada."

"Free will be so angry with me!" cried Anne. "He made me promise never to involve you in helping the runaways."

Jennet frowned. "Why should he make you promise that?"

Anne spread her hands wide. "He said it wasn't safe for you. He didn't want anything to harm you."

Jennet's heart jumped a strange little jump. Was that really Free's reason?

Anne sprang up and paced from the doorway to the fireplace and back again, her face flushed.

Jennet watched her with growing agitation. Something was wrong. Had something happened to Free that Anne was afraid to say? Jennet gripped the arms of the rocker. "Anne, what's wrong?"

Finally Anne sank to her chair again, her eyes boring into Jennet's. "Jennet, I need your help, no matter what Free said."

"What do you need?"

"My place is being watched too closely to be the drop-off spot. Can we use your barn?"

Relief washed over Jennet. It wasn't bad news of Free! "Of course you can use the barn!"

"Free will be very upset." Anne took a deep, steadying breath. "But right now getting runaways to freedom is more important. Jen, I cannot live with myself if I sit back and do nothing to help those people! I cannot!"

Jennet locked her suddenly icy hands in her lap. "I want to help. I'll do anything you say."

"I'll send word to my contact to use you until I let them know differently." Anne ran her fingers through her masses of dark hair, then flipped the curly tresses over her slender shoulders to let them cascade down her back. "When will this war end? I had a very disturbing letter from Wex last week."

Jennet waited for her heart to jump at the very mention of Wex's name, but nothing happened. "What did he say?"

"He was wounded again."

"Oh, no!" Marie would be beside herself. "How badly?"

"He might lose his left leg."

Jennet gasped, her hand over her mouth.

"It makes me feel terrible for helping him join." Anne nervously plucked at the sleeves of her gray dress, and tears welled up in her dark eyes. "I don't want anything to happen to him! But somebody had to stop the South!"

"Wex wanted to go," said Jennet.

"I know." Anne sighed heavily. "I tried to convince Free to go, too, but he wouldn't.

"Why wouldn't he go?" Jennet leaned forward slightly.

"He says killing people is not the answer. He has been helping with the Underground Railroad since he was about fifteen years old."

"I never knew that!"

"No one did but me. Most people think he stayed here when Wex joined just to get rich being a lumberman. He wanted them to think that so he could do more without getting caught." Anne studied Jennet thoughtfully. "Are you sure you're capable of keeping our secret?"

Jennet nodded.

"My contact Rafe, will bring the runaways about dawn. You're to leave a bundle of clothes, blankets, and some food in the hidden room. But don't let anyone see you do it."

"What hidden room?"

"It's under the floor in the tack room. You have to move aside the bench and lift up a hidden door." Anne told Jennet exactly how to find it and to take the things out there just after dark. "Rafe knows about the hidden room. Grandpa Clay had it built before he died, and he told Rafe about it. Grandpa never did know that I helped Rafe." Anne smiled, then sobered. "Rafe will leave the slaves about dawn, they'll stay hidden all day, and tomorrow night you'll drive them outside of town to Meek Arlan's farm." She told Jennet the route to take. "It'll take you about an hour there and an hour back. Can you manage that?"

"Yes."

"You won't be too frightened?"

"I'll be scared, but I can do it anyway."

"Good for you. You might want to take a ride past the Arlan farm during daylight just to get your bearings." Anne grabbed up her hat and set it at a jaunty angle on her head, then tied the wide bow to the side of her chin. "I feel much better. I'm glad you're willing to help."

"How will I know what clothes to leave in the room?"

"I brought a bundle in my buggy. Come visit me in a few days and I'll give you another bundle." Anne walked to the door, smiled, then hugged Jennet. "I'm glad you're going to help."

"I am too."

"I want to get to know you better, Jen. I was very surprised that Free married you when Wex wanted to." Anne's voice faded away and she flushed. "I'm sorry. I shouldn't have said that."

"It's quite all right. I am married to Free. And from what my sister Marie says, she is going to marry Wex."

"He told me in a letter, but I didn't know if I should say anything."

"It's all right. We can't set back time, can we?"

"No. No, we can't."

When Anne drove away, Jennet carried the bundle Anne had given her inside the barn and set it on the floor of her buggy. Calico rubbed against her ankle and purred. Dust particles danced in the sunlight. In the tack room Jennet glanced at the harness hanging on the back wall, the shelf that held saddle soap, brushes, and other things, then down at the wooden bench. She'd sat on the bench many times but never once knew a door was hidden under it. Even though she peered closely at the floor under the bench, she couldn't spot the hidden door.

"Jennet?"

She jumped, then turned to find Tunis Bowker standing in the open doorway, his hat in his hand. Wind ruffled his gray hair. She smiled and walked toward him.

"How're you making out with Freeman gone?" Tunis asked as he slipped an arm around her shoulders.

She shrugged. "He's only been gone a couple of days." Jennet saw the newspaper under Tune's arm. "How many Michigan men on the list this week?"

"Fifty."

"But not Wexal Havlick?"

"No. Thank God!"

"Anyone you know?"

Tunis nodded sadly. "A boy who once delivered papers for me."

"I am so sorry! When will this war end, Tune?"

Tunis sighed heavily. "I pray it'll be soon, but this war

will not be over when the end does come, Jen. It'll touch all of us for years to come."

Jennet led Tunis across the yard to the bench near the back door, and they sat down. The smell of wood smoke drifted on the warm breeze. Calico jumped up on Jennet's lap, curled up, and purred happily.

"Nina told me about your visit with your family. I'm glad you're free of all that anger."

"Me too." She and Tunis had talked before about her family, but she'd closed her ears to any advice he'd offered concerning them.

"Now you're ready to learn what God has for you. God has a purpose and a plan for every person. He wants to reveal His plan to you for your life."

Jennet had never heard anything like that before. "What purpose could God have for me?"

"God is a personal God, Jen. He doesn't look at the masses, but at each individual. He looks right at you and He knows you. He has something special just for you to do that only you can do."

Jennet's eyes widened. "What could it be?"

Tunis smiled. "One plan that God has for me is to help watch out for you and Free."

"Oh?"

"I promised Clay Havlick before God that I'd do just that. And I meant it, Jen. What's mine is yours." Tunis rolled the brim of his hat as he studied Jennet. "I also promised Clay that I'd teach you and Free all I know about God."

"I'm glad, Tune! I really do want to know Him. I learned a lot of Scriptures already."

"You can know the words without understanding their meaning. I want you to know that you have a covenant with God. He promised great promises to you, and He stands behind every one of them. He will answer prayer for you. He will meet all of your needs according to His own riches in glory. He will help you with your little problems and your big ones. He's your heavenly Father, and He loves you very much."

Jennet watched a bird fly around the zinnias in the Bowkers' yard. "Tune, I haven't been able to plan my life by myself." She was thinking of Free. "How do I know that I am not already out of God's plan for me?"

"Honey, you have to take your life as it is today and go from there. You can't go back and change things. It's impossible. But God can take your life the way it is today and show you what to do with it."

She thought of helping the runaway slaves, and she knew that God did indeed want her to help them to freedom. He would help her do that. "You are a good friend, Tune. A true friend."

"That's what I aim to be, Jen. I know you and Free had a weak start in your marriage, but that doesn't mean it'll be a bad marriage. You have God to help you."

Her face red, Jennet looked down at an anthill. It embarrassed her that Free had forced her to marry him. She wondered if Tune had guessed.

Jennet talked with Tunis a while longer. Then he said he had to get home for supper. She watched him cross the yard before getting up and going inside. The house seemed empty and quiet. Tonight she'd sleep alone for the first time since she was married in June. She realized the anger that she'd usually felt for Free was gone. An empty space remained.

Just after dark Jennet crept to the barn with a basket of food. There was no moon, but she could see well enough to pick her way without stumbling. Acorn nickered softly as Jennet slid open the barn door.

In the tack room Jennet moved the bench, lifted the hidden door, and dropped the bundle of clothes and blankets down. She heard them land with a gentle plop. She picked up the basket of food and carefully felt her way down the few steps. She wanted to look around the room, but she

couldn't see and didn't dare light a lantern. She set the
basket and the bundle of clothes to the side of the steps,
then crept back up and closed the door. Her heart thudded
loud in her ears, and she felt as if a dozen eyes watched her
movements. Calico mewed and Jennet jumped, then stifled
a nervous giggle.

"Go catch a mouse, Cal," she whispered as she bent
down and scratched Calico on the neck.

Several minutes later Jennet slipped into bed and pulled
the light cover over her. Last night she'd shared a room
with all of her sisters, and it had taken her a long time to fall
asleep with the giggling and whispering, then the gentle
snores of so many. Tonight the silence, interrupted only by
a cricket chirping outside her windows, kept her awake.

She reached out to touch Free's pillow and whispered,
"Heavenly Father, take care of Free tonight." She stopped
short. Had she actually prayed for Free?

Jennet frowned slightly. He was her husband, and she
really should pray for him just the way Ma had always
prayed for Pa. It was only right.

Hesitantly Jennet prayed, "Father, keep Free safe and
help him to forgive Roman for how he treated him. Help him
to love You and his family." She was on the brink of asking
God to help Free love her, but she couldn't get the words
past her suddenly dry throat.

With a sigh Jennet turned on her side and closed her eyes.

At camp Free awakened from a sound sleep. He lifted his
head and listened for an unusual sound that could've awakened him. He heard a wolf howl and smelled the wood burning in his stove.

Wearily he dropped his head on his pillow and closed his
eyes. He wished Jennet were beside him. Did she think
about him at all? Or miss him as he did her?

Just then a peace he hadn't felt in a long time settled over
him and he smiled.

CHAPTER

12

♦ With blood pounding in her ears, Jennet hitched Acorn to the buggy. The wind chilled her even through Free's jacket and pants. One of his hats covered her mass of hair she'd braided and pinned up out of sight. She'd decided it was safer to dress in Free's clothes and pass herself off as a boy.

All day long she'd tried to do her usual chores and not think about the runaways hidden in her barn. During the afternoon, she'd driven the route to the next station, making careful note of the road and the directions. Finally it was time to open the hidden door.

Jennet lifted the door and listened but heard only Calico purring at her feet and her own heart thudding. "You can come out now. It's time to go to the next station." She kept her voice low, but it seemed to boom out into the night. Slowly a man well over six feet with shoulders almost as wide as the opening climbed out. Right behind him were three children under the age of ten. None of them made a sound as they looked expectantly at Jennet.

She closed the door, and the man set the bench in place

as easily as if it were a feather duster. She led them to the buggy, and the children climbed in the back seat while the man sat up with Jennet.

Several miles out of town after she'd passed the road that led to the Havlick farm, Jennet heard a rider coming. She quickly pulled off the road and stopped behind a clump of trees. Nervously watching and waiting, she remembered that God was always with her and He sent angels to guard her. Silently she thanked God for His help and protection. "Father, please keep Acorn quiet," she mouthed.

The rider slowed his horse to a walk, and Jennet thought he was going to stop. Despite the chill in the air, perspiration pricked her skin. She heard the shallow breathing of the children and the man. Finally the rider passed them. She sat stiffly with her head up until she couldn't hear the hoofbeats. She jumped when a wolf howled and another answered. Acorn bobbed her head and moved restlessly.

Jennet flicked the reins, and Acorn circled the trees to the road and picked her way around the ruts. Moonlight silhouetted trees lining one side of the road.

"You are a brave boy," said the runaway. His voice was deep and cultured, and that surprised Jennet.

"Thank you." Jennet let him think she was a boy. She wanted to know who he was, but she rode in silence. Anne had stressed the importance of silence, especially since she didn't have a hidden compartment in her buggy to hide the runaways.

When Jennet reached the Arlan farm, she stopped in the woodlot and watched the house and barns for any activity. "It's safe," she muttered.

Before Jennet could lift her hands to slap the reins against Acorn, the man caught both her hands in one of his. He whispered, "Wait!"

She was suddenly frightened of the man. What if he wasn't a runaway slave? He didn't sound like one or act like one. No black man would put his hands on a white person. Maybe he was sent to spring a trap on the Underground Railroad.

The children were so quiet that she had to glance to the back seat to make sure they were even there. They were huddled together in fear.

"When that cloud passes over the moon, then drive ahead." The man's breath fanned her cheek, and she smelled the dustiness of his jacket.

Jennet looked up at the sky to see that a cloud was on the brink of passing over the moon. She felt weak with relief. Just as the cloud covered the moon she urged Acorn ahead. In a few minutes they reached the granary between two barns, and Jennet stopped Acorn near a half-open door just as Anne had said to do. "You're to hide inside," Jennet said in a low, tight voice. "Someone will get you tomorrow night and take you on."

"Thank you," whispered the man. "God bless you!" He eased out of the buggy, and it swayed under his weight. He lifted down the children, and they slipped like shadows inside the granary.

Jennet flicked the reins and Acorn stepped out, swung around, and walked back the way they'd come. Only when they were well away from the farm did Jennet breathe easily.

The night pressed in around her, and she started thinking about how she'd come to have enough courage to do such a bold thing. Free would be very angry if he knew.

Just why was he so concerned about her?

Abruptly Jennet pushed the disconcerting question aside and concentrated on the road ahead. The hour's ride seemed to take five.

She reached home without mishap, unhitched Acorn, then crept to the house. Soon dawn would break, and the birds would be twittering as they awoke.

Inside Jennet sank to a kitchen chair, her legs suddenly

too weak to carry her further. She rubbed her unsteady hands up and down the arms of Free's jacket. The faint smell of wood smoke and the distinct odor of vinegar from the pickles she'd canned helped calm her jangled nerves. Without warning tears filled her eyes and ran down her cheeks. She had accomplished a dangerous mission and returned unharmed! She had helped runaways on their way to Canada!

"Jesus, thank You for Your protection. Help the runaways reach freedom."

Just then she thought of Free. She wanted to tell him about tonight and explain why she'd helped. Maybe he'd understand.

A week later Jennet pulled off her bonnet and let the pleasantly cool September breeze blow against her hair. She looked at Tunis as he drove the buggy along the rutted road through the miles of stumps. What would he say if he knew that she had made two trips to the Arlan farm with runaways during the past week? Did he even know about the hidden room in the barn?

She smiled over at him. "Thank you for letting me tag along to Prickett with you, Tune."

"I'm glad for the company," he said.

A few days ago Tunis had mentioned that he was going to Prickett on business, and she'd asked to go along to see Eve and Joshua to beg Eve to leave Tait and move in with her. She'd thought of Eve often lately and had tried to think of ways to get her away from Tait. It wasn't right for Eve to live with such a hateful man.

Jennet patted the drawstring handbag on her lap. She'd asked Lem Azack for money so that she could pay Tait's debts if he still couldn't. She wanted him to be owing to her. She might even kick Tait out and turn the businesses over to Eve! The heady thought made her chuckle.

"What's making you laugh, girl?" asked Tunis.

Jennet pushed her coat off her shoulders and shrugged. "Do I have to have a reason to laugh?"

"I guess you're not going to tell me."

She patted his arm and smiled. "I guess I'm not." It felt good to have the freedom to say that to him. In the past she'd have answered just because she wouldn't have had the courage not to. She hadn't realized that she'd gained enough confidence to say what she wanted to say. She sat up straighter and looked off across the open field dotted with stumps.

Tunis waved his hand out wide. "I remember when all this land was covered with huge trees." His voice was sad. "Now look at it! Stumps as far as you can see!"

Jennet scanned the countryside, and for the first time she really noticed how ugly it looked. On the Havlick farm she'd seen stumps, but they'd been uprooted and burned to leave the land free to plant.

"Someday Michigan will be bare without a tree in sight."

She frowned at the stumps jutting up like giant pawns on a giant chessboard. Weeds grew here and there but couldn't cover all the bare torn-up earth. A few spindly pine trees remained.

"The lumbermen are turning the trees into lumber, and the farmers are turning the land into grainfields and orchards. To the farmers, the trees are a bother. To the lumbermen, they're money." Tunis shook his head sadly. "Your children and your grandchildren might never know what a forest is."

Jennet thought of her baby and frowned, barely able to comprehend that he might never see a forest. There would always be forests, wouldn't there? What if Tune was right? "How could we stop that from happening?" she asked as he drove off the road to keep the buggy wheels from falling into a rut over a foot deep, then around a few stumps.

Tunis drove back on the road before he answered. "Someone could buy this land, then let it set. The few trees that remain would grow and as time goes by reseed until once again the land would be covered with trees."

Jennet was silent for a long time as an idea popped into her head and grew into a plan. "I could buy this land," she said, sounding uncertain in her own ears.

Tunis lifted a shaggy brow. "Yes. You could if you wanted."

"Lem Azack told me how much money I have. He said it was enough to buy land, a big new house, and still have some left."

"Free might object to you spending the money."

"Lem Azack said it was my money. Not Free's."

"I see."

"But why should Free care? He'd want his children to see forests." Jennet flushed at the thought of children. It was hard to come to grips with the knowledge that she was expecting one child—let alone more. Each day she checked in the looking glass to see if she could tell that a baby was growing inside her, but she looked the same. She never experienced morning sickness like Ma had with Baby Vernon. Sometimes she tried to pretend she wasn't going to have a baby.

Tunis nodded thoughtfully. "You're probably right. Clay Havlick's grandson would want that. I'll help you check into buying this." Tunis waved a hand to indicate the vast area of stumps. "The owner is probably a lumberman, and now that the trees are gone he'll be willing to sell. Could be a farmer already bought it, though." Tunis shrugged. "I'll check tomorrow when we get back."

"It feels strange to have enough money to buy land." Jennet looked at the acres of stumps and imagined them to be giant pines and hardwoods again. She'd show her grandchildren the trees and tell them that she'd saved a forest for them to enjoy. "I never had enough money before to buy candy!"

"I guess we can all remember times like that." Tunis told

her about his lean years as a newspaperman, and she listened with interest. "Then I met Clay Havlick and we became best friends. He came to my office one day and said he wanted me to write about the beaver and how fast they were disappearing. I did, but it seemed nobody cared." Tunis sighed heavily. "Clay said he wanted to help me, so he lent me some money to invest in grain. I made enough to buy my house and have money for my old age." Tunis shook his head. "Yes, Clay and me were best friends."

That made Jennet think of Wex. He had been her best friend. She realized that she'd not fallen into the old habit of talking to Wex. She couldn't pinpoint the time she'd stopped. Come to think of it, she didn't touch the spot where once she'd worn his white hankie. Maybe it wouldn't hurt to see him with Marie when he returned.

Jennet and Tune rode in silence for a while as her thoughts returned to the disappearing forest. "Lem Azack said Clay Havlick left some tracts of white pine for me somewhere north of Big Pine."

"I've seen 'em. Beautiful. Tall and straight. Most of them are at least five foot through."

Jennet stared down at her handbag. "I could keep those trees. Not let anyone cut them down."

Tune studied her thoughtfully. "That you could."

Jennet looked at Tunis and nodded, suddenly determined to protect the white pines from the shanty boys' axes. "I don't want Michigan to be a land without trees. I want my children and my grandchildren to see a forest. Clay Havlick would have liked that, wouldn't he?"

"He would. He would at that."

As soon as Jennet could, she'd go see that land and those white pines that stood tall and straight and at least five foot through. She'd see for herself the forest that she was saving for future generations. She slipped her arm through Tune's and hugged it. "Maybe one plan God has for my life is to save the forest, Tune!"

"You could be right."

About five o'clock Tunis reached the river and followed the road along the bank until he reached Prickett. The smell of pine was mixed with the fishy odor of the river.

The terrible loneliness and fear that she'd felt when she'd come here with Tait swept over Jennet. How foolish she'd been to come with Tunis! Could she face Tait without turning into the cowering slave that she had been?

Tunis pulled around a team of workhorses hitched to a big wagon and stopped at the hitching rail outside the boarding house. Smells of fresh baked bread drifted from the dining room.

Jennet looked down the street past the shoe factory toward Tait's store. She *would* face Tait! She'd make him sorry for treating her the way he had!

Tunis stepped to the ground, rocking the buggy as he did, then turned to help Jennet down, even though she'd been jumping in and out of wagons and buggies all her life.

Tunis smiled at her. "We'll get rooms and carry in our luggage. What say we eat supper before we go about our business?"

Jennet's stomach flip-flopped at the thought of facing Tait. She couldn't eat a bite now if she tried. "You go ahead and eat without me. I'll check in, then walk over to see Eve." She'd visit Eve first, then Tait. Oh, what a shock he was in for!

Several minutes later Jennet walked along the wooden sidewalk to the far side of the shoe factory, then left it to follow the path that led behind Tait's store to his house in the woods. The clean smell of pine hung heavy in the air, and she sniffed deeply in appreciation. Jennet's skirts flapped about her ankles as she rounded a clump of blueberry bushes. Boys shouted from a raft on the river several yards away. Birds sang in the trees. Jennet shifted the paper-wrapped bundle in her arms; inside were a baby quilt for Joshua and a new cape for Eve.

Jennet walked through the gate of the white wooden fence, around the two tall pines, and stopped outside the house. For just a moment she thought of running back to the boarding house, but she squared her shoulders and walked to the door. The late afternoon air had a nip of fall to it, and she pulled her dark blue wool coat firmly about her. She'd left her hat in her room. She touched the silky strands of chestnut hair curling from her temple. She'd pulled her hair loosely back and pinned it in place on top of her head. Would Eve even recognize her without braids and the unhealthy, gaunt look she'd had when she'd lived here?

Jennet knocked gingerly. She waited for the sound of footsteps, but none came. Had Eve taken Joshua and run away from Tait?

A squirrel chattered noisily from a low branch of a pine.

Jennet knocked again, louder this time, then called out, "Eve. Are you home?"

What had Tait done with Eve? She had always been home this time of day. Tait wouldn't allow her out and about for fear someone would mock him for marrying a Pottawatomie, and worse yet having a child with her.

"She's not home," muttered a disappointed Jennet. She opened the door and called softly, "Eve?" Silence hung heavy inside the house. Jennet smelled the faint aroma of porkchops and saw a small wooden rocking horse beside the coat rack. Eve's old coat hung on the rack.

With a deep sigh Jennet laid the bundle on the chair just inside the door. She left the house where she'd had the only hint of happiness during her stay in Prickett.

Jennet's face hardened as she thought of Tait. If he'd hurt Eve or Joshua, he'd be sorry! She gripped her handbag that held her money. Tait would pay for every minute of agony he'd caused her and Eve!

Suddenly Jennet remembered that she'd forgiven even Tait, and she slowed her steps. She dare not be bitter toward him or do anything to get even! "Help me, Lord! Without You I can't stop hating Tait."

By then Jennet was in front of the store where she'd spent so many agonizing hours. She glanced in the wide windows, which were filled with merchandise just as they had been when she'd left. Smoke curled from the chimney. Who chopped the wood for Tait now that she didn't do it?

Pushing open the heavy door, Jennet noticed that the store smelled the same—leather, smoke, kerosene, and black licorice candy. A small woman stood behind the counter with her back to Jennet. At the sound of the door she turned and Jennet gasped.

It was Eve! Eve was dressed in a dark green wool dress, which showed off her slender figure. Her hair hung below her shoulders and was held back with a green band around her head.

"Eve," whispered Jennet as she stepped forward.

Eve's dark eyes widened, then with a cry of joy she ran to Jennet and flung her arms around her. "Jen! It is you! Oh, Jennet!"

Tears streamed down Jennet's flushed cheeks as she clung to Eve. Finally she pulled away and wiped at her tears with the back of her hand. "Eve, what are you doing in here? What will Tait say? Where is Joshua?"

Eve laughed softly and hugged Jennet again, then stepped back from her and looked her up and down. "You look so different! No sad face. No dark circles under your eyes. And your dress is grand!"

"You look different too! And you're here!"

Eve smiled and nodded.

Jennet looked around, expecting Tait to walk in with an angry roar. "Eve, should you be in here?"

Eve caught Jennet's hand and held it. "God has answered my prayer, Jen. Tait is no longer ashamed of me. I work here with him."

"No!" Jennet couldn't take it in.

"It is a miracle. I learned the business fast, he says."

"But where's the baby?"

"Asleep in the back room. Come. I will show him to you. I believe it was Joshua who softened Tait's heart enough to let love in."

Jennet followed Eve to the doorway of the tiny room that had once been hers. It looked and smelled clean. Fresh curtains hung at the window. No spider webs swung from the wooden ceiling. A baby lay on his stomach asleep on the same narrow cot where she'd slept. She wanted to run to him and hold him close to her heart, but she didn't want to wake him. "He's so big!"

"Nine months. Two teeth already. And he can say Da."

"He's beautiful, Eve! Such a lot of dark hair!" Jennet thought of her baby, and a gentle yearning to see him and hold him stirred inside her.

The two women went back to stand at the counter beside the cash register. "Where is Tait?" Jennet asked.

"At the mill. He'll be here soon."

Jennet's stomach knotted. Maybe she should leave without seeing him. "Eve, does he treat you well?"

Eve nodded. "He's not perfect, but he loves me."

"Does he beat you?"

"Not for a long time."

"If you had a chance to leave him, would you go?"

Eve shook her head hard. "He is my husband, Jen!"

"I was going to ask you and Joshua to come live with me."

Eve patted Jennet's flushed cheek. "I love you, Jen, but I won't leave Tait."

Jennet nodded. She told Eve about accepting God's love back in her life and about forgiving those who'd treated her badly.

"I prayed for you, Jen. That you'd let the Scriptures we learned work in your heart."

"Thank you, Eve.

"I got another Bible, and Tait has been helping me learn the Scriptures."

"Tait?"

Eve nodded and smiled. "One of these days he will let the Scriptures work in his heart. It is very hard for him to forget the pain of his childhood."

"What pain?"

"Did not your father talk about his growing-up years?"

"No."

"He and Tait grew up in Pennsylvania. Their father was a cruel, hard man, a farmer. He worked the boys long hours and whipped them even when they didn't deserve it. Their mother died when the boys were young so they had no soft woman's touch. Tait said I am the first one to ever love him. Joshua the second."

To her surprise, Jennet felt sorry for Tait and for Pa, but especially for Tait. Pa had seven daughters and a wife to love him. Jennet glanced down at her handbag. Maybe she shouldn't do anything to make more trouble for Tait.

Just then the heavy door opened and Tait walked in. He wore a white shirt and black tie and a dark suit. He stopped short when he saw Jennet. "What are you doing here, Jen?"

Jennet squared her shoulders and looked him in the eyes. "I came to see Eve and Joshua."

"You're not welcome!"

Eve touched Jennet's arm. "I will talk to him."

Jennet shook her head. "It doesn't matter." She smiled at Eve. "Good-bye. I'm glad all is well with you."

"Good-bye, Jen."

Jennet walked toward the door, but Tait caught her arm. The old fear returned as she looked up at him.

"I spoke too soon, Jen," Tait said gruffly. "If you came for a job, you can have your old one back. With pay," he added quickly.

179

"I don't need a job," she said evenly.

He dropped his hand. "Are you living with your pa?"

"No. I'm married to Freeman Havlick."

"Married, you say! So he bought himself a wife!"

Eve gasped but didn't speak.

Jennet's face flamed.

Tait rubbed a hand over his mustache and neatly trimmed beard. "I thought there was something funny about him taking you. I couldn't figure why a man like him would do that."

Jennet thought that Free had not considered marrying her when he'd taken her from Tait. But maybe in the back of his mind he had planned to wed her. An icy band squeezed her heart as Jennet started for the door, her steps as heavy as her heart.

"If you want to stay here instead of going back to your husband, you can keep my books."

"Jen belongs with her husband," said Eve softly.

"Even if he bought and paid for her?" Tait asked bluntly.

"Even then," said Eve, looking right at Jennet.

Jennet bit her bottom lip as she looked helplessly at Eve. Would God work the same miracle for her as He had for Eve?

"Miracles happen," said Eve as if answering Jennet's unspoken question.

"I couldn't pay you much since things are still tight, but you could have your old room back," Tait said.

"Did Swanson ever pay his account?" asked Jennet.

"No. Died before he could."

"What about Heppelink?"

Tait shook his head. "Joined the war."

"Betzer?"

"Got his leg tore off working as a river hog."

The money in Jennet's handbag suddenly felt too heavy to hold. She knew she didn't want Tait owing her, but she did want to help because of Eve and Joshua. She walked to

Eve, pulled open the drawstring bag, and handed the money to her. "This is for you. You pay those bills, and part of this business will belong to you if you want it to."

Eve's wide, dark eyes misted with tears. "How did you come by this money, Jen?"

"It is mine legally." Lem Azack had told her that when she'd hesitated about taking it.

"Hold on there!" cried Tait, his face red. "You can't do that."

Jennet's eyes flashed. "I can and I will. It's my money, and I am giving it to Eve as a gift. She can do as she pleases with it."

"Why would you give it to Eve?"

"She was my friend when I needed one badly. I love her. And Joshua."

Tait scowled until his dark brows almost met over his long nose. "She's Pottawatomie!"

"I know. She was good to me."

"When?" snapped Tait.

Eve told him, her voice steady and her head high.

Tait glowered at her and mumbled under his breath. Finally he turned to Jennet. "Since we're telling tales, I'll tell you about your letters from your family."

"I found them," said Jennet coldly.

"But you didn't take them."

"I read them, copied them off, and put them back so you wouldn't know." She gripped her handbag tightly. "How could you do that to me? Why did you?"

Tait ran unsteady fingers through his hair, leaving it on end. He looked old and haggard.

"He is sorry," said Eve softly.

"I can speak for myself, woman!" He rubbed his hair flat and tugged at his high collar. "It was wrong for me to do that. But it's done and I can't make it right." He cleared his throat. "I take back what I said before. You are welcome here. If you want to sleep at our place or here, you can."

"I already have a room at the boarding house." Jennet turned to Eve. "I left gifts in your house for you and Joshua. I thought you'd be there, so I went there first."

Eve hugged Jennet close. "For the gifts I thank you. And for this." Eve pulled away and held up the money. "I will give it to Tait to help pay his bills. But I do not need a part of his business. It's enough that Joshua will have it someday."

"When did I say that?" Tait shot the question at her.

"*I* say it," said Eve softly but firmly.

Tait glared at her, then shrugged. "Sure it'll be his. He is my son."

Eve smiled at Jennet as if to say, "I told you so."

With a soft good-bye Jennet left the store. The last of her hatred for Tait fell away, and she smiled.

At the lumbercamp Free stood outside his office and listened to the ring of axes. Smoke drifted up from the cookcamp where the cook and his helpers were making supper. Inside the office the bookkeeper whistled as he worked. The camp consisted of four principal buildings: cook and eating camp about sixty-five feet by thirty-five feet; the bunkcamp with sleeping room for about a hundred men; the barn and stable, which could hold eighteen teams and hay and oats to last the season; and a blacksmith and tinker shop where the massive sleighs were made and all the tools were repaired. Three smaller buildings were homes for himself, his foremen, and his cook. Near the office was the store where clothing and tobacco were kept for the men. Free looked around his camp and puffed up with pride. His dream was finally coming true! He would indeed make his mark in lumber!

This winter they would finish the trees in this area, then he'd move on to the huge trees that Grandpa had left him. Free frowned slightly. Grandpa had actually left them for Jennet, but he'd convince her to sign them over to him so that he could lumber them off. She didn't have enough spunk to hold out against him, even if she had a mind to. He hooked his thumbs around his suspenders and smiled. With those trees he'd be right up there with George Meeker and Abel Witherspoon.

Just then he caught sight of Jig walking into camp, his pack on his back and his muzzleloader in his right hand.

"Supper on?" called Jig when he spotted Free.

"Soon." Free strode to Jig and slapped him on the shoulder. "It's good to see you again, Jig!"

"I figured I could be the preacher man here of a Sunday. Unless you already got one."

"Not a one. You're welcome to stay."

"I knew Clay Havlick's grandson would say that."

"I'll rustle up a cup of coffee for you while we catch up on things and wait for supper." Free led Jig to his office as Jig talked.

CHAPTER

13

♦ Humming softly, Jennet stepped into the barn to look for Calico. He'd been missing all day. The bright October moonlight shone into the barn for Jennet to see to light the lantern. The match flared, sending out a smell of sulfur. It was warm for an October night, warm enough that she'd not grabbed a shawl to drape over her dark blue wool dress, which to her alarm had been almost too tight at the waist to button. She didn't want to be reminded that she was expecting a baby.

"Cal," Jennet called as she lifted the lantern high. She waited, expecting the cat to run to her, but he didn't come. "Where is he?"

Acorn nickered from her stall. Suddenly the hairs on the back of Jennet's neck stood on end. Was someone hiding in the barn?

Frowning at her foolishness, Jennet went to the tack room to look in Cal's special sleeping spot on an old rag rug. Just inside she stopped short and stared at the bench that usually sat over the hidden door. It was out of place! Her hand shook, and the light from the lantern bobbed. Anne hadn't sent a message to expect someone. Had someone entered the barn and moved the bench for some other reason? Only Tunis or Nina would come here, and they were gone to Detroit for several days. Should she open the hidden door and see if someone was inside?

When she heard a movement outside the tack room door, goose bumps covered her arms. Silently she prayed for help, then she slowly, cautiously, turned. Maybe it had been only Calico. But in her heart she knew it wasn't. She knew someone was there, someone was watching her.

With all the courage she could muster, Jennet walked out of the tack room. The light from her lantern caught the toes of black boots and the cuffs of gray tweed trousers. She sucked in her breath. "Who is there?" she asked sharply.

The man stepped forward. Blue Newmeyer! Jennet's blood turned to ice, and for a moment her legs trembled so badly she thought she'd fall.

"Jennet Havlick," he said with a low chuckle. "I might've guessed our paths would cross again."

Jennet forced back her panic. She wanted to run to the house, but she stood her ground. "What are you doing trespassing in my barn? I want you out of here now!"

Blue Newmeyer took a menacing step toward her, but she didn't move. "I followed a runaway to this here barn, and I won't leave till I have my hands on him!" Newmeyer called the runaway names that burned Jennet's ears.

A runaway! So, someone was hidden here! Perspiration dotted Jennet's forehead. She dare not let the man see how frightened she was. "Mr. Newmeyer, you have no right to sneak into my barn in the middle of the night. Now, get out before I scream for help." Jennet knew no one could hear her since Tunis was away, but she hoped Newmeyer wouldn't know it.

"You scream all you want, girl, but I'm finding me that runaway and you ain't gonna stop me!" Newmeyer grabbed the lantern and wrested it from Jennet's grip. Then he pushed her aside and strode toward the back of the barn. She ran after him, demanding that he leave.

Acorn nickered and pawed the straw-covered floor in her stall. Outside Newmeyer's horse answered.

"Mr. Newmeyer, you can't do this!" cried Jennet as she tugged at his arm to pull him away from Acorn's stall.

Newmeyer gripped Jennet's arm in a vise of steel. He pushed his face down close to hers, and she could smell his tobacco breath. "Don't cause me no grief, girl, or I'll bust your head wide open. When I find that runaway, I'm gonna hang him on the spot and you beside him." Newmeyer looked up at the hand-hewn support beam as if he could already see a rope dangling from it. Abruptly he flung Jennet away.

Jennet fell against the opposite stall beside the buggy and caught herself before she crashed to the floor. Pain sliced through her. The baby! Just how much of a fall would it take to harm the baby? She bit back a cry of pain and fire shot from her eyes, but she stayed away from Newmeyer. Trembling, Jennet watched Newmeyer thump on the back wall and the walls of each stall, even Acorn's. With the lantern in one hand he climbed up the ladder to the loft. Particles of dust and hay trickled through the cracks as he walked across the floor. Jennet heard him stab a pitchfork in clumps of hay. With an oath he flung the pitchfork from him, and it bounced down the ladder and landed with a thud on the barn floor.

Jennet pressed against the buggy wheel and watched Newmeyer drop down the last several rungs of the ladder. The lantern swayed, making shadows dance on the wall. Hay clung to Newmeyer's trousers. The second button of his blue shirt was missing, revealing his dirty-gray long johns.

Jennet's heart almost stopped as Newmeyer walked into the tack room. Free had been right! This was too dangerous for her.

Jennet glanced at the pitchfork, then stood outside the tack room door, ready to grab the pitchfork if Newmeyer found the hidden door. She watched him tug at the harness on the back wall. He knocked down the can of oil that she used on the harness and saddle. It landed on the hidden door, but even then he didn't see it. Swearing under his breath, he grabbed a shovel from the corner where several tools stood. He thumped the floor with the shovel handle to check for hollow sounds. He thumped the hidden door, but the sound was the same.

Swearing more vigorously now, Newmeyer hung the lantern on a peg. He jerked off his hat, wiped his sweaty forehead, and stabbed his fingers through his oily dark brown hair, then clamped his hat back in place. "I know he's in here! I saw him sneak in here. And he didn't run out the back door or I'd have saw him. You slave lovers make my blood boil!"

Jennet kept her back stiff as she walked toward the lantern. "I'm going to shut up the barn and go inside."

Just as Jennet reached for the lantern, she heard him move. He grabbed her from behind and she cried out in alarm. Was he going to kill her and the baby? He lifted her off her feet and swung her around, sending her sprawling. Her head struck the floor, and the pain almost made her pass out. Pins slipped from her hair, setting the long braid free of the coil at the nape of her neck.

Newmeyer grabbed her arm with his rough, dirty hands and hauled her to her feet.

"Take your hands off me!" she screamed.

"Where is he?" Newmeyer asked in a savage voice. "I'll break every bone in your body if you don't tell me."

"Let . . . me . . . go!" Jennet gasped, struggling to break free. Her head ached and she saw black dots before her eyes. She kicked out at Newmeyer's leg but missed.

Newmeyer gripped her left fist with his right hand and

squeezed, and she thought he'd crush the bones into powder. She cried out in agony.

Suddenly Jennet saw a huge shadow loom above Blue Newmeyer, and the scream died in her throat. It was the runaway!

Before Newmeyer knew what happened, the black man had him in a bear hug, making him lose his grip on Jennet. The runaway was the huge black man who had been with the three children Jennet had helped last month. He wore rumpled and dirty dark trousers and a wide-sleeved once-white shirt that had lost its collar.

The runaway shook Newmeyer like a rag doll, then flung him across the barn. He crashed into a stall with bone-jarring force.

The big black man looked into Jennet's face, and his eyes widened. "You are the boy," he said in his deep, cultured voice.

Jennet nodded. "Why are you here?" she whispered hoarsely.

Just then Newmeyer grabbed the pitchfork and lunged at the runaway. The black man leaped easily aside, as light on his feet as if he'd been a slight, wiry boy. He cuffed Newmeyer on the side of his head, sending him reeling. The fork fell to the floor. In a flash Newmeyer leaped up, gripped the fork, and flung it tines first at the runaway. He turned, but the tines caught his right arm. Immediately blood soaked his sleeve.

Jennet sprang forward to grab the pitchfork, but Newmeyer caught her braid and jerked her off her feet. Pain stung her head and tears filled her eyes. She lay in a heap against the tack room wall.

The runaway balled his fist and jabbed at Newmeyer. He ducked and danced away, then threw a punch that connected with the runaway's chin. The snap seemed to echo throughout the barn. The runaway grabbed for Newmeyer, caught his arm, and spun him around. The huge man

188

wrapped an arm around Newmeyer and pulled his back up against him, twisted his head, and snapped his neck. The toes of his scuffed boots an inch off the floor, Newmeyer hung limply in the man's arms. Finally he let Newmeyer slide to the floor. With a low, anguished moan, the runaway stood there with his broad shoulders bent and his head down.

Jennet ran to Newmeyer and knelt beside him. She shot a startled, frightened look up at the runaway. "He's dead," she whispered.

"I know." The black man helped Jennet to her feet and turned her away from Newmeyer's crumpled body. "Don't look at him."

"What'll we do now?"

"You go inside. I'll take care of the man, then be on my way."

Suddenly she saw the blood flowing from his arm. "But you're hurt! You're bleeding!"

"I will survive."

"You take care of Newmeyer, then you come inside and let me dress your wound and feed you," she insisted.

The man finally tipped his head in agreement. Gray streaked his mass of tight curls. He glanced around the stall. "Where will I find a shovel?"

"A shovel?"

"I must bury him."

"Here?" Jennet cried in alarm.

"If I drop him in the river, his body will be discovered and questions asked."

"You're right," Jennet said weakly. "I'll water his horse and put it in the stall beside Acorn. You ride it when you leave."

The man nodded, then peered closer at Jennet. "You look ready to faint. Go inside and let me tend to the dead man and his horse."

Jennet absently brushed dirt off her dress and whispered, "I'm fine. I can do it."

"You are brave and you are strong, but you let me take care of this." The huge man turned her and gently pushed her toward the door.

"You sit down inside and drink a glass of water. I'll be in as soon as possible."

Jennet walked to the house, filled a glass with water, and sat at the kitchen table, hardly aware of her movements. She ached all over and her head hurt. She gingerly touched her barely rounded stomach. Was the baby safe? Jennet frowned and downed the glass of water in two gulps, then leaned her elbows on the table and cupped her chin in her hands. Trembling started in her legs and moved up her body until she shook like the gold-and-red leaves on the giant maples and oaks in the pasture behind the barn.

Would the runaway bury Newmeyer in the pasture behind the barn? Jennet groaned and closed her eyes tightly.

Jennet pulled herself together, washed her face and hands, added wood to the range, and sliced ham and potatoes into a skillet. She brought a loaf of bread and crock of butter from the pantry. She felt as if she was in a dream, but as long as she concentrated on what she was doing, she couldn't think about the runaway and the grave he was digging.

Several minutes later the black man stumbled in and sagged against the back door. His shirt was wet with water, and water sparkled on his ebony face. Jennet knew that he had washed at the horse tank. He moaned, and she ran to him and helped him to a kitchen chair.

"I lost too much blood," he said as he looked down at his right arm.

She looked at the gaping wound, and her stomach turned at the sight of the torn flesh. "It stopped bleeding." She handed him a glass of water, and he drank it thirstily. "You eat and then I'll dress it."

"Thank you."

Jennet set the plate of food before him, sat across from

him, and watched as he bowed his head in prayer a minute, then ate quickly as if he hadn't eaten in a long time.

"You're not a slave, are you?" Jennet asked when he'd finished.

"No."

She sucked in her breath. "Who are you? What are you?"

"My name is George Washington Foringer, and I was a professor of English and journalism in a university in Pennsylvania."

"Then why are you here?"

"I had to do something!" George Washington Foringer said determinedly. "In the past year I've led several people to freedom. I'm on my way back again."

"But why did you stop here?"

"The man . . . ," Foringer motioned to indicate he meant Newmeyer, "the man got on my trail south of here. I showed him my free paper and he knew I was a free man, but he was out to kill any Negro he saw. I got away from him and hitched a ride in a lumber wagon that came to Grand Rapids. I thought I'd lost him, but I hadn't. He followed me here." Foringer held his large hand out to Jennet. "I truly am sorry for the trouble and pain I've brought to you."

"Don't give it another thought. I'll dress your wound and stitch up that tear in your shirt. You're too big to wear my husband's clothes or you'd be welcome to them."

"Don't trouble yourself with me."

"Please take off your shirt." Jennet sounded very firm, and it pleased her. She helped him off with his shirt, put it to soak in a dishpan of cold water, then carefully washed and dressed his wound. "How long has it been since you've slept in a bed, Mr. Foringer?"

He laughed a deep laugh. "A very long time."

"Tonight you sleep in one of the spare rooms. Sleep as long tomorrow as you can. When it's dark tomorrow night, you can be on your way again."

"I can't accept such a generous offer." He stood, swayed backward, and sat back down. "It appears that I shall accept your kind offer. I thank you, and I thank God for providing."

They talked a while longer, then Jennet led Foringer to the spare bedroom nearest to the kitchen. She returned to the kitchen to wash his shirt. Carefully she stitched the jagged tear and hung the shirt near the stove to dry. She banked the fire before finally going to bed.

The next morning Jennet peeked in to see Foringer sleeping soundly. She guessed him to be about Pa's age, but it was hard to judge because his face was full and unlined. Quietly she went about her chores and finally forced herself to go to the barn to tend Acorn and Newmeyer's horse.

Where had Mr. Foringer buried Blue Newmeyer?

Jennet let the horses out to graze, thankful that Nina and Tunis were not home to question her about the strange horse. She stood at the gate, shielding the sun from her eyes with her hand as she looked around. She couldn't find the terrible spot. Mr. Foringer obviously knew how to take off the sod, dig a hole, bury the body, cover it, and lay the sod back in place. No one would be able to find the body. Sighing in relief, she walked back to the house.

Just then Calico ran to her and rubbed against her ankle. Jennet picked him up, sat down on the bench beside the back door, and cradled Cal to her. "I see you have a bit of fur torn off, Cal. You'd better stay home after this and stay out of trouble." She laughed shakily. "I stayed home last night, but I didn't stay out of trouble, Cal. Oh, I missed you!"

Calico purred contentedly.

Just after dark, George Washington Foringer said goodbye and rode away. Stars shone brightly and a chilly wind blew down from the north. "God, bless him," Jennet whispered.

Jennet thought about George Washington Foringer off and on for the next several weeks. She tried not to think about Blue Newmeyer. She was glad when snow finally covered the pasture where he was probably buried.

After having Thanksgiving dinner with Nina and Tunis, Jennet watched snow swirl in the air as she sat near the window to stitch a quilt for the baby. The past several weeks had dragged by. Just last week when even her loosest dress no longer hid her secret, she'd told Nina about the baby. Nina had been delighted. She'd convinced Jennet to start sewing baby clothes and the quilt. Jennet had to admit that it helped pass the time.

Jennet had had one short letter from Free, saying that he was well and work was progressing as it should. He didn't mention the baby, and she was glad. Ma had written twice and Marie once. Even Pa had written, asking if she'd spend Christmas with them. He said he'd pick her up and she should plan to stay with them a week or so. She agreed to go, even though she knew they'd see that she was expecting a baby. She blushed scarlet just thinking about their knowing.

Just then the baby moved and Jennet smiled. The first time it had happened she'd been so alarmed that she'd run to tell Nina about it. Nina had laughed and said it was a good sign of a healthy baby.

Jennet touched her stomach. "Baby, I promise I'll get over being embarrassed about you. Nina says I have nothing to be embarrassed about, but I still am." A movement out the front window caught her eye, then a short time later she heard a knock at the back door. She laid the quilt on the rocker and went to the door. A gust of wind blew giant flakes of snow in on her. She pulled her shawl more tightly around her.

A ragged boy, no older than twelve, stood at the door with a younger girl just behind him. The boy smiled, but the smile didn't erase the haunted look in his blue eyes. His face was pinched and blue. He held a red wool cap in his dirty hands. "Ma'am, you got any wood that needs split?"

"I'm sorry, but I don't."

The boy stepped aside and pushed the girl forward. From under her red wool cap her light brown hair hung in ragged tails to her thin shoulders. Her dark green wool coat was full of holes, and her toes showed through holes in her shoes. She looked ready to cry. "She wants to know if you got any mending needs done or floors need scrubbed."

Jennet stood aside. She couldn't abide sending the children away without feeding them and letting them warm themselves in her kitchen. "Come inside and we'll talk about it."

The girl walked in and the boy reluctantly followed.

"I'm Jennet Havlick." They didn't offer their names, so she asked them.

"I'm Will and she's Meg."

Jennet had them hang their coats on hooks beside the back door, then led them to the kitchen table and asked them to sit down. She set out a plate of cookies that she'd planned to take to Tunis since he loved her oatmeal cookies with raisins. She filled three glasses with milk and sat at her usual place.

She held the plate of cookies out to Meg. Meg looked at Will, and he nodded slightly. She took a cookie and wolfed it down as Jennet held the plate out to Will. He ate his more slowly, but Jennet could see it took a big effort on his part.

From the pantry Jennet got some of the leftover turkey Nina had sent home with her. She sliced thick pieces of bread and set out butter. She made turkey sandwiches and gave them to the children.

"Where do you two live?" Jennet asked when they'd eaten.

"In town," said Will.

"We live in a box," said Meg.

Jennet was as much surprised at the answer as she was by Meg's speaking.

"She don't got to know that," said Will sharply.

"Where are your parents?"

"Dead," said Meg.

"Why don't you live at the Home for Orphans?" asked Jennet.

"Me and my sister can make it on our own," said Will, squaring his thin shoulders. The answer sounded as if he'd given it many times before.

Jennet couldn't stand the thought of the children being on their own. She decided to put them to work even though she really didn't need the help. "I could use someone to clean the barn."

Will jumped up, his blue eyes sparkling. He wore a threadbare red plaid flannel shirt and ragged black pants held up with old suspenders. "I'll get right to it."

"And brush my mare Acorn," said Jennet.

"I can do that too," said Will, nodding so hard his dirty brown hair flopped.

"I could do it," said Meg, jumping up to stand beside her brother. Her faded brown-and-yellow calico dress hung loosely on her too-thin body.

Will looked expectantly at Jennet. She shrugged and said, "She could do it, but I thought she might do the dishes and help me a little in here."

"Yes," said Meg quickly with a nod. "I can do that."

"Will, you come back inside when you're finished," said Jennet. "The calico cat you'll see out there is Cal, short for Calico. He likes to be petted and talked to."

"I like cats too," said Meg as she set water on to heat in the heavy teakettle.

The afternoon passed quickly and pleasantly for Jennet. She liked having Meg to talk to while she stitched the baby quilt and Meg dusted furniture that didn't need dusting.

After supper Jennet paid them both ten cents, and they acted as if she'd given them a fortune.

Jennet reluctantly opened the back door for them. Wind blew large snowflakes against the children as they stepped outside. It was already dark. "I could use you again tomorrow," Jennet said.

"We'll be here at six," said Will.

"Fine." Jennet smiled at Meg and wanted to ask them to stay the night, but she was sure Will would refuse.

Jennet watched until they were out of sight. She picked up the baby quilt and sat back in the rocker. Free had told her to hire someone to do the heavy work, so why not hire Will and Meg? She would hire them and give them a place to stay for the winter, maybe even find a permanent home for them! She nodded in satisfaction.

To Jennet's delight, after a week of coming to work every day, Will agreed that they could stay. Jennet gave them each a bedroom, laughing with pleasure at the joy on their faces. She introduced them to Tunis and Nina who were immediately taken with them. Nina went shopping for them and outfitted them in clothes like they'd not seen since their parents had died two years earlier. Each afternoon Jennet did with them what Ma had done with her and the girls—sat them at the kitchen table and taught them to read and write. Will was embarrassed that he didn't know how, but he learned quickly. It was harder for Meg, but she gradually caught on. Jennet read them Scriptures and helped them memorize verses. They went to church with her each Sunday and sat beside her as if they were family. Meg had been very excited when Jennet had told them about the baby, but Will hadn't said much at all.

The day before Christmas Pa arrived to pick up Jennet and take her home for a two-week visit. Nina begged Meg and Will to stay with her, but Will said they could take care of themselves, so Jennet left them at her house. Nina promised to keep an eye on them.

"We have a surprise for you, Jen," said Pa as he turned the sleigh into the drive on Roman Havlick's property. The sleigh bells jingled, making the snowy day seem even more like Christmas.

Jennet pulled her coat tighter about her under the heavy robe wrapped around her. "I have a surprise for you, too, Pa." She wanted to wait and tell all of them about the baby at the same time. How would her family take the news? Should she tell Free's family? She trembled nervously just thinking about speaking to them.

Pa drove past the huge main house. An evergreen bough tied with a wide red ribbon hung on the front door. Pa drove past the barn where Roman had whipped Jennet, past the granary. The large rock where Pa had sat to spank Jennet was covered with snow. Instead of stopping at the two-story cabin, Pa drove up to a big white frame house that Jennet had never seen before. "Here it is. The surprise," said Pa proudly.

Jennet stared at the house with the white clapboard siding and tall windows. Her breath hung in the cold air. "Whose house is this?"

Pa's beard moved as he grinned. "Ours. We built it. Three bedrooms upstairs and one downstairs. Even a bathroom. That was your ma's idea. She said we should all be able to take a bath in private."

Jennet remembered all the times when she'd said, "Turn your backs," just to have privacy when she needed it. They all knew the rule to keep turned until the person said it was all right to look.

"Do you like it?" asked Pa, sounding nervous.

"It's wonderful! It's left me speechless."

"Roman said he owed us a house for all the years of working all of us and not paying anybody but me."

"I'm shocked!"

"He's trying to set things right," said Pa.

"Has he written to Free and Wex?"

"Marie said he did, but he didn't have the courage to mail his letters. Lillian wrote, but he wouldn't send those either."

Just then the wide front door opened and Ma and the girls streamed out, crying a glad welcome. Granger ran from the barn, wagging his tail.

Jennet jumped to the ground and hugged Ma tight. Ma hugged her back, then held her away and looked into her eyes. Jennet flushed painfully. She knew Ma had felt the firm roundness of her stomach.

"Jen?" Ma whispered.

Jennet nodded slightly, and Ma hugged her hard again.

"I don't know if I'm ready for this," whispered Ma in her ear, and Jennet laughed. She knew *she* wasn't ready for it!

Jennet reluctantly pulled away from Ma and hugged each of the laughing girls, making sure she didn't hug them tight to her.

"We waited to put up our Christams tree till you got here, Jen," said Evie, jumping up and down. "I strung popcorn, and Nola made a silver angel for the top of the tree."

The girls all talked at once as Pa herded them indoors.

Jennet scanned the comfortable-looking room. The walls were covered with wallpaper of red roses and ivy. On the wall between two closed doors two sconces with red candles hung on either side of a large painting of red and yellow apples in a woven basket. Two rocking chairs were pulled up close to a potbellied stove on the wall to Jennet's left. To her right stood the kitchen trestle table with chairs instead of benches around it. The big cast-iron kitchen woodstove from their old house stood on bricks against the back wall covered with bricks. Nine people were not crowded in the big room. A doorway led to a bedroom, and another to the famous bathroom. The stairway was built in, but the door stood open for heat to rise to the upstairs rooms. "This is wonderful!" cried Jennet.

"Now tell us your surprise before I do my chores," said

Pa from where he stood near the front door, his hat in his hand.

Jennet reached out and gripped Ma's hand. She cleared her throat and kept her eyes glued to Ma. "I'm going to have a baby in the spring."

No one said a word for so long that Jennet wanted to dash from the house. Then they all exclaimed their delight. The girls tried out their new title of aunt, laughing as they did.

Finally Jennet found the courage to look at Pa. Tears glistened in his blue eyes.

"Your ma was about your age when she had you," Pa said. "I don't rightly know if I can see myself as a grandpa, though. Nor your ma as a grandma."

Jennet nervously plucked at her coat draped over her arm.

"You'll make a fine mama," said Pa, nodding. "A fine mama."

"You've had plenty of practice," said Ma, hugging Jennet again. She took Jennet's coat and handed it to Lois to hang on a hook near the door with the other coats. "Does Free know?"

"Yes."

"And is he happy?"

Jennet nodded. She knew his happiness came from inheriting more land at the birth of a child, but she didn't say so.

"Will you visit with Roman and Lillian while you're here?" asked Ma.

She looked helplessly at Ma. "I don't know."

"They'll be happy and proud about the baby," said Marie.

It was hard for Jennet to believe that, but she didn't say anything.

Ma turned to the girls. "Get supper started, girls. We don't want Jennet to starve, do we?"

"The sooner I get at them chores, the sooner they'll get

done," said Pa as he set his hat in place. "The temperature is dropping fast. Your tongue would sure stick to the pump handle today!"

They all laughed because they'd heard Pa's story many times: Tait had dared him to stick his tongue on the pump handle one winter day when he was six, and he'd done it. He had a sore tongue for a long time after. And he never took that kind of dare again.

As Jennet helped make supper she told them about Will and Meg. The little girls wanted Ma to let them live with them.

Ma rolled her eyes and laughed. "Find all the orphan kids and bring them here," she said.

"Do! Do!" cried the little girls together.

After supper Marie took Jennet aside and whispered, "Wex should be home next month! But we won't get married for maybe a year."

"Anne told me about his wound."

Marie's face blanched. "I hate this war!"

Jennet thought of all the runaways who had passed through her place, and she nodded. She hated it for more reasons than having Wex hurt.

"I learned something that will make you mad," whispered Marie.

Jennet didn't know if she wanted to hear, but she said, "What?"

"We didn't get the letters you wrote us when you lived with Uncle because Roman picked them up from town and tore them up. He told Pa just a week ago and he apologized, but it still doesn't make it right."

Jennet pressed her lips tightly together as anger rose in her.

"I wasn't going to tell you, but I thought you should know."

Jennet nodded.

"I hope Free doesn't turn into a mean man like Roman was."

Jennet gasped and felt faint. She'd never thought of that. What if that did happen?

CHAPTER
14

♦ Jennet lifted her flushed face to the warm spring breeze. She felt heavy and awkward and out of sorts. "April twenty-fifth! Just a few more days and I'll have this baby and be done with this misery." She'd always wondered why Ma had been so ornery during the last days before delivery. Now she knew.

Calico rubbed against her ankles, and she frowned down at him. "I'm not good company today, Cal." Jennet went outside to the bench and awkwardly, carefully, sat down. Immediately Calico jumped up and tried to find her lap.

"You'll have to settle for my knees, Cal." Jennet tried to laugh but couldn't manage it.

A forsythia bush in Nina's yard gave a pleasant splash of yellow against the tiny-leafed trees. Meg and Will's laughter floated over from Nina's yard. They were working together to ready the flower beds. Will had convinced Nina that they could do just as good a job as the man she usually hired. Nina had quickly agreed because she liked spending time with the kids, even though they were too noisy and rowdy for her at times.

Jennet smiled. Because of Will and Meg, the winter had

passed quickly for her. Both had learned their lessons well, though Meg was still a bit slower than Will. Jennet watched Meg twirl around. What a different girl from when she'd first come! Will yelled at her to get back to work, and she made a face at him but obeyed.

Jennet glanced up at the bright blue sky, thankful for the warm sun. She'd received two short letters from Free and had finally managed to write a short note back. She had not told him about the property that Lem Azack had purchased in her name, about the runaways, or about Will and Meg. She'd only told him that she was doing well and that she'd spent an enjoyable Christmas with her family. She didn't tell him that she couldn't find the courage to tell Roman and Lillian about the baby even though she'd seen them briefly when she and Marie were out walking.

Next month Free would be back.

Jennet jerked forward. Calico leaped off her legs with a yowl. What would Free do when he learned of all that she'd done? Should she say anything about Blue Newmeyer? She'd considered telling Pa, then decided against it. It was better that he didn't know. If anyone asked, he could truthfully answer that he had no idea about what had happened to the man.

Jennet had decided to tell Anne, then learned that Anne was expecting another child and not feeling well, so she had shared the terrible secret with no one.

Abruptly Jennet pushed herself up, then gasped as another pain shot through her. The pains had been coming off and on since she went to bed last night, but she'd kept it to herself. The baby wasn't due yet, and she didn't want Nina hovering around her, worried over a few false labor pains.

Just then Nina called out that she and the kids were going fishing at the river. "Would you like to join us, Jen?"

"No thanks. Go and don't worry about me. I'll be fine, Nina."

"We'll bring bluegills home for supper," said Will proudly.

"But I won't clean 'em," said Meg with a toss of her head.

Will jabbed her. "You will if Jen says so!"

Meg shrugged and finally agreed.

Jennet sank back on the bench and watched Nina and the kids walk toward the street. They had fishing poles over their shoulders, and Will carried a can of worms. Men had spread another covering of sawdust over the street early that morning, and the smell of freshly cut wood was strong in the air.

Calico settled back on Jennet's legs, and she absently rubbed his soft fur.

"Ma had false labor pains like this before she had Baby Vernon." Jennet gasped as another pain squeezed her. "Heavenly Father, thank You for an easy, quick delivery and a strong healthy baby," she whispered. It had been her prayer for the past two months, once she'd actually accepted that she was carrying her very own baby. She tried not to think about Free's part in her condition, but thoughts of their time together had flashed in her mind when she was least expecting it. Sewing the baby clothes and talking for hours about what he would look like with Meg had helped keep her mind off Free. Jennet and Meg always talked about the baby as a boy. Even though Ma had had seven girls straight in a row, Jennet had a feeling that she was going to have a boy.

"I really don't care if it's a boy or a girl, Cal," she said dreamily. "I'll just be glad when I can hold him."

Would he look like Free?

Jennet pushed the thought aside. This baby was hers! She loved him even though Free was the father.

Jennet eased herself off the bench, waited for another pain to pass, then walked to the back of the barn and leaned against the board fence. Acorn trotted over to her, a week-old foal at her side. Jennet had named her Cherry because her coat was almost as red as a cherry. Jennet rubbed Acorn's face, but the foal was still too skittish to be touched.

Jennet narrowed her eyes against the sun and looked over the pasture. She still could not see where Blue Newmeyer was buried. Maybe Mr. Foringer had buried Newmeyer beyond the pasture. Oh, she wished she'd learned where the body was so she wouldn't keep looking and wondering!

Jennet heard a rider stop at the barn, and she walked around to see who it was. She wasn't expecting anyone. Maybe Anne had sent a messenger to tell her about another runaway.

A man, dressed in a Union army uniform which had seen better days, swung off the horse and stopped short at the sight of her. He pulled off his cap and studied her, his dark brown eyes wide. "Jen?"

"Wex! Oh, Wex, is it you?" She reached for him and clung to him.

Wex hugged her and kissed her cheeks, then stepped back and looked her up and down. "Jen, it's so good to see you!"

Jennet brushed tears from her eyes so she could see him clearly. He had gotten taller and more muscled out across the chest. His face had thinned down, and he had the firm jaw of a man. Love for him rose inside her, but she realized it was the same love she felt for Will.

"Anne told me where I could find you."

Jennet knew Wex saw her condition but was too much of a gentleman to mention it. "How are you, Wex? You look strong and healthy!"

"It took a while, but I'm fit."

"What about your leg?"

"I still have it." He grinned crookedly as he tapped his left leg. "And a limp to go with it."

"Oh, Wex!"

"But I'm alive."

"Yes! And I'm glad! Do you realize that in just a few days it'll be your nineteenth birthday?"

Wex nodded. "Do you still have the hankie you made for my seventeenth birthday?"

"No, I don't," Jennet whispered. She forced back a flush as she remembered Free's anger when he'd seen the hankie and took it from her. She had never learned what he'd done with it.

"It was a very special gift to me, Jen," Wex said softly.

"But that was when we were children," Jennet whispered.

"Yes. Yes, it was. A lifetime ago."

Jennet squeezed his hand, then let it go. His hand was larger but softer than she'd remembered, and she knew the softness came from his weeks in the hospital. "Water your horse and we'll go inside for a cool drink of buttermilk."

Limping, Wex led his horse to water at the horse tank, then tied him to the rail beside the barn.

Jennet hated to see Wex limp. He'd always been so quick on his feet.

A false labor pain squeezed Jennet, and she couldn't move for a minute. Thankfully Wex was looking at his horse and hadn't seen. She managed to smile as he walked beside her into the house.

Jennet poured two glasses of buttermilk and set out a plate of oatmeal raisin cookies. Wex carried them to the front room for her, and they sat side by side on the sofa with the tray of cookies and buttermilk on the low table in front of them.

Wex drank half his glass of buttermilk before setting it back down. He turned to Jennet with a relieved smile. "The war is over at last, Jen."

"I heard rumors that it might be," Jennet said. Before

she could continue, another pain struck. The pains really were getting bothersome! "But I've heard the same thing for four years now."

"This time it's true. The South is defeated and cannot talk further of secession. I've heard that there are still a couple of battles going on, but when they hear that Lee surrendered to Grant at Appomattox, the others will stop fighting. And once again we'll be united."

"What wonderful news!"

As Wex talked, she stared at him as if he was a total stranger. He was not the boy she'd shared secrets with! He talked of places she had never seen and probably would never see. He talked about the politics of war and sounded like his pa.

"You're so grown up!" Jennet exclaimed.

"We both were forced to be," Wex said softly. "I'm sorry for all that happened to you. Marie told me in her letters."

Jennet fought back hot tears. "We both survived."

"Are you happy, Jen?"

Jennet thought of Will and Meg and the baby. "Yes. Yes, I suppose I am."

"It's strange that you married Free."

"And that you'll marry Marie."

Wex flushed. "I'm embarrassed at the way I once spoke to you of marriage."

"Oh, don't be!" Jennet caught his hand and gripped it tightly. She looked into his dark brown eyes that were so much like Free's. "Wex, you were my dearest friend!"

"And now we are brother and sister as well as friends." Wex smiled at her, and she felt his love flowing to her. Eagerly she received it and returned her love to him.

Jennet lifted his hand to her cheek and closed her eyes. He was the brother she'd never had! He would always be her brother. She opened her eyes to see Free standing in the doorway. His dark eyes smoldered with anger.

A muscle jumped in Free's jaw. Would Jennet ever look at him with the love that showed on her face for Wex?

Jennet's heart stopped, then thudded so hard she felt the room move. She dropped Wex's hand as if it had burned her.

Wex jumped up. "Freeman!"

Free saw the fear in Jennet's wide blue eyes. He fought against the urge to knock Wex across the county. "I came to talk to you about Grandpa's trees," he said hoarsely, his eyes never leaving Jennet's face. Even in her condition she looked beautiful! He knew he could've waited to see her until next month when he'd be home for the summer, but he'd felt a strong urge to be with her now.

A strong labor pain gripped Jennet. She closed her eyes and struggled not to cry out.

Free saw the pain on her face, and he thought it had to do with his breaking up her meeting with Wexal. Agony writhed inside him and spread until it turned to anger as it surfaced. He strode forward, his eyes boring into hers, and motioned at Wex. "Just how long has he been with you?"

"I just arrived," said Wex, frowning slightly.

Jennet started to speak, but another pain squeezed so hard she almost screamed aloud. When the pain lessened, she awkwardly pushed herself up and faced Free. "You said you'd be here in May. I didn't expect you yet."

"So I see."

Another pain seized Jennet, and she knew she'd been deluding herself. She was not having false labor. This was the real thing, and it was serious. "It seems you're just in time for the birth of the baby," she whispered as yet another pain gripped her.

"What?" cried Wex.

The color drained from Free's face. "I'll get the doctor," he said, starting for the door.

"No!" Wex caught Free's arm. "You stay with Jen, and I'll get the doctor."

Free told him the doctor's name and address, and Wex hurried out to his horse.

Perspiration dotted Jennet's face as another pain started. This one lasted much longer and was more intense. When it was over, she slowly made her way to the bedroom, and Free followed her. "You don't have to stay with me," she said stiffly.

"I won't leave you alone," Free said gruffly. He'd helped birth animals but never a human baby. He hated feeling frightened and helpless. "What can I do to help you?"

"Nothing," Jennet said. At another pain she reached out for the bedpost and gripped it until her knuckles turned white.

"Let me help you into bed."

Jennet shook her head, unable to move. From the pressure of the baby she knew it was time for the birth. She couldn't wait for the doctor or for Nina. She remembered how easily Eve had given birth to Joshua, squatting in the corner of Tait's house. Maybe she could do it the same way instead of in bed as Ma always had.

Jennet had to undress, but she knew she couldn't manage alone. She flushed with embarrassment as she realized Free would have to help her. She didn't want him with her, especially now with the baby coming.

Free saw the pain she was in and he wanted to take it from her and bear it for her, but he couldn't. "Help her, Lord," he whispered; then realized having Jig around all winter had helped him remember to call on God.

Her face red, Jennet swallowed her pride and whispered, "Help . . . me . . . undress."

Free gently helped her undress, then slipped the robe on her that was lying across the bed. He wanted to put his arms around her and hold her and soothe her, but he was afraid she'd push him away.

Jennet picked up the folded quilt from the foot of the bed and dropped it on the floor. A great pressure squeezed her, and she gripped Free's arm tightly. Another great pressure broke her water, then a pain almost took her to her knees. Jennet knew the baby was ready. Just as she had seen Eve do, she squatted down over the quilt and with a loud cry and a mighty push delivered the baby.

To Jennet's surprise, Free caught the baby in his hands and carefully lifted him up by his heels. The baby sputtered, cried a tiny little cry, then cried a lusty cry that made Jennet laugh and cry at the same time.

Free looked at the baby in his hands, and a love welled up inside him like he'd never experienced before. "It's a boy!" he said in awe.

Jennet laughed again as she looked at their wrinkled red son. "A boy!" She glanced at Free, and the love in his eyes for the baby melted her very bones.

Together they cut and tied the cord. Jennet pointed out a soft flannel blanket and Free wrapped the baby in it, laid him in the tiny cradle beside the bed, then carried hot water to Jennet so she could wash the baby and herself.

Much later Jennet lay in bed with the baby at her side. She smiled at Free, and he smiled back.

"A boy," Jen said softly.

"Our boy," Free whispered. He wanted to take Jennet in his arms and hold her close, but he couldn't find the courage. It would hurt too much if she pushed him away or, worse yet, only endured his touch the way she had before.

"What shall we name him?" Jennet asked.

Free hadn't thought about names, hadn't thought about having a baby or being a father. "I don't know."

"How about Clay? After your grandpa?"

A lump lodged in Free's throat, and he couldn't speak. He blinked back tears.

"If you don't want to name him Clay, we could call him Freeman after you."

Free was shocked that she'd even suggest naming the

baby after him. Finally he found his voice. "We could call him Clay Freeman Havlick."

She nodded and smiled down at the tiny baby. "Clay Freeman Havlick."

Free leaned over and kissed Clay's soft cheek, then his eyes locked with Jennet's. He wanted to kiss her, but he saw the sudden panic in her eyes and he stood up and turned away.

Jennet looked at his back. Had she seen pain in his eyes because she hadn't lifted her lips to his? She frowned. She was only imagining it. He had started to kiss her because as her husband he felt he should.

"I'll stay here with you a few days, then get back to camp," Free said in an unsteady voice.

"It's not necessary."

"Why?" He turned to her. Because of Wex?

"Nina will help me. And Will and Meg."

"Will? Meg?" He was puzzled by the names.

Before Jennet could explain, Wex and Doc Mundy rushed in. The doctor's face was red, and his usually well-waxed mustache drooped. He stopped short when he saw Jennet and the baby.

"It took me a while to find the doc," said Wex as he stared in surprise at Jennet and the baby.

"It seems I'm too late," Doc Mundy said, laughing

"It's a boy," said Jennet. "Clay Freeman."

"He's a real beauty," said the doctor.

Jennet smiled at Wex. "What do you think, Wex?"

He bent over Jennet and the baby and whispered, "He's a keeper, all right."

Jealousy ripped through Free. "We'll get out of here so you can rest, Jen. Come on, Wex."

"Good-bye, Jen," said Wex, smiling. "I'll tell your family the good news."

"I'd appreciate that," she said.

"What good news?" asked Free sharply.

"The baby," said Wex, looking oddly at his brother.

Free flushed and walked toward the door.

"I'll just check on mother and baby," said Doc Mundy.

On his way out Free caught Jennet's eye. She saw his haunted look, and she frowned questioningly. He thought her frown meant she was impatient for him to leave. Abruptly he closed the door and walked to the kitchen with Wex.

"Are you going to the farm now?" asked Free as he tried to push aside his jealousy and remember Wex was his beloved brother.

Wex nodded. "I meant to be on my way before now. I just got into town yesterday."

"I heard talk the war is over."

"That's right." Wex rubbed an unsteady hand over his eyes.

Free leaned against the doorframe between the kitchen and the dining room. "Anne told me you were in Tennessee."

Wex nodded as he sank to a kitchen chair. "In the fall of '63 I was with General William Rosecrans in Tennessee. We were pursuing General Braxton Bragg southward into Georgia after he evacuated Chattanooga. At a place called Chickamauga Bragg's army turned and engaged us." The color drained from Wex's face, and for a minute he couldn't speak.

Free had read about the battle without knowing Wex had been involved. Was this stranger his little brother?

Wex cleared his throat. "We hadn't realized he'd received reinforcements from Virginia. The sounds of rifles and cannons were deafening. All around me were the smells of gunpowder and sweat and blood. I couldn't stand the cries of the wounded or the smells of dying men. But I was there, in the battle, and I couldn't walk away." Wex looked unseeingly across the kitchen. "Our northern right flank crumpled and broke completely. The left flank fought on under General George Thomas. We fought hard, but we had to retreat into Chattanooga." Wex told Free about starving in Chattanooga for about two months because Bragg had them boxed in and cut them off from their food supply in Bridgeport. "All we ate was corn and gruel. Thousands of horses and mules starved to death." Wex's voice broke. "Finally Grant's army came from the west, floated down the Tennessee River, and overtook the Confederate troops guarding the river. Then food and supplies were brought in. Sherman arrived to help, and we took Lookout Mountain. Within days we were free. But not without losing many men."

Free could see the pain on Wex's face. "I'm glad you're back, Wex."

Wex was quiet for a long time, then said "When did you see Pa and Ma last?"

"Not for over a year. Are you home to stay?"

"Yes." Wex grinned and almost looked like his old self. "And I learned that Grandpa left a farm to me. Pa never said a word about it."

Free told Wex about the land and money that Grandpa had left him. He didn't tell Wex that he'd inherited only because of marrying Jennet.

"I hear Pa's changed," said Wex.

"That's hard to believe."

Wex shrugged. "I'll see for myself. If I leave now, I should be there just after dark. Want me to say hello for you?"

"To Ma."

Wex picked up his blue cap and ran his finger around the worn bill. "It doesn't pay to carry a grudge, Free." He kept his eyes on his cap.

Jig had talked to him all winter about forgiveness. Now Wex was trying to say the same thing. Free changed the subject. "Do you want something to eat before you go?"

"I have some food in my pack so I can eat as I ride." He smiled. "I'm anxious to get home."

Free clamped his hand on Wex's shoulder and suddenly realized that Wex had grown since last he'd seen him. "Wex, I'm glad you're back. And that you're in one piece."

Wex grimaced as he tapped his leg. 'I didn't lose it after all. But others did. Too many dead soldiers. I see 'em in my sleep, Free. I hear the screams of agony." His voice broke. "Only a miracle from God kept me alive!"

They talked a while longer as Free walked Wex outside. After they shook hands, Wex mounted his horse.

"Do you plan on coming back to see Jen?" asked Free, forcing his voice to stay light. He couldn't manage to rid himself of jealousy.

Wex nodded. "When I'm in town again."

Free's whole body tensed but he didn't speak.

"Tell Jen I'll see her," said Wex. He smiled down at Free. "Congratulations, Papa!"

Free smiled slightly, then stood in the yard as Wex rode away.

Just then Doc Mundy came out the front door with his hat in one hand and his black bag in the other. "She's doing fine, Free. Both are. I'll look in on them later. In eight days I'll circumcise the baby." Doc walked to his buggy and Free fell into step beside him. "You planning on being here long?"

"I have to get back in a few days. Jen told me she has help."

"So she said." Doc stepped up into the buggy. "That girl has a lot of strength, Free. A lot of strength."

Free didn't agree, but he didn't argue. For the years that he'd known her she'd needed protection and help from someone strong. Like him. "Thanks for coming, Doc. I'll take care of the bill before I leave town."

"No need. Jennet already did. She had it all tucked away and gave it to me just now."

That surprised Free, but he didn't let it show.

As soon as Doc Mundy drove away, Free walked inside. The house seemed very quiet after all the excitement. He peeked into the bedroom. Jennet and the baby were fast asleep. He stood in the doorway and looked at them. His heart swelled with pride and with a feeling he couldn't or wouldn't identify.

Jennet opened her eyes. "I thought you left," she said sleepily.

"I'll be here a few days," Free said stiffly.

"No need. Will and Meg will be home soon."

Free knotted his fists at his sides and a pulse throbbed at his temples. "Who are they?"

Jennet took a deep breath and told him.

When she finished, he said in a dead calm voice that alarmed her, "You mean to tell me you just let those orphan kids take over the house?"

"They lived in a box!"

"I know that's sad, but it's the orphan asylum's problem, not yours."

Jennet tried to sit up but fell back, too weak to move. "I couldn't let them live in a box during the winter!"

"It's not winter now."

Jennet turned her face from him and closed her eyes. He'd be gone in a few days, and she could do what she wanted.

Neither spoke again. Free couldn't stand the awkward silence, so he left the room. He resolved to take care of the orphans since Jennet couldn't bring herself to.

With his hands locked behind his back Free walked through the house. He stopped in the other two bedrooms and frowned. The orphans had really taken over. Why hadn't Nina or Tunis stopped Jen?

Free heard the back door open, and he hurried to the kitchen. Nina and two children walked in with a stringer of fish.

"Freeman!" cried Nina, throwing her arms around him.

Free hugged her and realized just how much he'd missed her. At camp he'd kept so busy that he hadn't realized he missed anyone. "Hello, Nina." He stepped back from her and eyed the children.

"Hi," said Will as he dropped the fish into a pail. "I'm Will, and this is my sister Meg."

"Where's Jen?" asked Meg, suddenly looking frightened.

"She's in bed."

"In bed?" asked Nina in alarm, heading toward the doorway.

Free caught her arm and stopped her. "She had a baby boy about two hours ago."

"No!" cried Nina.

"A boy!" said Meg, her face filled with excitement. "We knew it would be a boy. I want to see him."

"Hold it," snapped Free. "Jen needs to rest."

"But she'd want us to see the baby," said Meg in a small voice as she stepped close to Nina.

"She would," said Nina. "We'll just peek in."

Free gave in with a shrug.

"I'll take the kids home with me."

"That's not necessary, Nina," said Free.

Her brow cocked, Nina looked at Free. "Is something troubling you, Free?"

"You go ahead and look in on Jen and the baby."

"What did Jen name him?" asked Meg.

Free hesitated a second. "Clay Freeman."

Meg clapped her hands. "That's what I suggested!"

Disappointment washed over Free, but he wouldn't let it show. He'd thought Jen had chosen the name herself.

Nina led Meg and Will to the bedroom while Free trailed behind them. They were dirty and smelled of fish. But if Jennet wanted them as badly as Nina said, he'd let them visit her.

Jennet turned her head at the sound of the door. She smiled with delight at the sight of Nina and the kids. "It's a boy," she said. "Free probably already told you."

Nina kissed Jennet's cheek while Meg and Will stared down at the baby in the cradle.

"He's sure little," said Will. "When he's bigger, I bet I could teach him how to fish."

"He's so beautiful I think I might cry," whispered Meg. She turned to Jennet. "He sure looks like his papa."

Jennet saw the pleased look on Free's face. She'd already noticed that the baby did look a lot like Free.

Nina gently lifted the baby into her arms and kissed his soft cheek. "Clay Freeman Havlick, you are blessed of God! May you live your life serving Him and doing good to all mankind." With tears brimming in her eyes Nina looked from Free to Jennet. "May the two of you love and nurture this baby and help him to grow up knowing and loving his heavenly Father."

"I will," whispered Jennet, a promise to Nina, but to God first of all.

Free nodded, unable to speak around the lump in his throat. He'd never realized until just now that Clay Freeman Havlick was his responsibility. His and Jen's. It was up to them to tell Clay about God and to teach him to be honest and upright. It was an awesome, almost frightening duty.

Nina kissed the baby, held him out for Will and Meg to kiss, then gently laid him in the cradle. She bent over and kissed Jennet again, then led the children out.

Free turned to go, but Jennet said, "Free, don't go." She'd struggled with speaking to him but finally knew she had to.

Free walked to her side. "I'm sorry for upsetting you before."

Jennet nodded to acknowledge that she'd heard and accepted his apology. She had something to say to him, and she would say it! "Free, Meg and Will belong here." She would not let her voice quiver! "They are going to stay here with me."

Her forceful words surprised him. He'd never heard her speak that way before.

"I love them and they love me. We help each other."

"They're too much work for you, Jen."

"No. They are not!" Jennet looked Free squarely in the eyes. "Don't send them away and don't do or say anything to hurt them."

Free was too dazed to do anything but agree. Maybe there was more to Jen than he'd thought.

Jennet smiled and closed her eyes to sleep.

CHAPTER

15

♦ Jennet sleepily opened her eyes to see Free slipping into bed. She tensed, but he didn't touch her.

Free could tell she was awake, but suddenly he was tongue-tied. He wanted to turn on his side and lie with his arm across her the way he'd done the two and a half months he'd been home before. But he tucked his hands under his head and stared up at the ceiling. He heard little sounds from the baby in his cradle, and he smiled. Finally he said, "You awake?"

Jennet whispered, "Yes."

"I remember when I first saw you."

She smiled. This was a safe topic. "I was eleven."

"You tried to rob a bee tree, and you were running from a swarm of mad honeybees."

"And you caught my hand and ran with me to the creek and ducked down under the water with me."

"I almost drowned you."

"But I didn't get stung."

Free chuckled. "I did later."

"When we got the honey out." Jennet fingered the tip of

her braid as she watched the shadows dance in the moonlight. "It was good honey."

"That it was. I took some with me when I left." That was the first time he'd left home. Free could still remember his anger and his loneliness. "Even then Pa knew about Grandpa's money. But he didn't say a word."

Jennet heard the bitterness in his voice, and she turned her head to look at him. "Free, you've got to forgive him."

"I can't."

"With God's help you can."

Having her say that surprised him. Free moved but still couldn't find the courage to touch her.

"I remember the first time I saw you," she said softly. It was easier to talk to him in the semidarkness.

"Oh?" He'd thought it was when he'd first seen her.

"You were chopping down a tree. That big old wild cherry that stood next to the granary."

Free said thoughtfully, "Pa told me it had to come down because a branch fell off and wrecked the corner of the roof."

"You swung that ax and you hit the same spot every time. Chips flew right out from it."

"I loved that old tree. I used to climb it when I wanted to get away from Anne and Wex."

"I heard you call, 'TIMBER!' just like in the woods when it was ready to fall."

He grinned, remembering. "I didn't know you were watching."

"I was afraid to speak to you. You were so dashing and so handsome!" Her eyes widened at her admission, and she wanted to grab back the words. They had seemed to slip out on their own.

With a grin Free turned his head to look at her. "Handsome? Dashing?"

Jennet heard the laughter in his voice, and her heart jumped strangely.

They were quiet a long time, listening to the house creaking and the baby making funny little noises.

"Jen, thank you."

"For what?"

"Our son."

"He's beautiful, isn't he?"

"Perfect. He's perfect." Free found her hand, squeezed it, and let it go. "Good night."

"Night," Jennet whispered. The warmth of his hand on hers sent a tingle of awareness over her. She closed her eyes and listened to him breathe, then finally drift into sleep. In his sleep he turned on his side and wrapped his arm around her. Her eyes flew open, and she stiffened. His breath was warm against her face and his arm heavy on her waist. Slowly she relaxed and drifted off to sleep too.

At dawn Jennet awoke to the cry of the baby and slipped from under Free's arm and out of bed. Gently she picked up the baby and sat in the maple rocker beside the cradle to nurse him. Silently she praised God for His goodness and His help just as she did each morning. The only sounds she heard were the faint creak of the rocker, Free's breathing, and the baby's little noises. She burped the baby, kissed his fuzzy cheek, and put him to nurse again.

Jennet closed her eyes and worshiped God, her heart full of love for Him and her baby.

Just then she felt impressed to tell Free all that had occurred since he'd left. She frowned at the frightening thought, then tried to push it away, but it persisted. "Heavenly Father, I will tell him," she whispered.

Maybe she should tell him right now while her courage was high. She shook her head. No, she wouldn't wake him. Later she'd tell him.

When the baby finished nursing, she burped him, changed him, and laid him on his stomach in the cradle. She eased into bed and for one wild minute thought of moving close against Free. The desire was gone almost before the thought was over. She sank into her pillow and fell asleep. When she woke again, he was gone.

Jennet slipped out of bed and stood beside the cradle to admire her son. "You are a beautiful, precious baby," she whispered. Finally she turned away to dress.

Halfway through buttoning the front of her yellow-and-brown calico dress with the loose waist, Jennet stopped to press her hand to her racing heart. What would Free say when he learned about her work with runaways?

"I won't tell him." Yet she knew she had to tell him. He was her husband, and she should not keep secrets from him even if he'd be angry. "I can do it with God's help!"

Jennet glanced in the looking glass. Her stomach was not flat like she'd thought it would be. She felt very slim, but her reflection said different.

She brushed her long chestnut-brown hair, tied a ribbon around it, and left it to hang down her back and over her shoulders. She smiled in the looking glass, then stuck out her tongue and wrinkled her nose at her reflection. "I *will* lose that rounded stomach!"

Clay stirred in his cradle but slept on.

The door opened and Free walked in.

Jennet jumped guiltily.

Free stared at her. He wanted to stroke her shiny hair and kiss her moist lips.

The look in his eyes sent a trembling through Jennet, different from the fear she usually felt.

Free frowned. He wore dark pants and a light blue shirt with wide gray suspenders. "Why are you up?"

Jennet shrugged and managed a smile. Could he hear the unsteady beat of her heart? "It's a beautiful sunny day, and I couldn't stay in bed a minute longer!" She sank to the rocker and slipped on her shoes, unable to look at him without blushing.

Free stood beside the cradle. "Didn't the doctor say to stay in bed more than a day?"

Jennet waved her hand. "Ma was up and about hours after giving birth." Her face clouded. "Except for Baby Vernon."

Free wanted to insist she climb back in bed, but he didn't. "How is your ma now?"

Jennet told him about her family and how thankful she was that Ma was in such good health. Then she thought of Dacia, and that made her think of Blue Newmeyer.

"What's wrong?" asked Free, peering into her suddenly ashen face. "Maybe you should get back into bed."

"No. I'm fine."

Free sighed. She was not the submissive girl he'd left behind!

Jennet struggled against not telling him anything. "Where are the kids?"

He'd wanted to send them to the orphanage, but he didn't mention that. "At Nina's already. I didn't want them to wake you."

"That'll give us a chance to talk."

For some reason that frightened Free. He didn't know what to expect of her any longer. "What about the baby?"

"He'll sleep for a good while." Jennet stepped into the hallway. It felt strange to walk without the weight of the baby. "Let's sit outdoors."

Free didn't speak until they were side by side on the bench near the back door.

Jennet lifted her face to the warm sun. Calico jumped on her lap and curled up against her. She stroked his back and listened to the clip-clop of horses' hooves as two riders rode past.

"What did you want to say?" Free asked, surprised that his voice didn't quiver. He felt her tension, and it made every nerve in his body tighten. Was she going to tell him that she wanted to leave him to marry Wex? Surely she wouldn't do that! Divorce was wrong and she knew it.

"It started the day you left to go to camp," Jennet said in a low voice that she managed to keep steady.

"What started?" Free asked hoarsely.

Haltingly Jennet told him about Dacia and Colin, then about Blue Newmeyer. Free interrupted with questions and angry exclamations, but he was thankful she wasn't talking about going to Wex. She saved the details of Newmeyer's death until last.

"So, he's buried out there somewhere." Jennet couldn't look at Free but kept her eyes on Calico asleep in her lap.

Free groaned. "Jen, I don't know what to say!"

"I thought you should know."

Free looked at her as if he'd never seen her before. She was not the frightened, helpless girl he'd married. "Is there anything else?"

"Not about runaways."

Free stabbed his fingers through his dark hair. Now, was it about Wex? "What then?"

Acorn nickered, and Cherry squealed a funny little squeal.

Jennet took a deep breath and told Free about going to Prickett and about buying the land so the forest could grow again.

Free felt as if he was listening to a stranger. His own mother didn't have the courage to do anything unless Pa told her to.

"I don't want Michigan to be a land without trees," Jennet said.

Free frowned. "That can't happen."

Jennet turned to him in surprise. "How can you say that? It will if all of you keep cutting them down."

"Let us worry about that, Jen."

Jennet brushed back a strand of hair. "I'm not worrying about it, Free. I'm *doing* something about it."

Free lifted his brows questioningly.

Jennet's stomach tightened. "I bought the land, and I

won't let anyone touch it so that forests will grow again."

"Only to be cut down in another eighty years or so."

Jennet hadn't thought of that. "By then other people will know the importance of keeping the forest. Someone else will save tracts of land. I'll teach Clay the importance. I'll make a will that says they can't cut down the trees!"

Free didn't want to argue further with her. She was only a woman and didn't really know how things were. "Why'd you tell me all this now?"

Jennet moistened her lips with the tip of her tongue. For some reason this was even harder to tell. Silently she prayed for help. "This morning when I was praying, I felt I should tell you." Slowly at first, then gaining more confidence as she talked, she told him about rededicating herself to God and about learning to live as He wanted her to. "I had forgotten that God loves me and is always with me. He knows when even a sparrow falls, and He says I am of more value."

"You are," said Free under his breath.

"And so are you."

Free shrugged. At times he didn't think he had any value.

"Tune told me that Grandpa Clay was a strong Christian man the last few years of his life."

Free nodded.

"Did he ever talk to you about Jesus?"

"Yes." Free thought back on the talks and how much he'd enjoyed them. "When I was fourteen, I was born again."

"I didn't know that."

"This winter with Jig around I've been reminded of my promise to God." Last summer Free had told her all about Jig. "It's sure easy to let God fade away into the background of your life." Free laughed. "Except when Jig's around. Or Tune and Nina."

They smiled at each other. He studied the curve of her

pink lips, the line of her fine brows the exact color of her chestnut-brown hair hanging over her slender shoulders, and the depth of her blue eyes, and his gaze felt more intimate to her than a caress. She tried to look away but couldn't. He lowered his head to her, and she lifted her lips to him. Her pulse pounded in her ears, and she could hardly breathe. Before they could touch in a kiss the baby cried.

Flustered, Jennet jumped up, her face red. Her lips tingled at the thought of his kiss, and that sent another wave of crimson up her neck and over her face.

Free abruptly turned away from her, hurt because he thought she was relieved that she wasn't subjected to yet another unwanted kiss from him. Why keep asking for more pain? She loved Wex.

Free strode behind the barn and leaned against the fence to watch Acorn and Cherry and bring his wayward emotions into check.

Trembling with the strange feelings that Free had aroused in her, Jennet picked up Clay, sat in the rocker, and fed him. She touched his tiny fingers, his ears, and the dark hair on his head. "My baby," she whispered in awe. "Mine and Free's." She once again felt Free's eyes on her, and she flushed as she realized that she'd actually wanted his kiss.

Why should that embarrass her? She was Free's wife!

Jennet thought of the looks of love that had passed between Ma and Pa. Was it possible for her and Free to have that kind of love? It would take a miracle.

But God worked miracles. Jennet smiled. Maybe now that she'd gotten rid of her anger toward Free and with him here this summer they could really get to know each other and grow to love each other.

Maybe he isn't interested in love. The thought had never really occurred to her before.

Tears pricked her eyes, and she blinked them quickly away. Would they have to live their lives without love? She'd seen other couples live that way, people who had married for convenience or because the marriage had been arranged by parents.

Clay squirmed, and Jennet lifted him to her shoulder and burped him. She smelled his baby smell and smiled. A picture of Free catching Clay in his hands at the birth flashed across her mind. He easily could've walked away from her when she'd started giving birth. But he'd stayed at her side through it all. Pa could never stay at Ma's side during delivery. He'd always said he didn't want anyone to see a grown man faint dead away.

Jennet kissed the baby's soft cheek. "Clay, your papa's quite a man."

Outdoors Free sighed heavily, then turned away from the fence to walk back to the house. Before he reached the back door Tunis drove up in his buggy.

"Bad news, Free!" called Tunis as he jumped to the ground.

Free strode to Tunis s side. "What's wrong?"

"Your man Link stopped in my office to get a message to you."

"I told him that would be the best way to reach me. What'd he say?"

Tunis pulled off his hat and rubbed his thinning gray hair. "Link heard a couple of men telling about stealing your logs."

"When? Where?"

Tunis told him, and Free smacked his fist into his palm. Pirating logs was big business. All logs were struck on both ends with the heavy marking hammer that carried the lumberman's mark. Free had seen men steal logs two springs ago. The thieves hid along the stream, and as the logs floated past, they'd snake out their long pike poles, gaff a few logs, saw off the ends, and strike their own marks.

Free clamped Tunis on the shoulder. "Thanks for telling me. I better be on my way to check it out."

"Anything I can do to help?"

"Drive me to the stage." When logs were floating, the rivers weren't the safest mode of transportation. "I'll go get a few things and tell Jen."

"I'll be at home. Just give a holler when you're ready."

Free nodded. He walked into the bedroom just as Jennet was about to lay Clay in the cradle.

She turned and smiled at Free. "Would you like to hold the baby?"

Free hesitated, then nodded. A couple of minutes wouldn't hurt.

Jennet held Clay out to him, and their hands brushed as Free took the baby. Free's touch sent sparks flying through her, and she forced back a telltale blush.

Feeling awkward, Free held Clay to him. How he loved this little baby who bore his name! He nuzzled his cheek and whispered softly, "I love you, little Clay."

Jennet smiled at father and son.

Free caught a look of tenderness in Jennet's eyes that surprised him. But then he realized the look was for Clay and not him. "Jen, Tune just told me that someone stole some of my logs."

"Oh, no!"

"I've got to check it out. I hate to leave, but I must."

To her surprise, she realized she didn't want him to go. "When will you be back?"

"I don't know. I'll have to go on to Big Pine from Grand Haven."

"Two weeks?"

"Maybe more." Free peered closely at her. Would she miss him? Didn't she want him to go? His heart leaped at the thought.

He smiled, and the warmth of it wrapped around her heart. He kissed Clay, laid him carefully on his stomach in the cradle just as he'd seen Jennet do, then turned to her. He wanted to pull her close and kiss her, but he was afraid to in case he'd misread her softening toward him. "Tune will drive me to the stage."

"I wish you could be here when my family comes to see the baby."

"I do too."

"Once Wex tells them, they'll come as soon as they can." Jennet knew that would be after spring planting. "Your folks probably will come too."

Free frowned at that. "Don't let Pa boss you around."

"I won't."

Free gathered up his things and stuffed them in his backpack. He'd been home less than twenty-four hours, but he felt as if those hours had changed his life. He didn't want to leave Jen or the baby, but he had to.

"I'll walk you out," Jennet said, smoothing down her dress and buttoning the top button that she'd missed before.

Free gripped his pack tighter just to keep from reaching out to pull her close. With one last look at the baby he walked into the hall, to the kitchen, and out the back door.

Tears stung Jennet's eyes as she followed him. She wanted to put her arms around him and kiss him good-bye, but she couldn't find the courage. "Good-bye, Free," she whispered.

"Bye, Jen." Free stood before her, his hat in his hands, his pack on his arm. "Go back to bed for a while, will you?"

Jennet nodded. "You'll be very careful, won't you?"

Free nodded. He wanted to call to Tunis and walk to the buggy, but he couldn't move away from her.

A door slammed and Tunis called, "Ready to go, Freeman?"

The shout broke the spell, and Free hurried to the buggy.

Jennet sank to the bench, then waved to Tunis as he walked across his yard. Finally she looked at the buggy where Free already sat. She lifted her hand in a wave. He tipped his head toward her and waved as Tunis drove them away.

A great loneliness washed over her, leaving her weak and ready to cry. She forced herself to walk inside and fix something to eat.

Eventually Jennet stretched out on the bed with a quilt over her. She hadn't realized she was so tired. She closed her eyes and Free was there inside her head, imprinted on her eyelids. He smiled at her. She smiled back and then drifted off to sleep.

CHAPTER

16

♦ Jennet clung to Nina as the hot July wind blew against her. "Nina, it's so hard to say good-bye to you."

Nina stepped back and wiped tears from her eyes. "I'm going to miss you, Jen! But you're doing the right thing. You belong with Free."

Jennet nodded as she dabbed her tears with her hankie. She'd miss Tune and the house that had become a wonderful home to her and Clay. And she'd miss Meg and Will. Nina had talked Jennet into letting them live with her and Tunis. Meg and Will had agreed, with the promise that they'd visit her regularly wherever she and Free lived.

Clearing his throat, Tunis stood beside the buggy with his arms around Meg and Will. "We'd best be going, Jen." He was driving her to Big Pine, then he would take a boat back to Grand Rapids. "It's already daylight in the swamp."

Cherry whinnied from the pasture. She was staying behind, too, for Meg and Will to train. Hitched to the buggy, Acorn nickered, bobbing her head.

"Are you sure you have everything you'll need, Jen?" asked Nina as she looked over the bags in the buggy.

"I double-checked," said Jennet.

Tunis chuckled and patted Nina's arm. "We might call Big Pine the wilderness, Nina, but they do have a couple of stores there."

"I survived at Prickett," said Jennet, smiling as she adjusted the light blanket over Clay who lay in a basket in the buggy. "I can survive Big Pine."

"You certainly can," said Nina. "I know you can. God is with you even in the wilderness!"

Once again Jennet hugged Meg and Will and Nina. "I love all of you! And I will write."

"I'll write too," said Meg as tears trickled down her rosy cheeks. That was a big task for her since she hated writing.

Jennet spoke to Will. "I'm glad you decided to work with Tune at the paper."

"I'll work hard," Will said gruffly as he blinked away tears.

Jennet stepped up into the buggy, Tunis flicked the reins, and Acorn walked away from Nina, Meg, and Will and away from the house where Jennet had lived for over a year.

On her birthday in June her family had finally been able to get away from the farm and had come to see Clay. They were all proud of Jennet and pleased with the baby. Marie had whispered to Jennet that she and Wex were getting married right away so Wex could inherit the farm Grandpa Clay had left him. She said she hadn't told Pa yet. Jennet hoped she and Free would be able to make the trip for the wedding.

A week later Roman and Lillian had visited. They were formal but admired the baby and asked after Free. Jennet told them that he'd left home to check on men stealing his logs but had never found them. He had gone on to Big Pine and had been delayed there for one reason and another. She showed his letters to them, and Lillian read them aloud, eager to hear word of Free. Roman listened with interest but scowled until his brows almost touched over his nose.

He had voiced his surprise that Free really did seem to know the lumber business.

"You're sure quiet, Jen," said Tunis, swaying with the motion of the buggy as he drove along the rutted road between miles of ugly black stumps sticking out of the ground. "Are you sorry you're going?"

"Maybe a little."

"It's hard to leave people who love you."

Jennet patted his arm and smiled. "It's a little scary for me to go to Big Pine with Free not expecting me."

"He'll be glad to see you."

Jennet wasn't as sure about that as Tune seemed to be. He had learned that Free was having trouble with Willie Thorne over tracts of land, and that was keeping him in Big Pine, even though he'd planned to return home no later than the middle of June. If things kept going the way they were, it would be September and time for Free to go to the lumbercamp again. Jennet knew she belonged with him, but Nina had to convince her to take action.

"I know where his cabin is, so we'll go there," said Tunis.

The canvas top on the buggy shielded them from the hot sun. The buggy seat grew harder to Jennet as the day stretched on. Without asking Tunis to stop, Jennet changed and nursed Clay several times. She knew they had to keep going so they wouldn't be on the trail after dark.

Shortly before dark Tunis pulled alongside a small cabin tucked among tall white pines just outside Big Pine. "Here we are," Tunis said, sounding tired.

Her heart thudding, Jennet stared at the cabin. The door didn't open. "He must not be home."

Tunis climbed out of the buggy and helped Jennet down. Her legs felt stiff after sitting so long. She slowly approached the cabin while Tunis carried Clay in his basket. She saw a stick leaning against the door. Tunis had told her it was a sign to Indians to pass on because nobody was home. If the stick wasn't there, an Indian could walk right in and expect to be fed.

Tunis moved the stick and pushed open the heavy door. It was neat and clean inside and smelled of coffee.

Butterflies fluttered in Jennet's stomach as she stepped through the door onto the puncheon floor. Free probably had split the floor logs himself, and with a broad ax had cut the faces of them flat. The rounded side lay against the ground, and the smooth finished side was turned up. A trestle table with two chairs pushed up to it stood in the middle of the room. A cast-iron cookstove was against one wall and a bed against another. Light filtered in through two glass-paned windows. Pegs in the wall held clothes that she recognized as Free's.

Tunis quickly unloaded her things. "I'll put Acorn in the barn, then walk on back to Big Pine before dark. I sure don't want to run into a wolf." He grinned, but she knew he was serious. "Will you be all right even if Free doesn't come back tonight?"

"I will." She hugged Tunis and saw him on his way.

Jennet took in every inch of the small cabin. A peace settled over her, making her feel as if she had indeed come home. She closed the door and put the latch in place but did not pull in the latchstring in case Free came home. She lit the lamp in the middle of the table, then started a fire in the stove to keep out the chill of the night and to make supper.

Clay whimpered, and she knew it was time to feed him. She settled into a chair and hummed softly as the baby nursed. After a while her eyes drooped, and she yawned several times.

Jennet changed Clay and settled him in for the night. He'd sleep in his basket beside Free's bed.

I'll share the bed with Free tonight. To her surprise, the thought didn't frighten her as it had before. *After all, he is my husband!*

234

Just then the door swung open, and a redheaded man burst inside. He wore dark pants, black boots, a big-sleeved gray shirt, and wide black suspenders. He stopped short when he saw Jennet. "Who're you? Where's Free Havlick?"

As sure as she was born, Jennet knew the man was Willie Thorne. Fear pricked her skin, but she said calmly, "He's not here right now. I'm his wife, Jennet."

"Well, well." Willie walked around her, eyeing her and chuckling to himself. "His wife, huh? Well, well."

"Is there something I can do for you?"

"I came to see Free. But this is better."

The look in his eyes sent a chill through her. "He'll be home soon, I'm sure," Jennet said.

"I'm sure too. But he's gonna have a jolt, he is." Willie grabbed her arm and dragged her toward the door.

"Let me go!" Jennet cried, struggling to break his hold, but he was too strong for her.

"We're goin' for a walk. A nice little walk." Willie Thorne grinned, then laughed. "Free won't want to tangle with me once he sees his little wife was wolf bait."

The words turned her blood to ice. She struggled harder, but Willie snaked an arm around her and pulled her backward until she was tight against him. Silently she cried out to God for protection. She darted a look at Clay to make sure he was still asleep. She realized if Willie Thorne knew about Clay, he'd kill him too, so she stopped struggling. She dare not wake Clay!

Willie continued to chuckle as he pushed her out the door and closed it. There was still enough light to see several feet away.

"Please, just let me go back inside. Please!" Her voice broke.

"Not on your life, girl!" Willie Thorne walked her out of the clearing and into the tall pines. The fragrance of pine was heavy in the air, but over that she could smell Willie's sweat. She felt the heat of his body as he forced her onward. "I heard tell Free thinks he's gonna take some timber I want. This'll give him something else to think on."

Jennet bit back a moan. What if Free didn't return tonight? She'd be torn apart by wolves, and Clay would be all alone, maybe starve to death. Pain of losing Clay ripped through her body, and she jerked away from Willie, catching him off guard. She fled from him, but her skirt caught on a blackberry bush, trapping her. She ripped it free and ran as hard as she could.

"You can't get away from me," called Willie, laughing as he chased her.

Jennet ducked behind a pine, dashed to another and ducked behind that, then stopped, her breath coming in gasps. If she stood very still, Willie wouldn't find her. She listened but heard only the usual night sounds. Where was Willie Thorne?

"Gotcha!" cried Willie.

Jennet started to turn, but he struck her on the back of the head. Pain exploded inside her, and she crumpled to the ground. Her mind felt like it was crammed full of cotton, but she could still see Willie's black boots and hear him chuckle.

"Nobody'll ever know you didn't just run out here and get lost," Willie said. "Course I'll tell Free so he'll know I'm somebody to be reckoned with."

Willie mumbled something she couldn't make out as he walked away, leaving her in a heap at the base of a giant white pine. The smell of dirt and old pine needles almost strangled her. With a groan she pushed herself to her knees. Her head spun. Trees loomed over her and around her. Gingerly she touched her head until she found a lump the size of an egg behind her right ear. Her thick hair had given her enough protection to keep the blow from breaking her skin.

Jennet pushed herself up until she stood against the

trunk of the giant pine. She turned her aching head to look around. She couldn't see the light of the cabin. Before long it would be too dark to see anything. She fought against an urge to scream for help. If Willie Thorne heard her, he might come back and hit her again, this time hard enough to kill her.

Jennet pushed away from the tree and waited until the forest stopped spinning, then took a step forward. Which way was the cabin? What if she stumbled deeper into the woods? She'd heard many stories of people walking off the path to get lost and never find their way back. She sniffed back hot tears.

"Heavenly Father, You're with me even in this wilderness," she whispered. "Send help. Send Free to get me!"

Jennet walked forward, stumbled on a fallen limb, and caught herself before she pitched headlong to the pine needle-covered ground.

Suddenly she heard a low, menacing growl, and perspiration popped out all over her body, soaking her. A large gray wolf stood a few yards away, its teeth bared.

"Help!" Jennet cried, suddenly no longer fearful that Willie Thorne would hear. "Help! Help me! Free!"

The wolf sank to its great haunches and edged toward her, growling ominously. Saliva dribbled from the wolf's mouth.

"Free! Help me, Free!"

Muscles tightened in the wolf as it readied to spring. Jennet inched along, trying to put a tree between her and the wolf. The wolf leaped, and she jumped aside, screamed, tripped, and sprawled to the ground. The wolf landed where she had been standing. It turned and sprang again. A shot rang out, and the bullet caught the wolf in midair. It fell with a crash close to her.

She looked up and saw Free lean his rifle against the tree and reach for her. With a glad cry she clung to him, her arms around his waist, her face pushed into his neck. He smelled of sweat and pine and musky skin, and she never wanted to leave the safety of his arms.

"Jen," he said hoarsely, holding her tight, his face buried in her hair.

"Free, you found me. Oh, Free!"

"I saw Tune, and he said you were here. Clay was in his bed, and I looked all over for you." Free rubbed his hands up and down her back. "I knew you wouldn't leave Clay by choice." A shudder passed through Free, and his voice broke.

"I was so scared! But you came for me." Jennet moved so that she could lift her head and look up at him. "Will you always be around to save me?"

"Always," he whispered. He lowered his head and kissed her, a gentle, searching kiss.

She relaxed against him. Her eyelids closed, and she curled her fingers into the thick hair on the back of his head. He molded her body to his and the kiss deepened, igniting a passion in her that she'd never felt before. He lifted his head, but she pulled it down to kiss him again. Their hearts beat together, blocking out the sounds of the forest around them.

Suddenly, reason returned to her, and she tore her mouth from his and cried, "Clay! We must get back to him!"

Free caught her hand and picked up his rifle. They ran through the pines to the cabin.

Jennet rushed to Clay's basket and knelt beside it. He was sleeping soundly, but she touched him to make sure he was all right. She sighed in relief. Slowly she stood and faced Free.

As quickly as she could, Jennet told him what had happened. He leaped to his feet and she caught his arm. "What're you going to do?"

"Go after Willie Thorne," Free said fiercely.

She cupped his face in her hand and felt the hard stubble of his beard. "Please don't go tonight."

"I must."

"He might kill you!"

"He won't. He'll try, but he won't kill me!" Free pulled her close, glorying in the feel of her. Finally he held her from him. "You're taking Clay, and you're going back with Tunis in the morning."

"I'm staying."

Jennet shook her head and pushed away from him several feet. She squared her shoulders and looked directly into his eyes. Dirt streaked the side of her face and dress. "Free, I am going to stay here with you. You can't make me leave."

"We'll see about that." Free picked up the rifle that he'd leaned against the wall. "I'm leaving this for you. Keep it beside the bed with you, and if anybody but me comes, shoot 'em."

"Free, please, don't go!"

"I have to." Free wanted to hold her tight and never let her go again.

A tear spilled down Jennet's cheek, then another, and Free groaned. Once again he set the rifle aside and pulled her close to him. Jennet felt the thud of his heart against her. She wrapped her arms around his neck and lifted her lips to his. Having her willingly kiss him brought tears to his eyes. He'd never expected it to happen. His lips were feather soft against hers, then he kissed her with a passion that had been building between them. She returned his kiss, eager to give to him what she'd never been able to before.

Finally Free pushed her away, his face set. "I have to take care of Willie Thorne. But I'll be back. That's a promise."

Jennet managed not to cry out in fear for him.

"Pull in the latchstring when I leave."

Jennet nodded slightly. She knew she couldn't stop him.

Free closed the door, and Jennet lowered the wooden latch and pulled in the leather latchstring so no one could open the door from the outside. She stood there a long time, then finally walked to the bed and sank to the edge, her head in her hands. Oh, but she wanted to follow Free! But she couldn't with Clay. She clasped her hands tightly together, bowed her head, and prayed for Free.

Several minutes later Free strode into the saloon where he knew he'd find Willie Thorne. The noise rose around him, seeming to be extra loud after the silence of the woods. Men lined the bar, talking and laughing. Saloon girls, their bright skirts flapping about their legs, walked to the tables carrying trays with drinks.

"Willie Thorne!" Free called loudly.

Willie tensed, then slowly turned until his back was pressed against the bar. "Havlick," he said with an easy grin that didn't reach the cold steel of his eyes. "What brings you in here? Thought this was your idea of sin."

Men and girls laughed, but Free ignored them as he took two more steps forward. He smelled cigarette smoke and beer as well as the sweat from the many hardworking men standing around the stained and scarred bar.

"Willie Thorne, you took my wife into the woods, struck her over the head, and left her for wolf bait!"

Men murmured as they turned to stare at Willie. In this neck of the woods women were treated with great care and respect.

Free waited until the hubbub died down. "That's a coward's way to fight this battle we're in."

Willie shot away from the bar, his face as red as his hair. "You calling me a coward?"

Free nodded, the anger so great in him that he wanted to rip Willie limb from limb.

Jas Lotown, the owner of the bar, came around the bar, a

shotgun in his hands. "You boys want to fight, step out-doors."

Free glared at Willie, then stalked out of the saloon. He stopped in the middle of the sawdust-covered street and waited with his booted feet spread, his fists doubled at his sides. He watched men swarm out of the saloon, pushing Willie along with them.

Tunis was just leaving the boarding house, and he caught sight of Free. He hurried to him. "What's going on, Free?"

Never taking his eyes off Willie, Free answered, "Get away, Tune. I got a score to settle with Willie Thorne."

Tunis hesitated, then stepped away. "I'll watch your back."

Free nodded briefly to let Tunis know he'd heard. He'd told Tune about Willie, the lawyer, and George Meeker. They were shady enough to try pulling a fast one even though woodsmen demanded a fair fight.

Willie flexed his great muscles and walked toward Free. "It's not too late to call it off, Havlick."

"It's way too late," snapped Free, squatting slightly with his hands out and his feet spread wide. He knew anything would go in this fight—punching, gouging, kicking. And Willie Thorne was good at fighting dirty.

Willie leaped at Free, but he jumped aside. Willie kicked out, caught Free in the leg, and sent him sprawling to the ground. The roar of the crowd seemed to explode inside Free's ears as he rolled and leaped up just as Willie kicked at his ribs. Free shot out a fist and caught Willie below his left eye, sending his head back with a snap. Free shot out his other fist and caught Willie in the stomach. He stumbled back but didn't fall. Willie lunged again, this time catching him in a bear hug that almost crushed Free's ribs. They fell to the ground, rolling and writhing. Willie grabbed Free's hair, then tried to gouge out his eyes with his thumbs. Free bucked and twisted and sent Willie flying off. Before Willie could move, Free landed on him and pinned him to the ground.

The desire to kill Willie burned inside Free, and he pressed his thumbs against Willie's windpipe. From deep inside Free heard, "Don't kill him."

But Willie deserved to die!

"Don't kill him."

Free struggled but finally obeyed the still, small voice. Although the rage had seeped out of him, he didn't get off Willie. He pushed his face close to Willie and saw the panic in Willie's eyes. "Admit to what you did tonight!"

"No!"

Free pressed harder.

"Okay! Okay!" gasped Willie.

Free lightened his hold. "Talk!" He glanced over his shoulder. "You men listen to this!"

Willie shuddered and closed his eyes. "I took your wife into the forest, knocked her out, and left her."

The men muttered angrily. Tunis stepped closer to Free.

"Now tell about the crooked deals you made for George Meeker."

"George Meeker!" murmured the men who now formed a tight circle around Free and Willie Thorne.

Willie moaned. "Don't make me."

"Tell now!"

Willie muttered the story, but the men were close enough that they heard. They exclaimed in anger, many of them shouting out that they'd been cheated and robbed.

At last Free released Willie and struggled to his feet. Tunis wrapped an arm around him and held him up while they watched the crowd of men take charge of Willie. Several of the men congratulated Free, and he nodded in acknowledgment, too tired to do more.

"I'll take you home," said Tunis.

Free pulled away. "No, I can manage."

"If you say so."

Free weakly brushed dust off himself and gingerly touched a bruise on his cheek. He looked at Tunis. "Tomorrow you are taking Jennet right back where she belongs."

Tunis smiled and spread his hands wide. "She belongs here with you."

"It's not safe."

"With Willie out of the way she'll be all right."

"Maybe. Maybe not. She's going back."

Tunis laughed. "You'll have your hands full convincing her of that. If you haven't noticed, she's one stubborn lady."

Free had just started to notice that. "She said she won't go back."

"She won't."

Free sighed heavily, suddenly too weary to argue. "Will I see you before you leave?"

"I made plans to leave at dawn."

"Then I'll say good-bye now." Free held out his hand and Tunis took it in a firm shake, then Free hugged Tunis and slapped him on the back. "You're a good friend."

"So are you. Clay would be proud of you."

Free smiled through sudden tears. "Tune, I finally understand why Grandpa wanted me to have a wife and family. There's nothing more important."

"That's right, Free. That's sure right!"

Free trudged down the street and into the darkness beyond to where his cabin nestled among the trees. After a while he saw the soft glow of the light in the windows, and his heart quickened. Jennet was waiting for him. He thought of her warm response and her willing kisses, and he walked faster. This time she wouldn't push him aside or freeze him out.

Inside the cabin Jennet settled Clay back in his basket,

softly continuing to pray for Free. He had to come back safely. She heard a sound outside the cabin and she held her breath, her eyes wide and her hand at her throat.

"Open the door, Jen. It's me."

His voice left her almost too weak to move, but she managed to run to the door and swing it open. Free stepped into the lamplight, and she gasped at the bruises. "Oh, Free! Are you all right?"

He caught her arms and pulled her to him. "I'm fine," he said huskily.

Jennet gently touched her lips to his. "Let me clean your wounds," she said against his mouth.

"First take care of my heart," he whispered.

CHAPTER

17

♦ Free stopped the buggy and with a wide, proud smile turned to Jennet beside him. Clay lay sleeping in his basket at her feet. "Here we are!"

Jennet's eyes locked with Free's and she couldn't look away, nor did she want to. The past six weeks had been the happiest time of her life.

Free laughed low in his throat. "Your eyes are shining."

Jennet wanted to fling her arms around him, but she knew it was unseemly to do such a private thing out in public. "You make them shine," she whispered.

Just being with her gave him such pleasure! He'd liked sharing his cabin with her and Clay, and he'd spent most of his time with them. But soon he'd be too busy for them. He leaned toward her slightly. "We're here to look at the camp. Remember?"

Jen laughed, rubbed her hands over her print skirt, pushed back a strand of hair that had come loose from the braid coiled at the nape of her neck, and looked around at the buzz of activity. "So this is a lumbercamp?"

This was where Free would live in just a week. He planned to leave her at the cabin outside Big Pine. Somehow she had to find a way to stay here with him. She'd heard that some of the lumbermen, foremen, and cooks had their wives live at camp with them.

Free had already showed her the banking grounds where soon millions of feet of pine logs would be piled parallel with the river to wait for the spring thaw. Giant skidways were made by clearing off the brush and timber along a riverbank. After the thaw a key log would be dislodged, and the logs would roll down the skidways into the river to float down to the sawmill.

"There's the bunkhouse, home to all the shanty boys," said Free.

Jennet studied the log building. It was low and squat. The walls were chinked with clay and grass, and the roof was covered with tarpaper.

"I spent two winters in one." Free chuckled. "The bunks are spaced just far enough apart to slip in, and they're made of boards covered with spruce boughs. Rather tough on the back, but we were always so tired we didn't care what we slept on. We used our turkeys as pillows."

She laughed. "Turkeys?"

Free grinned. "We each had a grainsack filled with our personal stuff."

"I like my feather pillows."

Free's dark eyes twinkled. "Me too."

"Now that you're the big lumberman you don't sleep in the bunkhouse on spruce boughs with a turkey as your pillow?"

"Nope. See that?" Free pointed to three small wooden shacks standing in a row. "The first one is for me, the second for the foremen, and the third for the cook and his family." He waved his hand. "Over there is the office, there the barn that stables about eighteen teams of horses, and beside it the blacksmith shop, which carries everything from toggle chains to bridle bits. Over there the company store and the cookcamp. Sometime this week the tote teamster will haul in hay, grain, beans, molasses, tea, tobacco, salt pork, salted beef, lard, prunes, potatoes, flour, dried apples, blankets, candles, kerosene, kitchen stoves, and plenty of pots and pans." He thought of the cookies as big as stove lids that he'd eaten, and he told her about them. "I could go for a big mug of coffee and half a dozen cookies about now."

Jennet glanced up at the warm August sun. "It's almost dinnertime. Let's go home, and I'll cook dinner for you." Her stomach growled, and she realized she was hungry too. She knew Clay would awaken soon to be nursed.

Free turned away from Jennet. He hadn't told her yet that he had booked passage on a boat to Grand Rapids for her and Clay and that they'd leave early that afternoon. "We'll leave in a minute." He wanted their short time together to be pleasant. "I was able to hire on one of the best fiddlers in Michigan. One of the best cooks too."

"And will you sing for all of them?" Jennet asked, her eyes twinkling as she smiled. During the past six weeks, she'd learned that Free loved to sing and that he had a very good voice. He'd sung Clay to sleep almost every night.

With a grin Free nodded. "I've brought many a good man to tears with my songs."

Jennet giggled. "I thought they liked your singing!"

Free was always surprised when she teased him, and he laughed in delight.

"I've just had the most wonderful idea, Free!" Jennet said as three kids under eleven years of age ran past. "While I'm here with you I can have school for the kids just like I did for Meg and Will."

"I guess I best tell you."

Jennet had a sinking feeling. "Tell me what?"

"You're going back to Grand Rapids today. Going home."

Jennet's face fell, and it tore at his heart. "But my home is with you!"

"You can't live like this!"

"But I can! I survived living at Uncle Tait's, didn't I? And you'd be here with me. And Clay."

Tears welled up in her eyes. "Why don't you want me?"

"Want you? I can't survive without you!"

"I want to stay. Clay needs you. I need you."

Her words wrapped around his heart, and he suddenly knew he couldn't survive eight long months without her and Clay. "You know a woodsman's day starts about four in the morning and ends at dark."

"Like a farmer's day?" Jennet asked with a grin.

Free nodded and chuckled. "Can Clay take the snow and ice and cold weather?"

"Other babies have before him."

"You don't give up, do you?"

"I hope not."

Free wanted to pull her close, but he squeezed her hand instead. "I want to show you the prime lumber we'll do after this section is finished." He flicked the reins, and Acorn stepped forward and onto the deep trail that led away from camp.

Clay squirmed and whimpered a little but settled back to sleep with the sway of the buggy.

About half an hour later Free stopped the buggy and waved his arm in a wide arc. "All of that, Jen! This'll make me one of the wealthiest lumbermen in Michigan. We'll build a house bigger than the one Witherspoon has. And his house has fifteen bedrooms!"

Jennet clasped her hands, and her eyes sparkled as she looked. White pines reached a hundred and fifty feet in the air and were at least five feet across. "Free, the trees are massive! Oh, the beauty!" She turned to Free with a slight frown. "Don't you hate to cut them all down and leave only ugly stumps behind?" On their drive out to camp from Big Pine they'd passed section after section of stumps where once white pines had stood in all their grand glory.

Free said, "Jen, the country needs lumber. People are going West where there aren't trees for lumber. They need the lumber that I'll send West. Trees will grow again." Free knew it took about eighty years for a white pine to grow big enough to cut, but he couldn't be concerned with that now. "This will make us rich, Jen! Clay can have anything he wants."

Jennet locked her hands in her lap. "Free, Clay needs you and me more than he needs 'things.'"

"I know that."

"If I could choose between saving those trees and cutting them down, I'd choose to save them, no matter what the dollar loss."

"Jen, you're talking crazy."

Jennet shrugged but didn't argue further. She would save the timber that she could save, and Free could lumber out what he wanted. "When can we see the land that your grandpa left to me?"

Free frowned. Didn't she know? He was sure he'd told her. He cleared his throat and tightened the hold on the reins. "This is it," he said in a voice that he forced to sound normal.

Jennet gasped as she looked around at the massive, tall, straight white pines. These were the very trees that Grandpa Clay had left to her! These were the trees that she'd planned to preserve for future generations. Michigan would not become a state without forests! She turned to him, her blue eyes troubled. She must've misunderstood him. "But, Free, you can't cut these trees down."

Free's jaw tightened. "I can."

"But they belong to me!"

Free struggled against his anger and frustration. He'd make her understand the importance of lumbering these giant trees. He could build a house for her with twenty bedrooms! Then she wouldn't complain because he'd gone against her wishes. "Jennet, I *can* cut them and I *will* cut them."

Jennet didn't want to anger him or fight with him, but she couldn't let him cut down these trees. The forest was the heritage of future generations. Once all of Michigan was covered with trees, but no longer, not since the lumbermen had discovered the wealth. She moistened her lips with the tip of her tongue. "Free, please understand. I want Clay to be able to show these white pines to his children and know that Grandpa Clay walked among them, canoed down the stream that runs through them. These trees have stood here for hundreds of years! I want our children to take refuge in the trees like we both have."

Free's dark eyes narrowed as he looked at Jennet. "It's already in my schedule to cut them."

Jennet's face hardened. "Then change your schedule."

A muscle jumped in his cheek. "These trees are some of the finest around, Jennet!"

"All the more reason to keep them!" Jennet looked up, up, up to the tops of the straight-as-an-arrow white pines. The terrible thought of felling the giants and turning the section into stumps upset her more than she could say. She reached for Free's hand but felt him stiffen at her touch. She jerked back and locked her suddenly icy fingers in her lap. She stared straight ahead, her heart heavy. "I talked to Lem Azack about these trees."

"Nothing will change my mind," said Free hoarsely.

"He said under the law not even you can log them out unless I give you written permission." Jennet kept her eyes glued to her clenched hands. "I will not give you written permission."

Free thought he'd explode on the spot. "You're just like Pa!"

"How can you say that?" Jennet cried.

"You're trying to keep me from succeeding in the lumber business!"

"But you've already succeeded!"

"Am I as big as Witherspoon? Driscoll? No!"

"But why do you need to be that big?"

"I want to be," Free said grimly.

"To prove to your pa that you can be?"

Fire shot from Free's eyes, and she knew she'd hit a tender spot.

"Free, you don't have to prove anything to Roman. You know and I know that you're successful."

Without another word Free turned Acorn and drove away. He'd thought he loved her. Yes, loved her! No, he didn't! Right now he hated her with a passion that alarmed him.

Jennet felt his great anger, and she remembered her conversation with Marie at Christmas about Free turning as mean as Roman had been. Maybe it would be better for her to return to Grand Rapids. Hot tears burned her eyes, but she wouldn't let them fall.

Just as they were driving past the camp, Jig stepped out and shouted, "Free! I have a word with you." His Swedish accent made his words almost impossible for Jennet to understand.

Reluctantly Free pulled Acorn up. He did not want to face Jig today. Jig, like Tunis, could see into his heart, and right now he couldn't afford to let anyone see his heart.

Jesus saw his heart. The thought came instinctively now, but Free brushed it aside as he wrapped the reins around the brake handle.

Jennet looked at the tall rugged man carrying a muzzle-loader and smiled. She knew Jig from Free's description of him.

"You are Jennet, Free's little wife!" cried Jig, reaching up a dirty work-roughened hand to her.

"And you're Jig," Jennet said as she placed her hand in his.

Jig nodded as he helped her to the ground. "You are a beauty, Jennet. Is she not a beauty, Free?"

Scowling, Free walked around to join them. "I didn't expect to see you until later in the fall."

"I heard your Jennet was with you, and I had to set my eyes on her."

Jennet laughed. "Would you like to see Clay?"

"That I would like." Jig pulled off his cap and held it close to his heart as Jennet lifted Clay from his basket. "Clay Havlick's great-grandson is blessed of God through Jesus Christ our Lord. May he walk all his days upright toward God."

"Amen," whispered Jennet.

Free nodded, his lips pressed tightly together. He wasn't ready to give up his anger. He had to admit the sight of Jen holding Clay for Jig to admire softened his heart some.

"Watching this little one grow up will make my heart warm," said Jig.

"They are going back to Grand Rapids," Free said sharply.

Jennet shot him a startled look. She'd thought he'd decided they could stay. The icy look in his dark eyes and his aloof manner toward her locked her argument inside. She knew she'd burst into tears if she tried to speak. And she would not cry in front of Jig or Free!

Just then Clay started crying the cry that meant he was hungry and couldn't wait a minute to be fed. She excused herself and climbed in the back seat of the buggy with Clay.

Free led Jig away so that Jennet couldn't overhear them. She saw Free glance at her, and she knew he was talking to Jig about her. But what was he saying?

Free cleared his throat as he looked away from Jennet. "Jig, you said you'd do anything I asked. This is important. I want you to take Jen and the baby back to Grand Rapids tomorrow morning. I was going to send them by boat, but if you'll drive them in the buggy, it'll mean Jen will have the buggy at home. If you leave at dawn, you'll be there before dark."

"You said she does not want to leave here."

"I say she is." Free clenched his fists at his sides. "Either you take her, or they go by boat today."

Jig sighed. "Her I will take. Yes." But he didn't look very happy about it.

"Thanks Jig. You can come back by canoe or boat."

"No worry about that, Free. Jig will get back."

They talked until Free saw Jennet lay Clay back in his basket, then walked back to join her. She looked expectantly at Free.

Enough anger had drained away that Free felt bad for what he was going to do. He couldn't meet Jennet's eyes. "Jig will drive you and Clay back to Grand Rapids at dawn. You'll have the buggy and Acorn with you. Jig will come back by boat."

Tears filled Jennet's eyes, but she refused to let them fall. Without a word she climbed into the front seat of the buggy and sat staring straight ahead.

CHAPTER

18

♦ Jennet scowled at the ugly stumps as Jig drove south of Big Pine on his way to Grand Rapids. She glanced at Jig. "You know I'm right, Jig." For the past hour, since they'd left Big Pine at dawn, she'd tried to convince Jig to turn around and take her to the lumbercamp and Free.

Jig drove around a deep rut and almost struck a rock protruding from the ground. "My girl, Jennet, Free told me what to do with you."

"You know I belong with him! Grandpa Clay, your good friend, made his will to force Free into getting married and having a family. Grandpa Clay would want me with Free. And you know he would, Jig!"

Jig chuckled, reined Acorn around, and drove off the road to turn around among the stumps, then drove back on the road toward Big Pine. "Say no more. Clay Havlick said families are more important than anything. Time after time he said they belong together."

Jennet laughed as she patted Jig's hand. "Thank you."

"Free will be as mad as a bear with a sore tail."

"He'll get over it." But would he? The way things were

right now he wouldn't. Until he forgave Roman and let his anger go, he could not be free to live his life the way God wanted him to. Until then, his relationship with God was blocked, and it left room for Satan to cause trouble.

Silently Jennet prayed for Free. An idea flashed into her mind and she turned to Jig. "Will you do something to help Free?"

"That I will. Clay Havlick I promised. What is this you will ask of me?"

"Jig, Free needs to see his pa. They must have time together to talk." Jennet had remembered her talk with Pa, and she wanted that same thing to happen with Free. She knew he loved Roman but couldn't forgive him or couldn't set aside his anger.

Jig nodded as he slowed Acorn even more to keep the buggy from hitting the ruts too hard. He knocked a mosquito away from his matted hair, which hung down to his broad shoulders. Birds flew up from the branches of scrub pine trees and bushes. The sun glowed brightly just at the eastern horizon as Jig drove north to Big Pine.

"I want you to get a message to Roman to come see Free. You'd have to take it yourself because this is harvest time. A letter wouldn't be enough to make Roman come. If Free could see how much Roman has changed, and that he does want to mend the breach between them, maybe he'll be able to let go of his anger."

Jig shrugged. "I have not been out of the wilderness for a very long time. But for Clay Havlick, and for you, Jennet Havlick, I will go."

Baby Clay sneezed and cried. Jennet turned him in his basket, covered him, and patted his tiny back until he slept again. She looked at Jig. "Drive to the river in Big Pine and you can go yet today."

"And what of you?"

"I'll drive myself and Clay to the lumbercamp."

Jig scratched behind his ear. "Do you know the way?"

"It's a clear road, Jig, between Big Pine and there. I can't get lost."

Jig scratched his head, his arm, and his head again. "Jennet, my brain is working and spinning at your plan. Why would Roman Havlick listen to one like me? Here in these woods I am a part of all. People and animals knows me. But away from the trees . . ." His words trailed off.

With the tip of her finger Jennet tapped her lips and narrowed her eyes in thought as the buggy rolled closer to Big Pine. "You're right, of course, Jig. But he might listen to me."

"Yes. To you he would listen. Probably."

Jennet laughed breathlessly at a new and daring plan. "Jig, I'll go with you! We can go by boat from Big Pine to the farm! It's a lot quicker than by buggy. And we'll come back by boat with Roman, pick up the buggy, and drive to the camp. We'll be back in two days. Three at the most." Her face clouded. "If I can talk Roman into it." Free's pa had changed, but if he still had his bad temper, he just might beat her before anyone could stop him. She tightened her jaw. She would face Roman—no matter how afraid she was!

"This plan of yours will work. I think," said Jig, nodding.

The sun rose higher as they rode in silence the rest of the way to the dock in Big Pine. Jig booked rides for them on a small steamboat that was leaving immediately and left Acorn and the buggy at the nearby livery. Jennet took a change of clothes for herself and the baby from her trunk in back of the buggy, pushed them into a satchel, and handed it to Jig to carry for her. They walked to the crowded dock where the white steamboat was waiting.

Gulls swooped and cried above the calm gray water near the dock. With shouts of anger and loud teasing remarks dock workers loaded and unloaded three small steamboats and several canoes.

Clutching Clay tightly to her, Jennet picked her way along

the dock around coils of rope, barrels, and a tub of smelly fish. Her bonnet felt awkward on her head, and she wanted to push it off, but she knew she'd need its protection from the sun. Jig helped Jennet board the boat, and her stomach rolled as the boat moved in the water. Once she got her sea legs she knew her stomach would settle down. The captain called out to them and pulled the rope that made the whistle blow. Jennet settled into a seat in the stern of the boat and laid the sleeping Clay across her lap on his stomach. Jig joined the captain in the pilot house, and the boat chugged away from the dock.

Jennet smoothed the soft flannel cover over Clay's back. "I will do anything to save your papa, Clay. And if he keeps this anger and resentment inside him, he'll never be happy."

Much later Clay awoke and Jennet fed him, then made a pallet from blankets for him beside her feet on the deck.

Jennet watched two men outside the pilot house playing cards on an upturned wooden crate. They argued good-naturedly. Jig stayed with the captain, and at times Jennet could hear the sound of his voice. A yellow cat, its tail high, walked along the deck of the boat as if it owned the world. Jennet called to it, but it ignored her as well as the men playing cards.

The warm sun, the chug of the engine, and the gentle sway of the boat lulled Jennet to sleep. Last night she'd slept fitfully, always aware that Free lay cold and distant beside her.

A loud voice jarred her awake. The two men who had been playing cards were arguing and would've come to blows if the captain hadn't stepped in to stop them.

She noticed the sun was gone and dark clouds covered the once-bright blue sky. Wind whipped the river into small waves, rocking the boat slightly. Fear trickled over Jennet. She knew the waves couldn't sink the boat, but there was a real danger of the boat's running aground on a sandbar, hitting submerged logs, or catching fire. Just last month she'd heard the *J. W. Montrose* had caught fire and burned to the water line. No one had died, but several people had suffered injuries.

Jennet shook her head hard. No! They would not run aground or hit logs or burn! God was with them, watching over them! He had angels surrounding them to keep them safe. She let the Bible verse, "For God has not given us a spirit of fear, but of power and of love and of a sound mind," play over and over in her mind until she truly felt the words. *I will not be afraid!* she thought.

Jig sat beside her, his face pale under the dirt and whiskers. "My insides seem to be rolling like the water."

Jennet reached for his hand and clasped it tightly. "Tell me more about Clay Havlick." She knew that would take Jig's mind off his seasickness.

As Jig talked, Jennet had to listen closely to hear and understand because of his accent and the noise of the engine.

"When I first joined up with Clay Havlick, I spoke no English. He taught me while we canoed to the Indian villages to trade for the beaver pelts. The first word he taught me was *beaver*." Jig laughed. "Beaver was important to Clay Havlick. He was an honest man with hair and eyes as dark as his grandson, Free. Clay could talk to the Indians in their own language. He taught me a few words of Ojibwa and Pottawatomie. But English I learned the most."

By midafternoon the wind died down, and the river was calm again. Jig joined the captain to leave Jennet free to nurse the baby. When they reached Grand Rapids, Jig hired a canoe to take them down the Thornapple River to the landing near the farm where Tait had first taken Jennet. Jig rented a one-seater buggy with a black canvas top and drove them to the Havlick farm just as the sun set. Across the road from the main house a pig squealed and ran after other pigs. Horses and cattle were grazing in the pasture behind the barn. Flowers bloomed brightly along the front of the huge white farmhouse.

"What a grand place," said Jig as he stopped on the road and pulled off his cap to scratch his matted hair. "But no trees, Jennet. No trees!" He pointed at the cornfields stretching on and on. "What became of all the trees?"

Jennet shrugged. "Roman cut them to make room to plant. There's still a woodlot beyond the barns."

"A shame, a crying shame! But I will sleep in the woodlot and be happy." Jig slapped the reins on the bay mare's back and drove into the drive.

"There's plenty of room in Roman's house or Pa's. Even the barn," said Jennet.

"Can't sleep in the confines of walls."

She wanted to ask him why not, but she didn't. She looked longingly down the lane that led to her family's house, but she knew she must face Roman before seeing them. "Stop here, Jig."

Jig stopped in front of the big house. "Want me at your side when you speak to Clay Havlick's son?"

Jennet hesitated. She needed all the support she could get, but she shook her head. "Thanks anyway, Jig." Just then she spotted Tim at the barn. "Take the horse to the barn." She pointed. "Tim's inside. He'll show you where to park the buggy and where to water the horse."

Jig nodded and drove away as Jennet pushed open the gate and followed the walk to the huge house. Should she go to the front door or the back? Finally she decided on the back because she knew Kit or maybe even Marie would be in the kitchen making supper.

Baby Clay whimpered and wriggled, then settled back in her arms. Butterflies fluttered wildly in her stomach. She looked back toward Pa's house and longed to run to Ma's comforting arms.

Jennet hesitated, then knocked on the big white door.

Her legs felt almost too weak to hold her. To her surprise, Free's mother opened the door.

Lillian's face turned white, and she stared at Jennet with her mouth open. She plucked at the white apron covering her gray dress. Suddenly she burst into tears and tugged Jennet inside. "What's wrong? Why are you here? Is Freeman dead?"

"He's fine, Lillian. I promise, he's well. I came to speak with Roman."

Lillian's dark eyes widened fearfully. "Oh, my!"

Jennet realized she'd made a terrible mistake. She wasn't brave enough to speak to Roman. One harsh word from him and she'd turn tail and run.

"He'll be in for supper soon," said Lillian weakly.

Clay whimpered, and Jennet slipped the cover off him.

Lillian gasped in delight, looked around as if she were afraid her husband would walk in and see her, then held her hands out. "Could I hold the baby?"

Jennet laid Clay in her arms, and Lillian looked down at him with love like Jennet had never seen on her face.

"We'll go in the front room and sit," said Lillian, leading the way.

In the front room Jennet glanced around at the massive dark green leather sofas, walnut end tables, and a large walnut table covered with potted ivy, red geraniums, and pink begonias. Everything looked new, as if no one ever used the room. Jennet draped Clay's multicolored quilt over the arm of a dark green leather chair. Maybe she should leave now, go to her Grand Rapids home, and forget what she'd planned. The idea appealed to her more and more as she waited for Roman.

Lillian cooed softly to Clay but didn't speak to Jennet. Smells of frying chicken drifted in from the kitchen.

Jennet moved restlessly. Would she want to spend her life in fear of her husband as Lillian had? Jennet shook her head. But if Free couldn't forgive Roman, he might turn into a mean-tempered, money-hungry man she couldn't love or respect.

Jennet frowned slightly. Did she love Free as a wife was to love a husband? She had enjoyed being with him, but she hadn't thought about the change in her feelings toward him. She hadn't understood why she couldn't abide living eight months without him.

Indeed, she was in love with Free! Why hadn't she realized sooner that she was in love with Free like Ma was in love with Pa? She obeyed God and forgave Free, told him things she'd done even when she'd not wanted to, then went to Big Pine to live, but loving him hadn't occurred to her.

Did Free love her the way Pa loved Ma?

Jennet's heart gave a funny little jerk. He always took such good care of her, and he seemed to like to have her around. She frowned. Except now. And not just because he thought camp life was too rough for her but because she wouldn't allow him to lumber out the white pines that belonged to her.

Maybe she should give in to him, let him chop down the giants. Jennet shook her head. Loving him didn't mean giving him his own way, especially over such an important issue.

Just then Jennet caught Lillian's eye.

"You were deep in thought, Jen," said Lillian nervously. "I said I heard Roman come in."

Jennet trembled but jumped to her feet, leaving her dark blue bonnet beside Clay's quilt. Silently she called out to God for special strength to face Roman.

Lillian looked ready to run away as she stood with Clay in her arms. "I'll take Clay to the kitchen to show him to Marie while you talk with Roman."

"It's all right if you stay."

Lillian shook her head. "I couldn't! No. No, I couldn't do that!"

"Then take Clay to the kitchen."

Jennet heard footsteps coming toward the front room, but instead of feeling nervous a great calm settled over her.

Roman filled the doorway as he stopped to pierce Jennet with his dark eyes. He smelled of animals and outdoors. His graying hair was pressed down where his hat had been. A few pieces of straw stuck to his brown pants. "Why'd you come?" he barked.

"I'll tell you after you see Clay," said Jennet, proud of her calm voice.

Lillian held Clay out, and Roman looked at him, his face softening a fraction. Then he looked back at Jennet with a scowl. Lillian scurried from the room, the baby clutched to her.

Jennet walked closer to Roman, then stopped.

"You come to see Wexal?" he asked bluntly.

"No. You."

His brow shot up in surprise. "Me?"

"About Free."

Roman stiffened. "Is he hurt?"

"No." Jennet nervously fingered the top button of her dress. "He needs to talk to you. Get things settled between you. So he can get on with his life."

"Is he such a coward that he sent you to do his talking?"

"No!" Jennet's eyes flashed. "He doesn't know I came."

Roman looped one hand around his wide suspender. "I have nothing to say to you. What's between my son and me is no concern of yours."

"But it is!" Jennet doubled her fists at her sides, and her breast rose and fell. "You did Free wrong, and you know you did. But he must forgive you for it. He's all knotted up inside because of anger toward you." She brushed a strand of chestnut-brown hair off her cheek. "You could talk to him, tell him you care about him."

"He knows I do!"

"No, he doesn't. He believes you think he's worthless, a failure because he's not farming with you. He thinks you hate him because you kept his grandpa's inheritance from him."

Roman sank to a chair, his head bowed.

"Talk to him! Tell him how you feel!"

"How can I? He won't come to see me."

Jennet hesitated, then knelt at Roman's knee and looked into his face. She saw the fine lines that fanned from the corners of his dark eyes to his graying temples. Suddenly she caught a glimpse of how Free would look in twenty years. Jennet smelled Roman's sweat and dust from the fields. "Then you go see him," she whispered.

Roman frowned. "How can I?"

"Let Pa take care of things here, and you go back with Jig and me."

Roman shook his head. "I can't."

"You can! You know you want to see Free."

"But I got work here! I've never left during harvest."

"You can't wait until after harvest because of winter coming on." Jennet stood up and sat in the chair across from him. "Free needs you." She told him how obsessed Free was about succeeding as a lumberman because he wanted to prove to Roman that he could. She reminded him that Free loved God, but the sin of unforgiveness blocked his relationship with God. "I've been praying for him, and I think you have been too. I know God works miracles. I think you can help this miracle happen."

Roman sat in silence a long time. Finally he lifted his haggard face. "When do we go?"

Jennet's heart leaped, but she didn't let it show. "At dawn."

"How?"

"A buggy to the Thornapple, a canoe to Grand Rapids, and a small steamboat to Big Pine. From there we'll take my buggy to camp. It'll take the whole day if all goes well. You'd only be gone three or four days. I'm sure you'd want to stay a bit with Free to see his work." Jennet held her breath for his answer.

"I'll go. Me and Wex."

Jennet said, "Very well. I'll take Clay to see my family and be here at dawn."

Roman nodded but didn't get up.

Jennet hurried down the wide hall toward the kitchen to get the baby. Outside the kitchen door Wex stopped her with a glad cry. He caught her hands and squeezed them tightly.

"This is a great surprise," Wex said, grinning. His hair was damp from just washing up, and he was wearing clean clothes. "You see Marie yet?"

"Just on my way."

"We're getting married after harvest."

"That's wonderful!"

"Can you come? You and Free?"

"I'll talk to him and see." Jennet looked back toward the front room. "Your pa has something to tell you." Jennet touched Wex's arm. "How are things between you and Roman?"

Wex pushed back a strand of dark hair that fell over his forehead, a gesture she'd seen Free do many times. "There're still times we fight, but he doesn't even try to beat me and sometimes he even listens to my ideas." He lowered his voice. "I think he even cares about me. He never says so, though."

"What does he say about you leaving here for your own farm?"

Wex shrugged. "He didn't like the idea, but he's getting used to it. Your pa's here to take care of a lot of the work.

264

And it helps to have Tim around. He and Pa get on well together."

"How're things between Anne and your pa?"

"Right as rain! Pa even let Ma stay with her when she had her baby girl a couple of weeks ago."

Jennet leaned forward with a giggle. "If he's not careful, he's going to have folks complain because he's so perfect."

Wex laughed. "It's good to see you again, Jen. You have a glow in your eyes I never saw before."

Jennet flushed. "Do I?"

"Did Free put it there?"

"Yes," she said softly.

"You always did have a soft spot for him."

"I guess I did, come to think of it." Jennet laughed and wrinkled her nose. "I better go see about Clay and let you go talk to your pa."

Wex grinned at her and walked away.

Jennet smiled. So, she'd always had a soft spot for Free, and Wex had noticed! Had Free noticed? Maybe he'd rescued her so many times because of it. Or maybe he'd had a soft spot for her and had rescued her because of that!

Maybe God had planned for them to be husband and wife. Tunis had said that Grandpa Clay had prayed often for the wives of his grandsons and the husband of his granddaughter. When Clay had gone to be with the Lord, Tunis and Nina had taken over for Clay and had prayed for them, in fact, still continued to pray. Who would've thought that the little girl Free had saved from the honeybees would someday be his wife?

With a low laugh Jennet entered the kitchen.

CHAPTER

19

♦ Free walked inside his empty shack and sank to a chair with his head in his hands. The ring of the hammers as the men finished the last of the bookkeeper's shack along with the shouts of the men drifted in the open door. The smell of wood smoke from the cookcamp and the blacksmith's shop hung in the air.

A great loneliness filled Free. Jennet had been gone only two days, but it had felt like forever. Could he survive without Jennet now that he was used to having her around? He never should've taken her out to see Grandpa's trees! He should've lumbered them out, then told her what he'd done. But could she forgive him if he'd done that?

What difference did it make? She'd never forgive him for lumbering them now, permission or no.

What a mess he'd made of things. The past weeks they'd been happier than he'd thought possible.

Free closed his eyes and heard Jennet's laughter and smelled the soap she used and saw the twinkle of her blue eyes and felt the softness of her beautiful hair.

Why hadn't he let her stay? She'd wanted to, even though it'd be a hard life. Why had she wanted to? Was it possible that she'd grown to love him the way Nina loved Tune?

The thought knocked Free back, and he sprang to his feet to pace the tiny area. She had joined him because it was the proper action for a wife to take. When first they'd married, she'd been a *proper* wife. But the past weeks she'd acted as if she enjoyed being with him. She'd been warm and passionate and had told him her thoughts and feelings.

Did she love him with the deep, passionate commitment he'd always wanted?

Free stopped stock-still. Maybe he should go to her to learn the truth and leave Glory Be in charge. He was a good foreman and knew the business well.

Free stopped in the open door and rammed his fingers through his thick dark hair. What about Grandpa's pines? "They have nothing to do with love," he muttered. The giant pines were business, nothing more.

But Jennet called them their heritage. She wanted them left for all times. They were not *business* or *money* to her.

Free groaned from deep within. He wanted to lumber the trees, but he also wanted Jennet. Was it possible to have both?

Impatiently Free strode to the barns, saddled a horse, and rode through the tree-covered hills to Grandpa's white pines. "Jen's white pines," he muttered as he leaned low to miss a branch.

He tied his horse to a branch, then followed the stream several feet into the woods. Ground squirrels scurried under the layer of needles. Hundreds of birds rose with loud cries and flew away. A brown bear dropped to his haunches, and lumbered out of sight.

Free picked up a pine cone and tossed it as far as he could. It landed without a sound.

As a young man, Grandpa had walked here and had canoed down the stream to trade with the Indians. He'd been angry about the law that forbade the Indians to speak their own language and practice their native religion. They had taken Clay Havlick to their hearts because he had respected them for who they were.

Free stopped and watched a beaver swimming near its dam.

"From the beaver I made my money, Freeman," Grandpa Clay had said the first time he'd taken Free to the woods with him. Free was nine then.

"I thought there'd always be beaver, Freeman. They were everywhere. The beaver hat was the craze in Europe and so the craze spread here, and all the men wanted the tall beaver hat to show their importance." Clay spread his hands wide and shrugged. "Why not take advantage of it? I traded for all the beaver pelts I could get from the Indians and the French trappers. Soon the beaver were gone. Sure, some are around, but not like they used to be." Clay rubbed a hand over his stubbled face. "I was wrong, Freeman. The beaver didn't last forever like I thought. You can't keep killing off animals and expect them to survive."

"I want to be a fur trader just like you, Grandpa." Free had gripped Clay's hand as he looked up into his lined face. "How can I be if all the animals are gone?"

"You can't make it a big business, Freeman, but you can make a fair living at it. Me and John Jacob Astor and a few others made our fortunes off fur, but that's history. There were plenty of beaver, bear, mink, marten, fox, otter, deer, elk, raccoon, wolves, lynx. And there's more to be had, but not for a fortune like I made. No, not no more." Clay patted the trunk of a giant pine. "Here's the big money of your future, Freeman. Lumbering. It's already started, but in a few years it'll be bigger than beaver hats. But the trees won't last forever. Just like the beaver. Lumber out the forests, and the farmer will come in and plow the land. Your children might never see the forests of Michigan."

Free laughed. "Grandpa, I won't have no children. I won't never get married."

"Don't let your pa hear that poor grammar or you won't never grow up big enough to get married." Clay laughed and clamped Free's shoulder with his big hand.

"Grandpa, why don't Pa love you like I do?"

Clay brushed a hand over his eyes. "I was off trading when your pa was growing up. When I was with him, I took no mind of him."

"You take mind of me and Anne and even Wex."

"I do that. But I learned the hard way, Freeman. I love your pa, but he won't never believe it."

"I love you enough for me and Pa both, Grandpa."

"I love you, Freeman. Don't you never forget that! I love you more'n fur trading, more'n walking them woods, more'n sleeping between pine boughs under the stars at night."

Free's heart almost burst. Nobody else loved him that much. Ma loved him some, but not enough to take his side against Pa when he got mad and whipped the daylights out of him.

"You make me proud, Freeman. Just being you," Grandpa Clay had said with a firm nod.

Suddenly the beaver slapped its tail against the water and dived out of sight. The sound brought Free back to the present. He brushed moisture from his eyes and cleared his throat. Grandpa had loved him and had taught him many things.

Slowly Free walked on. He heard wild pigeons in the tops of the trees and looked up to watch them.

"Free, wake up," Grandpa Clay had whispered one morning when Free was ten. "The wild pigeons are back."

Free had rolled out of bed, still sleepy, but excited to go with Grandpa to see the pigeons. The spring morning was frosty but not cold like wintertime.

Together they walked away from the clearing to the trees. Thousands of wild pigeons filled the air and the tops of the trees.

"When I first walked these woods, pigeon droppings was about a foot deep," said Clay. "I aimed up in the air and shot and always got a few birds with each shot."

"Really, Grandpa?" Free knew there were times when Grandpa exaggerated a story to make it better or teased him to see how he would respond.

"Sure is. It don't take much to kill them birds. I'd feed 'em to the pigs." Clay laughed. "You should've seen them pigs fight over them pigeons." Clay leaned down to Free. "Tonight we'll come out and knock 'em out of the trees and give 'em to the pigs for breakfast."

That night just as Grandpa had promised they knocked the wild pigeons out of the trees and they fed them to the pigs. Then Grandpa Clay had gotten real quiet. "Freeman, there'll come a time when even them pigeons will be gone. In the future men'll look back and make fun of a person who says once the sky was full of wild pigeons."

Grandpa's prediction had come true. Free nodded. The wild pigeons were dying out because of the farmers and the lumbering.

Free sank down on the thick cushion of dried pine needles and leaned against the rough black bark. Had Jennet seen the wild pigeons when she was young? Maybe she'd knocked them out of trees too. He smiled at the thought, then a great loneliness swept over him.

Was Jennet at home now, visiting with Tune and Nina or catching up on all the news from Meg and Will? Maybe when she was settled at home she'd not even miss him. He groaned at the terrible thought.

If he wasn't too busy, maybe he could leave Glory Be in charge at least once a month and make a trip home to see her.

Free rubbed his face with an unsteady hand. His whiskers felt rough. If he kept thinking of Jen, he just might go home now and leave Glory Be in charge. No, he couldn't do that. He had to be here to see that everything got under way.

Free thought of his first visit to Fordham's lumbercamp just to see the setup. He and Grandpa had eaten in the cookcamp with the shanty boys. To Free's surprise, no one spoke during the meal. No talking was allowed, Grandpa had said. Free had yearned to own a wide red sash like each wore and be big and strong and swing an ax to hit the same mark each time.

Free smiled. He did get the wide red sash, and he'd worn it two winters. Now it was tucked away in a drawer in his cabin. Someday he'd show it to Baby Clay and tell him about his life as a woodsman. He'd already shown it to Jennet. Laughing, she'd slipped it on, picked up the ax, and gone to the woodpile to split a stack of wood.

"There," she'd said when she'd returned, handing it back to him, "I can say that I'm a shanty boy!"

Free had hugged her so tight she'd squealed, then they'd laughed together and he'd kissed her. "Grandpa would've loved her," Free muttered as he brushed off pine needles and walked further along the crystal clear stream.

The trees were full of thoughts of Grandpa Clay, full of the love they'd had for each other and the experiences and the memories.

Seven years Grandpa had been gone now. Free knew that Grandpa had gone to heaven and only his body remained to be buried beside Grandma in the special spot in the woods, but still at times the loss was great. Tunis had been there to fill the gap that Grandpa had left, but it wasn't quite the same.

Free kicked a stone in the water, listened to the splash and watched the whirlpool it made. It hadn't been a good idea to come here when he was feeling so low.

Free looked up at the trees around him. Would Grandpa

care if he lumbered out these white pines? It didn't matter. He was going to do it. Besides Grandpa had said lumbering was the way for him to make his fortune.

Abruptly Free turned and walked back down the stream to where his horse was tied. He let the horse drink, then mounted, and rode slowly back toward camp.

Maybe he'd change his mind if Jennet came back and begged him to leave the trees standing. He frowned. What a dumb thought. She wouldn't be back. She'd get so busy with her life in Grand Rapids that she wouldn't give him or the white pines a second thought.

CHAPTER

20

♦ Jennet stood beside the buggy and looked all around the lumbercamp. Was Free in his little shack on the other side of the cookcamp or off in the woods? Her hands shook as she reached to take Clay from Wex.

"Are you all right?" Wex asked.

"I think so." Jennet saw Jig talking to the blacksmith and heard his laughter. The cook's children peeked out from behind the cookcamp to stare at her. Hammers thudded against nails as men finished the roof on the bookkeeper's shack. Where was Free?

Wex patted Jennet's arm. "Relax, Jen. Pa will find Free and talk to him and get everything settled. You'll see."

"It all sounds so simple, and I know it's not. It was really a foolish idea!"

"It was a good idea," said Wex. "Don't give up so soon."

She held Clay close to her heart and looked around, then frowned. "Where did Roman go?"

"In the cookcamp where Jig suggested he start."

Jennet turned. As she did, her ankle twisted, and she started to fall.

Wex caught her and held her. "Are you all right?"

Before Jennet could answer, she heard a loud, angry bellow. Suddenly Free grabbed Wex and hauled him away from Jennet. He socked Wex in the jaw, sending him sprawling to the ground. His hat flew off his head and landed near Jennet's booted feet.

"Don't touch her!" roared Free, fire shooting from his dark eyes. His gray shirt tightened across the bunched muscles of his back and arms.

In shock Wex stared up at Free towering over him.

"What are you doing?" cried Jennet, tugging at Free's arm before he could hit Wex again.

"Stay away from my wife!" Free reached to haul Wex to his feet so he could knock him down again.

Wex rolled away and jumped up, his fists ready, his face red. "Don't do that again, Free!"

"I should've put a stop to this a long time ago," growled Free.

Jennet stared at them in growing alarm. Clay whimpered in her arms, then was quiet.

"You always wanted her, didn't you, Wex?" Free narrowed his dark eyes as he circled Wex, his fists ready, his temper rising even more.

Before they could attack each other, Roman grabbed Free from behind and held him in such a tight hold that Free couldn't break loose. "Stop it, boys!" barked Roman. "What's the meaning of this?"

Jennet glanced around to find the few people at camp watching. A red-hot flush crept up her neck and over her face. "Take Free inside his shack where we can talk in private," she said in a low, tight voice.

"Let me go!" snapped Free. He wanted to tear Wex into little pieces and feed him to the wildcats.

Roman twisted Free's arm harder. "You get that temper in check, and I'll let you go."

Wex brushed dust and pine needles off his pants, scooped up his hat, and dropped it in place. "You don't have anything to be mad at, Free," he said sharply. "What's got into you anyway?"

"Get in the shack," said Jennet in a low, angry voice. "We don't need everybody here to know our family business."

Free struggled, embarrassed that his workers witnessed the event. "Let me go, Pa," he said hoarsely. "I won't attack Wex. Just let me go!"

Roman released him, and Free strode to the shack and held the door wide for the others to crowd in. Jennet laid the baby on the narrow bunk and turned to face the men. Her blue eyes flashed, and her breast rose and fell. The high neck of her blue dress suddenly felt hot and tight.

"What're you doing back here, Jen?" Free stood with his hands on his hips.

Jennet faced him bravely, her chin high. "I said I intended to stay here with you. And I meant it."

"You're not staying."

"I am."

"No!"

"And I brought your pa so you could talk to him and settle this fight between the two of you."

"You think this will keep me from lumbering those trees?" Free's voice was cold.

"I want you to talk to your pa," she repeated.

Free realized that Pa *was* there, even though it was harvest time. His words died in his throat, and he numbly shook his head.

Roman pulled off his hat and tossed it on a peg beside the door. "Vern and Tim are taking care of things at home." He cleared his throat. "I thought it was time I saw what kind of work you do around here."

Jennet knotted her fists at her sides. "You did not come for that reason, Roman Havlick, and you know it! You came to tell Free you love and respect him and are proud of him."

Roman flushed and couldn't look at Free.

275

"Don't back down now, Pa," said Wex.

Free shot a look at Pa.

Roman cleared his throat and rubbed a hand over his red face. "It's time you hear me say I'm sorry about not telling you about your grandpa's will. I'm sorry for trying to keep you on the farm when you wanted to do this." He waved his hand and looked uncomfortable. The tiny space suddenly seemed even smaller. "This is hard for me, Free, but I'm doing it anyway."

"You ruined my life, Pa!" cried Free.

"He did not!" blurted Jennet.

Free pointed his finger at her. "You stay out of this!"

Jennet locked her trembling fingers together in front of her. "You have me."

He narrowed his eyes. "Not another word!"

"And Clay."

"Quiet!"

"And your lumber business!"

"Jennet!"

The color drained from her cheeks, but she wouldn't back down. "And God is on your side."

Free plucked at his suspenders as he stared at Jennet. "Will you forgive me, Free?" asked Roman gruffly.

Free turned his head to look at Pa. Was that really Pa looking so sorry and so humble? A strange feeling rose inside Free. He thought of all the times both Tune and Jig had talked to him about this very thing. He thought he'd carry his anger toward Pa for all his days, but suddenly he knew he didn't want to. He was tired of being angry, tired of struggling over his guilt for not forgiving Pa, and sorry that he'd put a wedge between himself and God. It took him a long time to find his voice. "I do, Pa," he whispered.

Jennet almost burst into tears.

Roman brushed a tear off his cheek.

"I need *you* to forgive me, Pa," said Free.

"Said and done," replied Roman.

Free felt a load lift and he smiled broadly.

Roman took a deep breath. "Now, how about showing me and Wex around your place here?"

Jennet sank to the bunk, her legs shaking so badly she couldn't stand another minute.

"Sure thing, Pa." Free held open the door and waited for them to walk out.

"I'll come too," said Jennet, jumping up.

"Stay here," snapped Free.

His look and his voice sent a cold dart through her heart. She would *not* allow her lip to quiver. "I have to feed Clay anyway, so I will stay here." She'd expected him to give her a quick hug and kiss for what she'd done for him, but he was still upset with her.

Free walked out, closing the door after him.

Jennet sighed and pressed her trembling hands to her flushed cheeks. She'd expected a long fight between Free and Roman, a great struggle, then a loud scene where they finally cleared the air. But it was settled at long last!

"Thank You, heavenly Father!" Jennet said fervently. "You worked another miracle today!"

But it wasn't over yet! Not until Free loved her the way a husband was to love his wife.

Outdoors Free forced back thoughts of Jennet and showed off the cookcamp where they had coffee and raisin cookies, the stable, the blacksmith shop, the company store, and the other buildings, telling them about each one. Free introduced Pa and Wex to his workers and made arrangements for them to have a place to sleep for the night. He felt like a little boy who had trapped his first beaver.

"You got quite a place here," said Roman, looking at Free proudly as they stopped at the rise of a hill overlooking the large camp. "I never knew it'd be like this. It takes brains and brawn to be a lumberman."

Pa's look and his words healed something inside Free that had been an open sore for a long time.

"It suits me," said Free.

"Like farming suits me," said Wex.

Free slapped Wex on the back. "I'm sure sorry about that punch. I saw red when you put your arms around Jen."

"She tripped and I caught her."

Relief swept through Free and he laughed.

"He's got eyes only for Marie," said Roman, pushing his hat to the back of his head.

"Is that right?"

Wex nodded. "We're getting married in November. We'd like you and Jen to be there."

"Jen will be home so she can be there, but I don't think I can make it."

"Jen's planning on staying here," said Wex.

"She is, is she?" The excitement that flashed through Free quickly turned to anger. He didn't know what to make of Jen with the change in her. "We'll see about that," he said gruffly.

"She told us about your grandpa's trees," said Roman.

Free stiffened. Had she brought Roman just to stop him from lumbering the trees?

"She's got a point, Free," said Wex.

"There's plenty of white pines," said Free with a shrug.

Roman pulled off his hat, wiped his forehead, and dropped his hat back in place. "I know your grandpa wanted the trees left standing."

"How do you know that?" asked Free sharply.

"We talked about it. He tried to get me to keep a stand of hardwood trees, but I was too pigheaded and wouldn't. He said it was important to keep at least part of the land the way we had found it."

Free remembered the talks he and Grandpa had had about that. Suddenly logging the trees didn't matter, having the money didn't matter, and not even being as big as Witherspoon mattered. "I can't fight you and Grandpa . . . and Jen too." Laughing, Free spread his arms wide. "I can see I'd better back down on this one."

"I'm proud of you, son."

A lump lodged in Free's throat and he couldn't speak.

"Jen plans to stay here with you, Free, and I think you should let her," said Roman.

"I can't give in on everything, Pa."

"She deserves to be happy." Roman looked uncomfortable. "And you make her happy."

He did? Free shrugged. "I'll talk it out with her," he said. Would he have the heart to send her away?

At dark after the men were settled in for the night, Free stood in his shack with Clay in his arms while Jen sat at the table. A wildcat screeched and a horse nickered, then all was quiet except for Clay's gurgles, Free's cooing, and the distant lament of a fiddle. The lamp on the table flickered, sending out a smell of kerosene. Jennet locked her hands in her lap as she waited for Free to lay Clay in his basket. Finally he did, then turned to her. She tried to read his expression.

"You went to a lot of trouble to get your own way," Free said. Just looking at her sent his pulse racing.

Jennet's heart sank, but she wouldn't give up. "We will have to get a bigger bed in here and a bed for Clay. He's getting too big for his basket."

"You think so?"

She met his eyes squarely. "I'm staying, Freeman Havlick!"

Free almost laughed aloud at seeing the stubborn set of her jaw. What a fighter she'd turned out to be! "Oh, all right! Have it your way!"

"But I want you to be glad!"

"You can't have everything," he said hoarsely.

She bit her lip.

"I can arrange for a bigger bed." Free sat on the chair across the tiny table from her. The night was warm enough that he hadn't started a fire in the small stove. A moth dived at the lamp. "What else will you need?"

She needed him! "A place to have school for the cook's three kids."

Free had expected her to say something different. "You can use one of the offices for now until we can figure something else out. Anything else?"

"No."

Free frowned. "You could ask for a bigger place to live."

"I said I'd be able to live here."

"So you did."

He wanted to take her in his arms and tell her he was glad she was there, but he couldn't.

Jennet stared at the flickering flame. She'd planned to fling her arms around him and tell him she loved him as soon as they were alone, but she couldn't find the courage.

Free stood up. "I'll be going now."

Jennet's heart froze. "Going?"

"You and Clay sleep here, and I'll bunk in with Pa and Wex."

Jennet struggled to hold back tears.

"See you tomorrow then. Right after breakfast I'm taking Pa and Wex out to the trees we'll be chopping first."

Jennet wanted to go along, but she didn't say so. "I'll get acquainted with the kids."

"Fine."

She moved restlessly. "Are you mad because I brought your pa and Wex here?"

"No."

She lifted her eyes to his. "Are you mad that I came back?"

"Yes. But I'll get over it." Free stood at the door and

watched the lamplight play over her. "Good night."

"Good night," she whispered.

He opened the door and closed it quickly to keep the moths out. He stood there a long time.

Inside Jennet covered her face with her hands and burst into tears.

For the next two days each time she was alone she cried, even though she'd try not to. If she couldn't see Free or even talk to him, why stay? Maybe she should return with Roman and Wex.

But Jennet couldn't leave Free, couldn't stand the thought of being so far away from him for such a long time.

The day after Roman and Wex left, Free pulled up in the buggy just outside the open door of the shack. "Jennet, bring Clay and take a ride with me," he called.

Jennet's heart leaped, and she scooped up Clay in his basket and walked to the buggy. She set the basket on the buggy floor and climbed in with a hand from Free. Her skin tingled from his touch, but she couldn't look at him.

Love for her rose inside him so strong it almost knocked him off his seat. When had he fallen so deeply in love with her? Did she know she was essential to his very being?

"Where're you off to?" called Jig from the outside of the cookcamp where he stood with a large mug of coffee in his hand.

"For a ride," said Free, so excited about having time alone with Jennet that he wanted to shout at the top of his lungs.

"You want me to keep Clay with me?" Jig asked.

Jennet giggled at the thought of Jig changing Clay. "No thanks, Jig," she called. She waved to him and he lifted a gnarled dirty hand to her.

"You sure stole his heart," said Free. *And mine,* he thought.

"I love him too."

Frowning, Free clucked to Acorn and flicked the reins. Would Jen ever say those words to him?

When they left the camp clearing, Free said, "I told Wex we'd try to make it to his wedding."

Jennet turned to Free with a cry of joy. "Oh, that's wonderful! Marie would be so happy!"

"I was pretty jealous of Wex and you."

Jennet flushed. "You had no reason."

"I know that now." Free watched an eagle fly high in the bright blue sky. How could he tell her he loved her? "You haven't asked me about Pa."

"I wanted to. But I figured I'd better let you tell me when you wanted to."

"It's fine between us now."

"Good." She'd already known it was by the way they'd acted together, but it was good to hear him say so. She wanted to ask how it was between her and him.

"I was wrong to hold a grudge. I told him so."

"I'm glad."

Free wanted to say so much more, but he couldn't get past the wall he felt between them. Had he built it—or had she?

They didn't speak again until Free stopped Acorn at Jennet's white pines. Her heart sank. Would they have to fight over the trees again?

Jennet jumped to the ground before Free could reach her side and help her out. Clay was sound asleep in his basket, so she left him in the buggy. She draped a light blanket over the basket to keep out the mosquitoes. When she turned around, she almost bumped into Free. Her pulse leaped and she couldn't speak.

"I have something else to tell you," Free said as he took her hand and led her away from the buggy to stand at the base of a nearby pine. He liked the way the soft blue of her dress matched her eyes. He wanted to touch the strands of hair that had fallen down her neck.

Just then Clay cried and Free ran to him and carried him to Jennet, talking to make him laugh.

Jennet's heart almost burst at the beauty of the two together.

When Free reached Jennet's side, he held Clay up high in both his hands. "Clay, you won't see the wild pigeons or the beavers in great numbers, but I promise you that you will see these white pines. They'll be here for your children and their children and their children."

Tears slipped down Jennet's cheeks.

Free looked down at Jennet and gently brushed away her tears with his thumb. "Jen, you were right and I was wrong. Grandpa felt the same as you. I remembered some of the things he told me. And Pa said they'd talked about it. Pa said he was too stubborn to save some of the hardwood trees around his farm, but he didn't want me to be too stubborn to save the white pines."

"Oh, Free," she whispered. A gentle wind blew the pine boughs, sending the clean smell of pine whirling around them.

"I've already sent out my timber walker to find more property for me. I can't quit being a lumberman, but I can let these trees stand forever."

Clay squirmed and started crying his hungry cry. Jennet took him and sat on the ground under the tree to feed him while Free talked to her about what the time with his pa had meant to him.

"I never thought I'd love Pa like I did Grandpa Clay, but I do. It's strange. A real miracle. I know God did it, Jen."

"I know too," she said with a catch in her voice. Silently she thanked God for answering her prayers. He had another one to answer, that Free love her as a husband should love a wife. It would happen because God was faithful to perform His Word. He never broke His promises!

Several minutes later Jennet laid Clay on his stomach in

his basket and walked back to join Free beside the stream. She heard the water rushing over the stones. Minnows darted in and out around the weeds and rocks. A frog croaked and hopped in the water with a tiny splash.

"I'm having a bigger place built for us," Free said without looking at her.

"You are?"

"It's behind my old shack. I'll show you when we return. The men are working hard on it, and they said it'll be done by tonight."

"It will?"

"Yes."

Just then white-tailed deer ran into sight, spotted them and leaped away, their tails high and waving like white flags.

She mustered up all of the courage in her and said, "I didn't want another night without you."

Her words curled around his heart. Slowly he turned to face her. A squirrel chattered at them from a tree. "I've missed you, Jen."

"You have?"

"I have." Free looked deep in her blue eyes, and the message in them sent his blood pounding. But he had to hear the words before he was satisfied. "Jen, do you . . . love me?"

Without hesitation Jennet said, "Yes. I do love you!"

He pulled her against his heart. "I don't know when it happened, but I fell in love with you." He held her away enough to look into her face. "I love you more than I've ever loved anyone." He cupped her face in his hands. "I love you with a love that will never end. All that I have belongs to you. I will love you and keep you and protect you all the days of my life."

Jennet slid her arms around his neck. "Freeman Havlick, I love you with a love that will never end. All that I have belongs to you. I will love you and keep you and protect you all the days of my life."

Free lowered his lips to hers, and she met his kiss with a passion that matched his own. He crushed her close, and she pushed her fingers through the dark thickness of his hair. The time for talking was over.

T H E
INHERITANCE

With love

to a man of his word

JOSHUA JAY STAHL

(number seven of seven)

◊   With special thanks to   ◊

The Freeport Public Library
Joanne Hesselink
Keith Kirkwood
Jeff Stahl
Norman Stahl

CHAPTER

1

♦ Trembling with sudden unexplained fear, Lark Baritt stopped short on the trail in the middle of the Havlicks' priceless white pine forest. A cool breeze flipped her taffy brown hair. She'd brushed it back into a smooth tail and tied it with a narrow blue ribbon at the nape of her slender neck. Her limp blue calico dress hung down over her leggings to the tops of her heavy boots. Her hand trembled as she touched the revolver in the pouch hooked to the leather belt at her narrow waist. She'd promised Jig, the old guard and her very best friend, she'd never set foot in the woods without the gun he'd given her for protection. There were people who would kill for the trees standing in the only virgin white pine forest left in lower Michigan. She lifted the cudgel Jig had carved from a branch of an American hornbeam. He had left a knot on one end the size of his fist. In his thick Swedish accent Jig had said, "This'll be of help to you when you're walking the line with me. You can bop a rattlesnake or a man. It'll work for both."

Lark blinked back tears as she thought of Jig. Twenty-five years ago Freeman and Jennet Havlick had hired the old woodsman to guard the 6000 plus acre forest they had inherited from Free's grandfather. Jig was eighty-three years old and growing weaker daily. He'd lived all his days as a woodsman since he'd come from Sweden in 1825. This year, 1890, when he'd grown so weak, the Havlicks had asked him to retire, but he'd refused. Lark had offered to walk the line for him until he was on his feet again, and he'd agreed because he knew he could trust her.

On alert, Lark glanced around. Had she heard the ring of an ax or the rasp of a crosscut against a tree? Or maybe it was the lack of sounds in the clearing that drew her attention. It was quiet, too quiet, unnaturally quiet. Was someone lurking on the trail ahead of her, waiting to pounce and kill her so he could steal some of the trees she was guarding? "I can't let my imagination run away with me," she muttered, trying to calm herself.

Many times in the twenty-two years she'd spent at the orphan asylum her imagination had run away with her. The worst time had been when she was six and Matron had locked her in a dark, damp room in the cellar for wetting the bed. Rats had squeaked around her and even had run across her bare feet. She'd pictured them eating her alive. She was sure that they would. They hadn't, of course, but the thought of it was as frightening to a six-year-old child as the reality would've been. The times after that when Matron had locked her in the cellar had been almost as bad, even when she was much older. Going to bed without supper or standing in the front hall for hours without moving or speaking while the other orphans teased her or tried to get her to talk had been horrible, but those times had been nothing like the dark cellar and the rats. The cellar room was Matron's favorite punishment and she used it liberally on all the orphans, but she had seemed to be especially fond of using it on Lark. Matron had never liked her. Lark was certain of that, but she didn't know why. She had always tried to stay out of trouble, but Matron seemed to find excuses to punish her on a regular basis.

Forcing away the agonizing memories, she lifted her chin and cocked her head slightly in order to hear better as she silently prayed for help. There were no unusual sounds to make her think there was someone waiting to leap out at her. Maybe she was nervous just knowing danger was possible.

Her eyes moving quickly from side to side, she studied the area around her. Mist rose from the bog to her left and marsh grass swayed in the breeze. Just beyond her in the pines birds twittered, ready to greet the day with song. Lark shivered and moved carefully in the tall grasses. After a deep, steadying breath, she started off again, walking the line she'd walked many times with Jig in the past fifteen years.

At first Matron had forbidden Lark to go, but Jig had talked to her and she had changed her mind. Lark had learned later that Jig had paid Matron to let her go. Just about everyone knew Matron hoarded money like squirrels do nuts. Apparently a little something to add to her stash could get Matron to agree to most anything. Lark was glad she'd had the freedom to walk these woods and be with Jig. Even if it had cost him several dollars it had meant everything in the world to her. He'd been the closest thing to a parent she'd known and he was her friend. She knew he loved her.

Lark stopped at the crest of a hill and brushed away a tear, then continued on. She must not let her thoughts keep her from being alert. She knew the west and north boundaries of the pines were hilly and inaccessible, but the east and south sides had to be guarded from dishonest lumbermen and tree robbers. The Blue River ambled along the east side of the pines, making it very easy for robbers to cut the trees and float the logs down the river before they were caught.

Lark paused briefly and surveyed the calm river at the bottom of the hill and the farms beyond. Then she headed south again through briars that made the trail barely visible. Suddenly birds filled the morning sky and insects buzzed around bright flowers at the edge of the woods. A blue racer a good five feet long slithered across the trail in front of her. She stopped to let it pass, and then walked on her way. At the swamp she looked closely for signs of water snakes before she waded through, the muck sucking at her heavy boots. In the heat of summer the swamp would be dry, sending the creatures living in it deeper into the woods. But now it was filled with wet muck and Lark knew to be careful. Jig had taught her that. She heard a bull frog croak a deep bass and several peepers answer with their high pitched peeps. The forest was alive with creatures. It felt like home to Lark, almost like an old house with familiar, friendly nooks and crannies. Still, there was danger in the forest and Lark could feel it.

The sun had turned hot and perspiration dotted Lark's face and dampened her dress as she walked up the long hill and then down. Her stomach growled with hunger. She'd been too tense about Jig to eat much breakfast at the asylum, but she'd packed a biscuit in her pouch. She dug it out and ate it, then drank water from the small canteen that hung from her belt. As she glanced ahead, her nerves tightened and her scalp prickled. She could sense danger, real danger, not something from her imagination.

Just then a tall man with a small brimmed hat covering most of his black hair stepped around the huge dry roots of a fallen tree and onto the path in front of Lark. He smiled at her, but his eyes looked as hard as steel.

Lark gripped her cudgel tightly, but she smiled as if she hadn't a care in the world the way Jig had taught her to put a thief off guard. Her feet felt like chunks of ice inside her heavy high-top boots. Her thin calico dress suddenly felt too hot. This was the very spot where Jig had been waylaid several times in the past. The huge tree root and the steep hill down to the river made it a perfect place for an ambush. "It's a surprise to see someone other than myself here," Lark said brightly, wondering if he could hear the wild beat of her heart.

"I'm Bruce Oliver and I seem to be lost," said the stranger, tipping his hat.

"Where is it you want to be, Mr. Oliver?" Lark forced her voice to stay calm.

"The little town of Blue Creek."

Lark saw the quick look the man shot past her and her nerves tightened. She noticed his clothes were dry and knew he hadn't forded the river on foot. "You'll have to cross back over the river and take the corduroy south and then west to find Blue Creek."

"Thank you. I guess I shouldn't have crossed the river in the first place." He licked his dry lips as he looked at her canteen. "I see you have a canteen." He motioned to it and said, "Would it be possible to have a drink?" He rubbed his damp forehead and dropped his hat back in place.

Lark unhooked her canteen while she listened for the slightest sound behind her. She watched the man's eyes and twice he flicked looks over her shoulder as if he were expecting someone. Her nerves tightened as she held the canteen out to him, and just as he took it she heard a footfall behind her. With lightning speed she turned, swinging the cudgel. A thickset bearded man lunged for her. The cudgel struck him on the side of the head and he dropped like a dead man at her feet. She turned back in time to see Oliver pull a gun from the belt under his jacket. She sprang forward and swung the cudgel again, striking Oliver's arm. The gun fell to the pine needle covered path as Oliver cried out in pain. Quickly she scooped up her canteen and Oliver's gun. Her legs trembled, and she locked her knees to keep from sinking to the ground. "Pick up your friend and let's go," she snapped.

"You broke my arm!" Oliver cried in shock.

"I'll crack your skull if you don't do as I say!" Lark kept the gun aimed at Oliver as he flung the unconscious man over his shoulder. He sagged under the weight. She longed to drop to the ground and burst into hysterical tears, but she snapped, "Now, walk!"

"Where?" asked Oliver with a groan.

Lark glanced around for sight of a wagon, then looked down at the river. She spotted a raft floating toward them. She'd get the men on board to help her. "Down to the river," she ordered. "You won't be stealing any trees today."

Oliver groaned again. "Page here said Jig was dead and the Havlicks didn't hire another guard."

Lark stiffened. "He's wrong! Jig's not dead! And *I'm* here to keep the trees safe." Lark followed Oliver down to the river, the gun held steadily in one hand, her cudgel in the other. She watched the raft float toward them, then when it drew close enough, she hailed it. She knew the two men in the raft were cooks who were following men searching for logs in the swamps.

"What's the problem, lady?" asked a huge man, leaning against the pole he used to guide the raft down the river.

"I'm Lark Baritt. This is Havlick property," said Lark, waving up behind her. "These men were trying to steal timber. I want them taken to the sheriff in Blue Creek. Could you take them for me?"

"Sure can, Missy," said the other man. "I cooked for Free Havlick some years back. He's a fair man and don't deserve to have his trees pirated."

"You got no proof we was trying to steal trees," said Oliver gruffly. The other man moaned and moved on Oliver's shoulder.

"Free Havlick will thank you for helping me," said Lark. "Take these men on in to Blue Creek with you and leave them with the sheriff. Tell him Freeman Havlick will be in to press charges."

"Get on board," ordered the cook as they poled close to the river's edge.

Oliver glared at Lark, and she smiled sweetly at him. He swore under his breath, and then stepped on the raft and dropped his partner in a heap.

Lark turned and on trembling legs walked back up the steep hill to the trail. She knew word would spread about what she'd done. Thieves would think twice before they tried to steal trees just because Jig was under the weather.

Suddenly Lark stopped and the short hairs on the back of her neck stood on end. Had she heard the rattle of a wagon and the jangle of harness? She ducked behind a massive white pine that could easily hide her as well as three of the little kids in the asylum. She rubbed her damp palms down her limp dress and touched the pouch where she carried the revolver. Was she hearing things or were thieves out in number because Jig was laid up? Maybe Oliver and his partner had a driver and a wagon across the river and she was hearing that, but she couldn't see any sign of a wagon.

A fly buzzed around Lark's head and she swatted it away. She pushed damp tendrils of brown hair off her face and patted her flushed cheeks. Everyone for miles around knew the ten sections of priceless trees were off limits. Still poachers tried to steal them. Through narrowed eyes Lark studied the tree trunks and underbrush. She wished Jig was with her. She couldn't afford another waylay or she'd be late getting back to Blue Creek Orphan Asylum where she worked as well as lived. She looked past the thick patch of violets and deep into the woods, but couldn't spot an intruder.

She leaned against a tree and looked up. The pine was about four feet across and stood arrow straight about a hundred and fifty feet tall. Its long, sweeping green branches began about a hundred feet above the ground. Its needles were over four inches long with five in each blue-green bundle. The gray bark was thick and deeply furrowed into narrow scaly ridges. The tree was worth a fortune with lumber being so dear. Lark couldn't imagine the value of the whole ten sections.

After lumbering the pines and the hardwoods of lower Michigan, the lumbermen had moved to the upper peninsula to rape the land of the giant white pines and uproot habitat for birds, animals, and insects, and ruin the rivers. Lark knew lumber was necessary to the growth of America, but she hated the waste the lumbermen left behind. Some replanted, but most left ugly stumps, deep ruts in the ground, and a spoiled countryside.

Freeman Havlick had given up lumbering to stay on his homestead near the white pines. He'd invested the money he'd made lumbering in real estate and businesses. Then he had turned to farming and buggy making. Lark was acquainted with the Havlicks because the community was small and Jennet was on the board of the asylum, but she'd never been close with them. But she was close to Jig, and she had to hurry and check on him before reporting to Matron. Lark needed to hurry, but she couldn't get her legs to move.

Birds sang and small animals scurried under the thick carpet of pine needles. From deep in the woods a bear growled, probably to protect its cub. Golden notes flowed from orioles flying at the edge of the forest. A flash of red caught Lark's attention and she watched a grosbeak land on a branch. It had a black back and cap and a red and white vest. Its gay song gave Lark the strength to step away from the tree and walk to the path that led to Jig's cabin at the south edge of the pines. Freeman Havlick had built the cabin for Jig and had finally convinced him to live in it instead of in the woods that had been his home all the years he'd lived in Michigan.

Once again Lark looked down the hill to the river. The raft was almost out of sight. She spotted a small boat tied to a tree root. *It probably belongs to Oliver and Page,* she thought, although she couldn't be sure, just as she wasn't certain they hadn't brought other thieves with them who were still hiding in the woods. She pushed back her fear, squared her shoulders, and walked quickly down the path.

The sweeping pine branches filtered out the hot June sunshine and mosquitoes buzzed around Lark's head, but she ignored them. Frogs croaked near the swampy bog that Jig had warned her against years ago when he'd taught her to walk the woods in safety.

She'd made friends with Jig when he'd visited the asylum. At first she'd been afraid of him, but after a few visits, she'd grown to care for him. Now he was father, brother, and best friend to her. She couldn't survive without him.

Finally Lark reached the hill that led down to the edge of the woods and the valley where Jig's small one room cabin stood. The pines in the valley made a wall behind the cabin and the pine covered hills behind it made the wall even higher. In front and to the sides of the cabin stretched a field where a few pines, oaks, maples, and hickory nut trees spread out to the edge of Freeman Havlick's farm. Two miles from there was the growing town of Blue Creek and about ten miles further on was Big Pine, the largest town in the area north of Grand Rapids.

Lark walked along the path flanked with yellow, white, and blue wild flowers to the cabin. She glanced at the bench near the covered well where she'd sat many times listening to Jig tell of his years with old Clay Havlick, the fur trader, and later with his grandson, Free Havlick, the lumberman. They'd talked of young Clay who would inherit the white pines on his twenty-fifth birthday. Even though Jig told her many things, he wouldn't talk about his life in Sweden before he came to America, leaving Lark to wonder about his early life. She knew his real name was Dag Bjoerling, but that was all she knew.

At the cabin Lark saw the stick at the side of the door, telling passing Indians they were free to stop in for food. The stick propped against the door meant "pass on by." The stick was an old Indian custom Jig still practiced to let the Indians know if they could stop in or not.

"Jig?" Lark called in a tight voice.

"Lark," answered Jig weakly, his voice muffled by the thick door.

Lark pushed the door open, then gasped at the closed-in smell. The fire in the cast iron cookstove, used both to heat the cabin and for cooking, was out. Light filtered through the dirty windows at either end of the cabin. Lark looked past the small round table to the low, narrow bunk built onto the wall. Jig lay on it, his muzzleloader on the floor beside him.

"I knew you'd come soon," he said, weakly lifting his shaggy gray head. His narrow face was grooved with wrinkles and his skin was dark and leathery from years of outdoor living. He wore the leather shirt and breeches he'd stitched together with rawhide.

With a strangled cry, Lark ran to him and dropped to her knees beside the bunk. She gripped one of his dirt encrusted, gnarled hands and whispered, "How are you, Jig?"

Awkwardly he patted her arm with his free hand. "Don't fret. I'm fine. Take me to the woods. I asked God to give me strength to see you and talk to you before I die. . . . He answered."

"Oh, Jig!" Tears burned Lark's brown eyes as she helped Jig sit on the edge of the bunk. He smelled as if he hadn't had a bath in weeks and Lark knew he hadn't. "Please, Jig, let me get Freeman or Jennet Havlick!"

Jig shook his head. "I said my goodbyes to them."

"What about Clay? I'll get him."

"Young Clay is in Detroit on business," said Jig as tears brimmed in his eyes. "I wanted to say goodbye to the great-grandson of my good friend Clay Havlick, but I won't get to." Jig reached for his boots and almost toppled over.

"Let me," said Lark as she helped Jig slip on his heavy walking boots over dirty, gray woolen socks. Then she helped him stand. His bones creaked and he moaned. Suddenly she realized how frail he'd become. She forced back a cry of agony.

She walked him across the puncheon floor and outdoors into the bright sunlight. He leaned heavily on her as she walked him to the bench and eased him down to rest before they made the last leg of the journey into the woods. She heard his labored breathing and she bit back a cry of alarm.

"I want your word that you will do what I ask of you, Lark Baritt," Jig said weakly.

Without hesitation she said firmly, "You have it, Jig." There was nothing he could ask of her that she wouldn't do. He was the only person she'd ever trusted. He'd taught her how to track, how to walk the woods without falling prey to the many dangers, how to shoot, but most importantly, he'd taught her about God.

Jig looked at the woods. "These woods belong to young Clay Havlick now that he's twenty-five."

Lark frowned. She hadn't realized Clay was already twenty-five. She didn't like to think of age. She was twenty-two and unmarried, and had no hope of being married. She'd probably spend the rest of her days at the orphan asylum. Maybe she'd become the matron, but she'd never marry, and she would never escape.

Jig held Lark's hand tighter. "I must tell you more of Willie Thorne."

"You said he's bad, that he almost killed Jennet and Free years back when Free was in the lumber business."

Jig nodded. "He's still trying to harm them. He bought a home on the outskirts of Blue Creek. He's come up with a new plan to destroy the Havlicks and those trees." Jig leaned back, struggling to continue.

"Don't talk," said Lark with a worried frown. She looked across the field toward the Havlicks' farm. Should she ring the bell at the corner of the cabin? It was there to call for help.

"I must tell you," said Jig barely above a whisper. "Willie Thorne wants his daughter to marry Clay, then have him give her the pines as a wedding gift. Once the pines belong to her, she'll let Willie Thorne lumber them."

"Clay would never marry Willie Thorne's daughter!"

"She is beautiful and she knows how to capture a man's heart," said Jig. "Clay has been working too hard and hasn't had time to look for a wife. If a woman sought him out, he might lose his heart to her."

Lark looked down at Jig's hand holding hers. She didn't want to admit it, but she was afraid Jig had slipped over the edge. No Havlick would have any dealings with a Thorne.

"You must believe me, Lark," said Jig hoarsely. "I speak the truth. I heard Willie Thorne and his daughter making plans. They didn't see me."

"Just how is she going to make Clay be interested in her?"

"Her first plan is to ride the train with him when he returns from Detroit. She will sit with him and engage him in conversation. She will use her wiles on him. He is too much of a gentleman to turn her away." Jig gripped Lark's hand tighter. "We must save Clay and we must save the trees. They're the only virgin stand left."

"Tell the Havlicks what Willie Thorne said!" cried Lark.

"I did, but they didn't think I heard right. They said they heard Willie forbid his daughter to even speak to a Havlick." Jig's voice broke. "But that was part of his plan. They are deceitful folks!"

Lark trembled. She hated to think her dear friend was imagining things, but she was afraid he was.

"Promise me you will stop young Clay from marrying Veda Thorne," said Jig urgently as he gripped her hand.

"How can *I* stop him?"

"You can do anything with God's help, Lark Baritt."

"Not this, Jig."

"Even this. I would do it, but it's too late for me." Jig lifted Lark's hand to his cracked lips and gently kissed the back of it. "My precious Lark. You have been a friend and a daughter to me for over fifteen years. It hurts me to lay such a task on you, but there is no other way. Back in '35 I promised my friend Clay Havlick I would look out for his people. I will not break that promise even in death. I will pass it on to you."

Lark bit her lip to hold back a cry.

"Young Clay would be hurt beyond all help if he marries Veda Thorne and she lumbers the pines the Havlicks have worked to save." Jig touched Lark's soft cheek. "Lark, *you* must marry young Clay."

"Me!" she cried. He'd never look at her. She was as plain as a post. She wasn't good enough for him or for any man of means. Matron had told her that for as long as she could remember. She wanted to argue with Jig, but she saw the pallor of his skin, and bit back the sharp words.

Jig frowned and his shaggy gray eyebrows almost met over his large nose. "Promise me, Lark. Promise that no matter what it takes you'll keep Clay from marrying Veda Thorne."

Lark's heart turned over. She didn't think the occasion would arise, but she nodded. She loved Jig too much to deny him anything. "I promise," she said around the lump in her throat. Sudden tears filled her eyes and slipped down her ashen cheeks. "I love you, Jig! I would do anything for you!"

"Thank you." Jig closed his eyes for a minute, then opened them. "I want to go home, Lark. I want to have strong legs again to run all over heaven. I want to see Jesus face to face. Be glad for me."

Lark's throat closed shut and for a while she couldn't speak. "I'm glad for you, Jig, but sad for me. I know I'm being selfish, but I want you with me."

Weakly Jig pushed himself up. "Help me to the woods so I can die in the shade of the pines I have enjoyed and loved and guarded all these years."

Lark pulled his arm over her shoulder and he leaned heavily on her. The smell of old leather and sweat burned her nose. Slowly they walked past the cabin and the covered well and into the woods to the narrow creek. She lowered him to a thick carpet of needles under a massive white pine. Overhead birds sang and beside them the creek rushed over rocks. A frog splashed into the clear, sparkling water. Lark sank down and laid Jig's head in her lap.

"Sing 'Blessed Assurance,' Lark," whispered Jig.

She lifted her chin and sang the hymn in a clear, melodious low soprano voice. At first her voice quivered with tears, then she sang in triumph the way she knew Jig wanted her to sing.

At Jig's cabin Clay Havlick looped the reins of his sorrel mare around the low branch of a bush, then lifted his head and listened to the joyous song that drifted out from the pines. He knew it was the orphan Lark Baritt singing. Clay had heard her sing at the asylum and in church. He knew she was singing for Jig. Clay pulled off his hat and stabbed his fingers through his thick, dark hair. He was tall with broad shoulders and lean hips and was well muscled from hard work. He wore the black traveling suit that he'd worn to Detroit. A muscle jumped in his suntanned cheek. Was he too late? Pa had said in his telegram last night that Jig might not make it through another day.

Clay frowned. Only Jig or his family could make him put aside his business to hurry home. But he had been able to find a bank to loan him the money he needed. He closed his eyes momentarily and groaned. Ma and Pa would have a fit when they learned what he'd done. "But I had to do it," he muttered, once again trying to convince himself he'd had no other choice. No one would loan him money to start his wagon business unless Pa co-signed or he had collateral. He glanced back toward the Havlick farm. He was twenty-five years old! Why should he have to have his pa sign for him? He looked toward the giant pines. The pines belonged to him. He'd used them for collateral and he'd borrowed the money to start his wagon business. His stomach knotted. Using the pines for collateral put them in danger and he knew it, but he'd done it anyway. "I'll keep up the payments no matter what it takes," he vowed firmly. "I won't lose the pines!"

Abruptly he pushed aside his thoughts of business and strode toward Lark's song, his steps quiet on the path. He tugged at the starched high collar of his white shirt as he stopped several feet from Lark and Jig to watch them. Lark had a glow about her that made her face almost beautiful. She finished the song, bent down, and kissed Jig's forehead. He touched her pale cheek with a trembling, gnarled hand. A lump rose in Clay's throat at the love he saw between them.

"Tell Clay goodbye for me," Jig said weakly.

"Tell me yourself," said Clay hoarsely as he walked to Jig and knelt beside him. Clay smiled at Lark.

Lark's heart jerked strangely the way it always did when he was nearby. She saw the pain in his dark brown eyes before he masked it.

Clay took Jig's hand and held it firmly. "Pa wired me to come and I came on the first train this morning." Tears filled Clay's dark eyes. "I'll miss you, my friend."

"I love you, young Clay."

"I love you, Jig." Adventurous times in the woods with Jig flashed through Clay's mind. Jig had been a grandpa, teacher, and friend to him. "Thank you for all the things you taught me down through the years."

Lark moved slightly. Should she give them time alone?

Weakly Jig pulled his hand from Clay's and reached for Lark's. He brought her hand to Clay's. As her hand touched Clay's, she tensed but didn't pull away. Shivers of awareness ran over her.

Clay looked down at the strong sun-browned hand that Jig had placed over his. Lark had always been around, but he'd never given much thought to her.

Jig whispered, "I pray God's best for both of you. Watch out for each other."

"We will," said Clay softly, willing to promise Jig anything, but not knowing why Jig would ask him of all people to watch over Lark. What could he do for her?

"I promise," whispered Lark, but she couldn't look at Clay because she knew what the promise really meant to her and Jig.

"Look in my special box when I'm gone," Jig whispered.

"We will," Clay answered.

Lark knew the special box Jig meant. She'd seen it in the corner of his cabin, but he'd never offered to let her look in it. At times her curiosity had almost overcome her, but she'd never looked no matter how badly she'd wanted to.

"Sing 'Safe in the Arms of Jesus,'" Jig said, his voice growing weaker and a faint smile on his face.

Tears burning her eyes, Lark lifted her head and began to sing. Clay joined with her and their voices blended in a harmony that sent a shaft of pure pleasure through Lark.

Before the song ended Jig's spirit left his body and soared to heaven to be with Jesus. Now Jig could run around heaven just as he'd once run in the woods.

Tears soaked Lark's cheeks and dripped down on her calico dress. She struggled to control her sobs, but couldn't.

Clay looked at her compassionately and started to reach out to comfort her, then drew his hand back. Finally he stood and brushed the tears from his eyes. "I'll carry him to the cabin and prepare him for burial. You go and tell my family."

Lark nodded. She sat still until Clay lifted Jig in his arms, struggling with the weight. She leaned weakly against a tree and waited for the strength to return to her legs. "Oh, Jig, how can I survive without you?" she whispered. She knew with God's help she would. That was another thing Jig had taught her—to lean on God.

She thought of her promise to Jig, and she moaned. Then she lifted her chin high. "I'll keep my promise no matter what it takes," she whispered hoarsely.

CHAPTER

2

♦ Lark wiped away her tears as she reached the driveway of Blue Creek Orphan Asylum. She'd helped Clay with Jig as long as she dared, but she had to return to the asylum to work on the books and teach deportment. She'd told Clay she'd see him late in the afternoon, then had run from the cabin to town. Maybe she could slip inside the small room she used for her office without Matron seeing her and docking her already low pay for being late.

Lark gripped the cudgel tighter as she walked toward the asylum. The large two story house with a full basement had been built years ago by a lumberman for himself, but he'd decided to move north with his business and had given the home to Blue Creek for an orphan asylum. Lark had lived there all her life, first as an inmate, then as an employee. The payment she received was room and board and a pittance of a salary. Fifteen boys and ten girls, ranging from infant to sixteen years lived there. In the past year Lark had been trying to have Matron Anna Pike replaced. She was too unbending and her punishments too harsh. Because she'd been at the asylum from its beginning, none of the board would listen to Lark, not even Jennet Havlick. Matron put on a good front with the board

17

members and the townspeople, but she was entirely different with the orphans.

Lark walked between tall maple trees up the wide brick sidewalk that led to the big front porch. Once the yard had been covered with grass and shrubbery, but now was bare from too many children playing on it. A barn for two cows and the mare that pulled Matron's buggy and the chicken coop stood behind the house. The house had been a good distance from the residents of Blue Creek, but in the past few years people had built closer and closer until homes now stood on either side and across the road. Lark could hear a man whistling as he did his chores, and she could see a woman working in her garden.

Lark walked up the wide steps and stopped on the porch. Straight ahead were the wide double doors that led into the huge front hall where she'd had to stand in silence as punishment. Across the porch to the left a door led to the offices and across the porch to the right a door led into the large front room. Lark took a deep breath and carefully opened the door to the offices. Hot, closed in air rushed down the hallway. The smell of fresh baking bread drifted from the kitchen. Lark heard the muted sounds of teachers teaching in the classrooms and a baby crying upstairs. She knew Zoe Cheyney, an orphan girl who had just turned eighteen but had no where to go, was attending the children too young to be in the classrooms. Lark and Zoe were friends, but they weren't as close as Lark and Jig had been.

Lark opened the window at the end of the long hall, then walked to her office. Inside were two desks, hers and John Epson's when he came in. She stroked his desk, flushed, and jerked her hand back. John was an attorney with an office on Main Street and a desk at the asylum for the work there. He handled the adoptions and any other legal matters that arose. He was in his early thirties and a bachelor. Lark had been attracted to him at one time, but Matron had seen the interest and had cruelly nipped it in the bud by telling Lark she was too plain and too low class to set her sights on a man of wealth and social standing. But the attraction for him was still buried in her heart, waiting for a sign from him to spark it into a flame of love.

Lark stood her cudgel in the corner near the coat hooks and stuck her pouch and canteen in a bottom drawer of her desk. She pulled off her heavy boots and leggings and slipped on her regular shoes. From the heavy pitcher on a stand in the corner she poured a bit of water onto a cloth and rubbed her face and hands. Listlessly she dried off, then hung the rough white towel on the wire hook near the stand. She brushed her hair and retied the blue ribbon. She scowled in the looking glass on the wall beside the hook. Her brown eyes were red rimmed from crying. Her face was too narrow, her mouth too wide, and her nose too pointed to be attractive. Jig had always said true beauty comes from within. Oh, what would she do without Jig? The ache inside of her was so great she almost cried aloud.

She sat at her desk and slowly pulled out the heavy dark red ledger. She sighed. Would this be her entire life from now on?

Just then John Epson walked in, his straw hat in his hand. Her pulse quickened, but she didn't let it show. "Good morning, Lark," he said, smiling. He sailed the hat onto a hook, then leaned back on his desk as he studied her. He wore a black suit that fit well across his broad shoulders and a white shirt and collar. He fingered his neatly trimmed black beard. "Is something wrong, Lark?"

His kindness brought tears to her eyes. She blinked them quickly away. "My friend Jig died this morning," she said with a break in her voice.

John shot up. He'd been waiting to hear the good news, but he didn't let Lark see how pleased he was. "I'm sorry to hear that, Lark. Will you be all right?"

Lark nodded. "I guess I have to be."

"Ask Matron to give you the day off."

Lark shook her head. "She won't."

"When's the funeral?"

"Probably tomorrow morning," whispered Lark as she locked her hands together on the ledger. "The Havlicks are taking care of everything."

"I figured they would. Jig seemed more like family to them than an employee."

Lark nodded. She picked up her ink pen as a hint for John to stop talking. She didn't want to break down in front of him. She didn't want him to see just how ugly she looked when she cried.

Just then Zoe Cheyney ran into the room. Tendrils of red hair clung to her damp, pale cheeks. Her hazel eyes were wide with fright. She gripped Lark's hand and tugged. "Hurry, Lark! Matron is locking Linda and Maggie in the cellar because they were swearing. You know there're rats down there!" She had been locked in the cellar several times just as Lark had been. "The girls are terrified! Help me stop her!"

Anger shot through Lark and she jumped up and ran with Zoe down the narrow hall to the foyer. Silently Lark prayed for the wisdom and strength to handle the situation.

In the hallway Matron held two skinny, frightened almost into hysterics, little girls by the arms. Matron was short and plump, dressed in a black wrapper and black shoes with pointed toes. Her brown hair was pulled into a tight bun. With steel gray eyes she glared at Zoe. "You can't stop me! So don't try, or you'll be punished too."

Zoe whimpered and stepped closer to Lark.

"Don't do this, Matron!" said Lark. Inside she was trembling because of the years of punishment she'd received from Matron, but outwardly she looked calm and in control. "Locking Linda and Maggie in the cellar won't solve anything."

"Please don't!" begged the girls. They were sisters who looked like twins and had been at the asylum for about five months.

"I will not tolerate bad language. They must learn!" snapped Matron.

"I will go directly to the Havlicks with this," said Lark, struggling to sound firm. She could feel Zoe tremble.

"Hummmp! Just stay out of my way!" Matron tried to push past Lark and Zoe while the girls dragged their feet and screamed.

"Let them go!" cried Zoe.

"Move!" shouted Matron, her round face brick red.

Lark wouldn't budge and Matron was forced to stop. Lark looked Matron straight in the eye and said, "The girls will learn to stop swearing as I teach them deportment. Locking them in a cellar won't work."

"It won't!" whimpered Linda and Maggie.

Matron narrowed her gray eyes into slits. "It worked for you two and it'll work for them."

Lark shook her head. "Times have changed. This is 1890!"

"I won't change my mind!"

Lark took a deep breath. "I will go directly to the Havlicks and bring Jennet here to witness what you've done. You know Jennet Havlick doesn't abide such treatment."

Matron sputtered with anger, then shoved the two girls toward Lark. "This is not the end of this, Lark Baritt!" Matron turned on her heels and strode to her office, slamming the door hard behind her.

The girls clung to Lark, sobbing against her. She patted their thin backs and talked gently to them.

"Matron will make it bad for us," whispered Zoe.

"I don't care!" cried Lark. "It's time we stood up to her! We are adults." She tried to smile at Zoe, but failed. "You'd better get back to the babies. I'll tend the girls and see that they get back to class."

"We'll talk later," said Zoe. She ran lightly up the wide stairs to the nursery.

The girls looked up into Lark's face. "Thank you, Miss Baritt," they said together.

"You're welcome." Lark's voice was gentle and she tried to

smile as she wiped their faces with her hanky. "I don't ever want either of you to say bad words again. You both know better."

"We won't," said Linda solemnly.

"Not even if we get mad," said Maggie.

"Good. Now, get back to class."

Maggie looked at Linda. "We should tell her, Linda."

"We should," said Linda.

Lark lifted her brow. "Tell me what?"

The girls looked quickly around to make sure no one was listening. In a low voice Maggie said, "We know where Matron hid your box of stuff."

Lark's knees almost buckled and for a minute she couldn't speak. She didn't pretend she didn't know what "stuff" Maggie meant. For as long as she could remember she'd tried to find the things the man who'd dropped her off at the asylum had left with her. Lark had been told her mother had died when she was born and her father couldn't manage a baby alone. A man, maybe her father, had left her at the asylum with a box of things. She'd been only a few days old. She'd not known about the box until she was seven years old and some of the other orphans had talked about their stuff that Matron kept in a closet. Lark had asked about her box of stuff, but Matron had said she didn't have anything for Lark. Just the same, the other children had said they knew she did have something. Allie, an older girl who had moved to Grand Rapids about eight years ago had said she was outside Matron's door the day a man had left Lark with Matron. He had also left a box of things—photos, money to help pay for her keep, and baby clothes. Matron insisted Allie had lied just to stir up trouble. Now, Maggie and Linda were saying they knew where Matron had hidden the stuff.

"You okay, Miss Baritt?" asked Linda in alarm.

"I don't know," whispered Lark hoarsely.

"Don't you want to know where your stuff is?" asked Linda.

Lark nodded weakly.

"It's in Matron's room," whispered Maggie.

"In a trunk," said Linda.

"How do you know?" asked Lark.

The girls flushed and shrugged.

Lark's head spun and she couldn't think what to do.

"Want us to show you?" asked Maggie.

Before Lark could answer Matron's office door burst open and Matron snapped, "Aren't you girls in class yet?"

"We're going right now," the girls said as they turned and ran down the hall and into a room.

Lark felt like her head was packed with cotton and her eyes wouldn't focus.

"What's wrong with you, Lark?" snapped Matron.

"I . . . I don't feel well," Lark whispered.

"You look ready to pass out. Get to your room and lie down! You have Deportment Class in two hours." Matron spun on her heel and slammed her office door behind her.

In a daze Lark walked to the open stairs in the wide hallway. As she climbed she clung to the bannister, her legs almost too weak to support her. Why would Matron lie about her stuff and hide it in her trunk? Lark hesitated. Should she go to Matron's bedroom to look in the trunk? Numbly she shook her head. She couldn't walk that far without collapsing.

The long hall seemed to stretch on and on. Finally Lark stepped into the room she shared with Zoe. She didn't notice the sun streaming through the windows or the shabby white muslin curtains fluttering in the warm breeze. A fly buzzed at the window, but she didn't hear it as she sank to the double bed. The carved mahogany headboard stood about four feet high and the footboard about two feet. A patchwork quilt Lark had quilted herself during her twelfth year covered the bed. Unable to contain her emotions any longer, she burst into tears and her slender shoulders shook with sobs. All those years Allie had been right! A man had left some of her family's things so that someday she'd have a sense of who she was! Why had

Matron kept them from her? Should she take them from Matron's trunk? Lark pushed herself up, shivering as if it were twenty degrees below zero. A sudden strength coursed through her body. She had to get her stuff! But how could she? Matron always kept her door locked.

Lark paced from the bed to the tall chest, to the trunk, over to the chifforobe, and back again. Somehow Maggie and Linda had gotten into Matron's room. If they could, she could. She couldn't wait to tell Jig what she'd learned! Tears burned her eyes as she realized Jig wasn't there to listen to her! How could she survive the trauma of the day? Jig was gone! She was all alone! She stopped and shook her head, then looked up. "I'm not alone!" she whispered, a feeling of calm spreading through her. "Heavenly Father, you're always with me! With your help I'll be all right. Thank you!" Lark clasped her hands together at her throat. "Dear Father, I need to know what to do about Matron hiding my things."

Wild ideas on what to do flashed through her mind, but she quickly rejected them. Somehow she'd find a way to look in Matron's trunk, and she'd do it yet today!

Suddenly she remembered that she hadn't told the Havlicks about the two men she'd caught in the pines. She'd have to tell them immediately. She pushed thoughts of herself to the back of her mind where she'd carried her own problems for years and rubbed her hands together with agitation. Perspiration dotted her face. "How could I forget to tell the Havlicks? What shall I do?"

She walked to the window and let the breeze blow against her damp face. Maybe she could get someone to teach her class so she could run to the Havlicks now. "Kaitland will do it without getting me in trouble with Matron!" she whispered, then rushed downstairs to the history class. She arranged for Kaitland to teach deportment, then ran the two miles to the Havlicks' farm.

A white picket fence surrounded the three story white frame house Freeman Havlick had built for Jennet and their six children when Clay, the oldest, was a small child. Outside the fence behind the house stood two large barns, several small sheds, and the large shop where Free and his sons built buggies by special order. Chickens scratched in the farmyard along with turkeys, geese, and ducks. Cattle grazed in a big pasture on one side of a barn and sheep grazed on another side. Far enough away to keep the smell from the house was a pen full of pigs. Lark took a step toward the house, then heard Freeman and Clay talking in the shop, their voices loud.

Lark hurried back through the gate and across the farmyard to the shop. Her limp dress clung to her damp body. A fly buzzed around her head and tangled in the loose strands of taffy brown hair. Impatiently she swatted the fly away.

"I don't understand you, Clay!" Free snapped angrily.

Lark stopped short just outside the open door. An unfinished buggy stood behind Clay and Free. Tools hung on the back wall of the shop. Free's face was dark with anger. In all the years Lark had known the Havlicks, she'd never heard Free raise his voice in anger. Maybe she should call out and let them know she was there. The men looked very much alike, even in their anger, as they faced each other. They were the same height and build, with the same dark brown eyes. Clay wore dark pants held up by wide black suspenders and a blue plaid shirt cuffed to his muscled forearm. Free wore overalls, faded from many washings, and a blue chambray work shirt. He could afford to dress like a city man and he had enough money to keep him and his family for years to come, but he chose to work and to dress like a workman. He wasn't one to have idle hands nor were any of the members of his family.

"Pa, I have every right to make my own fortune!" cried Clay as he jerked off his straw hat and jabbed his fingers through his thick dark hair. He'd been talking about going into business for himself the past two years. Now the time for talking was past. "Pa, I am going to buy the two big warehouses in town and I'm going to build wagons. There's a market for them and there'll be a market for a *long* time."

Free scowled as he stabbed his fingers through his gray hair. "Why can't you keep working with me? We make quality buggies."

"There are men already developing a gas-driven buggy. There will come a time when people won't use buggies pulled by horses, but farmers and freighters will *always* need wagons. I have a contract to supply Midwest Freighters with three hundred wagons before fall."

"That's out of the question, Clay. How can you do that?"

"By hiring men to work for me."

Lark's stomach tightened as she stepped even closer. It was very embarrassing to hear the argument. Flushing, she cleared her throat. "Freeman, Clay, I must speak with you," she called out. Her voice quivered and she flushed even more.

The two men stepped from the shop, putting their anger and argument aside.

"Lark," said Clay. "Did you come about the funeral?"

"It's in the morning," said Free, smiling gently at Lark.

"I did want to know that, but that's not why I came. I must speak to you about two men I caught in the pines this morning."

"What's that?" asked Clay in alarm.

"Were you hurt?" said Free.

Lark shook her head as she stepped into the shade of the shop. She quickly told her story with questions and exclamations from Free and Clay. "They're in jail waiting for you to press charges."

"I'll tend to it right away," said Clay. "I'll need you with me to identify the men."

Lark hesitated, then shrugged. She'd have to deal with Matron's anger if she was found out. "All right."

"How about a drink of cold well water first," said Free as he motioned to the windmill twirling in the breeze. Cold water flowed from a pipe into a big tank for the animals.

"That would be nice. Thank you." Lark smiled at Free, but suddenly felt too self-conscious to look at Clay again.

26

Clay filled a dipper with cold water and held it out to Lark. She took it thankfully and their hands brushed. A tingle went through Lark.

Clay noticed the sudden flush on Lark's cheeks and wondered about it. He wasn't a lady's man like his twenty-two-year-old brother Tristan was already and like his sixteen-year-old brother Miles was on his way to becoming, but he could recognize a blush.

Just then Tristan drove up in the buggy with Jennet and his two sisters Hannah, eighteen, and Evie, eleven. The other sister was married and lived in Grand Rapids.

Tristan leaped from the buggy and helped his mother down while Hannah and Evie climbed out unassisted.

Lark smiled at the girls and then at Jennet and Tristan. Lark knew Zoe Cheyney would give anything to be there right then. Zoe was madly in love with Tris Havlick, and he barely knew she existed.

Jennet slipped her arms around Lark and held her for a minute. At forty-one years old, Jennet was still slender. She had graying chestnut hair and wide blue eyes that didn't seem to miss anything. She and Lark were the same height. She held Lark from her. "I'm so sorry about Jig. I know how much you loved him. I pray God will fill your heart with peace and comfort."

"Thank you," whispered Lark. It had been years since she'd been hugged by any adult except Jig. It felt good to have Jennet hold her and speak comfort to her.

"Can you come in?" asked Jennet as she released Lark's hands.

"She's riding to town with me," said Clay. "Pa will explain what happened."

"You must come to dinner here tomorrow after the funeral," said Jennet. "I won't take no for an answer!"

"Now, Mother," said Clay with a grin. "Don't force Lark to do anything she doesn't want to do."

"No, that's fine," Lark said quickly. She had to grab the

opportunity to fulfill her promise to Jig. "I'd like to have dinner with you tomorrow."

"Good," said Jennet with a smile.

"We must be going," said Clay, cupping Lark's elbow with his hand.

His touch sent a shiver through her, but she didn't let it show. She climbed in the buggy and Clay sat beside her. They said their goodbyes and Clay flicked the reins. The buggy rolled easily along the dirt road and across the bridge to the rough corduroy, a road built of logs laying side by side across the road to keep it from becoming rutted. They passed Red Beaver's large farm, then reached the outskirts of Blue Creek. They passed the lumber mill, the train depot, and the livery before Clay headed down Main Street to the sheriff's office.

Lark gripped her hands tightly in her lap as a plan leaped into her mind. But could she voice it? "Clay," she said hesitantly. "Who will guard the pines now?"

"I'll find someone from the mill," he said as he stopped at the hitch-rail in front of the sheriff's office.

"I want the job," said Lark in a rush.

Clay cocked his dark brow. "You?"

"Yes! I've walked the trail with Jig and I know how to do the job." Lark bit her bottom lip. "And I'd like to live in the cabin."

Clay thought about her years in the asylum. If he had his way he'd put all the children in homes and do away with the asylum, but he knew that was impossible. "What of your job at the asylum?"

"I could go there every day after I walk the line," said Lark. Suddenly this was the most important thing in the world to her. She'd thought she'd never get to leave the asylum, but now she had a way out. "Please, Clay! I want the freedom to walk the woods and to live on my own. I know there's no reason you should give me, a woman and an orphan, such responsibility, but Jig trusted me, and I think you would too if you'd give yourself a chance."

"I don't know," said Clay, pushing his straw hat to the back of his head. He watched a horse and rider walk down the sawdust covered street. "I don't like the thought of you being in such danger."

"I know how to take care of myself."

"From your story of this morning's happenings, I can believe that. But why endanger yourself for my trees?"

Lark looked at him squarely. "They might be your trees, but they're our heritage for generations to come! We can't let anything happen to the pines!"

Clay laughed. "You sound like my mother." There was something about Lark that reminded him of his mother. Perhaps it was the stories Jennet had told of her involvement with the underground railroad and how she'd made him think of a gutsy young woman—something that Lark seemed to be. It was funny, but he'd never thought such things about Lark before. She did seem to have a certain gutsiness about her. Why hadn't he noticed it before? "I don't know, Lark. A woman all alone?"

"This is 1890, Clay Havlick, not the Dark Ages." Inside Lark was leaping with excitement, but on the outside she looked calm. "I want the job!"

Clay saw her determination and smiled as he nodded slightly. "I'll ask the hired girl to clean the cabin today," he said.

Lark's heart leaped. Clay had given her the job! "Jig wouldn't want someone else looking at his stuff. I'll clean it before nightfall." She took a deep breath. "Can I move in tomorrow?"

Clay shrugged. "Yes . . . yes, I suppose you can."

Lark laughed right out loud. "Do you know how wonderful it will be to have a place of my own?"

Clay smiled at her excitement. "I'm glad you don't have to live at the asylum any longer. But then you'd be moving out when you marry."

"I will probably never marry," she said stiffly.

"Some young man will come along and you'll change your mind."

Lark shook her head. She wondered how he could be so dense. "And how about you? Do you have a young woman friend?"

He thought of Veda Thorne. She'd stayed in the same hotel as he had during his business trip in Detroit and had ridden back on the train this morning with him. Her beauty and her courage to speak to him even though she'd said her father had forbidden her to had touched him. "I have decided to start seeing Veda Thorne."

Lark froze. Jig had been right! "Veda Thorne? But isn't she Willie Thorne's daughter?"

Clay frowned. He knew exactly what his parents would say when they learned he was taking Veda to dinner tonight. "What if she is?" he asked gruffly.

"Jig told me about Willie Thorne."

"Veda is different."

"She's a Thorne," said Lark. "She might be using you to get the pines."

A muscle jumped in Clay's jaw. "I see Jig has been talking to you. She would never destroy the pines. She loves them as much as my family does."

Lark bit back a groan. "You will be careful, won't you?"

"There's no need to be," Clay snapped.

Lark lifted her chin. "I'm sorry if I offended you, but I would hate to see the pines lumbered."

"So would I!" Clay stepped from the buggy and reached up to help Lark out. "We'd best tend to business. I'd appreciate it if you didn't say anything about me and . . . and . . . Veda Thorne."

"Who would I say it to? It's not my place, is it?" Lark bit her lip. She had made it her place with her promise to Jig!

After their business at the sheriff's office was finished, Clay drove Lark to the asylum. "See you in the morning at the funeral," he said stiffly.

She nodded slightly. "Thank you for the ride. I hope those men don't make more trouble for you."

"They won't, thanks to you." Clay tipped his hat and drove toward the empty warehouses. He felt a great urge to turn and look back to catch one more glimpse of Lark. He scowled and shook his head. She meant nothing to him, so why was he feeling a special warmth for her? It had to be because of his promise to Jig.

A picture of Veda Thorne with her mass of auburn hair, sweet smile, and tall, slender body flashed across his mind and he flushed with pleasure. He was glad thoughts of Veda pushed away thoughts of Lark.

Veda had acted as if she'd found him attractive—something no other woman had ever done. He'd been able to carry on a conversation with her—something else he'd never been able to do with a woman. She was Willie Thorne's daughter, but he liked her.

Clay reined in the team near the warehouses. He'd made a sound judgment in using his pines as collateral. As a boy he'd spent hours of pleasure running through the pines, knowing someday they'd be his. He and Tris had built a fort of pine boughs and played "war." Often Jig joined in. Clay chuckled, then grew serious as he thought of the time he'd found two baby bobcats in a den. They had tan hair dotted with lots of black spots. He'd known better than to stay near the den, but the kittens were so cute, he couldn't help himself.

He crouched down before the kittens and said softly, "I'd like to take you home." His sisters would love them.

At a sound on a tree branch above he looked up and his heart leaped to his throat. The mother bobcat stood on the branch and growled, ready to spring on him. He leaped back just as it landed a few feet from him. Immediately it sprang at him again. Sweat soaked his shirt as he jumped aside. He grabbed a big stick and held it as a weapon in front of him. His stomach knotted, and he prayed Jig would come to his rescue. But Jig didn't come. The bobcat sprang again. Clay leaped aside and jabbed at it with the stick. It growled, showing sharp teeth. Slowly he backed up, brandishing the stick in front of him. The bobcat tensed, but didn't follow him. Finally it turned and ran to the den.

Chills running up and down his back, Clay had gripped the stick tightly as he backed further away until he felt safe enough to turn and run back to Jig and Tris. He had spotted bobcat dens again, but had never stopped to watch the kittens. Years later Clay had told Jig and Tris about the close call, and they'd all had a good laugh.

The pines had brought adventure, danger, and enjoyment to his life. Now they were providing money for his business.

Grinning, Clay walked inside the first warehouse and his steps echoed in the empty building. The workmen could easily build several wagons at once in the huge buildings. During nice weather they'd leave the row of wide doors open to let in sunlight. He'd already talked to several men and had hired fifty to start to work the minute he had the business set up. He'd called it *Havlick's Wagon Works.*

Slowly he walked back to his buggy. Why was Pa being so stubborn about him starting his own business? He'd started to tell Pa about putting the pines up for collateral when Lark had interrupted them. He still had to face both Ma and Pa with the news. He wasn't looking forward to that at all.

Clay stood beside his buggy and looked at the long warehouses. He'd heard the stories about how Grandpa Roman Havlick had kept Great-grandpa Clay's money from Free when he needed it desperately to become a lumberman. Clay knew someday he'd inherit a fortune from Pa, but he couldn't wait for that day. He'd had to have money now for the wagon business. All he had was the ten sections of white pines and he'd never sell them, but they were collateral.

"I had to do it!" he cried, making his team bob their heads. Now he had plenty of money for Havlick's Wagon Works.

Clay drove to the bank and within a few minutes the paperwork was filed with them. He'd borrowed the money from a Detroit bank that had a branch in Blue Creek. He'd do his business from the Blue Creek bank from now on. He knew he'd be able to make the first large payment in three months without any trouble. He'd already ordered the lumber he'd need and had hired blacksmiths. Several of the men he'd hired didn't know wagon making, but he'd promised to teach them quickly. He'd offered them each $9.00 a week with a bonus at the end of the first three months if the wagons were completed on time. The men had been glad for the good pay.

At home again in Free's study Clay told his parents what he'd done.

Jennet jumped up from her chair, her blue eyes flashing fire. "How could you do that, Clay? Do you realize the jeopardy to the pines?"

Clay stiffened. "There's no jeopardy."

Free sighed heavily. "Clay, if you can't finish the wagons in time and don't get paid, you'll be in a financial bind. The bank could easily take the trees."

"Then sell them to the highest bidder!" cried Jennet. "Like Willie Thorne!"

"He's not interested in the trees," said Clay sharply.

"He'll do anything to get his hands on them!" snapped Free as he stabbed his fingers through his gray hair. "He could sabotage your operation just so he could take over the bank note."

Clay shook his head. "He's going to be too busy with his own business to worry about ours."

"What do you mean?" asked Jennet as she sank to her chair again.

"Since when do you know Thorne's business?" asked Free as he leaned back against his heavy walnut desk.

Veda had told him, but Clay didn't want to say that. "I heard he's opening a tavern in Blue Creek."

Jennet shot from her chair again. "A tavern? How dare he? Doesn't he know Blue Creek is a dry town?"

Free slammed his fist into his palm. "That man will do anything to create havoc!"

"I won't have him bringing liquor into our area," said Jennet.

Clay slipped quietly away. He knew his parents would immediately jump into action to stop Willie from opening his tavern. Maybe it would keep them occupied so he could go about his business without further objections.

CHAPTER

3

♦ In the middle of the afternoon Lark stood before Matron's desk with her chin high, her shoulders square, and her stomach fluttering nervously. "I would like the things that were left with me when I was brought here twenty-two years ago."

Matron scowled, but her hands lay still on her desk. "If you had anything, it was long gone before I came here."

Lark shook her head. "I know I have a box of photos and clothes. I want them."

Matron slowly stood and smoothed down her black wrapper. "You are getting high and mighty all at once, Lark Baritt. I could toss you out on your ear, you know."

Lark shook her head. "You can't. The board hired me to do the bookwork and to teach. You don't have the authority to fire me."

"But I can make life miserable for you," snapped Matron.

"I'm moving out tomorrow," said Lark. "I have a place of my own away from here."

Matron's eyes widened in surprise. "And good riddance, I say!"

Lark took one step forward. "Get my box of stuff or I shall bring Jennet Havlick in to help me get it from you."

Matron turned scarlet. "I did happen to run across a box that might be yours. I'll see that you get it."

"Right now," said Lark firmly. She was surprised at her courage.

Matron sniffed as she sailed past Lark to the door. "I'll be back with it, but don't expect much."

Lark waited until Matron was out of sight, then she sank weakly down on a highback chair that stood to the left of the large maple desk. Finally she was going to get to see her stuff!

Just then Zoe Cheyney slipped into the room. Her red hair was combed back neatly and held in place with a narrow ribbon. She was wearing the cream colored muslin dress she'd had since she was fifteen, and since she'd grown it was too tight across the bust. "Lark! Are you really leaving?" she whispered in alarm.

"Yes." Lark knew Zoe had listened at the door, something they'd both done many times in the past when they wanted to learn what was happening. Quickly she told Zoe about her plans. "I will move in the cabin tomorrow."

"That is so romantic, Lark! You'll be right close to the Havlicks." Zoe trembled. "You'll get to see Tris every single day, won't you?"

"I don't think so, Zoe."

"But you might! Oh, Lark, let me stay with you! Please!"

"You can visit and spend the night at times, but you can't move in with me, Zoe. I need this time alone. You understand, don't you?"

"Yes," whispered Zoe with tears in her large hazel eyes. "If I had a chance to get away from here in a place of my own, I'd do it as quick as a bunny."

Just then Lark heard voices. "Zoe, Matron's coming. Slip out quickly. She's bringing my box of things."

"Be sure to show me everything!" Zoe squeezed Lark's hand and left quietly.

Facing the door, Lark steeled herself for Matron's return. Soon she'd get to see her box of things. Soon she'd know something about her past, about the mother who'd died in childbirth and about the father who couldn't care for her.

Matron walked in empty handed and Lark's heart dropped to her feet.

"Just as I suspected," said Matron with a smug look on her face. "There is no such box! I thought I'd run across one that might've been yours, but I was wrong."

With a cry Lark ran out of Matron's office and back to the kitchen where she knew she'd find Maggie and Linda helping prepare supper. "Girls, come here," she said, motioning from the doorway.

"What's wrong, Miss Baritt?" asked Maggie.

"Did Matron beat you again?" asked Linda.

Lark gripped the girls by the arms. "I asked Matron about my box of stuff. First she said she had it, then she said she didn't."

"We have it," whispered Maggie.

Lark gasped.

"We saw Matron take it to the cellar just after dinner and we got it and took it upstairs," said Maggie.

"How do you know it's mine?" asked Lark weakly.

"We saw your name," said Linda. "Lark Baritt. Your parents were Matthew and Meriel Baritt."

Lark bit back a cry. "I want to see the box now."

"We can't leave the kitchen yet," said Maggie, "but we'll tell you where to find the box."

"It's hidden in a safe spot," said Linda.

"It's in the big linen closet on the top shelf way in the back," said Maggie. "It's about as big as a breadbox."

Lark ran down the hall to the stairs and up. Blood pounded in her ears as she reached the closet and slipped inside. No one was upstairs yet, so she had time to look in privacy.

She stood on the stepstool and reached to the back behind a pile of worn sheets, found the cardboard box, and pulled it out.

In her weakness she almost dropped it. She carried it to her room and sank to the edge of the bed with her box held tight against herself. Dare she open it and see who she was?

Shouts and laughter from the orphans drifted in through the open window. The box on her lap smelled and looked old. Slowly she opened it and looked inside. Her hands trembling, she lifted out a tiny dress and bonnet that once had been white but were now yellowed with age. Had she ever worn the dress and bonnet? She held the dress higher. A piece of paper fluttered to the floor. She picked it up and tried to read it, but her hand shook so badly she couldn't focus on the words. Finally she found her name: Lark Louise Baritt, born January 28, 1868. PARENTS: Matthew Quenten Baritt and Meriel Louise (Jakaway) Baritt of Big Pine.

Giant tears welled up in Lark's dark eyes. "Matthew and Meriel Baritt," she whispered around the lump in her throat. She lifted out faded photos and studied the faces of her parents. They looked very young but well dressed. She could see her own resemblance to her mother and even to her father. She read two letters that her mother had written to her father while he was lumbering in the Saginaw Bay area, then pressed the letters to her heart. After a long time she looked in the box, but it was empty. There was no money, just as Allie had predicted, and no mention of money.

"Why would Matron take my things?" whispered Lark, shaking her head. Oh, what did it matter now? She had them and that's all that mattered. To be safe she hid them in her drawer, carried the box down to the cellar, and left it where the girls had found it. Now she could go to Jig's cabin to clean and get it ready to move in to tomorrow.

Lark wiped away her tears, brushed her taffy brown hair, then retied the narrow blue ribbon. Life had suddenly become almost perfect. What could go wrong now?

Lark laughed as she walked out the front door of the asylum. This morning she'd felt lost and without hope, but suddenly she had a life to look forward to.

At Jig's cabin Lark stopped outside the open door. Clay was cleaning! He wore the same dark pants and plaid shirt that he'd had on earlier, only now he was dirty from cleaning. "Hello," said Lark with a breathless laugh.

Clay turned and smiled. "I thought I'd lend a hand."

Lark stepped inside and looked around in surprise. The windows sparkled, letting sunlight flow in. "It looks like you lent two hands! You've cleaned the windows, the stove, and swept down the walls! You're much too busy to do this! I planned to do it."

Clay shrugged. "I don't mind a bit. It makes me feel close to Jig."

Tears stung Lark's eyes and for a minute she couldn't speak. Just then she noticed a wooden box sitting on the table. It was about fourteen inches square and ten inches deep. It had her name on it. She touched it, then looked questioningly at Clay. "What's this?"

"I found it in that box over there." Lark saw Jig's special box that he kept closed and covered with a lap robe sitting with its lid open. She bit her lower lip.

"Jig left this for you," said Clay softly as he tapped the box.

Lark touched the latch on the box. "I don't think I can open it," she whispered. "Would you?"

A desire to comfort Lark rose inside Clay, surprising him. He pushed the feeling away and released the leather and wood latch and lifted the lid. Inside was a photo of Lark when she was about eight years old. With a laugh he lifted it out and handed it to her. "You'll like this."

Color washed over Lark's neck and face as she took the photo of the frightened little girl with skinny braids and a scratch across her cheek. She remembered Jig having the picture made when a traveling photographer came through town. For some reason it embarrassed her to have Clay see the picture. She laid it upside down on the freshly scrubbed table, then looked in the box herself. She lifted out a framed delicate, blue-green moth with touches of lavender and light yellow and white body. "I mounted and framed this for Jig when I was twelve," she whispered.

"It's a real work of art," said Clay in awe as he looked at the moth.

"Would you like it?" asked Lark.

Clay smiled at Lark, then once again gazed at the delicate moth. "I used to take moths home to Ma just because she found such pleasure in them. I'd forgotten about that until just now. I would like this. Thank you."

"Here's a note," said Lark, lifting it out of the box and opening it, then read it aloud. "My girl, Lark, I never had much, but what I do have I give to you. Take it and know that I love you as my own. I never told you I had a family back in Sweden. They could all be gone. I don't know. I want you to send the letter to them that I wrote. I could never do it. You do it for me, please."

"A family," said Clay. "We never knew."

Lark stopped reading and looked in the box for a letter and found the envelope addressed in ink with Jig's sprawl. She studied the strange words on the address, then handed it to Clay. She continued reading Jig's letter aloud. "I have money put away. Give $100 to the Blue Creek Orphan Asylum for taking care of you all these years when your Dad couldn't. The rest of the money is for you. Remember, God cares more for you than I could. Always keep Him first in your life. Love. Jig."

Giant tears welled up in Lark's eyes and slipped down her pale cheeks. "He left me his things, Clay. I never knew. Why would he do that?"

"He loved you," said Clay softly.

"But why? I'm nobody!"

"How can you say that? You're Lark Baritt!" Clay had always been loved and couldn't comprehend how Lark felt. He could see she didn't have the strength to rummage through the box more. "I'll find the money for you."

Lark sank to a chair and nodded, the note still in her hand.

Clay lifted out an envelope marked Orphan Asylum and another one marked Lark Baritt. He opened Lark's and counted $1500.00.

Lark helplessly shook her head. "I can't believe it," she said weakly. "That's a lot of money!"

"I can't believe Jig didn't put this in the bank in town," said Clay.

"I could buy a house or start a business," said Lark.

"You could," said Clay.

"I could buy a horse and buggy."

"You could use one of ours," said Clay.

"Oh, Jig! You've given me freedom," whispered Lark.

Clay looked in the box again and lifted out a heavy, awkward cap and ball pistol. His name was written on a paper around it. "Look what he gave me," said Clay as sudden tears blurred his vision. He could remember admiring the pistol from the time he was old enough to remember.

Lark looked in the box again while Clay studied the pistol. She lifted out Jig's tattered Bible, several rocks he'd found and thought were pretty, two books written in Swedish, two gold coins, a crystal paper weight, and a copper kaleidoscope she'd often looked through in years past. Jig had given her his treasures!

The next morning Lark stood in the white pines with the Havlicks and Jig's other friends while Pastor James said the last goodbyes before they lowered the wooden box into the ground. She stood aside from the family, but Tris caught her hand and tugged her close. She smiled thankfully.

Clay frowned slightly as he saw Tris and Lark look at each other. Would Tris try to make Lark another conquest? Right then Clay decided to warn Lark about Tris. He was quick to love and just as quick to leave.

Lark wiped away her tears and forced herself to stop crying as Pastor James walked to his buggy and drove away, leaving three men behind to cover the casket.

Jennet slipped her arm around Lark and said, "I'm glad

you're having dinner with us. We who've loved Jig need to be together."

Lark's heart warmed to the special motherly attention from Jennet. "I will never forget him! Did you know he left me his special things and money too?"

Jennet nodded. "Clay told me."

Lark shook her head. "I still can't believe he'd do that."

"He loved you very much," said Jennet softly.

Just then Hannah and Evie walked up. Jennet handed Lark over to them. "Take her home with you, girls, and see that she rests for a while before dinner."

Lark smiled at the girls. Hannah was eighteen and looked a lot like Jennet with her chestnut brown hair and wide blue eyes. Evie, eleven, had almost white hair and striking brown eyes.

"Jig was teaching me how to shoot," said Evie sadly as they walked across the field toward the farm. "I'll miss him a lot."

"Me too," said Lark.

Hannah looked wistfully behind her. "Lark, do you really know Red Beaver?"

Lark looked at Hannah in surprise. Hannah sounded like a girl in love. "Yes, I know him," said Lark. "Some of the orphan boys work on his farm." Red Beaver was a Patawatomi who owned the farm to the west of the Havlicks. He had been at the funeral. "He's a very nice man."

"Pa says Hannah can't talk to Red Beaver," said Evie as she skipped on ahead. She glanced back over her shoulder. "Pa says Hannah can't marry an Indian."

"Evie!" cried Hannah, flushing scarlet.

Evie ran on ahead, leaving Hannah and Lark to walk alone through the tall grass and wild flowers.

"Could you fall in love with an Indian, Lark?" asked Hannah in a low, tight voice.

Lark shrugged. "I never thought about it. Red Beaver's a fine man."

"Pa likes Red Beaver and admires him for being such a hard

worker, but he says no daughter of his can marry a Patawatomi. I don't think that's Christian, do you?"

"You can't disobey your pa," said Lark.

"I'm full grown, Lark. My sister was married at my age. So was Ma!"

Lark watched a bee buzz around a patch of daisies. "Hannah, you can't want to marry Red Beaver or any man if you don't love him."

Hannah sighed heavily. "I'll tell you a secret," she said quietly. "I do love him. I can't look at the boys who come to call on me because my heart is full of love for Red Beaver."

"I don't know what to say," said Lark. "I didn't know you even knew Red Beaver enough to love him."

"We've talked together many times."

"How does he feel?"

"I think he cares for me," whispered Hannah.

Lark looked helplessly at Hannah. "You do have a problem, don't you?"

"I told Jig how I feel, and he said to pray for Pa and for Red Beaver. Jig said God would help me know what to do."

"He will," said Lark.

"Do you love a man, Lark?"

She thought of John Epson. "No." Clay flashed across her mind and she flushed hotly. Why think of him? She wasn't good enough for Clay Havlick or Tris or even sixteen-year-old Miles. If she ever married, it would be to a poor widower with kids who needed tending.

"Red Beaver's a Christian," said Hannah as they walked around a large hickory nut tree.

"I know."

"His ma isn't. Silent Waters. Do you know her?"

Lark nodded and forced back a shiver. Silent Waters was usually very quiet and seemed full of anger.

"She scares me," said Hannah. "She hates me."

"I don't think she likes anyone except Red Beaver."

"Maybe. But she hates me because I'm a Havlick." Hannah

fingered the cameo at her throat. "I don't understand why she hates my family. It doesn't make sense. Do you think?"

"No. Jig said your pa lumbered out all the trees around this area except the sections he saved. Maybe Silent Waters lived in the woods he lumbered out."

"Maybe," said Hannah. "Between Silent Waters and Pa I don't stand a chance with Red Beaver." Hannah stopped and turned to Lark. "I feel him watching me at church and when he comes to bring grain. Every time we talk it feels like my heart will float right out of my body."

Lark laughed. "You sound just like my friend Zoe."

"I've met Zoe at the asylum. I like her." Hannah picked a flower and held it between two fingers. "Is Zoe in love?"

"Yes." Lark knew she couldn't tell Hannah that Zoe was in love with Tris. "I'm thirsty, Hannah. Could we get a drink from the well?" Lark really wasn't thirsty, but she wanted to get Hannah's mind off Zoe before she asked who Zoe loved.

Several minutes later Lark sat between Hannah and Evie at the large cherry table in the Havlicks' dining room. Clay, Tris, and Miles sat across from them with Jennet at the foot and Free at the head. As Free asked a blessing on the food, the aroma of fried chicken, potatoes, green beans, and freshly baked bread made Lark's stomach cramp with hunger. She'd barely eaten in the past two days.

As they passed the food and talked, Lark glanced around the large room. A cherry buffet with chinaware stood between tall windows covered with white curtains. A cherry sideboard was on one wall and a matching corner hutch filled with fancy serving dishes stood in the corner near the kitchen door. Lark liked the elegant hominess of the room. She knew she'd never have a home like this.

Lark found it easier to talk during dinner than she'd thought it would be. She'd had no experience with small talk during a meal. At the asylum they were forced to eat in silence, but she'd carefully studied deportment so she'd know what to do if she was ever invited out. She knew the Havlicks were trying hard to make her feel at ease.

During dessert of apple pie and slices of cheddar cheese, Free said, "Lark, I'm pleased you want to guard the pines, but it's too dangerous for you."

Lark stiffened. Would he convince Clay not to hire her after all? "I know it can be dangerous, sir, but I've been doing it a long time."

"And she has angels watching over her," said Evie with a grin at Lark.

Free smiled and nodded. "That's right. I guess I should keep my objections to myself."

"When do you move in to the cabin, Lark?" asked Jennet.

"Today," said Lark.

"I trust Anna Pike didn't cause trouble for you," said Clay. He had heard things about the matron that he didn't care about.

Lark fingered her napkin. "Matron wasn't happy at all, but she didn't say much."

"I know you care for the pines as much as we do," said Jennet as she cut a small bite of pie. "I want you to look on us as family now, Lark. Come here any time you want."

Lark smiled at Jennet. Had her mother, Meriel Baritt, been like Jennet?

"Any time," said Free, smiling.

"Thank you." Lark glanced at Clay, then quickly away. What would the family say if they knew of her promise to Jig?

CHAPTER

4

♦ Lark set her box of clothes and things on the bunk, then looked around the clean cabin with a pleased look on her face.

"Are you sure you'll be okay here alone?" asked Clay from the doorway. He'd driven her from the asylum to the cabin so she could be settled in before nightfall.

Lark turned with a smile. "I know I'll be all right! It'll be different sleeping here all alone, but I'll like it. I have never, ever been by myself!"

"You might want to get leather clothes like Jig wore to protect your skin from the briars," said Clay.

"I'll see about it right away. I know Red Beaver tans hides, so I'll check with him tomorrow."

"Good. And I'm going to get you a dog."

Lark beamed. A dog! "That's not necessary, Clay."

"I'd feel a whole lot better if you weren't entirely alone."

"Thanks. I've always wanted a dog."

"Good. Then that's settled." As though he were checking off items on a list, Clay asked, "Did you put the money in the bank?"

"Yes," Lark said with a slight smile. "And I mailed Jig's letter."

46

Clay nodded. "I must be going," he said stiffly.

"Are you taking Veda Thorne to dinner again?"

"Yes." Clay smiled, remembering the good time he'd had with her the night before. They'd talked about many things and he'd enjoyed their conversation. She was a woman of intelligence as well as a real beauty.

Lark noticed his smile and turned abruptly away. She had to do something to stop Clay from falling in love with Veda Thorne, but she didn't know what. Could she get him to ask *her* to dinner? She rolled her eyes. *That's a joke,* she thought. At the asylum she hadn't learned how to attract a man even if she wanted to. Finally she turned back to Clay. "Tomorrow after I teach my afternoon class I'll probably see Red Beaver about the leather."

"Don't go alone. Take one of my sisters with you," said Clay.

"Maybe Hannah?" asked Lark, studying Clay for any reaction.

Clay shrugged. "Probably not Hannah. But Evie would enjoy the trip."

"Do you think Red Beaver is beneath you socially?"

"No. But for some reason Pa does, I'm sorry to say."

"That doesn't sound like your pa, does it?"

"No. No, it doesn't. I've questioned him about Red Beaver, but he won't give me a straight answer. I like Red Beaver. He's a fine Christian and he works hard and stays away from strong drink."

"Speaking of strong drink, I heard Willie Thorne is opening a tavern in Blue Creek," said Lark.

"I hope he doesn't, but I heard the same."

"I belong to the Temperance League," said Lark. "I know our group will try to stop Thorne at any cost."

"Ma said the same thing."

"Does Veda Thorne belong to the Temperance League?"

Clay flushed. He hadn't learned how Veda felt about drinking, but she didn't seem to think Willie was doing anything wrong by opening a tavern. "I don't believe she does," said

Clay stiffly. He didn't want to talk about Veda to Lark. They were two such different women but, each in her own way, both were interesting.

After Clay left, Lark walked around the cabin that had become very quiet. Even the crickets, the frogs in the creek, and the night birds were momentarily silent. In the distance Lark heard a dog. Once wolves had been in the area as well as wildcats. There were still bears and a few other dangerous wild animals, but nothing like there had been years ago. Jig had said there were even fewer rattlesnakes. A big one lived near the bog, and it frightened her every time she saw or heard it.

Lark opened the door and looked up at the twinkling stars and the sliver of moon. All the night sounds from the woods were like a special orchestra. She smiled, feeling at great peace. This was her first night ever of not having to go to bed at a set time with sounds of children shouting or laughing. She didn't have to listen fearfully for Matron's footsteps or think Matron would punish her for something she'd done by accident or neglected doing, or because she blamed her for something she didn't do.

"Heavenly Father, thank you for this wonderful haven," Lark said, smiling up at the sky.

She closed the door and lit the kerosene lamp. The smell of kerosene and smoke waved out, then disappeared. She couldn't leave the door or windows open or moths would swarm in. She sat at the table and opened her Bible to read in Ephesians. Jig had shown her how to study her Bible. She knew her faith grew when she studied and heard God's Word. She also knew she could not survive without faith and trust in God. She thought of her blessings and smiled. She knew she'd once had parents who had loved her. She'd had Jig who had loved her and taught her many, many things. Now she had a home she didn't have to share with anyone unless she chose to. She had money in the bank and the guard job she loved.

When she was too tired to keep her eyes open, she crawled into the bunk, between the clean sheets Jennet had given her.

It felt strange not to have Zoe beside her, whispering to her as long as she could stay awake. Usually they both fell asleep within minutes of going to bed, dead tired because of their long work day.

Lark turned on her side and smiled in the dark. In the morning she'd walk the pines as the hired guard. She would be paid once a month and would live in the cabin free. Jennet had said that every day she'd send fresh fruit, vegetables, and meat over to Lark. "This will be a good life," said Lark. Her voice sounded loud in the great silence.

The next morning just after dawn Lark walked out of the cabin with her revolver in a holster and her canteen strapped to her belt, her cudgel in her hand, and wearing her boots and leggings. One of Jig's old hats sat on her head. At the thought of Jig the deep ache of missing him surfaced and tears filled her eyes. She brushed them away as her lips quivered with sobs.

She glanced up toward heaven and whispered, "Heavenly Father, thank you for your comfort! I'm glad I'm your child and that you love me. You're God Almighty, yet you know all about me. You are the God of the universe, yet you watch over me. Thank You, Father! I love you! Thank you for your protection. Please take care of the Havlicks today, and help Clay to see the truth about Veda Thorne. Keep these pines safe. In Jesus' name. Amen!"

Lark's heart felt light as she walked away from the cabin toward the trail in the pines. She swung the cudgel high in the air, then caught it. It had taken her a lot of practice to use a cudgel as a weapon, but with Jig's help she'd learned.

As Lark walked along the pine needle covered path, birds twittered in the trees and a crow cawed. Frogs and peepers blended with the sounds of small animals running under the thick carpet of needles.

Lark walked up the long hill and through the briars, using the cudgel to hold them back until she had passed through. The peaceful river was flowing down below. In the distance she could see a raft floating down stream. She looked up ahead to the spot where the tree poachers had waylaid her and her nerves tightened. Was someone hiding behind the giant up-rooted tree? She walked past it without a mishap, then relaxed slightly as she walked up to the northernmost tip, then on to the cutacross.

Just then some sound or smell sent a chill down Lark's spine. She slowed her steps on the narrow path and listened intently without appearing to do so. Jig had always said to act natural in case anyone was watching. She couldn't allow her actions to give away her sudden awareness of danger.

The birds were quiet and a squirrel deeper in the woods scolded loudly. Lark tightened her hand around the cudgel and rubbed her arm over the butt of her revolver. The feel of it reassured her and she walked just a little faster.

Suddenly a bear cub walked out on the path ahead of Lark. She stopped short, blood roaring in her ears. She knew the cub's mother was nearby. Lark turned slowly, studying the un-derbrush, the bushes, and the trunks of the trees. The sow could easily be hidden from view by the trunk of a pine. The cub stood on its hind legs and batted the air, then sniffed as if it had caught Lark's scent.

Lark took a deep breath as she silently prayed for protection and a way out of the situation. Should she leave the trail and try to walk around the cub? Lark looked across the trail to the swamp. Jig had warned her many times never to walk in that part of the swamp no matter what the time of year because she'd sink right down in it never to be seen again. He'd watched a deer disappear before his eyes. No, she couldn't take that way out.

Just then Lark heard a movement behind her. The hairs on the back of her neck stood on end. Her calico dress felt as hot as a wool coat. Slowly she glanced over her shoulder. Shivers shot up and down her spine and fear pricked her scalp. A mas-sive black bear stood on the trail on all fours! If it weren't for the cub, Lark knew she could get away without any problem.

Black bears usually left humans alone, but they were fearless when protecting their young.

Lark looked to her left and knew she couldn't walk into the swamp, nor would the bears. Lark looked to her right. She could walk off the trail to go around the cub, but to get back she'd have to fight her way through masses of wild roses that stood ten feet high and several feet thick.

The sow roared and reared up on its hind legs. Sweat soaked Lark's skin. The bear stood almost six feet tall. It looked around, then dropped to all fours and ambled along the trail toward Lark, sniffing with a snout that resembled a pig's.

Lark frantically eased her way toward the cub who was eating grubs from under a rotted log beside the trail. The cub stood half on the trail and half off. Maybe she could get around it and run like lightning away from the bears.

"Father, thank you for your help," Lark whispered as she drew closer and closer to the cub. She glanced back and could almost feel the sow's breath on her. She knew that was her imagination. She also knew that if she started running the sow could easily overtake her. Black bear could run fast and they also could climb trees.

The cub squealed in pain. The sow roared. Lark's heart stopped, then pounded so hard she could barely breathe. Her legs felt like two stumps held fast in the ground.

The sow roared again and ran awkwardly toward Lark. Lark leaped forward, startling the cub. She ran at a dead run, brushing past the cub. The sow roared fiercely, but Lark willed herself to keep her eyes on the trail ahead. She dared not stumble and fall or the sow would be on her in a flash and tear her to pieces.

Suddenly a shot rang out, missing Lark's ear by a hair's breath. Her cudgel gripped in her hand, she dropped to the ground, playing dead until she could analyze the situation. Dust tickled her nose and she held her breath to keep from sneezing. Her canteen felt like a hard lump under her. She heard men's voices, but she didn't twitch a muscle. An ant crawled over her cheek, tickling it, but she forced herself to ignore it.

"You got her, Bub," a man said gruffly.

"Or she's playin' possum," said Bub. "Go check, Dicky."

"Not me," said Dicky. "I heard how quick she is with that club of hers."

Lark's stomach tightened and her mouth felt cotton dry. She wanted to leap up, but she knew if she moved a hair the men would shoot her dead. Silently she cried out for God's help.

"Take a rock and bash in her skull," said Bub. "We don't dare shoot again for fear somebody might hear and check it out."

Bile rose in Lark's mouth and she almost gagged. She had to make a move. She heard footsteps coming toward her. Could she spring up, disarm the man, then move quickly enough to use him as a shield against the other man's bullet?

Further up the trail Clay Havlick crept forward. He'd heard the shot and wanted to make sure Lark was safe. He'd decided to walk with her on her first day, but she'd already left when he'd arrived at the cabin. Up ahead he could see two men and Lark face down on the trail. Shivers ran down Clay's spine. Was Lark dead? Why had he agreed to let her guard the pines? Why hadn't he brought his gun?

One of the men stepped closer to Lark, a large rock in his hand. Clay's heart caught in his throat. Silently he prayed for wisdom in dealing with the frightening situation. He knew he couldn't wait a second longer. In a loud, commanding voice he cried, "Drop your weapons and get your hands up before I shoot you both!"

Lark's heart leaped at the sound of Clay's voice. She peeked through her thick lashes at the boots a short way away. She saw the boots turn and she sprang to her feet. With a quick glance she saw Clay was not armed and that the men knew it now. Lark struck the man near her with her cudgel, dropping him to the ground in a heap, then she threw the cudgel at the other man, striking his arm and sending the gun flying from his grasp.

Clay sprang forward and scooped up the gun, then aimed it at the man still standing. "Are you all right, Lark?"

"Yes." Lark felt tears rising and she forced them back.

Clay smiled shakily. His relief was so great that she was unharmed, he couldn't speak for a while. Finally he ordered, "You men walk ahead of me. Lark, you keep your gun ready in case there's a third one waiting."

Lark nodded grimly.

Several minutes later they came across two horses tied to a bush. There wasn't a sign of an axe or a crosscut. Lark frowned. "They didn't come to steal the timber," she said, suddenly shivering.

Clay jabbed one of his prisoners with his gun barrel. "What brought you fellows out here to the woods this morning?"

"Sight seein'," snapped Dicky.

"We came to take care of her," said Bub gruffly, motioning to Lark.

Lark fell back a step. "Me? Why?"

Clay's heart almost stopped. Fear stung his skin. He had sent Lark into danger! "Why do you want her dead?" asked Clay harshly.

"We don't," snapped Dicky. "We got hired to do a job."

"Shut up!" snarled Bub.

"Keep talking!" commanded Clay. "Who hired you and why?"

Lark holstered her revolver and lifted her cudgel high. "I want answers now before I use this to break some bones."

Dicky rubbed the base of his skull and Bub rubbed his arm where she'd already hit him.

"A man at the mill asked us if we wanted some extra money. We said yes and he told us to get rid of the guard," said Dicky in a defeated voice.

"What man?" snapped Clay.

"We never saw him before," said Bub. "And we didn't get his name."

"Describe him," said Lark.

Bub shrugged. "Ordinary lookin'."

Lark swung her cudgel and the men cried out, but couldn't give any more information.

"You spread the word that I'm guarding the pines and that I'm not easy to kill," said Lark grimly. "And I won't let anyone steal a single tree!"

Clay looked at Lark in admiration. She was full of a fire he hadn't noticed before. He wouldn't be able to convince her to quit the job and go back to the asylum, but when the time was right, he'd try.

Later Clay rode one horse while the two men rode double on the other. He had left Lark to finish walking the line so she could get to her other job at the asylum. Once in Blue Creek he took the men to the sheriff, then checked at the mill for someone who might've seen Dicky and Bub with a man. Nobody knew anything.

Clay walked away from the mill in defeat. He glanced toward the asylum, then headed for the warehouse. Today the lumber and tools he'd need for building the wagons were coming by train. The men were already on hand to start to work.

Later in the day Lark forced away the dangers of the morning, changed her clothes, and walked to the Havlicks to get someone to go with her to see Red Beaver. The hot sun burned through her bonnet. A grasshopper landed on her arm, then jumped off onto a tall weed.

As Lark reached the Havlick yard, Tris stepped out of the shop and ran to meet her. He wore brown pants, brown suspenders, and a tan shirt without a collar. A straw hat covered his dark hair. Lark smiled as she thought what Zoe's reaction would be if she were there.

Tris tipped his hat and smiled. "Good afternoon, Lark. Clay said you'd be coming." Tris sobered. "He told us about this morning. I wish I could've been there!"

"You like excitement, don't you?" Lark laughed, then glanced around. "Is Clay here?"

"No. He had urgent business." Tris lowered his voice. "I

happen to know it has something to do with a woman named Veda."

Lark gripped her handbag tighter. "Doesn't it bother you for him to be seeing a Thorne?"

Tris shrugged. "Some. But he thinks Veda is prime, so how can I object?"

Lark let the subject drop, but she tried again to think of a way to keep Clay from continuing to see Veda.

Tris led Lark toward the barn where the buggy was already hitched to two matching sorrel geldings. "Evie," called Tris. "Lark's here and ready to go. Evie wants to get buckskin breeches and shirt too. She thinks she'll get to guard with you like she did at times with Jig."

"But of course she can!" Lark nodded, pleased to think she could teach Evie what Jig had taught her.

Her flowered skirt flipping around her stocking covered legs, Evie ran to Lark and caught her hand. "I'm glad you're taking me with you! Hannah wanted to go too, but Pa said she couldn't."

Tris tapped Evie on the head. "Don't tell all of our secrets, Evie."

Evie tossed her head and her white-blonde braids danced around her thin shoulders. "I never tell secrets!" She climbed in the buggy and smoothed her skirt over her knees, then impatiently rubbed at her puffed sleeves. "I just might get two buckskin suits! Pa said he used to dress that way because Great-grandpa Clay did when he was a fur trader. I wish I was a fur trader."

Tris helped Lark in, then started to climb up beside her.

"You can't come with us, Tris," said Evie sharply.

"Don't be obnoxious," snapped Tris as he settled in place and picked up the reins.

Her lower lip out in a pout, Evie turned to Lark. "Tell him to stay home."

"It's all right if he goes with us," said Lark, patting Evie's hand.

Evie shook her head hard. "He'll start making eyes at you and sweet talking you like he does all the girls, then you'll forget I'm even here."

Flushing, Tris jabbed Evie. "Stop that!"

Lark laughed softly. "Evie, I know what Tris is like. You don't have to be concerned about him sweet talking me. I won't let him. I don't like that kind of thing."

"You don't?" asked Evie in relief.

"You don't?" asked Tris in surprise. "But all girls do!"

"Not us," said Evie, taking Lark's hand. "We don't like sweet talk."

"We like straight arrow men," said Lark. "Men who don't flirt. Men who love from the heart in deed as well as in word."

"Like Pa," said Evie.

His face red, Tris jumped from the buggy with a self-conscious laugh. "I won't go with you. I'm just not straight arrow enough."

"You are in your heart," said Lark softly, looking deep into Tris's eyes.

"Thank you," whispered Tris, touched more than he thought possible.

He stepped back and waved them on. Lark flicked the reins and urged the horses over the dirt road that led to the corduroy. A short time later she drove up the long lane to Red Beaver's farmyard.

Cattle grazed in a field to the north of two large red barns and sheep grazed in a pasture to the west. Turkeys, chickens, ducks, and geese walked noisily around the yard. A short white picket fence circled the comfortable looking, well-kept white farm house. Several giant oaks shaded the yard.

As Lark stepped from the buggy, Red Beaver walked from the nearest barn. He was dressed like a white man except for a rolled red and gray scarf around his forehead to hold back his straight, shoulder-length hair. He was about Clay's age, but had a medium build where Clay was tall. Lark had heard Red

Beaver was part Patawatomi and part white, what most people called a *half-breed.*

Evie jumped down beside Lark. "Hello, Red Beaver."

Red Beaver smiled. "Hello, Evie. Hi, Lark. What brings the two of you to my place?"

"We came to get tanned hides for clothing to wear in the woods," said Lark.

"I have plenty of hides," said Red Beaver. "My mother, Silent Waters, could sew your clothes if you want. She is good with a needle and very quick." He named the price and Lark quickly agreed.

They walked to the house with Evie chattering happily beside them. A turkey gobbled and a donkey brayed. Flies buzzed around a bucket of slop near the back door. Red Beaver shooed away the flies and quickly opened the door, let Lark and Evie walk in, then he followed.

With Evie close at her side Lark stopped just inside the kitchen door beside a tall white cupboard that held white dishes. A tea kettle was boiling on the cookstove, sending steam whistling out. Silent Waters sat at the round oak table, a cup in her hand. She was slender, attractive, and dressed in white woman's calico with a rolled scarf around her forehead to hold back her long black hair. She glanced at Lark and Evie, then quickly down at her cup.

Red Beaver rested his hand lightly on Silent Waters' shoulder. They both had the same high cheekbones, wide foreheads, and deep brown eyes. Red Beaver's hair had a red cast to it while Silent Waters' was so black it almost looked blue. "Mother, this is Evie and Lark. I said you would sew leather breeches and shirts for them."

"I will," said Silent Waters with a curt nod.

"Thank you," said Lark, smiling. She'd seen Silent Waters in town, but had never spoken to her before. She had heard the gossip about her being a white man's squaw and Red Beaver their child. She was a woman who kept to herself.

"I'll go back to work while you women discuss the clothing," said Red Beaver. He squeezed his mother's shoulder, smiled at Evie, and walked out.

Lark felt at a loss for words as Silent Waters sipped from her cup. Should they sit down or remain standing?

"I want to look like a fur trader just like my great-grandpa," Evie said excitedly as she walked to the table to stand across from Silent Waters.

Lark stepped to Evie's side and slipped her arm around her. Silent Waters pushed herself up, eyeing Evie, then Lark.

"Your son said you are quick with the needle," Lark said when she couldn't think of anything else to say.

"Can you make me look like a fur trader?" asked Evie.

Silent Waters carried her cup to the dishpan at the back of the stove, dipped it in the soapy water, then faced Lark and Evie. Her eyes narrowed as she studied Evie. "Where have I seen you before?"

"I guess in town," said Evie, stepping closer to Lark.

"Where did your great-grandfather live?" asked Silent Waters sharply.

"All over lower Michigan, but his home was south of Grand Rapids," said Evie.

"He died years ago," said Lark. "You wouldn't know him."

Silent Waters flashed an impatient look at Lark. "Are you her mother?"

Lark shook her head as a shiver ran down her spine. The look on Silent Waters' face and the hatred in her eyes made her want to run to the buggy and drive quickly back to the Havlicks. Did Silent Waters hate all white people? Lark forced herself to say, "I'm Lark Baritt from the Orphan Asylum."

Silent Waters glared at Lark. "*You* I have seen in the pines where my grandfather's people once lived. You were with the old woodsman, Jig."

"I didn't know anyone ever lived in those woods," said Evie.

Silent Waters drew herself up haughtily. "We lived there

from the beginning of time. But the white man stole it from us."

"We didn't steal anything," said Evie sharply. "My great-grandfather bought it."

"And who is your great-grandfather?" asked Silent Waters sharply.

"Clay Havlick," said Evie, smiling proudly. "My big brother was named after him."

Silent Waters' face darkened with rage. "You leave my house now! I will not sew for a Havlick! Havlicks are evil!"

Lark gasped in surprise.

"Havlicks are not evil!" cried Evie, shaking her head hard.

"Evil! Wicked!" snapped Silent Waters. She shook her finger at Evie. "Get out of my house and never step foot in here again!"

Evie burst into tears and ran from the house.

Lark started to follow her, then whipped back around. "How could you hurt her? She hasn't done anything to you!"

"She's a Havlick!" spat out Silent Waters.

"She's an innocent child!"

"She's a Havlick!"

"But they're respected people in the community. They wouldn't harm anyone."

Silent Waters doubled her fists at her sides. Her breast rose and fell. "Freeman Havlick ruined my man! Freeman Havlick broke up my home!"

Lark stared at Silent Waters in shock. Free was never cruel. "What are you talking about?" asked Lark weakly.

"My man, Willie Thorne!"

Lark bit back a cry of surprise.

"Willie Thorne is father to Red Beaver, but Willie walked away from us and married a white woman to be part of the social community. He wanted to compete with Freeman Havlick!" Silent Waters spit the words out as if they'd been locked inside her for a long time.

Lark's head spun with what she'd learned. Did Free know

Red Beaver was Willie's son? Was that why he kept Hannah from Red Beaver?

Silent Waters jerked open the door. "Get out and don't set foot inside my house again!"

Trembling, Lark walked past Silent Waters, then ran to the buggy. She wanted to leave as quickly as possible. She stopped short. Evie wasn't in the buggy! Did Red Beaver have the same anger as his mother, and had he taken it out on Evie? Lark cupped her hands around her mouth and called, "Evie! Where are you?"

With a laugh, Evie stepped from the barn with Red Beaver beside her.

Lark ran to her and caught her hand in a tight grip. "Why didn't you go to the buggy?"

"She wanted to see the donkey," said Red Beaver. "She is safe with me."

Lark relaxed. She should've realized Red Beaver wouldn't harm anyone, not even a Havlick.

"You're my friend, aren't you, Red Beaver?" said Evie.

Red Beaver pulled a beaded band from his pocket and tied it around Evie's forehead. "We're friends forever. This will prove it to everyone."

"Thank you," said Evie in awe.

"If you ever need me, I'll come," said Red Beaver as if he were swearing a pact with Evie.

Evie pulled a pink ribbon off the tip of her braid and tied it around Red Beaver's wrist. "We are friends forever! If you ever need me, I'll come," she said as seriously as he had.

Lark smiled. Would Freeman Havlick object to the pact between Willie Thorne's son and his little daughter?

CHAPTER

5

♦ Late in June on a Wednesday after Lark finished teaching deportment, she walked to the only dress shop in Blue Creek. Sally Smith, a girl her age who Lark had seen in church, was the clerk. Lark knew she could trust Sally to help her find what she needed. She pushed open the door and the bell tinkled. The store smelled like new fabric and wild roses.

"Hello, Sally," said Lark with a hesitant smile. She'd never in her life bought a dress already made.

"Lark!" Sally was short and plump with a wide nose and mouth. She was kind to everyone and always thought the best of others. "What brings you in? Not that I'm not glad to see you! It's just you've never been here before."

Lark laughed. "I came to buy a nice dress."

"That's wonderful! What kind of dress?" Sally waved her hand around at the different displays. "Do you see anything that interests you?" Sally's voice dropped to a whisper. "How much do you want to spend?"

"I really don't know. You show me what the latest fashion is," said Lark. "I want to look like Hannah Havlick does when she's dressed up."

Sally showed Lark several ready made dresses, shirtwaists,

and skirts. Finally Lark chose a puffed-sleeved shirtwaist of medium green and white print with a black background and a black silk moire skirt lined with silk-finished taffeta and interlined throughout with canvas and extra fine velvet binding. Sally tied a hip-pad bustle on Lark, then helped her on with the waist and skirt. Lark marveled at the way the skirt hung straight down in front and swept wide in back. She stared at the puffed sleeves, the high collar, and the bustle.

"It looks so different from my old limp calico!" whispered Lark, hardly believing she was the attractive woman in the looking glass.

"The skirt has a full four-and-a-half yard sweep. It looks handsome on you, especially with that waist." Sally handed Lark a pair of fine kid shoes. "These will be perfect with it."

Lark pulled off her high top shoes and slipped on the others. How dainty her feet looked peeking from beneath the skirt!

Sally swept Lark's hair up and pinned it on top of her head. "See how wonderful you look? You're gorgeous!"

Lark wished it were so. "I'm as plain as a post, and we both know it, Sally. But these clothes do help."

"Here's a hat that would be perfect on you." Sally held up a small, medium green hat with three black feathers.

Lark tried it on, then gasped. She didn't look like Lark Baritt, the orphan! She looked as if she'd come from the Havlick's household. She pinned the hat in place and turned to Sally with a laugh. "I'll take it. I'll take the skirt and the waist and the shoes and the hat. And even the hip-pad bustle!" Lark patted her flushed cheeks. "And I'll leave them on and wear them home."

Sally laughed. "Good for you! You'll turn heads just like Hannah Havlick does."

Lark flushed with pleasure. "I don't know about that, but I do feel elegant." She thought of the money in her handbag and laughed breathlessly at her daring decision. "Sally, I want some other things too."

Lark bought a small looking glass, two fancy combs for her

hair, stockings, a flowered nightgown with a matching robe—the first new nightgown and robe she'd ever owned, a plain white shirtwaist, and a dark blue skirt. Sally showed her a variety of underclothing and she added some to her pile.

"That will be $22.50," said Sally.

Lark pressed her hand to her racing heart. She'd never spent that much money in her entire life.

"If you want to put something back, you may," said Sally softly.

"No. I can pay for it." Lark pulled out some of the money Jig had given her. How she longed to show him what she'd bought! Would he think she looked pretty all dressed up?

Lark handed the money to Sally, then silently watched as she wrapped the selections in paper and tied them securely. Lark considered throwing away her old dress, then decided to use it for a rag. She chuckled. A few days ago she had about one dollar to her name, now she was rich enough to buy ready made clothes.

A few minutes later Lark walked outdoors, the bundle in her arms and her head held high. Just then Clay Havlick left the bank and they almost collided. He tipped his straw hat and smiled, then his mouth dropped open. "Lark?"

She laughed breathlessly. "It's me, Clay."

"You look fantastic!" He couldn't believe this was the same Lark Baritt.

"Thank you." Lark flushed with pleasure. She was glad he'd seen her. It was as much a shock to him as it had been to her.

"Forgive my rude stare, but I can't get over it. I don't think I can let you guard the pines after seeing you like this."

Lark frowned. "I'm still the same woman, Clay Havlick! Clothes don't change who or what I am!"

"No . . . no, I realize that. I'm just . . . well . . . taken back." Clay ran a finger under his white collar, then checked to see that his dark blue plaid suit coat was buttoned.

"I'd better be going," said Lark, but she didn't move.

"Do you know Abe Nester?"

"Yes. His farm is near Red Beaver's." Lark considered telling Clay what had happened to them at Red Beaver's farm, then dismissed the thought.

"He has a Dalmatian for sale. I thought you might like him. He's a beautiful dog."

Lark had always wanted a big spotted Dalmatian. "I'll check into it."

"We could both go right now," said Clay. "My buggy's there." He motioned to the buggy and the gray mares hitched to it.

Lark hesitated only a fraction of a minute. "Let's go."

Clay took Lark's bundle and stuck it under the seat, then handed her in. She seemed small and frail and feminine. When he walked around the buggy and climbed into the driver's seat, she sat stiffly beside him, her hands clasped in her lap over her handbag. The canvas top of the buggy blocked the sun from her. Clay drove the team down Main Street, over the bridge, and onto the corduroy that led past Nester's farm.

For once Clay was at a loss for words with Lark. She seemed like an elegant, attractive stranger, not the little ragged orphan who'd hung around Jig. Lark peeked under dark lashes at Clay. She couldn't understand why he was suddenly so quiet.

She looked out at the farmland they passed that once had been the growing place of giant white pines. Jig had told her that before the lumbering began the entire area had been covered with trees. Off in the distance she could see a section of small pines about thirty years old. Jig had said it took eighty years for a pine to grow enough to be harvested for lumber.

Clay turned into Abe Nester's drive and stopped outside the fence near the barn. Nester walked out of his barn, wrapping his big, work-roughened hands around his wide blue suspenders. "How do, Clay. And who's the fine lady with you? A stranger in these parts?"

Lark laughed. "It's me, Lark Baritt. You know me."

Nester's eyes almost popped out of his head. "Well, I'll be dad-blasted! You clean up real good."

"Thank you," said Lark. She sat still in the buggy until Clay held up his hand to help her out. She stepped to the ground and stood with Clay. She thought they looked like they'd both just stepped from a catalog.

"We came for a Dalmatian for Lark," said Clay. He explained that Lark had taken over Jig's job as guard. "We want a dog that'll be of help to her."

"I got just the one," said Nester, nodding hard. "His name's *Sears* because he was always a tearin' up the wife's wish book when he was a pup. She swore she'd get rid of him first chance she got. He's trained well and would be a right good dog for Lark."

"Bring him out and we'll take a look at him," said Clay.

The *we* wrapped around Lark's heart and set her pulse fluttering. She couldn't look at Clay for fear he'd see her reaction. She watched Nester walk to his kennel, calling to Sears. He came back with a wide chested, spotted dog with pointed ears slightly flopped over. The minute Lark saw Sears, she knew he was the dog for her. She held out her hand and Sears licked it, then wagged his tail hard. She took his head between her hands and pressed her forehead to his. He wriggled all over, squirming until he was able to lick her face.

Clay paid for Sears and Lark stiffened. She would not allow Clay to pay for Sears and lay claim to him because of that.

"He's a fine dog," said Nester as he put Sears in the buggy.

"I'm sure he is," said Lark, holding her hand out to Sears. The dog sniffed her and flipped his white rope of a tail. Lark scratched Sears around the ears and down his spotted side.

"You got a friend for life," said Nester with a chuckle.

They said their goodbyes and Clay handed Lark into the buggy. When they were out of earshot Lark said, "I'll pay for Sears from Jig's money."

"No need," said Clay with a quick look at her. For some reason it had pleased him a lot to buy Sears for Lark.

Lark took a deep breath. "Clay, I will not allow you to pay for my dog! It's not your place to buy him for me."

"My place?"

"You're not my husband or my beau!" Lark flushed scarlet.

"Nor will I ever be!" snapped Clay, suddenly angry. "I gave you a gift and you throw it in my face."

"I didn't mean it that way," she said stiffly. "I just know I don't want you to pay for Sears."

"I can't imagine why."

"I don't want you to!"

"That's not a good reason," Clay said impatiently.

Lark lifted her chin stubbornly. "But that's the way I want it."

"You are a stubborn woman, Lark Baritt!" Clay slapped the reins on the team and they stepped forward so fast the buggy rocked hard, sending Lark bouncing against Clay. She flung her arm around him and gripped his muscled arm to keep from flying out of the buggy. Her touch burned into him, sending a shock through his body like he'd never felt before.

Her face on fire, Lark pulled away from Clay and braced her feet to keep from touching him again.

Even after she had righted herself, Clay felt the warmth and softness of her body. Finally he said, "Have it your way. You pay for Sears."

"Thank you," Lark said weakly.

They didn't speak again until Clay drove past Red Beaver's farm. "Did you and Evie get your tanned leather?" Clay asked in what he hoped was a normal voice.

"His mother refused to sew for us," said Lark.

Clay shot Lark a surprised look. "Why?"

Lark started to tell Clay, then shrugged. "She just said she wouldn't, that's all." Maybe he didn't know Red Beaver was Willie Thorne's son. She didn't know if she should tell him. "Are you as prejudiced against Indians as your pa?"

"No, I'm not prejudiced against Indians or anyone else. I

don't believe whites and Indians should marry each other, but I'm not prejudiced."

Lark bit back a sharp answer. He sounded prejudiced to her.

Clay drove Lark to the cabin and helped her stake out Sears until he got used to his new home. "I'll bring a dog house over tomorrow," he said, his voice quite stiff and formal.

"Thank you," said Lark, her voice equally stiff and formal.

Clay smiled. "I was almost afraid to offer."

Lark chuckled. "I'll pay for it."

Clay threw up his hands and let them fall in defeat. "I might've known."

Lark reached for her bundle under the buggy seat, but Clay took it from her and carried it into the cabin.

"Thank you," said Lark.

Clay tipped his straw hat and smiled. "You're very welcome."

Her eyes locked with his and she couldn't move or speak. His heart fluttered strangely. Abruptly he strode to his buggy, flicked the reins, and drove rapidly across the field to the Havlick farm.

Lark stood in the cabin doorway and watched Clay until he disappeared from sight behind a cluster of oaks. Sears barked and Lark dragged her gaze off Clay to see about her dog.

Several minutes later Lark stood at her table and unwrapped the bundle she'd brought from the asylum. She took a deep breath and once again looked through her things. She re-read the letters her mother had written to her father, then studied the photos a long time. Was her father alive or dead? If he was alive, why hadn't he come for her? How could she know if he was alive or dead? What steps could she take to find out? Maybe John Epson would know since he was a lawyer.

The next morning after her trip around the trail she hurried to the asylum, dressed in the new white waist and blue skirt. As she stepped inside the asylum, Matron was walking down the hall.

"May I help you, ma'am?" asked Matron with a polite smile. Then she recognized Lark and her face hardened. "Lark Baritt! My, aren't we putting on airs."

"Good morning, Matron," said Lark, determined not to lose her temper or be hurt by the cutting words.

"Jennet Havlick is in my office to see you," said Matron. "I allowed her to meet you there today, but don't let it happen again."

"What does she want of me?"

"Something about the Temperance League."

Lark knew Matron was totally against drinking liquor. "Did you hear Willie Thorne is opening a tavern on Main Street across from the dress shop? In fact, it's today!" Lark hadn't realized the time had crept up on her. She'd been too busy thinking about her own life and what was happening to her.

Matron clicked her tongue and shook her head. "We'll have him out by next week if I have anything to say about it! I'll set the children making posters to hang around town and a big one to stand right in front of his place."

"That's a good idea." Lark followed Matron to her office.

Jennet stood and walked forward. "Lark! You look wonderful!"

Lark blushed. "It feels good to have nice clothes."

"Clothes do make a nice covering, but Lark, we both know clothes can't change the person," said Jennet, squeezing Lark's hands. "You're the same fine young lady no matter how you dress."

Lark tipped her head slightly in agreement. She knew she was the same, only it did help her self-confidence to look better.

"I suppose we'd better get to the business at hand," said Jennet.

"Please have a seat," Matron said as she walked behind her desk, her black skirts billowing out behind her.

Lark sat on the chair beside Jennet and waited expectantly.

"We must discuss how to get the tavern out of town," said Jennet with a frown.

"I say one of the first steps to take is having a talk with Mayor Greene. How is it he agreed to give Willie Thorne a permit to have a tavern? It's in the bylaws of Blue Creek to be a dry town."

"That's a very good point, Anna," said Jennet.

Lark knew Jennet was the only person ever to call Matron by her given name.

"My husband has already spoken to Willie Thorne, but it didn't do any good. We'll contact Mayor Greene yet today," said Jennet as she jotted down a note on the pad of paper on her lap.

"I think we of the Temperance League should go right to Willie Thorne too," said Matron crisply.

"And his wife," said Lark, suddenly thinking about her promise to Jig. Maybe she could learn something from Mrs. Thorne about Willie's plan for Veda to marry Clay as well as learn Mrs. Thorne's feeling about the tavern. She'd read in the newspaper that other tavern owners' wives belonged to the Temperance League. Maybe Mrs. Thorne could help stop Willie from opening the tavern.

"Good," said Jennet, nodding. "Lark, you visit Agnes Thorne. Take someone with you if you want. Anna, you take a couple of women and visit Willie Thorne. I'll find someone to go with me and we'll see the mayor." Jennet stood to her feet, smiled goodbye, and walked out.

Lark glanced at Matron, and walked out, too, before any argument. She'd see Mrs. Thorne first, and then she'd come back to work.

A few minutes later at the Thornes' the maid answered the door. Lark gasped in surprise. It was Gert, the woman who had once been the housekeeper at the asylum. She was short and plump and wore a black apron over a gray dress and a black cap. She didn't look any older than when she and her husband,

Ray, had left the asylum six years ago. "Gert! It's good to see you! I thought you were in Grand Rapids."

"Lark Baritt, I believe!" Gert hugged Lark, then stepped back from her. Tears filled Gert's eyes. "You look like a real lady! It looks like Matron let you have some of the money left to you."

Lark gasped. "What money, Gert?"

Gert clamped her hand over her small round mouth.

"Please, tell me! I got my photos and papers and baby clothes, but there wasn't any money."

Gert fingered the brooch at her high collar. "It's not for me to say, Lark. But I will anyway! Matron does like to help herself to money not logged in. To my knowledge yours wasn't, and she more than likely took it and used it herself."

"How much was it?"

"That I don't know. But it was enough to keep you clothed and fed until your father could come get you."

Lark sagged against the heavy front door. "My father?" she whispered.

"Matthew Baritt. He was a naturalist and also worked in the lumber camps. He couldn't tend you, so he left you at the asylum to be taken care of."

"Where is he now?" whispered Lark.

"Last I heard he was in the Upper Peninsula, I believe."

"How could I get in touch with him?"

Gert frowned thoughtfully. "You might send a letter to Brackton at Driscoll's lumber camp. That might reach him."

"I'll do it," said Lark, barely breathing. Things were moving so fast she could hardly take it in.

"Are you all right, Lark?" asked Gert in concern.

"I don't know." Lark looked around the hallway, then remembered why she'd come. "Gert, I do thank you for the information. I almost forgot why I came."

"Did you come to call on Miss Veda?"

"Is she here?"

"No. You just missed her."

"I really came to see Agnes Thorne."

"Oh, I don't know," said Gert, suddenly nervous.

"Is there a problem?" asked Lark softly.

"She's in one of her vacant moods," said Gert. She lowered her voice. "I don't ever tell folks that, but I guess I can tell you. She's got a lot of strain on her what with that husband of hers treating her bad, I believe."

"I'm sorry about that."

"Me too. Mrs. Thorne is a nice lady. Gentle. Not like that Veda and Mr. Thorne. If I was a judging person, I'd say they're bad to the heart."

"Does Mrs. Thorne object to the tavern Willie Thorne is opening?"

"Yes, when she's in her right mind. But he doesn't care a whit about her feelings. He says he'll open it, and he will." Gert wrung her plump hands and looked ready to cry. "Me and my man don't drink and no liquor will ever touch our lips. If we could work somewhere else, we'd leave the Thornes tomorrow."

"You could go back to the asylum to work."

"Not as long as Matron is there," said Gert, shaking her head hard. "My man won't go back either. She accused him of selling a cow and keeping the money. No, he won't go back either."

"I'm sorry. You were always good with us kids."

"I never had none of my own, so you all became mine."

Lark brushed a strand of hair off her cheek and glanced toward the open door and the wide stairs. "May I please speak with Mrs. Thorne. I won't do anything to hurt her."

Gert nervously smoothed her black apron and touched the black cap covering most of her gray hair. "I suppose you can sit with her a while. But when she's in her vacant mood she doesn't talk to anyone."

"That's all right," said Lark. She had to try to speak to her anyway about Veda, about the tavern, and about the plans for Clay and Veda and the white pines.

Gert led Lark up the polished stairs to the first door on the right. The room was spotlessly clean and smelled like a flower garden. Agnes Thorne sat at the open window in a blue overstuffed armchair. The hot sun streamed in over her embroidery work and the breeze ruffled her gray hair. She looked up vacantly, then bent back over her work.

Gert fluffed a blue flowered pillow beside Mrs. Thorne and drew her footstool an inch closer to her chair. "Mrs. Thorne, dear, this is Lark Baritt. I've known her since she was little. She came to visit you."

"Hello, Mrs. Thorne." Lark smiled down at the woman, then turned to Gert. "I can sit with her if you have an errand you want to run."

"I do have some things I need to do. But it's asking too much of you to stay, I believe."

"I offered, Gert." Lark hugged Gert and turned her toward the door. "Come back in an hour."

"Thank you, Lark. You've always been such a dear!" Gert beamed with pleasure as she hurried out.

Her nerve ends jangling, Lark pulled a heavy oak armchair with a high back across the flowered carpet. She set it in front of Agnes Thorne next to her footstool, then sat down with her hands folded in her lap over her small pocketbook. She tried to appear calm.

"Mrs. Thorne, I want to speak to you about . . . Veda . . . and about Willie Thorne." Lark watched for a movement from Mrs. Thorne. None came.

"I promised my friend Jig that I'd save Clay Havlick and save the white pines. Does your husband still plan to lumber the Havlicks' pines?" Lark waited, but still there was no sign that Mrs. Thorne heard.

"Is Veda going to try to marry Clay to get the pines for Willie Thorne?" Again Lark waited, but Mrs. Thorne continued to embroider.

"Maybe Silent Waters would know," Lark said softly.

Suddenly Agnes Thorne jerked and her hands grew quiet on

72

her wooden hoop. Lark's heart raced. She'd said something that got through! She leaned forward and said, "Silent Waters. Willie Thorne's squaw."

Agnes Thorne looked up at Lark. "What does Silent Waters know of love?" Mrs. Thorne said sharply.

Lark almost jumped out of her skin. "I don't know. What does Silent Waters know of love?"

Mrs. Thorne flung her embroidery from her and jumped to her feet. "She knows nothing! If she did she would never have let Willie take her baby from her and give her to me!"

Lark pressed her hand to her heart. "What baby?" she whispered.

"Veda. My baby! But Silent Waters named her Laughing Eyes. Veda thinks she was born to me. That's what Willie wants her to think." Mrs. Thorne tapped her small bosom. Her black sateen wrapper with a small pointed collar made her skin look washed out and sickly. "Born to me? Ha! I couldn't have babies. Couldn't have babies!" Mrs. Thorne dashed away a tear. "But Silent Waters could. She had Red Beaver, then she had Veda."

Lark sat in speechless silence.

Mrs. Thorne tore at her gray hair, then dropped her hands to her sides, leaving her hair in wild disarray. "Willie Thorne was married to me, but he visited Silent Waters often." Mrs. Thorne folded her arms across her thin breast and rocked back and forth, back and forth on her heels. "Do you know how that made me feel? I wanted to kill both of them!" She spread her hands hopelessly. "But what could I do? I'm only a weak woman."

Lark knew Mrs. Thorne didn't expect an answer, and she didn't give one for fear of stopping the flow of words.

"Veda was born. Laughing Eyes." Mrs. Thorne moaned. "Willie loved her to distraction. He couldn't bear to be apart from her, but he couldn't go live with his squaw and still have the respect he wanted. So he brought her child to me." Mrs. Thorne tugged at her collar as if it was too tight against her wrinkled throat. "We lived in Grand Rapids and he took Veda from Silent Waters and he brought her to me. As a gift! A *gift!*"

"Does Veda know?"

"No! Willie says no one can know. He and I and, of course, Silent Waters know, but no one else." Mrs. Thorne stared through the window for a long time. A fly buzzed at the glass; the house creaked. "I'd been ill. So Willie just told everyone I had given birth to Veda. We hired a wet nurse to tend her. We raised her as ours."

Lark's breathing was so shallow she felt as if she couldn't get air into her lungs. "What did Silent Waters do?"

Mrs. Thorne turned to face Lark. She looked dead. "She came to take Veda, but Willie wouldn't let her. He said if she didn't leave us alone, he'd take Red Beaver from her too. So, she left us alone until we moved back here."

"Why did you move?" Lark waited, not moving, not blinking an eye.

"So Willie can destroy Freeman Havlick."

"How?" whispered Lark.

Mrs. Thorne sank to her chair and locked her hands in her lap. "He told Veda she must marry Clay Havlick, get the pines, and let him lumber them. Destroying the pines will destroy the Havlicks."

Lark knew it would hurt them deeply, but it wouldn't destroy them. "Can't you stop your husband and your daughter?"

"No, I can't. I'm too weak to do anything," Mrs. Thorne whispered.

"I'll help you," said Lark softly.

"You will?" Mrs. Thorne studied Lark questioningly. "But why?"

"Because I promised Jig I would do what it takes to save Clay Havlick and the pines."

"You can't do it. Willie is too strong for you too."

"No. I have the Almighty God helping me."

Tears spilled down Mrs. Thorne's pale cheeks. "What will

Willie do if he doesn't get his own way this time?"

"He will move away."

"He will keep trying. I know him."

"We'll pray for God to show us a way to stop him," said Lark softly.

"Yes. Pray. I once prayed. But it's been so long!"

"It's never too late to start again," said Lark. "Talk to God. He'll help you. He's always with you, Mrs. Thorne. He has comfort and peace for you. Just receive it from him."

Mrs. Thorne leaned back in her chair and closed her eyes.

Just then the door opened and Gert walked in. She looked flustered. "Willie Thorne just got home, Lark. You must leave before he sees you."

"Yes. Leave," said Agnes Thorne weakly.

Lark squeezed Mrs. Thorne's hand. "God is with you. Don't forget!"

Mrs. Thorne picked up her embroidery without answering.

Gert tugged on Lark's arm. "Hurry! Go out the kitchen door so Willie won't see you. Come with me. I'll show you the way."

Lark's stomach knotted as she followed Gert. And it stayed knotted long after she had slipped out of Willie Thorne's house through the kitchen door. She didn't breathe easily until she was almost at the asylum. As she walked along the dirt road all that Mrs. Thorne had revealed came back piece by piece until she sorted out the whole sordid story. She closed her eyes and moaned. Somehow she would have to think of a way to save Clay and the pines. She didn't have a moment to lose. Then she remembered what Gert had said about her father.

All thoughts of Clay and the pines left Lark's head as she wondered if her father was still alive. "If he is, how can I find him?" she whispered hoarsely.

CHAPTER

6

♦ After a fine supper that he couldn't enjoy, Willie Thorne paced his front room, his hands clenched at his sides, his graying red head bent. His dark suit fit snug across his shoulders and thickening waist. He'd always wanted to be tall and muscled like Free Havlick. Oh, how he despised Freeman Havlick! He seemed to have it all—an inheritance, a good wife, six children he could be proud of, and respect. Willie had a wife he didn't love and two children by a squaw.

Willie's pulse quickened as he thought of Silent Waters; then he frowned. How could he still love her? She was Patawatomi! With her he'd been able to relax and enjoy living without thinking about getting rich or making a name for himself. But that wasn't the real world. In the real world he had to have a name and he had to have wealth.

When he was young he'd been the timber walker for George Meeker, a lumberman without scruples. Willie smiled as he thought of those exciting days. He had been paid well to find the timber Meeker lumbered, and had been paid even better when he managed to find a way to get trees that another walker had already marked for someone else. Free Havlick had walked the woods with him to learn the business, but when Free had seen how dishonest he and Meeker were, he'd quit. Willie doubled his fists and narrowed his eyes in anger. Later Free had told what he'd learned about Willie, and from then on he hadn't been able to work in the lumber business.

He'd tried many things and finally had settled on living off Agnes and bootlegging liquor whenever possible. He'd already gone through most of Agnes's inheritance. She didn't know it yet, but soon she would. He'd tried to keep the truth from her. He didn't want Agnes or Veda to know how destitute they really were. It looked now that he'd be forced to tell her, unless he could get his hands on some money very soon.

The only way he knew to get rich quickly was to get Clay Havlick's trees and lumber them. Then he'd be *rich*. Then everyone in town would look up to him. Then he'd have the respect he deserved. He'd planned to open a tavern in order to tide him over until his plans could work out, but the Temperance League had delayed that and made him lose money. He slammed his fist into his palm and swore under his breath. Somehow he had to speed up his plans to lumber the Havlicks' white pines.

He'd tried stealing a few trees at a time during the past few years, but Jig had stopped him, and now Lark Baritt was standing in the way. But he'd get rid of her soon. No orphan girl was going to keep him from those trees. Still just getting rid of her wouldn't be enough. Stealing a tree or two now and then was not the answer. He needed to get *all* the trees.

For several months he'd toyed with the idea of having Veda marry young Havlick to get at the pines. Finally he'd concluded it was the only answer and without much trouble had convinced Veda to entice Clay into marriage. She didn't have to stay with him if she didn't want to, but she needed to get him to fall for her, and she needed to get him to give her the pines. Her charms seemed to be working on young Clay. Soon he'd get those trees—all of them. Soon he'd get the wealth he deserved.

Willie stopped at the wide window and looked out on the

77

flower gardens and the lush sweep of green lawn. He'd paid a small down payment on the place and struggled to make the bank payments each month. The price was much more than he could afford, but he'd had to keep up appearances. He growled deep in his throat. Free Havlick owed him for ruining his name and forcing him to live off a wealthy wife. "He'll pay for it all," muttered Willie as he paced from the sofa to the tall plant near the door and back to the overstuffed chairs.

Just then the door opened and Veda walked in. Her white and green shirtwaist was tucked in at her narrow waist. A silver and sapphire brooch was pinned at the high collar. Her dark skirt hung down straight in front and poofed out in the back over her bustle. Her dark eyes lit up as she smiled at Willie. "I wondered where you were, Papa."

Willie pulled her close and held her tightly. She was so much like Silent Waters he wondered how Veda could not notice. But she had no idea Agnes wasn't her real mother, so she wasn't looking.

"You are as beautiful as ever, Veda," said Willie against the rich auburn hair that smelled like lilac. He held her from him and studied her oval face, wide dark eyes, and perfectly shaped red lips. He and Silent Waters had produced a beautiful daughter! He pushed the thought aside and smiled. "Have you seen Clay today?"

"No." Veda pouted prettily. "He was too busy today, *again*. He isn't as easy to conquer as other men I've admired."

"He has his mind on his wagon business, but you keep at it. One of these days he'll see what a fine woman you are."

"Papa, are you sure you want me to marry him?"

Willie caught Veda's smooth, well-shaped hands in his. "He will make a fine husband for you, Veda. His family has a name and they have wealth. You'll want for nothing when you're his wife."

"I do think he's a fine looking man," said Veda. "And I could learn to care for him."

"Good girl!"

"Are you sure he'll want to give me the pines as a wedding gift?"

"Veda, since when has any man denied you anything?"

Veda laughed, then sobered. "Won't he hate me when I sign the pines over to you?"

Willie shrugged. "He might for a while, but with his Christian upbringing, he'll get over it. He won't hold a grudge or stay angry."

"I hope you're right, Papa." Veda kissed Willie's cheek, then sat on the edge of the sofa with her hands folded in her lap. Her dark skirt fell in graceful folds to the carpeted floor. "Already Clay and I have been out to supper several times since I rode the train with him last month. Tomorrow night we're going out again. But I don't know how to make him even consider marriage."

"Then you bring it up, Veda. You can do it without seeming to be forward. But you must act quickly. I've seen Clay with Lark Baritt on a few occasions. She doesn't have your grace or beauty, but she's a woman to reckon with. John Epson says she has a quality about her that's most attractive."

Veda waved her hand impatiently. "Lark Baritt is not competition for me even though she has learned to dress well!"

"Just be aware of her." Willie started to run his fingers through his carefully groomed hair, thought better of it, then dropped his hand at his side. "You talk marriage with Clay Havlick tomorrow night."

Veda nodded, then looked thoughtfully at Willie. "Maybe you should give up your plan for lumbering the pines."

Willie shook his head as he forced back his anger. Veda was the only person alive who could question his actions without knowing the sharp side of his tongue. "I told you I won't. *We must have them!*"

Veda sighed heavily. "Then I will do all I can to see that you get them."

The grandfather clock in the hall bonged seven times, and Willie glanced out the window just as a buggy stopped in the

drive. "John Epson is coming to talk business. Don't let him turn your head with his sweet talk."

Veda laughed softly. "He is a fine man, but I wouldn't marry any man you didn't approve of."

"Spoken like a true daughter," said Willie as he kissed Veda, then sent her out of the room. He couldn't let even Veda know about the plans he and John Epson were making against the Havlicks.

The next evening in the best restaurant in Blue Creek just after ordering the salmon dinner, Clay smiled across the table at Veda Thorne. Her auburn hair was piled becomingly on her well-shaped head. She was tall and slender and wore a floral design, black grenadine dress lined with yellow taffeta. Every time she moved he heard the soft rustle of the taffeta. There was something about the way she looked at him tonight that stirred his blood and made him very aware of her.

"You look very beautiful tonight, Veda," said Clay softly. He'd never said that to a woman before, so the words didn't slip off his tongue easily like they would have Tris's.

"Thank you, Clay." Veda smiled as she leaned slightly forward. "I know I'm not supposed to say this, but you look very handsome tonight. Any woman would be proud to have you as a companion."

Clay flushed and suddenly felt like a schoolboy. "Thank you." He wanted to run his finger around his stiff white collar and straighten his tie, but he kept his hands in his lap. Building the wagons was going so smoothly that Clay felt more relaxed than he had in a long time. Even Pa was starting to think he could meet the deadline.

"I still can't believe you're unattached, Clay." Veda widened her dark eyes and smiled. "I'm sure all the young ladies of the area have been making eyes at you. You're a fine looking, strong, intelligent man."

Clay liked to hear flattery, but he wasn't used to a woman saying nice things to him. Women usually stayed away from

him. Ma said it was because he was too formal and unapproachable. He wanted to reach out and run his finger down Veda's smooth, rosy cheek. He wanted to cup her face in his hands and kiss her full lips. He hadn't kissed a girl since the time he'd stolen a kiss from Tillie Rousch when he was sixteen. Tris couldn't count the number of girls he'd kissed, and Miles already had kissed quite a few. Suddenly Clay wanted more from life than working hard all day at the Wagon Works. His business was important, but he didn't want it to be his whole life.

"I'm glad you had time for me tonight, Clay," said Veda in a low husky voice. "I hope we can do it again."

"Tomorrow night," said Clay quickly before he lost his nerve.

Veda nodded, looking very pleased. "Tomorrow night. I would invite you home, but you know Papa would be very angry with me. I have to sneak out of the house to meet you." Veda patted her cheeks, then folded her hands in her lap. "Maybe you could invite me to your home sometime."

Clay hesitated, then nodded. "I'll see Ma about it."

"I know it's hard on your family because I'm Willie Thorne's daughter." Veda sighed heavily. "I trust that someday they'll accept me for myself like you have."

"They will in time," said Clay. But would they? Just then he glanced across the dining room and caught sight of Lark at a table with Zoe Cheyney. Lark was listening intently to Zoe but glanced up. Before Clay could look away, his eyes locked with hers. He felt as if he'd been caught with his hand in the cookie jar. He frowned and forced his attention back to Veda.

"Is something wrong, Clay?" asked Veda, glancing around.

Clay shook his head as he rubbed his damp palms on his pant legs. "Not a thing." Why was he so upset all at once? He glanced toward the kitchen. "I wonder what's taking the waiter so long."

"It doesn't bother me a whit." Veda sipped her water, then daintily patted her lips with her white linen napkin. "Time passes quickly when I'm with you. You always know just what to say and how to treat me. You make my heart beat faster and leave me light-headed."

He smiled, but didn't feel as good about her flattery as he had before he noticed Lark watching him, condemning him for spending time with a Thorne. "How do you feel about your father opening a tavern here in town?" Now, why had he asked that? He hadn't planned to, but seeing Lark had flustered him.

Veda lifted a slender shoulder and let it fall. "I can't stop Papa from starting a business. I'm against strong drink, of course, but Papa won't let me stop him."

Clay breathed easier. "I thought you'd be against it. I know the Temperance League stopped him for a while."

"I know. So does Papa, but he's ready to fight for his rights. He said the men around here are buying their liquor somewhere, so it might as well be from him."

Clay didn't feel like arguing the point. He was glad to see the waiter bring the plates of food and serve first Veda, then him. Steam rose from the salmon, sending out an aroma that made him realize he was very hungry.

Across the restaurant Zoe leaned toward Lark and whispered, "Why don't you walk over and say hello to Clay?"

Lark shook her head, sipped from her glass of water, and dabbed her lips with her napkin as her thoughts returned to her father. He was never far from her mind since Gert had told her in great detail about him. She'd said he was Matt Baritt, a man working his way up in the logging business. Lark laid her napkin in her lap and absently rubbed her hand over it. She'd sent off a carefully worded letter just after she'd spoken to Gert and had finally received a letter from Grant Evans in Saginaw, a man she'd never heard of, who said Brackton from Driscoll's lumber camp had forwarded her letter to him. He said Matt Baritt had worked for him five years ago after leaving the Upper Peninsula. Mr. Evans had suggested she contact Lucas Gotia in Grayling and had given her the man's address, but she'd been too impatient to send a letter. She had run to the telegraph office and had sent a telegram. That had been days ago. So far she hadn't received an answer.

"Lark," said Zoe impatiently. "Will you listen to me?"

"Sorry." With great effort Lark forced her attention back to Zoe.

"I wish Tris would come in. I'd say hello to him. I do think I would." Zoe stroked the sleeve of the new light blue shirtwaist Lark had bought for her. "And I wouldn't be ashamed to have him see me, now that I have this beautiful waist and skirt. Oh, Lark, it was so nice of you to buy me new clothes!"

Lark smiled. "If I could, I'd buy new clothes for all the kids at the asylum." She laughed softly as a great idea popped into her head. She should've thought of it sooner. She grabbed Zoe's hand and said, "I know what we'll do! I'll see that the money Jig gave to the asylum goes into the clothing account!"

"If Matron will allow it."

"Well, she'd better," said Lark grimly. "I'll fix it so she'll have no choice but to allow it." Once again she glanced toward Clay and Veda and all thought of clothing and the asylum vanished. Would Clay believe her if she told him what she learned from Agnes Thorne? She'd wanted to tell him, then all of her thoughts had been on finding her father and she hadn't mentioned any of it to him. She had to be careful how she told him. She didn't want to anger him and have him take her job away and send her back to the asylum. She couldn't give up the cabin after all those years of living in the asylum.

About an hour later Lark watched Clay and Veda walk through the heavy door of the restaurant. Clay's hand rested lightly on Veda's back. The sight of it made Lark grip her linen napkin so tightly she was certain there would be permanent wrinkles in it.

Zoe leaned over and whispered in Lark's ear, "Shall we follow them?"

Lark shook her head, though without meaning to she bunched her muscles to spring up and run after Clay. "They'd see us," she said stiffly. She had to admit to herself she really didn't want to see them together in the privacy of a buggy.

Outdoors Clay handed Veda into his buggy and drove slowly down the street toward her house. Unlike the first time he'd seen her in the hotel lobby in Detroit, he didn't want the evening to end. But he didn't know what else to do other than take her home. He could not take her for a long ride on such a bumpy road, and he would not park somewhere to spark like Tris always did.

The evening was pleasantly cool with a bright moon. The aroma of roses in bloom almost covered the odor of the river. Piano music drifted out from the house just before Veda's. A dog barked and another one answered. Clay stopped the team in the driveway. The harness rattled and the team snorted. Lights from the windows and the bright moonlight made it possible to see the flowers in the yard and the cat walking toward the barn. Clay stepped from the buggy, then helped Veda out. He moved away from her, suddenly at a loss for words—just as he had been at their first meeting in Detroit.

She'd stepped right up to him and said, "Clay Havlick, I know we aren't allowed to have anything to do with each other, but I think fate wants differently. Why else would we be in the same hotel at the same time? I've seen you the last two evenings and I couldn't walk away without speaking. I hope you don't mind. We shouldn't let our parents stop us from doing something we really want to do, should we?"

He'd felt a flush creep up his neck and over his face. "I suppose not."

"Can we sit and talk a while?" Taking his arm, she'd tugged him to a brocade sofa where they sat side by side. She'd done most of the talking, but he'd found himself actually relaxing and enjoying her company.

Tonight he'd enjoyed her company more than any other time.

Veda touched Clay's hand and he stiffened slightly. "I don't want the night to end," she whispered. "You're a dear, dear man and I care deeply for you."

84

Clay's pulse leaped. No woman had ever said that to him.

Veda leaned against him and looked into his face. "Do you care for me . . . just a little?"

"Yes," he said hoarsely. Oh, why couldn't he be as free with his speech as Tris?

"You may kiss me if you want," said Veda softly, lifting her lips to him.

Suddenly Clay wanted to do just that. He felt awkward as he slipped his arms around her and pulled her close. But before he could touch his lips to hers, she kissed him, and a shock went through him. Then he took control, kissing her as if he were accustomed to such things. Startled at his bold action, he pulled away slightly.

"You make me weak all over," Veda whispered against his ear. "Do I do that to you?"

"Yes," he said hoarsely.

"Could you ever care enough for me to marry me?" she asked softly.

"I might," he whispered.

"You could?" She kissed him again and he returned her kiss with a growing passion. Finally she pulled away, but kept her hands on his chest. "I know we haven't known each other very long, but I care enough for you to marry you."

He didn't know what to say.

"Do you think I'm too forward? Do you think less of me for saying that?"

"I like an honest woman." Her lips were so close to his he could smell her sweet breath. He pulled her closer and kissed her passionately. Desire stirred in him and he didn't want to let her go. He trailed kisses down her cheek and to the pulse throbbing in her throat, then kissed her moist lips again. "I can't get enough of you," he whispered against her soft hair.

"I know," she whispered. "If I had the courage, *I'd* ask *you* to marry *me*."

He hesitated a fraction, then held her away enough to look

into her face. "Will you marry me?" His question surprised him, but it felt right.

"Oh, Clay! Are you sure? Your family!"

"I don't care!" He was sure now. "I want you!"

"And I want you!" Veda's voice was low and whispery.

Clay felt a rush of emotion he'd never known before. He pulled Veda close and kissed her again. Finally she pulled away.

"I must go in," she said breathlessly. "I don't want you to get the wrong idea about me."

"I wouldn't."

"When shall we marry?"

"I'll let you decide."

She laughed breathlessly. "I don't want to live another day without you! Should we marry in August?"

"That's next month!"

"Then how about September?"

That still seemed too soon to Clay. "Let's have a Christmas wedding."

"But that's so far away! I don't know if I can wait that long." Veda ran her hands over Clay's chest. "But if that's what you want, then that's what it'll be."

Clay laughed softly. "Maybe we'd better make it sooner."

"Maybe we should elope so we don't have to listen to our families trying to break us up."

"Maybe so."

"Tonight?" she asked against his lips.

It was tempting, but he shook his head. "We'll think about the date and decide later."

Veda shook her head and pouted as she trailed her finger down his cheek and across his lips. "You said I could decide. And I will take you at your word. I say August."

Clay laughed. "All right. August it is. But it'll have to be late in the month to give me a chance to work on the wagons."

"Leave it to your men to do! I want a month's honeymoon in Europe."

"I can't be gone a month. Maybe next year, but not now. Maybe we should get married next year."

"I won't wait!"

"I can't be away from my business."

"I guess I understand." She tapped his lips with her fingertip. "But I don't like it a teeny bit."

"I'm sorry. My business is very important to me."

"I hope it's not as important as I am."

He didn't know what to say to that and he was feeling uncomfortable. "I'll walk you to the door."

Clay slipped an arm around Veda and walked slowly to the lighted front door. He kissed her one more time, waited until she slipped inside, then ran to his buggy. He slapped the reins on the team and drove away from the Thorne home. His head spun as he thought about the change in his life. He had his own business and soon he'd have a wife. His stomach knotted and he trembled. A month ago he'd never considered a personal relationship with a Thorne; now suddenly he was planning to marry one. Was he doing the right thing?

He slowed the team as he drove through Blue Creek, across the bridge, and onto the corduroy that led home. What would Ma and Pa say about his engagement? He hated to think about their anger. Borrowing against the pines had been the first thing he'd ever done in his life that they'd objected to. Marrying Veda would be the second.

Just past Red Beaver's farm, Clay spotted a buggy at the side of the corduroy. He stopped beside it and called, "Hello? Is there trouble? Could you use a hand?"

In the darkness Lark's heart leaped at the sound of Clay's voice. She stepped around the back of the buggy where she could see him. "Clay!" she said. "It's me, Lark. I'm so glad to see you! The lug nut fell off the wheel and I can't find it. Will you help me?"

Clay stared at Lark in surprise. He'd never expected to see her on the road alone after dark. "How long have you been out here?" he snapped. "Don't you know what could happen?"

She bit her lip, but didn't answer.

He jumped from his buggy and reached for the lantern in the back. He lit it and walked with Lark to look for the lug nut. He noticed she was still dressed in the finery that she'd worn in the restaurant. "What're you doing out so late alone?"

"Going to the cabin," she said. "I visited too long with Zoe."

"You could be in danger," said Clay sharply. "You can't forget the enemies you've made since you've been guarding the pines. This is no place for you to be by yourself."

"I have my revolver and cudgel in the buggy," she said stiffly.

Clay scowled as he walked back the way Lark had come, holding the lantern high to shed light on the log road. How could she think a cudgel and a revolver in the buggy would keep her safe while she was on foot?

Lark walked along beside him, her steps unsteady on the road. She could walk easily in her heavy boots, but her new shoes with the small heel made walking harder. Suddenly she tripped. With a startled cry, she flung out her arms and caught Clay's arm.

He stumbled slightly and almost dropped the lantern. The touch of her hands seemed to burn through his clothing and into his flesh. "What's wrong?" he asked sharply as he looked down on her.

She regained her balance and released her death grip on his arm. "Sorry," she muttered, barely able to breathe with him so close. "I tripped."

"Are you hurt?"

"No." There was a slight pain in her ankle, but not enough to mention.

"This is ridiculous. We'll leave the buggy here for the night and find a nut in the morning. I'll unhitch the team and tie them behind my buggy."

"I can't leave your pa's buggy for someone to steal!"

"He'll understand. He wouldn't want you to risk your life for a buggy. Get in mine while I unhitch the team." Clay's voice sounded angry even to him.

"I'll get my things," she said stiffly. She walked back to the buggy and lifted out the pouch carrying her revolver and her cudgel.

A few minutes later Lark sat beside Clay as he drove down the corduroy. Blood pounded in her ears and tingles ran over her body. "I'm sorry for ruining your night," she said with her hands locked in her lap over her pouch.

"You didn't ruin it. It just so happens this is a *fine* night for me." Clay hesitated a fraction. "Veda and I are engaged."

"What?" cried Lark in alarm as she turned to stare at him. "You're going to marry Veda Thorne? You mustn't! What about Jig's warning?"

Clay turned onto Havlick property and pulled the team to an abrupt stop. He glared at Lark as his temper rose even higher. The moonlight was bright enough for him to see her wide eyes and shocked look. "I told you Jig was wrong about Veda!"

"He was not! Even Agnes Thorne knows the truth!"

"Mrs. Thorne isn't well."

"She can't tolerate her life! She doesn't like to see what her husband and daughter are doing." Impatiently Lark told him what she'd learned from Agnes. Ordinarily Lark would've told the news carefully, but she was too upset at the moment to use care. Brutally honest words poured from her. She ended with, "If you don't think it's right to marry an Indian, then you won't marry Veda Thorne."

Clay gripped the reins so tightly his knuckles hurt. The team moved restlessly. An owl screeched. Surely Agnes Thorne was out of her mind and wasn't telling the truth!

"I *know* Veda wants the pines!" cried Lark.

"You're wrong!"

Lark struggled to calm herself. "I can't believe you've already decided to marry Veda. You met her only a short time ago."

"We've spent enough time together to know our feelings."

"And have you prayed about it?"

A muscle jumped in Clay's jaw. He hadn't prayed. "I know I want to marry her."

"And what will you do when she has your pines lumbered out?"

"She won't do that no matter what her mother said," Clay said grimly. He was angry enough to shake Lark until her teeth rattled.

"What if she does?"

"Drop the subject, Lark Baritt. It's not your affair."

"The pines are my affair! I won't let them be lumbered! I'll do anything to stop that from happening."

Clay gripped her arms and pushed his face close to hers. "Just what does that mean?"

"Just what I said." She felt his anger even as hers mounted. "You know Veda Thorne pushed herself on you."

"She did no such thing."

"She made the first move to speak to you in Detroit or on the train. She suggested you have dinner together. She probably even suggested marriage."

Lark spoke the truth, but just hearing her say it set Clay's blood boiling. "I suppose you don't think I can get a wife without my precious white pines."

"I didn't say that. I said Veda Thorne is after them."

"Don't say another word!"

"I suppose you'll kick me out of the cabin and take away my job."

"I'd like to, but I won't." Clay abruptly released Lark and flicked the reins against the horses. The buggy jerked, then rolled along behind the clip-clop of the horses. "I'll leave you at the cabin. If you say another word against Veda, I will fire you on the spot."

Lark clamped her mouth closed into a tight, straight line as she stared off across the field toward the cabin. She would not give up the cabin or her job as guard. Only in the woods could she find release from the tension she felt when she thought about looking for and finding her father. "You could settle it all by not giving Veda the right to the pines when you marry."

"I don't intend to give her the pines," said Clay stiffly.

"She'll ask for them."

"You don't know what you're talking about!" Clay braced his feet to keep from swaying with the movement of the buggy. He was afraid he would lose his temper if he so much as brushed against Lark.

Several minutes later Clay stopped the team outside the cabin. The smell of pine was heavy in the night air. Sears barked and strained against the rope holding him to the stake beside his dog house. "Quiet, Sears!" commanded Clay sharply.

Sears immediately stopped barking and whined a welcome.

Lark stepped from the buggy and retrieved her cudgel and her pouch. "The pines are as important to me as they are to your mother and as they were to Jig. I won't let them be lumbered. Not by Veda or Willie Thorne. Not by anyone."

Clay bit back the angry words burning his tongue, turned his team, and slapped the reins down hard. The buggy swayed dangerously as he drove toward the farm.

Lark slowly walked to Sears and patted his head. "Sears, we'll keep the trees safe, won't we?"

Sears licked Lark's hand as he wriggled his back end.

Lark looked toward the pines and said in a loud, ringing voice, "Willie Thorne, not you or anyone else will lumber the pines!"

At the edge of the pines a shadow moved. Lark held her breath as she watched. Was it her imagination or had she seen someone lurking among the trees? She shivered and hurried inside the cabin and locked the door.

The next morning at the Havlicks, Clay sat at the breakfast table with the family. They always ate breakfast in the kitchen around the round oak table. Wood burned in the cookstove.

The hired girl slipped outdoors to leave the family alone to eat the hash browns, fried eggs, bacon, thick slices of fresh bread, and applesauce, with coffee and milk to drink. Clay looked at his parents, his two sisters, and two brothers, and almost lost his nerve. He had to tell them before they heard it from someone else—especially Lark Baritt.

Jennet laughed as she looked at Clay. She knew something was on his mind. She straightened the collar of her brown calico dress. She wasn't wearing a bustle. She liked dressing plain when in her own home. "Out with it, Clay. You look ready to burst."

Clay took a deep breath, ran a finger around his collar, then blurted, "I am going to marry Veda Thorne next month."

Jennet fell back against her chair and stared speechlessly at Clay. The others sat in shocked silence.

Free pushed his chair so hard it fell backward as he jumped up. "You'll do no such thing!" he roared. "No son of mine will marry a Thorne!"

Clay leaped up, sending his chair flying. Sparks shot from his dark eyes. "I'm twenty-five years old, Pa. You can't tell me what I can or can't do."

"Stop it, you two!" cried Jennet as she ran to Free's side and caught his arm. "Don't say anything you'll regret later. We can't let this tear apart our family! Let's be calm. Don't we need to talk?"

Free shook his finger at Clay. "I'll go directly to Willie Thorne and tell him you won't be marrying his daughter."

"You can't do that, Pa," said Clay in a tight voice. "Veda is afraid he won't approve of the marriage as it is. But she won't listen to him. Just leave it alone and let me handle it. We'll marry no matter what anyone says."

"Then Jig was right," said Jennet hoarsely.

"No. No, he was not," said Clay between his teeth. "I don't intend to give Veda the rights to the pines. But I will marry her even if we have to elope." Eloping was beginning to sound like a great idea. He grabbed his hat off the peg near the back door and stormed out of the house. He couldn't listen to another word. He glanced across the field to Lark's cabin. She would already be walking the trail, but she'd be plotting ways to stop him from marrying Veda. More than ever he wanted to grab Lark and shake some sense into her.

"Nobody will stop me," he whispered grimly. His heart felt like an icy stone but he ignored it and ran to the barn to saddle Flame.

CHAPTER

7

♦ Clay stood at his desk and listened to the noise around him in the shop. July heat made the building hot even with the doors open. He watched Jay trim an axle, then smiled down at the new contract he'd signed to build a hundred more wagons for a company in Kansas. Clay advertised that they built wagons that would last. The wooden pieces were hand hewn out of white oak with an axe, an adze, and a drawing knife. The coupling poles were made from well seasoned hickory he'd bought from his uncle Wex. Clay's blacksmiths forged the standards, hound plates, and other metal parts, but he bought the actual nuts from a company in Chicago. He was certain that in the future someone would invent tools to make the building of wagons easier and quicker and he wanted to be in on any new method that would work.

As Clay dropped the contract back in the folder, he wondered where he'd find enough seasoned wood. Uncle Wex had said he didn't have any more and the mill in town didn't either. Clay scratched his head in thought. If he couldn't find it, he'd be in big trouble. Without more wood he couldn't build enough wagons to fill the order. He'd sent a man around to different mills to find more lumber. Was there a way to season wood quickly? He'd have to check into it. Pa might know. Clay sighed. Pa was still worried about losing the white pines. The memory of Pa's angry words and his warnings made Clay's stomach tighten. He knew if he couldn't fulfill the contracts and pay back his bank loan, he could indeed lose the pines. If he had to, he'd hire additional employees. He already had sixty men working. There wasn't a chance he'd lose the pines to Willie Thorne. He was certain of that but Pa didn't believe it.

Just then Tris walked in, his straw hat in his hand. He wore dark work pants and a black and white striped cotton shirt. He looked hesitantly at Clay. Clay stiffened. Tris hadn't spoken to him since he'd announced his engagement yesterday morning.

"Morning, Clay," said Tris.

Clay glanced quickly around to make sure his men weren't able to hear the conversation. They were all deeply involved with their work and making too much noise to hear. Clay nodded to Tris. "Don't try to talk me out of marrying Veda Thorne."

Tris grinned and shrugged. "I thought about it, and I wanted to. Then I decided against it. You get stubborn when anybody opposes you."

Clay scowled. "I do not."

Tris shrugged again. "I came to see what I could do to help you with your wedding plans."

"Why would you want to help? You're against it as much as Ma and Pa."

"I know. But you're my brother and I don't want hard feelings between us."

A lump filled Clay's throat and he couldn't speak for a moment. He clamped his hand on Tris's strong shoulder. "Thanks, brother. I won't forget this."

Tris grinned and settled his hat in place. "Could I help run your business while you're on your honeymoon?"

Clay considered the offer, then shook his head. "I'll have to delay the honeymoon until later. I just got a new contract for more wagons. I'll probably have to hire more workers. Know of any available men?"

"Not offhand. You could check in Big Pine or Grand Rapids. Maybe put an ad in the paper."

"I'll do that. . . . You could work for me."

"I would if I could, but I'm helping Pa finish the buggy he's working on and I have bookwork to catch up on." Tris leaned back against the wooden desk. "Who's doing your bookwork?"

Clay rolled his eyes. "Me. I tried to get Bob Jenkins, but he's too busy."

"What about Lark Baritt? She's good."

Clay hesitated, then nodded. He had thought about her, but immediately rejected the idea. She didn't approve of him seeing Veda. Now that he was engaged to Veda, having Lark work for him at the Wagon Works could cause a real problem. It was bad enough that she was guarding the trees and he had to see her about that.

"She's changed a lot in the past few weeks," Tris said.

"Really? I hadn't noticed." Clay tried to sound disinterested.

"Her appearance has changed and she's more sure of herself." Tris pushed his hat to the back of his head. "I heard from Zoe that Lark is trying to find her father." Zoe had been with Lark at the cabin when Tris had stopped by with fresh vegetables. He'd been surprised he hadn't noticed that Zoe had grown up. On impulse he'd invited her on a Sunday school picnic and she'd quickly accepted.

"I didn't know Lark's father was still alive. I thought, since she was raised at the asylum she was an orphan."

"Me too. Zoe told me what she knows about it." Tris looked out the open door to the street beyond. "Lark has had a lot of unhappiness and deserves to be happy. I hope she does have a father out there who wants her and will love her."

Clay didn't want to think about Lark. "How about dinner?" he said. "It's almost noon."

At the orphan asylum Lark closed the books with a frown. Why wasn't there an entry of Jig's hundred dollar donation. She'd given the money to Matron just after Jig died. At first Lark had thought she'd overlooked the entry since she was a little distracted. Her mind was full of plans to find her father—if he was to be found—and she could think of little else. Even the news of Clay's engagement to Veda Thorne had alarmed her only for a short time. Clay would have to take care of himself and his trees. She had to find her father before she could think about anything else.

Lark looked down at the books. Regardless of what was on her mind, she had to take care of the business at hand right now and see what Matron had done with Jig's gift. With a determined look on her face Lark walked to Matron's office.

Matron stood beside a bookshelf and scowled at Lark. Her office smelled like coffee and cinnamon rolls. She had a dab of white frosting at the corner of her mouth. "I'm very busy," she said.

"I can't find the record of Jig Bjoerling's donation."

Matron smoothed the skirt of her black wrapper, then fingered a pearl brooch at her throat. "Why are you speaking to me about it? You're in charge of the books."

"You took the money from me. I assumed you deposited it in the bank."

Color stained Matron's round cheeks. "What are you implying, Lark Baritt?"

Lark trembled at the tone in Matron's voice. "I want to know what happened to the money."

"I did deposit it. Check at the bank." Matron waved Lark from the room. "Don't bother me about it again."

Lark wanted to argue the point, but she slowly walked from the office. She would check at the bank. Just then the front door opened and Sally Smith from the store burst in, looking very angry.

"What's wrong, Sally?"

Sally's round face was red with anger and perspiration glistened on her wide forehead. "I just learned that Glenna must give Matron a percent of the money she earns from me." Glenna was the orphan who swept up for Sally. "Glenna says Matron forces her to hand over part of her money to help pay her own way in the asylum."

"So that's what she's been doing!"

"Glenna said the boys who work at the mill have to do the same thing. She said Matron told them if they tell anyone she'll lock them in the cellar for a whole week." Sally's breast rose and fell and her blue eyes blazed with fury. "I want to know what we can do about it."

Lark narrowed her eyes thoughtfully. "This is my chance to get her out of here. I'll talk to the kids and we'll call an emergency board meeting for this evening."

"Are you sure that's the right thing to do? I know how Matron has treated you."

Lark shivered, but nodded determinedly. "I won't let her continue to be cruel to the children!"

That evening Lark looked around the front room of the asylum at the board members she'd sent messages to about the emergency meeting. Her heart jerked when she saw Clay sitting with his mother. Lark hadn't expected to see him at the meeting. Was he still angry with her? She knew she didn't want to deal with him or his problems right now. Just then he looked up and his eyes locked with hers. She tried to look away, but couldn't. Her lungs ached from not being able to take in air. Finally he turned back to his mother and Lark was free.

Clay tried to concentrate on what his mother was saying to him, but he couldn't get his mind off Lark. She looked drained and her eyes haunted. Was she having trouble at the pines that she hadn't reported? He saw Lark stiffen as Matron walked into the room.

Smelling of talcum powder, Matron stopped beside Lark. "Call off the meeting or you'll never learn about your father," hissed Matron so low only Lark could hear.

Lark's heart zoomed to her feet. She pressed her trembling hand to her throat. "What do you know of him?" she whispered hoarsely.

"I know where he is."

Lark gripped Matron's arm. "Tell me!"

Matron pried Lark's fingers loose. "I'll tell you if you call off the meeting."

Frantically Lark glanced around the room. If she called off the meeting, she might not have another chance to remove Matron from her position. But if she didn't call it off, she might never learn her father's whereabouts. Lark trembled. Her blue plaid shirtwaist and dark skirt felt too hot.

"Tell them you made a mistake," hissed Matron close to Lark's ear.

Lark caught a glimpse of Sally with the orphans standing outside the door. Lark moaned. She wanted to call off the meeting, but she couldn't hurt the children. "I won't call it off," Lark said weakly.

"You'll be very sorry," said Matron, stalking to a chair, her black skirt rustling loudly.

Jennet walked to the front of the room and faced the others sitting on sofas and the chairs Lark had had the boys carry in. Jennet smoothed down her gray skirt and touched the cameo at her throat. "Shall we pray?" She bowed her head and prayed for God to help them. She lifted her head and smiled at Lark. "This is a special meeting called by Lark to settle an issue with Matron Anna Pike. You may have the floor, Lark."

Lark walked to the front and stood beside Jennet. Lark had so much she wanted to say, but she couldn't remember a thing. She saw the questioning look on Clay's face and felt Jennet beside her. Lark took a deep breath, but still she couldn't find the words she'd planned to say against Matron. "Sally Smith has something to report." Lark sat down while Sally walked in, the bustle of her black skirt swaying. Her face was flushed and her eyes bright.

Clay frowned slightly. What was wrong with Lark? She looked ready to pass out. He forced his gaze to Sally.

Sally stopped beside Jennet, smiled stiffly, then turned to the board members seated in front of her. "Glenna works for me and is paid every week. When she gets paid, Matron forces her to give her most of the money." Sally waited, letting the news sink in. Jennet gasped and Mrs. Pepper sucked in her breath. "Les and Joe work at the mill and Matron forces them to do the same. Even the boys who work at the Wagon Works have to give her some of their earnings."

Matron jumped up. "It's only right they pay for their own expenses!"

"Sit down, Anna," said Jennet firmly. "You'll have a chance to speak later."

Clay scowled at Matron's back. He'd always known there was something about her he didn't like.

Lark locked her icy fingers together. Had she lost all chances of finding her father?

"Come in, children," said Sally, motioning to them.

Lark moved restlessly as she watched the children file in and stand in a line in front of Sally and Jennet. All the children had on their best clothes and were scrubbed clean. Lark tried to listen to them tell what Matron had forced them to do, but her mind was on what Matron had said about her father. Had Matron lied or did she really know where Matt Baritt was? Lark's stomach cramped and the room seemed to spin.

When Matron stood to defend herself Lark wanted to shout at her to tell her about her father, but she clamped her mouth closed.

"The money these children earn must be used for their clothing and food," said Matron. "It's only right when we're so short of finances."

"But why are you short of money?" asked Mrs. Pepper. "The community supports the asylum."

"What about the money from Jig?" asked Clay. "That should've helped for a while."

Matron shrugged. "That money was used wisely."

"That money wasn't recorded," said Lark.

"Then how can I be expected to remember?" asked Matron.

"I don't think the children should give their money to Matron," said Sally. "They work hard for their wages."

"I agree," said Jennet. "And I will check to see what did become of Jig's money."

Just then two sisters, Linda and Maggie, ran to Jennet. The girls wore patched dresses and their faces and hands were dirty. Linda held her soiled apron close to her chest. Maggie pushed an envelope in Jennet's hand. "We found this in Matron's room," said Linda, her face red.

Lark recognized Jig's envelope and her eyes widened.

Matron gasped.

Jennet looked inside the envelope and saw several bills that added up to $100, then she glanced at the front. "This is Jig's writing," Jennet said, looking at Matron.

"I don't know anything about that money!" cried Matron. She glared at Linda and Maggie. "Those girls had no business being in my private room."

Maggie pressed against Linda.

"Here's more," said Linda, dumping the contents of her apron on the table in front of Jennet. Bills and coins scattered across the smooth surface and a few coins fell on the floor. "We found it all in a box in Matron's trunk."

"There's my special silver dollar!" cried Les as he picked up a silver dollar with a hole through the center. "Somebody stole it right out of my bag."

Just then Gert and Ray Moline walked into the room and stepped to the front of the room. "We heard about this meeting and we wanted to have our say," Gert said, wringing her hands as she looked at Jennet. "We worked here several years and we know Matron took money that didn't belong to her." Gert glanced at Matron and looked quickly away.

"I never!" snapped Matron angrily.

Gert swallowed hard and moved closer to Ray. "She accused my man of stealing, but he never stole anything. Matron took from the kids and kept donations when she thought she could get away with it."

Ray nodded, but didn't speak. Matron glared at Gert.

"Why didn't you tell us before now?" asked Jennet softly.

"Because it's not true," said Matron icily.

"We didn't have the nerve," said Gert, flushing. "It was wrong of us, I believe, not to report her. But we're telling now."

"She punished the kids even if they didn't do any wrong," said Gert. "And she never let me have enough to see the children got enough nourishing food."

"You're lying!" snapped Matron.

"We'll see who's lying," said Gert, looking smug as she walked to an empty chair and sat down. Ray sat next to her.

"Anna, there's a good bit of evidence against you, but I want to hear what you have to say," said Jennet softly.

Her face ashen and her chin held high, Matron crossed her arms over her ample breast. "I worked hard all these years."

"I know," said Jennet. "But did you steal from the orphans?"

Matron's face hardened. "Steal from orphans? You can't steal from someone who doesn't have anything." She waved her hand at the children. "Look at them! Why would I steal from them? I do admit I take the money they bring in, but it goes to pay for food and clothes for them. Why do they need cash money? All their needs are met."

"But the money was theirs to keep," said Jennet. "The county pays for food and clothing for them."

Matron patted her hair and cleared her throat. "You just don't understand, do you? I work hard. What do these kids do? Nothing! And they're mean, dishonest, little nothings! If I did happen to take their money, it's because I deserve it."

Lark sagged in her seat. Now the truth would come out and

Jennet and the others would finally learn of Matron's abuse, meanness, and dishonesty through the years. Now they'd know how the children had suffered. She had accomplished what she'd set out to do!

"Did you take their money?" asked Jennet firmly.

Matron's eyes blazed. "Yes! But I told you why. I need it and they have no use for it. They are nothings! They deserved every punishment I gave them!"

"How did you punish them?" asked Jennet, her face white.

Lark listened as Jennet pulled the confession from Matron. The room was very quiet as the others listened to the sordid details, their faces showing shocked surprise. The silence was broken only occasionally with a murmured "Oh!" and the sound of a gulp of air.

"Ask her about my father," Lark said in a weak voice.

"Your father?" Her eyes large and questioning, Jennet turned quickly toward Lark.

Clay leaned forward with interest.

"She knows where he is," said Lark around the hard lump in her throat.

"Tell Lark everything you know about her father," said Jennet, nudging Matron.

Matron shook her head. "I don't know anything. She's an orphan. There's nobody that wants her! Nobody ever wanted her!"

Lark trembled and bit back a cry of outrage.

Clay jumped to his feet. "That's a cruel remark, Matron Pike! If you know anything about her father, tell her now." Tears stung Lark's eyes at Clay's surprising intervention.

Matron lifted her chin. "Lark Baritt's been nothing but trouble for me from the day she arrived. Her father brought her here and left her and that's that." Matron turned and stalked from the room.

Lark trembled. Then she ran after Matron and caught her arm. Lark's breast rose and fell and for a minute she couldn't speak.

"Let me go!" Matron slapped Lark's hand away. "I have nothing to say to you!"

Clay hurried from the room after Lark and Matron. He saw the anguish on Lark's face and the anger on Matron's.

"Please, you must help me," said Lark with a sob.

Matron lifted her hand to slap Lark's face, but Clay caught her arm and jerked her back.

"Don't ever do that again to her," said Clay grimly.

Lark bit her lip to stop her sobs as she stared helplessly at Clay.

Clay leaned down to Matron. "You tell Lark all about her father right now or we'll press charges against you and you'll spend the next several years in jail. What'll it be?"

Shivering, Lark waited as she watched the anger drain from Matron to be replaced with defeat.

Matron leaned weakly against the paneled wall in the hallway. "The last I heard he was in Lansing."

"Lansing," whispered Lark. "So close!"

"When did you hear last?" asked Clay, surprised at the news.

"About a year ago," said Matron hesitantly.

"Last year?" cried Lark, her hand at her throat.

"Did you hear from him before that?" Clay's voice was even and hard.

"Occasionally," Matron said.

"How did you hear?" Clay asked. "Letters? Did he write?"

"Some," Matron said weakly.

"My father wrote letters and you didn't tell me?" Lark's voice was filled with pain.

"Did he ever come here?" asked Clay.

Matron shook her head. "No. Never."

"Why didn't he come here at least to visit if he's kept in touch?" asked Clay.

Matron trembled.

Lark struggled against fresh tears. "Does he want me?"

Clay narrowed his dark eyes. "We want the whole story, Matron."

"Did he ever say he would come for me to take me away from here to be with him?" whispered Lark.

Matron shook her head.

Lark sagged weakly. Suddenly she didn't want to hear what Matron knew.

"But he did write," said Clay. He hated to see the agony Lark was suffering.

Matron nodded.

"Where are the letters?" asked Clay.

"I destroyed them," said Matron weakly.

"What did he say in them?" asked Lark just above a whisper. She reached for Clay's hand. He held it out to her and she clung to him with all her might. He could feel her rapid pulse as she gripped his hand. The agony in her eyes made his heart ache.

Matron swallowed hard. "He . . . ah . . . he thinks you don't want to see him. And . . each time he wrote, he . . . ah . . . he sent his address for you to write to him."

Lark leaned weakly against Clay. The room began to spin and she gripped Clay's hand even tighter. Her father had wanted to hear from her!

"Give Lark the latest address," said Clay in a tight, hard voice.

"I burned it," said Matron.

With a moan Lark pressed her face into Clay's arm, and it seemed natural to him to put his arm around her shoulders and hold her close to him.

"You must remember something," said Clay.

Matron shrugged.

"Jail? Is that what you want, Matron?" snapped Clay. He gently patted Lark's back, but his eyes were hard and locked with Matron's.

Matron sighed. "He was in Lansing finishing a book. He's a

writer. It was a book about plant and insect life in lower Michigan."

"Was that last year?" asked Clay.

Matron nodded. "He said he wouldn't write again."

Lark turned to Matron. "Why not?"

"He thought you didn't want to see him and didn't want to hear from him again," said Matron.

"Did you tell him that?" cried Lark in horror.

Matron nodded.

"Why?" asked Clay.

Matron clamped her mouth closed tightly.

"You'd better tell me or you'll go directly to jail," snapped Clay.

"I couldn't let him find out about the money and all the letters he'd sent and why you hadn't answered."

"I'll go to Lansing," said Lark, trembling. "I'll find him and talk to him! I'll tell him I never knew."

"Lansing's a big city," said Clay.

"You can help me, Clay," said Lark. "You can help me find him. You promised Jig you'd watch out for me. You promised!"

"It isn't wise for us to go there since we couldn't begin to know where to look. But I will telegraph a man I know in Lansing and ask him to hire a detective to find your father."

"I want to go myself. You could hire someone from the mill to guard the pines for a few days."

Clay shook his head. "It's not safe for you to travel alone."

"I'm not a child or an invalid, Clay Havlick."

"Let her go," said Matron sharply. "Maybe we'll finally be rid of her. She's nothing but trouble anyway."

Clay frowned at Matron. "Go to my mother, Matron, and wait with her. I'll tell the board of the deal I've made with you. Then you'll have to find somewhere to live, somewhere away from Blue Creek."

Matron walked slowly away and into the front room. She stood quietly beside Jennet.

Clay turned toward Lark. He couldn't understand why he

wanted to help her or to protect her, but he knew he had to. It was probably because he had promised Jig he would. "Please, let me send a detective after your father first. Then if he doesn't turn up anything, you can do what you want."

Lark considered his advice and finally nodded. "But I'll only wait a week."

"Make it two weeks."

Lark sighed heavily and nodded. "All right. Two weeks."

Later at dusk Clay drove Lark home in his buggy. He hadn't wanted her to go alone. She'd sat quietly all the way from town. At the cabin he stepped from the buggy, then reached for her. Sears whined a welcome, but didn't bark.

Just then Lark noticed the cabin door stood open. Fear pricked her skin as she caught Clay's hand and gripped it tightly. "The door," she whispered, motioning with her head.

The hairs on the back of Clay's neck stood on end. Was this more trouble for Lark? "Wait here," he whispered.

Lark hesitated, then jumped down and followed Clay. He looked inside the cabin and frowned at the mess he saw. The pillow and quilt had been slashed into ribbons. Feathers covered everything like a first snow of winter. Jig's Bible lay on the floor with several pages wadded up on the floor beside it. Chairs were overturned and the pots and pans knocked from the cupboard.

"Who would've done this?" she whispered.

"I'll find out," said Clay grimly.

Lark ran to the bunk and dug out her cudgel and revolver and laid them on the ruined quilt on the bunk. The box Jig had left her was untouched in the corner where she'd put it. She opened the lid, then jumped back with a shriek as a rattlesnake rattled inside it.

The snake struck just as Clay pulled Lark aside, and the fangs missed them both. Clay grabbed up the cudgel and hit the snake a death blow before it could coil again.

Lark shivered, her hand at her throat. With a whimper she

sank to a chair and watched as Clay lifted the rattler with the cudgel and flung it out the door. He rested the cudgel next to the door and stood looking down at Lark, then looked back outdoors at the pines.

"What do you see?" she whispered fearfully.

"Come and look," he said around a lump in his throat.

Lark looked to where he was pointing and she cried out in alarm. An uneven ring of bark had been chopped off all the way around a giant pine near Jig's grave.

"Four giant pines have been ringed," said Clay gruffly.

"Whoever did that didn't want to lumber those pines. He wanted to kill them," whispered Lark as she walked toward the trees. She knew if chips had been chopped off the trees in one spot, rosin would ooze over the wound and eventually the bark would grow and cover the bare spots, healing itself. But a ring all the way around caused the tree to die.

"We'll have to get the crew to lumber them tomorrow," said Clay as he balled his fists at his sides. "I'll get someone else to guard the pines."

Lark whirled to face Clay. "What do you mean? You can't take this job from me!"

"It's too dangerous, Lark."

Lark's lip quivered. "Clay, please don't take this job from me! I can't go back to the asylum! I love the cabin and the pines!"

"It's for your own good."

Lark burst into tears and gripped Clay's arms. "I can't go back to my old life. I can't. Please don't make me, Clay."

His heart melted at the sight of her tears. Against his better judgment he said softly, "All right. We'll try it a while longer and see what happens."

"Thank you," she whispered, struggling to control her tears.

The temptation to take her in his arms made him tremble. How could he want to do that when he was going to marry Veda? Was something wrong with him?

Slowly Lark lifted her eyes to Clay. "When will they lumber the pines?"

"Tomorrow. It's better to put the lumber to use instead of letting it rot and fall later."

"You're right, of course."

The next afternoon Clay and Lark stood beside the mill foreman in charge of seeing that the trees were cut and felled to the best advantage.

"It won't be long now," said the foreman. "The saw is almost through. The tree will fall there." He pointed to an open spot where it wouldn't damage Jig's gravestone or the cabin. Immediately following his words there was an ominous grinding at the base of the tree. The powerful trunk trembled, then shivered. "Timber!" shouted the sawers.

Lark caught Clay's hand and gripped it with both of hers as she watched the top of the tree sway. "Oh, Clay," she whispered, close to tears.

Clay swallowed hard. He hated to lose any of the precious white pines. Cutting even a single one caused him grief.

Slowly the tree toppled, gained speed, and with a mighty crack the trunk broke from the stump. Sweeping limbs snapped against other trees, and the giant pine whooshed to the ground with a loud thud, sending dust high into the air. Broken limbs and twigs fell nearby.

Clay felt Lark tremble as she swayed against him. He thought she might fall too. He turned her to him and pressed her face into his chest, his hand spread across the back of her head. Her hair felt soft under his hand and she smelled like bayberry soap.

Lark felt Clay's heart thud against her forehead and she trembled harder, this time from the feelings that leaped inside her because of being held by Clay Havlick. She pulled away and said, "I can't watch the others fall."

Clay turned her away and they walked to the far side of the cabin where Clay had tied Sears out of the way. He barked a welcome and Clay patted his head.

"I'll find out who ringed the trees," said Lark grimly.

"Oh, no, you won't!" Clay caught her hands and held them tightly. "I won't let you put yourself in more danger. We'll leave it up to the sheriff. I mean it, Lark Baritt!"

She sighed heavily and finally nodded.

CHAPTER

8

♦ Clay held up a spoke and eyed it to see if it was oval-shaped instead of perfectly round. Oval-shaped spokes gave the wheels a tremendous amount of strength. Bailey and Timmers carved out the best spokes he'd ever seen. They used oak that had seasoned two years, and with a drawing knife shaped the base of each spoke to fit the slots in the hub. There were twelve spokes to a wheel. For the past week Clay had had Timmers training other men to carve spokes the way he did. And he demanded perfection. Timmers sometimes lost his patience if a man said a spoke was good enough when it wasn't really perfect. Clay was glad Timmers wanted the very best work, but at times Clay worried about perfection slowing production.

Just then a blond haired, blue eyed man about Tris's age called to Clay. Clay nodded, laid the spoke down, and walked to the wide doorway. A pleasant breeze blew in the door, making working easier on the men.

The man stuck out his hand. "I am Dag Bjoerling. From Sweden." He spoke with a heavy accent, but plain enough for Clay to understand him.

Clay stiffened, then shook the man's work-roughened hand.

"I had a friend with your same name, but we called him Jig."

"He is my grandfather."

"Did you receive his letter?" asked Clay.

"Yes. It was hidden away for many years, but I found it, and came looking for him." Dag nodded and smiled.

Clay frowned slightly. "Don't you know he died in June?"

"No!" Dag paled. "I came too late." Dag leaned against the doorway. "My grandfather left Sweden as a young man. He was deeply in love, but couldn't marry the girl he loved. They had a son, Erik. Her family put Erik in an orphanage." Dag swept a hand over his blond hair. "Erik was my father. As long as I can remember he's been looking for his father. He learned the story and he discovered my grandfather had come to the forests of Michigan. My father accidently found a letter written by his mother telling about a letter from Grandfather Dag. Father searched for the letter but did not find it until after he was married and had children. At that time he couldn't leave his family to search for his father in another country. He put the letter away and several months ago I found it. I came to America to find my grandfather."

Clay thought about the letter Jig had left for Lark to send to his family after he died. Dag would've been here in America by then. Clay decided not to say anything about that letter. "Where are you living?"

"I've been sleeping under the stars."

Clay thought Dag didn't look like a man who'd spent his nights outdoors. "There's a boarding house here in Blue Creek."

"Ah, but I have no job." Dag looked around. "I know much about making wagons."

Clay cocked a brow. "You do? Can you carve spokes?"

Dag walked to the men who were working on them, picked up a piece of oak and a drawing knife and carefully carved the beginnings of a spoke.

Clay watched him and knew he'd found a man he could use. "You have a job, Dag, if you want one. When can you start?"

"Right now," said Dag with a wide smile.

Clay introduced him to Bailey and Timmers, then walked away to supervise the men making the bolsters.

Dag watched Clay through his long lashes and hid a smile. It had been easy to get Clay Havlick to give him a job! Tonight he'd report everything he could learn about Clay's business to Willie Thorne and tomorrow their plan to start the workmen drinking and fighting would begin. Willie had not made a mistake in bringing him here to Blue Creek. He had been in Grand Rapids and Willie had seen him. Because of his looks, accent, and knowledge of wood, Willie had hired him to pose as old Jig's relative and to set himself up to do serious damage to the Wagon Works. His job was to see to it that Clay Havlick had so many problems he couldn't fill his contracts. The funny thing was although he was only posing as Dag Bjoerling, his name really was Dag. He had been given the surname of Gotland, but he had no idea what his real name was. He was tired of having nothing, so Willie's offer had been a godsend. Dag nodded. He wanted his own home, a business, and a wife and family. After his job was finished here, he'd have enough money to go back to Grand Rapids and get everything he wanted.

The next morning in the forest Lark sang as she strode through the briars and across the bog that sucked at her boots. Sears followed, coming out with muddy stockings. He was good company and never left the trail to chase an animal.

Suddenly Sears growled deep in his throat. Lark gripped her cudgel and rested her hand on Sears as they kept walking. She listened for any signs of an intruder, but heard nothing. Up ahead was the spot where she'd run into the bears. She brushed her hand over the butt of her revolver. Sears growled again and Lark silenced him with a gentle tap on the head.

From the corner of her eye Lark caught a movement in the woods to her left. Her nerves tingled, but she started another song, singing as if she didn't have a care in the world. She passed the huge root where she'd been waylaid, but no one jumped out to stop her. The movement had probably been her imagination. Or had Clay sent someone to guard her? She didn't know whether she should be angry or pleased if he had. She did know she was thankful he'd hired a detective in Lansing to find her father. Maybe by tomorrow they'd have word. She'd thought *maybe by tomorrow* for the last three days.

Lightning began to flash and thunder rumbled. Wind whispered in the pines. In the clearing Lark looked up through the trees at the gray sky. She didn't like being in the woods with lightning flashing so close. It could strike a tree and knock it down or even cause a fire. "We'd better hurry, Sears," she said, sprinting forward.

Thunder boomed closer and the sky grew darker. Lark listened for sounds of the intruder, but heard nothing other than a loud clap of thunder. She reached the cabin without mishap and her nerves tightened more. She tapped the bell once to signal the Havlicks all was fine, but longed to strike it hard twice to call someone to the cabin to keep her company during the storm.

Lark filled a pan with water for Sears and set it beside his doghouse. "Sears, I'm glad it's Saturday and I don't have to go to the orphan asylum." Thunder clapped and Lark jumped. Lightning zigzagged across the sky above the field. The wind whipped tall grasses and flowers and bent down the tops of the trees.

Lark ran into the cabin just as the rain began to fall in giant drops, soaking into the sandy soil. She closed the door against the storm, then sank to the chair to pull off her high top shoes. She pulled off her leather pants and tunic and slipped on the limp calico dress that she'd planned to use as a rag. It felt soft and comfortable against her warm skin. She looked longingly at her bunk. She hadn't slept well for several days, and she felt very tempted to take a nap. Finally she walked to the bed and sank down on it. She couldn't remember the last time she'd slept during the day. She closed her eyes and listened to the rain on the roof and the thunder cracking farther and farther away. The sounds of the storm became comforting as the thunder moved away. She drifted off to sleep with her arm resting across her forehead.

Silent Waters opened the cabin door and slipped inside. She crept to the bunk where Lark lay sleeping and carefully laid a rag soaked with chloroform over Lark's mouth and nose. When she was sure Lark was unconscious she removed the rag, tied on Lark's shoes, then eased Lark on her shoulder like a sack of potatoes, and carried her outdoors. The rain had turned to a steady drizzle and the temperature had cooled slightly.

Sears barked and strained at his rope, but no one heard him. Silent Waters had counted on that.

She carried Lark deep into the forest to a place near Red Beaver's farm where she would wait until nightfall to finish the last part of her journey with her unconscious prisoner. Willie would be glad to see she'd brought Lark Baritt to him. He'd been plotting a way to get rid of her. Now he'd have her at his mercy. Silent Waters smiled slightly. Maybe Willie would be so pleased that he'd let her see Laughing Eyes any time she wanted to.

Lark squirmed and moaned. The taste in her mouth made her gag, and the ground felt damp and cold under her. Where was she? Was it a bad dream? She forced open her eyes but couldn't see anything. She felt a cool breeze against her face and heard someone breathing beside her. She lifted her head, then moaned.

"You are awake," said Silent Waters.

Fear pricked Lark's skin. "Where am I?"

"Don't talk."

"Who are you? . . . I know you, don't I?"

"I am Silent Waters."

Lark gasped. "What do you want of me?"

"No more talk."

Lark clumsily pushed herself up and sat with her knees

drawn to her chest. She wanted to leap up and run, but she knew she wouldn't be able to get away while her brain was foggy and her legs trembling.

A bobcat screamed and Lark shivered. A great horned owl fluttered from a tree and swooshed up into the sky.

Without warning Silent Waters covered Lark's nose and mouth with the rag. Lark struggled, but the chloroform overpowered her. Once again Silent Waters flung the unconscious form over her shoulder and walked through the woods to a shed at Red Beaver's farm. She slipped inside, bound Lark's wrists and ankles and tied a rag around her mouth to gag her when she awoke.

Silent Waters eased open the secret door that she'd discovered a few years ago and pushed Lark inside. Silent Waters smiled, then closed the door and moved a potato planter enough to partially cover the door.

Much later Lark whimpered and tried to move to get comfortable on the chilly dirt floor. The rag in her mouth choked her and the ropes around her ankles and wrists bit into her soft flesh. Silently she prayed for Clay or Red Beaver to find her. Tears welled up in her eyes and she blinked them quickly away. It wouldn't do any good to cry.

When she heard a voice and saw a tiny flash of light she tried to yell, but the sounds wouldn't pass through the rag in her mouth. She bucked, but couldn't move enough to make a noise. Her pulse raced and perspiration soaked her face and blue calico dress. Again she shouted, but only a low sound came out, too low for anyone to hear. She whimpered and closed her eyes. How long would it take Clay to know she was missing? Would he even consider Silent Waters as the culprit? Lark moaned. Probably not. He'd assume it had been someone who wanted to steal the pines.

Lark's eyes widened. Had Silent Waters taken her to turn her over to Willie Thorne? Maybe he'd learned his wife had told her everything. Silently Lark prayed for someone to rescue her.

She heard a scratching sound and froze. Was it a rat? She bucked again and frantically tried to pull her arms free. Pain shot up her arms and down to her fingertips and she stopped struggling. She listened again, but couldn't hear the sound. She couldn't survive if rats came in to chew on her. She felt like the terrified child she'd been when Matron locked her in the cellar room when she was six years old. She balled up as tight as she could and waited for someone to come for her.

His stomach a tight, cold ball. Clay knocked on the cabin door again. A warm breeze ruffled his black striped shirt that was tucked into his dark work pants. The heavy walking boots felt awkward today after not wearing them for so long. He glanced at Sears straining at his rope. If Lark had left to walk the trail, why hadn't she taken Sears? If she was still here, why wasn't she answering the door?

"Lark? Open the door, Lark." Clay pulled off his straw hat, leaned his head against the heavy door, and listened for movement inside. None came. "It's me, Clay. I'm coming in." He hesitated a moment longer, then opened the door and looked inside. It was empty. "Lark?" He frowned as a shiver ran down his spine. "Where are you? Where is she?"

Clay glanced around the cabin. Lark's buckskins were draped over a chair, the cudgel and revolver lay on the table, and the bed was rumpled. "Something happened to her," he whispered as his heart turned over. She had a lot of enemies. Had someone who wanted to steal the trees killed her and carried her off? Would Willie Thorne take her? Or had Matron hired someone to get rid of her out of spite?

"Clay!"

He jumped, then hurried to the door to find his sister calling to him. She wore a heavy shirtwaist and skirt, leggings, and high top boots instead of the Sunday clothes he'd expected her to be wearing. "Hannah, do you know where Lark would be?"

"No." Hannah pushed her bonnet off her head to dangle

between her shoulder blades. "I saw Flame and wondered why you were here."

"Lark's gone." Clay showed Hannah the cabin. "She'd never leave without her revolver and cudgel or her work clothes."

"I was going with her this morning," said Hannah, fingering the long braid that hung over her slender shoulder. "I said I'd keep her company, then we were going to church together afterward."

"I came to tell her I'd walk the trail today," said Clay. "She's been under a lot of pressure and I wanted to give her a day off."

Hannah bent down and picked up a small red bead from the floor. Had Red Beaver been here? Her pulse leaped, then she shook her head. He'd never take Lark. But Silent Waters might. "Look, Clay." Hannah held out the bead on the palm of her hand. "Let's go talk to Red Beaver to see what he knows."

"He and his mother aren't the only Indians around here, Hannah."

"I know. But it's a beginning. And Silent Waters hates us. She might want to harm Lark."

Clay groaned as he stared off into the pines. Was Silent Waters really Willie Thorne's squaw? Was that why she hated the Havlicks? Had Agnes Thorne told the truth when she'd said Red Beaver and Veda were the children of Willie Thorne and Silent Waters?

"We'll take Sears with us," said Hannah as she walked toward the wide-chested Dalmatian. "He'll help us find Lark."

"We'll go get the wagon," said Clay, forcing himself into action after the paralyzing thoughts that plagued him. Could he still marry Veda if she really was part Patawatomi?

With Sears running beside them, Clay and Hannah rode double on Flame back to the farm. Clay hitched up the wagon, lifted Sears into the back while Hannah climbed on the high seat, then climbed in himself.

At Red Beaver's farm Hannah jumped from the wagon, her heart racing. The sun was bright in the sky already drying yesterday's rain. Chickens, turkeys, ducks, and geese walked around the yard looking for bugs or worms. A cow mooed and a donkey brayed. Wind whirled the blades of the windmill, pumping water into the big round tank in the barnyard. Hannah looked around for Red Beaver, then saw him run from the barn with his hired man, Dave Legg, behind him. Red Beaver looked tall next to the short, round hired man. Hannah's heart leaped at the sight of Red Beaver. She saw his eyes light up when he saw her, but he quickly masked his feelings.

"Is there trouble?" asked Red Beaver, looking from Clay to Hannah and back again. He couldn't trust himself to look too long on Hannah. He might give away his feelings for her.

"Is it me Cora?" asked Dave, rubbing a pudgy hand over his round face. Cora was Jennet Havlick's hired girl and Dave's oldest daughter.

"Cora's fine," said Hannah.

Dave breathed a sigh of relief.

"We're looking for Lark Baritt," said Clay. "Have you seen her, either last night or this morning?"

"No," said Red Beaver while Dave Legg shook his head. "Is something wrong?"

"She's missing," said Clay, stabbing his fingers through his hair. Sears whined from the back of the wagon.

"We found a small red bead on her cabin floor," said Hannah. "We thought you might know something."

Red Beaver frowned. "Do you suspect my mother?"

Hannah barely nodded.

"She hates the Havlicks," said Clay.

"I know and I'm sorry," said Red Beaver. He glanced at Hannah, then quickly away. White woman or Indian, he'd never met one he'd wanted to be his wife except Hannah Havlick. Silent Waters would object as much as the Havlicks, so he'd kept his feelings to himself. He knew Silent Waters' anger and bitterness were eating holes in her spirit and turning her into a woman he didn't know, but she wouldn't give up her hatred. "I'll speak to her. Wait here."

Hannah watched Red Beaver run easily across the yard to the white fence. Instead of going through the gate, he leaped the fence as if he'd done it thousands of times, ran to the back door, and disappeared inside.

"He won't find her," said Dave Legg with a long, tired sigh. "He don't know it, but she left last night and ain't returned yet."

"Why didn't you tell him?" asked Clay, frowning.

Dave shrugged his thick shoulders. "She disappears at times. But she always comes back."

His hands locked behind his back and his head down, Clay nervously paced the length of the wagon and back. Why did everything have to take so long? Lark could be hurt or even dead. Silently he prayed for her, but the weight stayed in his heart. He should've insisted she leave the cabin and the job. The asylum might not be a nice place to live, but she would've been safe there.

Her fingers laced together in front of her, Hannah watched the back door for Red Beaver. How she hated to see him hurting! It would be terrible to live with a hate-filled mother. Jennet Havlick was a wonderful mother, full of love and gentleness. She taught and lived the fruits of the spirit that Jesus had taught. Hannah bit her lip. Someday she'd be a mother just like her.

Finally Red Beaver walked back, his shoulders bent in defeat. "She's not in the house. If she knows anything about this, she could be hiding anywhere so she won't have to answer questions."

"I'm sorry," said Hannah softly.

Red Beaver glanced at her, but the love he saw in her eyes made him look quickly away.

"We brought Sears to help us find Lark," said Clay, helping Sears jump to the ground. "Can we look around?"

"Yes," said Red Beaver. "But Dave and I have been in most of the buildings already this morning."

"She's not here or we'd a seen her," said Dave, nodding hard.

Flags of red flew in Hannah's cheeks. "We'll take Sears and look anyway."

Red Beaver flushed hotly and nodded. He hated to think his mother had stolen Lark away, but he knew it was possible. Silent Waters knew the pines as well as she knew the woods around his farm.

Clay ran with Sears to the big barn. The others waited in the doorway as Sears zigzagged down the aisle, then back to Clay's side. He ran to the next building and the next, waiting just inside each one long enough for Sears to sniff it out. In the shed next to the chicken coop Sears ran to the back corner and scratched against a board.

"There's nothing back there but maybe a rat," said Red Beaver. "Dave, finish the chores while we look."

Dave nodded and walked reluctantly away.

Clay stepped around some stored machinery to where Sears was sniffing and scratching. "Did you find something?" Clay said.

"There's nothing there, Clay," said Hannah, her shoulders drooping with disappointment. She felt Red Beaver beside her and she wanted to reach out and touch him, but she kept her hands at her sides.

Sears barked and scratched at the rough board.

Behind the board Lark tried to shout and tried to kick, but she couldn't. Tears of frustration rolled down her face as she lay curled on her side unable to make a sound Clay and Hannah could hear.

Clay studied the board as Sears scratched harder. Clay patted Sears on the neck. "There's nothing there, boy. Let's look in the other buildings."

"We have to find her," whispered Hannah.

Clay began to walk away, but Sears wouldn't move.

"Red Beaver, what's behind that board?" asked Clay.

Red Beaver looked and shook his head. "It's only the siding."

"Can you pull off just that one board and see?" asked Hannah.

Red Beaver hesitated, then nodded. He'd tear down the whole shed if Hannah asked him to. As he started to pry it off he suddenly saw the hidden door. He pulled aside the potato planter.

"A door!" Clay bent to open it. Inside was a small hidden room, the kind that could've been used to hide runaway slaves. As his eyes adjusted to the darkness inside, he saw Lark bound and gagged. "It's Lark," he whispered hoarsely as he reached for her.

Hannah held Sears aside to leave room for Clay to move. "You found her, Sears," said Hannah with tears in her eyes as she patted Sears on the neck.

"Forgive my mother," said Red Beaver in a ragged voice.

"It's not your fault," said Hannah softly.

Red Beaver turned his head and bent his shoulders in anguish and shame.

Clay eased Lark out and pulled the gag from her mouth. Tears blinded her eyes as she looked into Clay's face. He gently untied her wrists and rubbed the red welts on her wrists. He untied her ankles. He lifted his head and tears stood in his eyes. "I'm sorry, Lark."

She wiped the tears from her eyes. "It was Silent Waters," she whispered. "Somehow she was able to drug me."

Red Beaver cried in agony as he knelt beside Lark and Clay on the dirt floor. "I'm sorry! Forgive my mother! Hatred has overcome her."

"You know I'll have the sheriff after her for this," said Clay in a hard voice.

"Clay!" cried Hannah. "Don't hurt Red Beaver more than he is already!"

"Let it be, Hannah," said Red Beaver. Her name fell off his tongue as easily as if he'd called her by name often. But always he'd called her Miss Havlick to her face. He'd spoken *Hannah* only in his daydreams.

"Don't blame Red Beaver," said Lark, struggling to her feet. She stumbled and Clay caught her and held her until she felt steady enough to stand.

"*I* blame myself," said Red Beaver sharply.

"Please don't," said Lark as she pulled away from Clay. Her taffy hair hung in wild tangles around her head and shoulders. She pushed it back off her face, leaving a dirt streak from her hand. "It doesn't do any good to talk of blame." She turned to Clay. "Please take me home. I must make sure the pines are safe."

A muscle jumped in Clay's jaw. "You'll do no such thing, Lark Baritt! I'll check *my* pines while you rest."

Lark cringed at his stress of the word *my*. She knew the pines were his, but at times she felt they belonged to her too. Finally she nodded. "All right. I'll rest for a while." She patted Sears on the head, then bent down and hugged him. "Thanks for finding me."

Clay swallowed a lump in his throat and blinked moisture from his eyes.

Outdoors Hannah turned to Clay. "I want to speak with Red Beaver. Take Lark home and I'll walk."

Clay frowned. "Pa wouldn't want you to stay by yourself."

Hannah lifted her chin. "I'm staying, Clay. I'll explain to Pa later."

"Go home with your brother, Miss Havlick," said Red Beaver sharply. "There's nothing for you to say to me."

"I will stay and I will speak my mind," Hannah said with more courage than she felt.

Lark smiled at Hannah, then let Clay help her into the wagon. Sears stuck his nose against her cheek and she patted his shoulder.

Clay slapped the reins on the team and they stepped forward.

"I'm sorry I worried you," said Lark.

"I'm just thankful you're alive," said Clay. "I am going to tell the sheriff." Clay shook his head. "But if Silent Waters doesn't want to be found, he won't find her. She's spent her entire life in the woods around here."

"She frightened me. I've never seen anyone with so much anger."

"She won't do anything to you again. She won't have another chance. You're moving out of the cabin and back to the asylum."

Lark turned on Clay. "No! I can take care of myself. I won't let her capture me again."

"I don't understand you, Lark. The pines don't even belong to you."

Tears blurred her eyes. She felt like the pines did belong to her! Around the lump in her throat she said, "I know, but I love them. I will do anything to keep them safe."

Clay heard the same passion in her voice that he heard in his mother's when she spoke of the pines. "I don't want anything to happen to you," he said with his eyes on the team and the road ahead.

Lark blinked away her tears and lifted her chin. "Someday I want my children and my grandchildren to see your white pines! I want them to have a part of what Michigan once was when Jig first came. I want the habitat left the way it is."

The passion she felt blazed in her eyes and through her speech. He knew he couldn't take the pines from her. She did indeed love them the way he and his family did. With a sigh he said, "I won't take them from you."

"Thank you," she whispered. Relief left her limp, but she held herself erect to keep from leaning against Clay.

At Red Beaver's farm Hannah squared her shoulders and turned to face Red Beaver. They had kept their love for each other locked inside long enough. It was time to speak up. After what had happened to Lark, she felt frightened about losing more valuable time. The sun felt hot against her head.

The fire in her breast felt even hotter. "We must talk freely about our feelings for each other, Red Beaver," she said with a catch in her voice.

Red Beaver groaned. "We dare not."

"I need you to tell me how you feel about me, Red Beaver," she cried.

A muscle jumped in his cheek. Behind him he heard the bray of a donkey and the squeak of the windmill. His heart pounded at the thought of speaking the words to Hannah that he'd only said in his daydreams. He shook his head. "I can't, Hannah, not after what Silent Waters has done to Lark."

"She doesn't blame you. Nor do I." Hannah clasped her hands to her heart. "I care for you." She saw his eyes darken. "Do you care at all for me?"

Red Beaver gripped her arms. "You don't know what you're doing, Hannah."

"I do! I want you to tell me how you feel about me. I've waited too long already."

Red Beaver moved closer to Hannah, but he dropped his hands to his sides. "What I feel for you is a love so intense it would frighten you. I want you as my wife. I want you in my bed, in my house, on my farm, at my side for as long as we live."

Hannah trembled and her heart soared at his words. She leaned forward until they touched. "I love you."

Red Beaver held her fiercely to him and she clung to him as if she'd never let him go. He smelled the clean smell of her hair and skin. She felt his heart thud against her and smelled his earthy smell. Finally he pushed her at arm's length and looked deep into her eyes. "But I can never take you as my wife. I will live out my days alone with the shame of what Silent Waters did to Lark and to the Havlick family."

Hannah shook her head. "No!"

"I am a man of honor."

"Red Beaver, I can't survive without you." Tears welled up in Hannah's eyes and slipped down her ashen cheeks.

125

"Nor I without you. But my shame is too great." Red Beaver knew how Freeman Havlick felt about him. Now there was one more reason for him to despise him. "You find a white man to love and marry."

"Never! I too will live all my days alone. You are the only man I want as my husband, the father of my children, my companion until we die. You have brought a lifetime of loneliness on me because of your pride."

A groan rose from deep inside Red Beaver. "You must forget about me."

Hannah lifted her chin and flames shot from her eyes. "Never! Do you hear me? I will love you forever."

With a low moan Red Beaver cupped Hannah's face between his work-roughened hands. He looked deep into her eyes, then slowly lowered his mouth to hers and kissed her with all the pent up passion in him.

Hannah clung tightly to him, returning the kiss while her heart raced.

Finally Red Beaver held her from him and said softly, "I love you."

"And will marry me before winter comes," she whispered.

Red Beaver shook his head. "I can't."

Hannah leaned weakly against him. "Then I shall die an old maid."

CHAPTER
9

♦ Clay leaned against the top rail of the fence beside Free and absently watched Evie train her pony to jump. Dust billowed out behind the pony's hooves. Clay's mind was on Veda and Silent Waters and Agnes Thorne's story. What was the truth and what was a sick woman's ranting?

Free chuckled. "Evie's like her ma. She won't quit even when she's tired." It was almost time for Evie to go inside for the night, but she wanted to take the pony around one more time.

Clay moved restlessly.

"What is it, son? You've been on edge since Sunday. Are you brooding about Lark's experience? She seems to be fine. Surely something like that won't happen again."

"She's a strong woman," said Clay. "I'm learning not to worry about her." He was amazed that she'd gone right back out Monday morning to walk the line, then had gone to work at the asylum as if nothing had happened to her.

"Then what's on your mind, Clay?"

"Red Beaver."

Free stiffened. "I'm not blaming you for Hannah's disobedience."

Clay faced Free. "Are you against Red Beaver because he's Patawatomi or because he's Willie Thorne's son?"

Free's eyes widened and he shot a look at Evie before he turned back to Clay. "I didn't know you knew."

"I found out a few days ago." Clay steeled himself to ask the next question. "Do Silent Waters and Willie Thorne have other children?"

"No. Willie went off to marry Agnes and left Red Beaver and Silent Waters on their own."

Relieved, Clay leaned back against the fence. Agnes Thorne hadn't been thinking clearly when she'd told Lark about Veda. He'd stayed away from Veda to try to sort out his feelings, but now it didn't matter. Veda wasn't Patawatomi. Clay cringed as he realized how prejudiced he was. He hadn't realized it before.

"Have you heard anything from the Lansing detective?" asked Free. He had been trying to find a way to help Lark find her father, but first he wanted to see what the detective discovered.

Clay shook his head. "He said he found a copy of the book he'd written, but couldn't find him."

"I think I'll send word to the lumbermen I know and see what they can find."

"Thanks, Pa. Lark will be glad to hear that."

"She's a fine woman, Clay."

Clay nodded. He knew Free was getting ready to compare her with Veda and he didn't want to hear it. "I have business in town, Pa. I'll be late getting home." Veda had stopped at the Wagon Works earlier in the day and wanted to have supper again tonight, but he'd said he couldn't until tomorrow night. She'd pouted at first, then she'd kissed him and walked away to shop for things for the wedding. He waved to Evie, then ran to the buggy he'd hitched earlier and drove away.

At Blue Creek Clay heard the last train of the day pull away from the station. The loud hiss, rattle, and clank covered all other sounds in the town for a while. He stopped the team to

128

the side of the street and waited. He watched two boys race their bicycles along the street. The wheel was becoming very popular around the country because it was cheaper than keeping a horse. He knew Miles wanted a wheel more than anything else. Pa said as soon as the roads were better he could get one. It was hard to keep a wheel upright on the corduroy.

Clay sighed. Sometimes he liked change and other times he didn't. Probably the wheel would take the place of riding horses and the gas buggy the place of a horse drawn buggy. Would anything ever take the place of a wagon?

Just then Willie Thorne stepped out of his tavern. It still wasn't open for business, but Clay knew men sneaked in from time to time for a "drink on the house." The Temperance League was still hard at work to keep the doors closed and locked. Clay frowned. Would Willie Thorne ever give up and leave town?

Just then Willie spotted Clay. Willie waved and strode down the wooden sidewalk to where Clay was stopped. Willie puffed out his chest and wrapped his hands around his suspenders. He wanted to ask Clay about Lark Baritt, but since no word had gotten out about her abduction, he couldn't. He'd told Silent Waters to let him handle the problems, but she'd wanted to do something to please him. Just seeing her pleased him, but he couldn't tell her that or she might take it on herself to get rid of Agnes.

Willie shook his finger at Clay. "I don't want you seeing my daughter again, young Havlick!"

Clay tightened his grip on the reins. "I'll see her if I want, Mr. Thorne."

Willie hid a smile. He'd already figured out Clay was the type who would try harder if he was told not to do something. "She won't get a dime of my money if she marries you."

"I have enough money without taking any of yours," snapped Clay.

"I won't have you eloping with her," said Willie gruffly. The wind ruffled his graying red hair.

"We don't plan to elope," said Clay.

"See that you don't!" Willie turned on his heels and stalked away. Suddenly he turned back and shouted, "And don't you marry my girl until winter!"

Clay wanted to shout that he'd marry her any time they decided, but he saw others listening. He slapped the reins on the team and drove to the Thorne house. He had a mind to elope with Veda that very day. His straw hat in his hand, he knocked on the door and Gert answered.

"Well, Clay Havlick, it's a real pleasure to see you, I believe," said Gert, opening the door wide enough for him to enter.

He heard the tick of the grandfather clock beside the tall green plant in the big hallway. He smelled oil soap and could tell someone had recently been at work cleaning and polishing the open stairway and the carved newel posts and bannister.

"How's your dear mother and father?" asked Gert with just a hint of nervousness in her voice.

"They're fine," said Clay, smiling down at Gert.

She touched the little black cap on her head and rubbed the black apron tied around her thick waist. "What brings you here?"

"To see Veda Thorne."

"But she's not here. She and Mrs. Thorne went to Grand Rapids on the afternoon train, and won't be back until tomorrow."

"I didn't know that."

"It was one of those spur of the moment things."

Clay fingered the wide brim of his straw hat. "I heard Mrs. Thorne wasn't well."

Gert spread her hands and shrugged. "She has her days, but she was fine today."

Clay watched Gert closely. "Lark said she came here and visited with her."

Nervously Gert rubbed her plump hands together. "It was to be a secret between me and Lark."

"I won't tell."

"Mr. Thorne would get up in arms if he knew his wife talked with Lark."

A shiver ran down Clay's spine. "Why?"

"Mrs. Thorne says things. Things that he doesn't want said, I believe." Gert patted her flushed cheeks and again rubbed her hands over her black apron.

Clay wanted to ask more questions, but he knew Gert wouldn't answer them. He talked a while longer, turned down the piece of apple pie she offered him, and walked back to his buggy.

He stopped at the Wagon Works and to his surprise found Dag still at work carving spokes.

Dag grinned. He enjoyed the work and he knew it wouldn't hurt to do extra work to get on Clay's good side. Dag wanted a key to the shop to give him the freedom to come and go as he wanted. He glanced toward a case of liquor partly hidden near the workbench, then smiled at Clay. "Caught me," said Dag.

Clay shook his head. "You should've stopped at six like the other men. Six to six makes a long day."

Dag carved off another strip of wood. "I think while I work, Clay. I have no family. What do I have to take up my nights? I don't drink and I don't gamble."

"Neither are allowed in Blue Creek."

Dag laughed. "Then it's good I don't do either." What would Clay do when he found his men drinking on the job tomorrow? Willie had dropped off the case of whiskey just a few minutes ago. If the men were drunk, they couldn't work well, and Clay wouldn't be able to fill the contract.

Clay picked up the spokes and eyed them one by one. They were perfect. "I'm glad you happened in when you did, Dag."

"It's like it was planned," said Dag.

"Ma says to bring you to supper one night. She and Pa want to meet you. Jig was like family to us."

The offer surprised but pleased Dag. "You name the day and I'll be there." Dag laid the drawing knife down and brushed shavings off his plaid work shirt and dark pants. "I would like to see the cabin my grandfather called home."

"I'll arrange it."

"If I can, I would like to live in it."

Clay shook his head. "The guard for my pines lives there."

"I didn't know. I would like to see it and touch what my grandfather touched."

Clay thought about Jig's muzzleloader, but he couldn't bring himself to offer it to Dag. There was plenty of time. Clay was sure he was being overcautious, but there was something about Dag that kept him from totally trusting him. Maybe given time he'd learn to trust Dag as much as he'd trusted Jig. "Sunday afternoon we could take a ride out there together."

"I could work Sunday."

"No. We don't work Sundays." Clay smiled. "But I like your attitude." Clay clamped a hand on Dag's shoulder. "Call it a night and I'll lock up."

"Timmers said he'd be by later to lock up," said Dag as he put away his tools and quickly cleaned the area. "I'll stop by his place and tell him you locked up."

"Thanks, Dag." Clay watched Dag walk to the main street and turn toward the boarding house. Clay started out the door, then remembered he hadn't logged in the wages. With a sigh he pulled the book from his desk. Suddenly the job seemed too much for him. Maybe now was the time to ask Lark to keep the books. "She's probably still at the asylum," he muttered as he quickly locked the large doors and walked to his buggy. Since Matron had left, Lark had taken over many of her duties until the board could hire a new superintendent. Often she stayed late. He flicked the reins against the horse, then frowned. Why was he suddenly excited about seeing her? It had to be because it would be so much easier to run his business if she kept the books.

A few minutes later Clay walked into the asylum and stood a moment in the wide front hall. Laughter floated down the stairs. The smell of cookies drifted out from the kitchen. He turned toward Matron's office that Lark had taken over until the replacement arrived. The door stood open and he saw her sitting at the big desk with her head in her hands. He frowned. Was she already too overworked to take on another job?

He tapped on the door and stepped into the room, taking off his hat as he did.

The color drained from her face as Lark jumped up and ran to him. Her waist and skirt were slightly wrinkled and the button at her throat was unbuttoned. Tendrils that had pulled loose from the pile of taffy brown hair on her head hung around her face. She clasped her hands at her throat and tried to steady the wild beat of her heart. "Did you hear word of my father?" She was sure that was the only reason he would come to the asylum looking for her.

"No."

Lark drooped just like a flower with no water. "What is taking so long?" she whispered brokenly.

Clay awkwardly patted her shoulder. "Don't give up," he said gently. He told her what his pa planned to do and she brightened.

Absently Lark brushed her hair from her cheek. "All my life I thought I had nobody of my own. Now that I know I do, I want to find him and get to know him. But oh, the waiting is agony!"

"I wish I could help." Suddenly Clay grinned. "I just might be able to."

Lark lifted a dark brow. "How?"

"By keeping you busier than you already are."

"I use that on the children here. Busy hands make time pass faster." Lark leaned back against the desk and smiled at Clay. Just having him stop in had brightened her day. "What do you have in mind?"

"I need someone to do the bookkeeping for the Wagon Works. Would you like the job? The pay is good and . . . the boss is nice." Clay chuckled and Lark laughed. He liked the sound of her laughter.

"I'll do it. When shall I start?"

"I'm already behind."

"Then I'll start tomorrow if that's all right with you. I can do it here or at the shop."

"Here would be better. I don't have an actual office there and you'd be a big distraction to the men."

Lark flushed. She knew Clay was only teasing. She was as plain as a post and wouldn't distract any man. "Does it look like you'll make your contract?"

"Yes. Thank the Lord."

Mrs. Pepper knocked on the door and ushered in a middle aged woman with light brown hair and big blue eyes. She was short and slight and looked on the verge of laughing. "Lark, Clay, I'd like you to meet the new matron, Mercy Kettering. Mercy comes highly recommended and is willing to start immediately."

Lark stepped forward with her hand out. "I'm happy to meet you, Matron."

"Call me Mercy." She shook hands with Lark, then with Clay. "I like your town and I know I'll like the Home." She smiled brightly. "I would rather call it a *home* instead of an *asylum*."

"That is better," said Lark, liking Mercy immediately. "I've been using your office, but I'll move my things to leave it free for you."

"That's very kind of you."

"Welcome to our town," said Clay, tipping his head slightly.

"Thank you," said Mercy.

"I've told her about the tavern," said Mrs. Pepper.

Mercy squared her shoulders and her eyes twinkled. "I've walked into many a tavern with my tambourine in my hands and a hymn on my lips to stop demon rum from destroying folks. I look forward to doing it again here in your pleasant town."

"My mother will be right with you," said Clay.

"And so will I," said Lark with a firm nod. So far she'd never stepped foot in a tavern to close it down, but she would if she had to.

They talked a while longer, said goodbye, and Clay helped Lark carry her things to her office. The evening breeze ruffled the curtains at the windows. The room seemed small to Lark after being in Matron's office the past few days.

"I'm thankful we have a matron again," said Lark. "I like her, don't you?"

Clay nodded. "She's different from Anna Pike, and thank the good Lord for that. I think she'll be wonderful with the kids."

"I had the same impression. She has a soft glove covering a hand of steel." Lark put her things away and closed the windows for the night.

"I'll drive you home if you're ready," said Clay.

Her heart gave a strange little jerk. "No need. I can walk. I'm sure you have more important things to do."

"Not at all."

"What about Veda?"

Clay shrugged. "She's away tonight."

"Oh." Lark pinned her small hat in place and picked up her handbag. She suddenly remembered the feel of Clay's arms around her when he'd rescued her and she flushed. She would not let herself care for Clay Havlick! She was not good enough for him even if he had been available. "I'm ready," she said in a small voice.

The next day after Clay left the building with the bookwork under his arm, Dag "accidentally" discovered the case of whiskey. He held up a bottle. "I don't know who this belongs to, but I say we break it and pour the foul drink on the ground."

"Hold it!" cried Clarence, grabbing the bottle from Dag. "You can't throw away good whiskey."

"You can't drink on the job," said Dag. "It's not right." He knew that was like saying "sic 'em" to a bulldog. He stepped away from the whiskey and watched the men crowd around it. Some of them tried to stop the drinking, but couldn't without a fight. Quietly Dag slipped to the other building. There he "found" another case of whiskey, pretended shock and outrage, and stepped aside so the men could greedily break open the bottles. By the end of an hour, about fifteen men were too drunk to work. A few others could work, but not up to the standards Clay had set.

Inside Dag was laughing, but he didn't let it show on his face or in his eyes. He'd learned that in the orphan asylum in Grand Rapids. While the drinking continued and the noise grew louder around him he carefully slipped a tenon he'd carved then shaped into the mortise. "A perfect fit," he muttered, pleased with himself. When he finished, the slope of the mortises in the hub automatically created the required dish shape. The dish curved toward the inside of the wagon so when the wagon was fully loaded the hubs were forced outward and the spokes would straighten up rather than bow out. If the wheels weren't dished, then as the load shifted, the wheels would bow outward and split apart. "Well done," he said. "Well done." He liked doing a job well.

Dag glanced up just as Clay walked in. Dag tensed, but he didn't let his tension show.

Clay looked at the men in horror. Several of them were sprawled across a crate, singing and laughing. Two had passed out on the ground. "Who brought drink in here?" Clay shouted angrily.

"Not me," said Higgins with a slurred laugh.

"Me kind angel did it," said O'Brian, lifting a bottle high.

Clay looked at the sober men and questioned them, but no one could tell how the whiskey came to be in the buildings. "You men go home and sober up so you can work tomorrow. If you ever drink on the job again, I'll fire you on the spot."

"But you can't meet your contract if you do that," said Mullins.

"I'll hire men from out of town," said Clay. "I will not allow drinking on the job." His head ached with anger. He'd report the whiskey to the sheriff, but he knew it wouldn't do any good. Had Willie Thorne brought the whiskey here? If the sheriff could prove that, he'd be able to kick Willie out of town. What would Veda think of that? Clay's head spun. Maybe Willie didn't have anything to do with bringing the whiskey in.

His fists clenched at his sides, Clay watched the men leave the shop. The ones left couldn't begin to meet production, but he'd keep them working anyway.

Dag watched Clay's control and was astonished. He'd expected Clay to rave with anger and maybe break a few bones or bloody some noses. If Willie Thorne expected to break Clay, he'd have to try harder.

Late in the afternoon Lark stepped from the dress shop where she'd stopped to talk with Sally and bumped into John Epson. "I'm so sorry," said Lark with a laugh as she stepped away from him.

"That's quite all right, Lark." John stroked his well trimmed beard and chuckled. He'd been waiting ten minutes already for Lark to come out of the dress shop. He pulled off his straw hat and held it between his hands. A slight breeze ruffled his black hair. "I don't get run into by a fine lady very often."

Lark straightened her hat and brushed a damp tendril of hair off her cheek. "I usually don't go around hitting men. Unless it's with my cudgel when they jump me in the pines."

"Would you leave your cudgel behind and join me for supper?" John smiled and his white teeth flashed through his black beard and his blue eyes crinkled at the corners.

Lark bit back a gasp of surprise. She'd never been invited to eat with a man. Several months ago she would've given anything to be with John. Even now she felt a flash of excitement as she nodded.

In the restaurant Lark looked around the crowded room.

She knew several of the people and she knew John did too. They spoke to several people as they walked around the square tables to an empty one near the back.

Smiling, Peg took their orders of perch for Lark and roast beef for John. She served them tall glasses of cold water, then hurried to the kitchen.

"I'm glad I decided to come to Blue Creek to live," said John. "I considered Lansing for a while."

"This is a nice place," said Lark. "The lumber mill and the farms provide good incomes. The economy is stable right now."

John cocked his dark brow. He hadn't realized Lark would know such things. "Do you approve of President Harrison?"

"He's a fine republican."

"What about the Sherman Antitrust Act?"

"A monopoly is harmful to the people. Competition keeps prices fair."

John leaned forward with interest. It had been a good while since he'd had a debate and he was looking forward to it. Willie had said to spend time with Lark and he hadn't wanted to, but now he was pleased he had agreed to it. He'd do anything to get her away from the pines so Willie could steal them. And a portion of every dollar Willie made belonged to him. Willie had first hired him to manipulate Agnes's wealth so he could have free access to all her funds, then when Willie couldn't pay him, he'd become a partner in stealing the Havlicks' trees. Maybe it wouldn't be so bad to work toward a close relationship with Lark Baritt. They'd been casual friends for a couple of years now, but he'd never considered her for more than that until Willie had made it part of his plans.

Over dessert of cherry pie John said, "I don't know how you can continue to guard the Havlicks' pines when you know it puts you in danger."

Lark gripped her napkin and her dark eyes flashed. "Do you know how much I love those trees? They're a part of my life! I will do anything to keep them the way they are!" She leaned forward. "They were a haven to me all these years! I won't allow them to be destroyed!"

"You are passionate about the pines, aren't you?"

Lark laughed and nodded. She sipped her lemonade, then patted her mouth with the white linen napkin. No one could begin to understand how she felt about the trees, least of all John.

He leaned forward, his eyes on Lark. "What of the money Clay Havlick would make if he lumbered the pines?"

"There are more important things in life than money!" she snapped.

"You mean health and happiness, I suppose."

She frowned. "Don't make light of it."

"You can have health and happiness and still have money."

"I know that, but there are other ways to get money. Cutting the pines would be terrible for everyone. Even you, John."

He shook his head. "The pines are nothing to me." He didn't add that they only meant money in his pocket.

"Don't you know God created the earth for our enjoyment?"

"I suppose I do," he said uncertainly.

"Have you ever seen a luna moth all dressed in green and looking like a royal princess? God created it; money can't buy it or produce it. Have you ever heard the golden notes of an oriole, an orange and black beauty? God created the oriole; money can't buy it or produce it. And the trees themselves! What beauties! Once most of the state was covered with trees. Do you realize the plant and animal life destroyed because of the lumbermen cutting the trees? These last trees must never be cut. I believe and the Havlicks believe God wants them left for others to enjoy."

John moved restlessly. If he wasn't careful he'd start to believe Lark. His mother talked that way. But he wouldn't let himself think about the heartbroken mother he'd left behind after the terrible fight with his father. "There's danger in the forest too, Lark."

"Do you mean the rattlesnakes this time of year? They can be dangerous, that's true. When it's this hot out you can't trust them to always rattle before they strike."

"Some people are like that," said John grimly.

"I know."

They talked a while longer and to John's surprise his respect for Lark grew. He'd have to guard against letting his emotions get the upper hand. He couldn't afford to get emotionally involved with Lark Baritt or it would ruin everything.

Outdoors John stopped Lark with a hand on her arm. "May I see you again, Lark?"

She stiffened. Had she heard correctly? "I'm sure you're joking, John. You know my background."

He frowned. "What do you mean by that?"

"You're a fine lawyer and probably had a good upbringing. I was raised at the asylum." Lark couldn't get used to calling it a "home." She looked down at her hands. "I'm not . . . not . . . good enough to associate with you."

A muscle jumped in John's cheek. How could she think that? She was modest and her standards high—two things the women he'd associated with didn't have. "Lark, I will take you to supper tomorrow night and every night after that!"

Lark laughed shakily. "We'll settle for tomorrow night, then. After that . . . well, we'll see."

John nodded. "Then I'll see you in the office tomorrow morning." He settled his white straw hat in place as he looked down the street. "I understand the asylum has a new matron."

"Yes." Lark laughed softly. "Mercy Kettering, a fine woman. Already the children have learned to respect her."

"I look forward to meeting her." John tipped his hat and walked away.

Lark walked slowly back to the asylum to speak to Zoe before she went home. Zoe wanted to talk to her about Tris Havlick and what she could do to make him interested in her even if she was only an orphan. Lark's mind was full of thoughts of her supper with John Epson. She frowned slightly. Why would he want to take her to supper and spend time with her? She stopped at the end of the brick walk in front of the asylum as she tried to think of a reason.

Her red hair flipping about her slender shoulders, Zoe ran down the sidewalk to meet Lark. "Thank goodness you're finally here! I'm so excited I'm ready to burst."

"What is it? Did Tris declare his undying love?" asked Lark with a laugh.

"It's not about Tris," said Zoe, fluttering a paper. "You got a telegram!"

Lark shivered and clutched Zoe's hand. "A telegram? Where is it? What does it say?"

CHAPTER

10

♦ Lark's hands shook as she opened the telegram. The collar of her shirtwaist seemed to bite into her soft flesh. For a minute her eyes wouldn't focus on the words. Finally she read, "Matt Baritt died of the fever December 18, 1889." Lark swayed and the telegram fluttered to the porch floor beside Zoe's feet.

"What's wrong, Lark?" asked Zoe anxiously.

Lark lifted her skirts and ran away from the asylum like a mad woman. Tears streamed down her ashen cheeks as she sped down the street and across the bridge toward the white pines, her haven.

Zoe picked up the telegram and read it. Tears burned her eyes. "I must find Clay. He'll know what to do," she whispered brokenly.

With her skirts held high, Zoe ran to the restaurant where she knew Clay usually took Veda. They were just walking to his buggy. "Clay!" called Zoe urgently as she ran to him, panting for breath.

He turned with a worried frown. Two men walked past and looked at them strangely.

"What's wrong?" asked Veda impatiently. She'd waited

several days for time with Clay and she was annoyed at Zoe's interruption.

Zoe pulled Clay aside and showed him the telegram. "Lark ran away crying," whispered Zoe.

"I'll find her," Clay said softly. He folded the telegram and pushed it into his suit coat pocket and turned to Veda. "An emergency has come up. I'll drop you at your home and see you tomorrow night."

Veda's face hardened. She wanted to shout her anger, but she knew she couldn't without upsetting Clay. "I hope it's nothing serious."

"It's nothing for you to be concerned about," said Clay as he handed her into his buggy. He turned back to Zoe. "You're a good friend. Run on back to the asylum and don't worry."

"Thank you, Clay." Zoe rubbed away her tears, tried to smile, and walked slowly away toward the asylum. A white cat ambled out of the corner store and rubbed against her ankles.

The buggy swayed as Clay stepped in. Absently he gathered the reins in his hands. Veda tucked her hand through Clay's arm and rested her head against his shoulder. Inside she was seething with anger. She'd planned to talk Clay into eloping tonight. "Will you tell me what happened?" she murmured, nestling close to him.

"Nothing that concerns you," Clay said, his voice even and unemotional as he drove toward her house. He couldn't bring himself to discuss Lark's business with Veda.

Veda's eyes blazed with anger as she sat up straight and folded her hands in her lap over her handbag. She had spent a fortune on the green silk dress she was wearing and the new green and black hat and Clay hadn't noticed. She dare not let him see how angry she was, though! "Everything that concerns you, concerns me," she said gently. "Is it your family?"

"No." Clay stopped the team outside Veda's door.

"Did something happen to the Wagon Works?"

"No." Actually, several men had gotten drunk on the job

again. He'd reported the illegal whiskey to the sheriff, but he hadn't been able to learn anything about it.

"Oh, Clay! Please tell me what's wrong or I'll imagine all kinds of terrible things." Veda stuck her lip out in a slight pout, something that always worked with her father.

"It's Lark," said Clay reluctantly as he helped Veda from the buggy.

Veda jerked away from Clay and her eyes flashed. "Lark Baritt! You cut our time together short because of that *orphan?*"

Clay jumped back in the buggy, tipped his hat, and drove away. He would have to deal with Veda's anger later. Right now he had to help Lark.

Veda stormed into the house, slamming the front door after her. She flung her handbag on a table outside the parlor door and ran to her father's study. She flung open the door, then stopped with a shocked cry.

Flushing with guilt, Willie jumped away from embracing Silent Waters. He'd thought it was safe for her to be in the house because Veda had gone out with Clay, Agnes was locked in her room, and the hired help was out for the evening. A warm breeze blew in through the open French doors. The tick of the mantle clock over the stone fireplace sounded loud in the quietness of the room.

Silent Waters looked hungrily at Veda, her eyes traveling slowly from Veda's head down to her beautifully clad feet. Oh, she was a beauty! What mother wouldn't be proud of her?

"Papa?" whispered Veda as she looked wide-eyed and helpless at him, then at the Patawatomi woman. It had never occurred to Veda that her father would be unfaithful to her mother.

"Why are you back, Veda?" asked Willie sharply. He desperately wished he'd turned Silent Waters away when she'd come knocking on his study door, but he hadn't been able to meet with her as regularly as he'd planned. Just seeing her at the door had left him as helpless as a lovesick boy.

"Clay went to help Lark Baritt!" Veda spit out the name as she balled her fists at her sides.

"Lark Baritt," muttered Silent Waters.

"Leave us, Silent Waters," said Willie briskly.

Silent Waters shook her head as she stepped toward Veda. "Laughing Eyes," she said softly and reached out to touch Veda's smooth cheek.

With a startled cry, Veda jumped back. "Don't touch me!" She shivered at the thought of an Indian touching her. Everyone knew they weren't like other humans.

Silent Waters stumbled back as if she'd been struck. Her own daughter wouldn't allow her to touch her! Tears filled her eyes and she turned helplessly to Willie. "What have you done to my child?"

Willie slapped Silent Waters across the cheek and the sound rang through the room. "Get out of here now!"

Silent Waters squared her shoulders. Her red calico dress fit snugly across her breasts down to her slender waist, then flared over her hips to fall in graceful folds at her moccasin covered feet. A rolled red scarf tied around her forehead held back her shiny, thick black hair. "If you force me to leave, I will take my daughter, my Laughing Eyes, with me."

Willie shook his head. He'd never been in such a tight spot. He saw the disgust for Indians on Veda's face. If she learned this Indian was her mother, what would she do? But he saw the determination on Silent Waters' face. This time she wouldn't be denied. Willie took Silent Waters' hands in his. He could feel the calluses on her hands and could see the look of love in her eyes. A pulse throbbed at her throat. Even though her body was rigid with anger, just touching her sent a wave of passion through him. "I'll take care of it," he said softly. "I promise you." He kissed her fingers, but she still didn't relax. "If you want to please me, leave us now. I'll talk to you later."

Veda pressed her hand to her racing heart. "Papa! How can you have anything to do with her?"

Willie turned to Veda with a frown and said sharply, "Don't

say anything against Silent Waters, Veda, or you'll have to reckon with me."

"Papa!" cried Veda in shock. He had never spoken to her in that tone before. First Clay cut short his time with her to run to that Lark Baritt and now this from her father who always sympathized with her. Her world was crumbling apart.

Willie pulled Silent Waters close and whispered against her smooth hair, "Come back tomorrow night."

Silent Waters trembled in his arms. How she longed to stay with her man and her daughter! "I will be back," she said softly.

Willie kissed her and didn't want to let her go. He walked with her to the French doors that opened into the garden and she slipped out. He watched until she was out of sight behind the barn, then he closed the door and with an unsteady hand lit the kerosene lamp on his desk. The flame burned high and he turned it down to keep the globe from blackening. Slowly he turned to face Veda.

"Papa, how could you hold . . . *her* and kiss . . . *her?*"

Willie ran his trembling fingers through his already mussed graying red hair. Could he tell Veda her real mother was an Indian full of love for her? How could he make her understand Indians are people, too, after all the years Agnes had taught her to despise them? "Sit down, Veda." He reached for her arm, but she pulled away. "Sit down!" he snapped as he pointed to the brown leather sofa.

Shocked again at his tone, Veda perched on the edge of the sofa, her hands on the smooth leather. Usually the smell of Papa's leather sofa soothed her, but tonight it turned her stomach. Why was he being mean to her? And why had he kissed that squaw?

Willie sat in the massive leather chair facing Veda. He tried to collect his thoughts, but his mind whirled with things to say to Veda and later to Silent Waters. "A man must make choices in his life, Veda," he said weakly. "Once I lived with Silent Waters. I loved her and she made me happy. But I knew I couldn't marry her. I needed a proper wife to help me make a name for myself. So, I married Agnes Groff." He gripped the arms of the chair. "Sometimes these things are necessary."

"Does Momma know about Silent Waters?"

Willie tipped his head to acknowledge that she did.

Veda's stomach knotted painfully. "Is that why she locks her bedroom door against you?"

Willie didn't want to go into that. "I want to talk about you and me and Silent Waters—not Agnes."

"I don't want to hear about Silent Waters!" Veda wanted to press her hands over her ears the way she had when she was a child when something unpleasant was about to be said. Her green silk dress suddenly felt hot and looked ugly to her.

Willie shook his head, then sighed tiredly. "Veda, I'd give anything if I didn't have to hurt you, but I must. It's time you knew the truth."

"Papa, don't . . . don't . . ." Veda saw the anguish on his face, but she hardened her heart toward him. He deserved her anger. "I don't want to hear anything about that Indian!"

"She is not *that Indian!* She is your mother."

Veda crumpled against the arm of the sofa. Had she heard correctly? "My mother is upstairs in bed."

"No. Agnes raised you." Willie ran a finger around his collar. "But she's not your mother."

The strength drained from Veda's body. "Do you mean the Indian woman is my mother?" she whispered hoarsely.

Willie nodded slightly.

"Is that why she called me Laughing Eyes?"

"Yes. It's your Indian name."

"I won't listen," she whispered, covering her ears and shaking her head.

He waited until she dropped her hands back in her lap. "You have to know the truth," he said crisply. He took a deep breath and blurted out the story of her birth and why he'd taken her from Silent Waters. "She didn't want to let you go, but I had to have you with me because I loved you so much. She already had my only son. I couldn't give you up too."

Veda gasped. "Red Beaver? He's my brother?"

"Yes."

Veda shook her head and moaned. She was part Indian! How could she survive the shame? She wanted to do something or say something that would hurt Papa as badly as she'd been hurt. "Clay Havlick will never marry me when he learns the truth."

"He won't learn the truth."

"But he might!"

"He's your chance for wealth and power," snapped Willie. "Don't ruin it."

Veda thought about it and finally nodded. "What if he does find out?"

Willie ran a finger around the snug collar of his shirt. "Then you'll have to talk him into eloping with you within the next few days before he can find out."

"I don't think I can."

"Don't lose your self-confidence, Veda."

"But Papa, I am no longer . . . whole."

Willie frowned. "What do you mean by that?"

"An Indian is not really human. You told me that."

Willie's face turned as red as his hair. "Agnes told you that and I was forced to agree even when I didn't. I know Indians are as human as white people even though others don't agree. Someday the rest of the folks in the United States will know it too." Willie pushed up off the chair and sat beside Veda on the sofa. "Now, what's this about young Havlick going to help Lark Baritt?"

Clay caught up with Lark at the edge of the Havlick property. She was running wildly and crying hysterically. Her hair had pulled loose from the bun at the nape of her neck and flowed around her shoulders and down her back. Dust covered the bottom of her skirt and her shoes. He jumped from the buggy and gripped her arm. Tears poured down her face as he turned her toward him.

"He's dead," she whimpered, looking through her tears into Clay's worried face.

"I'm so sorry, Lark."

"Dead before I could get to know him."

Clay wiped her tears away with his white handkerchief.

"I have no one," Lark whispered.

Clay pulled her close and held her tightly. He felt the flutter of her heart and the tension in her body. Wind blew her skirts around his legs and the intimacy of it sent a shudder through him. "You've made it through worse things, Lark. You can make it through this."

Lark shook her head and her forehead rubbed against the rough fabric of his jacket.

"God is with you, Lark. He never leaves you. He is your comfort and your strength."

She let the words sink into her heart until she was able to lift her head. She realized she was clinging to him and he was holding her. Flushing, she stepped away from him and tried to stop the wild thudding of her heart. She glanced up at the sky, surprised to find it already dark. "I must get home."

"I'll take you." Clay wanted to help her in the buggy, but she slipped past him and climbed in alone.

"Where's Veda?" asked Lark sharply.

Clay slapped the reins on the horses and they stepped forward. "I had supper with her, then took her home."

"Don't see her again." The words burst out before Lark knew she was going to say them.

Clay's jaw tightened. He turned off the road to cut across to the cabin. "Pa says Red Beaver is Willie Thorne's son with Silent Waters. Veda isn't, he said."

With trembling hands Lark pushed her hair back. She couldn't look at Clay. "The Thornes and Silent Waters know the truth."

"Don't you ever give up?"

"No."

The next morning Lark walked slowly through the pines with Sears beside her. She rested the cudgel on her shoulder as she walked. She tried not to think about all she'd missed by not meeting her father, but thoughts crept in anyway. The smell of pine seemed almost overwhelming. The heat pressed in on her and she wished she'd worn her old calico dress instead of her breeches. The buckskin kept her from getting too many scratches and gave her legs more protection in case a rattlesnake struck, but the leather was hot.

She walked through the briars while bees buzzed around her. Just as Lark caught a flash of movement to her right Sears growled low in his throat. Red Beaver had warned her Silent Waters wouldn't give up trying to harm her. Was it Silent Waters or was someone else after her? Maybe it was a deer or even a bear.

She scanned the area around the spot where she thought she'd seen movement. But she saw only tree trunks and underbrush. Her heart lodged in her throat.

Suddenly Silent Waters stepped onto the trail in the exact spot where the bear cub had stood weeks ago. Fear pricked Lark's skin and she stopped in the same spot where she'd stopped between the sow and her cub. Sears growled and Lark silenced him with a reassuring pat on the head.

Her eyes wild, Silent Waters brandished an old hatchet above her head. She'd found the hatchet in the shed the night before when she'd sneaked back to Red Beaver's farm. She'd hidden in the barn so Red Beaver couldn't lecture her again on her treatment of Lark. Silent Waters took a step toward Lark, then stopped. Her dress was torn in spots and pine needles clung to her long black hair. "You have hurt Laughing Eyes."

Lark gasped. "Veda Thorne? But how?"

"You are trying to steal her man!"

"I'm not!" Lark rubbed her arm over her revolver to reassure her it was still there.

"I hate the Havlicks, but Laughing Eyes wants Clay Havlick. You will not steal him from her."

"I'm not trying to steal him! Listen to me, Silent Waters."

"I will kill you. That will be my gift to Laughing Eyes. Then maybe she will love me as a daughter should love her mother."

"No! It's not me you should harm. I did nothing to you. And the Havlicks did nothing to you. It's Willie Thorne who hurt you. He cheated you of your daughter."

Silent Waters trembled and almost dropped the hatchet. "Laughing Eyes hates me. I am Patawatomi. Willie's white wife taught Laughing Eyes to hate Patawatomi."

"She could be taught differently. Look at Hannah Havlick. She was taught the same way, but she loves Red Beaver. She looked into his heart and saw a man like other men. She vows he is the man for her."

"I will kill you."

"It won't make your daughter love you."

Silent Waters tipped back her head and wailed. The sound spread across the swamp and lifted to the pines where the great boughs muffled it. Killing Lark would have to make Laughing Eyes love her! Nothing else would.

Lark gripped her cudgel. Should she try to strike Silent Waters with it? Lark knew she couldn't pull her revolver and fire quickly enough to disarm Silent Waters. The woman's great anguish kept Lark from doing anything.

Suddenly Silent Waters lifted the hatchet high and sprang forward with a loud yell.

Taking careful aim for the hatchet, Lark threw the cudgel sideways. It spun through the air, struck the hatchet, and drove it from Silent Waters' hand. The hatchet flipped back into the swamp. Sears growled and raced toward Silent Waters. She turned and lunged for the hatchet, caught her foot in a tangle of creeping thorny vines, and fell headfirst into the quagmire.

"No!" cried Lark, leaping forward to help Silent Waters.

Sears stopped at the very edge of the mire, growling menacingly.

Silent Waters struggled to stand, but her feet and legs sank into the muck. Wildly she looked for the hatchet, saw it, and grabbed it. The extra movement pulled her in to her waist.

"Grab my hand," cried Lark as she reached out to Silent Waters.

Silent Waters drew back her arm and hurled the hatchet at Lark.

Lark saw the feeble effort and easily dodged the hatchet. It landed in the mass of wild roses behind her. "Silent Waters, just fall forward and grab my hand," cried Lark. "The mire will support you for a while. Give me your hand and I'll pull you out!"

"I will sink," said Silent Waters in a defeated voice. "I will not put my hand out to you."

"If you fall forward toward me and stretch out your hand, I can pull you free. Please, let me help you. You don't have to die!" Lark's eyes burned with tears as she stretched out to try to reach Silent Waters.

"This has happened to me. It is my time to go," said Silent Waters tonelessly.

"I can't reach you and I can't get help fast enough." Lark dropped to her knees in anguish and Sears sank down beside her. "Dear God, please help us!"

"Don't call on your god for me," said Silent Waters as she sank lower.

"I don't want you to die without knowing God. Red Beaver has told you of God's love, of Jesus giving himself for you."

"I will not die. My spirit will walk these pines forever."

Lark groaned. "Your spirit will be doomed to hell for all eternity without God. You must know that."

Silent Waters didn't answer.

Great tears welled up in Lark's eyes and ran down her hot face. Sears licked her face, but she pushed him away. She picked up her cudgel and leaned heavily on it. She didn't want to stay to watch Silent Waters die, but she couldn't leave her alone.

Without a cry, a sob, or a sigh, Silent Waters sank below the muck and mire until not even a strand of hair was visible.

Lark covered her face and sobbed. Finally she walked back

to the cabin and weakly struck the bell twice. In minutes Tris and Hannah rode across in the wagon.

"What happened?" asked Tris in concern.

"Are you hurt?" asked Hannah, rubbing Lark's arm.

Lark told them Silent Waters had tried to kill her and had fallen in the swamp instead and was dead. She didn't tell them Veda Thorne was Silent Waters' daughter. "She wouldn't let me help her. She wouldn't hold out her hand to me."

"Oh, Lark! Don't blame yourself. It wasn't your fault," said Tris.

"I must go and tell Red Beaver," said Hannah.

Tris caught her arm. "You can't. Pa won't allow it."

Hannah pulled free. "I'm going, Tris. I love him."

Tris looked at her a long time and finally nodded. "Take the wagon," he said softly.

Hannah hugged him, then leaped in and shouted to the horses. The wagon bumped and swayed across the field.

Tris turned to Lark. "Are you all right?"

"No. It was awful." Lark sank to the bench with Sears at her feet.

Hannah found Red Beaver slopping the hogs. She threw her arms around him and told him what had happened. She didn't mind the sour smell of slop or the dirt on Red Beaver's hands as he held her tight.

"Did she hurt Lark?"

"No."

"I'm thankful for that."

Hannah stroked his cheek. "Your mother is gone and I'm sorry."

"I tried to help her."

"I'm sure you did."

"She didn't want anything to do with God."

"Don't torture yourself, Red Beaver." Hannah stood on tip-toe and kissed him. "Let's get married."

"What about your family?"

"They'll be upset of course, but I don't care! I want you. I'll make my family understand."

Red Beaver shook his head. He wanted to marry Hannah no matter what, but he couldn't have the Havlicks angry at her. Hannah couldn't live without her family. "They'll never accept me."

"Then it's their loss. I love you, Red Beaver."

He kissed her as if he'd never let her go. "And I love you. But that's not always enough."

Red Beaver rode to town on his gray gelding and stopped at Willie Thorne's tavern. It was noon and the front door was locked, but Red Beaver went around back and knocked.

Willie flung open the door, then whistled in surprise. "What brings you here?"

"My mother is dead. She tried to kill Lark Baritt and now she's dead. It's time you called off your revenge on the Havlicks."

Willie sagged against the door frame, the color drained from his face. "Silent Waters," he whispered. He was to see her tonight and tell her he'd settled the problem with Veda. He was going to tell her that soon her daughter would be able to speak to her, even get to know her and love her.

"Are you all right?" asked Red Beaver in concern.

"No. No, I'm not. I loved your mother."

Red Beaver didn't respond. He couldn't understand the kind of love that destroys lives.

"I want to see her. I want to hold her one last time before she's put in the ground," said Willie.

Red Beaver shook his head. "She is buried deep in the swamp. No one can see her ever again."

"I must tell Veda her mother is dead."

"Veda?"

Willie rubbed an unsteady hand across his face. "Veda is your sister. I took her to live with me and my wife as our own child."

Red Beaver shook his head as if to clear his brain. "I was seven when Silent Waters gave birth to Laughing Eyes. But she told me the baby died. I never knew you took her to your white wife."

Willie nodded.

"I ran to the woods and wept because my sister died." Red Beaver remembered the pain he'd felt at seven. Anger at his father rushed through him, then he refused to keep it. "Your hatred for the Havlicks brought all this agony on us, but it won't destroy me. I refuse to let it destroy me or the ones I love!" Red Beaver turned on his heel and strode to his horse.

Willie walked slowly inside the tavern, sank down on a ladder back chair, and buried his face in his hands.

Later Willie pulled himself together enough to go home. He found Veda sitting on the white bench in the flower garden, the cat on her lap.

Veda jumped up. "Papa, what is it? You look terrible."

Willie sank to the bench and pulled Veda back down beside him. "It's terrible news."

"Clay learned the truth and won't marry me!"

"No." Willie shuddered. "Silent Waters is dead."

Veda sighed in relief. "Now I won't have to think about having an Indian mother."

Willie jumped up and jerked Veda to her feet. "You will always be part Indian even if you choose to ignore it."

Veda trembled at his anger. "Nobody will have to know."

Willie raised his hand to strike Veda, then let it fall at his side. "The Havlicks will pay for this. Silent Waters died trying to help me get the pines. She will not have died in vain!"

Veda breathed easier. Papa was himself again.

Willie laughed wickedly. "After you and young Havlick are married I'll tell the whole Havlick family you are part Patawatomi. Then I'll tell the whole town! Those Havlicks will lose their high standing in the community as well as their precious pines."

CHAPTER

11

♦ Lark froze on the path in the pines. Sears stood beside her and Silent Waters crouched several yards away, a hatchet in her hand. More sunlight than usual shone through the boughs. The pine smell filled the air and took Lark's breath away. No animals made a sound.

Silent Waters lifted the hatchet high and sunlight glinted off its head. In a ringing voice Silent Waters cried, "My gift to Laughing Eyes is to kill you, Lark Baritt!"

"No!" Frantically Lark grabbed for her revolver, but the holster was empty. She gripped the thing in her hand, then looked to find both hands were empty. Where was her cudgel? She stared in fear at the wild look in Silent Waters' eyes. "Leave me alone. Please leave me alone." Lark sobbed.

Silent Waters threw the hatchet. It arched through the air and before Lark could duck, it struck her forehead and sliced through her head, splitting her skull. Lark screamed and grabbed her forehead.

She screamed again and sat straight up in her bunk, sweat soaking her nightdress and sheets. Moonlight streamed through the window and she sank back to her pillow, shivering uncontrollably. It had been a dream but it seemed so real she could feel the pain in her head. "A nightmare," she whispered. It was the same nightmare she'd had every night since Silent Waters died. Lark moaned. When would the nightmares end? When could she sleep again?

Lark pushed herself up and sat on the edge of the bunk with her damp face in her hands. A cricket sang in the corner. Sears whined and scratched at the door. Weakly Lark stood, her cotton nightdress sticking to her sweat-soaked body. What had happened to her good life? The cabin no longer seemed to be the haven it had been.

"I'm all right, Sears," said Lark as she opened the door. A hot breeze dried her skin as she stroked Sears. "It was just another nightmare." Since Silent Waters died Lark had let Sears sleep just outside her door instead of tying him at his dog house. "I'm all right."

Sears licked her cheek and the back of her hand. She hugged him, her head still pounding with pain.

Slowly she closed the door and heard Sears settle on the other side. She walked to the table and lit the lamp. The smell of sulfur and kerosene made her wrinkle her nose. She sank to a chair and clasped her hands together on the table. "I can't go on like this," she whispered and the whisper seemed loud in the silent cabin. Even the crickets had stopped singing.

She touched her Bible, then pushed it away. She didn't want to read God's Word now. It would tell her to forgive and forget, let go, but she would not forgive or forget that Anna Pike had kept her father from her. She would not forgive or forget that Willie Thorne was to blame for what she'd suffered and continued to suffer because of Silent Waters. It was Willie's fault that Veda was going to marry Clay and lumber the pines.

Lark doubled her fists and clenched her jaw. Anna Pike was gone, but Willie Thorne was still in Blue Creek within easy reach. "I'll get him if it's the last thing I do!" she shouted. The log walls muffled her shout, but the words continued to ring in her head.

From the corner of the shed behind the Thorne house Red Beaver watched Veda sit on the white bench in the flower garden and call to her cat. Red Beaver's heart raced and tears pricked his eyes. He could see Veda's resemblance to Silent Waters. Why hadn't he seen it before? If she'd worn her hair down with a rolled band around her head, he would've noticed immediately. But she'd always looked too much like a wealthy white woman. He knew her white gauze dress was very expensive.

Taking a deep breath, Red Beaver walked around the shed and through the flower garden. He'd changed from his work clothes to a nice pair of dark pants and a blue plaid shirt. He stopped beside a large patch of marigolds and waited for Veda to notice him. She looked sad and his heart went out to her. Was she grieving over the death of their mother? It had been a week since Silent Waters died.

Veda felt eyes on her and she glanced up from her cat, then stared in shock at Red Beaver. He seemed to be memorizing her.

"They said you died," Red Beaver whispered. "I was only seven and I mourned for a long time."

"What are you doing here?" Veda asked hoarsely, her hand at her throat.

"I was seven. Every day for weeks I went to the woods where no one could see me, and I cried. I couldn't let anyone know I wasn't man enough not to cry. I loved you, Laughing Eyes."

"No," whispered Veda.

"I did," said Red Beaver softly.

Veda bowed her head and swayed. Finally she lifted her eyes. "I was taught to look down on my own flesh and blood. That was a cruel thing to teach a child."

"Very cruel." Red Beaver knelt at the bench and looked into her face. "We can begin again."

"No."

"We are still blood."

"Don't say that!"

"No one can take that from us."

"They already have," Veda said woodenly.

"You have been wronged, Laughing Eyes." He reached out to take her hands.

"Don't!" Veda held her hand palm up against his touch. The cat jumped to the ground and ambled away. "Don't. Don't call me that."

"It is your name."

"My name is Veda Thorne. *Veda Thorne!*"

Red Beaver never took his eyes off her ashen face.

"I am Willie Thorne's daughter."

"Yes," said Red Beaver.

Veda bit her lip and laced her fingers together.

"And I am Willie Thorne's son."

Veda pressed her hand to her throat.

"Our mother hinted to me that you are helping our father steal the white pines from Clay Havlick. Is that true?"

A shiver ran down Veda's spine. Looking into Red Beaver's dark eyes made it impossible for her to lie. She just didn't answer him.

"How can you destroy the pines?"

"I didn't say I was."

"Look deep in your heart and see what is right, then no matter how hard it is, do it." Red Beaver reached again for Veda's hand, but she pulled away from him.

"Don't touch me!"

Red Beaver forced back the pain the words caused him. "You have been hurt, but you can choose your own path now. You can take your life and make it into something worthwhile."

Veda took a deep, steadying breath. "I will marry Clay Havlick." She moistened her lips with the tip of her tongue. A bee buzzed around a rose bush. Butterflies flitted around the row of blue bachelor buttons. "No one can stop me."

"What if Clay learns the truth?"

Veda scowled. "Get out of here!"

"I will go if I must, but I'll be praying for you, Laughing Eyes. God loves you just as you are—part white, part Patawatomi."

"No!" Veda clamped her hands over her ears and shook her head hard.

Red Beaver gently pulled her hands from her head and held them tightly. He smelled the clean smell of her skin and saw the rise and fall of her breast. "If you ever need me, my sister, I'll help you."

"Let me go," Veda whispered hoarsely, but she couldn't find the strength to pull free.

"You know where I live. You are welcome in my home any time."

Veda's heart turned over. His words and his touch burned her. "Let go of my hands."

"Please listen to me!"

"If you don't leave, I'll call for help."

Red Beaver tucked her hands back on her lap and stood before her. "I am your brother."

"No!" Veda shook her head hard.

"Nothing you can do or say will change that."

Veda stared up at him, her heart a block of ice in her breast. "Go," she whispered.

Red Beaver's eyes filled with tears. "You are my sister, Laughing Eyes."

"Go!"

He turned and walked away, his shoulders bent and his steps slow.

Veda sat for a long time without moving, her eyes on the path Red Beaver had taken.

Wednesday morning Clay left Flame at the livery, then walked to the Wagon Works. At the sight of the finished wagons parked outside the building in an empty lot he stopped dead in his tracks. The wagons they'd painted yesterday had splashes of black paint over the green. "Who did this?" His voice rang through the early morning and startled birds pecking in the grass. He ran to the first wagon and touched the black paint. It came off on his fingers. Who had splashed the black paint on the freshly finished wagon boxes? Anger raged inside him. He grabbed a rag from inside the shop and rubbed the paint from his fingers. August was almost over. The men had been drinking on the job, and that had cost precious time. Then several missing tools had caused further delay. Now this! If he couldn't fill the contract, he couldn't make the first large payment due at the bank. If the bank wouldn't give him more time he could easily lose the pines. Somehow he had to stop whoever was making trouble for him.

"I'll hire three more guards," he said sharply. The added expense frustrated him. Already he'd hired Dag as guard because he'd been willing and even eager to do it. Dag patrolled the area at night, slept until noon, then worked from noon until six in the shop. Clay had talked to the sheriff twice already and had gotten nowhere. The sheriff promised to look into it, but he hadn't learned anything.

His head buzzing with plans, Clay opened the doors of the two buildings and let the fresh air fill the hot interior. He glanced around at the parts of wagons laying where the men had worked on them. Today they would've been ready to assemble a few more wagons.

Clay paced across the front of the shop as he waited for his workers to arrive. He pulled off his tan straw hat and jabbed his fingers through his dark hair. Maybe he should've stayed in buggy making with Pa. Maybe he wasn't cut out to make his own fortune like Pa and Great-grandpa Clay had done.

Clay rammed his hat back on and squared his shoulders. He would not give up without a fight! Pa hadn't and neither had Great-grandpa Clay. Jig had told the stories often to Clay until he knew them by heart.

Maybe Pa would help make the bank payment. Clay shook

his head. Pa had plenty of assets, but often cash money was hard to come by. And he would not ask Pa to borrow money to help him!

At six when the sun was already turning warm, all the men came to work at once. Clay watched as they spotted the defaced wagons. All of them were outraged and wanted to know who'd done such a terrible thing. Clay knew they'd have to rub the excess black paint off, let the rest dry, then repaint the wagons. It would take valuable time.

"Somebody's out to get you, Boss," Leander said as he wrapped his fingers around the suspenders of his bib overalls.

"You got enemies?" asked Polaski as he scratched his head, then rammed his cap on.

Willie Thorne popped immediately into Clay's mind, but he rejected the idea that Willie was responsible for his troubles. Maybe Willie was so angry about him marrying Veda that he wanted to make Clay call it off. "It won't work," muttered Clay. He waited until the men quieted and shouted, "Men, gather round! I have something to say before you get to work." He stood before them, his feet apart and his hands resting lightly on his lean hips. "Men, it's obvious that someone is trying to sabotage the Wagon Works. I suspect it could be one of you or several of you." He saw their uneasy looks. Some of the men whispered among themselves. Some shifted their weight uneasily. "I'm not saying it is." Clay narrowed his dark eyes. "We have contracts to meet and we are going to meet those contracts on time, if not early! All these things that have happened are small things, but they've delayed production. Now, in the event that the culprit is here among you, be it known that when you are caught, you shall be prosecuted, and I'll see you sent to prison."

Clay looked around the crowd, sizing them up. Many of them met his eyes, but others stared at the floor. A couple of rough looking men glanced at the wagons.

"From what I've witnessed you're all hard workers. Meeting the contracts means your jobs, your livelihood. If we do not meet our contracts, we're all finished. Your jobs are on the line, so report any suspicious activity to me immediately. All these incidents are over and done with—they're behind us. Now, let's get to work. And keep your eyes and ears open!"

Just before noon Clay called Malda, Knegrave, and Von Tol to him. The three men looked nervous as they followed him outdoors to stand in the shade of a great oak. Clay cleared his throat. "Men, I need your help. I know I can trust the three of you."

They shrugged and looked pleased.

"I want you three to take turns guarding the Wagon Works."

"Dag's doing that already," said Von Tol with a nod of his blond head.

"I know," said Clay. "But things are still happening. It's too big a job for one man." Clay studied the men carefully. He'd known them most of his life. Two were his age and one was about ten years older. "I want this to be kept a secret between the four of us. I don't want to say a word against Dag, but things do keep happening."

"It's mighty strange how he's the one that keeps findin' the cases of whiskey," said Malda.

"He is my guard," said Clay, but he felt the same way. On the sly he'd look into Dag Bjoerling. Clay frowned slightly. He liked Dag and hated to think he'd do anything underhanded.

"You want us to keep our eyes and ears open?" asked Van Tol with a wide grin.

Clay nodded. "I want you three to work as guards. Split the time into three shifts and don't let anyone know you're guards for me. Let them all think you're still laborers." Clay assigned them the shifts and sent Malda home to sleep so he could be on guard all night. "Do your best to stay out of Dag's sight," said Clay as Malda walked away.

Later in the day Clay rode Flame to his forest to get away from the Wagon Works and have time to be alone. He leaned dejectedly against a giant pine looking down on the river. The oppressive heat burned through his blue shirt and gray pants.

How could he marry Veda in two weeks when he was so far behind in production? He lifted his head and looked at his great inheritance. Sometimes he wondered if it really was an inheritance or a giant weight on his shoulders. The pines were worth a fortune, yet he wasn't gaining any money from them. Was he wrong not to lumber them, even a part of them so he could be out of debt and out from under the pressure of meeting his deadline?

The morning sun burning through her yellow sunbonnet, Lark rubbed her hand over the smooth black buggy, then touched the green, machine-buffed leather. She wasn't in the mood to buy a horse and buggy, but she felt she had to have the freedom owning her own afforded her.

"It's a fine buggy," said Free as he watched Lark.

"I can see that," said Lark. Never in her life had she considered buying her own horse and buggy, but she had the money and didn't want to depend always on the Havlicks to loan her one.

"All the gear wood is made from the very best, carefully selected second growth Michigan hickory. The reaches are ironed full length with Norway iron." Free patted the wheel nearest him. "I use only the highest grade second growth hickory in the wheels too. Notice how the round edge of the steel projects over the felloes to protect the wood from wear."

"I do want it," said Lark. "For my sake I'm glad your customer couldn't take it after all."

Free smiled. He knew he could've sold the buggy to five different people, but he was glad to see Lark get it. He'd sold it to her for $65 even though he could've gotten $75 from Jake Spelling.

Lark touched the brass plate engraved with *Havlick Buggy*. She'd be proud to own such a buggy.

Free walked Lark to the pen where he had the bay mare. "Look her over and see if she's what you want," said Free.

164

Lark held out her hand and the mare walked to her. "What's her name?"

"Evie named her Star because of the white mark on her face."

"Star. I like that."

"She's trained to ride or pull a buggy. I have a spare saddle I can throw in too. It belonged to Grace, but she didn't want it after she got married and moved away." Grace was Free's married daughter. She and her husband had just had twins and Evie and Jennet had gone to Grand Rapids to be with them for a while.

Several minutes later Lark drove to town in her own buggy pulled by her own horse. She tried to feel excitement, but she couldn't. Since she'd learned her father was dead, the only emotion she'd been able to feel was anger at Matron. It seethed inside her. Matron had stolen her father from her just as she'd stolen the money he'd sent.

Lark drove the buggy around back of the Home, unhitched Star, and turned her into the pen. Lark slapped dust off the yellow gingham dress she'd bought last week from Sally and straightened her matching sunbonnet.

"You look like you lost your best friend," said John Epson as he walked up. He'd waited for Lark so he could have a few minutes of her time before she started to work.

Lark turned with a slight smile and he tipped his white straw hat to her. "Hi."

"You've turned down supper with me for several days." John took her hand in his and smiled into her eyes. His job was getting harder and harder because he'd come to care for Lark. When the time came to kill her, he didn't know if he would be able to do it. But Willie Thorne had insisted he get her away from the pines one way or another. John squeezed Lark's hand. "Today is the day you'll share dinner with me, won't you?"

"I can't, John." Lark liked the attention John had been paying her lately, but she couldn't find the strength to respond. She tugged on her hand and he reluctantly released it. "Maybe tomorrow."

John frowned as he rubbed his well-trimmed beard. "You've been saying that for over a week."

"I know." Lark couldn't imagine why he'd want to bother with her.

"I won't take no for an answer for tomorrow, Lark." John walked beside her through the back door of the Home.

Smells of roast beef and freshly baked bread filled the air. The cook and student helpers were already making dinner. All the windows in the Home were open to stir the hot air. Usually the temperature dropped at nights and cooled down the house, but the past two nights the temperature had stayed too high. Today Lark had dressed in the coolest clothing she had, and had even left off her bustle. She'd heard several women say the bustle would soon be a thing of the past. She hoped so, but wondered if that was true.

"You seem a long way off, Lark," said John as he opened the office door for her.

"I was thinking about bustles," Lark said. It was easier to think on that than on the harsh reality of life—on what Matron had done to her and on the death of her father.

John laughed. "I don't think I want to discuss bustles."

Lark flushed as she sat at her desk. She tried to keep her mind on the bookwork for the Home, but had to go over the same work several times. During Clay's bookkeeping her mind wandered and she pulled it back and started all over again.

Just before noon John stood up and brushed his hands together. "Well, that's that. I've finalized the adoption papers for Maggie and Linda. Their new parents should be here tomorrow to get them."

Lark frowned. "I didn't know they were going to be adopted."

"That's because you're living in a fog, Lark."

"I know." Lark sighed heavily. Maybe it was better to live in a fog where she had a cushion against pain. In the back of her mind she remembered God was her strength and help, but immediately she turned away from that thought.

John walked around her desk and sat on the edge of it beside her. "I want to help you, Lark."

"There's nothing you can do."

"Tell me what's wrong? Is your guard job too much for you?"

"No. It's nothing I can talk about, John."

He saw the dark circles under her eyes. "I care about you, Lark. Come back here where you can get your sleep. Ask Clay Havlick to hire someone else as guard. I happen to know someone who needs a job."

Lark shook her head. "I'll never come back here to live."

"Have it your way." John touched her cheek, then walked out the door.

Zoe slipped in, her eyes sparkling with unshed tears. She'd left Carrie in charge of the babies. "Lark, could I talk to you?"

Lark nodded absently.

Zoe pulled John's chair up near Lark's desk. Hot wind blew in the window and a coating of dust covered the furniture even though they'd dusted already this morning. "It's Tristan."

Lark didn't want to listen, but she nodded again.

"We went to the Sunday school picnic a while back and he hasn't asked me out again. I don't know what I'm gonna do!"

"I don't either."

"Please help me, Lark."

"Zoe, I can't even help myself."

Zoe jumped up and put the chair back in place. "I won't bother you, Lark. I'm sorry. I was only thinking of myself. Oh, but I love Tris! Why won't he love me back?"

Helplessly Lark shook her head. Right now she felt like there was no such thing as love.

Tears slipped down Zoe's cheeks as she walked around the

desk and hugged Lark. "I'm sorry I bothered you with my problem when you're feeling so terrible. Don't forget God is with you."

Lark's throat closed over and she couldn't answer. She absently watched Zoe leave the room, then turned toward the curtains fluttering at the windows. Laughter and the ring of an ax floated in from outdoors. Was God with her as angry as she was?

Just then a gray haired, blue eyed man walked into the office. He held a white wide brim straw hat against his broad chest. "Lark Baritt?" he asked.

She nodded.

"I understand you've been looking for me."

She frowned, searching her mind to try to remember who she'd needed to see. No one came to mind. She looked the man over and noticed his expensive dark suit and gold tie pin. "I'm sorry, but I don't know who you are, sir."

The man smiled as he stepped closer. "Matt Baritt."

"He died last year," Lark said in a wooden voice.

The man shook his head. "Not so!" he said and thumped his chest. "*I'm* Matt Baritt. And I'm very much alive."

The room spun and Lark gasped as she gripped her desk to keep from falling off her chair. What a terrible, terrible joke! "Why are you doing this to me? My father is dead."

Matt Baritt walked to the desk and bent down toward Lark. "I'm not dead. I am your father"

"No." Lark shook her head.

"I left you here twenty-two years ago with a box with a photo, two letters from Meriel, your mother, a little white dress and bonnet, and an envelope with $80 in it. Your mother died just after you were born and I couldn't take care of you and had no one else to turn to."

"I don't believe you," whispered Lark.

"I wrote and sent money regularly. Anna Pike knows I did." Matt rubbed a hand over his clean-shaven jaw. "I didn't think you wanted me to come for you. Then recently I started hear-

168

ing from every lumberman I knew asking if I'd contacted you They said you were looking for me."

Helplessly Lark shook her head. She wanted to stand, but she had no strength in her legs. "This is a dream."

Matt touched Lark's hand. "I am real. So are you."

"But I got a telegram saying you were dead."

"I don't understand that. Maybe someone was playing a cruel joke." Matt pulled out his wallet and handed her his identification. "I am Matt Baritt, your father."

Lark trembled as she took the paper. She studied it and held it to her heart. Who had sent the telegram? She couldn't think of anyone who would be that mean. Was it Anna Pike? Lark forced thoughts of Anna Pike from her mind as she looked at the man standing across the desk from her. "Why didn't you come to get me years ago? Why didn't you at least come to see me?"

Matt flushed. "I tried."

"Why didn't you try harder?"

Matt fingered his hat brim. "I was afraid."

Lark dropped his identification paper on the desk between them. "Afraid? What could you possibly be afraid of?"

"You," said Matt softly.

Lark was quiet a long time. "Me?"

"I thought you hated me for leaving you here. When Anna Pike said you refused to answer my letters, I was afraid you'd refuse to see me if I did come. In fact, she implied you would."

For a while Lark couldn't speak. Anger at Anna Pike raged inside her until she thought she'd explode. "I never even knew about you until a few weeks ago. Matron lied to you all those years. She took the money you sent and kept it for herself, and she never told me about the letters."

Groaning, Matt rubbed an unsteady hand across his eyes. "Oh! I never thought she was lying."

"Didn't you even suspect? Did you even check it out?"

Matt shook his head. "I should have. Please forgive me." He walked around the desk and stopped just inches from her.

"Yes. You should've."

Matt brushed a tear from his eye. "I've been without you for twenty-two years. Please don't send me away now. You're my daughter! I love you. I want to get to know you."

A sob rose in Lark's throat and escaped before she could stop it. She brushed at her tears, but couldn't wipe them away.

"Lark," said Matt softly. He caught her hand and rubbed the back of it. "We named you Lark after our favorite bird." His voice broke. "We wanted you so badly! Your mother fought to stay alive, but she was too weak. She kissed you, handed you to me, and died." Matt lifted Lark to her feet. He held her hand against his cheek and closed his eyes. "I tried hard to tend you, but I couldn't. Life was hard. There was no one to help me."

Lark trembled as she listened to her father. Did he really mean what he said? How hard it was to believe she had a father and he actually loved her and wanted her!

They stood in silence, studying each other. Children's shouts and laughter drifted through the open windows. Smells of dinner filled the room.

"Are you really Matt Baritt, my father?" whispered Lark.

Matt nodded.

"I don't know what to call you."

Matt shrugged and grinned. "Pop? Dad? Pa? Father? I don't know. Anything. What do you want to call me?"

"I don't know." Lark wiped her eyes with her hanky, then stuffed it inside her cuff.

"We'll wait and see. Right now I think we should go have dinner. I already asked your matron Mercy Kettering if you could have the rest of the day off. So, you're free if you want to be."

"I'll show you all around. Did you know I'm the guard for the Havlicks' white pines?"

"The guard? You're just a little girl!"

"But I can use a cudgel and a revolver. And I have a big Dalmatian at my side while I walk the trail."

"I'm impressed."

Lark smiled.

"I've heard of the white pines the Havlicks have saved. Everyone has, I think. I would like to see them."

"I'll take you around the trail," said Lark. She told him some of the adventures she'd had and he scowled and shook his head. She felt like she was talking double speed as she tried to share her entire life with Matt Baritt in a few minutes.

At the restaurant they both ordered perch, then laughed. Since neither of them liked coffee, they drank lemonade.

"Where do you live, Lark?"

She told him about the cabin. "How about you?"

"I travel around a lot, but I have a house on Mackinac Island." Matt leaned forward and his blue eyes twinkled. "I'd like you to go back with me. I could hire someone to take care of my business and we could have time together."

Lark's stomach knotted. Live away from Blue Creek?

"Does that frighten you, Lark?"

"A little. I've never been anywhere but here."

"We could travel. See the world! Have you wanted to see London or Paris or New York City?"

Lark balled her napkin. "I have wanted to see Grand Rapids. Or Detroit."

"Then we'll go!"

"Oh, my." Lark had thought she'd only experience distant places through the books she read.

Just then someone walked into the restaurant. It was very late for dinner customers. Lark glanced up to see Clay and Veda. He looked as if he hadn't slept well in a long time and her face was pale. Matt noticed Lark studying them.

"Who are they?" asked Matt softly.

Lark told him. "Her father wants Clay's white pines." Lark had already told Matt all about the Havlicks, Jig, and their years of friendship. "Jig asked me to keep them from marrying each other."

"That's a mighty big order," said Matt, shaking his head.

"I know." Lark glanced at Clay again. "He looks so tired and unhappy."

Matt shot a look at Lark. "Do you love him?"

Lark gasped. "Of course not! I just don't want him hurt by Veda or Willie Thorne."

"I see."

Lark flushed and looked down at the crumpled white linen napkin beside her plate.

Clay sighed tiredly as he looked across the table at Veda. He'd agreed to pick her up for dinner, but had forgotten until he'd gone back to work and found her there. He'd talked to her about his busy schedule, but she hadn't wanted to listen. "I know you don't want to postpone the wedding, but I don't have time to get married this month."

Veda's eyes flashed. Was he trying to get out of being married because he'd heard she was part Patawatomi? "It doesn't take long to get married, Clay."

"It's not fair to either of us to try to begin a marriage while I have to work twelve to fifteen hours a day."

"I don't mind a bit. I just want to be with you."

"We don't even have a house."

"I know one that just went on sale. It's not too far from your Wagon Works."

"I can't afford a house right now."

"Papa will pay for it."

"No!" Clay shook his head hard. "I won't be obligated to Willie Thorne for anything!"

Veda forced back the stream of angry words on the tip of her tongue. "I suppose I understand, Clay, so I won't suggest it again." She reached for his hand. "But please don't call off the wedding just because you don't have time for it. We could take a couple of hours anytime and get married. Tomorrow even! I just can't live without you!"

Clay's pulse leaped and he smiled. It felt good to be loved that much. "I don't want to live without you either, Veda, but I want to be fair to you. We shouldn't start off our married life this way."

"I can handle it if you can."

Clay squeezed her hand. "I'll give it some thought."

"I'll speak to Pastor James tomorrow and tell him we'll get married in a couple of days."

Clay's stomach knotted. Things were moving too fast for him.

"I'll make a good home for you, Clay. We'll have children and a house full of love." An icy band tightened around Veda's heart. Their children would be part Patawatomi. How would Clay survive that? Veda bit her bottom lip. How would she?

Clay glanced across the restaurant and caught sight of Lark and Matt. Clay stiffened. Lark was going out entirely too much lately. First with John Epson and now with a man old enough to be her father.

Veda followed Clay's gaze and jerked her hand free. "If you're going to look at her all afternoon, then let's leave!"

Clay flushed. "I only wondered who she is with. I feel responsible for her." Suddenly he longed to take back the promise he'd made Jig on the day he'd passed on.

Across the room Lark smiled at Matt, then glanced over at Clay. He looked upset again. Just what were they talking about?

"I'd like to meet that young man," said Matt, pushing back his chair. "Introduce us, Lark."

Hesitantly Lark stood up, her mouth suddenly bone dry.

CHAPTER
12

♦ Lark saw the anger in Veda's eyes as she and Matt stopped at the table. "I hope we're not intruding," said Lark stiffly. She suddenly remembered she wasn't wearing a bustle. Veda was wearing an organdy dress with a white background and lavender flowers with tiny green leaves. A small gold locket hung to her breast. Lark forced back a flush of embarrassment over her appearance and said, "My father wanted to meet you."

Clay jumped up in surprise. He didn't notice the stares of the four other occupants of the restaurant. "But I thought your father had died."

"Obviously not," said Veda crisply as she gripped the linen napkin.

"It was a mistake," said Lark. She introduced them, feeling awkward even though she handled the introductions the way she'd learned and taught in deportment.

Matt smiled at Veda and shook hands with Clay. "It's a pleasure to meet Free Havlick's son," said Matt.

"Do you know my pa?" asked Clay.

"Only by reputation as a lumberman."

"Are you a lumberman?" asked Clay, trying to size the man up.

Before Matt could answer Lark said, "He is a naturalist and had a book published on plant and insect life."

"How interesting," said Clay, wondering about Matt Baritt's expensive summer suit, starched white shirt, and polished manners.

Veda moved restlessly. She wanted to excuse herself, but she didn't want to upset Clay. She had convinced him to marry her soon and she couldn't take a chance on him changing his mind.

Seeing Veda's agitation, Lark felt her anger against Veda and Willie Thorne rise dangerously. She had to get away before she said something she'd regret later. She gently tugged Matt's arm. "We must be going."

Matt was aware of Lark's tension and wondered about it. "It was nice to meet you both," said Matt, tipping his head.

"You too," said Clay while Veda managed a small smile.

"I'd be interested in seeing your Wagon Works," Matt said.

"You're welcome any time," said Clay.

As Lark left the restaurant, Matt was close beside her. The street was empty except for a small black dog dodging around the wheel of a parked wagon. Lark heard the shout of a boy somewhere behind the bank. The heat pressed against her as she lifted her bonnet in place and tied the strings under her chin.

"Why are you so upset, Lark?" asked Matt in a low voice as they slowly walked toward Lark's buggy.

"I'll tell you later," said Lark in a tight voice. She waited until they were driving out of town, then told Matt about Willie Thorne, Silent Waters, her death, and the nightmares.

Matt shook his head and clicked his tongue. He waited until Lark stopped at the side of the corduroy so they could hear as they talked. "What kind of man is Willie Thorne?"

"A terrible one."

"Why don't Clay's parents stop him from marrying Veda?"

175

"Well, I haven't discussed it with them. I'm certain they are against it. I imagine they've even forbidden it. But he's very stubborn. That I know. Clay is about as stubborn as a person can be."

Matt thought for a minute, then said, "I think I'll see what I can do."

Lark looked closely at this stranger who was her father. Just what did he mean? She wanted to ask, but was afraid of the answer.

Clay rode Flame out of his yard, stopped, and glanced across the field toward Lark's cabin. He'd seen Lark recently with John Epson taking a leisurely stroll around town. In Clay's opinion Epson was entirely too cozy with Lark. Clay frowned. Just what kind of man was Epson? Why was he interested in Lark Baritt? She was out walking the trail in the pines or he would've ridden to the cabin to talk to her and demand some answers.

An eagle flew high in the sky. A rooster crowed on the top rail of the fence as Clay nudged Flame forward.

In town Clay left Flame at the livery and walked toward the Wagon Works. A few men stood outside the boarding house talking. Two dogs snarled at each other in front of the bank. The smell of smoke hung in the air. He frowned and his stomach tightened. The smell was unfamiliar and it grew stronger with each step he took.

Suddenly Clay broke into a run. He pulled off his straw hat to keep it from flying off his head. Sweat stung his skin and dampened his blue work shirt. He saw Dag looking at the finished wagons. "What happened?" called Clay in alarm.

Dag turned, shaking his head. His work pants and shirt were wrinkled and his blond hair mussed. "It's awful," he said. "Somebody tried to burn the wagons."

Clay could see scratched places on several wagons. He ran from wagon to wagon. It looked as if someone had splashed kerosene on the wagons and set them on fire They had burned only a while, then had gone out. But each wagon was left with deep scars. They were not fit to sell. Clay knotted his fists and shook his head helplessly. "How could this happen? Did you see anything? Did anyone?"

Dag shrugged and spread his hands wide. "I could only guard part of the night because I got sick and couldn't walk. But Malda was hanging around here, so I asked him if he could guard the rest of the night and I'd pay him from my own pocket. He agreed."

Clay glanced around. "Where's Malda now?"

Dag knew Malda was tied up and unconscious in the wagon bed in front of them, but he said, "I figure he went on home. I got here only a few minutes ago and didn't see him anywhere. But I wanted to tell you why I couldn't stand guard last night. I didn't want you to hear it from Malda." Dag rammed his fingers through his blond hair, leaving it mussed even more. "I take all the blame for this, Clay. I should've stayed instead of asking Malda to guard for me! I should've worked even as sick as I was."

Just then Malda groaned and hoisted himself up to the side of the wagon. "Help me," he said gruffly.

"Malda!" cried Clay.

"Help me."

With Dag beside him, Clay climbed into the wagon bed where he found Malda's hands and feet tied and a lump on the back of his head.

"Are you hurt?" asked Dag as he hunkered down beside Malda.

"Did you see who did this?" Clay asked as he untied Malda.

Malda shook his head, then groaned in pain. "I didn't hear or see a thing. Dag here asked me to take over for him, and I agreed." Malda looked at Clay trying to send a silent message. "I said I'd be glad to since I couldn't sleep no how."

Clay's frustration mounted as Malda described how someone had hit him on the back of the head during the early morning hours.

"When I came to the wagons were burning and I thought I was going to burn up with them." Malda shivered. "The flames burned bright for a while, then died down. The smell was terrible. I'm surprised it didn't bring folks out here. I don't know if I passed out again or fell asleep."

Clay patted Malda's shoulder. "I'm glad you're alive to tell about it."

"Me too," said Malda.

"Dag, take him to the doc, then see that he gets home."

They walked away and Clay leaned weakly against the wagon. He had to stop whoever was trying to ruin him. With the finished wagons scarred it was impossible to meet his contract. "Dear God, I need your help bad," muttered Clay.

"Having a bit of trouble here, I see," said Matt Baritt as he stopped beside Clay.

Clay jumped to attention, flushing that Matt had seen him almost in tears. "Sorry, I didn't hear you walk up."

His straw hat pushed to the back of his gray head, Matt frowned thoughtfully as he walked up and down the row of wagons. "Lark said you'd been having problems. I'd say it's mighty serious." Matt smiled at Clay. "I hope you don't mind that she talked to me about you."

Clay shrugged. It was too late to mind.

"I have a suggestion I'd like to make," said Matt, studying Clay carefully. "How about if we get together this afternoon to talk?"

Clay hesitated and finally agreed. He'd promised to meet Veda at Pastor James's office just after work, but he could take time for Lark's father.

"Some place private. How about your pines? Lark showed them to me yesterday."

"That'll be fine."

"I'll borrow Lark's buggy. We can ride together and talk," said Matt.

About two in the afternoon Matt stood in the pines near the stream with Clay beside him. Sears lapped water from the stream. Squirrels chattered high in the pine boughs and frogs croaked along the edge of the stream. Matt was in his shirt sleeves. He'd left his suit coat folded on the buggy seat.

"I can see you're in a hard place right now, Clay," said Matt.

Clay nodded. He hated to admit it, but it was true.

"Here's what I can do for you." Matt pushed his straw hat to the back of his head. "You have a payment due at your bank soon and no way to pay it."

Clay flushed. "That's right."

"I'll loan you the money to pay the bank off completely, and enough to hire more men so you can meet your contracts."

Clay felt as if his brain had stopped working as he stared in shock at Matt. "Why would you do that?"

"To tell you the truth it's because of Lark." Matt watched carefully for Clay's reaction.

"Lark? What does she have to do with this?"

"She told me about Willie Thorne and his daughter. They want the pines."

Fire flashed from Clay's eyes. "Well, they don't. Lark is wrong about that. But even if it were true, they can't get the pines."

"They can if the bank forecloses on you. The pines will belong to the bank and Thorne can buy them."

Clay's stomach knotted. "I don't want to think about it."

"You have to. It's a possibility."

Clay groaned and rubbed an unsteady hand over his face. The smell of pine was strong around him. He could hear small animals scurrying under the pine needles.

Matt reached down and patted Sears on the side. He didn't speak for a while. "I will loan you the money as I said. It would keep the pines out of Thorne's hands. I'll be willing to sign a contract with you, giving you extra time to pay, and with a statement that I will never have the pines lumbered in the event you can't pay me and the pines become mine."

"What's the catch?"

Matt folded his arms across his chest. "There is a catch."

"I thought so."

"You can't marry Veda Thorne until you have filled your contracts and given me the first installment of the loan."

Clay frowned. "That's a strange request. Is that it?"

"Yes."

"But why that?"

"Because I believe Lark. I think Veda is after the pines."

"She's not."

"Then you're safe, aren't you? Waiting to be married until December won't hurt anyone. If you're really in love, you'll still be in love in December."

"You're right." Clay trembled at the thought of facing Veda with the change of plans.

"And another thing," said Matt.

"What?"

"You can't tell anyone I'm holding your note. Not even Lark."

"She's my bookkeeper. She'll know."

"Change bookkeepers. You can tell her she's working too hard. She does work too hard. Besides, I want time with her so we can get to know each other." Matt pulled off his hat and ran his hand around the inside band. "And I'd like you to find another guard for the pines. It's too dangerous for Lark."

"I know it is, but she desperately wants the job. It won't be easy to take it from her."

"Do it anyway."

Clay tugged at his collar. Could he do it? Lark's tears made it impossible for him to refuse her anything she wanted. "I don't know if I can."

"Do your best and I'll do what I can." Matt looked deep into the forest, then up at the sweep of giant boughs. "I'm glad you saved these trees. I want my grandchildren to enjoy them someday."

Clay frowned. "Grandchildren? Is Lark planning to get married?"

"Of course."

"I didn't know." Clay thought of Lark with John Epson. "I hope she marries the right man."

"I'm sure she will. She has a good head on her shoulders." Matt slapped Clay on the back. "Let's get back to town and finalize our deal. I have to send a telegram. By Monday afternoon you'll have the money to pay the bank. Send out word today to bring more men to work. And if I were you, I'd hire trained guards. Take the men off who are doing it now and put on men who are trained to keep a place free of saboteurs."

"I'll do that," said Clay. He held his hand out to Matt. They shook hands and smiled at each other. Clay hadn't expected his day to take such a strange turn. "I feel like a big load has been lifted off my shoulders."

"I'm glad I could help." Matt's nerve tightened. What would Lark do if she ever learned of the deal he'd struck with young Havlick? Matt shrugged. What else could he have done? Saving Clay and the pines were important to Lark; therefore, they were important to him.

Clay tied Sears back up, then ran to the buggy. The flowers seemed brighter and smelled better. Clay patted Star's neck. He knew he could even face Veda about postponing the wedding.

Friday afternoon Lark stood at the window in her office and looked out at the children playing in the yard. Zoe had the babies on a large quilt and they seemed glad to be outdoors too.

John walked in quietly and smiled as he watched Lark watch the children. He stepped up behind her and slipped his arms around her waist. "You look happy today," he whispered in her ear.

She gasped and tried to pull away. "Don't, Jonn!"

He turned her in his arms and smiled into her eyes. "Have you ever been kissed by a man with a beard?"

Lark gasped and her pulse leaped. She'd never been kissed by anyone. She wanted to pull away, but felt too weak to move.

"Why are you doing this?"

He could say it was part of his plan to get her away from her job at the pines, or that he was trying his best to get her to trust him so totally she'd do anything he asked of her. Either was true. Instead with a low chuckle he said, "You're a desirable woman and I'm a man."

"Please let me go."

"I will." John stroked her cheek, causing her heart to flutter. "You're very special. I care for you more than you'll ever know."

"I . . . I didn't know," she whispered. She'd dreamed of this, and now after she'd given up all hope, it was happening.

John cupped Lark's face in his hands and gently kissed her lips.

His mouth felt strange against hers. She hesitantly returned his kiss and found she liked the feel of his lips on hers and his beard brushing her face. What did the kiss mean? Breathlessly she pulled back from him. "Please let me go, John," she whispered.

He tightened his hold on her. "I have a better idea."

"What?"

"Marry me and I'll never have to let you go."

Lark gasped. "You can't want to marry me."

"Why not?"

"I'm plain as a post!"

"Who said so?"

"Everyone! The looking glass!"

John laughed softly. "There's more to a woman than her looks. You are not as plain as a post. You're beautiful. And you have an inner strength that I admire."

Lark's head spun. Her pulse raced. Being held close to John made her have feelings she'd never had before. But could she marry him? Last year she'd have agreed without hesitation, but today she couldn't say yes so quickly. Maybe she wouldn't say yes at all. "I don't know what to say."

"Don't say anything. Think about what I said and we'll talk about it again over supper."

"I'm having supper with my father."

John stiffened. "Your father?"

"Yes." Lark pulled away from John and he let her go. "You don't know, do you? He came yesterday! He's not dead after all! Someone played a cruel joke on me."

"Are you sure?"

"What do you mean?"

"Maybe the man who claims to be Matt Baritt is an imposter. Maybe he's after something."

"From me? I don't have anything."

John shrugged. "Just be careful. Don't trust him."

Lark fingered the high collar of her green shirtwaist. She already trusted Matt. But maybe she should check him out further.

John sank back against his desk and crossed his arms. "I'd like to meet him. Could I join the two of you for supper?"

Lark thought for a minute, smiled, and nodded. "Yes. I'd like that. I want the two of you to meet. I think you'll like him, John, and he's sure to like you."

John doubted that, but didn't say so.

"We're having supper at my cabin about six," said Lark. "Does that suit you?"

"I'll be there." John stepped close to Lark, cupped her face in his hands, and kissed her again. "Think about what I said. I want you to be my wife."

Lark blushed. His wife! "I will think about it."

Clay walked around the Thornes' house with Veda's hand in his. Giant oaks shaded the yard, protecting them from the terrible heat. "Are you sure your pa won't be coming home?" asked Clay as they sat on the white bench in the flower garden.

"He said he'd be gone until late." Veda lifted Clay's hand to her lips. "Now, tell me why you didn't want to meet with Pastor James tonight."

Clay kissed Veda lightly while he searched for just the right words to say. "You won't want to hear."

Veda tensed. A bee buzzed past, but she ignored it. "Tell me anyway."

Clay held Veda's hands up against his chest. "We must wait until the end of December to get married."

Veda jerked her hands free. What had happened to her careful planning? "I don't want to wait that long!"

"That's sweet of you and it makes me feel good, but I've been having problems at the Wagon Works and I can't get married sooner."

Veda burst into tears. "You really don't love me, do you?"

"Don't say that!" Clay tried to pull her close, but she pushed him away. "Please try to understand," he begged. "All of my time and energy must go into filling the contracts. I must have workers from dawn until dark."

"What will I do with my time?"

"I don't know. What do other expectant brides do?"

Veda searched for something to say. "Get their homes ready."

"Then do that. I'll check into the house you were talking about. There might be a way I can get it."

"Do you mean it?"

"I'll see about it." Clay didn't know if he could, but he liked the idea of getting a home ready so they could move right in when they got married.

Veda snuggled close to Clay. "I'll like living with you."

Clay lifted her face and kissed her.

They talked about the house and what they both wanted in a home.

"I know what I want to buy you for a wedding gift," said Veda with a smile.

Clay hadn't thought that far ahead. "What?"

"A ring filled with diamonds just like Momma bought Papa." Veda's stomach knotted and she had to force her mind away from her parents and her personal problems.

Clay shook his head. "I don't want anything that expensive."

"But you're worth it!"

"I don't think I'd wear a ring."

"To business meetings and church you would."

"Maybe so."

"What will you give me, Clay?"

"What do you want?" Right now he thought he'd give her the moon if she asked for it.

"A month long honeymoon."

"I can't do that."

Veda laughed. "Oh, all right! I know you're busy with your business." She looked impishly at him as if thinking hard about another gift. "I know what you can do." She paused and smiled sweetly. "You could give me the white pines."

Clay pulled back, his body suddenly stiff. "The pines?"

Veda saw the startled look on his face and she knew she had to retreat. She managed to laugh. "I was teasing, silly! I don't want the pines. I would like an emerald brooch, I think."

Clay looked closely at Veda. Had she been even a little serious in asking for the pines? What if Jig had been right? Abruptly Clay pushed the terrible thought aside. "Then I'll get you an emerald brooch." He pulled her close and kissed her.

After supper Lark stacked the dirty plates. She would wash them later. She followed Matt and John outdoors to the bench. The tension between the two men filled the yard just as it had filled the cabin. Lark frowned as she sat down while they stood looking into the forest. Sears ran to Lark and she rubbed his neck. Maybe Sears felt the tension too.

John turned to Lark. "I'd like to come out early in the morning and walk the trail with you."

"I don't know if you should, John. There's a lot of danger out there this time of year with the terrible heat and all."

"You can do it, so can I." John sat beside her. "I want to see just what you do when you guard the pines. I want to have the experience with you."

Matt frowned. What was John up to?

Lark glanced at Matt, then back at John. "I leave here before five. Can you be here that early?"

John nodded. "Oh, wait! I have to go out of town until Tuesday, but I can make it Wednesday morning. Then we'll drive to work together."

"Sounds fine to me," said Lark. She couldn't look at Matt. She could sense he didn't approve. She already knew he didn't approve of her guard's job because of the danger.

John squeezed Lark's hand. "I'll see you sometime Tuesday. Take care of yourself while I'm gone."

Lark smiled. "I will. Be sure to wear heavy britches and boots when you come to walk the pines. The snakes are pretty bad this time of year."

"I will." John stood and shook hands with Matt. "I must be going. I'll talk to you soon. Probably Tuesday."

"I'm sure," said Matt.

John smiled at Lark as he took her hands in his. "Thank you for a wonderful supper and a very pleasant evening."

"I'm glad you came," Lark said, suddenly feeling light headed. If Matt hadn't been there, John would've kissed her. Her lips tingled at the thought.

Lark stood beside Matt as John stepped into his buggy and drove away. The rattle of the harness and the creak of the buggy faded finally. A whippoorwill called and another answered. "He asked me to marry him," Lark said softly without looking at Matt.

Matt sucked in his breath. "Uh-mmm. What was your answer?"

"I told him I'd think about it."

Matt wanted to tell her to drop Epson like a poison rattler. But he had a feeling Lark would take Epson even more seriously if he told her not to. "I'm sure you'll do the right thing," Matt said. Silently he prayed that she would do just that. "Did he give you a time limit to answer him?"

"No. Why?"

"I just think it would be good for you to take several days. This is a serious step."

"I agree."

"He might want an answer Wednesday morning."

"He might."

"Will you give it to him?"

"I don't know. If I've decided I will." Lark finally looked at Matt. "Would you like another glass of lemonade?" She still wasn't ready to trust him completely enough to tell him her whole heart.

Saturday afternoon Matt found Clay standing near a finished wagon at the Wagon Works. Sounds of men's voices, sawing, and hammering came from inside the buildings. Matt shook hands with Clay and smiled.

"I've hired ten more men," said Clay, rubbing back his damp hair. "And my brother Tris is scouting around for more."

"Good." Matt cleared his throat. "Did you know John Epson proposed marriage to Lark?"

"What?" cried Clay. "No, I didn't know that. I hope she turned him down."

"She's thinking on it," said Matt. Being a father was a little more complicated than he had thought. "Have you heard anything against him?"

"Not that I can think of."

"What do *you* have against him?"

Clay rubbed his hand down the side of his face. Too many sudden changes were taking place and he didn't like it. "Nothing I can put my finger on."

"I don't want to see Lark hurt," said Matt.

"I don't either."

"When will you tell her you no longer need her services?"

"Maybe tomorrow."

"Make sure it's not too late. I don't want her to know anything about our deal. It's between us."

"I understand," said Clay, but he wondered if he really did.

He watched Matt walk away, then Clay leaned against a wagon. Would he wake up and find he'd been dreaming a way out of his problems? It was too good to be true.

Clay's stomach was tied in knots when he met Matt outside the bank Monday morning. What if Matt had changed his mind and the deal was off? What if he still lost the Wagon Works and the pines? He'd planned to see Lark over the weekend to relieve her of her jobs, but when he wasn't at the Wagon Works Veda had kept him busy.

"Were you able to hire the rest of the men you need?" asked Matt after they shook hands outside the open door of the bank.

Clay nodded. "My brother Tris went to Grand Rapids and brought them back with him last night. They're all at work now. My lumber order came in this morning by train, so I'm all set." It all still seemed too good to be true.

Matt cleared his throat. "Not quite," he said, his eyes on Clay.

"What do you mean?" Clay's heart fell to his feet like a rock. He was in too far to have Matt back out now.

"I have one other thing to ask."

A shiver ran down Clay's spine even though the day was oppressive with heat. "What?"

Matt brushed a fly off the sleeve of his gray suit. Could he go through with his plans? This was harder than any business deal he'd ever made. He shrugged. "It's nothing you can't handle."

Clay stiffened even more. "Maybe you'd better tell me." Matt rested his hand on Clay's arm and urged him away from the doorway to the corner of the building. A horse and buggy drove past on the sawdust covered street kicking up a cloud of dust. Already Clay was having trouble breathing, he was so anxious about what Matt might say.

"First," Matt began, "let me tell you what I did shortly after I arrived here and met my daughter."

Sweat popped out on Clay's wide forehead. His suit coat suddenly felt hotter than long handled underwear. He had a premonition he wasn't going to like what Matt would say next.

"I listened to what Lark said about the Thornes. And I heard a few other rumors, so I hired a gardener to work undercover at Thorne's house."

"What?" cried Clay. It was even worse than he'd thought.

"I wanted to check for myself to see if Lark was right about Thorne and his daughter."

"You spied on them? You had no right to do that!"

Matt sighed heavily. "My daughter is involved and that gives me every right." Matt looked squarely at Clay. "My man heard Veda and Willie Thorne talking together in the flower garden. She said she couldn't convince you to elope or to sign over the pines to her."

"No," Clay groaned. He leaned heavily against the building, not trusting his legs to support him. "I don't believe it. There must be a mistake. Veda wouldn't do that—plot against me. Willie might, but not Veda. She loves me. She's told me many times." Clay felt as if his heart might break.

Matt reached out and gently touched Clay's shoulder. He understood Clay's disappointment and pain. He shook his head slowly. "I'm sorry, Clay. I'm very sorry, but you must know the truth even if it hurts you." He took a deep breath. "Thorne told Veda she had to do both. He told her to work harder to get you to elope with her *and* get you to sign over the pines to her. He said she should seduce you if she could find no other way."

Helplessly Clay shook his head. "No. No, I don't believe it."

"It's true, Clay. Thorne said you are an honorable man, that if Veda could get you in a 'compromising position'—as a last resort—you would marry her no matter what the consequences may be. My man overheard him say all of that. I'll let you talk to him to hear it for yourself."

Clay's face flushed with heat, then all the color drained away, leaving him white and trembling.

Matt waited until Clay had thought through what he'd just heard. The dusty town around them seemed to pause too. After several minutes, Matt said, "I told you Epson asked Lark to marry him. I know she doesn't love him and I doubt he loves her. There's something else going on there. I'm not sure what, but I know I don't like it whatever it is."

Clay frowned. Where was all this leading?

"Lark loves you, Clay."

Helplessly Clay shook his head. How could that be?

Matt tapped Clay's shoulder with his finger. "But since she knew you were going to marry Veda, she's considering marrying Epson."

Clay groaned and rubbed his hand over his face. Lark couldn't possibly love Epson. She'd never given him a hint of a special feeling for the man. Surely he'd know—he'd promised Jig he'd look after her. Had he been too distracted to notice or to listen?

Matt cleared his throat. What he needed to say next would be the most difficult part. He had no idea how Clay would react. He wanted to keep quiet, but it was too important not to say it. He forced out the words, his heart in his dry throat.

"Clay, I want *you* to marry Lark."

"What?" Clay jumped away from the wall of the bank, his back straight and his shoulders square. This was too much. "Me marry Lark? You can't mean it!"

Matt waited until two women walked past and out of ear shot. "Yes, I do. You won't have any problem sweeping her off her feet."

Sweep her off her feet? He wouldn't know how to begin. He wasn't Tris!

"She loves you. I'm sure of it. I think, if you would let yourself think about it, you'd know it's true."

"I can't listen to any more of this," said Clay, but he didn't move.

Matt rubbed his hands up and down his sleeves. This was almost as hard on him as on Clay, but he had to finish it.

"Marry her within the week and I'll tear up the loan papers. The money *and* the pines will be yours and Lark's together—free and clear."

"I can't believe this," said Clay hoarsely.

"It's my deal with you," said Matt.

"You're going to pay me to marry your daughter."

"It's not like that at all. We're both businessmen. I am offering you a business deal. If it weren't best for Lark, I wouldn't suggest it."

Clay ran his fingers through his dark hair, then smoothed it back in place. "How do you know she'll marry *me?*"

"I know. I've seen the way she looks at you. I hear the sound in her voice when she speaks your name. When we're together she talks mostly about you. It's as though she thinks about you all the time."

Clay blushed. He'd never thought about Lark loving him.

Matt took a deep breath. What would happen to him if Lark ever learned of this plan? She would be wildly angry. She might reject him. But for her sake he had to take the chance.

"You can convince her to marry you. Just ask her. If she hesitates, tell her you need her to marry you to get Veda Thorne out of your life. That'll work for sure. Lark will do anything to help you. And she doesn't want you to marry Veda."

Clay's heart jerked strangely. After a long thoughtful moment he nodded. "All right. I'll do it."

"This week?"

"Yes, this week. I'll ask Lark to marry me." The words sounded strange to his ears. Had he really said them?

Matt held out his hand. "Let's shake on it."

Clay looked at Matt's hand, then finally reached out to him. They shook hands, then Clay followed Matt into the bank.

CHAPTER

13

♦ Outside the bank after the business transaction Clay held his hand out to Matt. "Thank you. I hope I can do all that you asked of me."

Matt clasped Clay's hand. "You will. You're a man of your word."

Clay nodded. He was that.

Matt fell into step beside Clay. "I'd like to meet your family," he said.

"All but Tris are still in Grand Rapids with my sister. She and her husband had twins."

"Twins! That's wonderful. I'm sure you're all proud."

Clay hadn't given it much thought since he was so busy.

"Do you want children when you marry, Clay?"

"I suppose so."

"Maybe you and Lark will have twins."

Clay bit back a cry of shock. He hadn't thought that far ahead. Maybe it was time he considered just what he was getting into. He would be expected to be a true husband to Lark. A blush crept up his neck and over his face.

"I didn't mean to embarrass you," said Matt as they crossed the quiet street. "I'm looking forward to grandchildren, especially since I had to miss seeing my own child grow up." His voice broke and he brushed a tear from his eye.

"I'm sorry," said Clay. He knew his parents valued time with their children. Would he be that kind of parent? The idea was so new to him he couldn't begin to think of an answer.

Matt patted Clay's shoulder as they walked down the board sidewalk past the last store, then turned toward the Wagon Works. Several children ran down the middle of the road, shouting and laughing. Matt glanced at the children, then at Clay. "Have you spoken to Veda yet?"

Clay shook his head. "I was too angry. I want to face her when I'm in control." When he learned the truth, he'd wanted to rush to her house and throttle her until she admitted the truth.

"That's wise. She'll take the broken engagement hard and so will her father."

"Do you think they'll cause more trouble for me?"

"Yes, they will. You can count on it." Matt pulled off his straw hat, rubbed his handkerchief around the inside band, and settled it back in place. "If Thorne is snake enough to use his own daughter to try to get the pines, he'll try something else. Maybe violence."

Clay shook his head. "I have wondered if he's behind the treachery at the shop."

"I thought the same thing, but you can't do anything until you can prove it. Did you hire the guards?"

"Yes, men from Big Pine who've worked as guards at the lumber mills."

"What did you tell the men you were using?"

"I told them that I'd made other arrangements for security, but they could continue working as laborers. They all agreed to stay on." Clay narrowed his eyes thoughtfully. "Dag wanted to continue as a guard. In fact he was very determined. He said he felt a personal interest in seeing that the wagons are safe. But he gave in when I said he couldn't." Clay explained who Dag was, the suspicions he'd had, and the feelers he'd put out to check up on him. "He is a hard worker and very skilled. So far I haven't learned anything about him that's bad."

"I'll ask around about him, too, and see if I can come up with something."

"Thanks, Matt, but it's not necessary. You've helped me more than you should—more than I can ever repay. You've done enough."

Matt shrugged. Helping Clay really wasn't his aim. He wanted to take care of Lark, to help her. He'd missed all those years with her. He wasn't going to be denied any longer. "Have you seen Lark yet?"

"No. I must deal with Veda first." Anger rose inside Clay at the thought of Veda. How could he have let her trick him so easily? He'd been taught never to strike a woman, but he wanted to double his fist and punch her across the state, and then send Willie after her.

Just as they reached the Wagon Works, Veda stepped out of her buggy parked along the street and walked toward Clay. She wore a cream colored skirt with a large bustle and a cream and rose shirtwaist with wide puffed sleeves. Under the small flowered hat, her face was set with determination. Matt tipped his hat and quickly said goodbye. He stood off aways under a tree to see what happened.

Clay glanced toward the shop where the men were hard at work. No one seemed to notice Veda. He felt anger burning just under the surface of his calm facade as Veda stopped just inches from him. He smelled the clean scent of her lilac soap and saw a flash of anger in her dark brown eyes.

"Why have you been avoiding me, Clay Havlick?" she asked sharply.

Clay struggled to keep his anger in check as he gripped Veda's arm and led her back toward her buggy. "I'm very busy, Veda. I'll call on you this evening."

"No!" Veda jerked free and faced him squarely. Papa had said she had to make this look very good. "I don't want to see you this evening or any evening again! I am calling *off* the engagement." Her eyes flashed and she raised her chin in a pose of self-righteous indignation.

Clay stared at her in shock. He had planned to break the engagement. Now he was speechless. "I don't understand," he said weakly.

"You don't care one whit for me! I don't want to see you again as long as I live!"

Clay felt at a loss. Finally he said, "It is for the best. You'll find someone else to marry and so will I."

Veda looked as if she'd been struck. Papa had expected Clay to beg her to marry him even though he didn't have time. What had happened? "I will never marry," she said, trying to keep her voice from trembling. She stepped up into her buggy and without another word, drove away.

His head spinning, Clay watched her go. Had Matt lied to him about Veda? Clay saw Matt standing under an oak several yards away and strode to him. "Veda just broke our engagement."

Matt whistled in surprise. "What game is she playing this time?"

"Is it a game? How do I know I can trust you, Matt Baritt?"

Matt shrugged. "I guess you'll have to look in your heart and see."

Abruptly Clay turned away. He couldn't trust his own heart any longer.

"You have a Scripture to hang on to," Matt said softly. "The sons of God are led by the Spirit of God."

Clay remembered Jig telling him that same thing many times. He'd gotten so tangled up in his business and then with Veda that he hadn't taken time to pray or listen to God. It was past time to get back to spending time reading his Bible and praying. Jig had always told him he had an inheritance greater than the white pines—the promises in God's Word. All of God's blessings belonged to him, but first he had to know them. Then he had to claim them as his own.

"Is something wrong, Clay?" asked Matt.

Clay turned to face Matt. "Yes, it is! You just reminded me to let God's spirit lead me. I haven't been doing that lately, but I mean to do just that from now on!"

Matt smiled. "Good for you, Clay Havlick. Keep in mind you gave your word to marry Lark *this week*."

Clay nodded even though he didn't feel good about what lay ahead. He had given his word and he would keep it. He couldn't back out now and lose his business and his pines.

Just before leaving for the cabin, Lark ran to Matron Kettering's office. It felt closed in and stuffy and there was a strong smell of peppermint.

"Zoe said you wanted to see me immediately."

Mercy stood stiffly beside her desk. Her cheeks were flushed bright red and the fire of battle flashed in her blue eyes. "I just learned that the tavern on Main Street is opening at this very moment! We must march right down there and close it!"

"I thought the mayor refused to give Willie Thorne a business permit."

"I did too! But he's opening and we can't let the townspeople down by letting it stay open." Mercy picked up the tambourine that lay on the corner of her desk. She shook it hard and the jangle filled the room. "I've asked for others in the League to meet us outside the bank."

"I wish Jennet Havlick was here," Lark said, "but she's still in Grand Rapids. She'd want to march on the tavern." A shiver ran down Lark's spine. She'd never done such a brash thing in all her life. Could she push the doors open and walk right in and declare boldly that drinking was of the devil and that the men should get home to their loving families?

"Get your Bible," Mercy said as she tied her dark bonnet on over her light brown hair.

"It's at my cabin."

"Then take one of these." Mercy pointed to four huge

Bibles piled on a shelf behind her desk. "You can never have too many Bibles." Mercy struck her tambourine against her palm again and the jangles rang inside Lark's head.

Several minutes later Lark stood outside Willie Thorne's tavern with four other women. A dark green sign with shiny black lettering that read THORNE'S TAVERN hung above the swinging doors. Noisy piano music drifted into the street. So did a woman's squeal. Lark glanced at the others. The group didn't seem to be very big considering how many belonged to the Temperance League. Maybe some of the members found it hard to march on the tavern. Or maybe the women were too busy with their families.

Lark could see men stopping on the street outside the hardware and feed store to stare at them. A dog barked in the distance and a horse neighed.

Mercy held the big black Bible against her breast and the tambourine out from her hip; she lifted her chin and called, "Ready, ladies?" Mercy slapped her hip with the tambourine and marched through the door of the tavern singing "Onward Christian Soldiers." The other women marched in rhythm with her, their voices blending proudly with hers. Lark followed close behind, her voice a mere croak.

Inside, the tavern was dimly lit and smelled of beer and sweat. Several men at the bar turned at the singing. They shook their heads and swore. Other men sat at small round tables while girls in scanty red dresses walked from the bar to the tables serving the customers.

Angrily Willie Thorne pushed back his chair and strode toward the women. "Ladies," he shouted over the singing and tambourine, "you have no right in my establishment! Leave immediately or I'll call the sheriff." He saw Lark Baritt and three women he'd seen on the sidewalks with a woman he knew was matron of the orphan asylum.

Mercy stopped singing and, ignoring Willie, shouted, "You men! How can you waste your hard earned money on strong drink? Get home to your families. You are sinning against God and against your own bodies. Leave this den of iniquity now before you lose your everlasting souls!"

Lark tried to keep singing, but her throat closed over and no sound came out. Her cheeks burned with embarrassment. Then she looked at Willie and fresh anger rose inside her. She stepped toward him and shook her finger right in his face. "You have harmed enough people already, Willie Thorne. I was there when Silent Waters died. It was a terrible death and I shall never forget it. *And* it was all because of you and your greed. Leave this place and this town. You're not wanted here!"

Willie Thorne shrank back at the mention of Silent Waters and the horrible way she'd died. He turned to a large bearded man at a nearby table. "Get them out of here," Willie said hoarsely.

"We'll leave," Mercy shouted as Willie stalked toward his chair. Her voice was loud for such a small woman. "But if you don't close your doors and stop selling this evil liquor, we'll be back. And we'll come back again and again until you leave our good town."

"Sure, sure," said the bearded man. He gripped Mercy's arm and gestured toward the door. He towered over her and easily could have picked her up and carried her out. "You get out of here right now and stop making trouble."

Lark moistened her dry lips. The room was small and crowded. It had grown quiet. A cloud of embarrassment hung in the air as the customers and serving girls waited for the interruption to be over. Lark saw a blond haired man duck his head and turn away as if he was embarrassed for her to see him.

"Let go of me, sir," cried Mercy, trying to break free as the bearded man dragged her toward the door. The other three women rushed out of the tavern, leaving Mercy and Lark behind. Struggling to stay on her feet, Mercy looked all around the room. "I've seen you all and I will recognize you again. When I see you on the street or in church, I'll tell everyone who can hear that you were in here, in this evil place, drinking and carousing."

Lark walked toward the door with as much dignity as she could summon. She paused in the door for one last look and saw the blond man deep in conversation with Willie Thorne.

Outside the tavern Mercy smoothed down her skirts and tied her bonnet back in place. With her chin held high, she said, "They haven't seen the last of us!"

As the other women hurried away, Lark wondered if they'd ever follow Mercy into the tavern again. She knew it would be very hard for her to do.

"I know that young blond who sat in there," said Mercy as they walked toward the Home. "He was in the Home in Grand Rapids a few years ago when I taught there." She frowned thoughtfully. "His name escapes me right now, but I'll think of it."

Lark dabbed perspiration from her face with her small white hanky. She wondered what Matt would think of her latest exploit. Facing rattlesnakes, bears, and tree robbers seemed much easier than marching into a tavern with the Temperance League.

"I have it! His name is Dag. Dag Gotland! Yes, now I remember." Mercy nodded and smiled. "He was fourteen when I taught him arithmetic. I hate to see him take to drinking."

Lark listened numbly as Mercy talked about her days in Grand Rapids. The sun seemed hotter than the day before and Lark wondered when the hot spell would end. She longed to be back in her cabin in the forest.

When they reached the Home and she had listened to Mercy's promise to invade Willie's tavern again if he kept it open, she said goodbye to Mercy, grateful the experience was over. She was against drinking but she wasn't sure their march had done any good. She hitched Star to her buggy and wearily climbed in. "Let's go home, Star."

About to flick the reins, she heard, "Did you forget about our date for supper?"

Matt walked toward the buggy, his hat pushed to the back of his head. He was shaking his finger at Lark.

Lark laughed, feeling better at once. "I sure did. Sorry."

Matt frowned. "What's wrong? It's not like you to forget things."

He climbed into the buggy, then Lark told him about the visit to the tavern. She finished the story with, "It was awful."

Matt laughed. "I'd like to get to know your Mercy Kettering. She might be little, but she sounds mighty."

Lark laughed. "I happen to know she's walking among those maples over there." Lark pointed to the clump of trees between the Home and the house south of them. "You get acquainted with her while I go home and collapse. I'm tired all the way to the bone."

Matt squeezed Lark's hand. He'd decided to tell her about the loan he'd made to Clay and the rest of the agreement, but now he had a way out. It was probably best she didn't know anything anyway just like he'd first planned. "You go on home and I'll see you tomorrow," he said.

"Tomorrow? That would be nice. Just how long do you plan to stay around here?"

"As long as I'm welcome."

Tears pricked Lark's eyes. "I hope I don't get used to having you around only to have you leave."

"I promise that won't happen." Matt stepped from the buggy, then stood beside it and looked up at Lark. "I saw a house for sale in town. It's over near the Wagon Works. I was thinking about buying it. What do you think?"

"The one with lots of windows and at least six bedrooms? I love that house!"

"Then I'll buy it."

"Just like that? Do you have enough money to do that kind of thing?"

Matt nodded. "I have more than enough."

"Do writers make that kind of money?"

"No, but lumbermen do."

Lark stared at Matt in surprise. She didn't know much at all about this man who was her father. "Are you a lumberman?"

"Yes. I started out much the way Free Havlick did. Grant Bigalow and I went into partnership and we made a great deal of money in the Upper Peninsula. I invested my money and built up a nice nest egg for myself." He shrugged. "Some would call it a fortune."

"I didn't know," said Lark weakly.

"I want to share it with you."

Lark pressed her hand to her throat. What would it be like to have a fortune? She'd thought she had one when Jig left her $1500. She knew Matt was talking about a great deal more than that.

"I'm going to buy that house for you, Lark, and you can move in right away."

Lark gasped. "You can't do that!"

"I can if I want." Matt laughed. "I want to give you everything!"

"I wanted a father the past twenty-two years."

Matt's face fell. "I know. Fear wrecks lives, Lark. My fear kept us apart. I vow I will never again let fear keep me from doing what I want for my daughter. I will buy that house and I will furnish it just the way you want. You plan on moving in right away."

"What about my cabin?"

"Bring it with you!"

Lark began to laugh and Matt joined in.

With Sears beside her, Lark filled her canteen at the well just after dawn. "This heat has to let up, Sears. I can't take it much longer." Lark hooked her canteen to her belt beside the revolver and holster, picked up her cudgel, and headed into the pines. Her feet were hot inside her heavy boots and the leggings she wore made her legs itch. She was wearing her old blue calico dress instead of her leather pants and jacket because of the heat

A rabbit hopped into sight, then streaked away, but Sears ignored it. A deer drank at the stream. Nearby a raccoon sat watching. Lark flung her cudgel high in the air, then caught it deftly. She remembered the first time she'd done that. She'd almost broken her fingers as she tried to catch it. Now she barely felt the sting in her palm.

At the quagmire, mosquitoes buzzed over the top of it. Green and blue dragonflies flitted here and there. Several black crows teased an owl on a branch. The owl snapped angrily, but the crows kept cawing. She loved the early morning time in the forest.

As Lark pushed through the briars she heard the frightening whir of rattles and froze. Usually when it was this hot even the rattlesnakes didn't give a warning. She checked in front of her and saw a snake coiled and ready to strike. Sears stood without moving a muscle. Finally the snake crawled away through the pine needles.

"Close one, Sears," Lark said, her voice trembling slightly. Sears licked her hand and she felt better. Side by side they walked past the huge tree root. So many memories of dangerous encounters were connected with it, she had difficulty just passing by. She looked down on the quiet river. No one was on it yet. Men were still looking in the swamps for logs, so they'd be out and around later.

Sweat soaked Lark as she walked to the spot where she would cut across the pines and turn back to the cabin. She stopped and listened. She thought she'd heard the ring of an ax, but the only sounds she could hear were the normal sounds of animals and insects. It must've been her imagination.

Sears pressed his nose tight into Lark's hand. The short hairs on the back of her neck stood on end. Someone was nearby, she was sure of it. She brushed her arm across her revolver and gripped her cudgel tighter. The loud musical rattle of a sandhill crane startled her and she almost cried out.

Her senses alert, she walked fast to the cabin. Who had

been watching her in the pines? Had Matt hired someone to protect her because he knew of the terrible dangers?

Standing at the well, Lark studied the pines. Had someone followed her? She glanced at Sears. He was watching the pines also. Prickles of fear ran over her skin, but no one stepped out. Finally Sears ran to his bowl and lapped water. With a relieved sigh Lark struck the bell to signal the hired man at the Havlicks' that all was well. Clay would already be at the Wagon Works and Tris had left last night for Grand Rapids to be with the family.

Just as she was trying to relax Sears looked up and growled low in his throat. Lark stiffened.

"Lark Baritt, it's me. Dag Bjoerling. I came to see you."

Lark frowned, but didn't pull her revolver. Clay had told her Jig's grandson was working for him, but so far she hadn't met him. "Come on out from behind that tree," she called.

Dag stepped around a pine smiling hesitantly. He wore heavy boots, work pants, and a blue chambray shirt. He had a cap on his blond head. A revolver was stuck in his belt and he carried a long walking stick whittled from a sapling.

Lark recognized him as the blond man at the tavern who Mercy had said was Dag Gotland from Grand Rapids. He could not be Dag Bjoerling from Sweden as he'd said he was. Had Clay learned this man was an imposter? If he didn't know, she'd have to warn him. "What can I do for you?" she asked.

"Give me a ride back to town. I was trying to find Red Beaver's place and got lost."

Lark didn't believe that, but she didn't let it show. "I must change my clothes before I can go to town. You could go to the Havlicks to see if Clay has left yet."

Just then Sears lifted his head and whined. Lark frowned. Was someone else nearby, someone that Sears knew? Lark turned to Dag and whispered, "Someone's lurking about. When I shout, draw your gun and be ready to fire."

The color drained from Dag's face. He didn't want anyone hurt or killed. He pulled his gun and pointed it at Lark.

"What're you doing?" she cried.

"Drop the gun and the club. If your dog makes a move toward me, I'll shoot him dead." Dag knew he wouldn't shoot the dog, but he had to make Lark think he would.

Trembling, Lark dropped the revolver and cudgel on the ground. "What do you want?"

Just then John Epson walked from behind the cabin, his hat in his hand, his face red.

"John! I'm so glad to see you!" Lark cried, taking a step toward him.

"Stay!" snapped Dag. She froze, looking from John to Dag.

"Listen to him, Lark," said John, wiping his face with a large white handkerchief.

"John?" whispered Lark, trembling, suddenly too weak to stand. "What is it? Why are you here?"

"We have men ready to cut the trees," said John.

Lark stumbled back and sank down on the bench. Sears sank at her feet and laid his head on her heavy boots. "Cut the trees? You, John?"

He shook his head. "I'm only here to see that you don't stop them."

"You won't get away with it."

"We will," said John.

"What about me? What will you do with me?" Lark knew they couldn't let her go.

John flushed. He didn't want to think about that.

Dag held the revolver out to John. "Keep her here while I check on the men. We have a whole crew working. It won't take them long."

Lark groaned. While Dag and John talked she glanced down at Sears and whispered, "Fetch my cudgel, Sears. Fetch."

Sears padded to the cudgel and carried it to Lark. Her heart hammered so loud she thought the two men could hear it. She took the cudgel from Sears and stood it close to her, covering it with her skirts.

Dag glanced at Lark, then ran into the pines. Lark knew

they would begin at the easiest place above the river to lumber the pines. The sawers would cut a tree, others would chop off the limbs and branches, then they'd roll the huge trunk down the hill to the river and float it to Blue Creek. They'd put a log mark on each end of the log and no one would ever know it came from Havlicks' pines.

"Why are you doing this, John?" asked Lark.

He frowned at her, then down at the revolver. "Do you know how much money each pine is worth? It's more than most people make in a year! I had a chance to share the money and I took it."

"Is that why you paid attention to me?"

"Yes. I tried my best to get you interested in something besides the pines. I tried to get you away from here to keep you out of this. But you wouldn't listen. I'm sorry, Lark. I like and respect you. You deserve better than you're going to get."

"Just let me go, John. You know they'll kill me." Lark couldn't move without giving away the cudgel at her side. "Willie Thorne is behind all of this, isn't he?"

John laughed gruffly. "Willie Thorne? You've got it all wrong, Lark. It's Matt Baritt. This is how he made his fortune."

Lark cried out in searing agony. "You're lying!"

"Don't believe me if you don't want to. But I speak the truth." John's eye twitched. He rubbed his well-trimmed beard.

Suddenly Lark flung the cudgel, sending it spinning sideways. It struck Epson's elbow and the revolver flew from his hand. He cried in pain as he grabbed his arm. Lark leaped for the revolver, scooping it up before John could move.

"You won't shoot me," said John, his eyes hard. "I know you well, Lark Baritt."

"I'll shoot if I must," she said harshly.

John stared hard into her eyes, then bolted for the woods. Lark took aim, but couldn't fire. John was right. She could not shoot him. She caught up her cudgel and sprang toward the

bell. She struck it twice with her cudgel, then leaped after
John with Sears at her heels. She could hear John crashing
through the underbrush ahead of her. If he didn't stay on the
trail, he wouldn't last long among the swamps and rattlesnakes. Did he know enough about the woods to be on guard?
He was in good shape and he was a fast runner. That would
help him.

She thought of the men in the woods. If they heard the bell
they'd run off before anyone could reach them and capture
them. If they hadn't, she'd make John tell her exactly where
they were working.

Lark ran carefully, watching for every danger. The terrible
heat pressed against her, making it hard to keep going.

Up ahead John's dirt covered face was streaked with sweat
as he hesitated at a bog. If he didn't go through it, Lark would
catch him. If he did go through it, he might lose his shoes in
the muck. His heart raced as he looked back. He couldn't see
Lark but he could hear her coming after him.

He heard the sickening whirring of a rattlesnake. Fear stung
his fingertips as he caught sight of the huge coil. He sprang
back just as the snake struck, missing him by a hair's breadth.
He leaped forward through the bog. He sank ankle deep in the
mud but miraculously his shoes stayed on his feet. Reaching
the needle-covered ground on the other side, he thought he
was safe for the moment.

There was a sudden searing pain in his leg. He cried out,
stumbled, and sprawled to the ground. He saw the snake, but
he was too paralyzed with fear to move. Without a sound the
snake struck again, sinking its fangs in John's face between his
beard and his eye. He screamed and clawed at his face. The
snake struck again in his arm and he screamed again.

Lark leaped forward, caught up the snake with her cudgel
and flung it away. Sears growled deep in his throat as he
crouched near John. "Oh, John!" Lark cried as she knelt beside him. Tears burned her eyes as she caught his hand and
held it tightly.

John's eyes filled with tears. "This is it for me, Lark," he said hoarsely.

"I'm sorry." Tears slipped down her ashen cheeks. "God loves you and always has."

"You sound like Ma," whispered John, remembering even though he tried not to. "She always prayed for me."

"She prayed and God always answers prayer, John!"

"It's too late for me. I never thought it would end like this. Where did I go wrong?" His voice cracked. "I know where. I let greed take hold of me. I thought later, after I'd made myself rich, then I could straighten out my life. Maybe even repent. Now it's too late."

"Oh, John, don't give up!"

Great drops of sweat rolled down his face. A squirrel scolded nearby, then the raspy buzz of insects covered the chatter.

"It's too late for me. It's funny. I always thought I had plenty of time. I'll have to pay for my sins just like Ma always said. It's too late to call on Jesus."

"No, it's not! It's never too late to pray," said Lark with a sob.

"I'll die and spend all eternity suffering in hell." John moaned and his eyes glazed over from the pain.

"John, can you hear me? Ask Jesus to forgive your sins and become your Savior. He loves you, John! Think of your mother's prayers." Lark leaned down to John. "You must not die without God! He loves you! Call on him now before it's too late! Confess your sins, John. Ask him to forgive you. Claim his promises. Please don't wait another minute!"

"I can't pray," he whispered brokenly.

"You can! You must! God loves you and you know it. You've known it since you were a little boy at your mother's knee."

John's heart seemed to melt as he thought of the times he'd prayed with his mother. Life had been so simple then. But it suddenly seemed simple again. He could call on God! "Dear Jesus, forgive my sins," he whispered. "Forgive me for wasting my life. I accept you as my Savior. Forgive me for hurting Lark." John couldn't move his head, but his eyes sought Lark's and held them. "Forgive me, Lark," he whispered. "Please forgive me."

Lark bit her lip as tears streamed down her cheeks. "I forgive you." John stiffened. Then his body relaxed. His head rolled against her knees.

She stayed beside him on her knees for a long time. "Thank you, Heavenly Father, for hearing John. I do forgive what he did to me."

Finally Lark stood and Sears leaped to her side. She'd have to send someone to get John's body to give it a proper burial. Then she remembered that John had said her father was behind all the trouble, that he was the one stealing the pines. She clutched her throat and cried out in pain. She had found her father only to learn he was a thief. She looked up at the pines towering over her. Why couldn't everyone look at the trees the way she did? They were things of beauty, not just a source of money to line the pockets of the greedy.

With an anguished moan she looked down at John. Had he told her the truth about her father? Why hadn't she asked John before he died? He would've told her the truth. She bit her lip. She'd have to find out herself.

CHAPTER

14

♦ Her cudgel in her hand, Lark walked slowly back to the cabin. She heard no sounds of lumbering, but that didn't mean the tree robbers weren't at work somewhere. Her legs felt so heavy she could barely walk. She thought about John and groaned at the terrible pain he'd been in. Thankfully he'd accepted Jesus as his Savior before he'd died. As she reached the cabin, Matt rode up on a horse he'd hired at the livery. His tail waving, Sears ran to Matt.

Lark knotted her fists at her sides as anger raged inside her. Tangles of hair hung around her damp face and neck. Her dress was torn and dirty and an angry red scratch ran from the back of her left hand up her arm.

"Lark, what's wrong?" asked Matt in alarm as he stopped near her. He saw her anger and couldn't understand it. "You didn't get to the Home on time and I was worried about you."

"John Epson is dead!"

"Dead?"

Her voice rising at every word, Lark told Matt what had happened and what John had said. When she finished she was shouting, "How dare you come here and make me love you, then cheat and steal?"

Matt shook his head. "Lark, as God is my witness I am not after the trees or money from them. John was not working for me. Can't you see it was a lie?"

Lark raked back her hair and held it at her neck. "How do I know what's true?"

Matt helplessly spread his hands. "I don't know what to say. I love you, Lark, and I wouldn't do anything to hurt you."

Lark saw the truth in his eyes, but still she held back from him. "How can you love me? You don't even know me!"

"I love you anyway. You are my child."

Lark soaked in the words, almost daring to believe them.

"Willie Thorne is very deceitful. I learned that John Epson worked for him in the past." Matt didn't tell her that he'd had a detective check into John's background because of his association with her. "He was probably working for Thorne on this deal."

"Can I believe you?" asked Lark in a low, tired voice.

"Yes, you can." Matt took her hands and held them tightly. Because of the terrible heat he was in his shirt sleeves and lightweight gray pants. "You can ask about me anywhere in the Upper Peninsula and get a good report on me. Send telegrams around if it'll make you feel better."

Lark's anger slowly slipped away. She desperately wanted to believe Matt. "Do you really think John was working for Thorne?"

"Yes. I do."

Just then Clay rode up to the cabin and jumped off Flame before she'd stopped. Clay ran to Lark and gripped her arms. He saw the torn dress and the tangled hair, then the scratch on her arm. "Are you all right? Did anyone harm you?"

"John Epson was going to kill her," said Matt.

"What?" cried Clay as he fiercely pulled Lark close and held her tight. "I knew I shouldn't have let you stay as guard!"

Matt walked to the bench and called Sears to him. He smiled as he watched Lark and Clay. He had figured it right.

They did love each other. Maybe they didn't know it yet, but soon they would.

Lark clung to Clay. She never wanted to let him go. She smelled his sweat and dust and felt the thump of his heart. "Did you find the thieves? Did they get any pines?" she asked.

"They had one down, so my men are finishing it to float it to the mill."

"Didn't you catch anyone? Not even Dag?"

Clay held Lark from him enough to look into her face. "Dag was there?"

"Yes." Lark told what she'd learned from Mercy.

"He didn't come to work today. He sent word he was sick." Clay shook his head helplessly. "You will not stay as guard, Lark. It was never safe, but the danger is even worse now. You're coming home with me."

Lark shook her head. "I can't do that. I'm staying here!"

Clay suddenly realized this was the perfect time for his plan. "I won't let you! Do you know how much I'd worry about you?" That was very true. "I want you to marry me, Lark. I can keep you safe."

Lark's eyes widened in shock. "Marry you?"

Clay pulled her close again and touched his lips to hers. Just the touch of her lips sent waves of feelings through him that surprised him.

Lark felt his lips on hers and before she could stop herself, she returned his kiss with a passion she hadn't realized she could feel. She felt as if she'd waited her whole life for Clay's kiss. Wave after wave of passion swept over her until she was weak with a longing she'd never known existed. She loved Clay Havlick! When had that happened?

Finally Clay lifted his head. His heart thundered inside him. "Marry me now, today."

"Isn't this a strange time to be thinking of that?" Lark was sure he couldn't mean what he had said.

"What better time? I can't let you out of my sight for fear someone will try again to harm you."

Lark suddenly felt too weak to stand. She clung tighter to Clay.

"Will you marry me, Lark? Right now?"

"I will," Lark whispered in a daze. Suddenly she remembered Veda Thorne. "What about Veda?"

"We are no longer engaged. It's you I want to marry." The words rang true in Clay's heart and he was surprised. Maybe his admiration for Lark would someday turn into love.

"Oh, Clay!" Lark's eyes blazed with love. "We'll be happy together. I love you!" The words burst from her, but she didn't care. She did love him.

Clay pulled her close and kissed her again so he wouldn't have to say the words and tell her a lie. He liked the feel of her soft, but strong body. He knew his family would welcome her with open arms. He kissed her again. Maybe they would be happy together.

Two hours later Lark stood before Pastor James with Clay on one side of her and Matt and Zoe on the other. She wore a white organdy dress she'd bought from Sally and held a bouquet of pink and crimson gladiolus. Lark's face glowed with a happiness she'd never felt before in her life. She smiled at Clay as Pastor James read the marriage ceremony. Clay looked handsome in his light gray suit and white shirt with a black tie.

At the close of the ceremony Clay kissed Lark lightly on the lips, but he still felt it down to his toes. Lark blushed, then turned to hug Matt and Zoe.

Outside the church Matt said, "Clay, I'm giving you and Lark a house as a wedding gift. It's the big white frame and red brick near the Wagon Works. It is already furnished, but if you want to change anything, do it and I'll pay for that."

Lark's head spun. She couldn't imagine having a father with money.

"Here's the key." Matt handed Clay a skeleton key. "I had Mrs. Larsen from the boarding house take food there for you." He looked lovingly at Lark. "Zoe had three of the girls from the Home pack your things in the cabin and take them over. And I moved Sears and his house to your new home. I even took over your horse and buggy."

"You've thought of everything, haven't you?" asked Clay sharply.

Matt smiled, but he shot Clay a warning look. "I tried to. Now, I'm taking Zoe back to the Home and I'm spending the evening with Mercy."

"Have a wonderful life, Lark." Zoe hugged Lark tightly and whispered against her ear, "Wouldn't it be perfect if I married Tris?"

Lark laughed softly as she nodded. Today everything seemed perfect.

Clay took Lark's arm and led her to the buggy. Several boys were playing in the field beside the church barn. "I hope you never regret marrying me," Clay said as he handed her in.

"I won't," she said. "How could I? I love you."

Clay flushed with guilt as he kissed her lightly, then drove toward the very house Veda had wanted. He didn't tell Lark that.

Lark sat as close to Clay as she could as they stopped in the driveway. "I've admired this house a long time," she said. "When the Masters moved out, I'd dream it belonged to me. But I never thought about sharing it with my husband." She chuckled softly. "I never thought I'd have one."

Clay let her talk as they looked around. The wide yard was groomed nicely and brightly colored flowers were in full bloom. Star stood in the pen beside the big red barn and Lark's buggy was parked outside the shed where they'd put it later. Sears barked and whined as he tugged on the rope tied to his dog house. The house was two stories high with a black roof and dormers upstairs. The front was brick and the other three sides were wooden siding painted white.

"Isn't it grand, Clay?" Lark jumped to the ground and looked all around. She ran to Sears and patted his head. Some-one had filled his container with water and had even given him a bone to gnaw on. "This is our new home, Sears. We'll be happy here."

Clay laughed as he watched Lark dash from one thing to the next. He liked to see her so happy and full of excitement after being so frightened earlier. "We'd better go inside," he said, feeling a little hesitant.

"You're right." Lark ran to the door and waited while Clay unlocked it. This morning she had thought she was going to die. How different her day had turned out!

They stepped into the wide hallway with doors opening to different rooms and another to an enclosed stairwell. The home lacked a personal touch, but it was beautiful and grand. It smelled of roses. Lark ran from room to room downstairs while Clay followed behind her, enjoying her reaction. He would never be so excited about a house. But she'd lived in the Home and then at the cabin. No wonder she was so excited about the house.

In the kitchen Lark found the basket of food. "I'll fix us something to eat. Are you hungry?"

Clay shrugged. Suddenly he was hungry. "I'll eat and then I must get back to work. I have a change of clothes in the buggy."

Lark unloaded the basket as she talked about the Wagon Works to Clay seated at the round oak table. "It sounds like you won't have any trouble meeting your contracts."

"I shouldn't unless something else happens. But with the new guards I hired, they should keep intruders away." Clay told her about another new contract to be filled by March. "And I'll be hiring a new bookkeeper."

"You don't have to do that! I'll be glad to do it."

"You're my wife now and you don't have to work."

Lark gasped. "I never thought of that. I can't imagine not working!"

"You'll have enough to do here to keep you occupied. And if you want to continue helping at the Home, you can."

Lark sank to a chair and stared at Clay. "My life has changed so much so quickly that I can't take it in. I don't know what I want to do." Suddenly she thought of Willie Thorne. "But I do know I want to run Willie Thorne out of town!"

Clay caught Lark's hand and gripped it tightly. "Please leave him alone. He's a dangerous man. I don't want you hurt."

Lark smiled lovingly at Clay. "You're sweet, Clay. But I can't stay locked in this house and never face anything."

Clay ran his finger beside the scratch on her hand and arm. "Put salve on this scratch before it gets infected."

"I will."

Clay pushed back his chair and stood. "I'd better change and get back to work. I won't be home until after dark."

"You be careful. I don't want anything to happen to you." Lark circled Clay's waist with her arms and laid her cheek against his chest. She heard the thud of his heart and felt the smooth cotton of his shirt. Life was suddenly so perfect that tears filled her eyes. She lifted her face and looked at Clay. "I love you," she whispered hoarsely.

Clay bent his head and kissed her just as he knew she expected of him. He wrapped his arms around her and kissed her again, then again. He had to leave, but he found he couldn't let her go. She had a strange effect on him that he couldn't understand. He'd never felt this way when he'd kissed Veda. But then she'd never responded with passion like Lark was doing. "I don't want to leave," he said against her mouth.

"Then stay." Lark's stomach fluttered at the thought of sharing intimate times with Clay. It wasn't anything she'd learned in deportment and she didn't know what was expected of her.

His green plaid shirt open at the neck, Willie Thorne angrily paced his study. Veda sat on the sofa, her hands locked in her lap, her light blue skirt hanging gracefully over her slim ankles. Willie slammed his fist down hard on his desk making the pencil cup rattle. "The men didn't get a single tree! Dag said Havlick's men came too quickly and they all ran before they were caught. I don't know what happened to John Epson, but Dag said he'd nose around."

Just then the door opened and without asking Willie's permission Agnes Thorne walked in. Her face was pale, but her gray hair was neatly combed and she wore a dark green traveling dress. "I am leaving, Willie. I decided last night. I suppose I owe you the courtesy of telling you."

Willie frowned. "Go back to your room, Agnes. I don't have time now for you."

As though she hadn't heard him, Agnes turned to Veda. "I want you to come with me. I love you. You are Silent Waters' daughter by birth, but I raised you and in my heart you belong to me. Will you come with me?"

Veda slowly stood and took Agnes's hand in hers. "I love you, too, Momma."

"Veda, I forbid you to leave this house," snapped Willie. "I won't live without you."

"You will," said Agnes sharply. "You don't need anyone or anything. You have your greed and your desire for revenge. You need nothing more."

Willie lifted his hand to strike Agnes, but Veda jumped between them and pushed Willie back.

"I have some things to settle first, Momma," said Veda softly as she squeezed Agnes's hand. "But you go ahead and I'll join you in a few days. Maybe we can go to Europe again."

"I'd like that," said Agnes. "We had fun there, didn't we?"

Willie sank to the edge of his desk. How could he tell Agnes and Veda there was no money left to do anything? Unless he could get his hands on the pines, they'd be broke before the middle of September. He'd sold liquor several places illegally, but that didn't bring in the kind of money he needed to save their home. "Agnes, please don't leave," he said tiredly. "I need both of you here with me."

Agnes shook her head. "You only needed Silent Waters and

Veda. Now Silent Waters is dead. I will not let that happen to Veda."

Willie trembled violently. "Don't even speak her name!"

"You can live with your son if you get lonely," said Agnes. "If he'll have you."

Veda's head throbbed as she listened to her parents fight. She had never heard her mother stand up to her father before. Veda was afraid he'd strike her if she didn't stop talking.

The sky darkened rapidly outside the open French doors and thunder boomed. Within minutes the temperature dropped and rain lashed against the house. Willie paced his study like a caged animal. He'd planned to meet with Dag just after dark. Lightning lit up the sky and Willie cringed. He didn't mind getting soaked to the skin or the noise of thunder, but lightning could kill and he hated being outdoors where he was in danger of being fried to a crisp.

"Finally the heat spell has broken," said Agnes with a loud sigh. "Veda, I'll wait until tomorrow to leave. Can you be ready by then?"

Veda glanced at her father and finally nodded.

"You're not going," said Willie.

"I will go, Papa. I am tired of trying to get Clay Havlick interested in me."

Agnes looked from Willie to Veda. "You don't know, do you? Gert told me only a few minutes ago that Clay Havlick married Lark Baritt this afternoon."

Willie shot from his desk and Veda cried out in astonishment. "You lie, woman!" bellowed Willie, shaking his fist at Agnes.

Agnes turned on her heels and left the study, slamming the door hard behind her.

Veda pressed her hands to her cheeks. "I can't believe he'd marry that orphan when he could've had me!"

"I knew I should've had her killed last month when I talked to Epson about it. But he swore he could handle her."

"I suppose there's nothing more we can do," said Veda,

suddenly very tired. She touched the pearl brooch at her high neckline and thought of how nice it would've been to be married to Clay.

Willie slammed his fist into his palm. "I'll kill her myself! It was her fault Silent Waters died."

Veda frowned. "Papa, you can't go around killing people."

Willie gripped Veda and shook her. "Don't tell me what I can't do!"

"Papa, you're hurting me!"

Abruptly Willie released her and paced the room again. If only the lightning would stop so he could go to the tavern!

Veda trembled as she sank to the sofa. She'd never seen her father in such a state. "Why can't we just go back to Grand Rapids again? We were happy there. There were three men there who wanted to marry me."

"But none had the wealth of the Havlicks!"

"I know, but they had money enough."

"I should burn down the pines. Yes! If I can't have them, I'll burn them. I could do it now tonight and everyone would think lightning struck and started the fire." He seemed to be talking to himself. "It's been so dry, they'd burn fast. What would the Havlicks do then? This is my best plan yet! Burn down the pines *and* the Wagon Works."

Veda saw the wild look in her father's eyes and her stomach knotted painfully. Would he really set fire to the pines?

"I'll go as soon as the lightning passes. I will burn the Wagon Works and the pines! It'll serve the Havlicks right."

Helplessly Veda shook her head. Nothing she could say would help now. She slipped from the room and ran to find Gert.

"I need your help," cried Veda as she stopped just inside the kitchen.

Gert stood near the windows with a cup of tea in her hands. She glanced nervously at her black cap and apron folded neatly on a chair, then carefully set down her cup. "What is it you want?"

Veda laced and unlaced her fingers. Her cheeks were bright red and her eyes full of worry. "I must speak to Clay and Lark. Momma told me they were married this afternoon. Where do they live? How can I reach them?"

"It wouldn't do for you to visit them now, I believe."

"This will not be a visit! I must speak to them! It's urgent."

Gert wanted to refuse, but she told Veda where Clay and Lark lived. "You won't be going out in this storm, will you? It's as dark as midnight."

Veda grabbed her rain gear from the back porch and ran to the barn for her buggy. She found Ray Moline doing the chores and ordered him to quickly harness the buggy. As she waited she glanced toward the garden bench and thought of Red Beaver's visit. Maybe Red Beaver could stop Papa from burning the Wagon Works and the pines.

"You be careful, Miss Veda," said Ray as he stopped the black mare near Veda. "This weather ain't fit for ducks."

Veda nodded absently as she climbed in the buggy and drove away. Lightning lit up the sky and thunder cracked. Rain blew in against her, soaking her to the skin. She drove the black mare over the bridge and along the corduroy toward Red Beaver's farm.

Without warning the mare reared and a buggy wheel rolled off the side of the log road into the steep ditch. The sudden lurch threw Veda from the buggy. She landed in the ditch. Muddy water soaked her clothes under her rain gear. Mud squished between her fingers. Before she could stand, the mare raced away, the buggy bucking along behind it.

Slowly Veda pushed herself up. Her hair hung in wet tangles around her shoulders and her skirts clung to her legs. Mud sucked at her small kid shoes. She struggled back on to the corduroy, took three steps, bumped against something, and almost fell. She looked down at the hump and saw it was a man. "That's what startled the mare!" she muttered. She bent down to the man and in the flash of lightning saw he was in his twenties and wore a tweed suit, wet and muddy. She touched his neck to see if he had a heart beat and heard him groan. She sighed in relief. "Can you stand?" she asked over the noise of the rain and thunder.

"I think so," he said with a thick Swedish accent.

Veda steadied the man until he stood upright. He swayed and she caught him, supporting him the best she could. "My brother's farm is nearby," she said. Calling Red Beaver her brother made her weak in the knees, and she had to force strength back into them to keep walking. "We'll go there."

In silence they struggled up the long lane that led to Red Beaver's farm. Lightning flashed again, striking a lone maple several feet away. The crack of the breaking tree trunk struck fear in Veda. She'd never been in such danger in her life.

"Run!" shouted the man as he tightened his hold on Veda. He stumbled and Veda steadied him, her heart thundering. With one mighty effort they ran to safety. The crashing branches barely missed them. The ground shook under their feet.

"God is good to us," said the man weakly.

His words pierced her heart.

Finally they reached Red Beaver's back door. Wind and rain whipping her skirts tight around her, Veda knocked hard on the door.

Hoping against hope that it was Hannah Havlick, Red Beaver flung the door wide, then cried, "Laughing Eyes!" He took the weight of the man from her and helped them both to chairs in the warm kitchen. He gave them towels to dry with, then poured hot coffee for them.

Red Beaver leaned toward the man. The ties of his blue rolled headband swung forward. "I am Red Beaver. Who are you?"

"Andree Bjoerling from Sweden. Nephew to Dag Bjoerling. Jig to his American friends."

Red Beaver nodded. "I knew Jig well."

Veda stared in alarm at the dark haired man. What would

Papa do when he learned of this? Dag Gotland's impersonation of Jig's grandson would be found out.

"I am looking for Lark Baritt and the Havlicks." His Swedish accent made it hard for Red Beaver and Veda to understand him.

Red Beaver told Andree how to find the Havlicks' farm and that Lark lived in a cabin in the pine forest. Veda realized he didn't know Clay and Lark were married and had a house in town, but she didn't speak up.

"I came to see where Uncle Dag lived all these years and to meet the friends he made."

"You can stay the night here and see them tomorrow." Red Beaver stood. "We must get you into dry clothing. You're welcome to change into my clothes. They might be loose on you, but they'll be dry."

"That sounds very good to me." Andree smiled as he slowly stood. He winced and looked down at his bloody pant leg. "I have hurt my leg."

"I'll tend it," Red Beaver said as he helped Andree into his bedroom.

When she was alone in the kitchen, Veda looked around. Silent Waters once worked here. She had laughed and cried in this room. Papa probably sat at this very table and ate with Silent Waters and Red Beaver. Tears smarted Veda's eyes. She blinked them quickly away as Red Beaver returned. She jumped up and reached for Red Beaver, then dropped her hands at her sides before she touched him. "Papa needs your help, Red Beaver! He is making crazy plans to burn Clay's pines and the Wagon Works."

"Then I must stop him." Red Beaver grabbed his hat and rain gear off a hook near the door. "Stay here and take care of Andree. I'll be back as soon as I can. Is Willie Thorne still at his house?"

Veda nodded. "He won't go out until the lightning stops." She told him about Clay and Lark getting married and all about what she and her father had planned to do.

"He should've stayed with my mother," Red Beaver said. "They were happy."

Veda couldn't imagine what life would be like if she'd been raised half Patawatomi.

"Get out of those wet clothes, Laughing Eyes. You'll find our mother's clothing in her bedroom."

Veda nodded. The thought of dressing in Silent Waters' clothes made her uncomfortable.

In the barn Red Beaver saddled his spotted gelding and swung easily into the saddle. He galloped quickly to town in spite of the storm. He stopped first at the house Veda had described as Clay and Lark's new home. A pale light burned in a back window and he ran to the back door, leaving his gelding in the yard. He knocked and Lark flung the door wide, expecting to see Clay.

"Red Beaver, come in out of the rain!" cried Lark, stepping aside. "Is something wrong?"

"Yes. Is Clay here?"

"No. He's at the shop. Why?" Lark's stomach knotted in fear. "Why, Red Beaver?"

Quickly he told her and she ran to get her rainwear.

"I'll find Clay. You go see Willie Thorne," said Lark.

Red Beaver nodded and ran back into the lashing rain storm.

Lark knew it would be quicker to go to the Wagon Works on foot instead of saddling Star. She knew Clay was working late because of taking so much time with her after their wedding. She smiled as she remembered his touch and his kisses. It had truly been a remarkable day.

By the time she reached the Wagon Works, she was soaked. The doors were closed, but a light shone weakly from a window near where Clay had his desk.

Lark inched open the door to keep the rain from blowing into the shop. She could see Clay and Matt deep in conversation farther down near a half-finished wagon. Their backs were to her and they didn't hear her enter. She eased the door shut and walked toward them. Thunder boomed and she jumped. As she walked quietly toward them, her heart swelled with pride and love. *My husband and my father,* she thought with joy. They were speaking in low tones. As she drew nearer, she could understand the words.

"I feel terrible for not telling Lark the truth," she heard Clay say.

Lark froze. The truth? What could he mean?

"Just leave it be, Clay," said Matt tiredly. "I thought of telling her, but changed my mind. She doesn't need to know. She'd misunderstand. There's already been enough pain in her life."

Clay shook his head. "It's not right for me to pretend I married her for love. What if she learns you gave me enough money to save my business and the white pines on the condition I'd marry her?"

Lark's body shook so hard she could hardly move.

"She'll never know the truth," said Matt. "I love her too much to let her learn that."

"She's a fine woman," said Clay. Thinking about his time with her this afternoon sent his pulse racing. "We can be happy."

Lark slowly crept back to the door and out into the storm. She leaned against the door, her head spinning and her heart broken. Clay didn't love her! He had married her for money!

She stood for a long time. Finally when her head had stopped spinning, she remembered why she'd come. For one wild minute she considered not telling Clay, but she couldn't let his business or his pines be destroyed.

Taking a deep breath, Lark opened the door. Her face burned and her throat almost closed over. "Clay! I have news!" she called, her voice cracking.

Clay ran to her. "Lark, what are you doing out in this weather?" He put an arm around her, but she slipped away from him in the pretense of greeting Matt.

"What's the news that brings you out, Lark?" asked Matt.

Lark told them quickly, staying as far from Clay as she could without being obvious.

"I'll put out extra guards tonight here and at the pines," said Clay. "And I'll go see Willie Thorne myself."

Lark gasped. "What if he tries to kill you?"

"I'll go with you," said Matt. "He won't kill us both."

Clay and Matt began to discuss a plan for confronting Willie and while they were deeply engrossed in conversation, Lark slipped away. Slowly she walked back to the house that moments before had been her heaven on earth.

"Oh, God, help me," she whispered as she stepped into the warm, dry house. Water streamed from her clothes and made a puddle on the highly polished wood floor. "I can't survive on my own. Please, Lord, show me what to do." She wanted to grab her clothes and run back to the safety of the asylum but it wouldn't be home any more. She crept to the bedroom she shared with Clay and slowly undressed. Her head buzzed as she slipped on her nightdress. She sank to the edge of the bed that was still mussed from this afternoon and buried her face in her icy hands. Her joy was gone and her heart was broken.

CHAPTER

15

♦ Rain dripping from his raincoat and pants and his hat in his hand, Red Beaver stood in the middle of Willie Thorne's study. A lamp on Willie's large oak desk cast a weak glow over the room, revealing only part of the stone fireplace and the sofa. Rain lashed at the French doors and windows. Red Beaver ignored the puddle of water spreading around his feet as he squarely faced Willie. "You must stop your vendetta, Willie Thorne."

"Go back to your farm, Red Beaver. Leave my house."

"You have already caused my mother's death."

Willie winced.

"Do you want to die? Do you want to destroy Laughing Eyes too?" Red Beaver's voice was strong and deliberate.

Willie scowled as he raked his fingers through his graying red hair. "What about you, Red Beaver? What will I do to you?"

"I have Jesus as my helper," said Red Beaver. "Laughing Eyes doesn't. Nor do you. I can survive."

Willie wanted Red Beaver to leave so he could get on with his business. He felt the bulk of his gun in the shoulder holster under his jacket. He'd pick up kerosene and matches on the back porch. He'd already told his men to do any damage they could at the Wagon Works. "You go on back home, Red Beaver. There's no need to talk about this."

"Laughing Eyes is at my home," said Red Beaver. "I didn't want you to worry about her."

"She can take care of herself." Willie nodded, his head too full of his plans to consider Veda's whereabouts or her safety.

Red Beaver caught Willie's hand in his and gripped it firmly. "I have never stopped loving you, my father."

The words and the action penetrated Willie's thoughts and his eyes filled with tears. "I've missed you all these years, Red Beaver."

"I wanted you with us, Father."

"I'm sorry there wasn't room in my life for you." Willie looked at the strong young man before him and pride stirred in him. "Silent Waters raised you well."

Red Beaver didn't tell him that Jig had been the biggest influence in his life.

A rap at the French doors drew their attention. In the light from the lightning they could see Matt standing there. He had learned the location of Willie's study from the gardener he'd hired to spy on Willie's family.

"He won't want to see us," said Clay, hunched against the pouring rain. "Get ready for a fight."

Willie opened the door and stared in surprise at Clay and Matt.

Clay pushed inside and Willie was too weak to hold him back.

"Red Beaver," said Clay, nodding his head.

"Hello," said Red Beaver.

Matt pulled off his hat and rain poured from it. "We came to talk sense into you, Thorne. We know about your plans to burn Clay's place and his trees. You can't do it."

Willie grabbed for his gun, but before he could draw it Clay jerked his arm behind his back.

"Let me go!" shouted Willie.

Red Beaver pulled the gun from Willie's shoulder holster and emptied the shells into his hand. "No more killing, Father."

Willie strained away from Clay as he looked pleadingly at Red Beaver. "Help me get away, Red Beaver. You're my son."

"I won't help you destroy others," said Red Beaver with a shake of his head that made the ties of his rolled scarf dance around his head.

"You're going to the sheriff with us," said Clay.

"You have nothing against me," snapped Willie.

"There are men who'll testify against you," said Matt as he clamped on his hat. "We'll start with the men you hired to sabotage Clay's Wagon Works. Then we'll hear from the men you hired to lumber the pines. And young Dag, too. They'll all tell what they know. You don't have enough money to keep them quiet."

A muscle jumped in Willie's jaw. He didn't have enough money to buy silence from even one of them, much less all of them.

Angrily Clay gripped Willie tighter. "You sent John Epson out to destroy Lark, but he destroyed himself instead. Bit by a rattlesnake. You're lucky Lark didn't die."

"You've lost, Thorne." Matt jabbed Willie in the chest with his finger. "Earlier today I checked on your finances."

Willie cringed.

Matt crossed his arms over his chest as he eyed Willie. "I learned you're flat broke."

"Shut your mouth!" snapped Willie, swearing savagely. Clay stopped him with a sharp jerk on his arm.

"Why didn't you come to me, Father?" asked Red Beaver. "I would've helped you."

Suddenly Willie lunged, taking Clay by surprise. Willie spun around and grabbed Clay by the throat, sinking his strong fingers into Clay's neck. "The Havlicks did me in! You're a dead man, Clay Havlick!"

Clay gasped for air and struggled to break Willie's death grip.

Red Beaver caught Willie's wrists and squeezed. Willie screamed and released Clay.

Gasping for air, Clay sank back against the desk with Matt hovering over him to see if he was all right.

Willie kicked and swore, but Red Beaver held him tightly. Finally the fight drained from him and Willie sank weakly against Red Beaver.

Clay and Matt hung back, silently watching Willie and Red Beaver.

"Agnes and Veda have nothing," whimpered Willie. "I don't know what they'll do."

"They'll survive," said Red Beaver softly. "I'll do what I can to help them."

"Agnes won't accept help from you," said Willie. He knew how she felt about Indians. "She can go to live with her cousin in Detroit. But Veda . . ." Helplessly Willie shook his head.

"She's a fighter," said Red Beaver. "She'll survive."

Before Clay's eyes Willie Thorne turned into a whimpering old man. "Let's get him to the sheriff," said Clay gruffly.

The rain stopped just as Clay reached home. He smiled as he thought of the warm embrace waiting for him. How had he survived without a loving wife all these years? He opened the back door and found a lamp glowing brightly on a small table, towels, and the dry clothes he'd worn earlier in the day. He chuckled. Life was good!

He blew out the lamp and opened the door into the kitchen where he saw Lark at the stove. She wore a flowered print shirtwaist and a green skirt that brushed the floor when she walked. Her taffy brown hair hung in a long tail down her slender back.

"I made something for you to eat," she said tonelessly. She wanted to burst into tears and demand to know why he'd married her, but she didn't.

Clay waited for her to run to him with open arms, but she didn't move from the stove. Slowly he walked to her, but didn't touch her. "Willie Thorne's in jail."

"Good. That should be the end of most of your troubles." Lark tried to smile, tried to act as if her heart wasn't broken, but she couldn't manage it.

Clay saw the haunted look in her eyes, but thought it was because she'd feared for his life. He pulled her close and held her tightly to him. "It's good to be back home with you." He kissed her and waited for her to explode with passion in his arms, but she didn't. He looked into her face. "Is something wrong?"

"The food's getting cold." Lark pulled away from him and carried a bowl of stew to the table. She sliced thick slices of fresh bread and set them beside the butter. She wanted to scream at him that she knew he'd married her for Matt's money, but she couldn't force out the ugly words.

"It smells good," said Clay as he sat down. "Aren't you having any?"

Lark shook her head. She couldn't swallow a bite.

As Clay ate he told Lark about the evening and about Jig's nephew at Red Beaver's. "I want to meet him. He wants to meet us too. Jig told him all about us in the letter he left for you to send."

"What about Dag?"

"We couldn't find him. Maybe he left town when he heard Epson had died before he could kill you."

Lark trembled. "Life is cruel," she said hoarsely.

"At times," said Clay. But this wasn't one of them. He smiled across the table at Lark.

In October Lark sat in the buggy beside Hannah as they drove to Red Beaver's farm. A pleasant breeze ruffled Lark's gray bonnet and skirt. Overhead a flock of geese was flying south for the winter.

"You're quiet again today, Lark," said Hannah as she folded

her hands over her handbag. "Are you sorry you agreed to go with me to see Red Beaver?"

"Not at all! I'm glad I can help the two of you have time together." Lark couldn't say that it was hard for her to be at the Havlicks and see the white pines. Just seeing the pines sent a stab of pain through her heart. Clay loved the pines more than he could ever love her. But then he didn't profess to love her. He hadn't told her once that he did, not even in their most passionate moments. Abruptly Lark pushed thoughts of Clay aside and forced her mind back on Hannah. "It's a shame the family is still against Red Beaver."

"He's Willie Thorne's son and he's half Indian." Hannah looked toward Red Beaver's house as they stopped in his yard. "But I don't care about either. I love him! And he loves me."

Tears burned Lark's eyes. How she wanted that kind of love between her and Clay!

Red Beaver ran from the big red barn, his face glowing with happiness at seeing Hannah. He liked the black skirt and white and blue plaid shirtwaist she wore. Sunlight glinted on his shoulder length black hair, setting the red highlights blazing. He wondered how Hannah's dark brown hair would look hanging down straight with a rolled scarf around her forehead. But no matter what she wore or how she looked, he loved her. "Hello, Lark. Hannah." He lifted Hannah down and held her fiercely.

Hannah clung to him. She found it harder and harder to leave him at the end of her visits. She liked the smell of his skin and the feel of his red plaid, soft flannel shirt.

"Would you like a cold drink from the well, Lark?" asked Red Beaver to be polite. He wanted to take Hannah for a walk away from his hired hand and even away from Lark.

"No, thank you." Lark stepped from the buggy with Red Beaver's help. "Have you heard from your sister?"

"Yes. She is living in Detroit with Agnes Thorne. Laughing Eyes says she can't accept being part Patawatomi, so she and

Mrs. Thorne agreed not to tell anyone. She does write to me once a month."

"Veda doesn't know what she's missing by being away from you," said Hannah, snuggling against Red Beaver.

"Maybe someday she will appreciate her heritage," said Red Beaver.

Lark excused herself, walked away from them, and stood at the pen beside the barn to watch the donkeys. Evie had wanted to come with them to see the donkeys as well as Red Beaver, but she'd had to go to school in town. Evie and Miles went to school with the plan to stay with her and Clay during the snowy days of winter. Lark wondered if she could hide her pain from them. She had been able to hide it so far from Jennet and Free.

On their return from Grand Rapids, Jennet and Free had given Lark a big party welcoming her into the family. Clay had sent them a telegram, telling them of the marriage the day after the wedding. A week later they'd returned, happy for Clay and Lark. Jennet had been full of excitement over the twins and had told Clay and Lark she expected the same from them. Lark had flushed with embarrassment, but Clay had laughed and agreed. Lark knew Matt wanted them to have a houseful of children so he could enjoy them all. Lark found it very hard to talk to or forgive Matt. He had betrayed her.

Just then Clay rode into the yard and jumped off Flame before she stopped. Clay's blue jacket flapped as he ran across the yard to Lark. His hat was gone and his dark hair was mussed a little. "Lark, I knew I'd find you here! What do you think you're doing?" he cried as he gripped her arm.

Lark pulled free, her face white. "Don't yell at me, Clay Havlick!"

"You know Ma and Pa won't allow Hannah to see Red Beaver."

"Hannah is a grown woman and can see anyone she wants."

"I won't allow my wife to go against what the family wants."

Lark's brown eyes blazed. "I am your wife, but I'm also a free person. I have rights!"

"You've been listening too much to those speakers at the Temperance League talking on women's rights. I won't have it!"

"It's but a few months until 1891, Clay Havlick. You can't keep women in the Dark Ages forever."

Clay frowned and shook his head. "I don't know what's come over you, Lark. It seems if I say 'black,' you say 'white.'"

It was true. She jumped on everything he said. The anger and hurt were eating away on the inside of her. She couldn't really blame him for not loving her. She was as plain as a post and she'd been raised in the asylum. He would've never married her if it hadn't been for Matt Baritt paying him to do it. Tears smarted Lark's eyes. Sometimes she found herself hating Matt as much as she'd learned to love him.

Clay glanced around the neatly kept farm yard. "Where are Red Beaver and Hannah?"

"I don't know."

Clay gasped. "You mean they're off by themselves somewhere?"

Lark knotted her fists at her sides and her breast rose and fell. "Yes, Clay, they are. Don't you trust them at all? Maybe they should have a hurried wedding yet this afternoon so they can really be together. You're for hurried weddings, aren't you?"

"Ours was different," snapped Clay. He couldn't understand the anger that he felt just under the surface of everything she said. He could see by the set of her jaw that he wasn't getting anywhere with her. "I'm taking Hannah home. Get the buggy and go on home."

Lark shook her head. "I came with Hannah so she could see Red Beaver. I won't leave her to be taken home like a naughty child!"

A muscle jumped in Clay's cheek. "I won't have Ma and Pa upset!"

"They should understand true love. They are in love, aren't they?"

"Of course."

"Married people should be." Lark turned away and stared across the cornfield that Red Beaver would be picking soon. Would Clay ever learn to love her? Probably not.

Helplessly Clay moved from one foot to the other. Finally he said, "You tell Hannah I don't approve of what she's doing."

Lark spun around. "What does it matter if you approve or not? Who are you to judge what Hannah does?"

Clay's anger flared, then he saw the pain behind Lark's anger and his died down. He touched Lark's soft cheek. "I wish things were the same as the day we were married. You were tender and loving, but for some reason you turned into a sandbur."

"Does it matter? You have what you want—your business and your white pines."

Before Clay could say another word Hannah and Red Beaver walked into sight. They were arm in arm and both looked as if they'd just been kissed.

At the sight of Clay, Hannah stopped and frowned, but didn't move away from Red Beaver. "Hello, Clay. I hope you didn't come to play the big brother and try to send me home."

"You should go home," said Clay.

Red Beaver stepped toward Clay. "What must I do to get your family's approval? Cut my hair like a white man's? Change my name to a white man's name?"

"Don't, Red Beaver," said Hannah, catching his hand in hers.

Clay moved uneasily. He didn't know why his family wouldn't put aside their prejudice and accept Red Beaver.

"I do have a white man's name, but you wouldn't like it." Red Beaver squared his shoulders and looked at Clay. "My white man's name is William Thorne. But your family couldn't accept that either."

Lark bit her lower lip. She couldn't stand to hear Red Beaver called William Thorne. It would bring back too many bad memories.

Hannah hugged Red Beaver and smiled into his face. "I love you if you're called Red Beaver or William Thorne. I love *you*, not your name."

Clay saw the love on their faces and envied them. He glanced at Lark just as she looked at him, a look of great longing. Their eyes locked and Clay couldn't move. What was she trying to tell him? What was it she wanted from him that he hadn't already given her?

Lark longed to have Clay pull her close and declare his love, something he'd never once done. Abruptly she turned away. A turkey gobbled nearby and a donkey brayed. Lark watched a fly buzz around a donkey's long ears. Finally she had herself in control enough to turn and face the others. "We can go now if you're ready, Hannah," she said.

"I'm as ready as I'll ever be," said Hannah, looking tearfully at Red Beaver. "I wish you'd give in and marry me even if my family doesn't agree."

"You need your family, my Hannah," said Red Beaver softly. "They're important to you. It would break your heart to be without them."

Hannah sighed. "I know. I'll go home and talk to them again." She turned to Clay. "If you'd talk to Ma and Pa, they might see things differently. You could convince them to let me marry Red Beaver."

"I can't," said Clay.

Hannah turned to Lark. "You could."

"Red Beaver could buy you, I suppose," said Lark bitterly. "He could offer his farm in exchange for you."

Clay shot a startled look at Lark. Had she somehow learned about his deal with Matt Baritt?

Red Beaver shook his head with a laugh. "I could never get her in exchange for my farm. She is priceless. No amount of money could ever buy her."

"Thank you," said Hannah.

"But if I could *give* my farm to get her, I would do it. I would trade everything if I could have her."

"I would trade everything if I could have you," said Hannah softly.

Lark's eyes filled with hot tears. Clay would never give up anything of his for her.

Clay saw Lark's tears and cocked his brow questioningly.

With a muffled goodbye Lark ran to the buggy and climbed in. She blinked away her tears as she picked up the reins in her gloved hands.

Several minutes later Lark dropped Hannah off at her house. She would not look toward the pines and think of life as it had been.

"Will you come in a while, Lark?" asked Hannah as she stepped to the ground.

"I can't today," said Lark. "I'm going to the Home to take care of some bookwork."

"Thanks for going with me today."

"I'll come again tomorrow if you want."

"Clay will get angry at you again."

Lark shrugged.

Hannah laughed softly. "Tomorrow then, about the same time? I told Red Beaver I'd be there even if I had to go alone."

"You'll never have to go alone," said Lark.

Several minutes later Lark stopped outside the Home just as a man with a baby dismounted, left his horse near Lark's buggy, and walked to her.

"You work here?" he asked gruffly.

Lark nodded. The man was poorly dressed and had a day's growth of whiskers. "May I help you?"

"I'm Chase Henry and I got to leave my baby girl here. Her

ma died and I can't find no one to tend her while I work. I'll only leave her a few months while I look for somebody to help me."

Lark's heart stopped inside her and she felt as if she'd heard the words herself when she was a tiny baby. "Are you sure you can't find someone?"

"I tried, lady." Chase Henry brushed a hand across his rough face.

"How will she survive without you?" cried Lark.

"I heard tell this is a good home. I can get to visit her regular like. I'll send money when I can." Chase thrust the bundle into Lark's arms. "Take her. Her name's Ruth after her ma."

Lark looked into the infant's tiny pink face. Fuzzy light brown hair peeked out from the small white bonnet. "How can you leave her?" whispered Lark around the hard lump in her throat.

"I can't," said Chase with a break in his voice. "But if I don't, she'll die. I got to work to keep her fed and clothed. But if I work, she won't get no care. I can't leave her, but I got to or she'll die."

A tear ran down Lark's face. "Let me take her to my home. I'll love her and care for her." Lark explained to Chase Henry who she was and how she came to be at the Home. After careful thought he agreed to give Lark legal custody of Ruth until he could come for her. They drove to Lark's home and Chase wrote out the paper giving Lark custody of Ruth. He left a small bundle of clothes and a paper with family information. Lark wrote her name and address and he tucked the paper carefully into his pocket.

"Let me hold my little Ruth one last time before I have to go." Chase lifted Ruth from Lark's arms and held her tight against his chest. He kissed her cheeks and rubbed his face against her soft hair. "I love you, Ruthie. I'm your pa. Your pa will always love you."

Tears spilled down Lark's cheeks as she watched Chase

with Ruth. Finally he pushed Ruth back into Lark's arms and ran from the house to his horse. Had it been that hard for Matt to leave her at the asylum twenty-two years ago?

Ruth squirmed and gave a tiny cry. Lark's heart jumped and she smiled. She found a baby bottle, heated some cow's milk, and filled the bottle. She changed Ruth's diaper, then wrapped her again in a soft pink blanket and sat in a chair at the kitchen table while Ruth sucked the bottle.

"Ruthie, I will take good care of you," whispered Lark. "I'll never lock you in a dark cellar with rats or make you stand in the hallway while others call you bad names." Lark's voice cracked and she swallowed hard. "I will love you and everyday I will tell you how much your pa loves you. I'll teach you about God and about nature." Lark's voice trailed off. Would she teach Ruth to walk the pines without falling prey to the dangers? She knew Clay had hired Jig's nephew Andree Bjoerling as guard, but she still had the freedom to walk the pines if she wanted. So far she hadn't set foot in the pines since the day John died.

Just then Matt knocked on the kitchen door and walked in with his hat in his hand. He wore a dark suit and a starched white shirt. He stopped short when he saw Lark with a baby.

Lark quickly wiped her eyes with the corner of the baby's blanket.

"And who is this?" asked Matt as he dropped his hat on a chair and looked down at Ruth.

Lark told him the story and Matt whistled softly. "I couldn't leave her in the Home," she explained. "I just couldn't! I didn't want her to suffer like I did."

Matt sat down slowly as if he'd suddenly turned into an old man. "I've tried to make it up to you, Lark. But I can't no matter what I do."

Lark held Ruth to her shoulder to burp as she looked at Matt. "I understand now that you couldn't keep me with you. A man alone can't tend a baby. I saw how hard it was for Chase

Henry to leave Ruth behind, but he did it so she could live. I understand now that is what you did for me."

Matt stroked Ruth's head. "Your hair was this soft. You were this tiny. I was afraid I'd break you."

Lark touched Matt's hand. "You do love me, don't you?"

"Yes. I've been telling you that for weeks now."

"I started to believe it, then I didn't think it was true. I didn't think I was important enough or good enough or pretty enough."

"Oh, Lark," whispered Matt. "You are!"

"I don't feel like it." Lark settled Ruth in the crook of her arm and held the bottle for her to suck.

"Lark, God loves you just the way you are."

"Sometimes it doesn't feel like it," said Lark barely above a whisper.

"God knew you while you were yet in the womb. You are fearfully and wonderfully made. He knows your name and he knows the number of hairs on your head."

"I guess I forgot," whispered Lark. Those were the same words Jig had said to her many times. Silently she asked God to forgive her for forgetting such an important thing. Forgetting is as bad as telling God he is a liar.

"Since you're good enough for God, why aren't you good enough for me or for anyone else who wants to love you?" asked Matt.

Lark gasped. "I never thought of it like that." Once again she held Ruth on her shoulder to burp her. "If I am that worthwhile, why did you have to . . . to pay Clay to marry me?"

Matt gasped. "How did you find out?"

"I just did."

Matt stabbed his fingers through his gray hair. "I was so afraid the two of you wouldn't get together even though you were right for each other."

"How can I love him when I know he was paid to marry me?"

Matt searched for something to say. "I wanted you to have everything you wanted. You wanted Clay Havlick."

Lark flushed to the roots of her taffy brown hair. "I don't want him if he doesn't want me."

"He seems happy to me."

"Would he ever give up the pines for me?"

Matt lifted his brows. "That's a tough one."

"No. It's not tough at all." Lark held the bottle to Ruth's mouth. "If he had to choose, he'd choose the pines."

"You could be right, Lark. If I were you I'd do something about it."

"What?"

"The Bible teaches sowing and reaping. You sow love and you'll reap love."

Lark considered that and finally nodded.

"The white pines are Clay's inheritance. But you both have an even greater inheritance from God—his promises. Sowing and reaping is only part of your inheritance. Take it and turn it into a great wealth. Sow love, then reap love."

Lark held Ruth tight against her shoulder as the truth of God's Word leaped inside her. She smiled at Matt. "Thank you. Thank you, Papa."

Tears glistened in Matt's blue eyes as he bent over Lark and kissed her cheek. "You finally gave me a name. Thank you! I've waited twenty-two years to hear it."

"I've waited twenty-two years to say it."

After Matt left, Lark fixed Ruth a bed in a wicker clothing basket that she set on the kitchen table. "You'll have a real bed soon, little Ruth." Lark kissed Ruth, then started supper for Clay.

For the first time in weeks Lark hummed as she stoked the fire to keep it hot enough to cook the beef roast in the oven. Two hours later as she dished up the potatoes, gravy, green beans, beets, and corn, Clay came home.

He heard Lark humming and he smiled with pleasure. "You

sound happy," he said as he washed at the wash stand just inside the back door.

"I am. And I have a surprise for you." Lark waited until he hung up the towel, then she slipped her arms around him and kissed him.

Clay stiffened. She hadn't kissed him voluntarily since their wedding day. He wrapped his arms around her and kissed her as if he'd never let her go.

Suddenly Ruth cried a loud lusty cry.

Clay jumped and stared at the basket on the table. "What was that?"

"A baby," said Lark with a laugh. "Come see!" She took Clay's hand and pulled him to the table. She moved the tiny pink blanket so he could get a good view of Ruth. "Her name is Ruth and she's going to live with us instead of at the Home."

Clay stared at the baby a long time. Finally he looked at Lark. "So, is that why I rated such a nice kiss when I walked in?"

"No! I wanted to kiss you."

"Why today and not yesterday or the day before?"

"Let's eat first and then I'll tell you."

Later while Clay ate his dessert of sponge cake covered with sliced peaches and a dollop of whipped cream, Lark told him about overhearing his conversation with Matt that long ago day.

"I had thought you'd married me because you loved me," she said. "It hurt to learn the truth."

"I'm sorry," said Clay as he reached for her hand. "I didn't mean to hurt you. I wanted to make sure you were safe from harm and I thought if you were with me, you would be."

'Being safe is nice, but being loved is better.

"You're right, of course."

Clay squeezed Lark's hand. Their eyes locked and they sat for a long time in the stillness of the room.

During a beautiful Indian summer day Lark drove to the white pines near the cabin. She lifted Ruth from the basket and carried her to the edge of the forest. The pine smell engulfed Lark and she closed her eyes and breathed deeply. She heard the rustle of small animals running through the pine needles and heard the caw of a crow and the screech of a blue jay.

"Ruth, these are our white pines. We've saved them for future generations to enjoy. They've been standing since only Indians lived here. When you're a grandmother, they will be standing here still."

Lark walked along the stream where she'd once walked with Jig. In her mind's eye she could see him with his old muzzleloader, wearing his deerskin pants and shirt, with moccasins on his feet. It made her feel sad to know Ruth would never know Jig and listen to his stories of the wilderness or hear him teach about God.

Just then Clay rode up on Flame and left her tied to the buggy. Quietly he strode to the pines, then stopped to watch Lark with the baby. Lark's blue serge dress with a pink baby blanket over her shoulder was a bright spot of color in the browns and grays and greens of the woods. He watched as Lark looked down at Ruth and talked to her. He could hear the murmur of her voice, but couldn't hear her words. A rush of emotion rolled over him, startling him in its intensity. This woman standing before him was his wife! She would be the mother of his children. He loved her!

"Lark!" said Clay.

She turned to him and joy shone in her face. "Clay! I thought you'd be at work."

"I was, but I missed you so much I wanted to see you. You'd said you were bringing Ruth here today, so I came here to find you." Clay ran the last few steps, then wrapped his arms around Lark and Ruth. They felt good in his arms. How blessed he was to have them! "Someday we will bring our children to see the pines," he said softly.

"Someday," said Lark, smiling.

Clay lowered his head and kissed Lark gently. He said against her lips, "I love you, Lark Baritt Havlick."

The words warmed her heart. "You love me?" she asked in wonder.

"Yes! You're my life!"

"Oh, Clay, I love you." Tears pricked her eyes. "I will always love you."

"I would give up my pines for you."

"You would?" Lark looked deep into Clay's eyes and saw he meant what he said.

Clay kissed her lips, then nuzzled her cheek. "My darling, precious wife." He kissed her again, then lifted his head to look into her eyes. "Do you want me to give up the pines?"

"No." Lark shook her head. The love she saw in his eyes left her weak and trembling. "We want them for our children."

"We'll have lots of children and they will love these trees as much as we do," said Clay. He lifted Ruth from Lark's arm and stood with them under the sweeping boughs of the huge pines.

Afterword

◆

On December 10, 1891, Lark gave birth to twins. After much consideration, she and Clay named the two boys Justin Clay Havlick and Trent Freeman Havlick. Someday the pines would belong to them.

Dedicated with love and pride

to a man with a vision

MARK AUGUST STAHL
(number four of seven)

◇   With special thanks to   ◇

The Freeport Public Library
Joanne Hesselink
Keith Kirkwood
Jeff Stahl
Norman Stahl
Jane Jones

CHAPTER

1

♦ Her chin high and her fists doubled at her sides, Emily Bjoerling shouted up at the towering white pines deep in the Havlicks' forest, "I will not cry!"

But scalding tears welled up in her eyes and rolled down her cheeks. With a strangled sob she pressed her forehead against the nearest giant tree. How could she face her family and smile when they presented her with birthday gifts after supper? Could they understand how hard it was for her to be a year older and still an old maid? The tears fell faster and her throat ached with them. She should've married Bob Lavery before he went off to France to fight in the Great War no matter what Papa said!

She'd been in love with Bob since she was twelve. All she'd ever wanted was to be Bob's wife and raise a family with him. Papa had insisted they wait until Bob came home. Papa had said, "Emily, men return from war with only one leg or so injured their minds no longer work. I don't want that for you."

"I know I'll love Bob and he'll love me no matter what," she insisted. But eventually she agreed to wait, even though it was hard. Bob had been angry, but he'd agreed too.

She prayed for Bob every day, asking God to protect him and

bring him home safely. He hadn't written often in the two years he was away, at least not nearly as often as she wanted to hear. She knew that mail service in war time was irregular. Sometimes she wouldn't get a letter for weeks and then she'd get two at once. But never had more than two months gone by without a letter. Then she learned that Bob was on his way home. He was healthy and strong and excited about returning home. His ship had docked at a New York harbor and a few days later he had boarded a train. He was on his way home to Blue Creek!

She was all fingers as she dressed in her new lilac-colored dress. When would they be married and where? How would her wedding gown look? Where would they live? How soon could they have their first baby? She already knew the name—Bobby. They would be a family, Bob and Emily and Bobby. A year or so later they'd have Ned, and then Lilian and Betsy and . .

She dreamed and planned as she walked to the station. She stood waiting on the platform a little off to one side so that when he came to her they'd have a minute away from his family and friends who were all there.

As the train screeched to a stop, Emily locked her hands together and stood on tiptoe. Finally she saw him and she ached to run to him. How could she hold herself back until his family had all greeted him? There was such a crowd around him, she could just barely see the top of his head. Such rejoicing, and hugging, and kissing! Tears blurred her eyes. She felt a little lonely just watching, but soon he would see her and then their reunion would be wonderful.

Slowly, as she watched, something began to register—Bob wasn't alone. There was a woman with him and she was being hugged and kissed by his relatives and friends. They were saying, "Congratulations!" and "Welcome!" and "What a wonderful surprise!" Emily gasped and pressed her hand to her mouth to hold back a cry. Who was the woman? Then Bob and the woman wrapped their arms around each other and, surrounded by his family and friends, left the station. Emily took a step after them, then stopped, her heart dead in her breast. The sounds of their laughter floated back to torment her like a poisonous snake about to strike.

Somehow she'd gotten through the next days and weeks. Somehow she'd managed to go on living, to stop crying, to go for five or ten minutes without thinking about Bob. She was certain he would realize his mistake. He'd send the woman away (his friends said her name was Monique and Bob had married her just before leaving France) and beg her to take him back. She would hesitate a little bit to make him understand how he had hurt her; then, of course, she'd take him back. She loved him. They belonged together.

Then today, very early on this morning of her twenty-fifth birthday, a day when she was supposed to celebrate and feel special, she'd heard the news: Bob and Monique were expecting their first child.

Emily moaned. "Monique! Always Monique!" After several minutes Emily pushed away from the pine. A breeze dried her face and ruffled her black hair. "I hate her," Emily whispered hoarsely. Then she lifted her voice and shouted, *"I hate her!"* The ugly words caught in the great sweeping boughs of the pines and seemed to block out the sun as much as the branches did.

Listlessly Emily walked through the forest. Patches of snow lay against the north sides of the trees. It was the end of April, but the sun couldn't reach the snow to melt it. Unconcerned about snakes this time of year, she walked without watching every step. She touched her side, and her heart skipped a beat. She'd run into the woods without her revolver. Papa would have her hide! He had so carefully taught her how to be safe, but she'd broken almost all the rules. If he learned she'd gone off the path and deep into the woods, he'd forbid her to set foot ever again in the Havlicks' forest.

Papa's job was to guard the ten sections of virgin pine forest that had belonged to the Havlick family since the early 1800s. He had been protecting the priceless trees since before she was born. It was the only stand of virgin white pine left in lower Michigan—six thousand acres in a totally natural state. Papa knew the dangers well. And so did she!

The first rule of the forest was: Never go into the woods without a weapon.

But she had.

A strange odor wove in and out of the overwhelming scent of pine, taking Emily's mind off her heartache. She sniffed; then sniffed again. "What is that?" she muttered. She knew all the smells of the woods as well as she knew the smells of her family's farm. She walked in the general direction of the odor, but it was gone. "Probably my imagination," she told herself.

Just then she heard a low growl. She tensed as shivers trickled up and down her spine. Suddenly her blue wool dress seemed too hot. Were the bears out of hibernation? Or was it a wildcat? She caught a streak of movement to her left. Was it one of the wild dogs Papa had told them about? Why hadn't she remembered her revolver? But she knew why—her birthday plus the news that Bob and Monique were expecting a baby had caused her to forget everything else.

Emily bit her lower lip as she pushed at the mass of black hair flowing over her shoulders and down her back. For the past three years she'd thought of having it bobbed, but each time she decided to do it, she lost her courage. She laughed ruefully. She had the courage to walk in the woods, yet she couldn't have her long hair cut. Maybe if she did, Bob would take notice. She frowned. *It's too late for him to take notice.* Oh, if only her heart knew that!

Slowly she walked toward home, forcing her senses to be alert to everything around her. The hair on the back of her neck prickled, and she stopped to listen. What was the danger?

4

Years ago tree robbers had given up trying to steal the trees for lumber. If this wasn't thieves, then what? "My imagination again," she grumbled as she started walking again. Perspiration dampened her skin and the wool dress made her neck itch.

She stepped around a tree trunk big enough to hide four people and gasped. She was staring down the barrel of a shotgun. Holding her breath, she lifted her eyes to see Jennet Havlick, a shotgun steady against her shoulder.

"Emily! I almost shot you!" Jennet lowered her gun, her lined face gray.

"You gave me quite a fright!" Emily was so surprised, and relieved, she thought her legs might crumple.

Jennet Havlick was seventy-four years old, slender, and sharp in her mind, but not as steady on her feet as she'd once been. She wore a blue serge dress, leggings, and heavy boots. A brown hat covered her white hair that was pulled back into two buns on the back of her head. She had been the first to inherit the white pines from Freeman Havlick's grandfather. Now the inheritance belonged to her grandsons Trent and Justin, twin sons of her son Clay and his wife Lark. "What *are* you doing this far from home?" Emily asked when she found her voice again.

"I could ask you the same," Jennet said stiffly. She observed Emily's wool dress with the loose belt at her rounded hips, and noticed she wasn't wearing a hat or leggings. "And without a weapon for protection, I see."

Emily flushed. "Don't mention that to my folks, please."

Jennet smiled and the strain left her face. "I won't. But you know they are right, Em. You shouldn't walk alone this deep in the woods."

"And neither should you."

"I know. It's just that I am drawn to these woods now more than at any other time in my life. They're in my dreams at night, my thoughts during the day. Free doesn't understand it.

5

But he's busy with his buggy making." Jen wrinkled her small nose. "There are still those of us who want a horse-drawn buggy instead of the gas buggy that's so popular now, so he has plenty of work!"

Emily chuckled. "Free doesn't want to admit automobiles are here to stay."

"I suppose. He says he is waiting to see if they catch on."

Jennet's gentle laughter died as she glanced around, once again looking worried. She shifted the shotgun nervously. "I know there's someone or something nearby that doesn't belong," she whispered.

Emily nodded, straining to hear unfriendly noises. She felt the same way. "Let's get out of here."

"No," Jennet shook her head, "I want to investigate."

Emily caught Jennet's frail arm. "Please don't. Send Papa out."

Stubbornly Jennet tensed. "I'll look. You run on home."

"And leave you alone? No! I can't do that."

Emily fell into step beside Jennet. She knew Deep Lake was ahead. She'd been there with her papa, but never alone. Maybe it was the lake she'd smelled. Even as she thought it, she pushed the thought away. The smell hadn't been that of water or fish. She quickened her steps to stay beside Jennet. Because it was early spring, the brush wasn't thick yet and walking was easy. The pine needles were several inches thick and their heavy walking shoes sank in deeply.

Jennet stopped, cocking her head. She'd heard something.

Emily narrowed her eyes as she turned in the direction Jennet was looking. She stiffened at the movement of something brown. Then a huge dog sprang into sight. Emily's heart zoomed to her feet. This must be one of the wild dogs Papa had heard. "Do you see it?" Emily whispered.

"Yes." Jennet's mouth turned bone dry.

Growling, the dog leaped toward them, its great fangs bared.

"Shoot!" Emily cried.

Jennet trembled as she tried to raise the shotgun to her shoulder. Shivers ran down her spine and fear pricked her skin. She was hurdled back to the time when she was a young mother and Willie Thorne had dragged her to the woods and left her to the mercy of the wolves.

Emily saw the terror on Jennet's face. The wild dog was almost on them. With a strangled cry, she wrested the shotgun from Jennet, aimed it, and fired. Instantly she knew she'd aimed too high, but the dog stopped a short distance from them and sank to its haunches. Saliva dripped from its yellow bared teeth. Its brown hair was medium length and matted with burrs and its black eyes never left Emily's face. Jennet whimpered in fear, her breathing growing shallow as a band of fear squeezed her heart.

Her hands icy, Emily fumbled with the pouch hanging at Jennet's side, trying to open it and get another shell. Why wasn't the dog attacking them? What was it waiting for?

Suddenly the dog stood, its short ears pricked. Then it turned and loped away, its tail hanging limply against its back legs.

Jennet sank to her knees and, trembling, buried her face in her hands. "I thought it was gone—that terrible day. But it was buried deep in my mind to torment me when I wasn't expecting it. I'm sorry. I was suddenly in another place and I couldn't move."

Still holding the shotgun, Emily knelt beside Jennet. "The dog ran away. But we have to get out of here in case it comes back."

Jennet lifted her face and looked as if she'd aged twenty years in the past few moments. "I was younger than you when it happened. I had come from Grand Rapids with Baby Clay to be with Free at the lumber camp near Big Pine. We were tucked safely away in his tiny cabin while Free was working. All at once the door burst open and in walked the devil himself—

7

that redheaded Willie Thorne. He wanted to know who I was and I told him. Clay was sleeping and I prayed he'd stay asleep. I knew Willie would kill him like he planned to kill me. He took me to the woods. I ran, but then he caught me." Jennet sobbed as if that long ago experience were happening right then. "He struck me, but my thick hair kept me from being knocked out. He left me for the wolves. I prayed. Oh, but I prayed! Then a wolf came. It growled and leaped at me. I felt its breath and I could smell its foul odor. I jumped aside, and it leaped again. Then Free was there. He . . . shot . . . shot it dead at my feet. I grabbed Free and clung to him like I'd never let go."

Emily's eyes smarted with tears, but her muscles were tensed, ready to spring away. "Jennet, please, we must get out of here."

Jennet focused on Emily's face and after a long pause slowly stood. She opened the pouch and handed a shell to Emily. "Load the gun in case the dog returns."

Emily nodded, glad to see Jennet was herself again. Side by side they walked back toward old Jig's cabin.

Jig was Emily's great uncle. He'd guarded the pines from the time Jennet and Freeman inherited them until he died in 1890.

Shivering, Jennet looked back over her shoulder. "Andree will have to be on guard so he doesn't get attacked by that dog."

"He will. Papa always takes great care in the woods."

"I know. Still, I worry. So many dangerous things are possible."

Emily breathed a sigh of relief as they neared the edge of the woods. They stopped near the stream between two giant pines at Jig's grave.

Jennet brushed pine needles from the tall marble marker. "I loved him, Em."

"I know."

Emily had heard stories of the old woodsman many times while she was growing up, but she never tired of them. She had grown to love Jig just from hearing about him. He'd died several years before she was born, but all her life she'd wished she could have known him.

"Why, Emily," Jennet turned to Emily with a gasp, "I just remembered! It's your birthday!"

Emily nodded, her heart sinking. She really didn't want anyone to go on and on about her twenty-fifth birthday.

"Happy birthday." Jennet squeezed Emily's hand. "I hope you have a happy day after that terrible adventure in the woods."

"Thank you."

"And Em, please don't mention me being here alone." Jennet's eyes darkened. "I don't want my family to worry about me."

"You really shouldn't go in the woods alone."

"I know. But I find such peace in there. I can't hear the noise of those infernal machines that crowd the roads or see the sadness in Clay's eyes because his boy is still gone."

The "boy" was thirty-year-old Trent Havlick. He'd been gone ten years. They didn't know if he'd gone to war and been killed, or if he'd simply disappeared in his great sorrow. Sometimes Emily thought of him and wept for him. They'd been good friends.

Emily and Jennet walked to the edge of the pines and, turning, looked into them again. Birds flew in the trees, singing lustily. In spite of their encounter with danger, there was peace in the forest.

"I have a dream for this place," Jennet whispered. "It began a few years ago and has been growing stronger and stronger. One of these days I'll tell my family." She turned toward Emily. "And I'll tell you and your family. But not today. It isn't the time yet."

Emily saw excitement deep in Jennet's eyes. She wondered

about the dream, but didn't ask. She knew Jennet would tell when she was ready.

"Come on," Emily said, "I'll walk you home."

"No. I can manage. You go on home and enjoy your special day." Jennet smiled as she took the shotgun. "Oh, Emmie, I remember the day you were born. Andree and Martha had been married a year to the day. You weighed no more than five pounds, and you had hair as black as coal and a face as red as oak leaves in the fall. I loved you from that first minute." Jennet brushed at a tear. "I was glad to see your two sisters and three brothers arrive too, but you were always special to me. You always will be."

Tears glistening in her blue eyes, Emily kissed Jennet's wrinkled cheek. "Thank you."

"I always hoped you'd marry one of the twins . . ." Jennet's voice trailed away. "But it didn't work out that way, did it?"

Emily shook her head. "Trent did marry my best friend, Celine, and I've been taking care of their child these past eight years." Her voice broke. Celine had died ten years ago, but sometimes the pain still struck her.

"And Justin married Priscilla." Jennet looked across the open field without seeing anything. "Things aren't right with them. I can feel it."

Emily had sensed it too, but she didn't say anything. Mama had taught her not to gossip.

Jennet patted Emily's arm. "See you soon, Emily."

"Goodbye, Jennet."

Emily watched Jennet walk slowly across the field toward the Havlick farm. Her son Tristan and his wife, Zoe, ran a big dairy there and Freeman still built his buggies in the workshop. Tristan's sons Wesley and Reed helped on the farm. Emily knew all the Havlicks, old and young, as well as she knew her own family.

Slowly Emily walked along the edge of the pines to the farm-house the Havlicks had built for her folks when they were first married. She was born in that house, and had lived there all her life. Maybe she'd even die there—an unhappy old maid.

Tears stung her eyes, but she blinked them away.

CHAPTER

2

♦ With Rachel Havlick's small hand in hers, Emily stepped out of the drug store where they'd just had a strawberry ice cream sundae. She stopped short. Bob Lavery was walking toward her, his light denim jacket flapping against his thin body. Her heart lodged in her throat and shivers ran over her body. She wanted to pinch her cheeks to add color to them, but she didn't. She watched as he passed the dress shop and stopped at the millinery store to look in the window. The smells of the Feed and Grain directly across the street blended with the aroma of freshly baked goods coming from the bakery. Two women emerged from the general store and stopped to talk. In the distance a saw shrieked at the lumberyard.

Emily nervously fingered the collar of her white dimity blouse and rubbed with a trembling hand at the waist of her blue pleated skirt. The hem of her skirt reached just below the calves of her legs and barely touched the tops of her shoes. The blouse and skirt were birthday gifts from Mama two weeks ago.

"Why're we stopping, Emily?" Rachel asked impatiently.

"No reason," Emily said hoarsely. She couldn't drag her eyes away from Bob even to glance down at her ten-year-old charge. Bob stopped to talk to Austin Jentry. His voice drifted to her, then was covered by the sounds of a horse and buggy moving down the street with a noisy automobile behind. The smell of exhaust hung in the air even after the automobile passed by and turned the corner.

"I want to go home. Amanda is coming to play dolls with me." Rachel tugged on Emily's hand. "Why do you always have to stare at Bob Lavery? Grandma Lark says you have a crush on him."

Emily's face flamed as she stared in shock at Rachel. "She didn't say that! Did she, Rachel?"

Rachel shrugged and tugged at the white collar of her rose-colored poplin dress. "She didn't know I was listening. Sometimes she forgets I'm ten years old and know all about love and things." She ran her finger around the loose belt that hung just below her waist, then flipped her long red hair over her thin shoulder. "I'm very grown up, you know and it *is* 1922. But Grandma acts like I'm still a baby. I just wish she'd let me cut my hair. I want to have it bobbed like Aunt Priscilla's. I want to look like the modern girl I am."

Emily was thankful to get onto another subject. It would be absolutely terrible if anyone knew she was still in love with Bob. She'd be humiliated if people were talking. She forced her attention back to Rachel. "I don't have my hair bobbed either and I am a very modern woman." Emily touched the mass of black hair pinned in thick loops on her head.

Rachel looked around, then whispered, "Sometimes I even want to smoke cigarettes just like modern ladies do."

"Rachel! Don't you ever take up that terrible habit! Modern *Christian* ladies don't smoke."

"I know," said Rachel with a loud sigh. "But it might be fun to hold that long holder and wear a short dress and dance.

Amanda told me about the dances. She even showed me how to do some of them. And I want to see a moving picture show with Mary Pickford in it."

Impatiently Emily shook her head as she pushed back a stray strand of hair, but she dropped her hand to her side as Bob walked closer. Could he hear the wild thud of her heart even over the clomp of his workboots on the brick walk?

He tipped his cap, revealing a thatch of wheat colored hair, and said, "Afternoon, ladies."

"Afternoon, Bob," Emily said, feeling more like a flustered teenager than a mature woman.

Rachel frowned. "Afternoon, Mr. Lavery," she said and tugged Emily's hand again. "Now can we go?" she whispered.

Emily's face flamed. If Bob had noticed her blush, surely he'd think it was from the heat. It was the second week of May but almost as warm as a day in June.

Bob paused and looked at Emily. "Any news about Trent?" he asked. Lately that was the only thing he ever said to her.

Emily shook her head. Where was her tongue? Couldn't she pass the time of day with Bob without getting weak-kneed and speechless? "No word yet," she managed to say finally.

"Sorry to hear that." Bob smiled and walked on.

Rachel tugged Emily's hand harder. "*Now* can we go?"

"You will not be rude!" Emily frowned down at Rachel as they walked away from the drugstore and down the street past the millinery, the dress shop, and the general store. Rachel was usually a very easy child to tend, but she had finished school the week before. Emily was finding it hard to keep her entertained while she adjusted to the slower pace of summer.

"I know my dad is better looking than Bob Lavery." Rachel ran to catch up and Emily, forcing away her embarrassment and impatience, slowed her pace.

"Yes, he is." Rachel had never seen Trent, but Emily and the Havlicks often talked to her about him.

"Mr. Lavery has light hair and blue eyes and is as thin as a rail. But my daddy has dark brown hair like Grandpa used to have, and he has dark eyes. He's tall and strong and smart as a whip." Rachel's brown eyes softened and she smiled dreamily. "I've got the best looking, the very nicest daddy in the whole, wide world!"

"He's a fine man all right," Emily said. A lump filled her throat. How could Trent stay away from his own child? Was he dead? He had walked away from his parents and his baby the day they'd buried Celine. Emily slowed her steps even more. A sharp pain at the loss of her best friend shot through her heart.

"And my mamma was the best mamma in the world," Rachel said, looking up at Emily. "Tell me about her."

"I've told you about her almost every day for the past five years."

"But I want to hear it again."

Emily's face softened. "I know you do."

They walked past the street that led to Havlick's Wagon Works, the sound of saws and hammers following them. Trent would be working there right now with Justin and Clay if he were home.

"Your mamma, Celine, grew up in the Blue Creek Orphan Home. She never learned anything about her family, even though she tried, and even though your Grandma Lark helped her check."

"Cause Grandma Lark was raised in the orphan home, too, and when she grew up she found her pa. And she wanted my mamma and all the other children to find theirs."

"That's right. Celine and I met at Sunday school when we were young. I was about four years old then, and Celine was six. But it didn't matter to either of us that she was older. We loved each other and played together as often as we could."

"And you saw each other in school. She was in third grade when you started first. And she finished school two years before you did."

15

Emily smiled. "Then what?"

"It's the best part. My momma and my daddy fell in love. And they got married and had me. And I have red hair like Momma and brown eyes like Daddy." Rachel leaned her head against Emily's arm as they walked. "Then the worst part happened, the very worst part. Momma died. She went to heaven to be with Jesus. And Daddy ran away because his heart was broken."

Emily nodded. She'd known Celine was in love with Trent Havlick long before he'd known it. She'd known Celine was expecting a baby before Trent knew. But she hadn't known Celine was going to die, or that Trent and Justin would have a terrible fight. And she hadn't known Trent would leave his home and family. In the past ten years he'd sent three postcards to his parents to let them know he was still alive. The last one had come seven years ago when the United States declared war on Germany. Emily forced away the feeling of dread that often tried to overtake her. Only because she and Trent's family believed God answers prayer did they find hope enough to believe that someday he'd return.

As they walked past the Webber place, Rachel asked, "Why don't you tell Bob Lavery you love him?"

Emily stopped and stared in shock at Rachel. The aroma of coffee drifted out from the Webbers', and a cat meowed from the railing on the porch. "Rachel Havlick! You know good and well Bob is married! It would be a sin to speak to him about love!"

Tears welled up in Rachel's wide, brown eyes. "Don't scold me, Emily," she pleaded.

Emily bent down and pulled Rachel close. "I'm sorry, honey. I didn't mean to be so sharp."

Rachel touched Emily's arm. "Lots of times I have a wonderful dream about you. I dream Daddy will come home and marry you so you can be my momma."

Tears clouded Emily's eyes. "Honey, we all pray he'll come

home. And we all know God will answer. But I wouldn't marry him. We were always friends. We couldn't love each other as a man and a woman should when they marry."

"Why?"

"Because we were friends—your mamma and daddy and me." Emily didn't say she'd feel like a traitor if she married her best friend's husband, but that was what she felt.

Rachel brushed at her tears. "Will Daddy really and truly come home?"

"Yes. He will."

Rachel sighed loud and long. "You've been telling me that as long as I can remember."

"And I'll keep saying it until your daddy comes home."

Rachel gripped Emily's hand as they turned from Main Street onto Hickory. "Will he want me?"

A lump rose in Emily's throat. "Yes, he will."

"Will he love me?"

"Of course!" Emily squeezed Rachel's hand.

"You always say that," Rachel said with a catch in her voice.

"How could he not love you?" Emily asked. But what if something had happened to Trent, making it impossible for him to love anyone, especially his very own daughter, the only part of Celine that was left? Abruptly Emily pushed the terrible thought aside and smiled at Rachel. "We have to hurry. I have to help my mama and papa with the chores."

"Grandma Lark might not be back from the orphanage yet and Grandpa Clay will still be at the Wagon Works."

"Lulu will be there," Emily said.

Rachel sighed. "She won't let me in the kitchen when she's making dinner."

"Well, you'll be playing dolls with Amanda. And I'll be back in the morning. We'll make something special for Mother's Day for your Grandma Lark and your Great-grandma Jennet."

In silence they walked together from the brick sidewalk down the driveway leading to the large home Clay and Lark had lived in since they were first married over thirty-one years before. Lilac blossoms covered a row of bushes to the left of the driveway. Red tulips and yellow daffodils made a splash of color beside the brick walk leading to wide steps and up to the front door of the white frame and brick house. Emily's horse whinnied in the pen beside the large barn. Many of the barns in town had been torn down, but Clay wanted to keep his. He'd finally given up his milk cow when an ordinance was passed banning cows within the city limits.

Rachel ran up the steps onto the porch and looked down at Emily. "I will make something for you, too! And I'll pretend you're my momma."

Laughing, Emily shook her head. She'd heard this often. "Anyone would be proud to be your mamma, Rachel. You're a dear, sweet girl."

"And you will marry my daddy and be my momma."

"No, Rachel."

"You can't marry Bob Lavery. So who will you marry?"

Emily's heart turned over, and she thought of August Theorell in Sweden. She'd been corresponding with him for a long time. Maybe it was time to agree to marry him, move to Sweden, and begin a new life. "I'll see you in the morning," she said. Emily turned just as a dark haired girl, her arms filled with dolls, ran into the yard. "Here's Amanda. Have fun."

While the girls greeted each other, Emily ran around the house to the kitchen door and told Lulu, the housekeeper, she was leaving for the day. Then she hitched her mare to her buggy and drove along the brick paved streets lined with homes and trees, across the railroad tracks and the bridge, and into farmland.

She knew the entire area had once been covered with pine trees. Her great-uncle Jig had once walked the woods with old Clay Havlick, the fur trader. Later Jig had worked with old Clay's grandson Freeman Havlick, the lumberman. Now the land was farmland and in the areas that were too hilly for farming, second growth trees flourished. Papa had said that in another twenty years, the second growth would be big enough to lumber and he hoped lumbermen had learned the importance of replanting. Emily was thankful for the virgin pines still standing. Folks from all over came just to look at them, marvel at their size, and try to imagine that once the entire area had been covered with just such trees.

Emily turned off the road and onto the long lane that led back to her family's farm. The buggy creaked and swayed. She stopped near a shed and jumped to the dusty ground. Chickens, geese, turkeys, and ducks walked about searching for food. A colt nickered in a pen near the big red barn. In the field to the west of the barnyard Emily's brothers were discing. The ninety-five acres they farmed belonged to Freeman Havlick, but they lived there for free and kept the profit from the land. It was part of the deal to guard the white pines.

Emily quickly unhitched the mare and led her to the pen, then ran past several maple trees with tiny, new leaves just emerging to the back door of the house. The aroma of baking bread drifted out and her stomach grumbled with hunger. She walked through the enclosed back porch where a pile of wood was stacked against one wall and a wringer washer stood at the opposite wall. A round tub and an oval shaped copper boiler hung on the wall above the washing machine. She stepped into the warm, cheery kitchen and called, "I'm home."

Martha Bjoerling turned from the stove with a wide smile. Strands of gray hair had pulled loose from the bun at the nape of her neck and clung to her rosy cheeks. A plaid dress hung loosely on her slender frame and was partly covered with a flowered apron she'd made herself. Her blue eyes sparkled. "Another letter came for you today. From Sweden."

Emily wrinkled her nose and grinned. She glanced at the boiling teakettle, and then at her mama "Did you steam it open and read it?"

Martha chuckled. "I wanted to, but I didn't." She studied Emily closely. "Have you decided how to answer August's proposal?"

"Do you want to get rid of me?"

"Of course not! You know better."

"Does it embarrass you that your oldest daughter is still unmarried?"

"Not one bit!" Martha rubbed her hands down her flowered apron, then shrugged. "Well, maybe just a little. Your sisters are married and having their families. You are every bit as pretty and bright as they are. You could be married if you wanted to."

"I just haven't found the right man, Mama." Emily hoped Mama never learned she was still in love with Bob Lavery.

"Maybe August Theorell is the one. God knows if he is, and he will let you know."

"You're right, of course." Emily hugged Martha, then picked up the letter from the square table that stood in the middle of the kitchen. "I'll read it after I do the chores."

Martha threw up her hands. "Did I get all the curiosity in this whole entire household? I want to rip the letter open and read it right now!"

Emily laughed and tapped the letter against her hand. "I'll let you know what it says." She started for the door that led upstairs.

"Honey," said Martha softly.

Emily turned, then tensed at the look in Mama's eye.

Martha licked her lips and cleared her throat. "Honey, I heard some gossip in town. About you."

"Mother! You know not to believe gossip." Emily tried to laugh, but it died in her throat.

"They said you were making eyes at Bob Lavery."

The strength drained from Emily's body and she gripped the back of a ladder-back chair. "Mama! I never would do that!"

"Emily, if you still have feelings for the man, force them out of your heart before they cause trouble. Loving a married man is wrong, and you know it is!"

"I would never, ever do anything to shame myself or my family."

"I know you mean that, Emily, but at times our feelings can make us do things we wouldn't normally do. It's time for you to seriously consider marrying August."

Emily hung her head. Water boiled out onto the range and danced across the top of it. A floor board creaked as Emily moved toward the doorway.

"For your own good, honey."

"I'll think about it, Mama," Emily whispered.

When her chores were finished, Emily walked past the cabin where Jig had once lived and into the Havlicks' pine forest. She thought of the wild dog she and Jennet had seen, but brushed the thought aside. It wouldn't come this close to the edge of the woods. The letter from August was in her hand, and his proposal weighed on her heart. Could she even consider leaving Michigan . . . and Bob? Tears pricked her eyes as she sank to the pine-needle covered ground and leaned against a giant white pine. It stood arrow straight, about a hundred and sixty feet tall and was about five feet across. Its long, sweeping green branches began about a hundred feet above the ground. Its needles were over four inches long with five in each blue-green bundle. The gray bark was thick and deeply furrowed with narrow scaly ridges. Pines such as the one she leaned against covered the six thousand plus acres of Trent and Justin Havlick's inheritance. Down through the years the forest had always been her refuge. She pressed the letter from August Theorell to her heart. The scent of pine hung heavily in the warm May evening and birds sang all around her, but she didn't notice.

"Is this really the way out?" she whispered through trembling lips. She pulled her knees up to her breast and smoothed her blue skirt down over her long legs. Could she leave? What if she couldn't grow to love August after they were married? She'd loved Bob since she was twelve years old. It wasn't easy to stop loving him. When he'd come home from France with Monique she hadn't stopped loving him. When she'd learned they were to have a child she hadn't stopped loving him. What made her think moving to Sweden and marrying August Theorell would set her heart free?

"I must do something," she whispered hoarsely. August's letter crackled in her hand. He'd be overjoyed if she would marry him, but he wouldn't wait forever for her answer. He dearly wanted a wife—and soon. If she hesitated too long, he'd find someone else. He wanted her to set a time, hopefully before the end of the year. The Great War had been over four years already, so once again traveling was safe.

"Please, Father God, help me to know what to do," she prayed softly.

What would she do if everyone in Blue Creek was talking about her love for Bob? What if Bob learned her terrible secret? She pressed her hands to her blazing cheeks. He'd assumed her love for him had died as easily as his for her. And she'd let him believe it to keep her pride.

"I will marry August," she said harshly. "I will marry him just as soon as I can make arrangements to leave."

Her heart sank and she covered her face with trembling hands.

CHAPTER

3

♦ With a groan that tore through his tight throat, Trent Havlick stopped his 1915 Dodge at the edge of Freeman and Jennet's property and stared across the freshly plowed field toward the large white frame house where they'd lived since they were first married more than fifty years before. Were they still alive? Were they home this Sunday afternoon just as they had been every Sunday all the years he was growing up in Blue Creek? Trent narrowed his dark eyes and tugged at his dotted blue and white tie. He had to expect changes in the ten years he'd been gone. He rubbed an unsteady hand over his clean shaven jaw, then settled his plaid cap firmly in place. He'd given up his slanted high heeled boots and his wide-brimmed Stetson when he left the Rocking R Ranch in Texas to come back to Michigan. The clatter of his car engine seemed loud in the silence of the countryside. He leaned forward and switched off the ignition, then slumped back in the seat. The silence after the engine died seemed deafening. He felt like an intruder.

The warm May breeze blew against him, bringing the heavy smell of pine and newly turned soil. He glanced at the acres and acres of forest to his left where he and Celine had spent hours walking and talking and planning their future together, then he looked quickly away before the pain of remembering overwhelmed him. His mother had taught him to walk the woods in safety; then he'd taught Celine. She had loved the flowers and birds and wildlife and woods as much as he did.

"I won't think about her," he whispered hoarsely as he gripped the steering wheel until the knuckles of his sun-browned hands turned white.

Why had he come back? There was nothing in Blue Creek for him but heartache and a rage so deep it frightened him.

"It's Mother's Day," Trent whispered. "I've come to visit my mother." Why had he suddenly felt he should be home this Mother's Day? When he hadn't come for ten years? But he knew why. Several of the ranch hands he worked with had talked about their plans for Mother's Day and suddenly he'd longed to see his own mother. Would he find her happy and well? Would she be glad to see him after ten years with little contact? He'd stopped at his parents' house in Blue Creek, but no one was home. He figured they were at Grandma's for dinner just as they had been every Sunday for all the years he was home.

Trent groaned again. Ten years was a long time in one way. In another, only a flash. Could he find the courage to drive the rest of the way to the farm house and face his family? Would he be able to get the money he needed to buy the Rocking R? It was home now. When the opportunity came to buy it, he jumped at it. Now, all he needed was money—money that was rightfully his.

For the first time he realized the road was smoother. Once it had been a corduroy road made of logs, but now it was covered with gravel, making driving less bumpy.

He heard the caw of a crow, the melodies of many birds, and the bawl of a cow with a new calf. He dared not let the memories the sounds were threatening to resurrect get past the block in his mind. He'd see his family and stay a couple of days, just long enough to convince Justin to buy his share of the pines, then he would head back down to Texas and buy the Rocking R. He had a life there that was different from the one he'd lived in Michigan and he was close to being happy.

Happy? How does happy feel? If he reached back into his memories he could remember that once he'd been happy, very happy. Blissfully happy. But remembering that would mean remembering Celine and he'd walled off all memories of her when she died. The pain of losing her had been more than he could stand. If he remembered their happiness, retracing their life together and their dreams for the future—dreams that died with Celine—eventually he'd have to remember how he'd felt when she died. He'd walled off those feelings, too. He'd simply walked away, leaving the pain here, along with his family, his friends—his life.

That was why he left and that was why he hadn't returned. Now, sitting in the quiet, staring down the gravel road leading to his grandparents' home, he couldn't stop the memories filling his mind. Sweat broke out on his forehead and he struggled to breathe.

He had kissed Celine and said, "Are you sure you'll be all right for a few minutes? I'll be back in less than an hour."

"I'll be all right," she answered with a tired smile. Her red hair was splayed across the white pillow under her head, and her face was as white as the pillowcase. Beside the bed in the wooden cradle Grandpa Freeman had built lay their tiny newborn daughter, Rachel—her hair as red as Celine's.

"Are you sure?" Trent ran a gentle finger down her pale cheek. "I shouldn't be leaving you, the way you're feeling and all."

"I'll be fine. Your mom is coming later today, if she can."

"But I told her I'd be home all day. She won't know there's a need to come."

Celine smiled weakly. "Women have babies every day. Don't worry."

Trent lifted Celine's small hand to his lips and kissed it. "I love you." His voice broke as a wave of love almost sent him to his knees.

"And I love you." Love blazed from her eyes as she caught his hand and pulled it to her lips. "You gave me a beautiful home and a beautiful baby. It's more than I ever thought possible."

"You're no longer an orphan without a family." He bent down and kissed her warm lips. "We're a family. The whole Havlick clan is your family now."

Celine laughed softly. "And we'll keep adding to it."

"Yes! We will! I give you my word. But I must take a contract to Justin to sign so it can go out in today's mail. It really won't take me long." He bent over and kissed her again. "I love you."

"I love you," she whispered.

He touched the soft fuzz of red hair on Rachel's tiny head, then hurried to his buggy to drive to town to the Wagon Works. The two huge factory buildings were buzzing with activity. The wide front doors were open to give the men fresh air as they built and painted the wagons.

Justin hurried out of the office to meet Trent on the lawn in front. He looked worried.

"Here's the contract," Trent said, handing a folder to Justin.

Even though both parted their hair on the right, they often made an effort not to dress alike so others could tell them apart. But still they would find they'd chosen the same clothes accidentally. This day they'd both chosen the same blue plaid shirt and dark pants. The difference was that sweat stood on Justin's wide forehead and soaked the front of his shirt. Celine said she could tell them apart because Justin usually had a worried look and Trent a smile.

"Gabe Ingersol is trying to back out of his contract and we have over half his wagons built." Justin gripped Trent's arm.

"Will you talk to him? Right now he's at the boarding house but plans to be on the five o'clock train." Justin rubbed an unsteady hand across his face. "We can't afford to lose Gabe's contract. You've got to talk to him. He'll listen to you. You have a way with people that I don't have."

"I can't," Trent said. "I have to get back to Celine right away." Already he was turning away. It was a fifteen minute drive to their farm and he couldn't leave her alone any longer.

Justin stabbed his long fingers through his thick dark hair. Deep furrows ran across his forehead. "It won't take you long. It's really important."

"Yes, but Celine is more important. And we both know Gabe. He's a talker. If I have to cut him off, he'll drop us for sure."

"But you have to see him, Trent! We can't afford to lose this contract."

Trent sighed heavily and nodded. "All right. I'll go see him if you'll ride out and stay with Celine. Or get Mom to go."

"I'll take care of it. Mom's gone with Dad to Big Pine, so I'll ride out myself. I'll stay with her until you get home."

Trent looked long and hard at Justin who often forgot everything when he got busy. "You won't get busy and forget, will you?"

"No. On my word as a Havlick, I won't forget. I have to finish one thing. Then I'll go."

Trent laughed and clamped his hand on Justin's shoulder. "Then I'll do it and get home as soon as I can. Thanks, Just."

"Thank you, Trent. We make great partners."

"That we do."

They smiled at each other and the strain left Justin's face.

Trent drove to the boarding house, his mind on Celine. He forced it on business as he met with Gabe in the boarding house lobby. Their business did indeed take longer than Justin had thought. But finally Gabe agreed to honor the contract and Trent drove home as fast as possible on the rough corduroy. At times the buggy bounced so hard he had to brace himself to keep his balance. The buggy top shielded him from the hot sun.

At home he stopped the buggy outside the white fence in front of the house. He looked around with a frown. Where was Justin's buggy? Feeling a sudden unease, he ran into the house, leaving the door wide open. The anguished cry of the baby sent chills down his spine.

"Celine!" he shouted as he ran through the hallway toward their bedroom. The baby's cry faded to a soft whimper.

At the bedroom doorway, he stopped short. Celine lay on the floor in a crumpled heap. She was surrounded by a pool of blood. With a cry of anguish, Trent dropped beside her and pulled her into his arms.

"Celine! Oh, Celine, what happened? You can't be dead! No! No!"

The next two days were a blur. The doctor came and looked at Celine. He said she'd hemorrhaged and died from loss of blood. Someone came and cared for the baby. Someone else came and cleaned the blood from the floor. Others brought food. Mostly people stood around crying, talking to him, patting him. He went for long walks in the forest. But he never went back into the bedroom where she died.

On the day of the funeral, they buried Celine's body in the cemetery in Blue Creek, and then they gathered at Trent's place. Justin pulled Trent outside away from the house bursting with friends and relatives.

"I'm so sorry about Celine," Justin said.

"I know you are."

Justin's face paled and he trembled. "I intended to drive right out to stay with her like I said I would, but I got busy."

Blood pounded in Trent's ears. Had he heard Justin correctly? "You mean you didn't check on her at all?"

"I'm sorry." Justin blanched as he shook his head. "I planned to."

Anger ripped through Trent and he clenched his fists at his sides. "Celine would still be alive today if you had!"

"Don't say that," Justin whispered, trembling harder.

"It's true! You know that, don't you?"

Justin hung his head. "I know," he whispered in anguish.

Trent leaped at Justin and hit him in the face. Justin jumped back, holding up his arms to shield himself from more blows. Trent lunged at Justin. They fell to the ground and Trent pounded his fists into Justin while Justin tried to get away without fighting back.

Clay and Freeman heard the fight and ran to them. Clay grabbed Trent while Freeman held Justin.

"Stop it, boys!" Clay cried. "Fighting on this day of all days!"

Trent ignored his pa and glared at Justin. "I'll never forgive you for this as long as I live!"

"What are you saying?" Clay asked in alarm.

Justin stood in silence with his head down.

Without a word of explanation or goodbye, Trent had left on the train that day and hadn't been back since, until now. He shuddered as he forced himself back to the present.

"I can't face him," Trent said with a moan. "I'll kill him if I see him." He rubbed sweat off his forehead and a steel bar tightened around his dead heart.

The quiet shattered as he started the engine and shifted into reverse, grinding the gears. He would leave this place and *never* return. There was nothing here but pain and anger. Let Justin keep the forest and the Wagon Works. Let Justin keep *everything,* including his guilt. He'd find another way to get the money he needed to buy the ranch.

Just as the car began to move, another memory settled in his mind—a tiny pink face surrounded by a fluff of red hair. Rachel. Tiny, beautiful Rachel. Celine's baby. His child. He'd left her, too, and for ten years he'd blocked all thought of her.

He stopped the car again, helpless to stop the memories.

It was early morning when Celine's gasp woke him. Quickly he turned to her.

"It's all right," she said. "Our baby is coming."

"Now?"

"Yes," she said, a broad smile covering her face.

He jumped out of bed and drew on his clothes. "I'll get help."

"No," Celine said. "There isn't time. Please stay with me."

He sat by the bed, holding her hands, stroking her hair, gently wiping the perspiration from her face, kissing her, and feeling helpless, until she told him it was time and what he needed to do.

He saw the red fuzz of hair, cradled the tiny head in his hands—amazed at how small it was, and gently guided the shoulders until he was holding a new life. With his own lips he sucked the mucus from the tiny throat and then he watched the tiny body turn pink as she began to breathe. He laid her gently in Celine's arms and together they counted the toes and fingers and kissed the tiny nose and eyes. She was the most beautiful creature Trent had ever seen and the love he felt for her and Celine overwhelmed him until tears of joy ran down his face.

In time he drove into town to get his mother, and Lark had cried, too. She went to his home with him and, while Celine slept, Lark bathed the baby, wrapped her in a pink blanket, and gave her to Trent with instructions to sit in the rocking chair and get acquainted with his daughter.

He held her nestled in the crook of his arm and when she opened her eyes, he was sure she could see his face.

"Hello, Rachel," he crooned. "We've been waiting for you. I'm your daddy and I'll always take care of you and your momma."

That had been the most wonderful day of his life and the next three days the most awful. When he learned his brother was responsible for Celine's death, he'd left Rachel as though she had died, too.

I'll have to see her, he thought. *Maybe that's really why I came back.*

He shifted into first and drove forward slowly. He'd come this far. He would see the family, talk to Justin, and then leave immediately. He didn't know what he would do about Rachel. Probably nothing. He didn't know her and he didn't think he could allow himself to get to know her. He certainly didn't know anything about little girls. Most likely she was fine with his parents and ought to stay there. The only thing he knew with certainty was that he would never forgive Justin.

Trent glanced at the dirt lane that led to Andree Bjoerling's home. Giant pines made a wall along the edge of the field. Pines on the high hills behind made the wall seem even higher. He pulled his eyes off the pines and saw a woman walking in the middle of the lane, a bouquet of purple and white lilacs in her hand. Something about her looked familiar. Trent studied her; then his eyes widened. "Emily!" he whispered. "It's Emily."

Trembling, Trent stopped the car and stepped out beside it. She was fifteen when he left, so that would make her twenty-five—five years younger than he. She was wearing a calf-length blue dress with a darker blue belt at her hips. Her long black hair flowed over her slender shoulders and down her back. She was probably married with children. A picture of her and Celine laughing and talking together flashed through his mind. They had been best friends.

Emily saw him and waved. "Hi, Justin," she called. "You're late for dinner, aren't you?" She'd been invited to join the Havlicks for dinner, but had declined. She'd felt a tension lately that she didn't understand. It seemed to have something to do with Justin, and wasn't just that he worked himself into the ground without a thought of his wife and children. Jennet had mentioned she felt the same tension. When she was only a

31

few feet away, Emily said, "I see you've bought another auto-mobile. You and your gas machines. You change so often, I can't keep up!"

Trent's nerves tightened. She thought he was Justin. Nervously he rubbed his clean shaven jaw. Justin had always talked about growing a beard, so Trent had never grown one. But when he left he'd tried to stop looking like his twin. Evidently he'd failed.

Emily's breath caught in her throat, and her eyes searched Trent's face. Was she seeing things? "You're not Justin," she said cautiously. "Trent?"

He nodded.

The lilacs tumbled from Emily's hands and scattered in the dust at her feet. "Is it really you?"

"In the flesh." Tears stung his eyes. Her face looked almost the same, but she definitely wasn't the teenaged girl she'd been when he left.

"Where've you been all this time?"

"Here and there. In Texas on a ranch the last several years."

"Why didn't you write?"

"I . . . couldn't." He'd tried often but, except for the three postcards, had crumpled all the letters and thrown them away.

Her lip quivered. "Is it really you?"

He nodded. "Yes, it's really me. It's good to see you."

"I can't believe it. Ten years is a long time. You still look like Justin. But your skin is as dark as an Indian's, and Justin doesn't own a suit like that." Her head was spinning and she knew she sounded silly. She'd waited so long for him to return, had prayed earnestly for his return. Now, here he was.

"You look ready to faint, Emily," Trent said as he stepped toward her. "Maybe you should sit in my automobile."

"No, thanks, but I'll be all right." She swayed and he caught her arm.

"Please, sit down a while."

She gripped his hand for fear he'd vanish into thin air if she didn't hold on to him. "You caught me by surprise. We prayed for your return. Rachel needs you."

His head spun. "Ah, Rachel. How is she?"

"Oh, Trent. She's beautiful! She has Celine's hair and your eyes. She's curious, and smart, and funny, and serious, and well-behaved, and naughty. She's a wonderful child. And she's very anxious to have her daddy back."

"Does she . . . hate me?"

"Oh, no. I've tried to help her understand the pain you suffered when Celine died."

Trent trembled. The pain was still as great as it was ten years before, perhaps worse.

"Are you all right?" Emily whispered, patting Trent's muscled arm.

He breathed deeply and forced back the anguish. "I'll be fine."

She looked into his face. How dark and handsome he was! "Are you sure?"

He nodded. "Tell me about yourself. Did you marry Bob Lavery?"

Emily flushed hotly. "He married a French girl, Monique, while he was in France during the war."

"But you still love him."

Emily ducked her head. "I can't help myself. It shows, doesn't it?"

He nodded. "Just as I can't stop loving Celine."

Emily looked into Trent's dark eyes. "You do understand! No one else does."

"I do." Trent's face softened. Knowing Emily understood his love for Celine would never die somehow made him feel better.

"I've missed you," Emily whispered brokenly.

"I've thought about you a lot." Slowly he pulled Emily close and they clung to each other, sharing the pain of loss. He felt the softness of her body and smelled the scent of lilac in her hair. She was no longer the little girl he'd played with. She was a woman.

She pressed closer to him and felt the thud of his heart and smelled a hint of sweat and leather. His chest was broader and his muscles stronger than when he left.

Finally he held her from him. "Since Bob is married, what does the future hold for you?"

She clung to his work-roughened hand. "I'm going to marry a man in Sweden."

"You don't say!"

Emily told Trent about August and even about the gossip around town that she was still in love with Bob. She tried to sound excited about a marriage to August, even though she didn't feel excited. She didn't want Trent to think she had no other choices. He listened quietly until she ran out of things to say. Her voice caught when she finished with, "But I do hate to leave Rachel."

"Why her especially?"

"I've been taking care of her."

"I thought she stayed with Mom and Dad."

"She does, but they needed some help, and hired me. I've been taking care of her for eight years. Oh, wait'll you see her! She looks a lot like Celine, but she's like you, too."

A muscle jumped in Trent's jaw.

"She's smart, Trent! And she has a sense of humor like yours. Her giggle is just like Celine's!"

He forced back a groan of anguish.

"Now that you're back, my leaving won't be so hard on her."

Trent looked off across the field, then back at Emily. "I don't intend to stay."

She stiffened. "What?'

"I only came to see the family and get some money."

"But why won't you stay?"

"I can't."

"Rachel needs you."

"She doesn't even know me."

"I've told her about you. She has even tried to understand why you left her."

Trent's jaw tightened. "I'd best be getting to the house."

Emily gripped his hand with both of hers. "Please don't break Rachel's heart."

"It's none of your concern, Emily."

His words stung her. She lifted her chin as pink stained her cheeks. "I love Rachel."

Trent sighed and nodded tiredly. "I'm sorry, Emily. It's hard for me to be here. I'd rather drive back down to Texas without seeing anyone."

"Don't you dare! Your family wants you back!"

"I doubt that." Trent took a deep, shuddering breath. "I came this far, so I'll see them. But I won't stay. I can't stay here. And I can't suddenly be a daddy."

Giant tears filled Emily's blue eyes and slowly ran down her cheeks. "We've all waited so long for you to come home. Please, please don't leave again."

"I can't stay."

"Stay a week. Only a week. And if you still must leave, then you can go."

Trent shook his head. He couldn't take the agony for an entire week.

"Then stay three days! You can do that. Can't you, Trent?"

He saw the pleading in her eyes and weakened. Then slowly he nodded. He pulled out his handkerchief and gently wiped away her tears. "Okay. I'll stay three days. But that's all."

Emily hugged him and smiled. "Thank you! You'll be glad."

"I doubt that." He looked toward the big farmhouse and realized he couldn't go alone. He turned back to Emily. "I need you to do something for me."

"Anything!"

"Go with me. I can't face the family alone."

Emily hesitated. "But I'd be intruding."

"I need you. This is going to be very hard for me. Besides, Rachel might need you. It'll be a shock to have me suddenly turn up."

"Rachel has looked for you every single day since she was old enough to know about you. She'll be thrilled to see you."

"Don't do this to me, Emily!"

"I'm sorry. I was thinking about her."

"I've come this far on my own, but I can't walk into that house by myself. Will you go with me?"

"All right. I'll go."

"Thank you." Trent opened the automobile door. "I'm glad to see you haven't bobbed your hair."

"I'm considering it."

"Please don't. I like the way you look."

"Things can't stay the same forever, Trent."

"I know."

Emily stood beside the running board and studied him. Fine lines spread from the corners of his eyes into his dark hair. The great sadness in his eyes tugged at her heart. "What about you, Trent? Have you found someone else?"

"No. Celine was my life. When she died, I died, too."

"It's been ten years! You need someone. You can't live your whole life without love and companionship."

"I can try." He'd had other women, but he didn't tell Emily that. It would shock her to know how he'd lived.

She saw the harsh look in his eyes and knew he was no longer the gentle country boy who'd left home at twenty. Weakly she stepped up on the running board and slipped onto the seat.

CHAPTER

4

◆ Dust billowed behind the Dodge as Trent drove slowly along the road leading to his grandparents' home. Bright green spring grass covered the ditches and a few dandelions poked out bright yellow heads. The tires crunched loudly on the gravel. He glanced at Emily sitting beside him with her hands locked together in her lap. "I don't know if I can do it, Emily."

She tensed even more. He musn't leave after coming this far! "You can face them, Trent. They love you."

"I doubt that."

"It's true."

He slowed the automobile even more. "How are Grandma and Grandpa?"

"Just fine. Free is still building buggies. It takes him longer, of course. But you know him. He hates to give in to the automobile."

Trent chuckled. "Sounds like him."

"And Jennet spends a lot of time walking in the pines. She has been waiting for you to get home so she can talk to you and Justin about an idea she has."

"What is it?"

"No one knows. She says it's a secret that she can tell only when you're here."

"What do you *think* it is?"

"I think it is about the pines, but I don't know what she has in mind. She says it is her dream, the fulfillment of Great-grandpa Clay's dream. When she mentions it, her eyes shine and she gets a little weepy."

"There are only two things to do with them—leave them alone or cut them down. Which do you think she'd want to do?"

"Well, she'd never want to cut them!" Emily hadn't meant to raise her voice, but she was almost shouting.

"Hold it!" Trent said. "I'm just discussing the choices."

"Cutting them isn't a choice." Emily managed to control the volume of her voice, but she couldn't avoid the angry tone. Hearing Trent say the words, even in passing, made her very angry. And when she thought of the sacrifices his family and hers had made and the danger they'd faced to protect and pre-serve the trees, cutting them was unthinkable.

"Do you have any idea what those trees would be worth if they were lumbered?" Trent asked. "Why, we could give away half the money—do all kinds of charitable things with it—and still be wealthy for many generations. But just standing there, they're not worth anything but trouble."

Emily was seething inside. She'd never thought she would hear a Havlick speak of lumbering the pines.

"They're your inheritance," she whispered. "Doesn't that mean anything to you?"

"No, not any more. Nothing means anything to me now. I want to sell them and use the money to buy the Rocking R. And since they're half mine, I intend to sell my half. If not to Justin, then to someone else."

"That would break Jennet's heart and your mother's as well, Trent. I don't know how you could even think of such a thing."

"I'm just being practical. We have to do something with them besides let them just stand there."

Emily's head was spinning and for a moment she had forgotten where they were going and why, until Trent stopped the car.

"What's wrong?" she asked.

"How can I face them after all this time?" Trent rested his forehead on the steering wheel. The anguish on his face broke her heart and melted her anger.

"You can." Emily patted Trent's hand. "Your family wants you, Trent. They've missed you more than you'll ever know. Just promise me you won't mention this crazy idea until you've heard Jennet's plan."

"What about Grandpa Baritt?"

"He and Mercy are on an extended trip out east. Your mom was sad to see him go. And he'll be sorry he missed you, but he wanted to take Mercy on a trip since he didn't when they were first married. They planned to go a few years ago; then the war broke out and they couldn't. This time your grandpa said nothing would stop him from taking his bride on a trip." Mercy Kettering had become the matron at the orphan's home just before Lark and Clay married. She was responsible for turning the home into a happy, loving place, rather than the dismal, harsh prison it had been for Lark. And then she'd met Matt Baritt and they'd fallen in love and married. Matt was Lark's father who had left her at the orphanage when she was an infant. When they finally got together again, he'd tried to make up for all he'd missed with Lark by helping Mercy with the children in her care. Together they had made many homeless children very happy. "He still refers to Mercy as his 'bride' even though they've been married twenty years," Emily said. "It's very romantic."

"You and Celine were so alike—always ready for a good love story."

"You have a soft heart, too, Trent Havlick."

"Not any longer," he said coldly.

A chill ran down her spine at the sound of his voice and the look on his face.

Trent drove slowly up the lane between lilac bushes in bloom and some young pines. He noticed several fruit trees in the yard that hadn't been there before. The barns, sheds, and house looked in good repair. Dairy cattle dotted a large green pasture that had been a cornfield when Trent left. "Dairy cows?" he asked as he lifted his dark brow questioningly.

Emily nodded. "Tristan and Zoe live on the farm with your grandparents and they run the dairy farm. They've been here for the last five years. My pa helps raise feed for the cows and my brothers help with the chores."

"Are those little guys big enough to do that?"

Emily laughed. "They're not so little any more. Lars is eighteen, Neil is seventeen, and Dag is sixteen, and all are almost as big as you are."

Trent stopped the car behind a black Ford and sighed. "They're ten years older."

"We all are," said Emily softly.

Trent gripped the steering wheel more tightly as he stared at the three story white frame house with the wrap-around porch. He and Justin had played on the porch during rainy summer days. They'd worked in the fields spring, summer, and fall. The Havlicks believed in hard work. Even though they had the money to hire their work done, they did most of it themselves. He was glad for that. Hard work the past ten years had kept him from ending his life. Now he was back to face the family again. Could Emily hear the wild thud of his heart? Did she know just how frightened he felt? She'd always been able to understand him. "I can't go in," he said hoarsely.

"Yes, you can, Trent. I'll be right beside you." Emily opened the automobile door and stepped out, then walked around and opened the door for Trent. "Come on. You can do it. You didn't come all this way to back out now. You always had lots of courage. I expect you still do."

With a loud sigh Trent stepped to the ground and stood beside Emily. Chickens cackled and a turkey gobbled in a pen beside the chicken coop. Wind whirred the blades of the windmill pumping water into a large tank. A Dalmatian ran up to Trent and sniffed his hand. "Sears, Jr.?" asked Trent, bending down to the dog.

"No. Junior died several years ago. This is Betsy, his daughter." Emily patted Betsy's head while Trent stroked her side. Sears had walked the line with Lark when she'd guarded the pines for Clay before they were married. He'd saved her many times. He'd lived to be fifteen. Junior was his pup and he'd learned to walk the line, too. Both dogs had a special place in all their hearts. "Betsy belongs to Tris and Zoe. Your mother did have her in town, but didn't feel right about keeping her there where she couldn't run free."

At the sound of an automobile coming up the lane, Emily turned and recognized Justin's car. Sunlight glinted off the windshield. Shivers ran down her back and she locked her hands together as he stopped the 1921 black Duesenberg behind Trent's blue Dodge. She darted a look at Trent and saw the stubborn set of his jaw and the angry sparks shooting from his dark eyes.

"Relax, Trent. It's your brother," Emily said. She hoped whatever had caused their fight just before Trent left had been forgotten. But Trent stiffened as he watched his twin step from the Duesenberg. His voice failed him and all the strength seemed to leave his body.

Emily looked from Trent to Justin and back again. They were identical except that Trent was wearing a suit and Justin a white shirt open at the throat and dark pants. Trent was dark-skinned from working outdoors. Next to him Justin looked almost sickly from working indoors behind a desk. She felt the tension grow between them as they studied each other. Would

Justin break the ice and give Trent a bear hug? She hoped he would, but as his eyes narrowed she knew he wouldn't.

"So you decided to stop pouting and come home to your responsibilities," Justin said sharply, his eyes boring into Trent's. "It's about time."

"Murderer!" Trent snarled as rage boiled up and out of him.

Emily frowned. What could Trent mean?

With a loud bellow Trent leaped at Justin, his fists flying. Justin dodged the blows and threw a punch that connected with Trent's shoulder.

"Stop!" Emily cried, helplessly wringing her hands. "Stop it!"

Trent flung himself at Justin again and they fell to the ground, rolling on the dusty lane, punching and shouting angrily. Betsy barked frantically as she raced back and forth from the men to Emily.

"Sit, Betsy!" commanded Emily.

With a whine and her head at a tilt, Betsy sat on her haunches and watched the fighting.

Emily doubled her fists at her sides and shouted louder, "Trent! Justin! Stop it right now!"

Trent tasted blood and dust, but his anger was too hot to feel the pain of Justin's blows or to hear Emily's shouts. In his mind he saw the shovels of dirt falling on Celine's casket, filling her grave. He grabbed Justin's throat and pressed both his thumbs into his brother's windpipe.

Justin struggled and broke Trent's hold, then broke free enough to get in hard punches to Trent's jaw and stomach.

Emily shot a look toward the house, expecting any minute to see the door fly open and the family run out. Maybe they were in the dining room, still sitting around the table, laughing and talking, and couldn't hear the racket. Or maybe they were gathered around the piano singing the way they liked to do when they got together.

Should she run and get Clay or Tris? No. She'd find a way to stop the fight without them. She thought of the dog fights she'd stopped in the past and wondered if it would work on Justin and Trent. She ran to the water tank and filled a bucket with the icy cold water, then ran back to the men, water splashing onto her leg and foot. With a mighty heave she flung the water onto the fighting men. They parted with strangled gasps.

"Stop fighting right now," she commanded in a no-nonsense voice.

Water streaming down him, Trent glared at Justin. "I didn't come to fight. I came to sell you my share of the pines." Trent slowly stood in the grass beside Emily, his clothes wet and muddy, his breathing ragged.

"Your nose is bleeding," said Emily, pushing her hanky into his hand.

His chest heaving, he held the small white cloth to his nose, all the while watching Justin.

With a groan Justin stood. His once white shirt was soaked with water and covered with dirt and blood. The buttons had popped off and it hung open, revealing his undershirt. His left eye was already swollen shut, and his nose was bleeding. He pulled out his handkerchief and wiped his face and nose. "I won't even talk to you about the pines," he snapped.

Anger churned inside Trent, but he managed to control it. "You're going to buy out my share so I can get out of here."

"Not on your life!" Justin knotted his fists at his sides. "You're going to do your share at the Wagon Works. I've worked like a slave the past ten years while you were off wandering the earth. And I'm tired of it."

Trent growled low in his throat. He wanted to knock the air out of Justin, but he didn't move. "I'll never work with you again. You saw to that ten years ago."

Emily looked from one to the other. What had happened ten

years ago besides Celine's death? What caused the rage between these two brothers?

"What's done is done," snapped Justin. "I need help at the Wagon Works."

"Then hire somebody!"

"Nobody can do what you've been trained to do the way you can do it, and you know it."

"Then let the business fail!"

Justin trembled. "It's come close to doing just that because you weren't here. But I wouldn't let it. Nor would Pa."

Emily saw their rage was reaching the boiling point again. "Look at you two!" she cried, waving her arm. "You're both a mess! The family will see you like this. Is that what you want?"

Trent tore his eyes from Justin and looked down at himself with a scowl. He didn't want Rachel or Mom to see him in such a mess. "I have a change of clothes in my Dodge."

"Then get them," Emily ordered. "What about you, Justin?"

"Grandpa always keeps clean clothes in the buggy shop," Justin said, his eyes hard on Trent. "We can change in there."

"I'll change in the barn," Trent said stiffly. He didn't intend to be alone with Justin now or ever.

"Both of you get a move on," Emily snapped.

Justin limped to the buggy shop while Trent lifted his satchel from his automobile.

"I'm sorry you had to see that, Emily," he said.

"I'm sorry it happened," she said sharply. "You both know better. Fighting never solves anything."

"I told you I should leave."

"Well, you can't. You promised to stay three days."

Trent shrugged, then nodded. "Three days. It'll seem like three years." He limped across the yard to the barn. Horses nickered in the pen and a colt kicked up his heels and whinnied. The barn smelled just like it always had. He stopped just inside, waited until his eyes adjusted to the dimness, and looked at the clean-swept wooden floor and the thick hand-hewn support posts. He'd kissed Celine for the very first time on the very spot where he was standing.

"You can't catch me, Trent Havlick!" Celine had called, giggling as she ran to the far end of the barn. She was fifteen and he was eighteen.

He put down the fork he was using to clean the stall. "And why would I want to catch you, little girl? I have my eye on a full-grown woman I met in Big Pine."

Celine's eyes flashed. "I'm not a little girl! I'm almost a full-grown woman." She walked slowly toward him, looking ready to cry. "Who'd you meet in Big Pine?"

"Marlene van Tol."

"Does she come from a fine family?"

"Yes."

"So, she's not an orphan like I am?"

"No."

"You plan to marry her?"

"Did I say anything about marrying anyone?"

The sparkle came back to Celine's eyes and she giggled again. "I'll bet she can't run as fast as I can!" She tapped Trent's arm, then dashed away. "You're It! Can't catch me!"

He ran after her and almost caught her in the last stall, but she scrambled up in the manger and ducked across into the next stall.

"Can't catch me, Trent Havlick!" Celine jumped from the manger and almost landed in a pile of manure. "You didn't clean this yet. Better get a move on before your grandpa sees this and thinks you've been playing instead of working."

"Grandpa knows I'm a hard worker." Trent stood outside the stall and grinned. He acted as though he didn't care if he caught her or not.

Celine stepped a little closer to him. "Emily and I have a secret."

"Oh?"

"She knows who I love and I know who she loves."

"Are you going to tell me?"

"No! And you can't make me!"

Quick as a cat he caught her and pulled her hard against him. His pulse leaped as they touched, startling him. She was little Celine Graybill from the orphan home and he'd known her all his life.

"You can't make me tell," she whispered, her hazel eyes wide in her pale face.

He looked at her moist lips and wanted to kiss her. He lowered his head, then waited for her to struggle to get away. She stood quietly in his arms, her heart beating against him. He touched his lips to hers. Sparks shot through him and he jumped away, alarmed at how he felt.

"I'm sorry," he whispered, struggling to keep his desire from her.

"I'm not sorry a bit," she had said, flipping her hair with a soft laugh. She'd run to the open barn door, turned, then blew him a kiss.

Now he closed his eyes and felt the warmth of her lips and the softness of her body. It had been ten long years since he'd kissed her. And no other woman had ever filled the need in him that she had. "Celine," he whispered raggedly.

His shoulders sagged and tears burned his eyes. Slowly he walked to the room where the hired man slept when they had one. He changed into a wrinkled, but clean plaid shirt and faded jeans he'd worn many times at the Rocking R. He brushed his hair, wincing when he hit a swollen spot. Fresh anger at Justin flared. He was without Celine because of Justin.

"I hate him," Trent said grimly.

He left his bag and wet clothes, then strode out into the bright sunlight just as Justin walked out of the buggy shop. They stopped and stared at each other. Betsy ran to Justin and pressed against his leg.

"No fighting!" Emily cried, running to stand between them. "Let's go inside and see the family."

"If he has the courage," Justin said, glaring at Trent.

Trent took a menacing step toward Justin, but Emily caught his arm and held him back.

"Please, no more fighting! At least not now."

"I won't fight again," said Trent harshly.

"If you ever do, you'd better plan to finish what you start," Justin said gruffly.

Trent reached for all the willpower in him, found it, and was able to keep from tearing Justin in two.

Her hand through Trent's arm, Emily walked between the men up the steps and onto the back porch. She smelled ham, but she knew dinner would've been over long ago. They were probably upset that Justin hadn't made it on time. She knew he was often late. They walked into the empty kitchen. Dirty dishes were stacked on the table for the hired girl to wash later. The aroma of coffee came from a pot simmering at the back of the stove. The kitchen felt too warm from the fire in the wood-burning cookstove.

"Is that you, Just?" called Freeman. "We're in the front room."

"Grab a plate of food if you're hungry," called Jennet.

Hearing their voices sent shivers over Trent. Many times in his dreams he'd heard them call him, only to wake up and find himself with strangers in a strange place.

"I'm not hungry," called Justin, darting a look at Trent. He lowered his voice. "It's not too late to go back where you've been."

Trent stiffened. "I'm going to see the family." He groped for Emily's hand and held on tightly.

She wanted to ease his tension, but couldn't find any words to speak that would help. Instead she prayed silently for him and for Justin and for Rachel and the others in the front room.

Justin scowled at Emily. "You always did take his side. You should've learned by now you can't count on him."

"Please, Justin," she said softly. "This should be a happy time for the family. Both of you work to put aside whatever is wrong for their sakes."

"He won't," Trent snapped, jerking his head toward his brother. "He's always thought of himself first and only."

"Just a minute, now." Justin stepped toward Trent, but Emily touched his arm and shook her head. He glowered at Trent, but finally turned away and headed through the wide hall that led to the front room.

His stomach a hard knot and holding Emily's hand in a firmer grip, Trent followed. He was too nervous to notice if the house looked the same. He heard the heavy tick of the grandfather clock, or was the sound he heard the pounding of his heart?

Justin stepped into the front room. Someone said, "Well, you're here!"

"I'm not alone," he answered over the noise.

Trent paused in the doorway, gripping Emily's hand so tightly she almost cried out in pain. A hush settled over the room. His glance darted around until he found his mother. She looked the same—soft brown eyes that could see into his heart, her hair pulled back loosely and pinned at the back of her head, slender build, and a spirit that couldn't be dampened. She wore a pale green dress and black, one-strap slippers. "Happy Mother's Day, Mom," he said with a catch in his voice.

Lark gasped and, for a minute, couldn't move. Then she shot from her chair, ran across the room, and flung her arms around Trent.

Emily stepped quickly to Rachel's side, who was staring speechlessly at Trent. Rachel pressed her face against Emily's arm.

"Son! You're home! At last, at last!" Lark kissed Trent all

over his face, then clung to him. Finally she stepped back and looked him up and down. Before she could speak again, Clay grabbed him and hugged him tightly. Gray streaked Clay's dark hair and deep lines were etched down the sides of his nose.

"Is it my daddy?" Rachel whispered loudly as she looked up at Emily.

"Yes," Emily answered, giving Rachel a hug.

"It is," Clay said as he stepped aside and gestured for Rachel to come to Trent.

Trent stared in shock at the red-haired girl. He was looking at Celine when she was a child! His head spun. "Celine?" he whispered.

"No, Daddy. Rachel. I'm your daughter. And Celine's daughter." She cocked her head and studied him. "Emily says I have your brown eyes and Momma's red hair."

Trent bent down until his face was even with Rachel's. Before he realized what he was doing, he wrapped his arms around her and held her close. She smelled like lilacs and soap and Sunday dinner. Her body was warm and firm as she returned his embrace. It was hard to believe the fuzzy-headed infant he'd left behind had turned into a real live child. What had he missed? Skinned knees, chicken pox, hurt feelings, laughter, pictures drawn lovingly at school, good morning Daddy's, hugs like this? A little piece of his heart began to thaw.

Emily stood back and watched the family swarm around Trent, while Justin sank into a chair off in a corner, his face a study of resentment. Priscilla started toward him, but he scowled at her and she turned back to Trent with sadness in her eyes. She was twenty-seven years old, but she looked younger with her light brown hair bobbed and curled and a light dusting of makeup on her face. Her rose colored dress complimented her slender figure, and stockings covered her shapely legs. Her black leather sandals with fancy Junior Louis heels were the latest grecian style. Emily had wanted a pair like them, but she couldn't afford to pay $3.19 for fancy, impractical shoes when she could get black serviceable ones for half the price.

Justin and Priscilla's four children swarmed around Rachel, asking her all kinds of questions while Jennet and Freeman hugged Trent, their faces wreathed with smiles.

"Our boy's home, Ma," Free said, tears of joy in his voice.

Finally Priscilla had her turn at Trent. They'd always been friends and he'd often tried to help her understand Justin's moods when Justin was courting her. "I'm glad you're home," she whispered in Trent's ear. "I need you—desperately."

Trent smiled down at Priscilla. He saw the sadness in her brown eyes. Was Justin ignoring her again as he had years before? He'd always had a habit of getting involved in his work and forgetting everyone and everything around him. "So you married him, in spite of everything?"

"I loved him."

"We'll talk later," Trent promised, giving her a gentle kiss on the cheek.

She nodded, suddenly close to tears. She introduced him to her four children, seven-year-old Ted, six-year-old Ryan, four-year-old Faith, and three-year-old Chloe. Then she backed away and made room for Uncle Beaver and Aunt Hannah.

Emily sat quietly near the door as she watched Red Beaver and Hannah. She'd often heard the story of their courtship, and how the family had been against Hannah marrying a Patowatomie Indian. But true love had won out, and through the years their marriage had been strong and enduring. Red Beaver's farm was prosperous, and he'd provided well for his family. They had five children and fifteen grandchildren, all living on farms around Blue Creek. Of all the married couples Emily knew, she thought this one might be the happiest, perhaps even happier than Jennet and Freeman whose delight in each other seemed endless.

After a long time Freeman said loudly, "Let's let the boy

sit down. We don't want to wear him out his first day home."

Everyone moved away from Trent except Rachel. She stood before him, looking up at him in awe. "You really do look like Uncle Just. But you look different, too. Emily said you were handsome and smart and strong. And she was right. Now that you're home you can be my daddy all the time."

Trent's eyes glistened with tears, but he refused to let them fall. "I won't be staying here," he said hoarsely.

Emily's heart sank. She'd hoped that once he saw the family he'd want to stay. She peeked at Justin through her long lashes and saw the angry set of his jaw. No one seemed to have noticed Justin's swollen eye. In fact, no one, except Priscilla, seemed to have noticed Justin at all.

Rachel stared at Trent in horror. "But why? What will I do for a daddy?"

Trent wanted to say something to make her feel better, but he couldn't. He knew she'd be fine without him just as she had the last ten years.

"Why can't you stay, son?" Clay asked softly as he held Lark's hand in his to keep her from crying out. He knew she wanted Trent home more than she'd ever wanted anything in her life.

Suddenly feeling all alone, Trent looked around. He spied Emily sitting near the door with an empty chair beside her. She patted the chair and smiled. Relieved, he strode across the room and sank down beside her, his legs too weak to stand any longer.

Rachel ran after him and crawled onto Emily's lap. "Daddy's home," she whispered in Emily's ear.

Emily smiled and nodded.

"I'll stay for three days."

"Three days?" Lark cried in alarm.

"Shhh." Clay patted her hand. "Let him talk."

Justin bit back an angry retort. He wanted to make them see what a waster Trent was, but he thought that nothing he might say would make a difference. They'd have to learn for themselves. Trent had always been their favorite.

"I have to get back to Texas," Trent began. "I'm buying a ranch there." He told them about the Rocking R where he'd worked the past several years. As Emily listened, she sensed the excitement in Trent's voice was not quite genuine. He seemed to be trying to make the work sound fun and romantic, but later all she could remember was talk of tumbleweeds, dust storms, northers, long, lonely nights spent riding the range, stampedes, cattle rustlers, and weeks-long cattle drives. She thought Texas sounded hot, dusty, and very, very lonely. She wondered why Trent would want to leave a loving family to live in such a place. Something must be terribly wrong to make him want to do it.

"The owner wants to sell," Trent said, "and I want to buy it."

"What about your business here?" Justin asked angrily.

Priscilla frowned at Justin, but he ignored her.

"I don't want it," Trent snapped. "It's your business. You can have it."

Emily laid her hand over Trent's. She could feel his tension and anger, and again she wondered why.

"Boys!" Freeman said, keeping his arm around Jennet. "We don't want harsh, angry words spoken."

"We'll settle this peaceably," Clay said.

Rachel slid off Emily's lap and stood at Trent's side.

Lark brushed a tear off her pale cheek. "Will you stay with us while you're here?"

"Please do, Daddy," Rachel begged with her hands clasped at her throat and her eyes wide.

Trent nodded. It would be easier to stay with his folks than to go to the home he'd shared with Celine. There were too many painful memories there.

"I hired a caretaker for your place," Clay said. "Gabe Lavery."

Emily flushed. Gabe was Bob Lavery's brother.

"It's ready for you if you ever want to move back in," Lark said.

"Kill the fatted calf," Justin said bitterly.

"Stop it," Priscilla snapped, frowning at Justin.

Justin scowled at her, but said nothing more.

Trent tensed, ready to leap up, but Emily gripped his arm. Finally he relaxed. "I plan to stay three days. I came to sell my share of the pines so I will have the money to buy the Rocking R and stock it with a new breed of beef cattle I've read about. I'd like to sell to Justin."

Jennet shook her head hard and jumped to her feet. "No! No, Trent! You can't sell your share."

"Easy, Jen," Freeman said, catching her hand.

"Why?" Trent asked in surprise.

"I won't buy it anyway," Justin snapped.

"You can't sell it and Justin can't buy it," Clay said.

Trent sank back as a cold chill crept over his body.

"It's in the will that if you die or if you refuse the trees, or want to sell them, they go to your next of kin. That's Rachel. They can't be sold, son, only passed on."

Trent groaned. It had never occurred to him that he couldn't sell his inheritance.

"The pines are for all people to enjoy," Jennet said firmly as she sank down to the couch beside Freeman. "Your Great-grandpa Clay bought them and passed them to me to save for future generations. I passed them on to your parents and now they belong to you and your brother. But they are for saving, Trent, not for selling. When you and Justin inherited the white pines, you inherited Great-grandpa Clay's covenant to preserve them in their natural state. And that's what we're going to do."

Bright spots of color dotted Jennet's cheeks. "I have a plan to tell all of you. It's my plan to make the dream come true. It's about letting people everywhere see and enjoy our beloved white pines."

"What's your plan, Ma?" Clay asked softly.

Trent looked longingly at the door, but he knew he couldn't leave. If he couldn't sell his inheritance, he didn't care what anyone wanted to do with the forest. But since he was trapped, he looked at his grandmother and waited for her to speak.

Justin moved restlessly. He didn't want to hear Grandma's idea either, but he also knew he couldn't leave.

Emily glanced at Trent, then settled back to listen to Jennet's plan.

From the couch Jennet looked around the room at her family. How it had grown since she'd given birth to Clay fifty-five years before! If all the children and grandchildren had been able to be home today, the house couldn't contain them. With effort she pulled her thoughts together. Her stomach fluttered with nerves. "I want to turn the pines into a nature preserve and logging museum."

Justin thought about the money the trees represented and his heart sank. The Wagon Works needed money right away or he'd have to go to the bank for a loan. And he didn't like to do that with the economy the way it was. For some time he'd toyed with the idea of turning those trees into cash, just as Trent apparently had. He also hadn't known he couldn't sell his inheritance. The news today had been a shock. All he could think of now was that Grandma's plan would cost more money and he didn't know where that would come from. Still, it was a nice idea.

Jennet nervously cleared her throat. She saw the looks of shock on different faces. She turned to Freeman. "I want us to build a logging camp just like you once had, Free."

"That's a tall order, Jen," Free said.

"But not impossible," Clay said. The idea appealed to him, even though it was a major undertaking.

Emily smiled as her heart leaped with excitement. Jennet's idea was the best she'd ever heard. It was past time for others to get as much enjoyment out of the forest as they did. But what would Papa think of the idea?

Jennet continued as if she hadn't been interrupted. "I want folks to see how the trees were lumbered out and how precious the ones are that remain. I want trails made through the forest so folks can walk them with a guide and enjoy what we've enjoyed all these years. School children can take hikes there and learn first-hand about all the wonders of nature. Families can visit on their vacations." Jennet leaned forward earnestly. "There are still bears in our pines and all kinds of wild animals that left other areas because civilization took their homes. We'd tell the people how years ago the wild pigeons blackened the sky because there were so many as they flew up from the trees. Now they're extinct because so many of the trees were lumbered. We'll tell them of the beaver and all the other fur-bearing animals that once lived in the woods. We'll make it come alive for them just as it does for us." She took a deep breath as she looked around at her silent family. "And we'll call it 'Havlick's Wilderness' because it's the last true wilderness in Lower Michigan."

"Havlick's Wilderness," Clay said, smiling and nodding. Emily liked it.

Jennet tucked a stray strand of white hair into the bun at the back of her head. "It'll be hard work, but the whole family could work together. The small price we'd charge the visitors would help maintain the property and pay the taxes each year. We'd have benches scattered along the trails so folks could rest and enjoy the tranquility. We wouldn't allow anyone to pick a single flower or dig up any plants or kill any of the animals or birds. No one could leave litter behind, or take food to feed the birds and animals. We want the place left in its natural state. I want to know that fifty years from now folks will still be seeing the pines that've stood for hundreds of years. Our pines! Havlick's Wilderness."

Shaking his head, Free whistled softly. "That's a big dream, sweetheart."

"I know," she said, taking his hand. "But a Havlick always dreams big."

"You're right about that." Free looked around at the family. "What'd you think about your mother's dream?"

Emily blinked back tears. She wasn't part of the family, but she loved the plan. The trees had always been important to her. Sharing them with others was perfect.

Trent leaned back with a low sigh as he listened to the others all talk at once. He didn't feel a part of the discussion or of the decision. His name was Havlick, but he didn't belong here now. He belonged on the Rocking R in Texas. But how would he get the money to buy the ranch now?

Clay lifted his hand and called for attention. When everyone was silent he said, "Ma, I like your dream. I think my boys do, too. It'll take a lot of work, but I vote yes. Trent? Justin? What do you say?"

Justin shrugged. "It's fine with me."

Trent nodded. "Me, too."

"You boys are the owners of the pines," Clay said. "It'll mean working together to see it come to pass."

"No," Trent said gruffly. "I won't work with him. You'll have to get someone else."

"I'm too busy anyway," Justin said coldly. "I can help find someone to work the project, though."

"It'll have to be someone you both agree on," Clay said, studying his sons.

They both nodded.

Everyone started talking again, and Emily leaned close to Trent. "I'm going now," she whispered. "I'll see you tomorrow."

"Don't leave me," he said, gripping her hand. "Please!"

She sank back in her chair and let him hold her hand for comfort. Celine would've wanted her to do that.

CHAPTER

5

♦ His muscles tight from the stress of the day, Trent stopped his Dodge in front of Emily's house and slowly turned to her. "Thanks for your help this afternoon. I wouldn't have made it without you."

"I'm glad I could help."

He sighed. "If I remember right, you were always the one to help ease the way for me and for Celine."

She shrugged, but she was pleased that he remembered what she'd done for them. "I wish you would change your mind and stay."

"No." He looked down at his hands on the steering wheel. "Not with Justin here."

"What did he do to make you so angry?" Emily flushed. Of course that question had been on her mind all afternoon, but it slipped out before she thought. "I'm sorry," she said quickly. "It's none of my business."

Trent looked off across the farmyard without seeing the barns and sheds. He'd never told anyone that Justin was to blame for Celine's death.

"Don't answer that," Emily said as she fumbled with the door handle. "I had no right to ask."

He touched her shoulder. "You have a right to ask, and you have a right to know. But I can't talk about it. I doubt if I'll ever be able to."

Emily turned to Trent, her eyes full of compassion. "Have you asked God to help you with this, whatever it is?"

Trent's eyes pricked with tears as he shook his head. "Not even God can help with this."

She was shocked to hear him talk that way. He'd always had such faith. "He can help with everything. But we have to let Him."

Trent studied the curve of her chin, her rounded cheek, and the arch of her dark brows. He had forgotten her face. "You always did believe God is the answer to everything."

She locked her fingers together in her lap. "So did you."

"But that was a long time ago."

Emily's heart sank. She smelled the leather of the seats mingled with the pine scent that always filled the air. "You can't mean you no longer trust Him!"

"I guess I just haven't thought about Him."

"Then it's time you did. He loves you."

"When did you turn into a preacher lady?" Trent asked sharply.

"Don't get smart mouthed with me. I'm not Celine. She put up with it, but I won't."

He laughed, surprising himself. "And you never have. I'd forgotten that."

"Well, don't forget again." She lifted her chin and looked down her nose at him, then grinned. She caught a movement at the kitchen window and knew Mama had looked out. She was probably wondering what was going on. Most likely she'd think Justin was in the automobile with her. Wait 'til Mama learned the truth!

Trent watched a cat amble across the grassy road, then turned back to Emily. "You always could see right through me."

"And I still can."

"I hope not," he muttered.

"I know you're hurting badly inside. But for some reason you don't want to be free of it. You'd rather be in pain than ask the Lord to take it away and set you free." Emily shook her head. "From what you said, I can tell Justin did something that you won't forgive."

"You don't know the half of it!"

"Well, you have to forgive him, Trent." She shook her finger at him. "Unforgiveness eats away at you, and it will destroy you. It blocks your relationship with God, and with everyone else, too. That's why it's been so easy to lower your standards and live the way you do."

Trent flushed. "You don't know a thing about my standards."

"Yes, I do. I can see it in your eyes. Your parents and grandparents would be crushed if they knew what you've become. And it's all because you want to stay angry at Justin. It's not worth it, Trent."

He sighed heavily. "Some things can't be forgiven, Emily."

"*Everything* can be forgiven."

"No, not everything."

"If God can forgive us unconditionally the way He does, we can forgive each other. That's what it means to be Christ-like."

He considered what she'd said and after a long time he said, "I'll give it some thought."

"Don't just think about it, do it. Forgive Justin and get on with your life. And while we're talking about your life, don't forget you have a daughter. It's time you took responsibility for her." Emily pushed her mass of dark hair over her shoulder. "When I leave, what'll become of her? She loves me, and it'll be hard for her to lose me and lose you, too, especially now that she has finally found you."

Trent shrugged. "Then don't go."

"I have to." Emily flushed painfully. "You know that."

"Well, I have to go, too," Trent said impatiently. "And I have to find another way to get the money to buy the Rocking R."

"Then take Rachel with you."

"To Texas?"

"Yes."

The idea was new to him, and frightening. "What about her friends and the family?"

"She can make new friends." Emily tapped his shoulder. "But you're her family and she needs you desperately. Now that she's seen you, she can't survive without you."

Absently Trent ran his finger around the smooth black steering wheel. A pig squealed in the pigpen and a robin sang on the branch of a tree. Trent shook his head. "The Rocking R is miles out in the country. She'd be isolated. She couldn't get to school or even to church. There'd be no one there but me and the hands. She'd be all alone."

Emily smiled as she leaned toward Trent. "You'll figure out something." Having Rachel go with him was a brilliant idea, and she wouldn't let it go.

Thoughtfully Trent rubbed his cheek as he studied Emily. He grinned mischievously. "I just had a real good notion, Emily."

She cocked her brow questioningly, not certain she wanted to hear it. Already she sensed she wasn't going to like it. He'd always known how to aggravate her with his teasing.

Trent folded his arms across his broad chest. The grin grew wider and his eyes began to twinkle. He paused dramatically, his eyes locked with Emily's. She felt the color rising in her cheeks, and little flutters began in her stomach.

"I'll take Rachel with me if you come along."

Emily gasped, then, unable to look away, sat mutely, her face flaming.

Trent threw back his head and laughed heartily. "Ah, this is a first," he said when he'd caught his breath. "Always-ready-with-something-to-say-Emily is speechless!"

"I confess—you caught me off-guard," she stammered when she found her voice, trying to regain her composure.

"Excuse me." Trent reached for her hand, his voice gentle. "But I haven't had a good laugh like this in years.

"Well, how about it?" he asked.

"Me go to Texas with you?"

"Un-huh."

"You can't be serious. Why would you think of such a thing, even as a joke?"

Trent shrugged. "You're planning to go to Sweden with some other man. Why not go to Texas with me? Besides, Texas is a lot closer to home than Sweden is."

"I can't go anywhere with you. It wouldn't look right."

He laughed softly, thinking what he was about to say would, as they say in Texas, "throw her for a loop."

"It would if you married me."

Again she was speechless, and Trent chuckled as he tugged gently at a strand of Emily's dark hair.

"You planned on marrying that man in Sweden without loving him, without even seeing him before. You could marry me. At least you know me."

"Stop teasing me!"

A tingle ran down his spine. Why should this be a joke? Why not marry her? She already knew he would always love Celine, and he already knew she was in love with someone else. That wouldn't be a problem for either of them. "You could be Rachel's mother and see that she gets proper schooling and everything else she needs. Even though it hasn't shown much, I do want the best for her."

"This is just too ridiculous." Emily's heart raced and blood pounded in her ears. Was he serious? She couldn't tell. What had happened to her ability to read him like a book?

"It's perfect, Emily. We love each other as friends. That's all we need. But we'll give Rachel a whole lot more. And we'll both have answers to our problems."

Emily bit her lower lip. Was it possible? Would it work? "I don't know . . ."

"You'll have to decide fast. Remember I'm only staying three days."

"But, Trent, I can't make up my mind that fast."

"You did about this guy from Sweden."

"That's different."

"Sure. Because you've never seen him." Trent was pleased with his idea and his argument. "Talk to your parents about it and see what they say. They've always liked me and you said they love Rachel."

Helplessly Emily shook her head. "I couldn't marry you. We're good friends. We were best friends—you, Celine, and me. How could we be, ah, husband and wife?"

Trent saw her flush and understood the reason for it. "I didn't mean to embarrass you. We don't have to share a bedroom. We could live together as husband and wife without actually being . . . husband and wife. Does that sound better?"

"I don't know that it does," Emily said weakly. "I want children." And she wanted to know what it felt like to be held and loved by a man. But she couldn't say that to Trent without embarrassing herself even more.

He sank back against the seat. She'd surprised him. "Then we'll share a bed. You'll get the children you want and Rachel will get the mother she wants.'

All the strength seemed to drain out of Emily. Was she actually considering marrying Trent? "What about you?" she asked weakly. "What do you want?"

"Celine," Trent whispered. "I want Celine."

Emily's eyes filled with tears. "I wish I could bring her back for you. But I can't. No one can. And I can't take her place. No one can do that either'

They sat quietly for a long time. The evening breeze blew cool air into the automobile. Sounds of birds and farm animals seemed to grow louder. Finally Trent said, "So, will you marry me and go back to Texas with me and Rachel?"

Emily took a deep, shuddering breath, then let it out. Should she? It seemed more appealing than going to Sweden. "Why not? I would rather marry you than August Theorell anyway."

Trent laughed. "Thank you, Emily. I'll see that you're not sorry for it."

"And I'll try to get used to living in Texas. I hear it's vast and empty."

"It's big all right. But I like it." Trent pursed his lips in thought. "This is Sunday. We'll leave Wednesday. Can you be ready?"

"Yes," Emily said breathlessly. Oh, how could she possibly be ready? Suddenly she laughed. "Rachel has been praying that I'd marry you and be her momma. I said it'd never happen."

"I guess some prayers get answered." Trent looked off across the yard without seeing a thing.

"Prayers get answered all the time," Emily said, smiling. "We prayed you'd come home and you did."

Abruptly Trent pushed open the door and stepped to the ground. After not hearing about spiritual things for so long, he was feeling uncomfortable. "Let's go talk to your folks. They may want to talk you out of this." He opened her door and helped her out, then stood with his hands on her shoulders. "I don't want you to be sorry for agreeing to marry me. If you want to back out, do it now before we say a word to anyone."

Emily's stomach knotted and for a minute panic seized her. Then she shook her head. She felt this was right for them. "I won't change my mind. We'll tell Mama and Papa. They'll really be shocked."

"So will my parents."

They walked together into the house and straight to the kitchen where she knew her family would be. Emily was shivering, not knowing if she was excited or scared to death. Supper was already over, but the aroma of fried potatoes and pork chops still filled the air.

Andree Bjoerling looked up from his newspaper. Laugh lines spread from the corners of his blue eyes to his gray-streaked black hair. He was tall and thin and dark from years of working outdoors. He'd come from Sweden when he was twenty-two, hoping to learn about Jig, his uncle, and had stayed to work for the Havlicks. He'd never been sorry.

"Mama, Papa," Emily called. "Look who's here. It's Trent, home at last."

"Trent!" Martha covered her mouth and stared. The boys just stared.

"Welcome, Trent," Andree said, jumping up. He gave Trent a bear hug, then stepped aside to make room for Martha.

"You're home again at last!" Martha hugged him fiercely. This was the man she'd always wanted to be Emily's husband. Martha turned to her three boys. "This is Trent. You knew him when you were little." She turned toward Trent. "That's Lars, Neil, and Dag. They're almost grown men now—they were little boys when you left."

Trent shook hands as the boys greeted him boisterously.

Emily stood to one side and watched her family talk to Trent, trying to catch up the past ten years in only ten minutes.

Finally Trent moved to Emily's side. "We have something to tell you," he said with a smile.

Emily's heart raced as her mother's eyes widened and her father's brows lifted questioningly.

Trent took Emily's hand in his. "I'm going back to Texas Wednesday and I'm taking Rachel with me." He smiled down at Emily, then looked at her father. "I've also asked Emily to go as my wife."

Emily saw the shocked looks on their faces. "I've agreed to go," she said softly. "Is that all right, Mama? Papa?"

"Well, I'll be hogtied!" cried Andree, slapping his knee.

"I say it's good news," Martha said, blinking back tears as she tried to read Emily's eyes. "This is so fast. Are you sure, honey?"

Emily nodded and smiled. "Yes, Mama."

"Good," said Martha. She hugged Emily, then Trent. "I want the best for you children. Even though I'm surprised, I'm very pleased."

"I always loved you as a son," Andree said as he hugged Trent again. "Welcome to the family."

"Finally we'll be rid of Emily," Lars said with a laugh as he shook Trent's hand.

"Thanks for taking her off our hands," Neil said, winking at Emily.

"I get her room," Dag said, grinning.

"Wednesday, you say?" Martha's eyes widened in alarm. "I can't be ready to give up my daughter so soon."

"Yes, you can." Andree slipped his arm around Martha's shoulders. "We'll send her off with a smile just like we did Betty and Lucille."

Emily looked at Trent and grinned. Now that they'd told her parents, it looked like she was really going to marry Trent Havlick.

They talked about wedding plans for several minutes before Trent said, "Now we must tell my family. I'll bring Emily back later."

Emily squeezed her mother's hand, then walked to the automobile with Trent. In silence they drove down the dusty lane to the gravel road, then on in to Blue Creek. The town was quiet. Lights shone from the windows of several homes. Main Street was almost deserted. Emily knew Rachel would already be in bed, and probably was asleep.

Trent parked where Emily usually parked her buggy. The

sudden silence with the automobile turned off felt good. "I think Mom and Dad will be happy," Trent said. "Don't you?"

"I . . . I don't know. I hope so."

"You aren't going to back out, are you?"

"No." Emily trembled. "I am nervous, though."

"Don't be." Trent jumped to the ground and ran around to open the door for Emily. "We're old buddies, remember?"

Emily laughed breathlessly. "Yes, you're right, old buddy."

They found Clay and Lark in the front room listening to hymns on the victrola.

"We've come to tell you something," Trent said.

Lark lifted the needle, stopping the music in the middle of a note, and moved the arm off the record. She faced Trent and Emily, her pulse quickening. She'd changed into a comfortable cotton dress that reached almost to her ankles. She couldn't get used to short dresses. "When you didn't come for so long, I was afraid you'd left again," Lark said as she kissed Trent on the cheek.

"We were talking about Rachel before you came," Clay said as he wrapped his hands around his black suspenders. "She's not going to be happy here with us if you leave again now that she's met you."

Trent cleared his throat. "That's what we want to talk about."

"Let's sit down." Clay tugged Lark down on the blue sofa beside him and kept her hand in his.

Her legs weak, Emily sat on the blue, tapestry armchair across from the sofa. A cool breeze ruffled the white muslin curtains at the windows. A kerosene lamp with white frosted globe and brass base sitting on the end table cast a warm glow over the room.

"Have a chair, Trent," Clay said softly.

Trent sank to the arm of Emily's chair. His mouth felt as dry as on a cattle drive. He ran a finger around the neckline of his shirt. "I don't know how to say this."

"Just say it, son," Lark said gently.

Emily shivered. She felt the heat from Trent's body. Was she doing the right thing?

Trent cleared his throat. "I want to take Rachel back with me. I know you'll both miss her a lot, but you can visit us and we'll come see you."

Lark's eyes filled with tears. "We want you to stay, Trent. Please, stay here!"

Trent shook his head. "I'm sorry, Mom. I can't stay. I'm leaving Wednesday with Rachel. And Emily has agreed to go with us. As my wife."

Lark gasped and Clay laughed in delight.

"Rachel will be glad," Clay said. Nothing ever surprised him, not even this. "She's been pestering Emily for years to be her momma."

Lark jumped up, pulled Emily to her feet, and hugged her. "This is so sudden. Are you sure?"

"I'm sure," Emily answered.

"She's sure," Trent said.

"Welcome to the family." Clay hugged Emily tight.

"Thank you." Emily's head spun. She was going to belong to the powerful Havlick family!

"I think we should go and tell Rachel," Lark said. "She's probably still wide awake day dreaming about her daddy."

Emily hung back as Trent and his parents started toward the stairs. What could she say to Rachel after telling her so many times that she'd never be her mother?

Trent glanced back and saw Emily hesitating. He motioned to his parents to go ahead of him, then waited for Emily. He took her hand and squeezed it reassuringly. "You said Rachel wanted this. Why be scared?"

"You're right, of course." Emily smiled hesitantly. She gripped Trent's work-roughened hand as they walked to Rachel's bedroom. The room was decorated in a delicate pink and white—not at all the colors Emily would've chosen for her.

When she saw them at her door, Rachel sat bolt upright in bed, holding a rag doll tightly in her arms. Her red hair hung in two braids over her shoulders. She looked at Trent fearfully. "Are you going away already? Did you come to say goodbye?"

Awkwardly Trent sat on the edge of the bed and gently took Rachel's hand in his. She was so much like Celine it took his breath away. He managed to say, "I didn't come to say goodbye. We came to tell you good news."

"You and Emily are going to get married!" Rachel said, her eyes large and full of excitement.

Trent stared at Rachel in shock. Suddenly the child seemed very much like Emily.

Emily laughed. "What makes you think that, Rachel?"

"It's because I asked God to arrange it. And I asked Him to bring my daddy home. He did that and now you need to get married. That's what it is, isn't it?"

"Yes, that's what it is," Trent said, shaking his head in amazement. "I've asked Emily to marry me and be your momma. She said she would."

Rachel cocked her head and looked at Trent. "Then will you stay here and always be my daddy?"

With Emily beside him and his parents standing at the foot of the bed, Trent told Rachel that he would always be her daddy and that he was sorry he'd missed so much. "I've let my grief keep me from you and that hurt both of us. I hope you'll forgive me."

"Oh, I will, Daddy, I will." Rachel threw her arms around Trent's neck and hugged him hard. Lark had to ask Clay for a handkerchief. He gave her his after he dabbed quickly at his own tears.

Then Trent told Rachel they would live in Texas on the Rocking R Ranch and they would be a family. "So, Tuesday Emily and I'll be married and Wednesday you and Emily and I will leave for Texas."

Rachel hugged them all and after a long time settled back on her pillow. "I want Tuesday to come fast."

Emily kissed her cheek, then turned away as fear pricked her skin. All at once she realized she was afraid for Tuesday to come.

* * *

Late Sunday afternoon Priscilla Havlick drove herself and her children home from Freeman's place. Her family lived only a few miles from the elder Havlicks' home. She was bone tired and she knew the children were, too. Little Chloe was almost asleep against Ted.

Priscilla parked outside the small garage they'd built the year before when she bought her black Ford. Lilac bushes at the side of the gravel driveway were in full bloom sending out their fragrant aroma. Red tulips and yellow daffodils swayed in the gentle breeze. They covered a wide patch of ground between the picnic table and the two story white frame house Justin had built for them the first year of their marriage. Then it seemed too large, but now with four children it often felt too small. She quickly looked around for Noah Roswell, their hired man, but couldn't see him in the pen feeding the pigs, near the large red barn, or at the wood pile splitting wood. He was probably already milking the cows. He'd worked for them almost a year, but only in the past few weeks had her heart skipped a beat at the thought of him. Seeing him and talking to him made her days worth living. At times she longed for him to take her in his strong arms and kiss her senseless. Flushing at the turn her thoughts had taken again, she said over her shoulder, "Run inside. I want to speak to Daddy alone. You may have cookies and milk at the kitchen table. Ted, help Chloe and Faith."

"I will, Mom."

"I don't need help," Faith said with a toss of her dark hair. "I'm not a baby like Chloe."

"Run inside," Priscilla said impatiently.

With happy shouts, the children ran up the back steps and through the back door. The screen slammed behind Chloe, then all was quiet except for the squawk of the windmill and the gobble of a turkey. Priscilla fingered the strands of white beads hanging down the front of her rose-colored dress. Waiting for Justin to pull up beside her, she angrily pressed her lips together. Once again he had embarrassed her by being late for a family gathering. Then he'd had the nerve to come in with a swollen eye after an obvious fight with Trent. The afternoon had been a strain for everyone with Trent's unexpected arrival. Justin's angry mood had simply made things worse.

As Justin stopped beside her, she walked around her automobile to his, her short skirt flipping around her slender legs. He still wore Free's blue work shirt and denim pants. "I want to talk to you," she said sharply.

Justin groaned. Once again he'd have to listen to her lecture about being on time and not making her look bad in front of his family. "Don't even start, Priscilla!" he said impatiently.

Sparks flew from her dark eyes. "How could you fight with Trent? What kind of homecoming was that?"

"He started it." Justin stepped from his automobile and carefully closed the door. His nerves were coiled as tight as the springs in the automobile.

Priscilla folded her arms and narrowed her eyes. "You don't want him to stay, do you?"

"I don't care what he does!" Justin started for the house, but she stopped him with a hand on his arm. He looked down at her small, well-manicured hand. Once a touch from her had sent his senses reeling. Now it only irritated him.

"Well, *I* want him here! Maybe then you wouldn't work so hard or be gone all the time."

Here it comes, he thought as his heart sank. How he hated to fight with Pris, but that seemed to be all they knew how to do. Occasionally a few days of being pleasant with each other would go by, but those days seemed to be happening less and less often. "Maybe I'd be home more if you wouldn't nag so much," he shot at her as he walked past.

Her face flamed. "Oh, what's the use? You don't care about me or the children. You care only about yourself and the Wagon Works." Priscilla stamped her small foot in the dusty driveway. "I don't understand you at all! If you talked nice to Trent, maybe you could convince him to work there again."

Justin whirled on her and doubled his fists at his sides. Priscilla had no idea the depth of Trent's anger, nor his, for that matter. "I won't work with him!"

"You are so stubborn!"

"I don't want to talk about it."

Priscilla tossed her head and her short hair bounced. "Then maybe you'll talk about Grandma's plans for the pines. Do you really think it'll work?"

"Probably. What Grandma wants, she gets."

"But the pines belong to you and Trent."

"If we can't sell them, we might as well do something to generate money from them."

"I suppose." She sighed heavily. "It just means more work for you. And I see so little of you now."

"It gives us less time to fight," he snapped.

Tears burned her eyes and she blinked them away. "Justin, I need you! I get so lonely."

"You have friends."

"I want a husband who loves me and spends time with me. I want us to have fun together! Please, Justin."

He saw the pleading in her eyes and he wanted to reach out to her, but he couldn't. "You already take more of my time than I can give. I took off this afternoon because you begged me to. If you had your way, I'd close up the Wagon Works and spend every minute of my time with you."

"You know that's not true."

"Do I?"

71

"I hate you, Justin Havlick," Priscilla whispered as her breast rose and fell in agitation. With a swish of her skirt she strode to the house and slammed the door hard behind her. Sometimes she wanted to scream.

Justin walked slowly toward the picnic table and sank down on the bench with his head in his hands. He winced as he touched his swollen eye. He winced more for what he'd done to Priscilla. He did love her, but somehow he couldn't let it show. What had happened to their happiness? Deep inside he felt the agony that was always there when he allowed himself to think about his life and what was happening to it.

Seeing Trent again had brought a fresh wave of despair over him. He was to blame for Celine's death, and he could never forgive himself. He was worse than the worst murderer he'd read about. A groan rose from deep inside him and burned in his throat.

A bee buzzed around his head but he ignored it as it flew off to the flowers. He smelled the lilacs that covered the bush behind him, but even their perfume irritated him. He heard Noah Roswell whistling in the barn, already at work on the evening chores. Noah was twenty-one years old, handsome, and scot-free. He was always cheerful and friendly, without a care in the world. Justin looked toward the big red barn. "I'd trade places with him in a minute," he muttered. But he couldn't. He was a Havlick and Havlicks were expected to succeed at everything while keeping smiles on their faces and in their hearts.

When was the last time he'd had a smile in his heart?

CHAPTER

6

♦ Monday morning while the children were still in bed and after Justin had gone to work, Priscilla walked outdoors. It was a chilly May morning, but the bright sun promised a warm day. A cat ran to her and rubbed against her ankle, purring loudly. A rooster flew to the top rail of the fence and crowed with its head back and its beak raised to the sky. The cool breeze ruffled her hair as she walked across the dew wet grass that dampened her walking shoes. She knew Noah would be milking. Her throat closed over and she stopped, her hand at her breast. What was she doing? She was flirting with danger. She should walk right back into the house where she belonged and leave Noah alone. But, lifting her chin defiantly, she said, "I don't care! If Justin won't love me, someone else will."

She took a deep, steadying breath and patted her fluttering heart with a trembling hand. She moistened her lips with the tip of her tongue as she stepped inside the barn and waited for her eyes to adjust to the dimness. The pungent odor was as familiar to her as coffee perking in the early morning. She'd grown up on a farm, then had moved here when she and Justin were married. A few months after the wedding her folks had decided to sell out and move west to Oregon. They hadn't been back since. She bit her lower lip. Right now she needed to talk to Ma. But Ma was far, far away. Besides, Ma would tell her to keep her eyes and thoughts only on her husband and off other men.

Priscilla walked to the great hand-hewn beam in the middle of the barn. Noah was perched on a one-legged stool milking a cow. He had strong, dark, well-shaped hands. He wore denim jeans and a blue work shirt with the sleeves rolled almost to his elbows. Black hair covered his strong, sun-browned forearms. His brown hair was short and thick with a slight wave. He rested his forehead against the cow's flank. Foamy white milk streamed into the pail between his strong legs. The cat ran to him, mewing lowly. He squirted milk at it and it opened its mouth to catch it. Noah laughed, and the sound sent a thrill over Priscilla.

"Good morning," she said, stepping forward so he could see her. She rubbed her hand at the waist of her flowered cotton housedress that she'd hemmed at a length of two inches below her knees.

"Morning." He winked at her and grinned, but he didn't take his hands off the cow. His eyes were as blue as the morning glories that climbed the trellis on her porch. "You look mighty pretty this morning."

"Thank you, Noah" She leaned against the wooden partition and watched him. "My brother-in-law Trent came home yesterday."

"You don't say. The Havlicks must be real glad."

"They are. But he plans to leave in a few days. He wants to buy a ranch in Texas." Priscilla liked the way Noah's brown hair curled against his neck and around his nicely shaped ears. "Have you ever been to Texas?"

"Nope. Been to Arkansas. You ever been?"

Priscilla laughed and shook her head. "I've never been out of Michigan. Can you believe that?" She knew his parents lived in Flint and that he'd left home at seventeen to join the army and fight in the war. He never did join the army, but he did travel all over.

"You seem like a real lady of the world. I took you for a well-traveled lady."

"I've been to Detroit."

"That's some city, ain't it? But I wouldn't want to live there."

"Me either. I've read about New York City and Chicago. You ever been there?"

"Yup. Wasn't impressed. They got big trouble with bootlegging in Detroit and in Chicago." Noah stripped the cow dry, then stood and put away the milk stool. He picked up two buckets filled with milk and headed for the door. "But what can they expect when they say no booze at all."

"Yes, what?" Personally Priscilla was glad drinking wasn't allowed, but she didn't say that to Noah as they walked outdoors. He carried the milk to the milk house. It was a small wood-frame building with room enough for a cream separator, washstand with a sink and hand pump, ice box, and rack to set clean buckets on. He strained the milk twice just the way she'd asked him to when he'd first started working for her.

"A man should be able to decide for himself if he wants to drink or not," Noah said as he washed out the milk pail, soapy water splashing against him. "That makes bootlegging all right with me. But it does cause a lot of stir."

"Oh?" She didn't care about bootlegging, but she wanted to keep him talking.

"Sure does. They got troubles all over Michigan." Noah glanced around as if he thought someone might hear. "Did you know there's a bar right outside of Blue Creek?"

"But that's against the law!"

"It's there anyway." Noah poured the milk into the separator, turned the handle and watched while cream came out one spout and skimmed milk the other. He put the milk and cream to cool in the ice box. "And I heard tell there's lots of bootlegging going on in the area. It wouldn't surprise me none if there're stills hidden around here."

"It wouldn't surprise me either." Priscilla hoped he wouldn't realize she was only making conversation with him. Actually she hated to think bootleggers had stills in their area. How handsome Noah looked as he stood with his hands resting lightly on the wide belt of his pants! She managed to say in great concern, "Yet Blue Creek has a good sheriff."

"You're sure right about that. I know Sheriff Spud Lamont pretty well." Noah grinned at Priscilla, sending her heart racing. "We sometimes play cards together."

Priscilla fluffed her hair. "I once tried to learn how to play bridge, but I couldn't get the hang of it."

"We play poker."

"Oh." Pa had said often it was a sin to gamble and she knew poker was a gambling game. Somehow it didn't surprise her that Noah played poker. Maybe he even visited the illegal bar. "I hope you don't lose your money."

"Not me! But I don't gamble heavy." He took the separator apart and washed it as they talked more about gambling and bootlegging. "Bootlegging would be a swell way to earn big money."

Priscilla tried to hide her alarm. "I guess it would be," she said weakly.

He dried his hands on a white towel and hung it neatly. "I'd best get back to the barn."

Priscilla couldn't let him go. "I have coffee in the house if you want a cup."

Noah caught her hand and squeezed it. "You're a real darling! I would like a cup. I make bad coffee."

He'd told her that and that's what had made her decide to offer him a cup. She'd been trying for weeks to find the courage. She looked at their clasped hands, flushed, and tugged hers free. "I have pancake batter mixed up. I could fix you a few pancakes."

"You're a woman after my own heart," he said, smiling down on her.

Her pulse leaped and she smiled up at him. He was a man after her own heart, too, but she didn't say that. He listened to her and he talked to her. And that was a whole lot more than Justin did.

A few minutes later Noah sat at the square oak table in the middle of the big kitchen with a mug of coffee in his hands while Priscilla quickly fried a stack of pancakes. Heat from the cookstove turned her cheeks pink. Having Noah watch her and talk to her about what President Harding was doing made her eyes sparkle. Since women had gotten the vote three years before, she'd tried to keep abreast of what was happening in the nation. It was hard to keep her mind on Noah's words when all she wanted to do was have him pull her close and kiss her.

Yellow curtains fluttered at the open row of windows beside the back door. A large white sink with a red hand pump was against another wall. Beside it were wooden pegs for hanging towels and jackets and hats. Crocks sat on the floor near a tall white cupboard between the hall door and the dining room door. Fire crackled in the cast iron range against another wall. On the far side of the woodbox were a row of shelves and a door leading into the spacious pantry.

Priscilla set the plate of pancakes before Noah, poured herself a cup of coffee, and sat with him at the big table. It had been a long time since she'd sat at her table with anyone other than her children. Justin usually grabbed a bite in town. Abruptly she pushed away thoughts of Justin and watched Noah. She liked the way he smeared butter on each pancake, then poured maple syrup over the entire stack. The butter melted and dribbled down the sides with the syrup. She'd helped make the maple syrup last February.

Noah cut off a bite and stuck it in his mouth. He rolled his eyes in pleasure and said, "Ummmm."

"I'm glad you like them," Priscilla said, smiling with pride. While he ate she told him about Jennet's dream of turning the white pines into a nature preserve and logging museum.

"Sounds good to me," Noah said in between bites. "But there'll be some folks that'll throw a fit."

"But why?"

"They don't want strangers nosing around. Because of the bootleggers."

"You sound so sure of yourself. How do you know that kind of thing?" Priscilla asked in surprise.

Noah shrugged. "I heard it around town."

"If so many people know about bootleggers and about the places that sell liquor, why doesn't anyone tell the sheriff?"

"Folks like to drink. They're glad for a chance to buy the stuff."

"Jennet and Lark Havlick would shut those places down if they knew about them."

"Nobody's gonna tell 'em."

"They don't believe in strong drink."

Noah shrugged. "A lot of folks think different. They get a kick out of drinking and hanging around together at them places."

"Do you?"

"I been in some, but I don't drink much."

Priscilla bit her lower lip. She'd never thought about Noah doing anything really bad.

Noah took a long swig of coffee, then wiped his mouth with the back of his hand. "Thanks for the fine food, Priscilla. It felt good to an old bachelor's empty stomach."

She flushed with pleasure "You probably have women chasing after you all the time."

Noah grinned and shrugged. "I got my share."

Jealousy ripped through Priscilla and she quickly turned away to hide it. "The children will be waking up soon."

"Send 'em out later and I'll play ball with 'em."

Priscilla's heart almost burst with love. She turned back to Noah and smiled. "You're wonderful to play with them!"

"I figure kids need grown-ups to give 'em time or they have real problems when they grow up."

Why didn't Justin know that? She'd begged him to spend time with the children, but he was always too busy. "I'll send them out later, Noah. Thanks."

"You can come, too. Can you play ball?"

Priscilla laughed. "I haven't played in a long time."

"Then come on out." Noah caught her hand and squeezed it. Her very bones melted. His eyes softened and he squeezed her hand again. "Thanks for breakfast and for the fine talk. See you later outdoors." He strode out and she stood there with her hands pressed to her heart and her eyes sparkling.

* * *

Emily sank to the edge of her bed and groaned. She'd asked Lark to care for Rachel—Emily had a lot to do to get ready for her wedding the next day. Lark had quickly agreed. She was delighted that Trent was marrying Emily. "What have I done?" she whispered hoarsely.

The room suddenly seemed to close in on her. For twenty-five years this had been her bedroom. Three times she'd changed the wallpaper, curtains, and bedspread. Now lavender floral wallpaper covered the walls. White lacy curtains hung at the two windows. She'd made three small lavender pillows to use as decoration with the white pillows on her white bedspread. A large crystal vase full of lavender and white lilacs stood on her dresser, filling the room with their fragrance. After tomorrow this would no longer be her bedroom. Lars would change the room into a boy's room.

The door opened and Martha stuck in her head. "Can I come in?"

Emily nodded.

"You look like you've lost your last friend," Martha said as she sat on the bed beside Emily.

"I'm scared, Mama. Why did I agree to marry Trent?"

"Because you knew it was the right thing to do."

"Is it?"

"You wouldn't marry him if it weren't right."

"I don't know, Mama."

"He needs you, honey."

Emily sighed heavily. That was true. "But how can I get packed and ready by tomorrow?"

"That's why I'm here."

"You sure want to get rid of me, don't you?"

"No. I just want your going to be pleasant for both of us." Martha laughed as she walked to the dresser and pulled open the top drawer. "I'm doubly happy because you've given me a granddaughter without a waiting period."

Emily laughed and felt better. She opened the large trunk her brothers had brought to her room. "Mama, what do you really think about Jennet Havlick's idea for the pines?"

Martha turned from emptying a drawer. "I guess it'll work. I don't care for all those people that'll come traipsing around, though. Neither will your father. He likes his life the way it is."

"Sometimes change is good."

"Not when it makes you lose your privacy."

"I didn't think about that." Emily brushed a cobweb off the trunk.

"Jennet walked the line with your pa this morning. He's always glad for the company, but he says she's not as careful as she once was. Her reactions are slower because of her age. It's dangerous. But she won't listen to your pa."

"I heard Free tell her to take someone with her when she goes, but she usually doesn't."

Martha shook her head. "She loves the pines."

"That she does. It will be nice for others to enjoy the pines like we have all these years."

"I guess." Martha grinned as she held the blouse against her that she'd been folding. "I could take photographs of them with my new Buster Brown box camera and make pictures to sell. That way everyone could enjoy the view without coming here and bothering anyone."

"And we could send them pine needles so they could enjoy the smell," Emily giggled. "But that's not what Jennet has in mind."

"I know." Martha sighed and shook her head. "I think your pa might decide to take us all to Sweden to live to get away from the crowds of people."

"Who would guard the pines?"

"Who'll guard them once they're open to the public?"

Emily shook her head. "It will be hard to keep people from ruining the place. Jennet probably has it all thought out. She's a pretty bright lady." Emily pulled a box from under her bed and opened it. It held her treasures from childhood. She rummaged through the box, smiling at the memories its treasures brought back. She found a love note Celine had written to Trent when she was about thirteen years old. Emily pressed the note to her heart as she remembered the day Celine had written it. They were standing outside the school house after school.

"*You* give it to him, Emily," Celine had said breathlessly, her cheeks as red as her hair. "I just can't!"

Emily had laughed and had taken the note. "It won't bother me to give it to him."

"Then tell me exactly what he says and how he looks. Tell me every single detail!"

"I will."

Celine ran down the street toward the orphan home, then suddenly raced back. Her face was as white as the clouds in

the sky. "I changed my mind, Emily. Don't give it to him. He might laugh. Or hate me. I am only an orphan. And he's a Havlick!"

"He won't hate you. And you're every bit as good as a Havlick!"

"No, I'm only an orphan. Tear up the note. Please!"

"All right."

Celine breathed a sigh of relief. "You're my very best friend, Emily, and you always will be."

"You're my very best friend and you always will be." Emily tucked the note inside her grammar book as Celine dashed away. At home she'd hidden the note in her special box in case Celine changed her mind. But she never did.

Now Emily opened the note.

"What is it?" Martha asked softly.

"A note from Celine to Trent."

"Read it to me, will you?"

Emily took a deep, steadying breath. "Trent, you are the best looking boy in all of Blue Creek, probably in all of Michigan. Do you like me for more than a friend? Does it embarrass you to have an orphan for a friend? The next time we go for a walk in the woods, will you hold my hand? Would it embarrass you to hold an orphan's hand? I would be happy and proud to hold your hand. Love. Celine."

Martha brushed tears from her eyes. "She was a precious girl. Rachel might like to have the note."

"I'll save it for her." Emily refolded it slowly, her mind still on Celine.

Martha sat on the edge of the bed and patted a spot beside her. "Sit down a while, honey."

Emily hesitated, but finally sat down. She knew Mama wanted to say something serious, but she didn't know if she was ready to hear it.

"Honey, I know you and Trent love each other and have for years."

"As friends, Mama."

"I know." Martha took Emily's hand in hers. They both had callused hands from hard work. "Don't be afraid to open your heart to a deeper love."

Emily gasped and shook her head. "It wouldn't be right!"

"Yes, it would. Celine is in heaven with Jesus. She wouldn't feel hurt if you grew to love Trent as a wife should love her husband."

"Trent and I are happy to leave it the way it is."

"There'll come a day when you won't be happy with only friendship. Friendship is wonderful and it's important, but it's only the beginning. Passionate love should be part of marriage. Don't feel guilty when you find your love growing deeper."

Emily flushed painfully. "I don't want to talk about it."

"You're going to live a long way from me, Emily. I need to tell you things now so when it happens you'll be able to handle it."

"It's not going to happen. Trent will never stop loving Celine."

"I know that. But that love will change. It'll become only a memory." Martha frowned. "It should be already. I don't understand what's keeping him from getting on with his life."

Emily knew it was his great anger at Justin and his great love for Celine, but she didn't say so. She didn't say anything about her great love for Bob Lavery either.

Martha wrapped her arms around Emily and held her close. "I want God's best for you, honey. I'll pray for you every single day. You remember that when you're way down in Texas."

"I'll remember," Emily said with a catch in her voice. She clung to Mama, suddenly afraid to let her go. She smelled Mama's skin that often smelled like vanilla and felt her soft hair against her cheek. Finally she pulled away. "I love you."

"I love you, too." Martha jumped up and wiped away her

tears with the corner of her apron. "It's almost time for you to meet Trent in town to get the marriage license."

Emily's heart jerked strangely. A marriage license!

* * *

At the Wagon Works Trent forced himself to stand beside Justin's large oak desk without breaking Justin's nose. Most of the factory noise was muffled by the closed door. Justin poised a pencil over a pad of paper as he looked up at Trent.

"I'll agree with anyone you suggest," Trent said impatiently. It took all his willpower to keep his temper. "It doesn't matter to me."

Justin snapped the pencil between his fingers. It was hard to be in the same room with Trent. "You are as much responsible for the pines as I am! If I had my way, we'd lumber them and be done with it!"

"That's fine by me!" Trent snarled. The pines meant nothing to him at this time. All he could think about was getting away from Justin, away from Blue Creek, and away from his painful memories.

Justin slammed his fist down on his desk, making the pad of paper jump. "But we can't do that, can we? We must do what Grandma wants."

A muscle jerked in Trent's jaw. Justin shoved back his chair and stood. They both wore white shirts and dark pants. Trent's dark tan and Justin's lack of one was the only difference in their looks. The tension mounted.

"I think Andree Bjoerling would be the best man for the job," Justin said in a crisp voice.

Trent cocked his brows and nodded. "I wouldn't have thought of him, but I agree. I think the family will, too." He pushed his hands deep into his pockets and hunched his shoulders. "I told Mom and Dad this already; Emily and I are going to get married tomorrow. We're taking Rachel and going back to Texas Wednesday."

Justin whistled in surprise. "You and Emily. I always thought there was something between you two."

"There wasn't! Only friendship."

"But she agreed to marry you."

"It's convenient for both of us." Trent turned toward the door. "Let's talk to Andree and be done with it."

"I've sent someone after him already. He should be here shortly."

Trent shrugged. He didn't want to wait even a minute longer alone with Justin.

Justin strode around the desk. "Aren't you interested in the Wagon Works at all?"

"No."

"We build chairs now," Justin said impatiently.

Trent turned in surprise. "How come?"

Justin forced his temper down. "Wagons aren't selling like they did before the war. There are fewer farms, you know. Since we have men here who know how to work with wood, I decided to go into building chairs. Simple kitchen chairs made of oak. I've built up quite a business. Every family needs chairs whether they live in town or the country."

"Chairs. That's a good idea."

"We need more lumber to fill an order that came in a few days ago. Oak, we need. Lots of it."

"You'll find it."

Justin's eyes flashed with anger. "Sure I will. I always do, don't I? I always have the answer. I always have the money."

Trent cleared his throat. "I know I said I wouldn't take any money from the business, but since I can't sell the pines for the money I need to buy the ranch, I want to know how much money is mine."

"It's all in a savings account at the bank," Justin said gruffly. The first few years he'd gladly put the money away for Trent, but as time passed and he had to work long, hard hours because Trent was gone, he'd grown very angry at sharing profits with an absent partner. Several times he'd even considered using the money, but his pride wouldn't allow him to. "Ten years' worth of money is a good piece of change."

"I told you not to do that! I never wanted anything from you."

"Dad worked the business too, so don't think it's me giving you a hand-out. You don't deserve one! You don't even deserve the money I put away for you. But it belongs to you as a Havlick. It's in the bank in your name."

Trent desperately wanted to refuse the money, but it was the only way to buy the Rocking R. "I'll get it before we leave." He couldn't bring himself to thank Justin.

Someone knocked and Justin opened the door. Andree stood there with his hat in his hands. He wore denim pants and a blue plaid shirt with wide black suspenders. His blue eyes crinkled as he smiled.

"Andree, come right in," Justin said.

"I'm glad to see you boys together." Andree shook hands with them, then sat beside the desk. Trent sat beside him while Justin returned to his chair behind the desk. "What business is so important that it can't wait until daylight is gone?" He'd planned to work all day in the fields after his daily trip through the pines to make sure the trees were safe from vandals.

"Grandma has probably told you all about her plans for the pines," Justin said.

Andree nodded.

"We want you to be in charge of it," Trent said.

Andree's eyes widened in surprise.

Justin fingered the broken pencil. "We'll pay you well."

"Money's not everything, boys," Andree snapped as he stabbed his fingers through his graying hair. "Them trees are almost as important to me as to your family. I don't like the idea of letting folks traipse through them woods and destroy all that I've been protecting. Your grandma don't think folks would pick the flowers or carve initials on the trees or throw trash in the streams, but I know better. I've seen how people are. I sure don't like the idea."

Justin hadn't expected Andree to be against the plan. "If you were in charge of getting the place done the way Grandma wants, you'd be able to keep people from destroying the trees."

"You'd be able to hire guards to keep the trees safe," Trent said.

Andree scowled and shook his head. "I don't like to tell you boys no, but I must. I don't want folks to have free access to the trees!"

"They wouldn't," Justin said, forcing back his mounting impatience. "Nobody could go out without a guide. *You* can hire the guides. Men you trust."

"Talk to Martha about it," Trent said. "Let us know tomorrow."

Andree smiled in relief. "That's what I'll do. I don't know if I can think about anything but my daughter getting married and leaving us." He slapped Trent on the leg. "Why don't you stay here, Trent? This is your home. If you want to raise beef cattle, do it here. You have enough land to feed a lot of cattle."

Trent's stomach knotted. He couldn't stay even if he wanted. It was too painful. "I have my heart set on the Rocking R, Andree."

Justin locked his hands around the arms of his chair. He couldn't tolerate having Trent here to remind him of what he'd done to Celine.

"I sure wish you'd stay," Andree said.

Justin stood up "He's made up his mind. There's no changing it." He walked around to Andree and clamped his hand on his shoulder. "I hope you take the job. If you don't will you suggest someone? Grandma's set on having her way in this, so we'll see that it happens."

Andree sighed loudly. "You're sure right about her having

her heart set on what she calls Havlick's Wilderness. She was even talking about building cabins to rent out to folks who want to stay a week or two at a time. And a big resort cabin for rich folks with servants to wait on 'em."

"I didn't hear that part of the plan," Justin said.

"She even has the place picked out for the cabins," Andree said. "She told me this morning. It's by Deep Lake—the area covered mostly with oaks."

"I didn't know we had oaks," Justin said, alert and eager to hear more. "We need oak for chairs. I think I'll take a trip out there and check them out."

"Best way to go is drive up to Fromberg and take a boat across Deep Lake. You can get a clear view of the oaks and pines," Andree said. "I'd say there's about a hundred acres of oaks."

"I've never been in that part of the woods," Trent said. He and Celine had had a special spot near the creek where they sat and talked many times. A picture of them together flashed across his mind, and he bit back a groan of despair.

"We could use the oak," Justin said. He'd been wondering about cutting corners. Using their own lumber would save a fortune for them. Now with Grandma's plan for the woods, he wouldn't have to fight the family and Andree to cut trees. "We'll plan to take out only the trees that need removing to make room for the cabins."

Andree slapped his knee and stood up. "Boys, I've made up my mind. I'll take the job. I'd rather have the say about what trees come out than some stranger."

"Good!" Justin and Trent said together. They both reached to shake Andree's hand at the same time, and their hands brushed together. Both jerked as if they'd been snakebitten. They glanced at each other, then looked quickly away.

*   *   *

With a warm breeze flipping her long dark hair, Emily walked toward town, her head buzzing with what her future held. She stood on the bridge and looked down into Blue River. Water rushed between the tree-lined banks. Two ragged-looking boys fished off one bank, intently watching their lines. She'd learned to swim in the river when she was six. She and Celine had sneaked away when they were all having a picnic and Celine had taught her to swim.

"Just move your arms and legs like this," Celine shouted over the splashes she was making. "You can do it."

"I might drown." Emily was afraid of water because she'd fallen in over her head once when she was wading.

"I won't let you drown," Celine said. She held Emily around the waist. "Just lay down in the water and keep your face turned sideways. You can do it."

And she had. They'd both been proud, but couldn't tell anyone but Trent. They knew he wouldn't tattle.

After that they'd gone often. Many times Trent was with them. In her mind she heard their giggles and the splash of water. But that was a long time ago.

With a sigh she walked away from the bridge and past the lumber mill. The buzz of the saws cut off the sounds of the birds and even the sound of the train racing past. She glanced down the street that led to the orphanage where Lark had lived all her life until she'd married Clay and where Celine had lived until she married Trent.

"Oh, Celine. Do you mind that I'm marrying Trent?"

Emily walked down Main Street toward the courthouse. Lark and Clay had probably stayed home today to be with Rachel. It was going to be very hard on them to have Rachel leave them.

Emily's tan skirt flipped about her legs as she walked up the sidewalk to the large brick courthouse. Neatly trimmed grass wrapped around the building with flower beds scattered here and there, some in bloom and others waiting for summer. She brushed her shimmering raven hair over her shoulder with the back of her hand, then fingered the pearl brooch at the neck of her green blouse. She spotted Trent outside the courthouse. He looked handsome in his white shirt and dark pants. His hair was combed neatly. Should she tell him she'd changed her mind?

She considered it for a minute, but didn't. She walked to him, smiling hesitantly. She noticed the white skin showing near his sideburns. "It looks like you just came from the barber."

"Sure did," Trent said with a laugh. After he'd left Justin and Andree, he'd gone to the bank to see about his money, then right to the barber. He wanted to look his best for his wedding. His heart lurched, but he ignored it. He'd set his course and nothing would change his mind.

"Justin," called a man from the sidewalk.

Trent and Emily turned at the same time. Sheriff Lamont stood there with his hands resting lightly on his hips. He was in his forties and was beginning to get a paunch.

"Afternoon, Emily," the sheriff said, then he turned to Trent. "I'd like a word with you, Justin."

Trent frowned impatiently.

"This is Trent Havlick," Emily said. "Justin's twin. Trent, Spud Lamont."

"Trent, you say!" Sheriff Lamont lifted his hat to scratch his balding head. His hook nose was large on his narrow face. "Well, I'll be."

"Justin's at the Wagon Works if you want to speak to him," Trent said stiffly.

"You'll do just fine." Sheriff Lamont walked to them, his hazel eyes narrowed. "I heard a rumor a few minutes ago."

"What's that, Sheriff?" Emily knew he liked gossip as well as anyone. And he spread more than his fair share.

Sheriff Lamont settled his hat in place on his head. "About Jennet Havlick's plans for the pines."

Trent didn't want to take the time to talk about it, but he said, "We're going to make the woods into a nature preserve and logging museum. In fact, Grandma even plans on putting cabins in over by Deep Lake."

Sheriff Lamont clicked his tongue. "That sure sounds like more work for me, what with more people around. But I guess it means more money for the town merchants, so I can't complain. Just when will all this come about?"

"As soon as possible." Trent took Emily's arm as he turned to walk into the courthouse.

"Good luck," Sheriff Lamont said. "Nice meeting you, Havlick. It's always good to have another Havlick around."

Emily started to turn to tell the sheriff about them getting married and leaving, but Trent tugged on her to keep walking. She glanced at him from the corner of her eyes. He looked very determined. A shiver slipped down her spine.

The wooden floor of the courthouse was polished to a shine that reflected anything or anyone on it. Several closed doors lined the halls that went off the main entry. Voices drifted down the hall to Emily's left. A spittoon stood in one corner, a tall green plant in another. Pictures of lumbering in its heyday lined the walls.

Trent leaned his head close to Emily's ear and whispered, "If I hear another word about Grandma's plans, I'll belt somebody! I'm tired of the whole thing. I just want to get back to Texas where I belong."

Emily grinned. "You just didn't like being called Justin. Admit it."

Trent tapped Emily on the tip of her nose. "You think you're smart when you're right, don't you?"

"Of course."

"I was getting used to being the only Havlick around." Trent flung his arm wide. "Now here I am with Havlicks all over the place, and to make matters worse, there's one who looks just like me."

"No, Trent. You're much better looking," Emily said, laughing up at him.

He shook his head and chuckled. "You always know what to say, don't you?"

"Of course. The clerk's office is this way," Emily said, leading Trent toward it.

"I have news for you that might leave you speechless."

"Oh?"

"Your pa has agreed to head the project for Grandma. He said better him than a stranger who doesn't care about the trees."

"I am surprised," Emily said, her blue eyes wide. "Ma said he's against the whole thing. He'll do a good job, though. He loves those trees as much as the Havlick family does."

Trent's throat closed over. Once he'd loved the trees, but now he didn't care if he ever walked in them again. "Let's stop talking about the trees and get our marriage license."

Emily's stomach cramped, but she smiled and walked to the office with Trent, her head high and her shoulders square. She'd made up her mind and nothing was going to change it.

CHAPTER

7

♦ Jennet leaned against Free as they stood on the porch after supper, looking across the field toward the white pines. The temperature had dropped slightly and the breeze was pleasantly cool. The wind brought the constant aroma of pine along with an occasional whiff of the barnyard. The blades on the windmill squawked as they turned. A horse whinnied and another answered. Tears pricked Jennet's blue eyes as she looked up at Free. Sighing, she asked, "Is my dream too big?"

Free turned her to him and kissed her gently. "No, Jen. It isn't too big. It's a wonderful dream, and we're going to make it come true."

At seventy-four Jennet was as beautiful to him as she had been at sixteen. He'd bought her from a cruel uncle to whom she'd been indentured by her equally cruel father. Then when he'd learned he had to be married to inherit what his grandfather had left him, he'd married her. The marriage had started off rocky, but before the first year was over, they were deeply in love. They had six children; Clay, the eldest, had married Lark Baritt more than thirty years ago and she had given them the twins—Trent and Justin.

"I want to see Havlick's Wilderness finished before I die."

Jennet cupped her hand along Free's clean-shaven cheek. His sun-browned skin was etched with wrinkles and his once dark brown hair was gray. She saw the love in his dark eyes and it touched her deeply. He'd give her anything she asked for if he could. "Are you sure I'm not asking too much?"

"It'll take a lot of money—money we planned to leave to the great-grandchildren."

Jennet's blue eyes clouded. "I don't care how much money it takes! I want others to share the beauty we've preserved! Am I being selfish?"

"No, Jen. We all agreed to do it."

"Do you think any of the neighbors or the folks in town will object?"

"Why should they? We'll do our best to make sure nobody's privacy is invaded. And the merchants in town will be glad for the business. Tourism is growing in Michigan. Why not bring some of those folks here?"

"That's what I say!"

Free chuckled. "I know." They'd had the same discussion before, but Jennet seemed to need reassurance. She didn't want to do anything to cause harm to another person. "We'll call a meeting and talk to other farmers and the merchants. Then we'll know how they feel."

"Good idea." She stood quietly for a while. "The twins don't care about the pines." A tear slipped down her cheek. "But I *want* them to care! I want them to feel the same passion for the trees that we have!" She flicked away her tear and rubbed her hand down her flowered dress. "I thought working together on the project would do it for them. But they gave it over to Andree! I love Andree and I know he'll do a good job. But I want Trent and Justin to do it! Together! Oh, why can't they feel for the pines the way we do?"

Free held Jennet close and rested his cheek against her white hair. "They didn't get involved with them like we did and Clay and Lark did. Lark guarded the pines and grew to love them. She took the boys to the pines when they were young, and they seemed to love them. But something happened when Celine died that drove the boys apart. If they'd give themselves a chance, they'd learn to care about the trees again."

"Yes, I'm sure of it!" Jennet pulled back from Free and spread her hands over the front of his blue work shirt. "I'm thankful Trent's going to marry Emily. Maybe she can convince him to stay here.

"I have a wedding gift for them. That's why I asked them to come this evening."

Free glanced at his gold watch, then slipped it back in his pocket. "They should be here any minute."

Jennet walked to a white rocker and sank down, her legs suddenly too tired to support her. "I had an architect draw plans for the cabins I want over at Deep Lake. Did I show them to you?"

"Yes," Free chuckled. "Twice." He patted her hand as he sat in the rocker beside her.

She laughed and wrinkled her nose at him. "You'll have to be patient with me. Occasionally I forget little details, but I still remember the important things! It's strange that sometimes I feel only twenty, then other times, I think I'm way over a hundred. It's a good thing we live by faith, not feelings."

They rocked in silence a while.

"I want the main cabin to be a place rich folks from Chicago and Detroit would come to and spend a couple of weeks or even the whole summer. If city folks could stay in our pines and rest and relax and take in the beauty and the serenity, they'd go back refreshed and ready to work again."

Free had heard it all before. Jennet had begun to describe to him her dream of Havlick's Wilderness some time ago. He knew it had been on her mind most of the time as she gradually envisioned a plan. And he was certain she'd shared her dream only with him. But now that she'd told the family and most of them had gotten excited about it, she needed to talk and he let her. She liked describing the small cabins for folks with modest income and the big cabin for wealthy people. And when she did, he could imagine it, too. She liked talking about her big dream. Often they'd sat on the porch after dinner and talked about it, getting eventually to the past. Jennet had helped free slaves through the underground railroad when they were first married. Those memories of danger and struggle would live again as they talked and he would remember his struggle making it as a lumberman. They would remember Jig, the old woodsman who could spout Bible verses as easily as he could name trees and birds. And they often spoke of the covenant they had with God and each other. Although their life together hadn't always been easy, it had been a good life. As Free listened to the soft melody of Jennet's voice, he was content. If only Justin and Trent could come to terms with whatever had driven a wedge between them . . .

A cloud of dust billowed on the road leading to the farm, and Free shook his head at the sight of it. If he had his way, everyone would still be driving horses and buggies. The new gas buggies made too much noise and too much dust and they left unpleasant odors hanging in the air. He wondered briefly if they could ban automobiles from Havlick's Wilderness. Then he supposed the family wouldn't allow it. They were all busy becoming modern. He still hated to admit that Clay had been right to get out of the buggy-making business and into making wagons, something many people would still need even when use of the gas buggy had become popular

"It's Trent and Emily," Jennet said, smiling as she slowly stood, shaking her cotton dress so it fell in graceful folds to her ankles. She made sure the cuffs of the long sleeves were still buttoned, then tucked a strand of hair into the bun at the nape of her neck. She walked down the porch steps with Free close behind her and stood in the yard to wait for them. Silently she prayed for Trent. She wanted God's covenant to be as real to him as it was to her. She wanted him to know all of God's promises were true and were for him. She turned to Free. "Remember when the twins were about ten years old and they made a covenant with each other just the way the Bible tells about the one Jonathan and David made?"

Free smiled and nodded. "They even pricked their fingers with a needle and smeared their blood together. They vowed to fight for each other, take care of each other, and always love each other."

"I think I'll remind Trent of that."

"Better not. He's too angry right now to be reminded. Let's pray for them both, and when the time's right, we'll bring it up."

"You're always right, Free." Jennet smiled at him, then turned to watch Trent and Emily walk from the blue Dodge toward them. Trent was wearing a white shirt and dark pants and Emily a peachy-pink dress that Jennet thought was much too short. Her long hair curled over her shoulders. Jennet was glad Emily had sense enough to leave it long, and not get it bobbed like Priscilla had hers.

"Hello, Grandma," Trent said, hugging her. She smelled the same to him, like bayberry soap. "Grandpa." He hugged Free, too, as Emily went into Jennet's arms. Grandpa smelled the same too, like sawdust and sweat.

They talked about the pleasant May weather and how the plans were coming along for their wedding the next day. Then Jennet asked Trent and Emily to sit on the porch on the bench between pots of ivy facing the rockers.

"I want to tell you both about my wedding gift," Jennet said as she slowly sank in her rocker and smoothed her long skirt over her knees. She refused to wear the new short style, and sewed her own clothes so she could make the skirts as long as she wanted.

"We don't expect gifts," Trent said as he and Emily settled on the bench.

Emily nodded her agreement as she folded her hands in her

lap and crossed her ankles. Gifts would embarrass her since this wasn't a usual marriage. "Please, no gifts," she said.

"You might as well make up your minds to take this gift," Free said with a chuckle. "Your grandma is determined. I know—she told me." It had taken Jennet years to find the courage to speak her own mind. Now she had no trouble letting everyone know her thoughts. She was even known to raise her voice now and then.

Smiling, Jennet nodded as she folded her hands in her lap. "I am giving you two hundred acres of land that joins the property you already own, Trent."

He flushed and shook his head. "Don't do it, Grandma," he said sharply He knew she was trying to get him to stay. "I can't take it! I don't intend to live on that place again."

"Don't be so hasty, young man!" Frowning, Jennet leaned forward. "You don't know that you won't live there again. So, don't be so quick to turn down my gift. I am giving you that land."

Emily looked from Jennet to Trent and saw the identical stubborn set of their jaws. She knew Trent was sincere in refusing Jennet's gift, and she knew Jennet was sincere in saying she would give it.

"The gift is very nice," Emily said with a warm smile. "If we do take it, we'll sign it over to Rachel so that the land stays in the family."

"Do as you want." Jennet fought against tears of disappointment. "I just know I am giving it to you. It's almost covered with second-growth trees, and it has a wide valley that would be perfect for running beef cattle. And there's a spring-fed stream running through the place, so you'd always have plenty of water."

Trent tensed, but Emily's hand on his arm served to calm him. "Please try to understand, Grandma. I can't stay here. I have a life at the Rocking R Ranch. That's where I belong now."

"You're a Havlick!" Jennet jumped to her feet, her eyes blazing. Free tried to restrain her, but she brushed him aside. "You belong here, Trent! I don't know why you would ever think you don't."

Emily gripped Trent's arm so tightly she was sure she left nail prints in his skin. "We'll come back for visits," Emily said hastily.

Jennet shook her finger at Trent and cried, "This is Havlick land and a Havlick should tend it! Let Texas be tamed by someone who belongs there."

Free stood quickly and pulled Jennet firmly to his side. "Jen, calm down. Things are starting to get out of hand. Trent, accept the gift like a man."

Trent shook his head. "I will not take it! And I mean that. Give it to someone else."

Jennet's nostrils flared and she jerked away from Free. "All right. I'll do just that!" Her eyes locked on Trent's face, she studied him intently. After what seemed an eternity, she said, "I will give the land to Emily. She's going to be your wife, but a woman needs something of her own." Jennet had bought that very piece of land with money Free's grandpa had left her. She firmly believed other women should have the same opportunity. Jennet pointed at Emily. "It's yours."

Emily looked at Trent as if to ask what she should do.

"Don't you dare!" he snapped. How he longed to be back in Texas where he didn't have to face his family or his feelings.

Emily frowned slightly. His anger both alarmed and angered her. Why was he being so pig-headed? But telling her not to accept it was like saying "sic 'em" to a bulldog. She lifted her chin and turned to Jennet. "I'm honored to accept your generous gift, Jennet. Thank you."

Trent scowled at Emily. "What do you think you're doing?"

"Accepting your grandma's gift the way you should have."

He sputtered angrily, then stormed off the porch toward his automobile.

"He's angry." Emily fingered the brooch at her throat. Should she refuse the gift for Trent's sake?

"He'll get over it," Free said softly.

"He has to," Jennet said.

Trent stood beside his Dodge, his back stiff with anger. How dare Emily accept the land after he'd refused to? This was not the time to prove she had a mind of her own! Trent turned and impatiently called, "Emily! Are you coming or not?"

"She's not." Jennet caught Emily's arm. "She has papers to sign."

"I'll wait here." Trent slipped under the steering wheel, his head buzzing with sharp, angry words. He should never have returned home! He could've sent a telegram asking for money.

Emily followed Jennet and Freeman into their study where Jennet had spread out the papers to be signed and the deed for the land.

As Free held a pen out to her, she said, "Maybe I shouldn't."

Jennet tapped Emily's shoulder. "This is right, dear. Go ahead."

"Trent will get over it," Free said.

"You're right of course." Emily signed and dated the papers and put the deed in her purse. "Thank you, Jen. Free. This'll be Rachel's someday."

"No." Jennet shook her head. "It isn't for Rachel. I want it to go to your first son."

Emily turned crimson red. "As you wish." After today Trent might be so angry there wouldn't be a first son or any other children.

Several minutes later, Emily said goodbye and joined Trent in his blue Dodge. He drove away without waving to his grandparents. A huge cloud of dust billowed behind them, and the tires skidded as he turned on the gravel road.

"Why did you do it?" he asked through clenched teeth.

Emily shrugged. "Because it made Jennet happy." She jabbed Trent's arm. "It won't do you a bit of good to have a fit or pout or anything. The land is mine. So, that's that."

His nostrils flared in anger. "Have you always been this high-handed?"

"Probably."

He slapped the steering wheel with one hand. "How did Celine and I put up with you?"

Emily laughed, but it sounded strained. "You loved me. And I love you. That's how *I* put up with *you*."

"Emily, I don't know about you."

"Well, I certainly wasn't going to hurt your grandparents just because you're afraid you might be forced to stay here."

"I will not stay here!"

"I know. So relax, will you? Taking the land won't make us stay here."

His anger drained away and he chuckled as he carefully passed a pickup. "You're right, I guess."

"As usual."

He chuckled again. "I had forgotten"

"Don't let it happen again" She grinned at him and made a face.

"I think we just might end up having a very good marriage. Maybe friendship is more important than a grand passion."

"Maybe." Emily cleared her throat. Now was the time to discuss the delicate topic she'd been thinking about. She flushed as she said, "I want to say something but it's embarrassing to me."

"So?" He cocked his brow and glanced at her, then turned back to the road. "What is it?"

"Can we wait . . . to share . . . a bed . . . until we . . . get to Texas?"

He slowed the automobile, frowning. She never ceased to surprise him. "Why?"

"A new start in a new place." She fingered a fold of her skirt. "It'll be . . . easier for me."

Trent hesitated, then shrugged. "If that's what you want." Maybe it would be best. Maybe he wouldn't feel so guilty about sleeping with Celine's best friend once they were far away from here.

Emily sighed in relief. "Thanks."

He chuckled as he speeded back up. "You sure do embarrass easily, don't you?"

"Yes, about some things."

Trent laughed. "Good. Now I know just what to tease you about."

"Tease away. But if you can dish it out," she wagged her finger at him, "you'd better be ready and able to take it."

Trent laughed. She always could hold her own with him. "Bob Lavery was stupid not to marry you."

She turned away as sudden tears filled her eyes. For a while she'd actually forgotten Bob.

*   *   *

Tuesday at five in the little anteroom at the church Emily clung to a bouquet of lavender and white lilacs and lily of the valley. The Havlick and Bjoerling families along with a few selected friends sat in the sanctuary waiting. Organ music filled the air. Rachel, so excited she thought she couldn't wait, was squirming. Lark shushed her with a soft pat on her leg.

Clay smiled at Lark as he thought of their wedding day. He'd married her so he wouldn't lose the pines. He had mortgaged them to finance his business and was about to default on the loan. Willie Thorne was waiting to pounce when Lark's father turned up after a long, long absence and gave Clay the money he needed. But he said that to have the money, Clay must convince Lark to marry him. Feeling like a first-class cad, he'd done it. To his surprise, he'd discovered he loved her with a passion that startled him. He'd always wondered how Matt

Baritt knew something about him he didn't know himself. However Matt knew, Clay would be forever grateful. He couldn't imagine living his life without Lark.

Justin ran his finger around his collar and longed to be back at his desk working. He didn't want to see Trent or have to think about him. He glanced at Priscilla beside him and his pulse quickened. She looked beautiful and smelled like roses. After Trent left, maybe he'd make more time for Pris.

Priscilla moved closer to Justin as she remembered their wedding. They had married ten years ago, just after Trent left. They said their vows in this very church, and then went to Grand Haven for a honeymoon cruise. It was very romantic. Justin gave her his full attention and never once mentioned the Wagon Works. They were happy then. She'd almost given up hope they would ever be happy again. She glanced at their children to make sure they were sitting quietly. After the long lecture she'd given them, they were behaving.

With tears glistening in her eyes, Martha sat with her sons, leaving a space for Andree to sit beside her after he walked Emily down the aisle. They'd telephoned Betty and Lucille, with news of the wedding, but neither could come on such short notice. Betty's baby was due shortly and Lucille's husband couldn't leave his work. Martha prayed silently for her children, especially for Emily on this very special day.

Free slipped his arm around Jennet. He was remembering their wedding day. It had been a spur of the moment wedding and they were both dressed in work clothes. He prayed Trent and Emily would grow to love each other as much as they did.

Short and balding, Pastor Gray approached the altar with Trent walking behind him. Trent's spine tingled as he realized what he was doing, but it was too late to back out. The music swelled as the organist played the Wedding March.

Her stomach fluttering wildly, Emily slipped her hand through her father's arm and they walked down the aisle to join Trent. Emily had chosen a simple white dress and a roll brim,

white, silk-velvet hat. There hadn't been time to get an elabo-
rate gown even if she'd wanted one.

A pain shot through Trent as he thought of the day Celine
had walked toward him down the same aisle. He'd been happier than he'd ever thought possible. This time was different.
He wasn't expected to be happy. He wore a plain black suit
that he'd bought just that morning for the occasion. He managed to smile at Emily and she relaxed enough to smile back.

She listened intently as Pastor Gray read the ceremony and
then asked them to speak their vows to each other. Trent's
voice cracked twice, but Emily managed to keep hers even and
strong. Inside she was quivering, but she didn't let that show.
As they exchanged vows, she remembered that Trent and Celine had exchanged the same vows, and she paled. What was
she doing marrying Celine's husband?

At the correct time Trent slipped a wide silver wedding band
on her finger and she glanced up at him in surprise. She hadn't
thought about a ring, and she was surprised he had. Celine's
wedding ring had been gold with three diamonds. It was in safe
keeping for Rachel when she came of age. Emily stared at the
wide silver band. Trent had actually taken the time to buy her
a ring! A thrill shot through her.

At the end of the ceremony, Pastor Gray said, "You may
kiss the bride," and Emily tensed. Her eyes opened wide in
alarm as she met Trent's gaze. He stiffened, then brushed his
lips against hers so quickly she barely felt the kiss.

"I'm proud to present Mr. and Mrs. Trent Havlick!" Pastor
Gray said in a ringing voice. Organ music erupted in the silence, and Emily clung to Trent's arm as they fled down the
aisle to wait outdoors to be congratulated. Emily had planned
to drive right to Clay and Lark's home for wedding cake and
punch, but Martha had insisted they greet their families and
friends on the church lawn.

The guests swarmed from the church into the late afternoon

sunshine. Rachel dashed away from Lark toward Trent and Emily.

Suddenly a shot rang out. Rachel screamed and dropped to the ground. Women screamed and men shouted.

Emily swayed against Trent. Why had someone shot at them? What was happening? Maybe the shooter would shoot again.

Sweat soaking his body, Trent dragged Emily behind a giant oak. "Stay here!" he commanded and ran to Rachel, his heart racing, expecting a bullet to tear into his body. He scooped up Rachel in his arms and sped back to duck behind the tree with Emily while the others shouted to him to be careful.

"Is Rachel hurt?" Lark screamed as she huddled with the others at the side of the church building.

"We're all right," Trent shouted. Then he saw blood on Rachel and sank weakly to his knees. "She's been shot!"

Frantically Emily examined Rachel and saw she'd been wounded in her shoulder, her arm, and her leg. She was unconscious. Emily prayed that Rachel had only fainted from pain and fear.

"She's not dead," Emily called as she used her handkerchief to staunch the blood flowing from Rachel's shoulder. "But she needs a doctor."

"Oh, Rachel!" Lark screamed, struggling to run to her, but Clay held her back.

At the side of the church, Justin pulled Priscilla and the children close to him. "What is going on?" he wondered aloud. Who had shot at them and why? This was not the wild, wooly days of lumbering!

"Who shot that gun?" Freeman barked.

"I did!" a man shouted from behind a clump of bushes across the street from the church. "I didn't mean for nobody to get hurt. I just want all you Havlicks to listen to me!"

"Get a doctor! And the sheriff," Trent called frantically as he looked down on Rachel's pale face and the blood flowing freely. He couldn't lose his daughter now that he'd found her.

"Don't nobody move or I will shoot *to kill*," the man shouted.

"Everyone stay put!" Free cried.

"What's going on?" Justin shouted. "What do you want?"

"I'm tryin' to tell you!"

Trent looked helplessly at Emily.

She smelled his sweat and saw the pain in his eyes. "Who would shoot at us?" she whispered.

"I don't know, but I'll find out." Trent took a deep, steadying breath. "Then tell us so we can get my little girl to a doctor! She's bleeding bad!"

"I came to warn you not to build that tourist trap you're planning. We want things left the way they are."

"What business is it of yours?" Jennet cried, alarmed that anyone would want to cause them harm just because of her dream.

"I made it my business!" the man roared. He fired a shot into the air. It echoed; then all was silent. "Stop your plans or next time I'll kill me a Havlick or two!"

"You won't get away with this!" Jennet cried.

Free frowned at her and whispered, "Quiet! Don't antago nize him."

Jennet scowled at Free, but she was quiet, even though she seethed inside.

Emily held her breath and waited for a few minutes. When the man didn't speak again, she whispered, "I think he's gone."

Rachel opened her eyes and said with a sob, "I hurt all over."

"We have to get Rachel to a doctor," Emily said, patting Rachel.

Trent stood hesitantly and called, "I'm taking my daughter

to the doctor." When the shooter didn't shout or shoot again, Trent stepped from behind the tree. The others swarmed from the side of the church and filled the front yard.

"We're taking Rachel to the doctor," Trent said as he scooped her up. "Somebody go tell the sheriff what happened."

"We're going with you to the doctor," Lark said as she and Clay huddled over Rachel.

"I'll tell the sheriff," Justin said over his shoulder as he strode toward his automobile. "Pris, take the kids to Mom's."

Priscilla wanted to stay close to Justin where she felt safe, but she herded the children to her automobile.

"The rest of us will wait at Clay's too," Free said, his arm around Jennet to keep her from trying to follow the shooter. Fearful the shooter would return, he gestured for everyone to leave quickly.

Several minutes later the doctor bandaged Rachel's wounds. "She'll be just fine," he said. "Keep the areas clean and change the bandages every day. If you see any sign of infection, bring her right in."

"Is it safe for her to travel?" Trent asked.

"Safe, but not wise. Traveling's too dusty and too tiring. Rachel needs plenty of rest and her wounds tended regularly."

"Then we won't travel yet," Emily said.

His jaw set, Trent paid the doctor. Taking Rachel gently in his arms, he carried her outdoors.

"You'll be fine." Emily patted Rachel as she hurried along beside Trent. "We'll get you to Grandpa's and right to bed."

"I want wedding cake," Rachel said weakly.

Emily laughed softly. "We'll see."

Anger and resentment raged inside Trent. He should've taken Rachel and Emily and left yesterday. Whoever had shot his child was going to pay!

The sun had set and the temperature had dropped. Lights

shone from houses up and down the street. A dog barked and an automobile backfired.

"We'll have to put off the trip until she's better," Emily said.

"I know," Trent said grimly.

"You won't leave me behind, will you, Daddy?" Rachel asked, her eyes wide in her ashen face.

"No, I won't," Trent said around the lump in his throat. How long would it take Rachel to trust him not to leave her again? He set Rachel on Emily's lap on the front seat of his Dodge, then ran around the front and climbed in under the steering wheel. As he pushed the starter he said over the grinding noise, "We'll stay with Mom until we leave."

"That's fine," Emily said as he pulled away from the curb. She knew he wouldn't go to the home he'd shared with Celine. And she didn't want to. It didn't seem right. "Your mom has plenty of bedrooms for all of us."

Trent shot her a look of surprise. "Bedrooms? Who can think about that at a time like this?"

Rachel moved restlessly on Emily's lap. "I hurt," Rachel said, sounding close to tears. "Did somebody really shoot me?"

"Yes," Trent said grimly. "But we'll find out who did it so he can't do it again."

Emily shivered at the rage in Trent's answer.

Several blocks away Justin stood beside Sheriff Lamont as they looked around the area where the man with the shotgun had stood. The sheriff had picked up two empty shotgun shells, and they'd found footprints too obliterated to see clearly.

"Looks like you Havlicks will have to watch your step." Sheriff Lamont scratched his head, settled his cap in place, and rested his hand on the butt of his gun.

Justin shook his head. "Grandma won't give up her dream just because of this. I know her!"

"I don't know her all that much, but I bet you're right. If she wants, I can assign a man to keep his eye on all of you. It'd be a tall order, though."

"We can watch out for ourselves." Justin squatted down to look again for clues. The streetlight was too dim for him to see clearly. Tomorrow in the daylight he'd look the place over. He stood slowly, his eyes narrowed thoughtfully. "Why should anyone care what we do with the pines?"

Sheriff Lamont shrugged. "Might not be the pines at all. Could be the local farmers don't want strangers trespassing on their land."

"Grandma already talked to them. Nobody objected enough to want to shoot at us."

"Well, we'll find the man and put a stop to him shooting anyone. I sure hope the little girl will be all right."

"Thank you. So do I." Justin told the sheriff good night and strode to his Duesenberg. What would he have done if one of his children had been shot? His stomach knotted and he quickened his pace. Maybe he should try to talk Grandma out of her plans. He shook his head as he started his automobile. Grandma was stubborn. She wouldn't let tonight's shooting scare her.

But what if someone was killed next time?

"Then let it be me," he whispered hoarsely.

* * *

Emily pulled the covers up to Rachel's chin, then kissed her cheek. The lamp on the dresser cast a soft glow over the pink and white room. "Sweet dreams."

Trent knelt at the side of the bed and gently pushed strands of Rachel's red hair off her forehead. "Close your eyes and sleep tight, honey. Daddy won't let anything hurt you."

"You won't leave me while I sleep, will you?" Rachel asked, barely able to keep her eyes open. The medication the doctor had given her so she'd sleep soundly through the night had taken effect.

Trent kissed Rachel's cheek. "I won't leave you. I promise."

"We both promise." Emily knelt beside Trent. "Close your eyes, Rachel. Your heavenly Father is watching over you. He never leaves you. He loves you more than we do."

"I know," Rachel whispered as she finally closed her eyes. A few minutes later she was fast asleep.

Trent kissed her cheek again, then stood and lifted Emily up with him. He kept his hand on her arm. "She's so beautiful."

"Just like Celine," Emily whispered with a catch in her voice.

"She looks like Celine, but she sure acts like you."

Emily chuckled softly. "She does have a very strong will."

Just then Lark and Clay stuck their heads in the door. "Can we come in?" Lark asked.

"Of course," Trent said. "But she's already asleep."

"I'd like to stand by her side a while." Lark dabbed tears from her eyes.

"I'm thankful she's all right," Clay said hoarsely as he blinked moisture from his eyes.

"We all are." Trent kissed Lark and hugged Clay.

"I'll take my things to my room," Emily said. She'd explained to Lark that she wasn't sharing a room with Trent until they got to Texas. Lark had been surprised, but hadn't said anything.

"Your brothers already brought your trunk in," Clay said.

"Oh, good," Emily said. They were sure to tease her about not sleeping with Trent and she didn't want to face them.

"We'll see you downstairs later." Trent led Emily out so his parents could be alone with Rachel. Clay and Lark's room was directly across the hall from Rachel's. His was near the top of the steps and Emily's across from his.

She carefully pulled off her hat as they walked to her room.

The door stood open, but her trunk wasn't in sight. She dropped her hat on the flowered bedspread and looked around. "Where's my trunk?"

"I told them to put it in my room," Trent said.

Emily turned on him, her eyes flashing. "In your room? How could you do that? You promised! Did you forget?"

"Oh. Oh, yes." His temper flared. He'd told the boys to put the trunk in his room just to keep them from teasing Emily, but he wasn't about to tell her that now that she'd gotten so angry at him. "I guess I did forget."

"A person's word is his bond, you know," she said, keeping her voice soft so it wouldn't carry down the hall.

"You always were too trusting," he said, grinning.

"You always kept your word," she said stiffly.

"That was then. This is now. Times change People change."

Was it possible he'd changed so much that she couldn't see right through him the way she had in the past?

"I told you people change. *I* changed!"

"I guess you have! You used to give your word and nothing could make you break it!" Emily knotted her fists at her sides and her breasts heaved in agitation. Spots of Rachel's blood streaked her wedding gown. "Do you think you can force me to share your bed?"

He gripped her arms. "I'm stronger than you are. I can make you do anything I want."

"No. No, you can't! You could make Celine do anything you wanted, but not me!"

He dropped his hands and stepped back from her. "You're the one who wanted this to be a real marriage. But this time, lady, you won't get your own way! It's either start our marriage tonight, or never!"

"Then it will be never!" She wanted to pound him with her fists or pull his hair out by the roots. "Bring my trunk in here and be done with it!"

He spun on his heels and strode across the hall to his room. He lifted the trunk to his shoulder easily, carried it to her room, and set it down with a thump. "Now, let's get downstairs and listen to our families wish us a happy life together."

With her head high and her cheeks flushed red, Emily walked ahead of him down the wide stairs.

CHAPTER

8

♦ Trent laid down his fork and patted his mouth with his white linen napkin. He'd changed from the denim pants and shirt he'd worn during the day, while looking for clues for who shot Rachel, to a white shirt and dark wool pants. He managed to smile at his parents, but he didn't bother looking at Emily. They'd barely spoken since the night before. When they had, Emily's anger was still evident. Rachel had eaten earlier and was already in bed.

"Fine meal, Mom," Trent said.

"How would you know? You barely touched your food." Lark frowned slightly. "And I made roast beef the way you like it."

"He has his mind on who shot Rachel, no doubt," Emily said. Her eyes were cold when she looked at him.

Trent flushed. Pete at the Wagon Works had talked about Gilly's Place where a guy could relax, get a drink, and find a girl. Without being too obvious, he had learned Gilly's Place was north of town, hidden among a stand of pines. Could Emily know he was planning to go there? "We still don't have a lead on who shot Rachel," he said. "The sheriff said he's been working on it, too."

Clay set down his glass of water. "I've heard some whispers

around town that it's the bootleggers who're worried about the tourists. From what I've heard, they think more people will bring more law. And that could shut down their illegal establishments and the sale of liquor."

Trent stiffened slightly. He had to be very careful of his reaction around Emily. She was too observant! "Have you heard about a speakeasy around here?" Was Gilly's the place Dad was talking about?

Clay shrugged. "None around Blue Creek, but I did hear there's one in Fromberg. And that's too close!"

"I'm thankful our family doesn't darken the doors of such places," Lark said with a shudder.

"Very thankful." Emily looked right at Trent. Would he go to a speakeasy?

"When I was a very young lady I belonged to the Temperance League and our group marched on a tavern that was trying to open right here in town. It was a terrible experience, but I'd do it again to close down those places." Lark's eyes flashed with indignation. "To think of people drinking and carrying on! I'm glad we're a dry state. I pray prohibition becomes a way of life for our country!"

"I'm afraid it won't," Clay said with a shake of his head. "There're too many people who want to have their liquor— right or wrong. That's why bootlegging is going on and that's why so many people are sneaking off to these places called speakeasies."

Lark lifted her chin high. "If I ever learn of such a place around here, I'll shut it down with my own hands!"

"And I'll help you," Emily said firmly.

Struggling with his conscience, Trent pushed back his chair and excused himself. "Don't wait up for me. I don't know how late I'll be."

"Where're you going, son?" Clay leaned back in his chair. "I could go with you, if you want."

Trent's heart lurched. "No need, Dad. You're tired after all that's happened the past two days. I'm used to being on my own."

Emily saw the guilt on Trent's face. What was he going to do? She wondered if he was heading out to his farm so he could reminisce about Celine and the happy times they'd had together.

"Good night." Trent kissed his mother's soft cheek, clamped a hand on his dad's shoulder, and gave Emily a brief nod.

Emily wanted to leap up and demand he stay home so they could talk and get the problem settled between them, but she sat very still and watched him leave.

Trent strode through the darkness to his Dodge. The night was pleasantly warm. Wood smoke from houses all around and the perfume of apple blossoms on the trees next door filled the air. Trent glanced back at the soft light shining from the windows. Did Emily suspect where he was going? "Forget her! She's too stubborn and unforgiving, and she deserves whatever I do to her."

Impatiently he opened the door. Maybe he should get a Duesenberg before he headed back to Texas. He could spare the money. Slowly he slid under the steering wheel. There was enough money in his bank account to buy the Rocking R and stock it with the cattle he wanted. He'd drawn it all out before the wedding, then had put most of it right back in when he learned they couldn't leave for a while. He took a deep breath and looked back toward the house. Should he go back inside? He thought of Emily's anger and his jaw tightened. He wouldn't spend the evening with her accusing eyes!

His mouth bone dry and his palms sweaty, Trent drove north out of town. He slowed as he neared the cemetery where Celine was buried. He groaned in agony. Without knowing he was going to do it, he pulled off the road and stopped. Slowly he walked through the cemetery. A twig snapped under his foot and he jumped. Moonlight gave him enough light to find the grave. Dad told him they'd added a monument after he left. He ran a finger over the engraved name. "Celine," he whispered and his voice broke. "I wanted you to live so we could grow old together." He knew only her body was buried there and that she was in heaven, but that didn't make her being gone any easier. Did she know the anger and bitterness he felt toward Justin for what he'd done to her?

He pushed the agonizing thoughts aside. He didn't want to think about that. He wanted to remember the fun they'd had together.

He squatted beside the grave and thought of Celine, but Emily's face kept getting in the way. And he could hear her speaking. "You're a man of your word, Trent. You must forgive Justin. Rachel needs you. God loves you. You're a man of your word, Trent."

He leaped to his feet, his fists doubled at his sides. "I gave my word to hate Justin forever! Is that the word you want me to keep, Emily Bjoerling?"

"Not Bjoerling. Havlick."

Her voice was as clear to him as if she were standing at his side. He whirled around, but of course she wasn't there. Like a mad man he ran from the cemetery to his automobile. He pushed the starter, and the noise exploded in the silence of the cemetery.

His wide mouth set in a grim line, he drove north until he found the turn off that led to Gilly's Place. He parked his Dodge away from the vehicles hidden behind a stand of pines. He didn't want anyone to recognize his automobile.

As he stepped to the ground, he saw the dark outline of Gilly's. It was a long wooden building without windows. The sight of it caused a chill to run through him. Did he really want to be here?

He stood in the shadows of the pines as three men who worked at the Wagon Works headed in. Already drunk, they were laughing and talking. What would he do if they saw him?

Of course, they'd think he was Justin. Four women in short dresses with several strands of beads draped around their necks stood in the lighted doorway, smoking and talking and laughing.

Maybe he should go home, but he'd come this far. He'd drink until he forgot his agony over Celine, over being home, and over getting married to Emily when he shouldn't have.

Trent took a step forward, then stopped. What would his family think if they knew he was here? He knew what Emily would think! She'd shake her finger at him and remind him he'd been raised with high standards. She'd say he was to abstain from even the appearance of evil. In his mind's eye, he could see her face and hear her words. He frowned.

"I don't care!" he whispered. "I'm going in!" He walked toward the entrance, but stayed in the shadows. He smelled liquor and heard laughter and bawdy talk. He would go in! So what if the family found out? So what if he spent the night with one of the girls just to show Emily that she couldn't run his life?

Then he heard Rachel say, "Daddy, where were you last night? I wanted you," and he hung his head. He couldn't go into such a place, especially one so close to Blue Creek where the story would spread like a forest fire. In Texas he'd been able to live like he wanted, but here things were different.

Deep inside a small voice said, "I saw you in Texas, too."

Trent felt hot all over. He knew the voice, but he'd stopped hearing it years ago. Being back home where everyone was always talking about spiritual things must have made him hear it again.

A man shouted, "Get your hands off me!"

Trent looked toward the door of the speakeasy. A large, burly man had a smaller man by the scruff of the neck and the back of his trousers. Trent recognized the smaller man was Lars Bjoerling, Emily's eighteen-year-old brother!

"Don't you never set foot in this place again, kid!" The big man tossed Lars through the door. He landed in a heap and rolled over on his side. The bouncer threw Lars' cap after him.

Lars leaped to his feet. "Send Suzie out and I'll leave."

Trent tensed, ready to spring to Lars' aid.

"Suzie don't want to leave." The bouncer's voice was sarcastic.

"Then I'm going in after her!" Lars lunged at the burly man, but was stopped by a powerful jab in the stomach and another on the chin. Again Lars fell in a heap.

"And don't come back!" The big man brushed off his hands and walked back inside, closing the door behind him and cutting off all but a faint sound of the music and laughter.

Trent ran to Lars and gently lifted his head. Lars moaned. "I'm taking you out of here," Trent said grimly.

Lars opened his eyes. "Justin?"

A muscle jumped in Trent's jaw. "Trent. Can you walk?"

"I guess so." Lars gasped with pain as he stood.

"I'll take you home where you belong."

"No! I got to get Suzie."

Trent gripped Lars' arm. "Hold it! You'll get tossed out again and maybe with a few broken bones this time."

"I can't leave Suzie."

"Who's Suzie?"

"My girl."

"What's she doing in a place like this? What're *you* doing in a place like this?"

"I heard Suzie was coming here with Ray Brookside. He doesn't know she's only seventeen. She said she wanted to go dancing, and she thought Gilly's was only a dance hall. But I'd heard different. I warned her this was no place for her to be. But she was mad at me, and she said she'd do what she wanted."

"Then leave her here."

Lars shook his head, then groaned and gingerly rubbed his jaw. "She wants to leave, but Ray won't let her go. He says

118

she's staying with him until he's ready to leave. He's already soused to the gills, and he's a mean drunk."

Trent looked at the closed door. "Tell me where she is and I'll go in and get her."

"But you don't want to be seen in such a place, Trent." Lars looked at Trent sharply. "What are you doing here, anyway?"

"I heard about it and thought I'd check it out." Trent was thankful it was too dark for Lars to see his red face and neck.

"It's not the dance hall they say it is. It's a speakeasy and they sell bootleg liquor in there. I told Sheriff Lamont and he raided the place a couple of weeks ago."

"Then why isn't it closed down?"

"Because he didn't find any liquor. The folks were just dancing and having good clean fun. He said he ought to arrest me for giving him a false lead."

"Tell me where Suzie is and what she looks like and I'll get her."

"She's at a table to the right of the door. She has straight blond hair cut in a bob and is wearing a wide beaded band around her forehead. Her dress is blue and kind of shimmers when she moves. It's real short. Too short, but she doesn't care. She's out to have a good time."

"Who's the big guy who tossed you out?"

"Pork Lanski."

"You wait over under that tree. I'll be out shortly." Trent picked up Lars' cap. "I'll wear this."

"Take this too." Lars handed Trent a long, lightweight black coat. "I had the cap and coat so nobody would recognize me. I sure don't want Mama and Papa to know I been here!"

Trent chuckled and slipped on the coat. "I know what you mean." He pulled the cap down low on his forehead and turned the collar of the coat up. He was going to Gilly's and he was going to get a girl, but it sure was different from what he'd planned. "I'll be out as quick as I can."

"God is with you," Lars whispered.

Trent's heart jerked. He strode to the door and pushed it open just enough to slip inside. The room was dimly lit and filled with smoke and noise. Several people in the middle of the long room were dancing to the loud music. Two rows of round tables lined the walls and most of them were occupied by four or more people. The smell of liquor was strong, in spite of the heavy smell of cigarette smoke.

He spotted Suzie immediately. She looked lost and close to tears. The man beside her had his arm around her and was trying to get her to drink from the glass he was holding to her tightly closed lips. Trent saw the big man, Pork Lanski, who'd tossed Lars out. He was standing near the dance band, tapping his toe, with his arms folded as he watched the dancers.

Trent inched his way through the crowd until he stood behind Ray Brookside. He leaned down and whispered, "Pork Lanski wants to see you about bringing a minor in here."

Ray Brookside put his glass down so hard the liquor splashed up and out. He turned to look back at Trent, but Trent moved so that Ray couldn't see his face.

"Pork says if you pay him enough, he won't say anything. He wants you now." Trent moved again.

Ray shoved back his chair and started through the crowd.

Trent gripped Suzie's arm. "Come with me. I came to get you out of here. Lars is waiting outdoors for you."

Suzie gasped, her eyes wide with fear, but she jumped up and walked out with him. Just outside the door, she whispered, "Who are you?"

"Never mind. We have to hurry." Trent glanced down at her feet and knew she couldn't run on the rough ground in those shoes.

Lars leaped across to them. "Suzie! Are you all right?"

She stared at him, then threw her arms around him, sobbing hard.

"Get out of here fast," Trent snapped, clamping the cap back on Lars' head.

Lars scooped Suzie up in his arms and half-ran, half-walked to the shelter of the nearest pine.

Hurrying along beside them, Trent peeled off the coat and draped it over Suzie. "How're you two getting home?"

"I caught a ride here, so I don't have a ride back," Lars said.

"I'll take you then." Trent glanced back to see the door of the speakeasy fly open. Ray Brookside stood there, angrily looking around. Trent whispered, "We have to hurry."

Lars ducked around a pickup truck and broke into a run.

A few minutes later they climbed in Trent's Dodge and he drove away, the noise of the engine loud in the silence behind him.

"Suzie lives at Red Beaver's farm," Lars said. "Her pa works for Beaver."

"Is that Justin Havlick?" Suzie whispered.

"No. Trent," Lars whispered back.

Trent's stomach knotted. Justin indeed! Would it always be this way?

Trent drove into Beaver's lane and stopped when Lars asked him to. The moon was bright in the sky. An owl hooted. The smell of a pigpen was in the air.

"I'll walk Suzie the rest of the way so we can talk and she can pull herself together. I'll run home from here. Thanks, Trent. We appreciate all you did."

"I'm glad I could help."

Suzie climbed from the car and stood at Trent's window. "Thank you. If I can ever help you with anything, let me know."

Trent smiled. "No need. Just don't go to that place again. It's not for girls like you."

"That's what I told her," Lars said, putting his arm around Suzie.

"I believe you now," she said weakly.

"Don't mention about us being there," Lars said.

121

"I won't." Trent knew they wouldn't say anything about him being there either. They couldn't.

Trent made a turn-around, then drove slowly back to Blue Creek. Gilly's Place wasn't for him either.

Yawning, he parked the Dodge outside the shed at his parents' house and walked quietly to the bedroom he slept in alone. The house was quiet. The smell of coffee lingered.

He pushed open his door, then glanced back at Emily's. He saw a line of light beneath it. He hated being on the outs with her. Should he tell her the truth about the evening before—that he'd had her trunk put in his room just to keep her from being teased by her brothers?

He took a step toward her door, then stopped. Why bother? What did it matter if she treated him like a stranger? An enemy, in fact! For some reason it did matter.

Slowly he walked to his dresser and lit the lamp. He closed the door, then opened it, and stepped across the hall. He knocked before he lost his nerve.

Emily opened the door, the light glowing behind her. She wore a pale blue nightgown and a darker blue wrapper. Her feet were bare. She bit back a gasp. She'd thought it was Lark. "Yes?"

"I just wanted to let you know I'm back," he said stiffly. What was wrong with him? Was that the best he could do?

She tightened the belt on her robe. "Rachel will be glad. She asked about you."

"I'm sorry I wasn't here."

She suddenly realized her feet were bare, and flushed.

"Now what's wrong?"

She lifted her chin. "Nothing!"

"You're embarrassed about something."

She flipped back her mass of black hair. "If you must know, it's my feet. They're bare."

"I've seen you many times without shoes."

"Not since I grew up."

He chuckled under his breath. "I guess you're right about that."

She felt awkward. "Did you want something else?"

"I don't like it when we fight."

"Neither do I!"

"Let's forget what happened the other night and get back to normal." He waited for her answer, willing it to be what he wanted to hear.

She knew she should forgive him, but she couldn't. She wanted him to be a man of his word like he once was. Finally she said, "I'll try."

That surprised him. He'd thought she'd leap at the chance. "Don't make such an effort," he snapped and strode to his room, closing the door with a sharp click.

She stood with her head down. Her heart was racing. What was wrong with her? She knew Jesus said to forgive. Taking a deep breath she walked across the hall and tapped on Trent's door. "Can we talk?"

He sprang to the door, but didn't open it. "It's up to you."

"What'd you mean?"

"Come in all the way or not at all."

She whirled and ran to her room.

He pressed his ear against the door and listened. He heard her door click. Just as he thought. She had to have everything her way. Well, he didn't work that way, and she might as well find that out now.

*　*　*

Early the next morning Trent dipped the oars into the cold water and pulled, sending the rowboat gliding over Deep Lake, away from the dock at Fromberg toward the shoreline where their property began. Andree sat in the bow and Justin in the stern. Mist drifted up from the cool water. Quacking ducks flew low across the early morning sky. Men on the dock shouted to each other, but the sounds of their voices grew faint

123

as the rowboat glided through the water toward the other side. Trent kept his eyes on the shoreline at Fromberg. He would not look at Justin, for if he did he knew his anger would erupt. Because of Grandma and the shooting a few days ago, they'd agreed on a truce while they investigated the shooting. Today they were going to check the oaks and help Andree mark the locations of the cabins.

Justin's stomach knotted so tight that pain shot through him. He knew he should've gone to work as usual instead of agreeing to go with Trent and Andree. At work he could forget everything except making wagons and chairs. As he braced his feet and gripped the seat on either side, he glanced at Trent, whose jaw was set. He looked ready to explode. Andree seemed relaxed as he studied the cloud formations. The silence in the boat pressed against Justin. He liked the noise at the Wagon Works. During a silence it was too easy to let his mind drift back to the failed areas of his life.

Trent dipped the oars deeper and pulled harder. Sweat popped out on his forehead and a dark cloud seemed to surround him.

Andree looked from Trent to Justin. Both had faces of stone. Silently Andree prayed for them. Trent was a far cry from being a happy newlywed. It was hard to get used to this angry young man being his son-in-law.

With a sigh, Andree looked over his shoulder at the approaching shoreline. Havlick trees looked like a solid wall beginning almost at the edge of the water. Pine tree covered hills jutted up to the right of where they'd land the boat. Giant oaks with leaves still as small as a mouse's ear covered several acres. Oak, maple, and walnut trees were mixed in with white pines in another area. It would be hard to decide which trees to cut. How could anyone saw down one of the giants that had been standing for hundreds of years? He turned back and the expression on Trent's face reminded him of something that had happened when the twins were about eight. He chuckled.

"Boys," he said with a hearty laugh. He didn't care that they were thirty years old—they were still boys to him. "I just thought about the time you went canoeing by yourselves for the first time. Remember?"

Justin shook his head. He didn't want to remember.

Trent remembered, but he didn't acknowledge it.

"You boys always did everything together," Andree said. "It was a great day to be on the river in a canoe. Your ma thought I would be with you, but you didn't let on none to her or me. I helped you with the canoe and you two got in and paddled away. You looked too little to do it, but you did it together. You boys always did everything together."

Trent bent over the oars, digging deep into the lake water. He would not think about that day! He'd close his ears to Andree's story!

Justin gritted his teeth as he recalled the day Andree was talking about. They'd tipped the canoe and he'd almost drowned, but Trent caught his shirt and held on tightly until he flipped the canoe and they could crawl back in. Even Andree didn't know he'd almost drowned. Scalding tears burned the backs of his eyes as Andree finished the tale.

Trent refused to listen and refused to see in his mind's eye two little boys paddling down the river. He glanced over his shoulder to see how close to shore he was. To his relief, land was only another minute or two away.

He rowed to the few feet of the shoreline where access was easy. Most of it was lined with rocks and trees. Birds sang in the tall branches and squirrels scolded.

Justin jumped into the cold water and tied the rope around the base of a young tree. He shivered as water seeped through his boots. He heard twigs snapping and the rustle of animals as they ran deeper into the woods. He caught a movement and watched closely until he made out a deer running away.

Trent waded to shore and stopped on the sandy beach, his boots waterlogged. He saw several animal tracks. Once he could identify every animal by its tracks, but he didn't know if he still could.

"Look at the beauty around us!" Andree cried, spreading his arms wide. Wet feet and pant legs didn't bother him. "The trees! The lake! And white clouds up above in a picture-perfect blue sky! It seems a shame to ruin this beauty by putting in cabins and a landing dock for boats."

Trent didn't want to notice the beauty around him, but he couldn't ignore it. The trees were indeed beautiful giants. He'd forgotten how big and magnificent the old-growth trees were. They were a far cry from Texas sand and sagebrush.

Justin walked several feet away to an oak and touched the rough bark. It was too large for the three of them to reach around. Its lumber would make many chairs after it had cured. Something stirred inside him as he looked up at the spreading branches covered with small leaves. High in the top he saw the large nest of a red-tailed hawk. He remembered that it came back each year to the same nest, repaired it, and raised its family. Could he destroy the tree and leave the red-tailed hawk without a home? He frowned. What was he thinking? Oak for lumber was more important than a nest.

The strong smell of pine made Trent think of the time he and Celine had brought a picnic to the side of the stream several yards past Jig's grave. They'd been married only a few months. They had spread the blanket on the pine needles, and he'd kissed her for a long time. They'd forgotten the picnic basket.

She'd curled tightly against him and said softly, "I have good news, Trent."

"You love me?"

"Always!"

"I love you?"

"Always!"

She lifted her head and looked into his eyes. "We're going to have a baby."

"A baby?"

"Yes. Are you glad?"

Tears had filled his eyes. "I want a girl just like you." And they'd had a girl just like her!

Trent knotted his fists as he struggled against the rush of tears he felt. He wanted to run back to the boat and row away. "Let's get on with it," he said sharply.

"You boys remember what I said about the wild dogs. Keep close watch." Andree led the way into the woods. He shook his head and clicked his tongue. "How can we cut any of these trees?"

"We have to," Justin snapped. He felt guilty about his tone of voice and tried to soften it. "Let's just mark a few, and then get out of here. I have work to do."

Trent bit back a sharp retort that surely would've brought on another fight. Sometimes it was very hard to be a Havlick and still be a man of his word. Was he a man of his word even though Emily didn't believe he was?

The massive branches blocked out the sun as they walked deeper into the woods. Trent smelled a strange odor. He sniffed and wrinkled his nose. Maybe it was his imagination.

Andree stopped in a small clearing and looked around. The ground was almost covered with pine needles. "This is a fine place for a cabin. It'll mean taking out only those two trees " He pointed to a maple and an oak.

Justin pulled a red marker out of his pocket and drew an X on each tree.

Farther in the woods Trent spotted a deep ravine with branches growing over it like a roof. It would be dangerous to build a cabin too close to it. He found another small clearing and called, "This is a good spot. It's far enough from the other for privacy." Grandma had said she didn't want the cabins on top of each other. She said folks deserve privacy while on vacation.

Several minutes later Andree found the right location on the side of a hill for the large cabin. Several trees would have to be removed, but the view of the lake would be perfect.

Justin marked the trees. To his surprise his heart sank lower and lower at the thought of cutting them. Once he'd loved the woods as much as the rest of the family, but then he'd gotten too busy to walk through them and enjoy them. Would he be able to stand seeing the area torn apart while the building was taking place?

While Andree and Justin walked around the area, Trent leaned against a maple. He and Justin had gone with Grandpa many times to tap maples. They'd never tapped this one, but he knew it would give gallons of sap to be made into maple syrup. When the Indians lived in these woods maybe they'd tapped this very tree. Red Beaver's people had lived in the area before they were sent to Oklahoma to live on a reservation.

"Does it hurt the maple to drill holes in it, Grandpa?" Justin had asked one chilly morning in February.

"It can't hurt," Trent had said. He and Justin were bundled up in the same kind of winter coat, warm red caps with ear flaps, and boots with wool socks to keep their toes from freezing. "If it did, Grandpa wouldn't do it."

"That's right. God made these trees so we could get sap from them to make maple syrup. Hang the buckets on these spiles." Grandpa had lifted Justin high so he could hang a bucket, then had done the same with Trent.

The first year he'd been tall enough to hang a bucket without Grandpa lifting him had been a milestone in Trent's life. And Justin had hung a bucket himself that same year. They'd looked at each other and grinned. They both knew it was a great occasion.

Impatiently Trent pushed away from the maple and strode through the trees to join Andree and Justin. He'd had enough of the forest and enough of the memories it brought back. He expected Justin had too.

Trent scowled. He no longer *knew* Justin's thoughts like he had in the past. The bond had been broken when Justin let Celine die. "Let's get out of here," Trent said gruffly. He'd had more than enough of the woods and the terrible memories.

He strode toward the lake with his shoulders bent and his head down.

CHAPTER

9

◆ Her black skirt swirling about her legs, Emily paced from one side of Lark's porch to another. Rachel and Amanda sat in the shade of a maple tree playing dolls. Clay was at the Wagon Works and Lark was inside talking to Lulu about supper. Emily brushed aside a gray and white cat winding around her feet. It leaped off the porch and ran to Rachel. Emily flipped back her mass of dark hair and continued pacing. For two weeks Trent had barely spoken to her except to tell her they had not learned the identity of the man who shot Rachel.

Emily bit her lip and swatted away a fly. She'd tried to tell Trent she was sorry for getting angry, but he wouldn't listen. She'd almost given in and moved into his room, but couldn't bring herself to. And he hadn't asked her to again. He'd been gone every day working with Papa on the plans for Havlick's Wilderness. Today he and Papa were planning the trails through the woods.

Lark stepped onto the porch and said, "Emily, I've been watching you for the last hour. You act like a caged animal. I think you need something to do."

Emily leaned against a support post and sighed. "I don't

know what's wrong with me." But she did know. She and Trent were no longer friends. He'd changed more than she'd known. Marrying him was a mistake. She thought he needed her. She thought she could save him—make him into the man he was before he left Michigan. How wrong she'd been!

Lark tucked a strand of gray hair behind her ear and smoothed the flowered apron covering her green dress. She hated to see the tension between Emily and Trent. "Why don't you take a trip out to the property Jennet gave you? It's a pleasant day for that."

"Oh, I don't know. . . ."

"You can drive my auto."

"I don't know how to drive."

"What? I thought you were going to learn!"

"I was." Emily didn't want to admit she was actually afraid to learn. Usually she didn't fear new things, but the gas contraption was beyond her powers of reasoning. How could it keep going? And how did a person know when to push down on what thing on the floorboard?

Lark shook her head and clicked her tongue. "I'm going to teach you to drive, or have Trent teach you."

Emily stiffened. She didn't want Trent to teach her anything. But she couldn't say that to Lark. "I don't know if I can learn."

"Priscilla did. She's a good driver."

"I'll think about it."

"Modern young ladies should know how to drive," Lark said, wagging her finger at Emily.

"I suppose."

"Take the buggy then."

Emily smiled and agreed. Maybe she did need to get out alone. She might even stop and see Mama.

They talked a while longer. Emily told Rachel goodbye, then she hitched a horse to the buggy and drove out of town toward Free's farm. The top of the buggy was down and the sun was warm on her bare head. She should've grabbed a hat, but once she'd decided to go, she didn't want to take the time to run upstairs for one. She turned on a tree-lined gravel road just before the turn off to Free's place. In the past she'd come this way often to see Celine. She'd spent a lot of time at the farm with Celine, but hadn't been back since she died. It would be hard to see it again.

The two hundred acres Jennet had given her butted against Free's place to the south and Trent's place to the west. She'd seen the property from the road many times before, but had never stopped to look it over. She waited for excitement to bubble up inside her, but she couldn't muster even a drop. If Trent were with her, it would be different.

"Oh, Trent, I miss you," she said loud enough to make the horse prick its ears. Trent was right—friendship was better than a grand passion. When Trent got home tonight she'd make him listen to her. She wouldn't let another day go by with them at outs with each other.

Several minutes later she turned onto her property and drove along a wagon trail winding around a hill covered with second growth pines and various hardwood trees. The oak leaves were small and the black walnut trees were covered with tight buds. Giant pine branches blocked the sun. The harness shook and the buggy rattled as the horse picked its way along the trail at the base of the hill. With loud cries birds flew up from the branches. After several minutes of driving through thick growths of trees she came upon the most beautiful valley she'd ever seen. She sucked in her breath as she stopped the horse, then gazed at the valley, her hand over her heart. The valley stretched on and on and was covered with lush green grass and yellow and white wildflowers. A deer grazing in the grass lifted its head, then leaped away with its foot-long white tail held high. It sailed over a stream running along the east side of the valley and disappeared among the trees. A bluebird flitted across in front of Emily and a robin sang nearby. A warmth spread through her. She felt as if she'd just come home after years away. It was a strange feeling, one she couldn't understand, nor did she try to. After a long time, she slapped the reins on the horse's back and headed for the stream. She pulled up beside a deer trail leading down to the water. Sparkling blue water rippled over stones and tree roots. A frog jumped off the grassy shore and landed in the water with a splash. She breathed in the heady scent of pine and the faint smell of the stream. She gazed around, holding firmly to the reins. In her mind's eye she could see cattle scattered across the valley, growing fat for market. It would be easy to fence the valley for cattle to graze. Her eyes widened and she gasped as she realized where her thoughts had taken her. She wanted to stay and make her home here, not in Texas. Could she convince Trent to consider staying?

"He'd never agree," she muttered. Then she lifted her head high. "But I'll try to convince him anyway!"

After a long time, she drove slowly out of the valley and through the trees onto Trent's farm. From the crest of a hill she looked down on the house and buildings. She knew Free had hired Gabe Lavery as a caretaker for the place. He was probably there right now. Smoke drifted up from the chimney and disappeared in the fluffy white clouds.

What if Bob Lavery was visiting his brother this afternoon? Emily's pulse leaped. She hadn't seen Bob lately. Truth to tell, she didn't think about him as often as she once had. His farm was one place over from Trent's, at the bend in Blue River. She'd dreamed often of living on his farm, tending to his needs, and becoming a mother to his children. Her muscles tightened. Monique was doing all that.

Abruptly Emily pushed away thoughts of Monique as she looked down on Trent's house.

The house was a four-bedroom, two-story white frame house with a wrap-around porch on the south and west sides. Trent and Celine had planned on a large family and had built the bedrooms large. Emily brushed away a tear. "Oh, Celine, I wish you were still here."

To the north of the house was a huge white barn. White sheds and a granary stood east of the barn. All the buildings were in good repair. Pigs rooted in a large muddy pen. It had rained hard two days ago. About twenty head of cattle grazed in a field in back of the barn. Chickens scratched in the yard and a turkey gobbler strutted from one shed to another. Maybe Gabe would let her look around inside the house for old time's sake. Lark had said Celine's things were still there.

Emily urged the horse down the hill to the road leading to the driveway. The buggy swayed and Emily braced her feet to keep from pitching out. Just then she saw a black Ford pickup truck pull into the driveway and stop. To her surprise Bob Lavery got out of the pickup truck and waved for her to stop. A blue chambray work shirt and heavy denim pants hung loosely on his thin frame.

Her breath caught in her throat and her heart hammered wildly as she pulled back on the reins. Was her hair a mess? Oh, why hadn't she grabbed a hat before she left Lark's? "Afternoon, Bob," she said with a slight catch in her voice.

He smiled and tipped his sweat-stained blue cap, showing his damp wheat colored hair. "Afternoon, Emily."

Emily struggled to keep from falling out of the buggy in a dead faint at Bob's feet. What had started out as a miserable day was turning into the best day of her life! "What brings you out here?" she asked, trying to keep her voice from cracking.

Bob rested his hand on the side of the buggy as he smiled up at Emily. "I came to see my brother, Gabe. He's taking care of Trent's place."

"Oh, yes. I heard that." She glanced up the long driveway to keep him from reading the love in her eyes. "I thought I'd take a look around. It's been a long time since I was here."

Bob cleared his throat as he squeezed the bill of his cap. "Is it right what I heard about you and Trent Havlick?"

Emily trembled. "Yes. We got married."

"Congratulations." Bob rubbed his calloused hand over his suntanned cheek and scratched the side of his thin nose. "It sure came as a shock to me."

"It did?" She looked deep into his eyes that were the color of the sky above. Just what did he mean?

"A terrible shock!"

"It was, ah, sudden."

"I heard about his daughter getting shot outside the church. How is she?"

"Fine. She was frightened more than hurt."

"I'm glad to hear that."

"Me too! It was frightening."

"I suppose you and Trent will be heading to Texas before long."

"I guess. Now that Rachel's well enough to travel."

Bob looked off across the field, then back up at Emily. "I sure was surprised about you getting married."

Emily moistened her dry lips with the tip of her tongue. "It was . . . sudden." She flushed as she realized she'd already said that.

He looked up at her, then off across the field again. "I heard . . . heard gossip about . . . about you being . . . in love . . . with me."

"Oh, dear," she whispered as her cheeks turned bright red. How she longed to sink to the sandy floor of the buggy and disappear from sight! She trembled so hard she dropped the reins.

He caught them, sprang up beside her, and looped the reins around the wooden brake handle. He turned to face her and caught her hands in his.

She stared at him in surprise, shivers running up and down her spine.

"I don't know if I can live knowing you're married," he said hoarsely.

135

Shock waves rippled over her as she swayed weakly. She felt the rough calluses on his hands. She smelled the tangy sweat of his skin as he leaned closer. "How can you say that?" she whispered weakly.

"Your love is real important to me, Emily."

"I . . . I didn't know. . . ."

He caught her close and kissed her roughly.

She gasped and pulled away, her eyes wide with shock, her mouth tingling from his touch. "You mustn't do that!"

"I couldn't help myself! You're a beautiful, desirable woman. I want you! I've always wanted you."

Her heart raced and the words sent her reeling. "But you married Monique."

"I was away from home. Lonely. And I couldn't live just on thoughts of you."

"Oh, dear."

"I hated myself for doing it." He ran a fingertip over her lips.

She groaned and leaned toward him for another kiss, but deep inside she heard, "Don't do it, Emily." She jerked back before their lips touched again. "I'm sorry," she whispered. "This is . . . wrong."

"How can love be wrong?" he asked in a voice hoarse with emotion.

Her eyes widened. "Love?" she whispered.

"Between us, Emily! You can't say no to it!"

Her pulse leaped. Since he'd returned from the war she'd longed to hear his declaration of love for her and feel his lips against hers! "I can't believe you're saying this." She'd dreamed of this very conversation. Or was *this* a dream? Maybe she'd fallen asleep. But no. Bob's face was indeed close to hers. She could see the splash of freckles on each cheek and the dark shadow of whiskers on his jaw. She could smell the tang of his skin.

"One more kiss and I'll let you go," Bob said, tugging her close again.

"No! Oh, we dare not!" Emily pushed against his chest until he let her go.

He rubbed an unsteady hand over his narrow face. "What will we do now?"

"Nothing!" she cried.

His face fell and he sighed unhappily. He sat in silence a long time. "Are you going back to town now?"

She nodded, not really knowing what she was planning to do.

He cupped her flushed cheek in his rough hand and leaned forward to kiss her.

She jerked back and his hand fell away. "Please. Don't. It's not right."

Bob sighed and nodded. "I know, but I couldn't help myself."

Emily pressed her hand to her racing heart. He couldn't help himself! Was it possible?

He tugged his cap low on his forehead. "I'll go about my business so you can get back to town. But I *will* see you again."

"I don't know   "

"I must!"

She hesitantly unwound the reins and gripped them tightly.

He jumped to the ground and stepped away from the buggy. "Goodbye, my love. Until we meet again," he said softly.

"Goodbye," she whispered. She turned the horse and buggy and drove toward town, her mind in a daze. Would she let there be a next time?

His Adam's apple working, Bob stood quietly until she was out of sight, then he sprang in his pickup truck, drove to the house, and screeched to a stop, sending sand spraying. He jumped to the ground, startling chickens that were scratching in the driveway. "Gabe!" he called. "Get out here now!"

A shotgun in his hand, Gabe ran out the back door, slamming it behind him. He had the same wheat colored hair as

Bob, but his eyes were hazel instead of blue. His chest and arms were thick with muscles and his hips narrow. "What's wrong? Who was that?" He motioned toward the road with the shotgun.

Bob scowled at the gun as he said, "Emily Bjoerling. Emily Havlick now."

Gabe stood the shotgun on the ground and rested it against the pickup truck. "I had my gun on her when she came down the hill. I pretty near shot at her. And I didn't want to do that."

"It's a good thing you didn't!"

"It was bad enough hitting the little girl outside the church the other day." Gabe rubbed an unsteady hand over his day-old whiskers. "I still have nightmares over that one."

"Emily says the little girl's doing fine."

"It's a good thing. I'm no killer."

Bob slapped Gabe's thick shoulder. "I know you're not."

"It don't bother me none to break the law to make and sell liquor."

"The law's wrong," Bob snapped. "We already agreed it was."

Gabe leaned against the fender of the pickup truck. "Why was Emily here anyway?"

"She came to snoop, but I stopped her cold." Bob laughed wickedly. "I made a pass at her and scared her silly."

"You made a pass at that old maid?"

Bob nodded as he wrinkled his long, thin nose. "I had to do something to keep her away."

"All in the line of duty," Gabe said with a chuckle.

"It wasn't so bad," Bob said. "I planned on marrying her before I went to war. I could get her to warm up some if I worked at it long enough."

"Not if Monique ever heard about it. You'd be a dead man!"

Bob grinned and nodded. "She sure would get mad, but she won't hear nothing about it." Bob frowned. "Unless you tell her."

"Me? Never! She'd have my hide too."

Bob nodded. "I'm sure glad I was able to stop Emily from coming up to the house."

"She would've seen our cases of liquor and smelled the stuff cooking."

"It was a close call, all right." Bob hiked up his denim pants on his lean hips. "I came to pick up ten cases and take them to Gilly's Place."

"What about the sheriff?" Gabe asked as they headed for the house.

"He's gone for a while."

"How about Leroy? Is he having trouble with the still in the Havlicks' trees?"

"No." Bob stopped outside the back door. "But he will if the Havlicks keep on with their plans for the nature preserve. The place they want to build the cabins is too close to Leroy's still."

"He told me Jennet Havlick and Emily almost stumbled on it a while back." Gabe opened the screen door and the squack it made was a better alarm than anything else he could've planned. "He said he'll shoot anyone who gets too close. And he means it It don't bother him none to kill. He's done it before."

Bob stopped just inside the back door and wrinkled his nose at the smell of brewing mash and the heat pouring out from the kitchen stove. A hundred pound bag of sugar leaned against a wall beside gunnysacks of ground corn. The smell of malt turned Bob's stomach. They'd had the sprouted corn ground by Logan Piper and paid him in finished liquor. Gabe had learned from Gilly which miller he could trust with his sprouted corn. Logan would keep his mouth shut for a regular supply of liquor. "I don't like working with Leroy, what with his quick temper. But he makes the best stuff and it brings high dollar."

"We don't want no killings," Gabe said.

"We only got to do this a few more months to pay off our farms, then we can quit. Maybe make just enough for our own use." Bob hoisted a case of liquor on his shoulder, steadied it, and carried it to his pickup truck. Gabe was close behind with another case.

In silence they loaded the cases, then pulled a black tarp over the back and tied down the corners. Bob gave the rope one last tug. It was easy for him to deliver the liquor because no one would ever suspect him—a good family man with a farm of his own. Since the Great War the farm wasn't paying enough to keep up his bank loan, so he'd taken to bootlegging. Gabe had started first to help pay off his farm, then brought Bob in on it when he'd seen his brother's need for extra cash.

Gabe pulled off his cap and wiped sweat from his forehead. "Is there any chance Trent Havlick will decide to stay in Michigan and want to move back here?"

"Not the way I hear it. Emily said they'll be going soon. If Rachel hadn't been shot, they'd already be gone."

"It almost did me in when I heard her scream and seen her fall."

"I'm just glad she didn't die."

"Yeah, me too. We don't want to do anything to make Trent stay!"

"I don't think Emily will come back here again," Bob said with a laugh. "I scared her too bad."

"I sure hope so. I wouldn't want to shoot nobody."

Bob stiffened. "Don't you dare shoot anybody! I mean it, Gabe."

"Only if I'm forced to, Bob. You would, too."

Bob shook his head, but he wondered if what Gabe had said was true. A few years ago he wouldn't have considered bootlegging, but times were too rough not to. Bob walked slowly to the cab of the truck and stepped up inside. "I almost forgot to ask you about Noah Roswell. I saw you talking to him at Gilly's Place the other night. Did he tell you anything important?"

Gabe grinned. "Give him more than two drinks and his tongue flaps at both ends."

"Did you learn anything?"

"Nothing worth knowing, but you never can tell when he'll tell us something important. I told him the Havlicks were trying to shut down Gilly's Place and we needed to know what they had planned. He says Priscilla Havlick is a real beauty." Gabe laughed and slapped his thigh. "I told him to play up to her and learn all he could about their plans. He said he'd be glad to. He'll do anything for a little money."

"When will you see him again?"

"Tonight. I set up a meeting twice a week. He knows how to get in touch with me if he learns anything important."

"It was a lucky day when you met him."

"You never know when a man working for the Havlicks will come in handy." Gabe scowled. "The Havlicks are too high and mighty for my blood. Always have been. They don't have a clue to all that's working against them to make them fall."

"Cut it out, Gabe. We agreed we ain't in this to ruin the Havlicks. We're in it to get out of debt."

Gabe shrugged. "If the Havlicks fall while we're getting ahead, well and good."

Bob sighed heavily as he started the pickup and drove away.

*　*　*

Emily's face burned with shame as she slapped the reins harder on the horse's back. It quickened its pace, making the buggy sway dangerously on the dirt road. How could she face anyone now that she'd allowed Bob Lavery to kiss her? She felt the kiss again and her blood surged and her lips tingled. With a frown, she gripped the reins tighter. How could part of her like the kiss and want more and part of her abhor it and be determined never to put herself in that situation again?

Without warning an automobile pulled from a side road onto the road directly in Emily's path. The horse neighed and reared, its eyes wild. The driver swerved in time to miss the horse's hooves. Emily sawed on the reins, trying to bring the horse under control. Shaking its head, the horse reared again and twisted enough that the buggy tongue snapped. Emily's heart thundered in fear as she pulled the reins harder. Finally the horse calmed. She wrapped the reins around the brake handle and jumped to the ground. Dust puffed onto her high-top walking shoes.

A woman jumped out of the open black automobile and walked angrily toward Emily. "You broke a lamp on my auto!" she cried, shaking her fist.

"Aggie?" Emily stared in shock at the woman she hadn't seen in two years. "Aggie Beaumont!"

"Emily Bjoerling!" Aggie stopped short and stared at Emily. "Imagine running into you this afternoon." Aggie waved a hand at her headlamp. "Just look at the damage you did. I expect you to pay me for it."

Emily lifted her chin and knotted her fists at her sides. "You pulled out in front of me. The accident was your fault and I will not pay a cent!"

"I see you're as sharp-tongued as you were in school!"

"I won't allow you to take advantage of me, if that's what you mean."

"And you call yourself a Christian." Aggie looked at Emily sharply. "You still claim to be a Christian, don't you?"

"Of course."

"Well, you'd still call me a sinner," Aggie said with a sharp laugh. She flipped her long strands of pink beads and patted her bobbed blonde hair that hung just below her soft pink hat with a wide turned-up brim. She wore a white middy trimmed in pink and a white skirt.

"I don't have time to argue with you." Emily unhitched the horse from the broken buggy. "I have to get back to town and send someone out for the buggy before dark."

Aggie swished her skirt and tilted her head. "Aren't you even wondering why I'm back?"

"No."

Aggie frowned. "I've moved back to Blue Creek. My dear husband died."

"I'm sorry to hear that," Emily said stiffly as she started to lead the horse past Aggie.

"Gossip around town is you married Trent Havlick for his money."

Emily stopped short as she held back her temper. "Not everyone marries for money."

"You and Celine made it hard on me for doing it." Aggie lifted her rounded chin and batted her dark lashes. "I'm not a bit sorry. But he didn't have quite the wealth I'd thought. I used his money to train to be a nurse. It'll give me a chance to find another rich man, this time one my age. And I will do just that!"

"Who could you possibly want in Blue Creek?"

"Maybe your husband."

"We're moving to Texas."

"Too bad. I could've taken him away from you. I've stolen my share."

Emily shook her head. "Don't brag about such a terrible thing, Aggie. You make it sound no different from when you stole mine and Celine's dolls."

Aggie shrugged and flipped her beads. "It's just as easy." Her short skirt swished around her long legs as she walked back to her car. She said over her shoulder, "I just might steal both the Havlick twins."

"How can you even say that? You and Priscilla were once good friends."

Aggie laughed softly. "All's fair in love and war."

Emily pressed her lips tightly together and gripped the lead rope as Aggie started her auto and drove away in a cloud of dust. "Now that she's back I'm glad we're going to Texas," Emily muttered.

She walked along the side of the road leading the horse. Since she was closer to Free's place than town, she stopped there and asked if she could leave the horse. Then she ran to her place and asked her brothers to get the buggy. As they hitched up their team she stood in the yard and told her mother what happened with Aggie.

"Are you sure you're all right, Emily?" Martha asked as she rubbed a hand down Emily's arm.

"I'm fine, Mama." Emily forced back a flush as she thought of Bob's kiss. Mama would never understand that. Actually, she didn't either.

"I hope Aggie doesn't try to make trouble for you the way she always used to do."

"We won't be here long enough for that to happen."

Martha narrowed her eyes thoughtfully. "I have this feeling that you won't move to Texas."

Emily's heart turned over. Mama's feelings often came true. "You're probably wrong this time."

"Would you be upset if you didn't move to Texas?"

Because of Bob's kiss she would, but she couldn't say that. "I looked at the land Jennet gave me. The valley is a perfect place for cattle. While I was there I actually wanted to stay. It was peaceful and very, very beautiful!"

As the boys drove the team and wagon down the lane, Martha walked to a bench under a maple tree and sat down. She patted the bench beside her and waited until Emily sat down. "Honey, God knows what's best for you and Trent—whether here or in Texas. Your papa and I are praying you'll both know."

Emily hugged Mama. "Thanks." All her life her parents had prayed for her and her brothers and sisters. Their prayers were as important to her as the food and shelter they'd provided. "I know Trent's mind is set."

"I'm sure he'll listen as God speaks to him."

Years ago Emily would've agreed, but now she couldn't.

They talked a while longer, then Emily walked toward town, her head buzzing with all that had happened. Once again she heard Bob's declaration of love and felt his lips on hers. She stopped on the bridge and leaned weakly against the railing. Water rushed down below and the smell of fish drifted up.

Bob had kissed her! Emily trembled and touched her lips. Her cheeks flamed at the shameless thing that had happened. "God, help me," she whispered weakly.

* * *

Priscilla leaned against the fence and watched Noah feed the pigs. His shirt sleeves were rolled almost to his elbows, revealing strong brown forearms covered with black hair. His gray shirt and dark pants were stained with dirt and sweat Mud and manure covered the soles of his high-top work shoes. Just watching him work left Priscilla weak in the knees. "Did you have fun last night?" she asked. He'd told her he was going to the speakeasy near Blue Creek, and she was immediately jealous, thinking he would be with another woman.

Noah carried the bucket to the fence and easily jumped over. He landed beside her and smiled right into her eyes. "Sure did. Did you miss me?"

Priscilla stiffened and stepped away from him and the fence. He'd never been so forward and it startled her. "Why would I miss you?"

Noah grinned as he set down the bucket and leaned back on the fence, his arms crossed over his broad chest. "I hoped you would. I missed you."

Her legs weakened and she thought she'd fall. "You did?" she whispered.

"Sure did."

"You're just saying that. You probably had all kinds of pretty women hanging on you."

"None as pretty as you, Priscilla."

145

"Yes. Well. Thank you." She was at a loss for words. He'd never said anything like that to her before.

"How're the plans coming for the great Havlick's Wilderness you told me about?"

Priscilla shrugged. "All right, I guess. Justin's been working on the plans. He's going to have some oak trees lumbered out near Deep Lake and use them to make chairs in his factory."

Noah dropped his arms to his sides and stepped forward. "And when's he going to do that?"

"Soon, I guess. Why?"

"It'll give us more time together."

Priscilla's pulse leaped. "Oh?" she whispered.

Noah ran a finger down the side of her face, leaving a trail of sparks along her skin. "I don't like to see you so lonely all the time. Your husband is crazy for leaving you alone so much."

"He does have to work hard," Priscilla said weakly.

"Sure he does. He's a Havlick and he's got to make something of himself," Noah said dryly. "But he shouldn't ignore you or the children."

She knew that, but it felt strange to hear Noah say it.

"If you were my wife, I wouldn't leave your side," he whispered.

"Don't," she said weakly. But hadn't she wanted this very thing?

Just then Faith opened the back door of the house and shouted, "Momma, Chloe's being naughty again! Momma! Can you hear me?"

"I'd better go," Priscilla whispered.

Noah caught her hand and squeezed it. "We'll talk again."

She nodded, then ran to the house, her cheeks flushed pink and her heart racing. If Justin didn't come home on time maybe she would ask Noah in for coffee. She put the kids to bed early and put on her new green dress.

What was she thinking?

A black cloud settled over her and she whimpered.

CHAPTER

10

◆ Emily sank to the edge of the bed and stared at the half-packed trunk in the middle of her bedroom floor. It was going to be harder to leave Michigan than she'd thought. Absently she twisted a strand of blue beads around her fingers. Her mind flashed to Bob's kiss and she moaned. Getting away from the temptation would be the best thing in the world for her. She wouldn't have the strength to resist Bob if they stayed. She bit her bottom lip. She'd miss her family! She'd never been away from them.

A rag doll dangling from her hand, Rachel slowly walked in and leaned against Emily. "Amanda can't go to Texas with me."

"I'm sorry." Emily kissed the top of Rachel's head. "You know her parents couldn't get along without her just like I couldn't get along without you."

"But I can't get along without her either!" Rachel rubbed her hand up and down Emily's arm. "What friend will I have at Daddy's ranch?"

"I don't know. We'll have to wait and see. But your daddy will be there and so will I." Emily's heart turned over. Would Trent continue to be cold toward her?

"Grandma Lark and Grandpa Clay won't be there. I'll miss them a whole lot, Emily. And Grandma Jennet and Grandpa Free won't be there." Rachel went down the list of all the Havlicks who wouldn't be there. "And the Bjoerlings won't be there. What will we do without all of them, Emily?"

"I don't know." Loneliness smote her and she held Rachel close, resting her cheek on Rachel's head. "I guess we'll have to find new friends and new people to take the place of family."

"I wish I'd get shot again."

"Rachel!" Emily held her away and looked into her face. "Don't even say that!"

"But if I did, then Daddy would let us stay here longer. He might start liking it enough to want to stay forever."

Hesitantly Trent poked his head around the corner of the door. He was wearing a plaid shirt and denim pants. His heart jerked at the picture Emily and Rachel made. He walked in and even managed a smile. "Hey, why the long faces?"

Rachel ran to him and wrapped her arms around his waist.

Emily stood, her legs trembling. Was Trent ready to be friends again?

"Daddy, we're afraid to move to Texas. We won't have any friends or any family."

Trent shot a look at Emily, then knelt down to look eye to eye with Rachel. "We'll have each other. And you'll like my friends there. You'll have a pony to ride and a dog I named Cricket because he's as quick as one. You'll like Cricket."

"I guess I might."

"You'll like riding your pony."

"I guess I will."

Trent hugged her, then stood up. "Run downstairs and see Grandma so I can talk with Emily, will you?"

Emily's nerves tightened.

Rachel ran out and the room was quiet. From the open window distant sounds of the Wagon Works drifted in with the closer sound of a dog barking.

His dark brows cocked, Trent took a hesitant step toward Emily. "Are you afraid to move?"

She shrugged. "A little."

"You'll like it there." Trent folded his arms across his broad chest and frowned at her. "I heard you went out yesterday to look over the property Grandma gave you."

Emily's cheek turned bright red. Had he also heard Bob had kissed her? "I did." Her voice was sharp and she forced it to sound normal. "I thought it was beautiful land."

His eyes flashed. "I thought you'd have more sense than to ride out alone. After what happened to Rachel."

"I never thought about that."

"You could've been shot!" He dropped his arms to his sides and clenched his fists.

Suddenly it was hard for her to breathe. "But I wasn't."

He gripped her arms. "I don't want you shot, too! I don't even want to have to worry about where you are and what you're doing!"

"You don't need to." She twisted to free herself, but he was too strong. His fingers bit through her sleeves into her arms.

"Did you see anyone out there?"

Her face flamed.

He saw her red cheeks and let her go. "Just who did you see that makes you look that way?"

Her stomach fluttered. "Does it matter?"

"Bob Lavery!"

She flushed again.

"And you talked to him!"

"Yes," she whispered.

He felt her tension and saw her agitation. "Suppose you tell me about this meeting with the great love of your life."

Words caught in her throat but she finally managed to say, "He asked about Rachel. And wondered when we were leaving Michigan."

"Don't tell me he's sorry he married the French girl and now wants you?"

She lifted her chin defiantly. "Am I so unlovable that you think that's impossible?"

"Of course not!"

"Then what do you think?"

He nudged her trunk with his toe. "I think I'll be glad when we're in Texas. And I'm glad to see you're getting the packing done. We'll leave tomorrow morning as early as possible."

"Tomorrow morning? So soon?"

"Not soon enough for me!" He cleared his throat. "Mom said she'd get the family together to say their goodbyes. Your family too, of course."

The tension seeped out of her. "I hate to leave, but I will be glad to get to Texas where we can start our life together."

He gripped her arms again and looked into her face. "You think it's going to be that easy, do you?"

She stiffened. "Isn't it?"

"You're treating me like a Bolshevik and you think I'll be willing to take you as my wife with open arms?"

Flushing, Emily lifted her chin high. "I am not treating you like a Bolshevik! I've tried to apologize to you for not being your true wife, but you won't let me. You won't even take time to talk to me the way we used to."

He stepped away from her and looped his thumbs in his pockets. "Things are different now."

She bit her bottom lip and took a hesitant step toward him. "Why can't we be friends again? Like we were . . . before?"

His heart jerked. "I'll think about it."

"I miss you."

He'd missed her too.

"I wanted you to see the valley yesterday." Then she thought of Bob and her legs gave way. She dropped to the edge of her bed.

"What's wrong?" he asked sharply.

"Nothing." She forced a smile. "The valley is perfect for cattle just like Jennet said."

Trent waved the words away in exasperation. "Let somebody else put cattle on it! We're going to Texas and that's final." He strode to the door, then turned to face her again. "Don't go out alone again."

She pressed her lips tightly together and clenched her fists as he strode away, his footsteps loud in the hallway and on the stairs.

* * *

Jennet sat in the bow of the boat as Abel Grant paddled across Deep Lake. He was wide chested with thick muscles and ebony colored skin. His voice was deep and cultured and reminded her of the huge black man, George Washington Foringer, who'd saved her life when Blue Newmeyer, a slave hunter, had tried to kill her for helping in the Underground Railroad. She'd hired Abel this morning to guard this side of the forest without telling anyone else, not even Freeman. He wouldn't understand why she needed more than Andree Bjoerling. She couldn't understand it herself, but she'd felt compelled.

"Free would be very angry if he knew I was here," she said as Abel expertly dipped the oar in and shot the boat forward.

"You're safe with me, Mrs. Havlick," Abel said.

"I know I am." Jennet smiled. She'd met Abel purely by chance at Fromberg last month and had taken an immediate interest in him. When she'd decided to hire another guard, she'd sought him out and asked for his help. He was a thirty-five-year-old schoolmaster on summer break and had gladly accepted.

Effortlessly he rowed to shore, then tied the boat down. The water was cold on his feet and ankles. He waded back as Jennet stood. "Let me carry you so you don't get your feet wet."

"That's not necessary at all, but thank you." She rested her hand lightly on his shoulder as he swung her easily up into his arms. He took a step forward, then froze. He'd caught a movement and heard a low growl.

"What?" Jennet asked, looking around. The smell of the water mixed with the smell of pine. Birds flew from the trees.

He waited, but nothing moved. "Nothing, I guess." Slowly he waded to shore and put Jennet on dry ground covered with pine needles. He touched the butt of his revolver as he looked around.

"I think somebody will try to stop us from putting the cabins up," Jennet said as they slowly walked away from the lake and into the forest. She'd told him her dream. Several feet into the woods she stopped and turned to him. "I need you to watch the place, keep all intruders out, and destroy the wild dogs."

"I'll do the best I can."

Without warning a huge wild dog sprang at them, brown hair bristling, a mad glitter in its eyes, growling deep in its throat. Abel knocked Jennet aside, sending her sprawling to the ground just as he jerked sideways and frantically reached for his revolver. The dog barely missed him, then seemed to whirl in mid-air and hurled itself forward. Snarling, it struck Abel in the chest, knocking him to the ground. Abel felt the hot breath and saw the sharp fangs ready to sink into his throat.

Jennet pushed herself up, grabbed a branch, and whacked the dog hard across the back.

It turned from Abel with a ferocious snarl and, ears laid back, snapped at her. She jumped back, tripped, and fell down hard, knocking the air out of herself. With a deadly growl the dog turned back on Abel, ready to sink its teeth deep. He caught the dog by the throat in a deathgrip. Its coat was tangled and filthy, its breath like a rotted dead animal. Abel's heart roared in his ears as he tried to press the dog's windpipe to shut off its air. Its muscles contracted spasmodically. Its saliva dripped down on him. He pressed its windpipe harder while the dog jerked and growled deep in its chest.

Her breathing ragged, Jennet struggled to her feet and swayed over Abel and the dog. If she tried to strike the dog again, Abel might lose his grip and the dog would be at his throat with its razor sharp teeth.

Abel felt the strength of his arms waning. His face and chest were wet from the dog's foamy saliva. He heard the dog's breath rattle and he pressed tighter. All at once the dog went limp in his arms. With a cry he threw the dog from him and struggled to his feet. The dog lay in a ragged heap at the base of a pine. Abel swayed. Blood oozed from his face and arms where the dog had torn his flesh with his fangs.

"Are you all right, Abel?" Jennet whispered hoarsely as she plucked at his torn sleeve.

"I've been better," he said weakly.

"Thank God we're alive. Let's get out of here before we get attacked again."

Abel nodded. His legs felt almost too weak to walk, but he forced them to move. "Do you know how many wild dogs are in the pack?"

"No. But I've heard stories from the farmers who've had sheep killed. Maybe five dogs." Jennet stepped around a branch, then quickened her pace to stay close to Abel. "I don't want you to feel you must take the job after what just happened."

"I want the job," he said grimly. "A dog gone wild is very dangerous." He stopped at the edge of the water. The boat rocked gently, tugging against the line. He carried Jennet to the boat and sat her down, pulled the line free, and climbed in himself. Would he have the strength to row back across the lake? It stretched smooth and clear for what seemed miles.

Jennet looked back into the woods. Should she give up her dream? There were too many dangers to face, too much opposition. Softly she said, "Heavenly Father, thank You for Your help, Your strength, and Your wisdom to do what's right."

Taking a deep, steadying breath Abel started rowing toward Fromberg.

Jennet saw the pain on Abel's face. "I can take over," she said hesitantly.

"No need." Could he keep rowing? Muscle spasms made him jerk his arms. "I'll take it slow and easy." The boat barely crept forward.

Jennet wanted to demand to take over, but she knew she would have a hard time rowing. Oh, why had her body grown so old! Why wasn't she strong like she'd been during her childhood when she could chop wood all morning and still have strength to do the chores?

The morning sun burned down on her, making her head sweat under her bonnet. Her dress was dirty and ripped at the hem. Her mouth was bone dry.

At the dock Abel climbed from the boat and secured it, then reached to help Jennet

Her legs trembled and she clutched Abel's muscled arm to keep from falling.

"You need a doctor, Abel." She glanced around to find someone who'd help, but the dock was empty.

He looked down at her and saw her wan face and felt her tremble. "Are you all right?"

"I'll be . . . fine." She tried to walk, but collapsed against him.

He lifted her easily and carried her to the first building, a warehouse with an office. He set her on a bench in the shade and found a drink of water for her.

She drank thankfully. "Please, sit down, Abel. You look ready to collapse."

He shook his head. His wounds hurt unbearably, but he didn't want her to know.

"Leave me and go get yourself taken care of."

"I can't just leave you!"

"You must! Look at yourself! You'll get infection in your scratches if you don't tend to them."

He touched his cheek gingerly and his fingers came away bloody. He sank down beside her.

"I must call my grandsons. They'll help us without worrying Free. Is there a telephone here?" She stood and the world seemed to spin. With a gasp she collapsed back on the bench. "I don't believe I can make it."

"I'll call for you."

"No. I must. Could you help me to the telephone?"

He lifted her again and carried her to the office where she got permission to use the telephone from a man too busy to notice the condition they were in. She had the operator ring the Wagon Works for her. Justin answered and for a minute she couldn't speak.

"Justin, I need you."

"Grandma?"

"Yes." She told him where she was and about the attack. "Bring Trent and come right away. Don't say a word to your pa or anyone else."

In his office Justin ran his fingers through his hair. What more was going to happen to them? He grabbed his hat and hurried into the factory where he knew Trent was talking with Dad near the outside door. Justin ducked around a finished wagon that had just been painted green. How could he get Trent without making Dad suspicious? In the past to get Trent to follow him without alerting Dad, he'd salute and keep on going. They'd made up the signal when they were seven years old and had used it until Trent had left. "I'll try it again," Justin muttered. He caught Trent's eye and saluted, then hurried out to his automobile.

Trent saw the salute and stopped talking mid-sentence. Had

he seen right? Did Justin want him? Justin had looked more upset than usual. "Dad, would you excuse me? I have to check on something. See you at home later."

"Is something wrong?" Clay asked, frowning.

"Not that I know about. I'll see you later."

Trent tugged his cap lower on his forehead as he dashed outdoors and looked around until he saw Justin just getting into his Duesenberg. A pain of anguish shot through Trent and he almost stopped. How could he be alone with Justin?

Justin motioned to him to hurry and Trent sprinted across to the auto. "What's wrong? Is it Rachel?"

"It's Grandma. Get in quick." Justin started the auto and backed out even as Trent was closing the passenger door.

"What about her?"

Justin told Trent what Grandma had said as he drove as fast as possible out of Blue Creek and north toward Fromberg.

"This is getting out of hand," Trent said, shaking his head as he braced his feet to keep from being thrown against Justin. "Why won't Grandma stay home where she belongs?"

"I say we drop this whole Havlick's Wilderness idea." Justin cut the air with his hand to emphasize his point, then gripped the steering wheel with both hands. "I never did like it. It's not too late to drop it."

"But we both know Grandma won't." Trent stared out the windshield at the road ahead.

"Maybe she will after this. I hope she's not hurt. You know how she understates things."

Trent had forgotten that about her.

Several minutes later they found Jennet sitting in the shade of the factory with a black man in bad shape beside her. Trent and Justin exchanged startled looks.

Jennet hugged Justin, then Trent, and said briskly, "This is Abel Grant. We must get him to a doctor immediately."

Abel was too weak to object. He greeted Trent and Justin with a wan smile.

Trent's head spun with questions, but he kept quiet as he helped Abel to his feet.

Justin swung Jennet up in his arms and carried her to his auto. She seemed very frail. He wanted to suggest she see a doctor too, but he knew she'd object.

There wasn't a doctor in Fromberg so they drove Abel to Doctor Kyle Mewsac in Blue Creek and waited while he dressed the wounds. Medium height and leaning toward fat, the doctor was in his thirties with neatly brushed reddish brown hair and blue eyes. The office was quiet and smelled like medicine.

"What happened to you, Grant?" Dr. Mewsac asked when he finished.

"Got in the way of a dog," Abel said. He didn't want to give information Jennet Havlick didn't want known.

"Keep the bandages changed regularly." His white coat flapping around his thick legs, Dr. Mewsac walked Abel to the waiting room where the Havlicks waited.

Trent jumped up. "Doc, take a look at my grandma, would you?"

"Now, Trent," Jennet said with a frown. "I'm all right. Just tired."

"Did you get in the way of the same dog?" Dr. Mewsac asked with a laugh.

"I sure did." Jennet nodded. She'd known Dr. Mewsac for almost three years and admired him for his hard work. "But how about Abel? Will he be all right?"

"He's a strong man and shouldn't have any problem if he takes care of himself." Dr. Mewsac took Jennet's pulse as they stood there.

"That's enough of that," she said sharply, pulling away from him. "I'm fine, I tell you."

"Grandma, we want to make sure," Justin said.

"It won't take long to have the doc look you over," Trent said.

"There is no need, boys!"

They shrugged, knowing it was the end of the discussion.

"Just where was this dog?" Dr. Mewsac asked.

Abel shrugged as he looked to Jennet for the lead.

Jennet brushed back a strand of white hair. "We're having a problem with wild dogs in our old growth. We were there today and one of the dogs jumped us."

"I'm surprised you got away with your lives," Dr. Mewsac said sharply.

"Abel throttled the dog," Jennet said proudly.

Abel flushed.

"Let's go, Grandma," Trent said. He didn't want her to tell all their business outside the family. It wasn't safe.

"I trust folks will stay away from your woods after this," Dr. Mewsac said sharply.

"I hope so too," Jennet said. "We're going to be clearing out a few trees so we can start building cabins."

Trent tried to hurry her out, but she wouldn't be hurried.

"I thought you'd given up on that idea," the doctor said, his reddish brown brow lifted.

"I don't know where you heard that," Jennet said. "It's just not so. We will continue with our work."

"I hope no one else is hurt because of your stubbornness, Mrs. Havlick. First your granddaughter shot, now this."

"They are hardly connected," Justin said impatiently.

"Well, no. I don't suppose they are. But they both caused harm."

Trent looked at the man shrewdly. Was he warning them about continuing? Surely not! Trent relaxed slightly. He was seeing enemies where none existed. "We have to get you home, Grandma. And you too, Abel."

Justin shook hands with the doctor, paid the bill, and followed the others out to his car. "Where shall we take you, Abel?"

Before he could speak Jennet said, "To the farm. He has no family and he's staying with us."

Trent and Justin exchanged looks, but knew not to argue.

Abel shook his head. "I can't impose on you, Mrs. Havlick."

"You were hurt in my employ and I won't send you off by yourself. There'll be no more argument." Jennet smiled and patted his arm. "Let us do this for you, Abel. It'll help ease my conscience for what happened to you today."

Abel grinned and nodded. "You're very kind."

"Never argue with a Havlick woman," Trent said, laughing. He thought of Emily—now a Havlick woman—and the laugh died. She was probably the most stubborn one so far. What in the world was he going to do with her?

Justin helped Jennet into the front seat while Trent and Abel sat in the back. Justin patted Jennet's knee. "I'm glad you're all right, Grandma. But in the future you stay home where you're safe and let us make Havlick's Wilderness a reality. We don't want anything to happen to you."

Jennet caught Justin's hand and squeezed it. "I'll be more careful, but I won't sit at home and do nothing to accomplish my dream."

Trent shook his head. Just what was going to happen next?

Later as Justin helped Jennet to the house, Abel laid a hand on Trent's arm.

"I didn't tell Mrs. Havlick this, but I saw a man in the woods just before the dog attacked us."

Trent sucked in his breath. "Why didn't he help you?"

Abel looked worried. "That's what I was wondering myself. I think it'd be better to keep her away from the woods. She hired me to kill the wild dogs and keep an eye on the land around Deep Lake. I'll do that. But I don't want her in danger again."

"I agree," Trent said as a shiver ran down his spine. But

why was Abel so concerned? He barely knew Jennet Havlick.

Later as they drove away from the farm, Trent told Justin what Abel had said. "I say we should report it to the sheriff."

Justin nodded. "I wonder who could've been out there? Not Andree. He would've jumped to their defense. Maybe we should go have a look."

"Maybe so. It's a little late to go today, but we could do it first thing in the morning."

"I thought you were leaving tomorrow."

Trent groaned. "I was. But after what happened today, I can't "

Justin gripped the steering wheel tightly. He'd been holding his feelings in so Trent could leave without a big blow up. How much longer could he do it? "This could take a while," he said stiffly.

"I know." Trent's stomach knotted. Could he stay around Justin even a day longer and not kill him?

Justin slowed the auto as he glanced at Trent. "What about the ranch you're going to buy?"

"Cactus Pete said he'd give me until the end of summer."

Justin burst out laughing, surprising himself as much as Trent. "What kind of name is Cactus Pete?"

Trent grinned "I had a chuckle over that one, too." He sobered "I think I'll hang around another month to see Havlick's Wilderness get started. Then I'll head on down to Texas."

Justin bit his tongue to keep from crying out in agony. A month! Could he survive a month with Trent?

Just then Trent saw Gabe Lavery beside his pickup truck at the Feed and Grain. "Stop here, Just. I'm going to tell Gabe I'll be moving back home. You don't have to wait for me."

Justin pulled up behind the pickup truck and waited until Trent climbed out, then drove away in a daze. Trent had called him Just! Was Trent forgetting? Was it possible for them to work out their problems after all?

Trent walked to the man beside the black pickup truck, nodded, and said, "Afternoon, Gabe."

Gabe looked toward the departing auto and back to Trent. "Justin? Trent?"

"Trent. I wanted a word with you about my place."

"I've kept it up good." Gabe smiled even as he tensed for the worst. "You plan on selling it since you're moving to Texas?"

"Can't say yet. But I do plan to move back in. I'll be staying on here for a while."

Gabe paled. "And how soon do you plan to move back?"

"As soon as possible. Is tomorrow too soon for you?"

"I do have a few things to clear out of the house and some livestock to take over to my place. How about giving me a couple of days?"

Trent thought for a while. "Tell you what. I'll come out and help you move your things. I want to be in there tomorrow."

Gabe's temper flared even as fear smote him. "Don't trouble yourself on my account. I'll be out tomorrow afternoon. You can move back in then."

"Fine." Trent held out his hand and finally Gabe took it and shook it. "If you can't get your livestock out tomorrow, don't fret about it. Move it when you can." Trent felt the tension in Gabe and wondered what it was all about. Trent tipped his cap and walked away.

Gabe flung himself in the pickup truck and roared away. How was he ever going to get all his stuff out by tomorrow? Where would he move the still? He struck the steering wheel with his fist. Trent Havlick was going to be very sorry for booting him out like that!

Trent walked slowly down main street. A few buggies and automobiles stood outside the stores. Three women stood in

161

front of the general store, talking and laughing. They smiled at him and called him Justin. He didn't correct them.

What would Emily say about staying on another month? He knew Rachel would be pleased. Would Emily find ways to be around Bob Lavery?

Trent doubled his fists. She was his wife and Bob Lavery had better stay away from her!

CHAPTER

11

♦ The smell of bread baking for supper followed Trent up the stairs. He stopped just outside Emily's closed bedroom door. Mom had told him she was there even though she'd finished packing. He wanted to tell her they were staying before he told anyone else. He reached for the doorknob, but stopped, afraid to walk in. Frowning at his own lack of courage, he knocked.

"Yes?"

"I need to talk to you"

"Trent?"

Impatiently he pushed open the door and strode in past the locked trunk. She was standing beside the bed, her hands at her throat. She wore a white blouse, a mid-calf length blue plaid pleated skirt, and ankle strap shoes with a low heel. Her red-rimmed eyes and sad face left him weak. "What's wrong?" he asked gruffly.

"Nothing," she said in a tiny voice.

"I can see there is."

She turned her face away, her black hair falling across her cheek. "You wouldn't want to listen anyway."

"Try me." He caught her hand and held it as he smiled.

She looked in his eyes and her pulse quickened. Was he ready to be friends again?

"Come on, Emily. Tell me what's wrong. Please."

"I . . . don't know if I can . . . leave my family. When will I see Mama and Papa again?"

Relief washed over him. He'd thought she was going to say she wanted out of the marriage. "Texas is a lot closer than Sweden."

"I know." Her voice rose in a wail. "But it's still a long way away."

"I'll make sure you get to see them."

"But it's still hard to leave them!"

"I'm sorry." He rubbed her wedding ring.

"Everything is different now." Tears filled her eyes. "And you're angry at me."

"Not any longer."

She opened her eyes wide in surprise and looked at him closely. "Aren't you still mad at me?" she whispered.

He shook his head.

"Are you sure?"

"Very sure."

"I am so glad!" She flung her arms around him and hugged him tight.

Startled, he just stood there, then hugged her and buried his face in her mass of black hair. He liked the apple smell of it and liked the feel of her soft body against him. "I have news that'll make you even happier."

His voice was muffled, but she'd heard him clearly. Trembling, she pulled away from him, but kept her hands on his shoulders. His hands at her waist felt warm and comforting. "What is it?"

"We're going to stay a while longer." He'd never noticed how dark and long her lashes were or how pretty her eyes were. "Maybe another month."

"Oh, Trent!" She laughed breathlessly. "I'm so glad!" She

hugged him again. She smelled the tang of his skin and felt the thud of his heart against her. Flushing, she jumped back. "Why'd you decide to stay?"

He pushed her hair off her damp cheeks and smoothed it down as he told her about Jennet, Abel, and the wild dog. He didn't tell her about the man Abel had seen or that Justin had gone to report it to the sheriff. "I told Justin I'd stay until Havlick's Wilderness gets under way."

"Are you sure?"

"I'd rather leave, but the family needs my help."

"You will be careful, won't you? I don't want a dog to attack you."

He smiled, pleased she cared. "I'm too tough anyway." He caught her hand and held it. "There's more."

Her pulse quickened. "Oh?"

"We're going to move to the farm tomorrow."

"To the farm? Oh, Trent! Can you handle that?"

A shudder ran through him. "Sure. You and Rachel will be there to help me."

"And that's a promise!"

He fingered the blue beads around her neck. "What about you? Can you handle running into Bob Lavery from time to time?"

She sucked in air. For a moment she'd forgotten about him. Could she keep him at arm's length if he wanted to be closer? She lifted her eyes to Trent. "If you'll help me."

He smiled gently. "I will. You can count on it."

Fresh tears filled her eyes. "Oh, Trent! I'm so glad we're friends again."

"Me, too, Emily. Me too." He'd missed her more than he'd realized and more than he thought possible.

"When do we move in?"

"Tomorrow afternoon."

"What about Gabe Lavery?"

"He's leaving right away."

"It'll be strange living at the farm."

Trent stiffened. Could he walk back in the room where he'd found Celine dead?

Emily saw the look on his face and knew what he was thinking. "Rachel and I will be right beside you, Trent. We'll help you."

"I haven't been there since the funeral."

She rubbed his arm. "I know. I know."

He bent his head as the agony swept over him again. She pulled him close and held him, soothing him with soft words. "Comfort his heart, Jesus," she whispered.

At last he stepped back, self-conscious for crying on her shoulder when it should've been the other way around. "I guess I'd better go."

"Does Rachel know we're staying?"

"No. I wanted to tell you first."

That pleased her. "Can we tell her together?"

"Sure. I know she'll be glad. She hates leaving Amanda and the family."

"She'll like living on the farm. She's pestered me often about going to the farm to see where she was born. And to see Celine's things."

Trent turned away. "Maybe you should take her alone for the first time. I don't think I could listen to and answer all her questions without crying like a baby."

"She'd understand."

"But I won't break down in front of her! I am her father, not some child!"

Emily cupped his cheek with her hand. "I know and so does she. If it'll help you, I will take her there by myself."

Trent covered her hand, locking it against his face. "Thank you." He liked the feel and smell of her skin. "I guess I'd better set you straight about our fight the day of our marriage."

She flushed and tugged at her hand, but he wouldn't release it.

"I had your brothers put your trunk in my bedroom so they wouldn't tease you."

Emily's eyes widened in surprise. "Why didn't you tell me?"

"I planned to, but you made me mad."

"So all this time we've been upset because of a misunderstanding!" She jabbed him with her free hand. "I don't like that a bit! I've been miserable without you, Trent Havlick!"

He caught her other hand, then held them both firmly in his. "I felt pretty bad myself. I guess all our secrets are out in the open now."

Bob's kiss flashed across her mind and she flushed scarlet. To cover up she quickly said, "You don't think I can tell you all my little secrets, do you?"

He chuckled. "You're an innocent girl. What secrets could you possibly have?"

"Not as many as you, I'm sure." She tugged him toward the door before he pursued the subject further. "Let's go tell Rachel and your mother."

* * *

The next morning, just after sunup, Trent picked up Justin at the Wagon Works and they drove to Fromberg. As they agreed, they both carried revolvers. Justin told Trent about his visit to Sheriff Lamont.

"He said Abel probably was only seeing things and to leave it up to him."

"Does he know we're heading there this morning?"

"No. I didn't figure it was any of his business. It is Havlick land."

"Maybe we'll run into him while we're there."

Justin shrugged. "Maybe."

167

Several minutes later they rowed across Deep Lake without talking. In silence they tied the boat securely and walked into the woods where Jennet said she and Abel had gone. Birds twittered in the high branches of the trees.

"Here it is," Trent said in a low voice. The ground was bare where Abel and the dog had fought. The broken branch Jennet had struck the dog with lay near the base of a pine. Wind whispered through the tall branches.

Trent shot Justin a startled look. "Where's the carcass?" he asked just above a whisper.

His nerves tight, Justin glanced around. No wild animal would eat a dead dog. A buzzard might pick its flesh off but the bones would be left behind. "Maybe Abel didn't kill the dog." His voice was low and terse. A shiver trickled down his spine. He turned to Trent. "Would Abel lie about killing the dog?"

"Why would he? Besides, Grandma saw it all." Trent walked away from the spot, his eyes on the ground for footprints or other signs to show that someone else had been there. He couldn't see anything. He glanced at Justin and shrugged. Would Abel lie about seeing a man here? Or had he been mistaken?

"Maybe the sheriff did something with the dog's body."

"Why would he?" Trent shook his head. "I doubt if the sheriff's been here yet. It's early."

"You're right. It sure is a mystery."

"Sure is." Watching his step in case of snakes, Trent slowly climbed a hill with Justin close behind him. They stopped in a spot where one of the cabins was going to be built. He heard a stream trickling through the woods to his left. It meandered down into a ravine and out of sight.

"I don't like this one bit," Justin said as he pushed his cap back.

"Something's going on. That's for sure." Trent looped his thumbs over his belt as he slowly looked around. He saw bushes leafed out, the ground covered with years of pine needles and leaves, and trees as far as the eye could see. He caught a flicker of movement and stood stone still. Had it been a deer? A bear? Or was it a man? Trent motioned in the direction and whispered to Justin, "I thought I saw something."

Justin narrowed his eyes, but couldn't see a thing. "Let's check it out." He led the way, his heart racing.

Just then a man stepped from behind a tree, shotgun pointed right at Justin's heart. "Hands up!" the man commanded. He wore high-top walking shoes, heavy pants, and a gray shirt. Black hair hung below a dark gray cap.

Trent wanted to grab for his gun, but he lifted his hands high as he stopped beside Justin.

Justin's hand itched to jerk his revolver out of the holster, but he also slowly raised his hands.

"Who are you and what're you doing here?" the man snapped. A white scar stood out boldly on his left cheek. "This *is* private property."

Trent narrowed his eyes. "And we happen to own it!"

"You're the one trespassing," Justin said coldly.

The man studied them several minutes. "Are you two Havlicks?"

"Justin and Trent," Trent said, motioning to himself and Justin as he said their names.

The man blew out his breath. Finally he lowered his gun. "Forgive me, men. I'm Pierce Lorraine, federal agent."

"What're *you* doing *here?*" Trent snapped, resting his hand on his revolver.

"Did our grandma hire you without telling us?" Justin asked sharply.

The man shook his head. "I'm a federal agent." He shoved his badge out to them and held it while they looked at it. "I work for the government to stop the making and selling of alcohol."

"But why are you here?" Justin waved his hand to indicate where they were.

Pierce Lorraine narrowed his eyes and a muscle jumped in his jaw. "There's a still in your woods."

"What?"

"That's impossible!"

"A man by the name of Leroy Bushnell operates it and several others around Fromberg and Blue Creek. He supplies liquor to Gilly's Place and a few other speakeasies on this side of the state."

Trent's stomach knotted. "How do you know this?"

"I followed him here. But I lost him before I could find the still. He's from North Carolina and he knows about moonshine and stills and revenue men."

Justin pushed his cap back. "Does he know you're here?"

"No. I don't think so. And I want to keep it that way."

Trent told him about the wild dog and the man Abel had spotted. "Did you see that happen?"

"No. But I did see Leroy Bushnell bury the dog. It belonged to him. He trained it to attack at his command, and return at a whistle."

Justin and Trent exchanged shocked looks.

"Why didn't you arrest this Bushnell?" Justin asked.

"He's working with someone in Blue Creek. I want them all, not just Bushnell."

Impatiently Trent brushed a bug off his sleeve. He wished he could rid the woods of Leroy Bushnell as easily. "Have you spoken to the sheriff?"

"No. In my business I can't trust anyone. I've told you fellas because I need help. You're Havlicks. If you know these woods you could help me find the still."

Justin moved restlessly. "Then what?"

"I'll keep an eye on it and on Bushnell so I can see who else is involved."

"How'd you get here?" Trent looked down toward the lake. "I didn't see a boat."

Agent Lorraine chuckled dryly. "I rowed out from Fromberg

like I was going fishing, then rowed close to the bank along your woods. I hid the boat behind an outcropping of rocks and climbed up there. Bushnell hides his boat near where yours is tied up. He's got it hid so well it took me a while to find it among the bushes. He takes a different route to the still so he never makes a trail."

"Smart man," Trent said, shaking his head.

"We heard tell about a pack of wild dogs. Have you seen them?" Justin asked.

"No. I think it was just a rumor Bushnell spread. But keep your eyes peeled in case he has more than one dog." Agent Lorraine explained to them what they were looking for and that Bushnell's still would be near a stream or creek. "Whatever you do, don't jump the man. He's dangerous. I'll be in the boarding house in Blue Creek tonight, Room 10. If you learn anything, stop in and tell me. I checked in as Joe Bent, a salesman."

Nodding, Trent and Justin walked silently away, watching for signs of trespassing.

About two hours later they found the still hidden in a ravine with branches growing across to make a natural hideaway. The smell turned Justin's stomach. Trent watched a tiny trickle of smoke rise and dissipate in the tree branches.

Cautiously they crept away from the ravine and back to their boat. They didn't speak until they were in the middle of the lake.

"I plan to tell Andree what's going on," Trent said as he dipped in the oar.

"Good. But we'll keep it from Grandma. First thing she'd do is come here and try to capture Bushnell. She'd do it, too! Can't you just see her filling him with buckshot?" Justin chuckled and Trent joined in.

They looked at each other and laughed harder.

* * *

Priscilla walked restlessly back and forth in front of the picnic table while the children shouted and laughed and played in the yard. Her short blue skirt flipped about her knees. She ran a finger around the neckline of her plaid blouse. The hot afternoon sun burned down on her, putting her temper on the verge of exploding.

"Want some company?" Noah asked with a grin.

Her heart leaped and she nodded. How handsome he looked in his light gray shirt and dark trousers! His brown hair was parted on the right and slicked back above his ears and back off his forehead. "I thought you were gone for the day."

Gabe Lavery had paid him to come back and play up to Priscilla. He smiled into her eyes. This was going to be an easy, pleasurable job. "I came back early."

"Oh?" She fingered her bobbed hair. "Why?"

"I missed you too much."

His words turned her to jelly and she sank to the bench. "You did?" she whispered.

He sat beside her and took her hand in his. Gabe had said Justin Havlick and all the Havlicks were going to have Gilly's Place and all the other speakeasies shut down, so they had to do everything they could to get the Havlicks' minds off bootlegging and illegal drinking. "Make family problems and they'll soon forget all about other things," Gabe had said. Noah leaned close to Priscilla. "I'm fed up with the way your husband ignores you. I want you to leave him and go away with me."

She gasped. "But I can't!"

"Sure you can."

"But I'm married to Justin."

"So what?"

"I couldn't . . . leave him!"

"Sure you could." Maybe this wasn't going to be as easy as he thought. "You and me and the children could have some good times together."

"Oh my."

"I got some money. We could go far away."

Priscilla's heart fluttered as pictures flashed across her mind of the fun she could have with Noah. "I don't know," she said weakly.

He lifted her hand to his lips and kissed her palm. He liked making her heart beat faster.

A thrill ran through her.

He pressed her hand to his cheek as he looked at her tenderly. "You're a beautiful lady and you deserve to be loved and cared for. You deserve it all! You think about it and let me know."

"I will."

"You're important to me. So are the children. I want to show you the world!" He lowered his voice to a husky whisper. "I want you to know how it feels to have a real man love you."

Her heart lurched. Wasn't this what she'd wanted from him? Then why was she afraid to take what he was offering?

* * *

It was three in the afternoon. Emily took a deep breath and opened the back door to Trent's farmhouse. Rachel stood at her heels. For once she wasn't chattering.

Emily stepped into the enclosed porch that held the washing machine and stack of split wood, then on into the kitchen. A strange smell hung in the air. A breeze ruffled the curtains at the windows. Gabe Lavery had probably left them open to air the house. The room was clean except for a fine dusting of what looked like ground corn in the corners nearest the cast iron range. An oblong oak table with four chairs around it stood in the middle of the large kitchen.

"Did my momma Celine cook at this stove?" Rachel asked, her eyes wide.

Emily nodded.

Rachel touched the tall cupboard with glass doors, the pie

safe, the sideboard, the washstand with a red hand pump. "Celine touched all of this."

"Yes, she did." Emily blinked tears away. Many times she'd worked side by side with Celine in this very kitchen. They'd canned together, baked Christmas goodies together, cooked meals together.

Rachel ran into the dining room just off the kitchen through wide oak pocket doors. She rubbed a hand over the cherry table and counted aloud the eight chairs around it. She patted the matching hutch, buffet, and corner hutch. She studied the fancy dishes and the white china pitcher and bowl with red cabbage roses painted on it sitting on top of the buffet. "I like Celine's things, Emily."

It was hard to speak around the lump in her throat. "So do I."

Rachel slipped her hand in Emily's as they walked into the parlor, the front room, the den, then up the wide stairs to the four huge bedrooms. A wooden cradle stood beside a large bed in the first bedroom.

Rachel touched the cradle and lifted wide dark eyes to Emily. "Was this mine?" she whispered.

Emily's tongue clung to the roof of her mouth and she could only nod. She saw the bed where Celine had given birth to Rachel. She walked around the spot where Celine had crumpled to the floor.

"Is this where Momma died?" Rachel whispered, standing beside the huge bed and looking down at the wooden floor.

"Yes. But she's in heaven now, Rachel."

"I know. She's with Jesus."

Emily stood at the window. She would not have this for the master bedroom! She'd make this into a pleasant sitting room and play room. She'd change the drapes and put in a sofa and rocking chair.

Rachel led the way to the other bedrooms down the wide hall. Two of the bedrooms were empty and the fourth had a four poster walnut bed and dresser that looked old and cherished. It was a bed Freeman's grandfather had passed down. Free had given it to Trent. This would be the bedroom she'd share with Trent. She flushed, turning away quickly before Rachel noticed.

Emily looked out the window, waiting for her brothers to arrive to help her.

"Where will I sleep?" Rachel asked, leaning against Emily.

"You can have the room across the hall from this or the one beside it."

Rachel ran to look out the windows of both rooms. She stayed in the one across the hall. "I can see the river from here. I'll take this room."

"Good. We'll make it pretty for you."

"But not pink!"

Emily laughed. "No, not pink."

Several minutes later Emily's brothers arrived and she had them move the furniture where she wanted it. She took the drapes off the windows in Celine's room and put up the blue and rose floral drapes that had hung in the front room. The boys carried a sofa from the front room and set it against a wall with a low coffee table in front of it. They carried a rocker in from the parlor and Emily laid a rag rug in front of it. She set Rachel's dollhouse and several of her dolls near the window. She found pictures throughout the house that would look nice in the room. Soon the room looked so different it was hard to imagine it had been a bedroom.

The boys put Celine's bedroom furniture in Rachel's room. With a different spread and a different color around it, even the furniture looked different. Rachel lined up three dolls on the pillows, then stood back, satisfied. Her small rocker stood in one corner beside a short table with a kerosene lamp on it.

While Emily worked upstairs Martha, Zoe, and Hannah worked downstairs. They were glad Trent was staying even if only another month. Martha had reminded Emily of what she'd said a few days ago about Trent never leaving. Emily had brushed the idea aside once again.

Soon the house smelled of pie baking and beef stew boiling.

Emily's brothers did the chores, then left for home to do their own chores. Shortly afterward the women said goodbye and left.

Later Emily and Rachel stood in the kitchen at the window. Fire crackled in the range. Outdoors a turkey gobbled.

"Are you sure Daddy's coming?"

"I'm positive."

"What if he goes to Texas without us?"

"He won't." Emily pulled Rachel close as they stood at the window and watched the lane for Trent's blue Dodge. "Maybe we should eat. I'm hungry."

"I guess we could. I did want to wait for Daddy."

"Me too, but he might be really late." Emily dipped stew into two bowls and sliced the bread Lark had sent with them. With Rachel talking only a little, they ate. The stew was delicious, but Emily couldn't enjoy it. She jumped at every little sound.

They walked to the parlor and Rachel tried to play the piano "I remember hearing Celine play the piano," Rachel said.

Emily smiled gently. "You remember me telling you about her playing."

"I know. I wish I could really remember it."

Several minutes later Trent drove in and stopped near the back door. The last time he'd lived here, he'd driven a buggy instead of an auto. He gripped the steering wheel. Could he get out and walk to the door as if this was just any old house?

Emily and Rachel stepped out the back door and waved.

"Hi, Daddy! I like our house!"

Emily's stomach tightened. She knew it was hard for Trent to walk to them so they walked to him. "We ate supper without you. I hope you don't mind."

"Not at all."

"We waited and waited," Rachel said. "And we got too hungry."

Trent bent down and kissed Rachel's cheek, then turned to Emily. "Sorry I wasn't here sooner. I got held up in town." He and Justin had reported to Agent Lorraine and they'd learned what he planned to do next.

"I like our house, Daddy." Rachel tugged on his hand. "I like the animals, too."

Trent hesitated, almost too weak to step through the back door.

"Everything's in order," Emily said cheerfully as she nudged Trent from behind

He walked in and stopped near the table. The room was familiar, but also different.

"Your Aunt Hannah baked an apple pie for us," Emily said, pointing to the still warm pie on the top shelf of the pie safe.

"Smells good," Trent said around the lump in his throat. Celine had made delicious apple pies. She favored making cherry pie, but she'd made apple especially for him.

They walked through the house Outside the master bedroom Trent broke out into a sweat. Emily caught his hand and held it firmly, then pushed open the door and followed Rachel in.

Trent looked around in surprise at the changes. The dull ache of losing Celine was there, but the stabbing agony was gone. "Thank you," he whispered to Emily.

She smiled and nodded.

"Come see my room, Daddy!" Rachel ran down the hall and stopped in the doorway of her room. She pointed across the hall. "You and Emily have that room and I have this one."

Startled, Trent turned to Emily. "Is that right?"

She barely nodded.

A muscle jumped in his jaw. Was he ready for this? He strode down the hall to look in Rachel's room, but his mind was on Emily and on Celine.

Long after Rachel was asleep, Emily slipped into bed, her nerves as tight as the ropes that held the mattresses. Would Trent come to bed with her or stay downstairs? The lamp burned a low flame on the stand beside the bed. She heard every creak in the house and every sound outside the house. She closed her eyes, but they popped open the minute her eyelids covered her eyes.

Finally Trent walked in, blew out the lamp, undressed, and slipped in beside her. He didn't reach out for her or turn to her. "This is hard for both of us," he said in a tight voice. "I would've stayed downstairs, but the couch was too small and the floor too hard."

Emily breathed a sigh of relief. "When the time is right we'll become man and wife."

"Yes. I thought you'd understand." He turned on his side facing away from her and fell asleep.

She listened to him breathe and almost reached out to touch him. Her face flamed and she kept her hands at her sides and her back poker straight.

The next morning when she woke up he was gone.

CHAPTER

12

◆ Yawning, Justin looked through the pile of bills on his office desk. Early morning sunlight shafted through the window behind him. A cup of coffee he'd made himself was at his elbow. He wore a white shirt with a figured tie and dark pants. The bills in his hand crackled. If they didn't get oak for chairs soon, the Wagon Works would be in bad shape—worse than last year. He heard the first men arriving for work. He yawned again. Priscilla had been in one of her moods again last night and wouldn't let him get to sleep.

She'd rested her head on his arm and put her arm across him while he lay on his back. "Justin, let's get somebody to watch the children and then ride the train to Grand Rapids. We could stay a couple of days at the hotel and spend time together, eat in a nice restaurant, and maybe even go to the theater. Could we do that, Justin?"

"I have too much going on," he'd answered, already half asleep.

"Then how about if you come home from work early tomorrow? I'll feed the children early and put them to bed. We could have the whole evening together—just the two of us. Please, Just?"

"I'm bone tired, Pris. Let me get some sleep, will you?" He turned away from her and pretended to sleep. She sobbed quietly into her pillow for a long, long time. He'd almost gathered her in his arms, but he couldn't make himself move. He'd gone to sleep while she was still crying.

Now at his office desk, he yawned again. Things weren't right between him and Priscilla, but he couldn't spend time thinking about it. He had to keep the Wagon Works going, even while he worried about bootleggers and Grandma's dream of Havlick's Wilderness.

The door opened and Trent walked in, his cap in his hand. His blue chambray shirt was buttoned to his throat and at the cuffs. A wide leather belt circled his hips and held up his denim pants. "Anything new from Agent Lorraine?"

Justin stifled another yawn. "Nothing that I know about."

"It's been two days!" Trent paced the small office. He'd slept soundly the night before, just as he had the first night with Emily, and woke at the crack of dawn with his arm around her, just as he had the first night. For a split second he'd thought she was Celine. He'd crept out of bed, dressed, and hurried away before Emily stirred. She did look pretty when she slept—her cheeks rosy and her hair in two braids. Abruptly he pushed thoughts of Emily aside to take care of the business at hand. "I think we should get Bushnell ourselves so we can get the crew out there."

"Maybe so." Justin rubbed a hand across his face. For two nights he hadn't slept well. Priscilla had tossed and turned and even mumbled in her sleep. Well, he couldn't think about her or his lack of sleep now. He had more important issues at hand. "Know where we can get oak right away?"

"Did you try the Havlicks south of Grand Rapids?"

"Yes. Cousin Steven doesn't have any. I've tried all my other sources, but the prices are way out of reach. We can kiln dry the oak in the old growth that we'll cut down, but we can't wait that long. This is serious, Trent. We have orders to fill before the end of July and if we don't get them filled, we might lose the accounts."

Frowning thoughtfully, Trent perched on the corner of Justin's huge walnut desk that was cluttered with papers, drawings of chairs and wagons, a telephone, and a cup of coffee. "Remember old Sam McDaniel near Caledonia?"

Justin narrowed his eyes thoughtfully. "I don't. What about him?"

"We sometimes got oak from him. I'll contact him and see what he has to say."

Justin smiled. "Thanks. It's great not to carry this alone."

Trent shot up. "Don't get used to it. I won't be here long."

Justin's nerves tightened. "I know." He looked back at the mail in his hands. He flipped through it, stopped at an envelope that looked soiled and was addressed with a pencil in a scrawl that could be a child's. "What have we here?"

"What?" Trent leaned over the desk to look.

"It's addressed to both of us." He turned the envelope for Trent to read their names written in inch tall letters. "Somebody dropped it off."

A shiver trickled down Trent's spine. "Open it."

Justin pulled a piece of lined paper from the envelope. He unfolded it and read aloud: "You Havlick twins think you have everything. But you don't. Ask Priscilla how she likes Noah Roswell's romantic attentions." Justin's mouth dried to dust and the letter fell to the desk. His face turned a chalky white.

With an angry cry Trent scooped up the letter and read, "Ask Emily about Bob Lavery's kisses. You Havlick twins are losing your wives and you don't even know it." Trent sank to a chair, his whole insides on fire. He flung the letter to the floor. The words looked bold on the white paper and seemed to jump up for him to see all over again. "Lies!" he said hoarsely.

"What if it's not?" Justin raked his fingers through his dark hair.

"It has to be!"

The door opened and Clay walked in dressed in dark work pants, held up by wide black suspenders, and a green plaid shirt, his cap in his hand. He stopped short. "What's wrong?"

Justin struggled to pull himself together, but couldn't.

Trent turned his face away.

Clay saw the paper on the floor, picked it up, and read it, then savagely balled it up. "Lies! You boys can't believe those lies!"

They looked at each other, at their dad, then nodded.

His brow knit, Clay hauled a chair up near the desk and straddled it. "Tell me what's going on, boys! It seems I've been missing something. Justin, you start."

He flushed, feeling like a boy again. He had to admit it felt good to have Dad take over. Justin talked, too numb to know what to do. "I know Pris likes Noah. He takes time for the children and he talks to her. But I never thought it would go this far."

"Maybe it hasn't!" Clay cleared his throat. "But I have noticed you've been neglecting her."

"But . . ."

Clay lifted his hand to stop Justin. "You know you have. We've talked about this several times already."

Justin raked his fingers through his dark hair. "It doesn't give her any right to two-time me with the hired man! And a kid at that! He's twenty-one years old and she's close to thirty!"

"Don't let your temper make things worse."

Justin growled. If he had Noah Roswell here right now, he'd beat him within an inch of his life!

"Let Trent talk now." His gray brow lifted, Clay turned to Trent. "I know there've been rumors about Emily and Bob Lavery. But that's all it was. I know Emily."

Trent thought of the look on Emily's face when he learned she'd talked to Lavery the day she looked over the property Grandma gave her. That had been a guilty look if ever he had seen one. "You don't know her as well as you think, Dad." A hurt stabbed deep within as Trent told his story.

Justin jumped up, almost spilling his cup of coffee. "I'm going home right now!"

"Sit down!" Clay barked.

Surprised, Justin sat.

Trent sat on the edge of his chair, his muscles bunched, ready to spring up.

Clay's gaze softened. "It's not going to do a bit of good to rush home with your tempers flying and demand an explanation. We got to think this through. We got to pray for wisdom."

Trent sprang up, his fists doubled. "You pray, Dad. I'm going to get the truth out of Emily now!"

Justin shot around the desk and shook his fist at Trent. "It's your fault this happened! If you'd stayed home to help me run the business, I would've had more time."

"Boys! Boys!" Clay gripped Trent's arm and reached for Justin, but he backed away. "You boys have been spoiling for a fight for weeks now. But fighting's not the answer and you both know it. God is the answer."

"I don't want to hear it," Trent snapped, twisting free of Clay. "Preach to Justin. He's the killer of the family!" Trent strode out, slamming the door behind him.

Justin's face was as white as his shirt. Killer! That's exactly what he was. Yet the words burned him, especially coming from Trent after the past several days of working together without fighting.

"Killer? What does Trent mean?" Clay asked, frowning.

"It's between him and me, Dad."

"I want to know so I can help you!"

Justin shook his head. His face set, he grabbed his cap off the peg near the door and stormed from the office, leaving the door wide open.

Clay moaned. Hot tears stinging his eyes, he covered his face with his hands and prayed.

Outdoors Justin ran toward his auto, his mind reeling. He didn't deserve a wife and family, but he couldn't let Noah Roswell steal them!

"Justin!" Trent shouted frantically from his Dodge parked on the side of the street under a maple. "I need you, Justin!"

He looked toward the street to see if he'd heard right. Abel Grant stood at the side of Trent's car while Trent sat in the driver's seat. They were motioning wildly to him. Fear shot through Justin. He veered away from the parking lot and ran to the street, his collar suddenly feeling too tight. "What's wrong?"

"Your grandma took another walk by herself," Abel said in agitation, his ebony face glistening with sweat, his hand on the butt of his revolver.

"And she went to the woods!" Trent slapped the steering wheel in frustration.

"I tried to talk her out of it, but you know your grandma."

"Let's go get her," Justin said gruffly as he ran around and climbed in the passenger seat.

Abel climbed in the back seat of the Dodge and was barely seated when Trent took off. "She was gone this morning when I came down for breakfast She left me a note That's why I came after you I knew I couldn't find my way around the woods like you two can. Your grandpa went away with Tris and Zoe, so I couldn't tell them."

Justin groaned as he braced himself to keep from falling against Trent as they turned a corner. Would Grandma walk to the area where Bushnell had his still? Maybe Agent Lorraine was watching him and would be there to protect Grandma. Justin tried to pray, but the words stuck in his throat. He hadn't been able to pray since the devastating day of Celine's death.

Trent gripped the steering wheel so tightly his knuckles hurt. Would they get to the woods in time to keep Grandma safe? Maybe she wouldn't walk in the area of the still. His heart sank. She'd want to stand where the cabins were going to be built. Bushnell's still was in the ravine several yards from the very spot where one cabin was to be. Driving to Fromberg and rowing across the lake was much quicker than trying to run through the woods with the swamps and briars, not to mention the wild creatures that always meant danger. Grandma would take a gun; she always did. Trent glanced at the glovebox. His revolver was in it. He knew Abel carried one, but Justin didn't.

After what seemed like hours, but was only part of an hour, they tied the boat at the edge of the white pine forest. Trent led the way as they ran silently through the woods from tree to tree like Indians toward the ravine and the still. It had rained the night before and their steps were muted on the fallen leaves and pine needles. They stopped behind a clump of bushes and peered around them down at the ravine. The wind carried the smell of the corn liquor away. No smoke drifted up that they could see. Honey bees swarmed on a low hanging limb of a wild cherry tree. Deeper in the woods a crow cawed. A heckling bluejay darted from bough to bough. The smell of damp leaf mold rose around them.

"Maybe the sheriff or Agent Lorraine already arrested Bushnell," Justin whispered.

Trent caught a movement in the ravine. His nerves jangling, he nudged Justin and Abel and pointed. As they watched, Sheriff Lamont walked into sight, deep in conversation with the man they knew from Agent Lorraine's description was Leroy Bushnell. His face was almost covered with wild, uncombed whiskers and a mustache that hid his mouth. Long shaggy dark hair hung below a wide brimmed hat that looked like he'd worn it since the turn of the century. Why was the sheriff talking to Bushnell as if they were in cahoots? Trent frowned. He and Justin exchanged puzzled looks.

Abel jabbed Justin and motioned to their right. A walking

stick in her hand, Jennet Havlick stepped into full view of the sheriff and Bushnell. She was looking down and didn't see them. A blue bonnet covered her white hair. A revolver hung in the holster strapped around her waist. Her blue and white dress made a splash of color against the dull gray bark of the trees.

Bitter gall rose in Justin's throat, almost choking him as he forced himself to hold back a shout.

A knife-sharp pain stabbed at Trent's stomach. He wanted to call to her, but pressed his lips closed and bunched his muscles, ready to leap to her defense.

Groaning from deep inside, Abel drew his revolver.

Jennet looked up and caught sight of the sheriff and Bushnell. She frowned, then waved, and called, "Sheriff! What brings you out here? And who's that with you?"

The sheriff growled something to Bushnell that Trent couldn't hear, then strode up the incline to where Jennet stood while Bushnell disappeared in the ravine.

"You here alone, Mrs. Havlick?" Sheriff Lamont asked, his face red.

Jennet laughed softly. "I know I shouldn't be, but I have protection."

Lamont wiped a thick hand over his hook nose "Where's the Negro you hired to guard this side of the woods?"

"At home. He's feeling much better after the dog attacked him, but I didn't want him coming here until he's a little better." Jennet looked down at the ravine. "Who's the man you were talking to? Why's he here?"

"He's working with me to catch the bootleggers. Now, suppose you head back to your place."

A shiver ran down Trent's back. He lifted his brows as he looked at Justin and Abel.

"Liar!" Justin mouthed, his face a dark thundercloud.

Trent and Abel angrily nodded in agreement.

Just then Leroy Bushnell strode up out of the ravine with a double barrel shotgun at his shoulder. He stopped several yards from Jennet and Lamont. "Step aside Lamont."

Trent's blood ran cold as he drew his revolver. He felt fear in Justin and Abel. He saw Abel lift his gun. They didn't know what to do, what with the sheriff there to see that the law was upheld.

"Bushnell, you fool!" the sheriff cried "You can't shoot her!"

"Who sez?" Bushnell's whiskers bristled and he waved the barrel of the shotgun. "Step aside 'less you want shot deader 'n a skunk!"

Jennet cried out, her hand at her racing heart. She wanted to reach for her revolver at her side, but she knew there wasn't time. Silently she prayed for a miracle. That's what it would take. The man was indeed planning to shoot her, but she didn't know why and she didn't know why the sheriff wasn't doing something about it.

"There's another way, Bushnell!" the sheriff cried, holding out his hand as if he could ward off a slug

Bushnell sighted the shotgun on Jennet

The sheriff jumped away from Jennet

Abel fired at Bushnell The shot whizzed past Bushnell and he jerked back. The shotgun exploded just as Jennet dropped to the ground.

Jennet's head whirled and she was too frightened to reach for her gun. She lifted her head in time to see the sheriff aiming his gun right at her. "No!" she screamed.

Trent leaped around the bushes, his revolver pointed at the sheriff. "Don't make a move, Lamont, or I'll kill you where you stand!"

"Trent!" Jennet cried, too weak to move.

His face black with anger, Lamont dropped his gun and raised his arms high.

Cursing angrily, Bushnell lifted his shotgun. Abel fired again. The bullet plowed into the man's chest, knocking him back. The shotgun flew from his hands and landed on the ground.

With a strangled cry Justin raced to Jennet and pulled her tight into his arms. She clung to him, trembling.

"Get that gun off me!" the sheriff shouted at Trent. "I'm a law man. I was here to protect your grandma."

"We saw it all," Trent snapped as he strode toward the sheriff. "No story you tell will do you any good." He turned and looked down at Bushnell. "It looks like he's dead."

With lightning speed the sheriff scooped up his gun, but before he could fire at Trent, Justin caught up a branch that looked much like the cudgel his mother had carried while guarding the pines years ago and flung it at the sheriff. It struck his shoulder and the gun fell from his hand.

Justin grinned. He'd thought he wouldn't remember what his mother had taught him. But he had. He'd never been as good as she was with the cudgel, but he'd been good.

"Good move, Just," Trent said, grinning.

Justin smiled back. "Thanks."

Abel found the sheriff's handcuffs and locked them on the man's wrists and sat him against the base of a pine.

"Abel, you stay with Grandma while we check out the still and Bushnell," Trent said.

Abel nodded, his eyes on Jennet.

Trent and Justin walked away, talking about what had just happened.

Jennet shivered and wrapped her arms around herself.

Abel stepped closer to Jennet. "You all right, ma'am?"

Jennet smiled and nodded, then shivered again. "I should've listened to you."

"I know." Abel holstered his gun.

Jennet touched Abel's arm. "You saved my life."

"Now we're even"

"What'd you mean?" Jennet studied him thoughtfully. "You've been acting as if you know me from the time we first met. Suppose you tell me what's going on."

Abel pulled off his cap and looked down at Jennet. "Years ago you helped a slave named Dacia find freedom—Dacia and her newborn baby, Colin."

"Dacia! Yes, I remember. I hid Colin in my laundry basket and had Dacia dress in Freeman's clothes. I took them to my pa and on the way we got stopped by a slave hunter, Blue New-meyer."

"You gave him a paper he thought was Dacia's identification papers and the only word the man could read was *free*."

Jennet gasped. "How did *you* know!"

Abel laughed. "Colin is my daddy and Dacia, my granny."

Tears welled up in Jennet's eyes. "Your granny?"

"I came to find you to thank you for what you did for us."

Jennet held her hands out to Abel.

"I promised Granny I'd find you no matter how long it took and that I'd stay until I helped you to partly repay you for what you did all those years ago when you were no more than a girl yourself."

"I want to hear everything!" For the moment Jennet pushed aside thoughts of Bushnell near the ravine and the sheriff handcuffed several feet away. "How is Dacia?"

"She's doing just fine for her age. She married when she was about eighteen and had eight more children. All of 'em born free just like she wanted." Abel brushed at his eyes.

"And baby Colin?" Jennet whispered around the lump in her throat.

"Grew up to be a fine man—a blacksmith by trade. I know the trade too, but I went to school and became a school master." Abel's voice broke. "All the family got schooling. Even Dacia learned to read and write."

189

Jennet wiped away a tear. "I never expected to hear from any of the slaves I helped. Thank you for finding me to tell me your story."

While Jennet and Abel talked, Trent and Justin walked down to the ravine. Trent bent over Bushnell. "He's dead."

Justin's stomach rolled and he looked quickly away.

They walked down in the ravine and stood at the side of the still. Behind the still stood a small cabin—four walls and a roof. It housed the sugar and ground corn as well as a cot, a blanket, and a tiny stove with a pot of coffee on it.

"We'll destroy the still and save Agent Lorraine a trip out here," Trent said.

Justin shook his head. "I figure prohibition will be over someday and the tourists that come to Havlick's Wilderness would like to see this still. We'll ruin it so it won't work, but otherwise leave it."

Trent chuckled. "You're always thinking of the angles, Just. I always did admire you for that."

Justin's heart jerked. Once they'd loved each other, been best friends, now they were enemies. All because of him! Couldn't they go back in time and be friends again? With tears in his eyes he turned to Trent. "About that day Celine died."

Trent's jaw tightened. "Don't bring it up. Not ever!" He strode away, blood roaring in his ears.

Justin hung his head, feeling as dead inside as Bushnell. Slowly Justin put out the fire with a couple of shovels of dirt, then tore off a piece of copper tubing that looked like it might be a vital part of the operation. The smell turned his stomach. Nobody would have a chance to rebuild the still and work it again since men were coming to cut down some nearby trees.

Slowly Justin walked up out of the ravine, past Bushnell's body, and to the spot where Abel and Jennet stood. Trent leaned against a tree several feet away with his back to all of them.

Much later Abel walked Jennet home, telling her more of Dacia and Colin and the family.

Ignoring Justin, Trent unlocked the handcuffs and jabbed the sheriff in the back. "Pick up Bushnell and carry him to the boat."

Cursing, Lamont struggled with the body and finally flung it over his shoulder and carried it to the boat.

His mind reeling from Trent's rejection, Justin rowed while Trent kept his gun on the sheriff. The sun beat down on them, glaring off the mirror-smooth lake.

A tight feeling in his chest, Trent looked at the gun in his hand, then at Justin. It would be so easy to point the gun at him and pull the trigger. Then they'd be even. But he couldn't do it. He cursed his own weakness.

He had to get away from Justin—away from his family! He'd take Emily and Rachel and leave for Texas today! With Bushnell dead and the sheriff in custody, the men could build Havlick's Wilderness without a catch.

Agent Lorraine was at the dock ready to get in his boat. Justin handed the sheriff over to him while Trent told him about Bushnell.

"I had my suspicions about you, Lamont," Agent Lorraine said.

"You'll be sorry you interfered," the sheriff barked.

"Nobody will ever know what became of you," said the agent with a chuckle. "I'm taking you away where you can't get in the way of my work here."

"I hope that's the end of this," Trent said grimly.

Agent Lorraine shook his head. "Afraid not. But I can't expect you to do more for me. I appreciate your help with these two."

"We're taking a crew out to start cutting trees tomorrow," Justin said.

"Go right ahead. I hope someday my family and I can visit your Havlick's Wilderness. In the meantime, I've got more bootleggers to find around Blue Creek and a few speakeasies to shut down."

Justin turned to ask Trent about their next move, but the icy hatred in his eyes stopped even the first word.

Rage erupting inside him, Trent ran down the dock to his auto and drove away, leaving Justin behind to find his own way home.

CHAPTER

13

♦ Trent drove like a wild man toward Blue Creek, the rage against Justin seething inside him. Why hadn't he killed that murderer when he'd had the chance? Were either of them thinking the last few weeks together had made a difference? He would not now or ever forget what Justin had done! And he would never forgive him. He would take Emily and Rachel and go to Texas, even if it meant leaving before construction of Havlick's Wilderness was under way.

The thought of Emily brought the note to his mind, and his blood ran cold

"Emily!" he growled through clenched teeth

He sped toward home, the Dodge swaying dangerously. Several agonizing minutes later, he jerked to a stop in a cloud of dust near his house. Chickens scattered, squacking and flying low across the yard. He leaped from the auto and strode toward the house.

Alone in the house, since Rachel had gone to Lark's for the day, Emily had heard the automobile approaching. Alarmed at its speed, she ran out the back door. "Trent! What's wrong?" she shrieked. "Has something happened to Rachel?"

Trent gripped Emily's arms, his eyes like smoldering

chunks of coal. "How could you let Bob Lavery kiss you?"

She sagged like a rag doll and her forehead fell against his chest. She could smell his sweat and feel his anger. How had he found out? Had he read her mind? If he had, he would also know she had asked herself the same question many times— how could she let Bob kiss her and how could she enjoy it? The shame she felt seemed boundless.

Trent glared down at Emily and a shudder passed through him. In his heart of hearts he'd believed the note was a cruel hoax, but now he could see it spoke the truth. Emily, the last pure woman he knew, had been dallying with another man. "But she's *my* wife," he thought "How could she do this to me?"

His silence alarmed her. Weakly she lifted her head and looked into his pale face. His fingers bit through the sleeves of her flowered blouse into her arms. "I . . . didn't mean . . . for it . . . to happen," she whispered.

"I'll kill him." Trent's voice was ice cold steel.

"No!" She gripped the front of his shirt, almost tearing off the buttons. "How can you say such a thing?"

"I . . . will   . kill . . him!"

His words sounded like the snarling roar of a wounded bear, and Emily was cold with fear.

"No, Trent! No!"

Their eyes locked and Emily was unable to look away. She'd never seen such pain and rage on a human face.

"Please, Trent," she whispered, her blue eyes wide with pleading. "Please." She stroked his face with her fingers. "Please, don't."

"You love him that much?"

"No. I don't love him." And she realized she'd spoken the truth. She no longer loved Bob. "I don't love him at all."

Trent groaned from deep within and a weakness crept over him. His gaze fixed on a hairpin holding the coil of black hair in place. "Such pretty hair," he thought and longed to remove the hairpin and run his hands through the luxuriant mass as it cascaded down her back. Slowly he wrapped his arms around her and held her close. She pressed her face against his neck and clung to him, her arms tightly around him. He felt his rage drain away. The closeness of her body and the feel of her breath on his skin reminded him of another time, years before, when he had held her close.

It was just a few months after he had caught Celine in his grandpa's barn and kissed her. Since that day, he'd managed to "run into" Celine as often as possible. Emily was always with her The three of them had become good friends, sharing secrets, laughing, and teasing each other until the girls' faces were red with embarrassment. This day he'd found them walking toward the orphanage, talking and laughing. He reigned up his horse, jumped to the ground, and fell into step with them.

He tried to be nonchalant, not wanting to admit that for more than an hour he'd galloped all over town searching for them. Something very exciting was about to happen to him and he wanted to tell his good friends, Celine and Emily. They were always interested. He was certain they'd be excited when he told them he had a date to court Marybell Astor, the most pursued young lady in town.

But when he proudly lifted his chin, squared his shoulders, and told them his news, they weren't glad. Celine gasped and Emily frowned. Then, her face very pale, Celine turned and ran as fast as she could toward the Orphans Home. Emily remained in front of Trent, her hands on her hips and her face red with anger.

"I don't understand," he said. "I thought she'd be happy for me."

"How could you do that?" Emily shrieked and flew at him, pounding his chest with her fists.

He caught her tight against him to keep her from hitting him again. "What are you talking about?" he asked, completely confused.

"You'll hurt her if you court another girl. Please don't do it."

"But I like Marybell."

Great tears welled in Emily's eyes. "I thought you liked Celine!"

"I do, but Marybell's so pretty."

"So is Celine."

"I know."

"And Celine's a whole lot nicer."

"She is nice."

"I thought you'd wait until she grew up. Then you'd marry her."

Trent was speechless.

"Please don't break her heart. Please!"

His heart was touched deeply. He held Emily close, and promised, "I won't court Marybell Astor. I promise."

Emily smiled. "Thank you, Trent! You won't be sorry!" She hugged him fiercely, then ran off after Celine.

Chuckling, he'd swung up onto his horse. He never did court Marybell Astor. But he did court Celine and, as soon as she was old enough, he married her. On their wedding day he made sure he thanked Emily for helping him.

Now he looked down at Emily, realizing that once again she was helping him. She'd done it many times. Suddenly he was aware of just how much he'd missed her while he was away. He didn't want anything to separate them again. She was his friend, a real friend.

Gently he held her from him and tipped her face up to his. She sighed in relief.

"I don't ever want to see you even passing the time of day with Bob Lavery."

"I won't ignore him on the street, but I won't go out of my way to see him. I promise."

"And if he tries to see you here or anywhere else in private, you'll refuse to see him?"

She nodded, determined more than ever that she would never be alone with Bob.

Trent brushed a strand of her hair off her cheek. "You've always been able to talk sense into me, Emily. Thank you."

She flushed with pleasure. She wanted to talk sense into him about his anger toward Justin, but this wasn't the time to bring it up. "You're a wonderful man, Trent. A man of your word."

Chuckling, he tapped her nose with his finger. "You always could get me to do exactly what you wanted."

"I could?"

"Don't act so surprised. You know you could." He turned her toward the house, his arm around her lightly. "Do you have anything to eat? I'm hungry. I missed breakfast and dinner."

She slipped her arm around his waist as they walked. "I could fry you a steak."

"Or two." He grinned down at her.

Later after they'd eaten and she'd stacked the dishes, she stood beside him at the kitchen window. He was holding a cup of coffee in his hand.

She reached deep for the courage she needed, then asked, "How did you find out . . . about Bob kissing me?"

Instantly Trent was angry again and set the cup on the table with a bang. "From a note left at the Wagon Works."

"Who left it?"

"I don't know." He told her what the note looked like and what it said.

"Priscilla and Noah? I can't believe it!"

Trent nodded.

"Does Justin believe it?"

"I think so. He acted like he did."

"Somebody was certainly trying to cause trouble by sending that note." Emily frowned thoughtfully. "I wonder who and why?"

"Good questions," Trent said grimly.

"Who would know both about me and about Priscilla? Did someone spy on the two of us because we're married to you and Justin? Maybe we should talk to Priscilla and Justin."

Trent stiffened. "I don't want to see him again."

"We have to get to the bottom of this, Trent. If we don't, who knows what else will happen? The Havlicks are fighters, not quitters!"

Trent laughed. "Well, you sure fit right in, don't you?"

She laughed with him. "I guess I do."

"Think what our kids will be like!"

The laugh caught in her throat, and she flushed crimson.

Trent tweaked her chin. "Don't you go getting all embarrassed on me now. Married people do have kids, you know. You are such an innocent!"

"I am not! I know where babies come from."

"But you don't know the pleasure of making one. I'm going to show you about that."

"Can we change the subject, please?"

He chuckled. "I'm sorry, but teasing you is so much fun."

"Oh, you!" She managed to laugh even as she struggled against the strange feelings going on inside her.

Abruptly his mood changed. He strode to the kitchen window and looked out. Wood snapped in the stove. "I wonder who sent that note. Why would someone want Justin and me to know about Lavery and Roswell and our wives?"

Emily sat at the table, her hands folded in front of her. "From simple power of deduction, I'd say it has something to do with Havlick's Wilderness. If your mind is on me, it won't be on getting the project under way."

"Think so?"

"That's why we have to talk to Justin and Priscilla. Instead of drawing apart, the family needs to get closer, stop the enemy, and accomplish our goal."

Trent turned to face Emily and smiled tenderly. "Come here, you. What did I ever do to deserve such a wife?"

His words wrapped around her heart, turning her limp. Slowly she walked to him.

He pulled her close and held her.

She felt the thud of his heart as her own heart beat faster. She smiled up at him and rested her hands at his waist.

A desire to kiss Emily rose in Trent, surprising him. He lowered his head and touched his lips to hers.

The kiss took her by surprise. She kissed him back, surprising herself even more.

He pulled away slightly and looked into her eyes, then down at her trembling lips. "Emily," he whispered hoarsely. He kissed her again, savoring the taste and the feel.

She returned his kiss with a fervor. Never had she experienced such a rush of emotion! Just as she thought she would drown in it, she heard the ugly ooh-ga of an auto horn.

Trent heard it too and reluctantly pulled away, his breathing ragged. He peered out the window, then frowned. "It's my dad! I wonder what he wants."

"Maybe he's bringing Rachel home." Emily struggled to sound normal. But her heart was beating so wildly she was sure it would rattle her words.

"No. He's alone." Trent strode outdoors with Emily hurrying fast to keep up. The sun shone brightly in the blue sky. "Dad, this is a surprise!"

Clay smiled, but his eyes were serious. "Trent, Emily, we are all meeting at the home place at seven tonight. Please come!"

"What's it about?" Trent asked.

"The family," Clay said.

"We'll be there," Emily said.

Trent shot her a look, grinned, and said, "We'll be there. What about Rachel?"

"If it's all right with you, we'll leave her with Lulu in town."

"That's fine."

"Would you like a cup of coffee, Clay?" Emily asked.

"Not this time." Clay smiled as he turned back to his auto. "I'll see you two later."

They stood together and watched Clay drive away, then slowly walked back inside, not touching, both trying to forget what had just happened.

Trent sighed heavily. "I had myself convinced to leave for Texas and forget all about the family."

"I'm glad you changed your mind. We will not let some evil force tear apart the Havlicks!"

* * *

Justin thanked Ben Dreski and dashed toward his Duesenberg. He was outraged at Trent for leaving him without a way home. He had walked for over an hour, getting madder by the minute, looking for someone heading toward Blue Creek who would give him a ride. But now that he was back, he intended to confront Priscilla about the contents of the note. The thought of it made his blood boil again. She would have to give him an explanation—even for a hoax!

As he reached for the doorhandle, a woman's voice called, "Oh, Justin, wait!"

Impatiently he turned.

"You are Justin, aren't you? Not Trent? Someone told me this is your automobile. I've been waiting for you."

She walked toward him, her hips moving provocatively. A short skirt swished around her knees, and a wide brimmed hat rolled in front covered her short, straight blonde hair. Her legs were shapely and her low cut dress hugged her. Heavy makeup covered her cheeks and lips, and he could smell her perfume before she reached him. She looked familiar.

"It's me, Justin—Aggie! Your old flame."

It was Aggie! "I heard you were back in town." Justin forced himself to be polite.

"Yes. My dear husband died and I've come home." She fluttered her eyelashes and toyed with her beads, showing off a large diamond ring.

"Sorry about your husband," Justin murmured. He didn't have time for Aggie, of all people.

"Thank you. But now that I'm back, I expect to see a lot of *you*. In fact, I thought this afternoon I would drive out to see Priscilla. Do you know if she's home? She was always such a dear friend of mine."

Pictures of Priscilla watching Noah flashed through Justin's mind and he tensed, the color draining from his face. He'd been aware of something between them, but he'd been too preoccupied to care. "Today isn't a good time, Aggie," he said, feeling a dread building inside. "Maybe another day. Excuse me; I must hurry." He reached again for the door-handle.

"Is something wrong?" She put her hand on his arm and moved closer to him.

"No, of course not. Why do you ask?" he said as he stepped back.

"You look worried."

"Oh, well, business, you know." He shrugged. "Excuse me." He tried to turn away, but she stepped between him and his automobile

"I wanted to talk to you about that, too. I hear you need oak for your company, and I know where you can buy some at a good price. Let's go to the cafe. We'll have a cup of coffee, and I'll tell you all about it. Besides, it's been a long time and we need to get reacquainted." She slipped her arm through his and began to move toward the cafe.

Justin took a step and then stopped. He desperately needed oak for the Wagon Works but it was even more important that he get home to Priscilla. And he had the feeling that wouldn't wait.

"I can't," he said.

"Oh, Justin," she cooed, running a finger down his cheek. "I've missed seeing you, and we have so much to talk about." Her voice dropped to a whisper. "I can make you forget all your problems."

His pulse quickened. The burden he was carrying was killing him. He would like to forget it, even for a little while.

"I've returned to Blue Creek to put the sparkle back in your eyes. I'm gonna put fun in your life."

He looked down at Aggie, remembering the carefree days when they were in school. She'd been wild—a girl with a "reputation," the kind of girl that men dally with but never marry. He had found her both appealing and repugnant—appealing because she seemed to have fun and repugnant because she had loose morals. He was looking for a good girl then, one he could truly love and marry, one who had Christian values and would be a good mother to his children. He had found Priscilla And now he needed to make certain she was still with him

"Sorry, Aggie. I'm a married man. You'll need to find some other man and put a sparkle in his eyes " He disentangled his arm from her clutch.

"Oh?" she said. "You're turning me down? Well," she fluttered her eyelashes and slowly moistened her lips with the tip of her tongue, "there are other men who appreciate what I can do for them." She paused and trailed her fingers up and down his neck. "Noah appreciates me." She paused again and opened her eyes innocently. "Do you know Noah? Noah Roswell? He's very handsome and young and, ah, vigorous. Of course, he is a teeny bit distracted right now with another woman. . . ." Her voice trailed off and she smiled.

Justin felt like someone had socked him in the stomach. He

stammered, "Gotta go," yanked open the door of his automobile, and jumped in. As the door shut, he could hear Aggie laughing. He switched on the ignition and roared away, her taunting laughter ringing in his ears.

When she was out of sight he slowed. How did Aggie know about Noah? Was the whole town gossiping about his wife and his hired hand? It must be true, else how would Aggie know? The pictures began to flash in his mind again: Priscilla gazing longingly at Noah; Noah winking at Priscilla; Priscilla giggling as Noah whispered in her ear; Priscilla's face flushed and her eyes shining as Noah embraced her; Noah and Priscilla kissing, their arms wrapped tightly around each other.

"No!" he growled. Rage began in his toes and rose until it consumed him. "Cuckold me, will you! I'll kill you, Noah Roswell!"

Justin mashed the accelerator to the floorboard and the Duesenberg careened through curves and around corners until it screeched to a stop behind Priscilla's black Ford.

As he dashed toward the house, he was aware of the windmill squawking, a piglet squealing in the muddy pigpen, and the horses standing quietly in a pen near the barn. Chickens pecking in the yard scurried away from his pounding feet. He threw open the door, yelling, "Priscilla!"

He ran to the kitchen, through the dining room, and into the parlor. The rooms were neatly clean and empty. In the front room, a rag doll lay in a heap beside the rocking chair. He snatched up the doll and roared, "Priscilla!"

He ran to the hall and took the wide stairs two at a time. His steps ringing loudly on the wooden floor, he dashed in and out of the boys' room and the girls' room. The beds were made and the toys lined up neatly on the shelves.

In the bedroom he shared with Priscilla, he stopped. The creamy-colored crocheted spread neatly covered the brass bed. A breeze ruffled the muslin curtains at the open window.

On the dresser, yellow roses were in a milk glass vase next to a framed photograph of Priscilla in her wedding gown. "Priscilla?" he whispered. "Where are you?"

With a groan he opened the chifforobe. Her clothes hung there next to his. He touched the sleeve of her pink robe and pulled it to his face. The scent of her perfume clung to it and he breathed deeply, filling his lungs with Priscilla's perfume. His eyes filled with tears. "Oh, Priscilla, I'm sorry. Please, don't leave me."

Slowly he walked back downstairs, through the open door, and into the yard. As he touched her car, he noticed he was still clutching the rag doll. He set it gently on the hood and gazed across the yard to the big red barn.

Noah! Justin clenched his teeth and strode purposefully toward the barn. He'd find that philanderer, beat him within an inch of his life, and send him packing!

In the barn, pigeons flew among the rafters, and dust particles floated in beams of sunlight. A cat rubbed against Justin's ankle. Noah wasn't there or in his room. Justin found only a pair of denim pants hung on a hook beside the steel-frame bed and a bright afghan, folded neatly at the foot of the bed. Angrily he strode from the barn to the sheds and to the milk house. Noah wasn't anywhere.

Justin stopped short in the middle of the barnyard. The wagon and the work horses were gone! Again pictures of Noah and Priscilla in each other's arms flashed through Justin's mind. He slammed his fist into his palm. A groan of agony rose inside him, leaving him weak.

He'd been a terrible husband. He'd ignored his children and neglected his wife. He'd been surly and short-tempered, angry and sarcastic. He'd been consumed with guilt—that he wouldn't measure up, that he wouldn't succeed the way his father and grandfather had, that he would senselessly cause harm again the way he had caused Celine's death. He had been afraid and had buried himself in the Wagon Works, trying to block all his feelings He had pushed his wife into the arms of another man.

Standing in the barnyard, looking at his house—the house he'd built for Priscilla and their children, where they would live together all their lives, where they would love each other—he felt bereft.

The sounds of jangling harness and laughter floated across the field. Justin ran to the side of the garage and peeked around it. He saw Noah driving the wagon with Priscilla on the high seat beside him. Blood roared in Justin's ears. Where was his gun? He'd kill Noah Roswell!

He tried to push away from the garage to go after his gun, but his legs wouldn't move. He peeked around the garage again and saw his four children riding in the back of the wagon, laughing happily. Pris hadn't been alone with Noah! Relief swept over Justin.

Noah stopped the team near the barn and jumped to the ground. He reached up to help Priscilla down, then held her by the waist and looked into her smiling face. He held her while the children jumped up to stand in back of the wagon. He held her while the team shook, rattling the harness. He held her while heat washed up over Justin, then washed back down, leaving him icy cold.

"That was a fine picnic," Noah said, still holding her.

"It was fun." Laughing, Priscilla stepped away from him, flushed and pretty.

Justin bit back a groan.

Noah laughed and winked at Priscilla. Then one by one he lifted the children to the ground. And a fire exploded inside Justin.

He stepped into sight and stood perfectly still, his feet apart, his fists on his hips. He saw the shock on Priscilla's face and the look of surprise on Noah's.

"Daddy!" Faith shouted happily and ran to him. Chloe tumbled after her, trying to keep up.

"Daddy! We had a picnic!" Chloe called. They hugged his legs. "It was fun. Noah took us."

Justin patted their backs and the tops of their heads, then squatted down and hugged them.

"Run on in the house," he said, his voice catching. "I need to talk to Mommy. Ted," he called, "take your brother and sisters in the house. You're in charge until we come."

"Yes, Dad," Ted said, sounding very grown-up for his seven years.

Priscilla watched the children until they reached the back porch, then said stiffly, "What brings you home in the middle of the afternoon? Is something wrong?"

"Yes!" Justin barked, his anger rising again at the sight of Priscilla, her face flushed and her hair mussed from the wind, standing with Noah.

Noah moved nervously. "I'll take care of the horses."

"Don't move!" Justin's muscles bunched as he walked to Noah and Priscilla. Without warning, he knotted his fist and struck Noah on the chin, sending him sprawling in the dust. The team moved uneasily, rattling their harness.

Priscilla stifled a scream. She caught at Justin's arm. "What's wrong with you?"

He brushed her aside and hauled Noah to his feet and punched him in the stomach, knocking him hard against the side of the wagon. Justin caught Noah by the front of the shirt and pushed his face close. "Leave my wife alone!"

Priscilla trembled, her hands at her mouth and her eyes wide with fear.

Noah struggled, but couldn't break free. "Let me go! You got no right to hit me!"

"You're fooling around with my wife! I have every right to kill you!" Justin pulled back his fist to strike Noah again.

"Wait!" Noah cried. "Don't hit me again. It was innocent. We just took the children on a picnic."

"I saw you! Smiling at her, winking at her, touching her!" Justin dropped his fist, but continued to glare at Noah.

The color rose in Priscilla's cheeks. She forced herself to look at Justin, at his white skin—pale from spending every day inside, at his shoulders—slightly stooped from bending over his desk for long hours at a time, at the lines in his forehead—put there by worried frowning. She hadn't meant to hurt him, not really. Or had she?

She'd been so lonely and hurt that Justin didn't seem to be aware of her. Noah had made her feel alive, giddy, like a schoolgirl. His winks and whispers had told her she was still attractive, that someone wanted her. She needed to be wanted.

Noah laughed, shrugging. "It was just a joke."

"A joke?" Justin roared.

Noah nodded. "I was spying on you, getting information about you and your brother and what your family's up to with the forest. I didn't want her," he jerked his head toward Priscilla. "I only wanted news and her tongue wags at both ends."

Priscilla gasped. She'd made a fool of herself, and it had been meaningless. Noah hadn't been interested in her. Her heart froze and she couldn't move or speak.

"Why would you spy on us?" Justin asked, balling his fists and tightening his hold on Noah's shirt. "Explain!"

Noah tried to laugh again, but the rage on Justin's face made him blanch. "I don't know for sure, but I think it has to do with bootlegging. Gabe Lavery and his brother Bob been running a still out of Trent's house, and they wanted to keep up with Trent—if he'd want his house back, you know. There's a lot of money in running liquor, you know. They've been paying me for information I got out of your wife. That's all there was to it. I had to keep her happy so's she'd talk."

Humiliated, Priscilla sank to her knees and buried her face in her hands.

"You're fired," Justin growled. "Get out of here before I break you in little pieces and feed you to the hogs."

Noah eased himself away and stumbled toward the barn. He broke into a run and disappeared inside. Justin stared after him until, a few minutes later, Noah ran from the barn with his shabby suitcase, jumped into his pickup, and roared away.

Justin looked down at Priscilla kneeling in the dust, sobbing quietly. He took her arm and gently raised her to her feet. Their eyes locked.

"Priscilla, I'm . . ." Justin's voice was low and she strained to hear him. But his words were drowned out by the noise of an automobile churning gravel in the lane, the horn blowing repeatedly

Clay drew up beside them and called, "There's a family meeting tonight at Pa's place. Martha Bjoerling will watch your children. Be there at seven!" He jammed the automobile in gear and drove away, leaving behind a cloud of dust.

CHAPTER

14

♦ Her hands locked in her lap, Emily sat beside Trent on Free's front porch, looking at the others. Nervously she rubbed her slightly flared skirt over her knees and touched the beads hanging down on her white blouse. It had a rounded collar embroidered with tiny yellow and blue flowers. Trent had changed into a white shirt and dark pants, the very thing Justin was wearing. Emily watched Trent and Justin exchange frowns before she turned her gaze on Priscilla, who wore a red middy and a knee-length white skirt. Justin and Priscilla looked as tense and nervous as she felt. Clay and Lark were talking softly to each other. Free stood near the screen door, his hands looped around his wide suspenders, a thoughtful look on his lined face. Jennet sat in her white rocking chair, her dark blue cotton dress covering her crossed ankles. Her hands were folded in her lap. She wanted to meet on the porch to catch the cool evening breeze.

The sun was low in the west and had lost its heat. In the pigpen at the far side of a shed, baby pigs squealed and their sow grunted to calm them. A horse nickered behind the big barn. The constant smell of pine filled the air.

Emily glanced down the lane. Were Beaver and Hannah

coming? Where were Tris and Zoe? This was a Havlick family meeting, but not all the family was present. She moved restlessly. She'd sat in on Havlick family meetings before, but this was the first time as a member of the family.

Free cleared his throat and stepped away from the screen door. His pants hung loosely on his lean frame. A gentle breeze ruffled his gray hair. "We didn't ask the whole family to come tonight, because this is something for just the eight of us to settle."

Trent moved uneasily. He hadn't been to a family meeting in ten years, and he dreaded this one. He felt tense and very uncomfortable

Justin glanced at Trent, then quickly away He sensed Priscilla's tension and suspected she wished she were at home, away from all of them. He'd often wished the same thing. Frequently he was the target at meetings called to discuss his over-involvement with his work and his under-involvement with his family. He would usually get mad, eventually promise to try harder to be a good husband and proper father, but afterward there would be little change. He glanced again at Priscilla. This time it would be different, regardless of the topic of the meeting

Free pushed his hands deep in the pockets of his dark pants. "I've told you this many times in the past, but I want to tell you again." He looked at Jennet and she smiled reassuringly. His gaze rested lovingly on each of the others before he continued. "When I was a boy I worshiped the ground my Grandpa Clay walked on. That's why I named my first son after him."

Free smiled at Clay, and Clay smiled broadly in return. At times, when he was working hard to make his own fortune, it had been hard to live up to the image of Great-grandpa Clay, a man of impeccable integrity who was respected by all who knew him.

Free looked off across the field toward their beloved white pines. "Grandpa walked the woods around here when this area was completely covered with timber. With the money he made as a fur trader, he invested in businesses in Grand Rapids and in Detroit, and he bought this land. In his later years he accepted Jesus as his Savior. He began to study the Bible and talk to Jig, his friend, about God. Grandpa learned that through salvation he'd entered into covenant with God. Jesus cut the covenant with God for him and for us and for all mankind. And the most wonderful, comforting promise we know from God is that He will never break it!"

Free's voice faltered and he cleared his throat. "It took me years to learn that, but I finally did, and I taught it to my children, and they to theirs. Trent and Justin, you are to teach it to yours. We are in covenant with God!"

Trent and Justin squirmed guiltily. They had failed to teach their children.

Free smiled. "A covenant is two people filling each other's shoes all the time. All that God is, I am. All that God has is mine. All that I have is His. *I* am His!"

Free brushed moisture from his eyes.

"Every one of you has confessed Jesus as Lord and Savior and, therefore, is in covenant with God and heirs to His promises.

"So," he paused and looked intently at Justin and Trent, "what's going on here? We have had differences of opinion in the past, but this is much more than that. This is deadly! Someone in this family has opened a door and allowed the devil to come in to work against us."

Trent's stomach tightened, and Justin forced back a groan.

Free sighed heavily. "As a result of strife and unforgiveness and our preoccupation with it, we haven't been living in the covenant promises. Strife and unforgiveness are tearing this family apart." Free sank to the edge of his chair and looked around at his family.

Emily bit her lower lip and peeked at Trent. She knew he didn't want to hear what was coming, but she also knew he wouldn't walk away. He respected and loved Free too much for that.

Free motioned to Justin and Trent. "I should've talked to you boys about this long before now." Free reached over and touched Justin's shoulder and tapped Trent's knee. "You boys had a falling out that you must set straight. You two are in strife and have been for ten years. As a result you haven't been living in the blessings of God, and it has affected the whole family. It's killing you! And the family!"

Justin sat very still, his eyes on the gray porch floor. Inside he was crying out to settle the agony he felt, but he didn't let it show on the outside.

A muscle jumped in Trent's jaw. Grandpa had no idea. It wasn't a falling out. It was murder. Justin's self-centeredness had caused Celine's death. Trent tensed. He couldn't forgive that and he couldn't forget it. Justin would have to pay. Trying to pretend it no longer mattered, saying "I forgive you, Justin, for the pain and heartache you've caused, for taking my life from me," would mean that it didn't matter, that Celine's life wasn't important. They'd forget her. It would be like she'd never lived and loved him. She'd given meaning to his life. Without her he was empty, nothing. "No, Grandpa," Trent thought in his mind, "there'll be no setting straight. You'd understand if you knew."

Free leaned forward earnestly. "We're going to build Havlick's Wilderness. But look at the trouble we've faced already. Look at what happened to Rachel and to your grandma. Now today I learned someone is trying to make trouble between you, Trent, and Emily. And between you, Justin, and Priscilla. We can't let the enemy destroy our families!"

Free jumped up, his eyes blazing. "Your marriage vows spoken to each other are a covenant between you. Don't break that covenant! Love each other. Love God with all your beings. We have a dream—to build Havlick's Wilderness for folks everywhere to enjoy. You boys have the Wagon Works to keep going. We each have a family to keep together. Every part of our lives is affected by what's in our hearts. When your heart is right with God, it'll be right with each other. Your marriages will be blessed and happy. *You* will be blessed and happy."

Emily bit her lip to keep from sobbing. She hadn't thought of her marriage as a covenant with Trent. That wasn't why she'd married him.

Free's eyes filled with tears. "If you have unforgiveness in your hearts, forgive. Ask God to help you forgive and to help you be forgiven. If you are harboring bitterness and hatred or are suffering from a broken heart, rely on God's grace. He can do in you what you can't do yourselves." Free studied his grandsons closely.

"Do you love each other?"

Trent kept his eyes down. Justin bit back a groan.

"Justin, do you love Priscilla?" Free asked softly.

Without hesitation, Justin answered, "Yes, Grandpa, I love Priscilla." His voice was level and even. He forced himself to continue. "But because I haven't given her time, I may have lost her."

"Son, have you told her?"

Justin turned to Priscilla. "I've hurt you. I've raged and moaned, and I've neglected you. I've been very selfish. I'm so sorry. I cannot express how sorry I am. Please try to forgive me."

Tears stung Priscilla's eyes.

"Priscilla," Free said, "do you love Justin?"

She hesitated, her eyes locked with Free's. Then she whispered, "Yes, I do. I always have. But I was hurt and lonely and angry. I believed he'd stopped loving me, and I . . . did something that makes me very ashamed."

She dropped her eyes and tears rolled down her cheeks. Justin took her hand in his, kissed her fingers, and held her hand to his heart. She leaned against him weakly.

Free turned toward Trent and Emily.

"You've been married only a short while. There'll be much joy and happiness, some sad and troubling times, too, but God will see you through.

"The most important thing you need to remember is that a marriage is a commitment to honor, respect, and care for each other every day of your life together. It's part of the covenant you've made with God and each other. You honor God and each other and keep the covenant. You'll know a love for each other you've never thought possible. But this won't happen without God."

Free paused and studied their faces: Emily, struggling inside, biting her quivering lower lip; Priscilla, her head down and tears flowing freely; Justin, the anguish on his face tearing at Free; and Trent. His body tense, his hands balled into fists, his jaw set, Trent stared straight ahead through dark, clouded eyes.

"Trent, son, if you leave us, do it because it's what God wants in your life, not because you're angry or grieving or want to run away from pain."

Free cleared his throat. Had he said enough or gone too far? It was hard to know when a parent, or a grandparent, moves from compassionate, loving involvement to meddling. In his heart, Free prayed for guidance.

"Now, we're going to pray about this," Free said. "We're going to ask God to help us with it. Without Him none of us will make it." Free closed his eyes and, his face lifted toward the heavens, began to pray.

"O God, maker of all things, creator of the universe, thank You for being with us here, right now. . . ."

Priscilla bowed her head and listened to Free in his gentle way ask God to heal their hurts and bless their marriages. She hadn't prayed for a long time. She'd thought she'd forgotten how. But Free's simple words encouraged her to try. Silently she begged for patience and the kind of love that forgives.

As Free asked that God give them wisdom, Emily silently confessed that she had been foolish in dreaming about and longing for a man she couldn't have. She had let that disappointment interfere with her daily walk. She asked God to take away her feelings for Bob. "Forgive me, Lord," she breathed. "I was wrong. Now show me how to love Trent the way a wife should."

When Free begged that their sins be forgiven, Justin knew he wanted forgiveness. In his heart, he asked God to help him make amends for the hurts he'd caused Priscilla. But when he thought of Celine, he knew that could never be forgiven—not even by God.

Trent's heart and mind were troubled. He hadn't prayed since Celine died. He hadn't wanted to talk to God. But he couldn't shut out Free's prayer asking God to open their hearts and dwell in them. In his mind, Trent heard a soft voice, saying, "My child, I am with you," but he couldn't respond.

The voice said, "It's time to let Celine go."

"No!" Trent felt it like a scream, exploding through his body, reverberating through the fields, echoing through the forest. "I can't let her go! She's my life!"

"I will give you new life."

Free ended his prayer by saying, "As always, Father, thank You for Your great love."

"Amen," Clay said, and together Jennet and Lark said, "Amen."

Free blew his nose and Jennet and Lark dabbed at their tears.

"God is good," Clay whispered.

"And faithful," Lark said.

"Yes, yes," Jennet murmured.

They sat in silence, each lost in personal communion.

"We must talk about this note." Clay took the folded paper from his pocket. "We need to figure out who sent it to Justin and Trent and why. Each of you look at the handwriting to see if you recognize it."

"Emily may have guessed the reason behind this," Trent

said as they passed the paper from one to another. He looked quickly at her and a smile passed between them. "If I have my attention on trouble with my wife, I can't pay attention to building Havlick's Wilderness."

"But why would anyone want to stop you from building a nature preserve?" Lark asked. "That's a good thing and will benefit everyone."

"I think it has to do with bootlegging, Mom," Justin said, a new fire in his eyes.

"Bootlegging?" Jennet's face was a study in shock. "There's no bootlegging around here, and if there were, what would it have to do with our family?"

"It isn't just bootlegging, Grandma," Justin said gently. "It's illegal stills, too! And it's been happening on Havlick property."

Jennet gasped and looked at Free who threw up his hands and said, "I don't know what the boy is talking about."

"Grandpa, this afternoon we learned from Noah—by the way, Noah Roswell is no longer working for us!—that Gabe Lavery, while he was caretaking at Trent's place, was operating a still in Trent's house. He and Bob have been running liquor all over the area.

"Naturally they didn't want Trent to stay here—he'd want his place back and they'd have nowhere to hide their still. So they paid Noah to play up to Priscilla and get information from her."

Priscilla's face flushed beet red as she remembered the humiliation she'd felt when she learned Noah had made a fool of her.

Emily was so shocked to learn that Bob—the man she'd tried so hard to love—was involved in such evil, she thought she might faint.

Trent remembered Martha had mentioned, after she helped Emily move into his house, that the place was in good order and clean, except for mysterious piles of grainy dust in the corners of the kitchen. "Corn," he thought. Anger surged through him.

"But Trent and Emily and Rachel are living there now," Clay said.

"I expect they want them to leave again," Free said.

"As bad as all that sounds," Jennet said, "what would it have to do with Havlick's Wilderness? The man that shot Rachel said not to build it."

"Our forest is very big, Grandma. Someone hid a still there, too. If we were to bring in loggers and construction crews, we'd be sure to find it. They had to stop us. But we found it and the man who was running it. And we learned the sheriff was involved."

"Get us fighting among ourselves and maybe we'd have to give it up!" Free slapped his knee. "I believe you've got it, Justin. But is it only the Laverys and the sheriff? Is there anyone else involved?"

"Until we know, we've got to be very careful," Clay said. "Like Pa said, this is deadly business."

"Whoever they are," Free said, "they've picked on the wrong family! No one will destroy the Havlicks."

"Anybody recognize that handwriting?" Clay asked.

"I think I do," Priscilla answered. "There's something about the *i*'s and the *e*'s that is familiar. The *i*'s are open when they should be closed, and the *e*'s are closed when they should be open. Aggie Karin used to write notes to Gabe when we were in school, and she would show them to me. I think this looks like her handwriting."

"Aggie?" Justin asked, remembering his encounter with her that afternoon. "I saw her today. She was definitely trying to work on me."

"Gabe and Bob and Aggie and the sheriff," Clay said. "I wonder who else is involved."

Emily looked up at the full moon as she walked toward their house with Trent. A dog howled in the distance. A horse nickered in the pen beside the barn. The quiet sounds of the forest added to her sense of peace. She wanted to ask Trent why he hadn't settled his quarrel with Justin, but she couldn't bring herself to speak of it. She wondered if he felt the peace, too?

Trent stopped near the back door and rested his hands on Emily's shoulders. "Do you think you'll ever stop loving Bob Lavery?"

She looked in her heart and found the feeling was gone. "I've stopped loving him already."

"For a fact?" Trent asked in surprise.

Emily laughed breathlessly, glad to be free of her guilt. "I don't know when it happened, but it's gone." She rested her hands on Trent's waist. "Tonight I asked God to take that away and forgive me for it. And I also asked Him to fill me with love for you—the love a wife should have for her husband."

Trent's heart jerked. Emily's honesty always took him by surprise. "I wish I could love you the way a husband should love his wife."

"Your grandpa said marriage is a commitment. And you're committed to me. Now all you need is the feeling."

Trent pecked Emily on the cheek. "Sometimes I think my feelings are dead."

"God is a God of miracles," she whispered.

They walked into the kitchen and Trent lit the lamp. The smell of sulfur and kerosene stung his nose. He turned down the flame to keep it from blackening the globe. The lamp cast a soft glow over the room.

"I wonder how long it'll take to get electricity out in the country," he mused, but he didn't want to talk about electricity. He wanted to ask if she was ready for them to become truly married now that her love for Bob was gone.

"I heard that someday in the future every farm and every home would have electric lights. That's hard to imagine."

Trent chuckled. "Well, that subject's boring. How about talking about something we're both thinking about." His pulse quickened "Us."

"All right. You start."

He walked to the window and stood looking out at the bright moon, his back to Emily. "I don't know how to start."

Emily's heart sank. He didn't want her near him! "Since Rachel's not here I could sleep in her bed tonight if you want," Emily said just above a whisper.

"Is that what you want?" He held his breath, waiting for her answer. Slowly he turned to face her.

She hesitated, then with her cheeks crimson, she lifted her chin and said, "No. We are married and we should share a bed. That's what I want."

Once again she'd taken him by surprise. He'd expected her to be too shy to agree to share his bed after their kisses that afternoon.

Gently he took her in his arms. He thought of his wedding night with Celine, how shy she'd been and how he'd had to tenderly, gently coax her out of her fear.

"You're the only man for me," Celine had said in the safety of his arms.

"You're the only woman for me," he'd whispered with his lips against hers.

Abruptly Emily pulled away. "You're thinking of Celine, aren't you?"

He nodded slightly.

Emily locked her fingers together in front of her. "I thought I could handle this, but I can't. I can't have you touching me, holding me, kissing me, while thinking about Celine." Tears filled Emily's eyes. "I can't, Trent."

"You knew how it'd be when you married me."

"Yes, but I didn't know it'd be too hard for me."

"I'm sorry. I don't want to hurt you."

"I know." She gripped the back of a chair. A cricket sang in a corner in back of the woodbox. "Maybe it'll be different in Texas. Maybe we should wait until then."

"If that's what you want."

"It's not, Trent, but I can't take Celine's place in your bed." She moistened her dry lips with the tip of her tongue and lifted her chin. "I will share your bed the way we've done the last two nights."

He picked up the lamp and silently they walked side by side up the wide stairs to their bedroom.

She pulled back the spread, then turned down the sheet and cover. She took her nightgown from the chifforobe and dropped it on the bed. Too shy to undress in front of him, she said, "You can blow out the lamp now."

He smiled as he turned down the wick and blew out the flame. He walked to her and slipped his arms around her. He reminded himself that he really should feel guilty, but he didn't. He wanted her.

She stiffened and gasped. "Trent! We agreed."

He laughed gently. "You said it, but I didn't agree."

She struggled to free herself.

Catching her face with his hands, he looked deeply into her eyes. "I'm not thinking about Celine now. I'm thinking only about you. Celine's gone." And she was. He could see her face and hear her laughter. But his longing for her was gone.

Emily stood very still, her heart thundering.

He lifted her face with his fingers under her chin and kissed her.

She swayed against him and clung to him. She returned his kiss. A fire she never knew was locked inside her burst into flame. Her passion ignited his.

"Emily, Emily," he whispered huskily as he gathered her closer.

* * *

In his stocking feet, Justin paced the bedroom. Priscilla walked into the room and stopped short. She was ready for bed, wearing a long yellow nightgown. She'd checked to see that the children were asleep and covered and kissed them tenderly. She had prayed silently for them. She hadn't heard Justin come into the house or walk upstairs.

"I thought you were going to sleep in the barn."

"I changed my mind."

"Oh." Trembling, Priscilla set the lamp she was holding on the dresser beside her silver brush and comb set.

Justin raked his fingers through his hair. "We can't let our marriage crumble because of what either of us has done. We're a family. We can't let anything or anybody break us up."

Priscilla sank weakly to the edge of the bed. "I didn't think I'd ever hear you say that! I fell in love with you and married you because you believed so strongly in the Lord. I wanted a marriage like your parents and grandparents had. After Celine died and Trent left, you changed so much you were someone else. A stranger."

He knelt beside her and rested his head in her lap. "Forgive me, Pris. I know I get caught up in my work and forget everything and everybody. I am going to try to do better. With your help and with God's help, I'm going to change. I'm going to try to make it up to you."

She stroked his head. His hair was as soft as their children's asleep down the hall. "We'll all help you remember us. We need you." She bit her lip. "I said I wouldn't say that again, but it's true. I love you and I need you."

He stood and pulled her into his arms. "I almost lost you. I don't know what I would've done if I had."

"Forgive me for turning to Noah."

"I already have. Grandpa showed me the way." Justin stroked her hair. "I'm sorry for what I've put you through. Please forgive me."

She smiled and nodded. "I already have."

"Oh, Pris! I do love you!" He kissed her as if he'd never let her go.

CHAPTER

15

◆ Trent hesitated at the office door. He knew Justin and Dad were waiting for him inside, eager to get things under way for Havlick's Wilderness. He heard a voice he didn't recognize and slowly opened the door. Agent Lorraine sat beside Clay. He was talking about closing down Gilly's Place. He stopped when he saw Trent and nodded with a smile.

"Come in and sit," Clay said, motioning to the only empty chair.

"Sorry to interrupt your story, Agent Lorraine." As Trent sat down, he glanced at Justin. Once again they'd dressed alike in dark pants and plain shirts. Their eyes locked; then they looked quickly away.

Agent Lorraine, looking very pleased with himself, held his hat in his hands. "We've closed down a couple of other places in the area even though we couldn't close Gilly's place. I went there again last night to shut it down, but the patrons were only dancing. No one was drinking. I couldn't find a drop of liquor on the premises. Somehow they knew we were coming. Too many folks around here are against prohibition." He shook his head helplessly. "The deputy sheriff, Steve Brison, will take over the sheriff's job. He can be trusted to stop any small-scale bootlegging going on. I told him to keep an eye on Gilly's Place. He said he would."

"What about the lead we gave you?" Trent asked.

"On Gabe and Bob Lavery," Justin said.

"Sorry, but I couldn't get anything on them." Agent Lorraine stood. "So, I'll head back to Lansing. But if you ever need me, call." He shook hands all around, clamped on his hat, and said goodbye. At the door he said, "I'll bring my family to visit Havlick's Wilderness when it's finished."

"You do that," Clay said, smiling.

Agent Lorraine left, closing the door after him. Sounds of hammering and sawing seeped in around the door. The faint smell of paint drifted in.

Clay smiled at his sons. "We aren't going to do anything about Gabe Lavery at the moment, but we'll always be on the lookout in case he tries anything."

Trent wanted to do something about the Laverys immediately, but he couldn't say that to his dad. As Clay continued talking of their plans for the morning, Trent turned to Justin and lifted his hand in a salute, their secret message to meet together without Dad knowing. Justin saluted at the same moment. They grinned at each other, then quickly looked away.

Clay stood. "And we're going to take a crew to the forest this morning to begin the work on Havlick's Wilderness."

"I have some business to take care of before going out," Justin said. He didn't look at Trent, afraid he would chuckle.

"Me too," Trent said, holding back a laugh. It had been a long time since he and Justin had had the same thought at the same moment. He knew their business was the same—Gabe and Bob Lavery.

"Then I'll get the men and be on my way," Clay said, smiling. "Ma and Pa are going to meet us there. They want to watch the first tree fall that'll mark the beginning of Havlick's Wilderness. Your mother's not really looking forward to it. It hurts her deeply to see a tree cut." He put his cap on and opened the door. "See you later."

The minute the door closed behind him, Trent said, "What's the plan?"

"To knock Gabe into next week." Justin jumped up.

Trent chuckled and Justin joined in. "Your auto or mine?"

Justin shrugged as he lifted his hat off the hook. "This time let's take mine."

Side by side they walked outdoors toward Justin's Duesenberg. The sun was already warm in the sky even though it was early. A pickup truck drove past, briefly covering the factory noises. Trent opened his door. "But we won't drive up his lane and give him warning. We'll park along the road and walk to his farmhouse. And after we're finished with him, we'll go after Bob Lavery."

Justin nodded. "They'll both be sorry they messed with the Havlick twins and their wives!"

"You bet!" Justin started the engine and Trent burst into song as they drove away from the Wagon Works. "The yanks are comin', the yanks are comin'!"

"You're in a good mood," Justin said, chuckling. He longed for it to last.

"That's because I have a wonderful wife and I'm off to defend her honor."

"Well, then, let's keep singing." Justin sang "Yankee Doodle Dandy" and Trent joined in. It was like old times and Justin didn't want it to end.

Several minutes later they pulled off the road into the underbrush. A cottontail rabbit frantically hopped for cover in taller grass. Trent turned to Justin with a serious look on his face. "We don't know what we're up against, so be careful."

"I will. You be careful, too."

Trent nodded as he climbed from the auto. Further up the dirt road, crows sat in the middle pecking away at a dead animal. A hawk soared in the summer-blue sky.

Instead of walking down the lane to the farmhouse, they cut across a pasture. They ran from tree to tree, pausing behind each and looking out carefully to see if they'd been spotted. As they got closer to the farmyard, Trent noticed Bob Lavery's pickup in the yard beside Gabe's. "We'll kill two birds with one stone," he whispered grimly.

Justin hesitated. "You can't kill them, Trent."

"No, of course not. I didn't mean it that way. But I can make their lives miserable."

Trent ducked behind a large maple and peered around it while Justin hid behind an oak. The house was small and needed paint. The big red barn and the sheds around the place were in good repair. The windmill blades whirled in the wind as water gushed from a pipe into a horse watering tank. Chickens scratched around the yard. Pigs rolled in the muddy pigpen. Cattle and sheep grazed together in a pasture behind the barn.

"Is Gabe married?" Trent asked in a whisper.

"No. He never got married. Maybe he's still hung up on Aggie."

Just then, Gabe and Bob walked out of the house, talking loudly and angrily.

"Let's go," Trent whispered.

He ran across the space with Justin beside him.

Gabe and Bob stopped in surprise.

Justin shot past Trent and knocked Gabe down hard.

"What the . . ." Bob cried.

Trent slammed his fist into Bob's face, bloodying his nose. "That's for touching my wife! You stay away from her!"

Bob stumbled back against his pickup, holding his nose. He made no effort to fight back.

Gabe rolled away from Justin and jumped to his feet, his fists doubled and fire shooting from his eyes. He lunged at Justin, but Justin stepped aside and landed a blow to Gabe's eye.

Trent wanted to jump in and help Justin, but he knew Justin

could take care of himself. Trent kept an eye on Bob even as he watched the fight.

With one mighty blow to the stomach, Justin knocked Gabe to the ground, then stood over him, daring him to get up. "We know what you did!" Justin snarled. "I ought to kill you right here!"

"No, don't." Gabe's face was white with fear. "I didn't mean to shoot the little girl. It was an accident!"

Aghast at what he'd heard, Trent leaped forward and hauled Gabe to his feet. He slammed his fist hard into Gabe's stomach. "That's for Rachel!"

Gabe crumpled to the ground and groaned in pain.

"We want the whole story, now," Trent said grimly as he stood over Gabe with Justin beside him.

The back door of the house burst open and Aggie Beaumont ran out. "Get away from him!" She yelled, and flung herself at Justin "Don't hurt him!"

Justin pushed her away.

She dropped to her knees beside Gabe and cradled his head in her lap. "Are you all right?"

"He won't be if he doesn't start talking right now," Trent said sharply

"We didn't mean for your girl to get hurt," Bob mumbled through his bloody lips.

"I only wanted to get your attention," Gabe said, struggling to sit up.

Trent and Justin stood over the Laverys and Aggie as the brothers told about bootlegging to pay off their farms.

"Aggie said she'd marry me once my place was paid off and making money," Gabe said. "She would've married me years ago if it hadn't been for you Havlicks! You and your money!"

"Money's not everything," Trent and Justin said at the same time. They looked at each other and quickly away. In the past they'd often said the same thing at the same time. Were they connecting again the way they had long ago?

"What're you going to do with us?" Bob asked as he slowly stood.

"We'll let the law deal with you," Trent snapped.

Bob shook his head. "Don't! I got a baby on the way. We've stopped bootlegging. The federal agent working the area made that too dangerous, and when you took your house back, we didn't have a place for the still. We're out of business now and we'll leave you and your family alone."

"You'll leave my wife alone, that's for sure!" Trent growled.

"I only kissed her so she wouldn't snoop around the house where we had the still going."

Trent rammed his fist into Bob's stomach. "That's for taking advantage of that innocent woman!" And he slammed his other fist into Bob's chin. "And that's for using my house to make liquor!"

Justin stood with his hands on his lean hips. "We're not going to turn you in this time, but we'll keep an eye on you. If you ever cause any problems for our family or if you start bootlegging again, we will turn you in. Is that clear?"

Gabe nodded and Bob muttered, "Yes."

Several minutes later Trent and Justin climbed back in Justin's auto. They looked at each other and chuckled. "We took care of them," they said together, then laughed, sounding just alike.

"Think we should have turned them over to the deputy?" Trent asked. "After all, they were doing some serious things, especially when they shot at us. They might have killed Rachel."

"I think they've learned their lesson," Justin answered. "Greed's a powerful teacher. I think we ought to give them a chance to redeem themselves." As he thought of giving Bob and Gabe a second chance, he wished that were possible for him.

"Then let's get out to the forest and watch history being made," Trent said.

"Havlick history," Justin said with a nod.

* * *

At the edge of the forest, Trent and Justin left the boat and walked uphill toward the family. Four men were sawing a huge oak with a crosscut. The tree had already been notched with a deep undercut so it would fall where they wanted it to. Justin hurried on ahead and stopped beside Priscilla. He slipped his arm around her waist, and she smiled up at him. His pulse quickened.

"I'm glad you made it," she said, snuggling close to him.

Trent glanced over the cluster of people watching the workers until he found Emily. She was wearing a plaid blouse and green skirt and hightop walking shoes. Just as he spotted her, she turned toward him. Her face lit up and she smiled. The rush of emotion he felt surprised him. She ran to him and caught his hand.

"Hi," she whispered, her eyes glowing with happiness.

"Hi." He felt awkward as he walked her back to stand with the family. Her hand in his felt warm and pleasant.

She leaned close and whispered, "I missed you."

He smiled at her, not knowing how to reply. The feelings for Emily surging in him were new and strange.

"Timber!" a sawer shouted. The great oak trembled, swayed, and with a loud crack and swish fell to the ground, breaking branches from nearby trees. As the tree slammed against the ground, twigs and dust shot high into the air.

"I can't bear to watch," Lark said tearfully as she turned her face against Clay's arm.

"That's the beginning of our dream," Jennet said with a catch in her voice.

Emily barely noticed the tree falling. Her heart was singing. The night before had changed her. Passionate love for Trent had burst into full bloom. She'd never known love could be so all-consuming. This morning as she'd worked in the garden, milked the cow, and fed the animals her heart had been so full of love for Trent that she'd told every living creature around her. When she'd met Free and Jennet to ride into the woods with them, she'd told them, and they'd been overjoyed.

Now he seemed shy and distant. Did that mean he didn't really love her even though she loved him with every fiber of her being? She tugged her hand free in the pretense of brushing back her hair, and she didn't slip her hand back in Trent's. She thought he didn't seem to notice.

Trent felt Emily pull away, and, thinking she'd suddenly turned shy, he smiled. She'd been far from shy during the night. He didn't reach for her hand or slip his arm around her the way he wanted to because he didn't want to embarrass her in front of the family. He turned his attention back to the men cutting the branches off the fallen oak. He knew Justin was figuring how many chairs he could make once the lumber was dried. The smaller oaks they'd selected for cutting would be used to build the log cabins.

A thrill ran through Trent. Havlick's Wilderness was actually getting under way! He'd thought it didn't matter to him, but it did. The log cabins would have fireplaces made of stones taken from the ground right here in the forest. Each cabin would have front and back windows, a loft, and puncheon floors. Grandma wanted the doors made from split logs and hung by leather hinges just like they were done in the past. Maybe he and Emily and Rachel could come for a visit sometime and stay in a log cabin.

He chuckled under his breath, thinking about the first time he spent a night in a log cabin. He and Justin were nine years old and, both pretending to be brave, they'd spent the night in Jig's old cabin. They'd heard every sound in the woods and some that they'd only imagined. They didn't sleep, but that hadn't mattered. They'd made it through the night. They had spent the night in the log cabin and they'd survived!

Trent glanced at Justin to see if he was having the same

remembrance, then frowned. Their fight together with the Laverys would not make a difference in how he felt about Justin. He and Justin would never have the same thoughts again if he had anything to do about it. Justin had ripped them apart ten years ago and nothing could put them back together.

He waited for the familiar rise of rage to wash over him. When it didn't come, he reached for it. But he felt only peace. He frowned thoughtfully, remembering Grandpa's prayer and the voice that spoke to him.

The voice spoke again. "I told you I would give you new life."

Trent bent down to Emily and whispered, "Come with me." He held out his hand and she slipped hers in his. He squeezed her hand and bent down and kissed her.

Her heart leaped and she hugged his arm as they walked together toward the water. In the boat he told her about the meeting with Gabe and Bob Lavery.

"I'm surprised Aggie wants Gabe. She said she was going to marry another rich man. She even said she was going after you and Justin."

"Too bad for her." Trent chuckled as he dipped the oars. "We're both married men."

"And don't you ever forget it," Emily said sharply.

Trent laughed with his head back. His laughter floated out over the blue lake and up to the blue sky.

* * *

Early in the morning on the last day of August, Trent stood on the spot where the cook camp would be built. The other buildings would be nearby, just as in a real lumber camp. The sun was already hot, even in the shade of the forest. He and Justin had agreed to meet to make their inspection. They'd worked together all summer, planning and supervising the construction, laying out paths through the forest, listening to Grandma Jennet describe her dream for Havlick's Wilderness in greater detail, and trying to make the dream a reality. They'd also worked side by side at the Wagon Works, each running the part of the business he knew best. They'd done it mostly without speaking unless they had to. But there had been times when they'd had the same thoughts or when something made them laugh together. There were times when they felt like brothers again, but that didn't happen often. But times change and circumstances alter, Trent thought.

He put his hand in his pocket and fingered the letter. When he'd stopped at the post office that morning it was waiting for him. Trent didn't need to look at it to remember what the letter said. He had memorized it.

"Dear Trent, I've had a good offer from a man up in Abilene to buy the ranch. He wants to take over right away, but I told him the place is yours if you still want it. I'm not putting pressure on you, but I need to know what you're planning by the first of October. I don't want to lose this chance to sell if you've changed your mind. I know you are a man of your word, but sometimes things don't work out the way we thought they would. Your friend, Cactus Pete."

"Morning," Justin said, stopping a few feet from Trent. His face bore the agony that had become so familiar.

Trent's heart lurched at Justin's grief, and he remembered two ten-year-old boys, pricking their fingers, pressing blood to blood, and vowing a covenant with each other. Just like Jonathan and David in the Bible, they vowed to take care of and love each other all the days of their lives.

"Ready?" Justin asked.

"In a minute," Trent said. "I have something to show you." Trent took the letter from his pocket, offered it to Justin, and waited quietly while Justin read it. Justin's shoulders sagged and he took a ragged breath, then his temper flared.

"You got the oak I needed to make the chairs and now you think your duty is over at the Wagon Works! It's not! I need you there."

"You knew we'd be leaving."

"I thought you'd accept your responsibility and stay!" Justin had really thought they were finally going to be brothers and friends again, especially after Grandpa's talk and prayer. He and Trent had gotten along well the past few weeks. He looked Trent squarely in the eyes. "I thought you were over Celine's death."

"Death? Murder, you mean!" His fists doubled, Trent sprang forward to strike Justin, but he couldn't do it. His hand fell to his side. What was wrong with him?

Justin doubled his fists, but he didn't move. His mind flashed back to when they were ten and they had pricked their fingers and pressed blood to blood and vowed a vow that they'd take care of each other forever, that they'd love each other forever. He opened his hands and pressed his palms against his legs.

Trent remembered the covenant again. Justin had said he was Jonathan and Trent had said he was David—blood brothers. He'd forgotten the promises they made. With a strangled cry Trent bowed his head and wept, the tears coming from deep inside where he'd locked them ten years ago.

Justin groaned in agony, then tears filled his eyes and poured down his cheeks. He laid his hand on Trent's shoulder and sobbed harder. After a long time Justin said hoarsely, "Trent, forgive me! I'm sorry, so sorry for killing Celine! I am so sorry! Forgive me!"

Trent flung his arms around Justin. "I do!"

"Thank you," Justin whispered hoarsely. He held Trent as if he'd never let him go.

Finally they broke apart and looked searchingly at each other.

"I guess this means you'll be leaving soon," Justin said.

"That's always been my plan. You know that. Just yesterday I hired Emily's brother Lars to take care of my place—live in the house and share the profits from the land—and I told Emily and Rachel to get ready to leave Saturday morning."

Justin's eyes sought solace deep in the forest. "I'd hoped you would stay. I need you at the Wagon Works."

Trent studied Justin's face. All the agony was gone from inside Trent—all the hatred. "I went over and looked at the land Grandma gave Emily and I could see cattle grazing there, and drinking from that clear stream. I could see us harvesting the second growth trees and using the lumber at the Wagon Works, then replanting for future Havlicks to harvest, or leave if they want. I could see my children growing up with yours and learning to love and care for Havlick's Wilderness and each other, but I refused to accept it. But now, Just, I can't imagine not being here. I'll send Cactus Pete a telegram and say, 'If it's a good deal, take it. If it's not, I'm still a man of my word.'"

"But I'll be here." Justin's throat felt like he would strangle. "Will you be able to stand that?"

Trent's eyes sought Justin's but Justin couldn't return the look. "Of course, you'll be here."

"Can you stand it, seeing me every day, knowing what I did?"

"Yes "

Pain tightened Justin's stomach, then his temper flared. "You're just going to stay here and make me as miserable as possible, punishing me every day."

"No, that's not it. I want to stay." Trent raked his fingers through his hair.

"Something much bigger than I am has been working on me." Trent's voice was low. "I vowed I would never forgive you for Celine's death, and I vowed I would never forget what you did. I intended to hate you with a vengeance for the rest of my life. I would hate you and torment you until you wanted to die, but I wouldn't let you die. You had to live and suffer!

"Then God began to speak to me. The first time was during

233

Grandpa's prayer at that family meeting. That time I thought I could hear it the way I hear you when you talk to me. But it was just in my mind. Then later it was like thoughts coming to me. It's so clear to me now!

"It honestly was God, Justin—teaching me, caring for me, loving me, and telling me that my hatred for you was killing me.

"And it was. It separated me from Rachel and I lost ten years of her life. It separated me from my family and my friends who could have helped me with my grief. It separated me from you. It separated me from my Lord. Until that night on Grandpa's porch when he prayed for all of us, I hadn't prayed—not once, and I hadn't read one word in my Bible. Grandpa was right. I'd broken the covenant. But most of all, it separated me from myself.

"As long as I could hate you and blame you for Celine's death, I didn't have to face my part in it. I didn't have to admit that I was to blame, too."

"You? What did you do?"

"I left her. Knowing full well that a contract wasn't worth her life, I left her. Then you asked me to talk Gabe Ingersoll out of cancelling the contract, promising you'd go out and stay with her, and I knew you would forget. But I got a little puffed up with pride. I was the brother who could save the contract and save the company!

"I was as much to blame as you were."

Justin put his arm around Trent's shoulder. "You're being too hard on yourself. It was my fault."

"No. We both did it."

"Are you trying to make me feel better?" Justin was angry again.

"I'm trying to tell you that me forgiving you won't work. You have to forgive yourself. I know God will forgive you."

"How could He, for something so bad?"

"I don't know. I just know that He will if you let Him. Actu ally He's already forgiven you. You just don't know it. And He'll help you forgive yourself. That's what He's done for me. He's given me new life. I guess I was like the prodigal son—I was dead and now I'm alive again.

"I want you to know that peace, too."

Justin struggled with the agony that had gripped him for years and finally released it. He smiled at Trent.

"You're free, Just!"

Justin pointed toward Jig's cabin. "Remember when we spent the night? We were scared of everything and trying hard to be brave. It was the next morning, right there by the door, that we made our covenant."

"I remembered it while I was waiting for you."

"Let's make a new covenant and this one I'll never break!"

Trent hesitated, then nodded. "Brothers again, Just!"

Later they walked their rounds together. They chuckled. Throwing their heads back, they laughed, the sounds ringing out in the clearing and echoing through the forest. At last they were free!

"Brothers again," Trent said again just as Justin said it.

"What will Emily say when you tell her you're staying?" Justin asked.

"I don't know. Be happy, I hope."

*　*　*

Later Trent climbed in his Dodge and drove slowly to his farm, singing at the top of his lungs. He parked in his usual spot and looked around. He'd work at the Wagon Works, but he'd raise cattle, too. He'd have Lars work the farm as they'd planned. Lars and Suzie were talking about getting married, and they'd need a house. They could build one south of his home with a lane of its own.

"Daddy!" Rachel called as she ran from the garden where she'd been working. Her red braids bounced on her shoulders. Her legs and hands were dirty. A smear of dirt covered her cheek, but she didn't seem to care. She liked working as much as the other Havlicks.

Trent gathered her close and kissed her clean cheek. "Where's Emily?"

Rachel frowned and shook her finger at him. "Mom, you mean?"

Trent grinned and nodded. "Sorry, I'm having a little trouble remembering her new name."

"Children don't call their mothers by their names," Rachel said. "She's my mom."

"That she is. Where is she?"

"In the house. She's packing and crying."

Trent stiffened. "Crying? How come?"

"I don't know."

"You go back to the garden to work and let me talk to her alone, will you?"

"Sure. But I'm almost done."

"Stay out until I call you."

"I will." Rachel squeezed Trent's hand. "You can make her feel better."

"You think so, do you?"

"Of course! She loves you."

Trent's heart leaped. "Did she tell you that?"

"Yes."

She hadn't told him in words yet, but maybe now she would. He'd longed to hear her say, "I love you." He kissed Rachel again. "I'll give you a call when you can come in."

She nodded and ran to the garden. The chickens squawked and ran out of her way.

Trent took a deep breath and slowly walked inside. The kitchen smelled like fresh baked bread. He hung his cap on the peg near the door. "I'm home, Em!"

She ran from the front room and flung herself in his arms, sobbing hard.

Love for her rose inside him until he thought his heart would explode. When had he started loving her this way? It had snuck up on him and caught him unaware. He gathered her closer and held her fiercely. "What's wrong?" he asked softly.

She lifted red-rimmed eyes to him. "I know I said I wouldn't ask again, but I have to! Please, please, let us stay here to live! Don't move us to Texas. Please!"

He held back a chuckle.

"All right," he said, trying to look serious.

She gasped and her tears dried instantly. "All right?"

"All right. We'll stay."

"Oh, Trent!" She hugged him again and kissed him all over his face in between her thank you's.

He held her close, enjoying every kiss. His lips burned to kiss her. He caught her face between his hands and kissed her deeply, hungrily.

She grew still, sensing a difference in him.

He lifted his head and smiled. "Emily Havlick, I love you."

Her eyes widened. "Oh, Trent!"

"I love the way you smile, the way you walk, the way you kiss me. I love *you*. You fill me with happiness." Gently he kissed her again.

The world was spinning and she had to hold him tighter to keep from falling. He loved her! Her prayers had been answered! "I love you, my darling Trent," she said against his lips. She pulled away slightly and said again, "I love you! I will always and forever love you!"

Afterword

◆

May 27, 1923, Emily stood beside Trent with all the Havlick family nearby. It was the family's day to go through Havlick's Wilderness and the next day it would open to the public. Already people from as far away as Washington, D.C., had made reservations. Smoke drifted up the chimney of the cookshack where two men were cooking dinner for the family. The bunkhouse, with rows of bunks built so close together the lumberjacks, once called shanty boys, had to slip in them like a slice of meat between two pieces of bread, stood closer to the forest. Farther away were the stable, the blacksmith shop, the company store, and the small shacks where the foreman, the bookkeeper, and the cook lived. The furnishings inside the buildings were exactly like they'd been when Freeman had been a shanty boy back before the Civil War. His red sash, enclosed in a glass frame, hung for all to see with a write-up about how all the shanty boys/lumberjacks wore the red sash to show who they were.

Emily stepped closer to Trent as Freeman made the speech ne'd make tomorrow about lumbering. Trent smiled at her just as the baby moved inside her. In the fall they'd have their first child. She wanted a boy and she knew Trent did, too, but they really didn't care. They'd love a girl just as much.

Rachel leaned against Emily and whispered, "Mom, I'm hungry."

Emily bent down to her. "As soon as Grandpa Free is done talking we'll all have the giant raisin cookies he told us about." They were as big as stove lids and the lumberjacks loved them. Emily felt hungry enough to eat two of them.

Emily saw Ruth and her family. Clay and Lark had adopted Ruth when she was left as an infant at the orphanage. She'd come from Grand Rapids with her husband, Tom, and their seven children. Their daughter Nan was Rachel's age and they'd become best friends instantly. They reminded Emily of Celine and herself.

Celine. Emily smiled. She, Trent, and Rachel talked about her freely. There was room in their hearts for Celine just as before.

Emily dragged her attention back to what Free was saying. She knew he was happy that all his children were present along with their children and grandchildren. Freeman's brother Wexal and sister Anne had come with their families.

"There are a lot of Havlicks here," Trent whispered.

Emily laughed softly. "Think what it'll be like in twenty years! Fifty years!"

"We're leaving our mark, that's for sure. And I don't mean just Havlick's Wilderness. I mean this whole enormous family is making a difference in our part of the world." Trent gently touched Emily's stomach. "And this new Havlick will make a difference too."

Emily leaned her head on Trent's arm and smiled proudly.

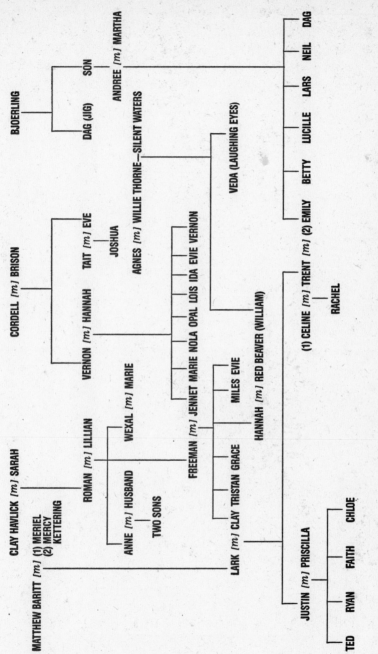

About the Author

Hilda Stahl was a writer, teacher, and speaker. She was born in the Nebraska Sandhills and grew up telling stories to her five sisters and three brothers. After she married and had her first few children, Stahl began her writing career. She published 92 fiction titles and 450 short stories and was a member of the Society of Children's Book Writers. In 1989 she won the Silver Angel Award for *Sadie Rose and the Daring Escape*. Stahl died in March of 1993.